READER'S DIGEST

CONDENSED BOOKS

FIRST EDITION
Published by
THE READER'S DIGEST ASSOCIATION LIMITED
25 Berkeley Square, London W1X 6AB

THE READER'S DIGEST ASSOCIATION LIMITED
Nedbank Centre, Strand Street, Cape Town

Typeset in 10 on 12 pt. Highland Lumitype Roman
and printed in Great Britain by Petty & Sons Ltd., of Leeds
on paper made by Kymmene, in Finland.

Original cover design by Jeffery Matthews.

ISBN 0 340 161221

READER'S DIGEST
CONDENSED BOOKS

SARAH WHITMAN
Diane Pearson

THE RUNAWAYS
Victor Canning

NUNAGA
Duncan Pryde

THE WINDS OF WAR
Herman Wouk

COLLECTOR'S LIBRARY
EDITION

In this volume

THE WINDS OF WAR *by Herman Wouk (p. 305)*

"A splendid epic . . ." *(Daily Express)* ". . . in the tradition of *Gone With the Wind*" *(Evening Standard)* . . . . Twenty years after *The Caine Mutiny*, Herman Wouk returns to World War II for his biggest novel yet. On the one hand the deeply personal story of an American family, of new loves and old loyalties tested by the stress of war, on the other, it is a giant canvas of living history.

With chilling authenticity Wouk describes America's gradual wakening to the terrible dangers of Nazism. The gilded panoply of Hitler's Reich, the piteous lines of Polish refugees, the fire-bombs raining down on London . . . in a world gone mad slowly the pattern of terror and greed becomes clear.

Here, through the eyes of his characters, Wouk presents historic confrontations: the Siege of Warsaw, the Battle of Britain, the German assault on Moscow. Here too he presents the simple joys and agonies of people swept along in a turmoil of great events. It is a big book. To present it in Condensed Books and still remain true to Mr. Wouk's grand design, the editors have devoted more pages to it than have ever before been given to a single work. We are convinced that this is a right decision. In *The Winds of War* America's most gifted storyteller has produced a novel of epic proportions and matching narrative power.

NUNAGA
by Duncan Pryde (p. 207)

Twenty years ago the Eskimos of Perry Island were following unchanged the ways of their Stone-Age ancestors. Their customs were primitive, sometimes harsh. This is the true story of a Scotsman who went among them, learnt their ways, and came to love them. He writes it as it was. Today civilization has touched them, given certain things, taken others away. Today the way of life described in this rare book no longer exists.

THE RUNAWAYS
by Victor Canning (p. 117)

The policeman grinned. "Wanted: Chief Sitting Bull," he said. "Height five feet two, fair-haired, age fifteen, wearing a red and yellow blanket." He paused. "Wanted person's face is heavily freckled." On that particular night there happened to be a second runaway as well. Yarra: seven feet one from the point of her nose to the tip of her tail. The boy and the cheetah were to meet. They both wanted one simple, difficult thing: freedom.

SARAH WHITMAN
by Diane Pearson (p. 11)

She was a country girl, a young schoolteacher come up to live and work in the slums of the big city. London in the 1920s was an exciting place to be young in: ugly maybe, but alive and warm-hearted. She was not looking to fall in love. There was too much else to be got on with. Least of all was she looking to fall in love with someone her family would see as a dangerous influence, a foreigner, and a nasty Bolshevik foreigner at that. . . .

SARAH WHITMAN
Diane Pearson

SARAH
WHITMAN

a condensation of the book by
Diane Pearson

Illustrated by Jack McCarthy   Published by Macmillan, London

Sarah wasn't a looker, not like her ma had been. But Charlie loved her in his own quiet way, and all his fat, jolly Billingsgate relations were sure that quite soon—just as soon as times got better—he and the gentle young schoolteacher would wed. But those were the Depression years, and times didn't get better.

Not that being single worried Sarah. She had her family, she had her work, she had her dreams . . . of the wonderful things that might happen, of the exciting places she might visit. And if Charlie had no place in these dreams, well, neither did the attractive David Baron, for all his foreignness and dangerous socialist ideas. She knew, anyway, that dreams were only dreams. Life was for living. And to be poor was not necessarily to be miserable.

Sarah's story begins in the 1920s, when a visit to the cinema meant two pictures, a stage show, and an organ in the interval, all for sixpence; when scratchy gramophones played "Ramona", and a day on the river was a golden time to remember and cherish. It was a time of great hardship, but a time too when dreams, if you didn't fuss about them overmuch, had a way of coming true.

CHAPTER ONE

There was to be another public thrashing in the Hall.

Throughout the morning an air of hysteria had been growing steadily in the classroom. Sammy Alexander had been sent for at playtime by the headmistress, and he was now locked in the staffroom cupboard, awaiting his punishment.

Sarah found the atmosphere infectious. To be thrashed by Miss Bennett was terrible enough, but a public thrashing took on the sanctity of capital punishment. It was reserved for such depravities as stealing, bad language, or other crimes which came under the general heading of "filth".

The last lesson before the dinner bell should have been arithmetic, but as Sarah found it difficult to control the mounting panic in the classroom she gave up trying to teach the ambiguities of nine apples cut in quarters and distributed among three boys and three girls. Instead she passed round paper and coloured chalks and drew a map of the world on the blackboard for the children to copy. As she sat down at her desk she could hear the concentrated breathing of thirty-seven children and the occasional snap of a chalk-stick as someone pressed too hard. She could also hear sniffling and stifled whispering.

"Stop whispering, Gertie," she said, without looking up. Gertie Alexander, sister of the condemned Samuel, began to cry. The two children usually fought with one another so much that they had to be seated at opposite ends of the room, but in an emergency

11

family unity brought them together. "Bring your map to me," Sarah said gently.

Gertie came up, sobbing miserably, and Sarah caught the smell of her. It was the smell of the whole class: the aroma of malnutrition, chalk, and dung from the farrier's yard that ran alongside the playground.

This farrier's yard was the cause of the present trouble. The school liked playing "running up the dunghill". This involved a long, speed-gathering flight across the farrier's yard, and a final leap to the top of the dunghill. Sammy Alexander was so good at this sport that he had become bored. A mixture of bravado and goading from the other boys had compelled him to plaster dung all over Miss Bennett's bicycle.

Sarah stared down at Gertie and hoped that her tears would not spread to the rest of the class.

"Show me your map, Gertie." She held out her hand, wishing that Gertie's mother wouldn't dress the child's head with a butterfly bow. It didn't match the dingy blue-grey smock and the boots with splitting seams. Gertie continued to cry.

"That's very good, dear," Sarah said. "But you've crayoned all of Africa red. It should be *nearly* all red, but not quite. It's India that is *all* red."

Gertie sniffed and wiped the sleeve of her smock along her upper lip. "What's going to happen to Sammy, Miss?"

"He will have to be punished. He was very, very naughty."

Secretly she admired Sammy's courage. At eight he had dared to do what she, at twenty-one, dared not. He had challenged the terrifying authority of Miss Bennett.

"Now Gertie, go back to your seat and re-do the British Empire in red. Copy what I've done on the board."

Tense silence settled again. Sarah wondered gloomily if the morning and the thrashing would ever be over . . . .

On the window sill stood Class Three's attempts at gardening— flaccid runner beans growing out of wet blotting paper. Sometimes, when she looked at them and thought of the green, lush runner beans in her pa's garden, she wanted to run away and get a train back home to the village. She thought of the clean sky and the wind, and her father cutting logs. She hated the runner beans on the blotting paper.

There were times too when she looked out of the classroom window, and watched the clouds being blown to the south. She imagined them drifting over her pa's cottage in Sussex and away over the Downs to the sea, and in her mind she would travel to Spain and Egypt and down through Africa. The classroom would become smaller and stuffier and she would be filled with impatience for all those strange countries, the colour, and huge wild horizons, all the exciting things she had read about but never seen.

But someone was knocking on the classroom door. It opened, and Miss Enderby scurried in, plucking nervously at her jumper-suit and trying to smile without letting her top denture slip. "Miss Whitman," she whispered. "You are to report to the Head's room. *At once.* I will look after Class Three for you."

Sarah felt the blood drain down to her feet. Class Three was silent with dread, pupils and teacher united in terror. Sarah smoothed her hair—worn low, one coil over each ear—and left the classroom. She was only in the second term of her first year's probation, and the way things were going Miss Bennett could not fail to give her a bad report. She would almost certainly be out of work at the end of the year.

The post had been incredibly difficult to find. It was 1926 and any work was hard to find in those Depression years. Her training had been unorthodox. She had left school at fourteen to go into domestic service. Then, at fifteen, thanks to her village school-master who deplored any waste of talent, she had gone to work in an East London Church School. In return for caring for a class of thirty infants she had been given her keep and intensive evening tuition. Eventually she had qualified for a teachers' training college where she had lived on small grants and whatever money her father could spare from his narrow income.

At twenty-one, when at last she qualified, Sarah was flushed with the success of her six-year fight. But she waited for weeks with many other unemployed teachers in the office of the local education committee. Finally the teacher at her old church school had recommended her to Miss Bennett as a good girl, from a poor but Christian home. Thus Sarah had a double responsibility to perform well—as justification for her father's years of unselfish economy, and because Miss Bennett had taken her as a favour to her friend. Every time she was rebuked or humiliated by Miss Bennett her fear of a bad report to the committee grew worse. There were nights when she found it impossible to sleep for worrying about it.

The door of the headmistress's room had a panel of pale grey glass, the same colour as Miss Bennett's eyes, and as cold. Sarah knocked timidly.

"Enter."

As Sarah came into the room she saw that Miss Bennett was seated, but Miss Bennett's sitting—like her walking and her talking—was tense, barely controlled. She was in her late forties, hard and vigorous, and today her mouth was even more rigid than usual.

"Miss Whitman," she said, "I am beginning to wonder if you have any idea at all of how to discipline children. Have you any idea what that miserable, filthy Sammy Alexander has done now? He has climbed out of the cupboard window and run away, Miss Whitman." Miss Bennett lifted a register from her desk and crashed it down hard. The pen tray rattled on the desk top.

Sarah swallowed. "I think he was probably afraid."

"And so he should have been."

"Yes, Miss Bennett." Sarah stared at the floor.

"That child will either be brought back to the school by the school inspector or he will be brought back by you. I need hardly tell you that if the inspector has to bring him back it will read very badly in your report to the committee." Miss Bennett stared contemptuously at Sarah. "And one other thing, Miss Whitman. It has been observed that a man waits for you occasionally at the staff entrance. I would be obliged if your . . . followers could wait elsewhere. It gives the school a bad name."

Sarah felt humiliated and ashamed. "He's a friend of my family," she said angrily. "He just comes to see me sometimes." She realized how feeble the excuse sounded. Also it was untrue. She was very fond of Charlie Dance.

Miss Bennett picked up a pen. "You may go, Miss Whitman."

Her stare had said everything. That Sarah was here as a personal favour, that her blue woollen dress was old-fashioned, that her stockings were of black wool instead of fashionable beige silk, that she was the daughter of a village postman and that she did not know how to behave like a schoolmistress. Feeling sick, Sarah left the room.

SARAH had large hazel eyes, high cheekbones, and the rich cream and pink complexion of a country girl. She was well built—too well built for the styles of the twenties, so that even if she could have afforded the fashionable, narrow-hipped frocks, she would not have looked right in them. She walked badly because she thought she was big and unattractive, but on the rare occasions when she forgot this she had an eager swinging stride; and sometimes she would wear a flower or a scarf in a certain way, and would look vivid, and somehow different. She appealed especially to older people, because her face was young enough to register hope but humble enough to register compassion. Above all, she had perseverance, which drove her—sometimes miserable and afraid—through whatever ordeal awaited her. So after school that day she set out grimly for the Old Kent Road.

The Alexanders lived six floors up in a prison-like block of three-room flats, with a sink on each landing which was shared between two families. She paused at the bottom of the stone stairs to gather courage, and a man with a fish barrow walked past her shouting "Shrimp-o! Shrimp-o!" When he saw her waiting on the bottom step he said, "Wanna buy some shrimps, luv? You get a live crab with every pint."

Sarah looked into his enamel tray and saw the small brown crabs lying in half an inch of water. Several were dead and the remaining ones moved feebly.

"No thanks," she said, shuddering.

Taking a deep breath she began to climb the stairs. On the fifth flight she passed Gertie Alexander, sitting on a step eating bread and dripping. Gertie's eyes grew round when she saw Sarah.

"Good afternoon, Gertie," said Sarah, pretending a confidence she did not feel. "Is your mother in?" Gertie gulped and nodded, and Sarah continued on up the steps.

On the sixth landing a man in a vest was washing at the sink. He stared at Sarah. She knocked on the Alexanders' door. She could hear voices, shouting, inside.

"It's no use knocking," he said. "They'll think it's the tally man come for 'is money and they won't answer." He pushed her out of the way and beat on the door with both fists. "George! George! Shut up talking and open the door."

The hubbub inside stopped abruptly and the door was opened by a thin, tired-looking man. "Yes?" he said quietly.

"I'm the schoolteacher," Sarah said. "I wonder if I could have a word with you, Mr. Alexander . . . . It's about Sammy. A little spot of bother at school."

"The wife takes care of all that kind of thing," said Mr. Alexander, unruffled. "All right then. You'd better come in."

They went into a tiny room, crowded with men all sitting round a table. "This 'ere's the schoolteacher," explained Mr. Alexander, and there was a scraping of chairs as the men stood up, mumbling, "'Evenin', Miss. Pleased to meet yer, Miss . . . ."

She was acutely embarrassed. They had the servile, humble look she had occasionally seen on her father's face when he was talking to the village gentry. It was as if her official position somehow made her superior. "I'm sorry to disturb you," she said nervously.

"The wife's in the kitchen," said Mr. Alexander. She nodded, and walked towards the kitchen door. Then she noticed that one of the men, a young one at the head of the table, had not stood up. Illogically she was annoyed. As she passed him he said "Good evening," and returned to the study of some papers. He had intense brown eyes and a pale serious face. Before she could close the kitchen door behind her she heard him saying, "Let's waste no more time. We still have a lot to decide . . . ."

Mrs. Alexander was tall and thin and gave the impression of a woman who expected the worst and usually got it. Her face was white, her hair simply hacked off. She gave Sarah a small half-twitch of her mouth, a tired courtesy of a smile. "I thought someone would be along ever since Sammy told me. Sit down then."

Sarah sat, feeling faintly surprised. She was sure that if she had run away from a thrashing at school, she would not have told her mother.

"So he nipped off before she could cane him then?" Mrs. Alexander was putting slices of bread on to plates.

Sarah began to think Mrs. Alexander was so unruffled about the whole thing that there would be no difficulty about getting Sammy back to school. "The headmistress feels her authority has been flouted," she said. "She's sent me to persuade you to send Sammy back."

Mrs. Alexander began to take cups down from the dresser. "Thought that's what you'd come for," she said kindly.

What a nice woman Mrs. Alexander was! "So you'll send him back tomorrow?" Sarah asked.

"No." Mrs. Alexander smiled. "He's a little horror, I grant you that. His father'll wallop him for his dirty ways. But I can't send him back to school. He's too terrified of those public beatings." She reached for a teapot. "You know, that Miss Bennett . . . she enjoys the beatings. There's something wrong with her. I've watched her. She never did it to me—I made sure I never did nothing wrong. But I've watched her beating the others."

Shocked, Sarah realized that Mrs. Alexander was only a few years older than herself. Probably only twelve years had elapsed since she had been at Miss Bennett's school.

Mrs. Alexander measured three spoons of tea into the pot. "Of course, I know the school inspector can *make* Sammy go back. But I'm not sending him back to that, whatever he's done."

It wasn't the school rules that Mrs. Alexander was flouting. It was the something in Miss Bennett that made her coiled hair come unwound when she thrashed children, that made her hands shake with rage when anyone defied her. Sarah knew she had no right to make terms. But, "If I promise to persuade Miss Bennett to thrash Sammy privately," she said, "will you let him come back tomorrow?"

Mrs. Alexander stared anxiously into her eyes. "Oh, it's not going to be easy," Sarah went on quickly. "I'm new to the school, and she doesn't like me very much. But I promise to do my best . . . . You see, if we leave this to the inspector we'll all be in trouble and he'll get the thrashing anyway."

"Oh, I wouldn't want to get you into trouble." Mrs. Alexander twisted her apron, then faltered, "All right. If you think you can persuade her, I'll send him back in the afternoon."

"I'll go to see her in the morning," said Sarah, and stood up.

In the next room the men were standing now, and the young one was stuffing papers into a carrier bag. Sarah nodded as she passed, said "Goodbye," and hurried to the door.

Mr. Alexander smiled. "'Bye then," he said kindly. "Hope it's all sorted out."

As she started downstairs, feet pounded after her, and she drew to one side for the men to pass. "G'night, Miss . . . G'night, Miss . . . ." Finally the young one came, engrossed in conversation with his companion. "It will work," he was saying, "if we organize properly." The way he pronounced "work" wasn't quite right, and she wondered if he were foreign.

She pressed against the wall to let them pass abreast. "Good evening," she said.

His companion's cap came off and he mumbled, "'Night, Miss." But the young one stared at her without even seeing her, even though to get past her he had to twist sideways and change his bag from one arm to the other.

His indifference was the final depressant in a day that had been disastrous. When she reached the bottom of the stairs she had to fight a strong desire to sit down and rest her head against the dirty wall. Tomorrow she had to face Miss Bennett. She felt tired out, and already a failure.

I want to see Charlie, she thought suddenly. If I go and see Ma Dance this evening, Charlie may be there . . . . As she went out on to the pavement her foot knocked against something. She looked down and saw one of the shrimp-man's crabs. It was dead. "I want to see Charlie," she said aloud, and her eyes filled with tears.

AFTER tea that night she went upstairs to her room, rummaged at the back of her underclothes drawer, and brought out a small box of neutral-coloured face powder. She rubbed a little of it carefully across her nose, then hid the box again and blew the telltale traces from the dressing table top. She knew Aunt Florrie herself wouldn't care if she used face powder, but she was bothered that the next time Florrie saw her pa she might mention it. She was grateful to her stout Aunt Florrie Dance and her even stouter Uncle Max for having her as a boarder, but she wished they didn't take their chargeship so heavily.

She put her hat and coat on and went downstairs. She opened the front door. "Just going round to see Ma Dance," she called, closing the door and running quickly away down the street.

The evening was cold, but there were tight green buds on the trees in Trinity Square. The sky was rosy and the wind had dropped. At last she could smell spring. She swung out of the Square and past the pub on the corner where someone was singing "Always" in a rich porty voice. I wonder if I can afford a new dress this spring, she thought, cream, with a sailor collar and a sash round the hips. She felt breathless with excitement because spring was coming and something *must* be going to happen to her.

Charlie opened the door himself, and when he saw her his round good-natured face beamed. "Luvly," he said. "I didn't know you was coming round, Sary. Luvly!"

Charlie thought she was wonderful. That was why she had wanted to see him so badly. She managed a smile. "I thought I'd better see how Ma was," she said.

"Always better when you come round, Sary. Wish you boarded with us instead of Maxie. Love to 'ave you we would, only there's such a lot of us."

There were so many of the Dances in fact, that Sarah had never really worked out the ribald, red-faced, generous total. In the same street, and in adjoining streets, were settled Dance daughters and sons and grandchildren, all living in and out of each other's houses. Dances who died were wept over. Then their photographs were prominently displayed on mantelpieces and charabancs were hired on the anniversaries of their deaths to take the family, smothered in floral tributes, to the cemetery. Then they all went back to Ma and Pa's for a slap-up tea. When a Dance fell out of work or a husband died, the rest of the family moved in to help and everyone cut back on expenditures. If a Dance had a win on the horses there was a party after which at least two Dance wives got pregnant again.

Ma Dance presided over the tribe, though seventy and huge and bronchial, with dropsical legs. Beloved by all, she was still able to tell a daughter-in-law exactly what she thought of her, the way the children should be reared, the husbands managed. Her grandchildren adored her, though she couldn't remember all their names. She had for them all an inexhaustible supply of interfering, noisy, insensitive love.

Sarah had only just stepped inside the door when Ma's thick gravelly voice rasped down the stairs. "That's our Sary then! Come on up and see old Ma Dance, darlin'."

Sarah climbed the narrow stairs between walls papered in a brown fruit-and-flower pattern. The bedroom door was wide open.

"Come in, darlin'. Come and give old Ma a kiss then!"

Ma, wearing a pink flannel nightgown, lay smothered in two feather mattresses on a brass bedstead surrounded by large mahogany pieces of furniture. When Sarah bent over her, two mammoth arms brought her face down to Ma's. "How you bin, Sary love?" She held Sarah away from her, looking into her face, then hugged her again. "Always cheerful you are, Sary." She released Sarah and heaved herself up on her pillows. "You ain't a looker like your ma was, Sary, but you're always cheerful!"

Sarah was used to being told she wasn't pretty like her ma. "We can't all be beauties," she said, sitting on the bed.

She was unusually abrupt, and this must have registered with Ma Dance for she suddenly put her swollen hand over Sarah's and clumsily patted her. "Don't you worry, gel. You may not be a looker, but my Charlie thinks the world of you."

Sarah wriggled uncomfortably. She knew that all the Dances took it for granted that one day she and Charlie would be married. Admittedly, Charlie's devotion was balm to her: she had never been transparently worshipped before, and besides, Charlie was nice to look at, blue-eyed and tall, making her feel small and feminine. But the thought of becoming a Dance and losing her identity in the teeming family depressed her. Too many things are going to

21

happen to me, she thought. I can't become a Dance, not just yet. She smiled weakly. "He may not want to marry me, Ma."

"'Course 'e will, love. Can't marry you till 'e finds 'imself a job, can 'e? That's why 'e's not said anything."

The Dances gained their living largely from Billingsgate, but there were too many Dances now for the fish market to provide employment for all of them. Charlie had to find work as and when he could: as temporary porter, drayman or roadsweeper. At least he was more fortunate than over a million of his fellows, for he had a home and sufficient food.

Suddenly Sarah felt suffocated . . . in Ma . . . in Charlie . . . in Dances. "I've got to go," she said, rising. "I mustn't be late."

"Charlie will walk you 'ome," said Ma confidently.

Sarah escaped from the room. Charlie was waiting downstairs in cap and overcoat. "Let's go for a walk, Sary," he said.

"I'm going home," she snapped, and immediately felt ashamed when she saw the hurt on his face. "But you can walk home with me. I'm sorry, I didn't mean to be rude."

Outside, Charlie fell into step beside her. "You all right?" he asked anxiously. "You seem tired . . . . Ma's a bit much at times, ain't she?"

"Oh, Charlie!" She was filled with delighted surprise that Charlie had realized what she was feeling. He didn't often follow her moods. She seized his arm and hugged it. "She's lovely, Charlie. It's me that's bad tempered. I've had a dreadful day at school. Miss Bennett's said you're not to wait there for me any more. Said it gave the school a bad name. Then I had to go and see some parents and a man there was rude to me."

He stopped walking and frowned at her. "What man?" he asked.

"There was a meeting going on—this young man seemed to be some kind of leader. And I could tell he didn't like me."

"Oh, Sarah," said Charlie. "You're always imagining things about people. Why shouldn't he like you?"

"He didn't," she said stubbornly. "He was foreign, I think. He looked foreign."

"Ah," Charlie's frown cleared. "Well, that explains it. A foreigner would behave like that."

She felt the irritation and frustration that often occurred when Charlie completely missed the point. "Let's not talk about it any more," she said, and Charlie smiled and patted her shoulder, having solved the incident to his own satisfaction.

When they reached her gate Charlie bent and kissed her cheek. "Don't worry, Sary. Not about that foreigner."

He watched her pull the string with the key on it through the letter-box and when she went in he waited for a moment. Sarah saw him standing there, looking up at her window. Dear Charlie, she thought affectionately, and then she turned away from the window and forgot him . . . . That man *was* rude to me, she said to herself. Yes, he definitely was.

THE FOLLOWING morning was Sarah's day for handing out the hot milk and malt to the children classified by the school doctor as suffering from malnutrition. She hated milk duty because it meant that every sick or undernourished child in the school was gathered together in one classroom. There were days when Sarah felt courageous, and handed out the milk cheerfully, trying to imbue the children, not only with vitamins, but with hope. There were other days when she just felt depressed. The weak, quiet children would grow up into weak, quiet men and women. On these days there didn't seem any point in trying.

Today, with the knowledge that she must face Miss Bennett about Sammy Alexander, the children seemed unbearably slow, moving in a long shuffling line and each one taking an unconscionably long time to lick the malt from the spoon and sip the milk from the enamel beakers. When she finally got away, the morning break was nearly at an end.

She found Miss Bennett sitting in her room, sipping tea from a bone china cup. She set the cup down. "Miss Whitman?"

Sarah swallowed. "Excuse me, Headmistress—it's about Sammy Alexander. I went to see his parents, and Mrs. Alexander promised me that he would come back to school this afternoon."

Miss Bennett poured more tea. "I am delighted to hear it."

Sarah's legs began to feel weak. "I'm afraid getting him back to school was not simple," she said. "His mother agreed to it only if

23

the public thrashing was waived. So I . . . I've promised Mrs. Alexander that there would be no public thrashing."

She dared not look at Miss Bennett. The room was so quiet she could hear her own heart thumping. Then there was a violent crash. Miss Bennett had pushed her cup off the end of the desk.

"You did what?"

Sarah dared to look up. Miss Bennett's face was white, and her eyes were concentrated into small brilliant points of fury.

"I had to promise," Sarah gabbled in terror. "Otherwise Mrs. Alexander would never have let him come back. She agrees that he must be punished, but privately."

Miss Bennett's face did not change. "I shall send Mr. Janning to collect Samuel Alexander as soon as he arrives at school. On your way back to your classroom please tell the rest of the staff that I want a full assembly after the dinner-break."

Sarah was terrified—of Miss Bennett's eyes, of the violence she had always sensed in this woman. But she was also shocked at the significance of Miss Bennett's words.

"I gave my word," she said. "I know I had no right to give it, but that means *I* should be punished, not the boy."

"Miss Whitman," hissed the headmistress, "your entire conduct in this matter is impertinent and undisciplined. I shall expect you to sit on the platform and, if necessary, hold the boy."

"I'm afraid I can't do that," said Sarah coldly. Suddenly she wasn't afraid any more. She stared with loathing directly into Miss Bennett's face. "I shall stay with my class."

She turned and walked out of the room. And when she heard Miss Bennett scream, "Come here, at once!" she took no notice.

She walked slowly back to her classroom, making calculations on how the money she had saved could see her through unemployment. She'll have to report me to the committee before I'm sacked, she thought. So I'll have at least another week's salary, if I'm lucky . . . . But what am I going to tell pa?

WHEN Sarah led her class into the assembly hall she was aware that Miss Bennett was looking at her. She stared coldly back, daring the headmistress to call her up on to the platform where

Sammy stood. Miss Bennett looked away, recognizing something implacable in her youngest teacher. Then she picked up the cane and turned to Sammy. "Hold up your right hand," she ordered.

Sammy was small and weedy. One sock was wrinkled down over his ankle and his face was very frightened. He extended his fingers towards Miss Bennett. Sarah saw her swing her whole body back with the cane. Sarah closed her eyes.

"Now the other hand." She opened her eyes. The coil of hair had come unwound from Miss Bennett's head and swung every time she threw her body violently back with the cane. On her face was an expression of delight. Sammy was white and his teeth were chattering, but he did not cry.

Miss Bennett finished, and replaced the cane on the table beside the Bible. She lifted her hands and recoiled her hair. "Let nothing of this kind occur again," she said. "School dismissed."

Feeling tired and old, Sarah led her class from the hall.

ALL the way to the Alexanders' she prayed they would be out—though that would only delay facing Mrs. Alexander until another evening. Her steps grew slower as she mounted the stone stairway.

She knocked on the door. It opened almost immediately and Mr. Alexander stared coldly out at her. "Yes?"

"Could I speak to your wife, Mr. Alexander?"

"Didn't you say quite enough last time you come?"

She could feel her face colouring. Then the door opened wider and Mrs. Alexander stood there. When she saw Sarah she wiped her hands nervously down her overall. Mr. Alexander put his arm round his wife's shoulder. "It's the schoolteacher, come to make more trouble," he said.

"Well, there's no need for all the neighbours to know about it." Mrs. Alexander opened the door wider. "Come in if you must."

Miserably Sarah stepped inside. When she saw the foreign young man sitting at the table she realized she was going to be spared nothing.

"I'm sorry," she said. "I didn't know you had company, Mr. Alexander. I'll come back another time."

"No. You say what you've come to say. I'm not ashamed of my

friends knowing the kind of treatment my son gets from his schoolteacher."

"Yes . . . but . . . as it's a private family business, I—"

"It's a bit more private than my boy had when he was wallopped, ain't it?" Mr. Alexander shouted. "You've only got one witness. My son had the whole school."

Mrs. Alexander put her hand on his arm. "You'll only make it bad for Sammy, George," she said, tremulously.

Sarah realized that in Mrs. Alexander's eyes she was a monster to be classified alongside Miss Bennett! Deeply hurt, she said, "I never wanted him thrashed. I tried to stop it."

"Looks like it, don't it?" said Mr. Alexander nastily.

Her temper flared. "I didn't have to come here, Mr. Alexander. I did my best to stop the public punishment, and I failed. I should not have made promises I could not keep, so I came here to say I'm sorry. And if it'll make you feel any better, I can tell you that I'm likely to lose my job over the whole business." She was nearly crying. "I'll go now." She strode to the door and opened it. "Good day to you. And I hope you and your friend there have enjoyed being unpleasant to me."

She darted a brief glance back at the young man who was staring down at the table. Then he was blotted out by the figure of Mrs. Alexander. "Don't mind Mr. Alexander," she whispered. "He didn't mean to be rude. It's just he's got a lot on his mind at the moment, with a strike coming and all."

Sarah tried to smile. "I really did try, Mrs. Alexander."

Mrs. Alexander nodded. "That's all right, dear. I know what Miss Bennett's like. And I hope you don't really lose your job . . . ."

Sarah walked away down the stairs. She hoped, fervently, she would never have to come up them again.

TWO DAYS later she was putting her books together in the staff room when Miss Enderby twittered in. "Miss Whitman, a man is asking for you at the staff entrance. And really—Miss Bennett—you know she doesn't like it."

Since Sarah's trial of strength with Miss Bennett the headmistress had simply ignored her. She supposed it was just a case of waiting until the report to the committee filtered through. Sarah tried not to think what would happen after that. Once she was blacklisted, it would be almost impossible to find another post. Frantically she stuffed the last of her books into her bag. Drat Charlie! She forced her arm into one sleeve of her coat, jammed her hat down and ran for the door, trying to put the other arm in her coat as she ran.

There was no sign of Miss Bennett in the passage, and she quickly slammed the outer door of the staff entrance behind her. Then—when she saw who was waiting for her—she stopped.

It was the foreign young man, bareheaded, leaning against the railings. His hair was dark and very curly. "Hello," he said. "I've something to say to you."

Desperation finally got her arm into her coat. "Well, say it somewhere else, please, not in front of the school. I'm not supposed to have people wait for me outside the school."

She walked away towards a side road. The studs in the young man's boots made a ringing noise on the cobbles. He was watching her and although he wasn't smiling—did he ever smile?—for once he wasn't absorbed in his own thoughts either. Automatically she began to follow her normal route home.

"I decided I had to say something to you," said the young man. "You see, I know you're a bourgeois do-gooder who is grinding down the faces of the poor, but I thought it was morally very brave of you to go and see the Alexanders."

She was astonished. "A bourgeois do-gooder? What *are* you talking about?"

He began to walk faster, waving his hands excitedly. "Bourgeois," he said. "Middle-class bourgeois education, and you come into poor people's homes to interfere with their children. You think you're being kind, but you treat poor people as you would a dog or a horse—give them enough to eat and lots of discipline and they'll be all right."

Sarah took a deep breath. "I think you're the rudest, most objectionable young man I have ever met. You were rude to me the first time you saw me. You don't know anything at all about me. You're . . . you're *rude!*"

He stopped walking and faced her, looking surprised. "*Was* I rude?" he asked. "I mean, how was I rude?"

Angry and astonished, Sarah fought for words. "You don't tell people they're bourgeois and face-grinders when you don't know anything about them. You don't even know my name!"

"Yes I do," he said imperturbably. "It's Sarah Whitman. And I know lots about you from the young Alexanders. You're always talking about Africa and India and places where there are mountains and deserts. You're good at reading but nobody in the class really listens because they like watching your face when you read. They like you, even though you're bourgeois. They're too young to know you're one of the enemy."

"Good-bye!" said Sarah, quickening her stride. So did the young man, and almost at once they came to Aunt Florrie's and she had to stop and fumble with the gate.

He looked at the three feet of concrete that separated the gate from the narrow terraced house. "You live *here*?" he asked.

"Yes," she answered savagely. "I sit in my little upstairs room and brood over new ways of grinding the faces of the poor."

He looked very uncomfortable. "Well, I still think you're bourgeois," he muttered. "All the same, you were very brave, going to see the Alexanders."

There was definitely something different about him, his accent and the way he used his hands when he was talking. "You're not English, are you?" said Sarah.

She hadn't meant to sound patronizing, but he flushed. "I was born two days after my family landed here and that makes me just as English as you."

He seemed to be sensitive about it and impulsively she put her hand up and touched his arm. "Don't be hurt." She could see that, for him, being called a foreigner was far worse than it was for her being called bourgeois. "I was just interested because I love talking about countries over the sea."

At that he smiled—a warm, bright, exciting smile that completely changed him, making him seem young and full of fun.

"You've a lovely face, Sarah Whitman." He gazed down at her for a moment, and then she became aware that Aunt Florrie's lace curtains were stirring. But because his smile was so wide and infectious she had to smile back. "I must go in now," she said.

"Good-bye." He stuffed his hands into his pockets and walked jauntily away down the road. When he came to the end he looked back, then vanished round the corner.

"And I quite forgot to ask his name," she said dreamily to a curious Aunt Florrie as she opened the door. "I completely forgot to ask his name."

CHAPTER TWO

She made up her mind that if she saw him again, the first thing she would ask would be his name. But when the time came she was so agitated that she forgot everything but the need to get him away from the school gates as quickly as possible.

She had come out of the staff room just in time to coincide with Miss Bennett and in silence they had walked together to the staff entrance. But when she followed Miss Bennett out into the yard, with a sinking heart she recognized the figure waiting for her by the railings. "I have told you about this before, Miss Whitman," said Miss Bennett stonily.

"I'm very sorry, Miss Bennett, I will see it does not happen again." She hurried to the gate. "I told you not to wait for me here," she whispered fiercely. "That's the headmistress."

She took hold of his arm and tried to push him away along the road. Stubbornly, he refused to be hurried. "A typical example of upper-class autocracy," he said airily. "You have allowed yourself to be victimized. You should fight for your rights."

"Oh, don't talk rubbish!" She hadn't been in his company a minute and already she was annoyed. "There are too many school-teachers and not enough vacancies." She had begun to hope that perhaps her dismissal wasn't as imminent as she had feared. Five weeks had elapsed since the thrashing with no letter of dismissal, so she was trying hard not to antagonize Miss Bennett any further.

"You are a typical cog in a capitalist society," he answered.

"A bourgeois oppressor of the poor who is, in turn, oppressed by a tyrannical headmistress."

"And what do *you* do for a living?" she retorted. "That's what I'd like to know."

"I'm a railway clerk," he said. "But I'm not always going to be one. One day I'm going to lead the people into a perfect society."

"Stuff," said Sarah. "You're a rude young railway clerk, and one day you'll be a rude old railway clerk. What do *you* ever do about leading the people into a perfect society?"

His brown eyes studied her seriously. "I do a lot. I'm a delegate for my branch of the union, organizing our part in the big strike for the whole of this area. That's what I was doing at the Alexanders. A national strike—it's coming, you know."

"But that's wicked!" Living and working in a district where nearly everyone was poor, where many were unemployed, she still had never had a personal encounter with a Bolshevik.

He waved his arms. "What's wicked about trying to stop a miner's pay from being cut? What's wicked about that, eh?"

She'd expected him to say something silly about grinding the faces of the poor. The fact that he came out with a reality that a lot of people were feeling bad about made her a little uncertain how to argue. "It's the *way* you're trying to stop it," she said earnestly. "Making everyone stop work won't solve anything."

"So you tell me a better way!" he shouted.

To be truthful, she didn't know very much about the miners. "They can settle it by discussion," she said feebly.

"They've been discussing for five years. And what has happened?"

"I don't know," she flared back at him, tired of being made to feel stupid. "All I know is that sensible, God-fearing people wouldn't start strikes just because of a lot of Bolshevik talk."

"That's a stupid, bourgeois thing to say! Only middle-class people like you talk about God. Believing in God is ignorant suspicion."

He had gone too far. For Sarah, with her strict non-conformist background, this was more than blasphemy—it was a negation of everything in her life . . . of her pa, of all the others in the village, and of her own achievements, brought about by people who believed in God and therefore wanted to help her.

"I'm sorry," she said quietly. "I have to go now. Good-bye."

The animation left him. She had closed herself away behind English politeness. "Could I see you? I mean, I would like to talk to you again—"

"I'm sorry," she said. "But we don't really believe in the same things, do we?" She walked away and left him. She still didn't know his name but now it didn't matter, because she wouldn't be seeing him any more.

HIS NAME was David Baron. In the old country it had been Baranowicz, and his parents hadn't intended to change it. They were proud of being Baranowicz because in the old country it was a much respected name. But when David's father had come to England as an escape from the pogroms of the Tsarist régime, the English registrar had merely entered "Baron" on the form because that was the nearest English sound. Two days later, in January 1900, David had been born, the first of the Barons' "British" children, the one most dear to their hearts.

To his beloved David, old Jacob Baranowicz had imparted his sense of a new freedom, his belief that in England anything could be done if one desired it strongly enough. He could have trained the boy to be a shoemaker like himself—there was a good living in the trade—but he wanted to prove that his family could now work at any kind of trade. He would say to his friends, "My son, he has an important, responsible position! A post on the railway. Like an Englishman. Can you see that in the old country?"

David had studied at evening classes and absorbed all kinds of ideas that were beyond his father. And then, one day, Jacob found that the boy had absorbed the idea of freedom to the exclusion of everything else, even God and the Jewish Law. His son was a Godless rebel.

David had denounced God to Sarah almost as a mark of defiance, knowing it would shock and offend her. He despised her for her ignorance and for her assumption that what she believed was right. But Sarah's serenity, her strength that came from the soil, her face, her secret smile, had captured his imagination. She was so . . . English.

Her rejection wounded him deeply. "She's nothing," he muttered as he stumped unhappily along the pavement. "Arrogant, and a snob. She's nothing, just an ignorant, bourgeois nothing . . . ." But he knew in his heart that it wasn't true.

HE SAW Sarah again in the early days of the General Strike. He hadn't really felt happy since the last time he'd seen her, but he thought that for the present he had no *right* to be happy. He was busy organizing a social revolution. Unfortunately this particular revolution was proving more difficult to organize than he had expected. *His* strike was running beautifully, but in other parts of the country things weren't stopping as efficiently as they should have.

He was on his way to do picket duty at the station when he saw Sarah, happy and excited, riding on the back of a red motorcycle. When it pulled into the kerb ahead of him she climbed down, straightened her hat and waved, laughing at the cheerful young man in front, as the cycle roared away. David hurried up to her. "What were you doing on that bike?" he burst out. "This isn't your way home."

Sarah looked sheepish. "I know. But I may never get a chance to ride on a motor bicycle again. And today everyone is giving everyone else rides. It's quite respectable, because of the strike."

David wished he could afford to buy a motorcycle and go roaring· down the road with Sarah on the back. Because he wished it so very much he said stuffily, "This strike is a serious business, you know. Too many people are treating it as fun."

"I know." She was a little ashamed. Here he was, wearing an armband and looking very responsible. But then she remembered the way he had spoken about God. "Good-bye," she said swiftly, and began to walk away.

"Sarah!" She stopped, but didn't look at him. "Please. Can't I see you again? Perhaps we don't believe in the same things, but that's what's interesting about people, the way we're all different."

He had struck the right note. Sarah could not resist anything "different". "You're very different," she said reluctantly. "I never met anyone like you before . . . . All right, I'll see you again. But not outside the school. At the Elephant. This time next week." Then she remembered something. "But I don't know your name."

"David. David Baron."

"David Baron . . . ." It sounded nice the way she said it. "Good-bye, then."

He watched her walk away—tall, well-built, and walking awkwardly because she knew he was looking at her. She seemed to carry a bright warmth with her: everyone around her looked dull and ordinary.

When she had disappeared he began to run down the Old Kent Road, dodging in and out of the masses of people. Suddenly everything was wonderful again. If necessary he would even go to Wales and run their strike for them . . . . At Willow Walk Station the other pickets were already on duty and some students were in the shunting yard messing about ineffectually with the engines. "Come on lads," he said excitedly. "Up to the bridge over the line!" He felt so happy he had to stop himself from laughing out loud as he grabbed several lumps of coal from the siding and raced up over the bridge.

"Scabs! Blacklegs!" he shouted joyfully to the students below, and threw the coal down on their heads.

THERE was a family meeting that night in Ma Dance's room and Sarah attended, squeezed in between two over-sized Dances by the door.

"Me and Dad've decided that the family must stand by the country like we did in the war," wheezed Ma. "Ain't that right, Pa?"

Pa, in a collarless shirt with a brass stud at the front, nodded heartily. "'T'ain't that we don't feel sorry for the miners. I've said to your ma many times, those poor kids in Wales ought to come down 'ere and 'ave one of your good feeds. That's what they need. 'Aven't I said that lots of times?"

"You 'ave, Pa. You 'ave. But feeding the poor little devils is one thing. Threatening to murder the King and Queen is another."

This was too much, even for the Dances. Charlie looked

bothered. "Who said anything about murdering the King and Queen?" he said.

"That's what they did in Russia. And when things like strikes start 'appening 'ere, it's time the family put a stop to it."

There was mumbled assent in the room, and Ma went on, "All you boys what are not working at the moment, you get up to Whitehall tomorrow and sign on for doing your bit for the country. That's what we think is right, don't we?"

There was an affable pause, a complacent sense of everyone knowing they were right. Sarah felt a sudden urge to annoy them. "What about the miners?" She was horrified as soon as she had spoken, when they all turned and stared at her.

Ma breathed heavily. "We all know it ain't easy when the money stops coming in, but striking ain't the way to settle things. They ought to 'ave a good talk with Mr. Baldwin."

"But they've been talking for five years. And nothing's happened." Then she remembered where she had heard these words. That wretched David Baron had made her say something stupid in front of the family.

Ma stared at her. "Where d'you get these Russian ideas then?"

"I . . . I was just talking to someone, and—"

Charlie was watching her now, with hurt reproach on his face. Remembering her promise to meet David, she was aware of a double disloyalty: to the family ideals, and to Charlie.

"You want to go against the family?" asked Ma.

"No, of course not."

"Right. Then let's 'ear no more nonsense. It's all decided."

The serious business was over and Ma relaxed. "Let those kids come up, Maxie. I got some 'umbugs for them."

IT WAS a strange week that followed, a warm week of long, soft, early summer evenings. London was packed: with strikers, people forced to walk, strollers out to see the fun. Sometimes the streets were pleasant to walk in, at other times not. Buses were stoned or pelted with eggs and refuse, and a bunch of "gay young things" acting as special constables received the contents of some Whitechapel chamber-pots on their heads. After a determined effort in Hull to get a train service working again, trains were turned over and burned. In Leeds an angry crowd gathered round buses used to take wool workers to their factories, and a union leader pulled a revolver on the depot inspector.

But the day before Sarah was to meet David, rumours began to circulate that the strike would soon be over. Somehow, things had become a little half-hearted. Men were drifting back to work, and discussions were reinstated. When she met David in the crowds at the Elephant she was shocked to see how ill he looked.

"Are you all right?" she asked, and was embarrassed when his eyes filled with tears.

"It's off," he choked. "We've lost . . . . All for nothing, all that working and planning to help the miners. The first time people did something for someone else, without thinking what they were going to get out of it, and it's all been for nothing."

She pushed her hand beneath his arm, trying to comfort him with physical contact. "Come on," she said gently. "Let's get away from the crowd."

They walked on down the Old Kent Road, but instead of fewer people they found more, and finally they were unable to move at all except in the direction everyone else was moving. A lorry, guarded by policemen, appeared from the direction of the docks, moving carefully, right in the middle of the road between the tramlines. A brick flew over Sarah's head and smashed into the lorry. "We'd better try and get out of here," David said urgently.

Sarah tried to move, but they were hemmed in, trapped by the surging crowd. Sarah's hat was knocked from her head and lost. She felt David's arm wrenched away, and she turned to see him scrambling to his feet after having been thrown to the ground.

"David!" she shouted. She began to claw her way through the crowd towards a shop doorway. A loud cracking noise broke through the shouting of the crowd and she saw the window of a shoeshop spring into a myriad silver lines and fall in a shower of glass. Two men began to snatch shoes from the display and the crowd milled faster, anxious to disperse before the police moved in.

She had started to run with them in panic when David appeared in front of her, put his arms round her waist, and held her tightly against him. "Stand still," he said quietly, "and look innocent. If you run, the police will be after you in seconds."

They came almost immediately, whistles blowing, pounding through the thinning crowd, straight past those who were standing still, following the people who had taken flight. A sensation of warm excitement welled in Sarah. David's face was only a few inches from her own. His arms were strong and warm and . . . alive. A shiver ran over her as she looked into his face and saw what a beautiful mouth he had.

Suddenly he pushed her away, into the doorway of a cobbler's next to the shoeshop. She saw two mounted police bearing down on them. As David tried to follow her into the doorway a policeman's baton caught him on the side of his head.

He lurched to one side, and she saw his face change, saw disappointment and angry frustration well up in his eyes, to be centred on the policeman who had hit him. "You bloody rozzer!" he shouted. He flung himself forward, clutched the bottom of the policeman's tunic and pulled him down with all his strength. Then he jumped up and clutched the man round the neck. "I'll get you down, you bloody rozzer!"

Thinking about it later, Sarah decided that the blow hadn't even been meant for him, that he'd simply intercepted a clearing thrust of the baton. But now he clung to the policeman in such agonized fury that it took three constables to drag him off and away through the crowd. The last she saw of him he was fighting every inch.

She waited for twenty minutes—twenty minutes in which she became slowly aware of embarrassment at the dreadful spectacle she had just been part of. Supposing Miss Bennett had seen David holding her close, and then fighting a policeman on a horse! It was degrading, losing her hat and having to stand still by a broken window so that the police would not arrest her for breaking it. David was dangerous: already he had brought her confusion and trouble. She felt an urgent need to go home, to sit in Aunt Florrie's kitchen drinking tea, nice and safe.

When the crowd had thinned more, she hurried away. In an alley one of the men who had taken shoes from the shop was kneeling on the ground rummaging among them. "All bloody left shoes!"

she heard him say. "Not a single pair in the whole bloody window."

It was as futile as everything else on this miserable day.

THE STRIKE was over, but everything had to go on just the same. Empire Day was just over a week away. The flagpole must be erected in the playground, the Union Jack unfolded, the children selected to represent the different countries.

Sarah, still trying to atone to the Alexanders for the Sammy incident, called Gertie out and told her she would be Britannia. Gertie's face brightened: no Alexander had ever been chosen for the Empire Day parade or the Nativity Play.

But on the morning of the great day—May 24—Gertie arrived at school with swollen eyes and—as usual—no handkerchief.

"We can't have Britannia crying on Empire Day," Sarah said gently. "You've got to lead the procession, dear." She took her quietly to a corner of the classroom. "Now, what's the trouble?"

"It's me dad," Gertie sobbed. "He's got the sack. He was one of the leaders in the strike. No one will take him on now. . . ."

Sarah felt a laden weight descend on her heart. It was the same old nightmare that hung over all of them.

"What about that Mr. Baron?" she asked slowly. "What's happened to him?"

"'E's got the sack too. Only 'e's in prison for three months so 'e won't 'ave the sack till 'e comes out."

From the playground came the sound of Class Four leading the school out into the procession. Sobbing bitterly, Gertie put on her robe and helmet and picked up her trident.

When they had all gone Sarah remained kneeling on the floor. She put her head down on the nearest desk and let tears soak into the sleeve of her blue dress.

She could hear them all outside, the chanting voices of children wearing drab costumes of made-over clothes and crêpe paper.

> "Today's the Empire's birthday,
> The 24th of May.
> Salute the Flag, salute the King,
> On glorious Empire Day!"

CHAPTER THREE

Sarah's cousin May was slight in build, with her father's dark blue eyes. She was also, as he had been, a giver—generous sometimes to the point of foolhardiness. Partly it was wanting to be loved, but mostly it was just the pleasure of making people happy.

May had never been out of the village. Her father had been killed at sea when she was twelve. She bore her unhappiness with silent stoicism and accepted bravely her inevitable employment in domestic service with dirty old Mr. Fawcett. Though she was human enough to feel envious when her sister was apprenticed to the village dressmaker, she knew very well that there was not sufficient money now for her dear, anxious mother to give two daughters a trade.

And of course there was Peter, Sarah's half-brother. He was very dear to May. He wasn't really her cousin—only by marriage—but he *was* a sailor as her pa had been and had loved her pa as much as she did. She waited eagerly for his shore leaves.

May was content enough in her life until she saw her cousin Sarah, changed by city life into what seemed to May a smart, elegant young woman. Then for the first time in her life May wanted something for herself. She wanted to be like Sarah, so that next time Peter came on leave she would have something nice to give him—herself, made-over and renovated. She decided to get a job in London.

May's search followed exactly the same route as Sarah's—from their old school teacher to the church school, and on to Miss Bennett.

May couldn't believe her luck! To get a job not just near Sarah, but actually working for Sarah's headmistress! She travelled up to Victoria for the interview, her hands spread on the seat on either side of her so that her nervous perspiration would not stain her cotton gloves. Sarah was waiting for her at the barrier, looking anxious. "Do I look all right?" asked May. "Do you think I'll suit?"

Sarah steered her cousin through the station crowds. "I wish you'd think about this, May. I don't know what the brother who lives with her's like, but Miss Bennett's a terrible woman."

Sarah had reckoned without May's quiet determination. "I don't care what she's like. Just one lady and a bachelor gentleman to look after—it can't be worse than Fawcett's."

They began walking towards the river, since May was early for her interview. She stopped and clutched Sarah's arm. "Oh look, Sarah! Big Ben and everything. It's going to be wonderful working in London!"

"I hope so," said Sarah glumly, wondering what refinements of cruelty Miss Bennett would inflict on Cousin May. She could not understand Miss Bennett and indeed she had given up trying. Nothing had happened at the end of her probationary year, and the expected committee letter had never arrived. She did not realize that she was as necessary to Miss Bennett as the public thrashings, simply *because* she had received the post as a personal favour and was mostly too poor and unsure of herself to rebel. The delightful part for Miss Bennett was that sometimes Sarah *did* rebel, and the rebellion could be held over her as a threat. Taking May on as her own domestic would make Sarah doubly indebted to her.

When they arrived at the large, early-Victorian Bennett house in Kennington Road, Sarah watched her cousin disappear inside with extreme anxiety. The anxiety had not lifted when, half an hour later, May came clattering down the front steps. "I've got it! Thirty-six pounds a year, half a day and two evenings a week off. Starting next month. And the house is beautiful, Sarah. It's electric! And there's a telephone in Mr. Bennett's study!"

"Did you see him?" asked Sarah curiously. She had often tried to imagine what Mr. Bennett was like and failed. Miss Bennett seemed above normal relationships.

"No, just his study. He's awaiting the Call to teach the heathen in foreign parts. He was out in Ceylon but had to come back because of ill health."

Ceylon! Beautiful women in saris . . . white elephants trampling disobedient slaves to death . . . gods with eyes made of rubies!

"Fancy living in Ceylon," Sarah said. Her gloom dispersed. She grinned at her cousin and gave her a hug.

"Come on," she said, "let's take the tram down to Brixton market."

They began to run, holding on to their hats and whooping with laughter as they arrived at the tram stop just in time. "Perhaps it's a good thing you're coming to London," huffed Sarah as they collapsed on to a seat. "You won't like Miss Bennett, but you can have fun with Charlie and me on your evenings off."

Since the shaming evening with David Baron she had been virtuously spending most of her spare time with Charlie and the Dances. Although David was out of gaol he hadn't tried to see her again, and she was glad. With his dangerous ideas and his lack of self-control, he wasn't reliable, not like Charlie.

May was clutching her bag tightly. "Could we buy presents to take home?" she said.

"Oh, May! You're *always* spending your money on other people. Let's get you something pretty to wear, a hat or some material for a dress." She twisted round and stared at her cousin through screwed-up eyes. "Blue marocain . . . . With a lace inset down to the hips."

At Brixton the Saturday crowds were so thick that people had overflowed into the gutter. Underfoot was orange peel, tram tickets, and an occasional cigarette card to be pounced on by small boys. Sarah paused by each stall to feel the quality of the fabric. She was idly flicking through a rack of blouses when she heard her cousin say, "There's a man selling purses over there, Sarah. I'll get one for Aunt Florrie."

She became dimly aware of a familiar voice shouting, "Purses, purses made from genuine leather! A quality bargain at sixpence each!" Then she looked up and saw him standing on the other side of the covered lane, a box in front of him with a case resting on it. He looked thin and bent and undignified, and his jacket was frayed at the cuffs. No one should look that . . . that defeated, not when they had led a strike and fought three policemen and held her tightly in a public street. Her eyes filled with tears.

"What's the matter, Sarah?" she heard May ask, but she couldn't answer. David looked across and smiled, a warm, delighted smile. Then he remembered, and the smile faded. He banged the lid of the case down and rushed away through the crowd. "David!"

she called, but he had vanished, and if he heard her he pretended not to. Tears began to run down her cheeks.

"He didn't want to speak to you," May said gently. "Was he a friend?" When Sarah couldn't answer, May continued, "I think he was embarrassed. He looked as if he was out of work, and you know how dreadful that is."

Sarah pulled her shoulders back. "Well, it's over now. Let's go and buy your marocain."

IT WAS the best summer May had ever known. It was the summer of the blue marocain dress, the wonderful summer when Peter's ship was berthed at Gravesend for refitting. Peter seemed to be on leave all the time—coming up to London, handsome, smiling, joking in his droll way and encouraging them to do terrible things like smoking a cigarette. And then there were the four of them, Sarah, Charlie, Peter and herself, going to the zoo, crying over Ronald Colman in *Beau Geste*, and running furiously for the tram so that she could get indoors before 9.30 when Miss Bennett put the bolt on. Anyway, working for the Bennetts wasn't nearly as bad as Sarah made out. Mr. Bennett was no trouble, and though she did occasionally glimpse Miss Bennett's violent temper, it was usually Mr. Bennett who provoked the rages, not May.

The best day of all came in September. Aunt Florrie made up a basket of sandwiches and a bottle of cold tea, and the four of them took a bus to Richmond. There they walked down to the water's edge and Charlie and Peter went into a whispered consultation. Then Peter came back to the girls. "We're going to take a skiff for the afternoon," he said.

"But Charlie can't afford . . ." Sarah began, and then stopped as Peter frowned at her. Charlie led the way to the boathouse and jumped down into the boat. He took off his jacket and rolled it carefully against the back of the seat. "There's a cushion for you, girls," he said importantly. "Peter will see you in and I'll be here to steady you."

Sarah was touched by Charlie's expression. Poor Charlie, she thought, he so loves giving things to people, just like May, and he can't afford to do it very often. She obligingly gave a little squeal as she left the bank, and clutched Charlie's arm, giving him an affectionate hug.

"Cast off forrard, cast off stern!" shouted Peter, and the skiff moved away from the bank.

It was hot and hazy and soundless. Sarah trailed her hand languidly in the water, the way she had seen a lady do it in a magazine illustration. When Charlie was rowing, drops of water would spray off the oars every so often on to the other three, and they would shout at Charlie, not really meaning it but just enjoying being four friends together, having fun, not worrying about things. Four people, safe for one afternoon and feeling sorry for everyone who was on his own.

"Don't we look nice together?" said Sarah dreamily, and they saw themselves with her eyes: two girls in cream sailor dresses and white stockings and canvas shoes, and Charlie and Peter tall and strong. Charlie's hair was bleached nearly white by the summer sun, and Peter brown-skinned and smiling as always.

They pulled into the bank and lodged the skiff against the root of a willow. Up the river someone had a gramophone and, through the heat, came the lazy strains of the "Sweetheart Waltz". It was a green and golden afternoon—green river, green banks, and gold in the sky, in the girls' dresses, and on Charlie's hair.

"I wonder where we'll all be ten years from now," murmured Sarah. "Do you think we'll get the things we want?"

May flicked water into Peter's face, hoping to rouse him, but he only smiled and lay back with his eyes closed. Charlie said, "All I want is a job." This afternoon he was able to say it without shame. "Just a job and I wouldn't want anything else." He stared at Sarah. "Not for a little while, anyway . . . ."

The water lapped gently against the side of the skiff. "What do *you* want, Peter?" Sarah was playing her favourite game, and making everyone else join in with her dreams.

"I don't *want* anything. When my time is up I'm going to leave the Navy. With the money I've saved I'll be able to go back to the village, settle there and make a living."

The music upstream had changed to "Ramona". "That's what I want too," agreed May eagerly. Sarah and Peter glanced at each

other over her head. Poor May, said Peter's face. Don't hurt her, answered Sarah silently.

"What about you, Sary?" demanded Charlie hopefully.

"I want to go to the places Peter has been to, to wander round the world, talking to strange people, and having . . . adventures!"

"But you can't do that for ever," said Charlie. "Even Peter is going to settle down one day."

Sarah waved a hand in the air. "Oh, I'll settle down one day. But I want to *do* things first."

"And I want my tea. Where are the sandwiches?" asked Peter quickly, because he could tell that Charlie was getting upset.

After tea they wandered along the bank for a little way. Charlie held Sarah's hand and May walked behind with Peter. And because it was summer, and the river made soft noises against the bank, because May was so very pretty and her eyes were so adoring and so hopeful, Peter leaned forward and kissed her.

That was the happiest day of May's entire life.

THROUGHOUT the next autumn and winter Sarah watched the condition of the Alexander children steadily deteriorate. It was a dreary winter anyway, with Peter gone for perhaps two years and May trying with pathetic courage to be composed about it.

But all through May's martyrdom and the glumness of Charlie, who was unable to pick up much casual work, Sarah had to watch Gertie Alexander turn into a wizened facsimile of her mother— thin and white-faced, with tired shoulders, for Gertie, as the eldest girl, was the one who suffered most. She was the one who had to run down to the corner shop for a pennorth of tea and please put it on the slate. She was the one who had to look after the children while ma was out cleaning, and answer the door to the tally man and the rent man and tell them no one was in.

Sarah asked the school doctor to authorize free milk and malt for the Alexanders, and got them three free dinners a week as well. She had done the best she could, she assured herself. But her concern only grew worse every time she looked at Gertie. In the end she went round to see the Alexanders.

The woman who answered the door was almost unrecognizable.

"Oh, it's you, Miss," she said tiredly. "Come in."

Sarah could not believe that in two years any woman could have changed so much. Mrs. Alexander was still only in her early thirties, but she was waxen yellow, she walked bent forward, and she was thin to the point of emaciation. Though three of the children were at home, the flat was extraordinarily quiet. Maud and Georgie sat on the floor folding paper spills out of old newspaper, and Teddy, the youngest, was on a chair by the window, staring listlessly down into the area well. It was the wrong kind of quietness.

"Sit down," said Mrs. Alexander. She sagged into a chair by the table. The flat was filled with the watery, stale smell of poverty.

"I don't want to interfere, Mrs. Alexander," Sarah said, sitting down, "but is there anything I can do? Perhaps see the Board of Guardians?"

"We're no worse than many others," Mrs. Alexander said. "We've got the dole and Sammy does a paper round. And Gertie's got herself a Saturday job at the Seven Bells, doing brasses."

"It's just. . . . You look so ill, Mrs. Alexander. Are you having another baby?"

Mrs. Alexander jerked upright. "No! I'm not having another baby. We wouldn't be able to manage." She began to cry and suddenly the colour of her face, the dragging way she moved, became explanatory.

Sarah didn't ask how it had happened. She wanted to pretend to herself that Mrs. Alexander had just had a miscarriage. "Have you been to the doctor?"

Mrs. Alexander shook her head. "I can't," she whispered. "He'd find out what I've done and I'd get into trouble."

Sarah wasn't shocked. But she was encountering for the first time the lengths to which a desperate woman would go. "You'll *have* to go to the doctor," she said quietly. "You can't go on like this."

"I'll be better in a while. It gets better."

Sarah took ten shillings out of her handbag and pushed it across the table. "It's not charity. You can pay me back one day."

Mrs. Alexander clasped a terrible, clawlike hand round the money and began to cry again. "You're so kind. I forget you're their teacher. You're just like us."

Sarah stood up to leave and Mrs. Alexander dragged after her. "Don't let it happen to you, dear. Keep your job, no matter what happens. And be careful about getting married . . . ."

TWO MONTHS later Mrs. Alexander collapsed in the street. She was returning from her cleaning job—three shillings for a morning's scrubbing at the Seven Bells—and had just spent a shilling of it on a marrow bone, some potatoes, and two pennorth of pot-herbs for a broth. When she collapsed the potatoes rolled all over the pavement. Her first words on regaining consciousness in hospital were, "Did someone pick up the vegetables?"

Gertie received permission to stay away from school and look after the family. They grew even scruffier, more pallid, more apathetic. Then one afternoon Sarah was surprised to see Gertie waiting outside after school. "Hello," she said. "How's your mother?"

Gertie's face, tense and grey, stared up at Sarah. "She's come home from hospital and she wants to see you, Miss."

They were now so much her family that she was glad something was happening where she could be of help.

In the flat the bed had been brought into the living room and there were clean, patched sheets over the mattress. Mrs. Alexander lay propped up on several pillows. Her face resembled, exactly, a skull. She smiled when she saw Sarah.

Gertie put her arms round her mother's shoulders, mercifully covered in a flannel nightdress, and kissed her. "She's getting better now," she said.

A lump in her chest, Sarah crossed to the bed. "How are you?" she said.

Mrs. Alexander nodded gently. "It's nice to be home."

Then the door to the kitchen opened and Mr. Alexander came in with a plate of bread and butter and a cup of tea. "A nice cup of tea, love," he said. Mrs. Alexander took the cup from him. "She'll get better now we've got her home again," he said. Suddenly tears began to stream down his cheeks. He stumbled across the room to the kitchen. Mrs. Alexander whispered something to Gertie, and the child followed him.

"I'm going to die," she said to Sarah when they were alone.

"They told me at the hospital. It's all gone wrong inside me and I'm going to die." Sarah did what Gertie had done, put her arms round the thin shoulders.

"When I'm gone," Mrs. Alexander went on, "the Board of Guardians will try to put the kids in homes . . . George won't know what to say. You'll help, won't you? You'll go see them and tell them how important it is? The family's just got to stay together. That's all people like us have . . . just each other." She raised a corner of the sheet and wiped her face. "Oh God," she murmured. "I don't want to die."

I mustn't cry, Sarah thought to herself. She's enough to bear without that. She held her ribs taut and stared out of the window at the flat on the other side of the well. There were the sounds of other people all around them, families bawling up the area well through the warmth of the July evening.

"There's someone at the door," said Mrs. Alexander, all emotion now drained away. Sarah stood up, and as she turned away from the bed her control broke and tears flooded out.

When she opened the door David Baron was standing there. He was shabby, his shabbiness emphasized by the magnificence of the carnations and the large bunch of black grapes he was holding. "Come in and see her," Sarah said.

He walked over to the bed. "These are for you," he mumbled, putting the flowers and fruit on the bed.

Mrs. Alexander smiled. "That's nice," she said.

"Do you need anything? You just let me know what you need and I'll get it for you. You just let me know. . . ." He sat down awkwardly on the bed.

Sarah felt sorry for him. He wanted to show compassion but he didn't know how. When Mr. Alexander came back into the room he jumped to his feet.

"I'll go now, George," he said, relieved. "Just brought a few things round. And I'll come on Friday. You let me know, George, anything at all you want. . . ." And he was out of the door and away from the dying woman and the small sad man.

Mrs. Alexander was leaning back on the pillow, her eyes closed. "Will you go now, Miss?" said Mr. Alexander politely. "The wife's tired, see, and she ought to 'ave rest." His eyes were red-rimmed. "I got to build her up again, like she was before."

"If you need me, send Gertie round." Sarah didn't look back as she left, for she knew what she would see: Mr. Alexander holding his wife's hand and staring into her terrible face.

David was waiting for her on the stairs. Whatever their personal memories, they were all unimportant compared with the dying woman upstairs. For a moment neither of them knew what to say. Then, "Where did you get the money for the fruit and flowers?" Sarah asked abruptly, and equally abruptly he answered, "I stole them."

They began to walk. He annoyed her by staying apologetically just half a pace behind her, but she didn't want him to go. "Have you got a job?" she asked, meanly. "The last time I saw you, you were selling purses."

"I'm working with my father," he said defensively.

So he had gone back to his family, having nowhere else to go. After prison he had needed the reassurance and strength family gave him, even when they scolded him.

"You look dreadful," Sarah said. "Are you ill?" She knew she was being nasty, but she wanted to hurt him for that day in Brixton.

"It's been a bad year, that's all," he answered.

And then she felt ashamed, and miserable about him and about the whole terrible evening. "I'm sorry!" she burst out. "I'm being spiteful and I don't really mean it. I was worried about you when the police dragged you off."

"Can I see you, Sarah? Can I see you again? Please!"

She began to cry. "Yes. Of course you can see me."

"Oh, Sasha, Sasha! That's my own name for you, Sarah." He took her hands and brought them up to his mouth. Feverishly he kissed her palms and twisted them against his cheeks. She could hardly bear to be so close without embracing him.

"You mustn't do that," she cried.

"When shall I see you? I must see you soon."

"I can't. Not often. I don't have time." Already she was afraid of the violence in him, of the strength of his emotions.

"You must see me!" he shouted.

People outside a pub had turned to watch. "Stop shouting," she pleaded. "Everyone's looking at us." Her emotion was a confused tangle of his warmth and violence, and beneath that the memory of Mrs. Alexander. "We'll go and see the Alexanders together," she said, inspired. "Every week. Then you can walk home with me afterwards." She felt tremendously relieved. Somehow helping the Alexanders set a seal of respectability on their meeting.

He quietened, as though the Alexanders and their troubles stilled his own passions. "Yes, Sarah," he said humbly. "If that's what you say, then that's what we'll do."

And so the pattern of their meetings was set. She felt no guilt at using the harrowing respectability of the Alexanders. Their misery, their grief, their poverty were all a part of David and herself.

And when, in November, the tired, sad woman finally died, the habit of seeing each other had become too strong to break. So, while Sarah worked to get Gertie through the labour exams and the younger children back from foster homes, she and David continued to meet every week outside the grim flats off the Old Kent Road.

SECRETS in the East End were hard to keep. Sarah and David were soon seen by one of the Dance family, and immediately Ma Dance went into devious action . . . . When May called round to see Sarah on her next half-day she found four of the Dances trying to push a large horse through the front door and out into the back yard. Florrie was holding a carrot before the horse's nose while Pa, Maxie, Bert and Sid pushed and heaved at the animal's behind. Flies buzzed fiercely over the sweating heads of both men and animal.

May watched with interest while the difficult corner by the kitchen door was handled. At last the horse was tethered to the lilac tree and tentatively chomping at a wisp of hay.

"I don't know why Aunt Florrie has to have a horse in the back yard," said Sarah irritably when May came up to her room.

"It's to do with setting Charlie up in a fish round," May said cautiously. May had got on well with the Dances. At first she had been shocked by them—they were so vulgar, and fat, and sweaty, and *marvellous*. More recently, however, she had even attended a family conference, one from which Sarah herself had been significantly excluded—in the hope, Ma said, that May might be able to *do* something.

Sarah flung herself down on the bed. "Charlie was well enough as he was. He's been getting enough casual work to tide him over."

"He wants to get settled," said May slowly. "You know he's hoping to marry you, Sarah."

Sarah jumped off the bed. "Why does everyone take it for granted I'm going to marry Charlie? I don't *want* to get married."

May took a deep breath. "Is it something to do with David Baron?"

A slow flush spread up Sarah's neck. "Of course it's nothing to do with David Baron! I just see him when I go to visit Gertie, and he walks me home. That's all." She stared at May defiantly.

May twisted her hands nervously together. "You've been so funny lately. The Dances have noticed it. I thought it might be something to do with him."

"Well, it isn't." How could she explain to May the delight, the violence of her meetings with David? Every week they quarrelled, about Karl Marx, or the coming election. And every week David made her feel that she was living in a world where things were happening, where anything was possible. He would surprise her with his sudden changes. Once, in the middle of a heated fight, he had grasped her face between his hands and kissed it. Often he would snatch her hand and hold it against his face. She was glad they were always in public where even he had to control himself. She was quite sure that if ever they were alone together, the tide of emotion between them would flare into something violent and uncontrollable.

"You like him, don't you?" asked May doggedly.

The temptation to confide in someone was too strong. "Oh May! He's so interesting. So *different*!" She flung her arms out in the air. "He makes me feel . . . he makes me feel the world is so big!"

May had been sorry for the Dances, and especially for Charlie, but now she was really worried about Sarah. "If he's that special," she said, "you ought to take him home to meet your pa."

"I can't. I just can't."

David would be completely alien in her village. And there were things about him that frightened her. He stole. Every time he went to the Alexanders he took groceries or clothes or meat, and when she asked him where they came from he simply said, "I stole them." When she protested he told her she was a servant of capitalist dogma. "In our society of plenty, the Alexanders should go hungry?"

His wild words and violent actions would shock and frighten her village. And she loved her village.

Dimly from the back yard came the neighing of the horse. It was a reminder of the Dances and Charlie. "What are you going to do about Charlie?" May asked.

"Charlie's all right. I like Charlie. He's very nice."

"Oh, Sarah!" The distress May felt registered in her voice, and she looked so doleful that Sarah began to laugh.

"Come on, May," she said, not wishing to talk about David any more. "There's nothing to worry about, truly. You forget about David Baron." She put her arm round May's shoulder. "Come on. We'll go and buy some carrots for the horse."

They descended the stairs, and May allowed herself to be cheered by Sarah's gaiety. But she wasn't really satisfied. She decided to write to Peter, enlisting his aid.

THE LETTER caught up with Peter in Haifa. All through the Suez Canal Peter had thought longingly of the rest period in Haifa, but when the time came to go ashore he was suddenly too tired. Increasingly in the last few months this tiredness had beset him so that even the simplest tasks required a superhuman effort.

When he was put on first watch while the others went ashore, he watched them donning their tiddly suits without any resentment. He had four letters from home. One from his father, one from Sarah, and two from May. He opened his father's letter first because it told him about the village and the land which every year away at sea made more valuable to him. Fifteen years of life at sea had convinced him that he was, in fact, a countryman like his father.

Quietly he had planned his future, saving as much of his pay as he possibly could. He intended to buy the meadow that his father rented, turning it eventually into a profitable holding. At night, swaying gently in his hammock, he would design in detail the functioning of the meadow: where he would put poultry houses, how many hives he could accommodate, the soft fruits, the greenhouses and cold frames.

His father's letter was reassuring. The family were well, and no one else had bought the meadow. He turned to Sarah's letter, which was full of ideas and comments on people they knew. It made him grin because it was so much like Sarah—frustrated yet funny. When he read May's letter about Sarah he felt even more sorry for his half-sister, not because she was going out with a "foreigner" but because she was hemmed in by kind, well-meaning people who wanted to keep her in their own safe world.

When I'm home again, he thought, I'll talk to Sarah. Then I'll begin negotiating the sale of the meadow and persuade pa to let me do what I want with it. We might start with some of the soft-fruit bushes . . . . He felt tired again, just thinking about all he had to do.

Towards the end of the watch he began to sweat, great spasms of perspiration that saturated his clothes. He couldn't understand this because the evening was so cool. When his watch was over he went down to his cabin and tried to unstow and sling his hammock, but couldn't manage it. Two of his messmates did it for him. He supposed he ought to report to someone, but then decided it could wait till morning. All he wanted to do was sleep.

He didn't really feel ill—just hot and strange, and terribly tired. And in the morning he felt fine again. He couldn't believe he had been so feverish. When divisions were sounded he went up on deck feeling light-hearted because he was not after all seriously ill with some kind of tropical fever. They stood to attention on deck, the offshore breeze lightly lifting the backs of their collars, and the captain made the inspection in an easy, relaxed way.

He was nearly up to his division when Peter felt the cough rising in his throat. He held it back, waiting for him to pass, but the captain stopped right in front of him. "Your uniform's too big on you, man. Have it altered."

He opened his mouth to say, "Aye Aye, sir," but the cough came out instead. Only the cough was a bright jet of blood that showered out on to the deck and he could feel himself beginning to choke.

His messmates on either side caught hold of him and he heard someone shouting for the doctor.

AFTER the conversation with May, Sarah's relationship with David Baron changed. She could no longer pretend that he was "just a friend". The arguments, the ideas they had together were important, but now she had to admit that more important were the swift kisses, the way her stomach knotted every time she saw him.

At the end of April he took her to a concert and, with their friendship now unbearably intense, she found the music almost painful, aware as she was that he sat beside her. When they left the concert hall he didn't speak to her, just walked her to the tram stop and pushed her on in front of him. "It's going the wrong way," she faltered.

"No," he said. When they changed on to another tram she didn't ask where they were going. She was frightened by him, but excited also. They got off the tram somewhere near Bow, and when they came to a street of terraced houses with doors opening on to the pavement, he took a key out of his pocket and walked up to one.

She began to tremble. "Where are we?"

"My home." He opened the door, drew her into a tiny hallway, and closed the door. "None of my family are here this evening," he said abruptly. Then he kissed her.

It was the most terrible feeling she had ever had, unlike any time he had kissed her before. This was like drowning, her hair released by his hands pouring over her neck, his muttered, "Sasha! My beautiful Sasha . . . !" There must have been a door just behind her, for she felt it open and somehow they were in a small room which was lit very dimly from a distant street lamp . . . . Her coat was on the floor and the top of her dress was unbuttoned and her old-fashioned chemise and "sensible" vest were pushed away from her shoulders.

"Beautiful, my Sasha. Oh, so beautiful!"

And she knew she was beautiful. She freed her arms from her dress and raised them over her head, and she knew her hair was soft by the way he kissed it and wound it round his face.

She found she was capable of things she had not believed possible

53

—she was able to undress with grace, she was able to smile at him without shyness or humility. Her gracefulness made him clumsy and awkward. He fumbled with shaking hands at his coat and shirt. When his arms locked round her, when his chest met her breast, there was a quick indrawing of breath.

But her eyes had grown accustomed to the dimness and now over his shoulder she could see the heavy furniture, the ugly china and ornaments, the photographs standing on a table just behind the sofa. He sensed her sudden withdrawal from him.

"Sasha?" She didn't answer—she was looking at the big photograph of David with his family, suddenly burningly aware of where she was and what she was doing. Her gracefulness vanished. With ugly movements she tried to put her clothes on and hide her body from him at the same time.

"No, Sasha! No!"

She was crying quietly. "This is your mother's house. This is her parlour, her sofa." She tried to fasten her dress and found that some of the buttons had been torn off. "I'm sorry. I should not have done the things I did. I want to go home now."

"I can't let you go home. Not like this!"

She buttoned her coat. She wanted to tell him how sorry she was, how wrong to make him want her, how cruel to provoke his desire by her shameless behaviour. How could she explain that when she saw the photograph of his parents, so like her own, so tired and poor, she had suddenly felt that her own father was watching her.

"I don't want you to come home with me," she said. "I want to go home alone." She fumbled for the catch on the front door and turned back before she opened it. "I'm sorry. Please forgive me. But it's your mother's house, you see."

She went on crying all the way to the tram.

HE CAME and knocked on Aunt Florrie's door the following day after school. Florrie wouldn't ask him in, and when Sarah came out to him he was waiting nervously a little way up the street.

"Walk up to the river with me. I must talk to you." He was white, and there were heavy shadows under his eyes. He grasped her hand when they were only just round the corner from Florrie's and turned her to face him. "Sasha," he said hoarsely, "you must marry me as soon as we can arrange it. Then we'll move away to a new part of London. Our families won't want us, and we'll have to make new friends. But it will be all right because I'm the only one you've ever met who's right there with you all the time."

It was as wild and unpredictable as everything else about him. "You know we can't do it like that," she said. "People like us are too—*ordinary* to do things like that."

He gripped her hands so fiercely that the bones scrunched. "Sarah, if we try to work everything out in the proper way we'll never be able to marry. It has to be done first and thought about afterwards."

"My pa," she faltered, "it would hurt him so dreadfully."

"Sarah—once you start thinking of all the reasons why we shouldn't marry, you'll never stop! There's my family too. Do you know how terrible it is for a Jewish family if their son marries a Gentile?"

"If we leave our jobs, what shall we live on?"

"Stop it!" he shouted. "You're destroying it all. If we stop to think about this, it will be more than we can manage. If you want to marry me, you must marry me now, without thinking. And Sasha," he smiled suddenly, a wide smile that made her heart ache with loving him so much, "you know it will be all right. With us it will never be dull or stale like it is with everyone else. Sasha, you've never lacked courage before. Marry me, Sasha!"

"Yes . . . perhaps you're right. But you must let me think." She wrenched her hands away. "You must let me think for just one night, David. You had last night to think. Give me one night too."

He caught her in his arms and held her tightly. "When you're thinking, Sasha, remember how much I love you. No one will ever love you like this again. You mustn't throw it away, Sasha!"

She threw her arms round his neck and kissed him without thinking about the people she knew who might be walking by. "I love you, David. I love you so much."

He held her hard for one more moment and then he let her go. "I'll come round tomorrow evening," he said.

She turned and walked back towards the house. She had to know if the guilt of walking out on the Dances would be bearable. She had to know if she could face up to a future in which neither of them might find regular employment. Once she had faced these things she could tackle anything.

But at home she found a telegram from her father. Peter had been taken seriously ill with advanced tuberculosis. He had been rushed to the Victoria Park Chest Hospital. Would she come at once.

Wearily she sat down and reached for a pen and paper. There was a letter that had to be written, an impossible, necessary, terrible letter to David Baron. Her guilt at walking out on the Dances she could have faced. But not the guilt that would burden the rest of her life if she walked out on her brother, and her pa.

CHAPTER FOUR

The Chest Hospital bristled with efficiency and an air of comprehensive knowledge. Peter wasn't frightened because he knew he wasn't really as ill as they seemed to think. He had no pain; he was just very tired.

Sarah and May visited him as often as the hospital permitted, May, even more than Sarah, spending her meagre salary on expensive presents. At first, when other people were present, she just sat quietly looking at him, but then she grew bolder and held his hand all the time she was there. And the strangest thing happened: he found himself watching the door of the ward, hoping for the sight of May's small worried face over her shabby clothes, her soft hair wisping out from the ugly cloche hat. She came on her days off, and sometimes she chanced snatching a few hours she wasn't really entitled to. Once she hurried in all out of breath, with her apron still on under her coat.

Sometimes, when he was expecting her and for some reason she couldn't come, his sense of deprivation was all out of proportion to the fact that it was only little May who was coming to see him. Because she didn't talk very much her visits usually meant that he talked instead. He told her about the meadow, and his plans, and he showed her his post-office book with the money he had saved. Her love had ceased to be a gentle burden to him. Now her love was what stopped him from being afraid in the night when, foolishly, he wondered if he was going to get well.

Late one afternoon the doctor arranged to see Peter's father and sister. Sarah promised to telephone May from the hospital afterwards, to Mr. Bennett's special private telephone. It would be her first telephone call ever.

Sarah's father, Jonathan, was waiting outside the hospital main door when she arrived, wearing his best suit and Sunday hat. His shoulders were stooped, his face far older than his years.

"Hello, pa." Sarah held her face up and he kissed her. They smiled brightly at one another, pretending that everything was normal. She put her hand on his arm and they walked along the corridor to the sister's office. They sat on wooden chairs, Jonathan turning his hat between his fingers, till the doctor came out.

"Mr. Whitman?" Jonathan stood up. Beside the white-coated doctor he looked what he was—unsophisticated, a countryman. "Please sit down." They all three sat as the doctor went on, "I expect you know, Mr. Whitman, that we haven't been very happy with the progress of your son." The doctor looked down at the folder in his hand, marked "Peter Whitman". "I'm afraid both lungs appear to be badly affected, so there's no use trying to collapse one for healing. Your son has had two haemorrhages. The next may prove fatal."

There was no sound at all in the room. "I'm very sorry," said the doctor. He fumbled with the folder again. "I don't wish to add to your distress at this time, but we can no longer keep him here. We are short of beds and we are concerned with treatment, not intensive nursing. We have arranged for him to be transferred to the Infirmary tomorrow. Every care will be taken of him there."

"No!"

The doctor looked startled. "I beg your pardon?"

"He'll come home. He'll die at home, among his family."

"But you can't do this," said the doctor. "The disease is highly contagious. Nursing a consumptive patient demands the strictest care if the bacillus is not to spread."

"We've had sickness and trouble before," Jonathan answered simply. "You tell us the rules and we'll obey them."

The doctor looked from Jonathan to the girl sitting beside him, reflecting the same obstinate assurance. Their stubbornness was irritating. But they were good people, he thought suddenly. And they were fighters.

"All right," he said. "You can take him this afternoon. Sister will get him ready."

He rang for the sister, had a quiet conversation with her in a corner of the room, and then said to Jonathan, "Come with me, Mr. Whitman, and I will go through the things you must do. Sister here will call a taxi for the three of you."

Sarah watched her father follow the doctor out of the room. She remembered May. "Please," she said to the sister, "would you help me make a telephone call?"

She gave her Mr. Bennett's number. The sister lifted the earpiece down from the hook and called the operator.

May's voice sounded odd. "What's happened, Sarah?"

"There's nothing more they can do for him here, May. Pa's going to look after him at home." May didn't say anything. "May? Are you all right?"

"Yes."

"I'll have to go now. I've got to see about a taxi and everything. You'll be all right, won't you?"

"Yes."

"Good-bye then, May." There was no answer. Just the click of the replaced receiver.

WHEN Sarah finally arrived home, physically and emotionally exhausted from the strain of seeing her brother on the first lap of his journey, May was sitting on Sarah's bed in her hat and coat. On the floor was her papier-mâché suitcase, tied round with string.

"I'm going home, Sarah," she said. "Back to the village. You see, he might die at any moment." Her thin face was calm. She was as resolute as Sarah's father had been.

"Uncle Jonathan will need help," she went on quietly. "I'll work in the village, and the rest of the time I can help look after him."

"No," said Sarah. "Pa and I have worked it out. I'm to ask Miss Bennett for unpaid leave of absence and go home to help."

"It doesn't need two of us," said May practically. "And it's more sensible if you go on earning money. You earn more than me. And anyway, it doesn't matter what you or your pa decide to do. I'm going home to Peter."

She sat very quietly, her feet tucked neatly together and her hands, all stubby and red from housework, folded over her handbag. She had had nothing from life except her own capacity for love, and now even the object of that selfless love was to be removed.

"There's just one thing," May continued, taking a note from her handbag. "The Bennetts were out when you phoned, so I left without waiting to tell them. I want to get the evening train, you see. I've written my notice." She held out the note. "I'll have to forfeit my month's pay, of course. I was going to leave my notice on the mantelpiece but I thought it looked rude so I wondered if you'd take it round there for me. I know I shall lose my character, but I'll worry about that after . . . ."

A terrible sob burst from her and she stood up. "I'll miss the train if I don't go now."

Sarah followed her down the stairs. Florrie came out of the kitchen with a packet of sandwiches, her face full of concern. "There you are, luv," she said, pressing the packet into May's hand, together with a ten-shilling note. "That's from your Uncle Maxie to buy something for the boy."

She kissed May on both cheeks and then May went out of the door and Sarah watched her trudge up the street. Now I'll go to the Bennetts', she thought. Get that done and then this dreadful day will be over.

SHE HAD to ring twice before she heard someone moving inside, and then the door opened and a strange little man stood there. She couldn't see him properly because the light was behind him. "Yes?"

"I'm sorry to trouble you. I'm May's cousin. I wondered if I could speak to Miss Bennett."

He tutted fussily. "She isn't back yet, and I don't know where May is."

"I'm afraid May has left—a sudden family emergency."

He stared hard at her. "You'd better come in," he said suddenly, turning and leading the way towards the stairs so that she was left to shut the front door and follow him through a huge hall papered in brown lincrusta. She watched him walking up the stairs ahead of her. He had one leg shorter than the other and he wore a heavy surgical boot. Fancy May never telling me that, she thought.

"In here," he said, opening a door on the landing, and Sarah recognized the room from May's description as Mr. Bennett's study: the books, the carvings and the brass statues, the umbrella stand made out of an elephant's foot, the inlaid table and the japanned fire screen.

"Sit down," he said. "You teach at my sister's school, don't you?"

"Yes, Mr. Bennett. My name is Sarah Whitman." Now that she had a chance to look at him in the light she saw that he had curly hair of a nondescript brown that grew to a wiry point on the crown of his head. His face was small, but not thin. She handed May's note to him. "This is May's notice. She had to leave very suddenly because of my brother. He's going to die."

"I'm sorry," said the little man. He limped over to a lacquered cabinet and pulled out a bottle. "I keep a little brandy for medicinal purposes. I shall join you if I may." He handed her a glass, and poured one for himself. It scalded her throat but almost at once she felt better.

"I've had to give May one or two of these since your brother's been ill," he said, smiling, and a warm sense of gratitude spread through her.

He bounced up and down on his chair several times, obviously trying to make himself comfortable. She realized that as well as having one leg shorter than the other, he had a very slightly twisted spine.

On the walls were several photographs—groups of Indians with Mr. Bennett seated in their midst, the veranda of a bungalow with Mr. Bennett standing on the steps, a huge banyan tree with Mr. Bennett resting in its shade, and a painting of the Himalaya.

"Have you actually *seen* the Himalaya?" asked Sarah.

"No. My Calling was in Ceylon. The painting was given to me by a very dear pupil of mine who had served up near the frontier. He was later called to a mission on the edge of the Kubanga marshes. A very primitive people."

The front door slammed. Sarah was amazed at the speed with which the little man moved. In one galvanized action he had pushed the bottle of brandy to the back of the lacquered cabinet, opened a drawer of the desk, placed the glasses inside, and returned to stand by his chair.

"Up here, Amelia," he called.

Miss Bennett came into the study and froze, staring at Sarah.

"Miss Whitman? How extraordinary."

"Miss Bennett, my cousin has been called home suddenly on a serious family matter. She apologizes for the inconvenience. Here is her notice."

"You mean to tell me, Miss Whitman, that your cousin has had the temerity to walk out of this house without any notice whatsoever? How dare she?"

She strode across Mr. Bennett's study with a wild, man-sized stride, and the little scholar leapt well back to keep out of her way.

Suddenly Sarah felt she could take no more. The day had been too much. She muttered "Good evening," and then walked away downstairs as quickly as she politely could. While she was fumbling with the latch she heard a bobbing little walk behind her, accompanied by a furtive "Psst!"

"Good-bye, Miss Whitman," Mr. Bennett said. "My kindest regards to your cousin. And I hope the Lord comforts you in your distress."

"Thank you, Mr. Bennett. You've been very kind."

He smiled, leaning heavily against the frame of the door. "Perhaps Miss Whitman, when your tribulations are eased a little, you would care to come to one of my magic lantern evenings? They are considered entertaining, you know."

"I should like that," said Sarah politely.

A door upstairs slammed violently and Sarah heard Miss Bennett's voice. "Bertram! I wish to speak to you at once!"

He blanched, whispered "Good-bye" once more, and quickly shut the door. In spite of her terrible day Sarah still had sufficient compassion to feel sorry for him.

JONATHAN did manage all right. The bed was put by the front parlour window so that Peter could look out and see the hedgerows and the fields. The life of the house centred round the dying man, and the extra work and money needed in caring for him was a therapy that helped to exorcize their grief. Every evening the soiled handkerchiefs, the bed linen and Peter's night clothes were boiled with soda and disinfectant. His cup, saucer, plate, knife and fork, were scalded in hot water after every meal. He had visitors, but no one with young children.

Peter knew now he was dying, but he fell into a euphoric condition of sleep and peaceful contemplation. He still felt no pain.

May was the one he would cry out to in the night, "Help me, May! Help me! Don't leave me!" With everyone else he knew he must not show his fear, but with May he did not have to pretend. With her arms round him he could cry and tell her he was afraid . . . . "Hush, my dear, hush. You won't die yet. I won't let you."

When Sarah came down he gave her his post-office book—all the money he had been saving. "For pa," he said. "One day when he really needs it."

He watched the winter pass, the bare shapes of the trees and then the snow, and a fire burning in his room. He watched the seagulls that came in when the weather was bad on the coast. And then spring came, the hedgerows yellow with lambs' tails, and the breeze blew through his window smelling of flowers and new grass. May dug up celandine and violets and planted them in an old egg crock for him.

It was May's idea that they should buy the cane bed. When June came, she and Jonathan would wrap a blanket round him and lift him out to the cane bed and he would lie in the meadow he loved so much.

Towards the end of June it became hot, and one day he found that he couldn't bear the heat any more. "Take me in, pa. Take me in," he called fretfully. But as his father started to lift him he felt the blood come up again. He saw the blanket stain red, and specks of blood on the grass of the meadow. He saw his father's face turn white, and over his father's shoulder he saw May begin to run towards him, her hands full of flowers.

Then he died.

SARAH saw May at the funeral, but they were so hemmed round by family and friends that she didn't have time to talk to her properly. Sarah didn't cry at the burial. She had done her crying upstairs in Florrie's house where no one could see her. She wept mostly for Peter, but a little for herself and David too.

The telegram had been more than a simple summons to her dying brother. It had been a reminder that she was still part of a family unit—a unit where custom decreed that its members did not plunge into wildly unsuitable marriages. Even then she had hoped that David would answer her hasty letter with some promise for the future. Instead his reply had been hurt, accusing. "If you had wished it as I do, we would be married now. I would not have stopped you nursing your brother." And finishing, "If you want me, you know where I am."

That was over a year ago. Could anything be the same after a year? If she wrote, not now but when the family were more settled and she herself ready and healed from the agony of the last months, would he answer? She made no conscious plans, but the thought was there, lying beneath the tiredness and sorrow.

In the scullery, when they were refilling teapots for the funeral feast, she said to May, "Are you all right, May?" It was a foolish question, but somehow she had to let May know she was aware of the extent of her loss.

May threw the old tea leaves away. "I'm all right," she answered, without expression.

She was so stiff, so distant that Sarah made no effort to continue the talk. May said good-bye to Sarah at the end of the day almost as though she disliked her cousin, and in the weeks that followed she made no effort at all to see her.

So it was with surprise that Sarah returned from school one afternoon to find May waiting in her room. She sat small and cowed, a piece of helpless flotsam dressed in black, beside her papier-mâché suitcase.

"I've run away," she said. Suddenly tears began to run down her face. "I'm going to have a baby. I think I'm going to have it in November. I'm not quite sure . . . . You see, I couldn't go to the doctor at home. The village would all find out."

"But you can't be, May! You can't be . . . ."

"At night he was so afraid, Sarah. And he needed me so much."

Beneath Sarah's shock she felt a deep, aching admiration for May. Admiration—and envy, because May had not been dissuaded from her chosen path. She had loved Peter more completely, more fully, than Sarah had ever loved David Baron.

"May, you'll have to tell your mother."

"I know, but I can't go back to the village. You know what they're like. Help me, won't you, Sarah?" She wiped her wet cheeks and the black from the dyed gloves came off on her face. "And Sarah, I want to keep the baby. I don't want it to be sent away."

"I'll help you. We'll get a small flat, and between the two of us we'll be able to manage." She thought, Peter, I'm going to have to use the money you meant for pa.

"I can take in sewing and washing until the baby's old enough to be left," said May eagerly. "It won't cost much at first, will it? Not a tiny baby?"

Later, when May had finally been soothed to sleep, Sarah lay awake, facing up to the realization that any lingering hope she had ever had of loving David Baron again was gone. She was now fully committed to her family.

CHAPTER FIVE

They were bad times, the thirties. The depression grew worse and salaries were cut. Even schoolteachers' pay was cut by fifteen per cent, which didn't help Sarah and May and young Anna very much. But somehow they managed. They should, by rights, have been miserable and crushed. They had very little money, and May had been ill for a long time after the baby was born. They lived in an attic flat in Brixton. May was in disgrace at home, and to a certain extent Sarah was too. May had been home once with Sarah and Anna, but the giggles and stares had reduced her to tears. She never went home again. Even worse than the gossip was the silent guilt of her uncle Jonathan who felt that May's situation was somehow his responsibility because Peter had been his son.

But, strangely enough, they managed to be happy. The flat had a bedroom, a living room, and a windowless kitchen. When they were cooking or boiling the washing they couldn't see across the room for steam, and green mould kept growing over the walls. But still, it was a nice flat. Their families contributed a few bits of furniture and Charlie got them some second-hand pieces and brought them round on his fish-cart. They just about managed to skate along on Peter's savings, on the money that Sarah earned, and the little that May could pick up from time to time.

May tried many ways of earning money: evening cleaning when Sarah came home from work; taking in washing; going out as a daily cook and taking Anna with her. Anna (May had called her that after seeing Garbo in *Anna Karenina*) was no problem: she had been born old, and she knew she must be unobtrusive when she went with her mother to work.

Then May, who had thought she was incapable of anything but housework, found an unexpected talent. She saw a notice in the sweetshop window asking for a dressmaker to make costumes for the Butterflies-in-the-Rain Dancing Academy. After a frenzied interview with Madame Parker who ran the academy, she and Sarah unwound fifty yards of pink tarlatan and began to make twenty-five dresses for twenty-five fat fairies. May would be paid ninepence a dress, and they had to be ready the following Friday. By midnight on Thursday, Sarah and May felt ill every time they looked at anything pink, but the dresses were delivered on time and May returned with an order for ten black satin tap-dance dresses embroidered with spangles.

So the money came in fairly regularly, and they were happy. It's hard to be miserable indefinitely when you are young. Charlie distempered the living room for them. He bought them a wireless and charged the accumulator for them every fortnight. He brought them at least one free fish dinner a week, and more towards the end of the month when Sarah was waiting for her pay. He still thought of her as "his girl", though he could see she couldn't leave May and Anna and get married yet awhile.

They were happy too because they were free, free to do as they pleased and go where they wished, subject to the limitations of finance. The place they went to most was the Trocadero—two pictures, a stage show, and the organ in the interval, all for sixpence. And then out to the delicatessen on the corner to buy pease pudding and faggots for supper. Young Anna went with them, fascinated by the screen, and the theatre organ. When she grew tired she went to sleep: by the time she was three she was a connoisseur of the picture palace.

The pictures were their escape. There was Chaplin, and Myrna Loy, and Jeanette MacDonald, and Anna Neagle—*Goo-oodnight Vi-enn-a!*—and Garbo again, in *Grand Hotel.* There was Charles Laughton staring out of the window looking very sad because Anne Boleyn was going to have her head cut off, and then looking angry because Elizabeth Barrett wouldn't drink her porter.

For Sarah, the pictures soothed her desperate sense of wasting life. Sometimes at night she would wake and stuff the edge of the sheet into her mouth to stop from crying. "I'm nearly thirty," she thought. "Nearly thirty, and nothing has happened to me! One day I shall be a Miss Enderby, twittery and terrified of losing my job before I qualify for a pension." She would look across at May's bed, and then at Anna's. "I'm trapped!" she would scream silently to herself. And in the morning her guilt would be so bad she would get up early and bring May her breakfast in bed.

The passing of time was marked by the events at school. Gertie had left at thirteen, and the Alexander family was reunited. Once a week Gertie spent an evening with Sarah and May. Sarah was touched when she saw how important this evening of freedom from drudgery was to Gertie—how the girl dressed up and made an exciting outing of her visit. Gertie spent two mornings a week charring for Miss Bennett. She said she didn't mind it because Miss Bennett was usually out at school and Mr. Bennett was ever so nice.

One evening in the summer of 1934, she turned up with an envelope addressed to Sarah and May. "It's an invitation from Mr. Bennett," she said. "He's put me in charge of Refreshments."

Inside the envelope Sarah found an embossed invitation card for an illustrated lecture on Ceylon at St. Stephen's Hall, by Bertram Bennett, B.A. (Cantab). And on the back, in spidery elegant writing:

> My dear Miss Whitman:
>   Perhaps you will remember my invitation to you at the time of your family bereavement to attend one of my Evenings. In view of your further Family Trouble I have hesitated to do so before, but as I am now accepting another Calling, I presume to invite you and your cousin formally to the occasion described overleaf. I am sure you will find the lecture most edifying.
>
> Bertram C. Bennett.

May took the card from Sarah and read it. Her face went blank. "I don't want to go," she said. "I think magic lantern slides are very old-fashioned."

Gertie's face clouded with disappointment. Not knowing the turmoil in May's heart at the reference to Family Trouble, she felt rejected.

"I'd like to come, Gertie," Sarah said. "You can take a note to Mr. Bennett on your next cleaning morning." Her acceptance was only partly to soften May's words—she was curious about funny little Mr. Bennett: so frightened of his sister, so eccentrically kind.

ST. STEPHEN'S Hall had a raftered roof and rows of narrow wooden chairs. Mr. Bennett was wearing an old-fashioned alpaca jacket. When he saw Sarah he turned pink and a gratified smile spread over his face. "Miss Whitman! How nice! I hardly dared hope . . . I know your duties are onerous." He led her down the aisle. "Please sit here in the second row, where you will see the slides clearly." He ushered her in with a little bow, then bustled back to the projector.

The slides were indistinct and colourless, but the lecture, to Sarah's surprise, was enthralling. It was obvious that, although Mr. Bennett had been sent to Ceylon to teach the people about God, he had actually spent most of his time studying the history, languages and customs. As Sarah listened, her image of Mr. Bennett as a crippled eccentric began to fade and in its place emerged a rather wild little man, plunging through jungles, avoiding crocodiles and elephants, all the while taking copious notes, and then rushing back to the mission to teach the heathen.

When the lecture and the refreshments were over, Mr. Bennett drew Sarah to one side. "I am walking in your direction, Miss Whitman. If you would delay your departure for just a few seconds, I should very much like to discourse with you on one or two points in my lecture."

She was a little embarrassed, but her natural good manners, and a sense of pity, made her stand on one side while the rest of the visitors filed out into the street. He crossed over to Gertie, who, her face furrowed with responsibility, had presided over two large tea urns and several plates of paste sandwiches and rock buns. She saw him press a ten-shilling note into Gertie's hand and she felt again, as she had when she learned he had been giving brandy to May, a glow of gratitude.

Outside he made a point of walking on the outside of the pavement, and every time they crossed a road or turned into another street he would dart about, tripping and bumping into her till he was again on the outside.

"I couldn't mention everything in my lecture," he said. "So many things to describe: the birds, and the turtles, and the flowers! All so beautiful. And the people are beautiful too. They wear sarongs, you know, not saris, blue and white and green sarongs. You see them bathing in the river, their hair and the colours of the sarongs all shining and wet."

"But the lecture was wonderful, Mr. Bennett. All the things you've done—so interesting and exciting." She was no longer sorry for him. Just envious of all the things he had seen.

He flushed. "How kind!" He stared intensely at her. "I wonder, Miss Whitman, if you would care to accompany me to a lecture on China at the British Museum given by a friend of mine."

She paused, because although she wanted to go to the lecture, she felt awkward about going with him. He quickly said, "I shall

not have many more opportunities for lectures in this country. I am accepting another Calling, you know."

"Are you going back to Ceylon?" she asked wistfully.

"To Baluchistan, on the Northwest Frontier. Pathans. The desert of the north. An old colleague runs a small mission there. It has long been my ambition to join him and now a small inheritance has enabled me to fulfil my wish."

To Sarah this was a world one only read of—a world where people were left "small" legacies that enabled them to travel half-way round the globe. It was then, just as she was feeling painfully envious of Mr. Bennett, that she suddenly saw David Baron. He was walking towards her. He looked fatter, and well-dressed, and held a small child by the hand.

He stopped in front of her and stared. "Sasha?" he said at last. "You look well, Sasha. Are you well?"

She nodded, and colour came into his face. He seemed guilty, happy, confused, uncertain. "This is Mr. Bennett. Mr. David Baron." Mr. Bennett stared at David and muttered, "How-de-do," and relapsed into silence.

"I joined my uncle in his leather business," David blurted suddenly. "Quality handbags and handmade shoes and gloves. We have a factory now, the whole family. My father and mother are very happy now." He smiled nervously. "I was a firebrand. I caused them a lot of worry." He saw Sarah looking down at the child. "My son," he said faintly. "My uncle's wife had a younger sister . . . ."

"How really wonderful," she said gaily, "that all your bad times are over. I still see the Alexanders, and they're doing well too! I'll give Gertie your regards, shall I? Now we must go on. It's been lovely seeing you again."

"Sasha . . . ." His eyes were as warm as they had ever been.

"Good-bye!" she sang brightly. "I hope everything goes well for you." She strode on, her eyes so blurred she couldn't see where she was going.

"Miss Whitman! You are going in the wrong direction."

She smiled brilliantly at Mr. Bennett. "How silly of me!" They turned down the next side street and once again he hopped round so that he was walking on the outside. "It's many years since you've seen Baron, isn't it?"

She shrugged, and made the bright smile come back to her face. "Oh, yes. Some time, I suppose."

"You mustn't mind too much," said Mr. Bennett quietly. "When everyday life is difficult it's natural for a man to lean on his family, let them guide his life. You who have such a loving family can surely understand David Baron's family too."

"It's not that. It's not just his marriage. It's all his ideas, the things he made me believe in. He didn't mean them."

"He meant them, Miss Whitman. He probably still believes in them. But it is hard to go on fighting, especially alone."

"But I couldn't do anything else," she cried. "My family needed me. I couldn't go off and leave them!" She turned to stare entreatingly at this man who evidently knew so much more about her than she had realized. Then she said abruptly, "I'll get a tram here."

Quickly he withdrew behind his shell. He held out his hand and made a little bow. "The lecture at the British Museum is two weeks from tonight. I shall take the liberty of ordering a ticket for you. If you will wait for me on the steps at six o'clock I shall be delighted to introduce you to the Land of Green Ginger!"

"Thank you." She wasn't sure whether she would go or not.

For the first time that evening he looked nervous. "I think, with your permission, it would be as well if my sister were not acquainted with our forthcoming expedition. She is highly strung, you know. There is no need for her to be bothered with such a trivial matter."

"No, of course not. And thank you, Mr. Bennett, for a very interesting evening." She was thankful to see a tram coming. He was kind and interesting, but she wanted to get away. She climbed on to the tram and sat staring blindly in front of her, feeling old and ugly and somehow betrayed.

When she got back to the flat, Charlie was there. Dear, dear Charlie who was a part of his family, but still remained loving and faithful.

"Pack your bags," he cried. "You three are off to Brighton for the week. One of the blokes in the market, his sister's been let down and she's got a last minute vacancy. My treat. You goes on

Sunday and I've fixed me fish round with Maxie to come down on Thursday and spend the last three days with you."

"It's worked out right!" said May excitedly. "You've this week before the new term starts, and I'm up to date with the costumes."

It *had* worked out right. In a different place she could forget all about David. It was time she started thinking sensibly, like the Dances were always telling her. She smiled at Charlie and saw his blue eyes brighten because his girl was so happy.

IT WAS a scorching week. They went to the beach every morning, white canvas hats pulled forward to shade their eyes, and their shoes, newly whitened each night, leaving little showers of blanco on the pavement. By Tuesday, greatly daring, they had left their stockings off. They bought Anna a bucket and spade, and when they saw her face brighten with pleasure they both wanted to cry— she was such a funny little girl, and most of the time they forgot she was a little girl at all because she had learned, of necessity, that the most important thing in life was not being a nuisance to people.

By the time Thursday and Charlie came, they all had glowing faces and arms. He bought them cockles and whelks and candy-floss, and took them to Madame Tussaud's, and the Regent's Palace. On their last day he bought May an emerald green taffeta evening dress. Sarah wouldn't let him buy her a dress because there just wasn't anything she looked right in. May, in her emerald dress, looked just like Myrna Loy.

That afternoon May tactfully disappeared from the beach for some "last minute shopping", leaving Charlie and Sarah together. He fidgeted in his deckchair, and she wondered if at last the moment had arrived when he would actually give their marriage a time and a place. She was going to say yes. She had dreamed for too long. But the day was too hot and relaxed for anything unusual to happen, and they simply lay back in their chairs, dozing, and listening to the waves.

They went to the Palace Pier that night, although neither Sarah nor May knew how to dance. Charlie, undeterred, jogged alternately with each of them, and May, in her green dress, found when it was her turn to sit out that she was approached more than once by young men wanting her to dance. She didn't, of course, but it was lovely to be asked.

"Hasn't it been a lovely holiday!" she breathed when they were walking back in the evening air, the lights of the piers effervescing behind them. Charlie and Sarah were strangely quiet.

"A lovely holiday," May said again.

SARAH did go to the lecture, and the week after that she went to another, on the ancient people of the Tigris. Then Mr. Bennett took her back to the British Museum to show her the Egyptian rooms. She felt sorry for Mr. Bennett, but her pity was not the sole reason for accepting his invitations. She had a sense now that the best and most intelligent years of her life were coming to an end. Soon, she thought, she would marry Charlie, and Anna and May would probably live with them, and they would settle down into a comfortable pattern as another unit of the vast Dance tribe. But before that happened she must grasp at every opportunity life offered. And Mr. Bennett offered one such opportunity.

After the first lecture she was surprised to find herself invited to a house in Bloomsbury where people drank China tea and conversed about Ming dynasties. She was fascinated, but appalled at her own ignorance. Mr. Bennett, however, seemed unaware of her shortcomings and after that she was always included in the invitations that followed the various talks.

Sometimes she wondered why Mr. Bennett kept inviting her to things, considering the risk he ran that his sister might find out. She concluded that he was lonely, in spite of all his scholarly friends.

Once he had astonished her by asking if she and Mr. Baron had had occasion to communicate. "No," she had snapped, angry because she didn't see it was any of Mr. Bennett's business.

In fact, there *had* been communication, through Gertie. Gertie had reported that, after all these years, David had been round to see them. "And he asked after you, Miss," she said with interest. "He said he'd like to come round with me one evening."

"I don't want to see him again! Not ever." Sarah had jumped up and gone into the dark old kitchen where she took a long time getting the supper, long enough for the panic to subside. David brought nothing but trouble into people's lives. Charlie was a giver. David was a taker and would always be a taker.

At the beginning of November she had a letter from Mr. Bennett, asking her to stop by his house the following Saturday to discuss "a certain matter". His sister, he added, would be at a Christmas bazaar from half-past two until five.

She showed the letter to May. "I know we were all going to the matinée at the Troc, but I think I'd better go as he's asked me so specially. I'll get Charlie to take you."

Mr. Bennett answered the door even before she had time to knock. "Miss Whitman! How nice!" He led her upstairs into his study. "Sit down, Miss Whitman." He walked over to the fireplace, clasped his hands behind his back, and cleared his throat.

"Miss Whitman. Over the past months I have been watching you very closely, and have been impressed with your ability to learn. I have further noted that you have excellent health and a tidy mind. In addition, you do not shy from accepting responsibilities, heavy responsibilities."

Without knowing why, Sarah began to feel nervous.

"I have thought long and seriously, and have spent much time in prayer, before coming to a decision . . . . Miss Whitman, how would you feel about accompanying me to Baluchistan?"

Obviously, with his legacy and his friend's private mission, he had lost sight of the basic requirements for a qualified teaching missionary. Touched, she said gently, "I am most flattered, Mr. Bennett. There is nothing I would rather do than be a part of your mission team. But I have no knowledge of the language, and no experience at all of mission work."

A slow flush spread up his face. "You misunderstand me, Miss Whitman. I was asking you to come as my wife."

Through her shock and incredulity, something said, Accept! This is your chance, the only way out of the trap. You can see all the things you've ever wanted to see . . . . Accept!

"Of course, I am not a young man," he said, suddenly very humble, his pomposity replaced by stumbling sincerity. "I'm forty-seven, and you are only thirty. I know that." He flushed even brighter and held his hands tightly together. "And I'm not a strong man, not a man you could be proud to look at. But if you would be my wife I would try to make you happy."

He was eccentric and pathetic, but he had dignity too, and sincerity. She was shocked at her own greedy thoughts. He did not deserve them.

"I'm sorry . . ." she said softly, but before she could continue, he interrupted.

"I don't want your answer right now. If you think about it, you may see it's a good idea. Please go away and think about it."

"It would be unfair. You might think I would change my mind."

"But you might!" he answered eagerly. "Now you know that Mr. Baron is married." She stared at him aghast. He was hopping up and down, red-faced, all self-control gone. "And you'll never marry the fat one with the fish-cart. You'd be wasted on him, Sarah. Wasted, I say!"

He reached out to her and she pulled away. She couldn't believe it was Mr. Bennett—all his control, his pedantic eloquence had vanished. She opened the door. "I'm going, Mr. Bennett!"

"Don't say no!" he shouted over the banister as she ran down the stairs. "Think about it, Miss Whitman!"

On the way home she began to giggle, pretending it was all a joke—fancy being asked to be a missionary's wife! She stopped on the way to buy a tin of baked beans as a treat for Saturday tea.

When she opened the sitting-room door, Charlie and May were sitting together on the sofa holding hands.

THEY sat up until three in the morning, talking, crying, trying to explain what had happened, how it wasn't anybody's fault. Sarah's sense of loss was bewildering. For so many years Charlie had been *her* Charlie that she couldn't assimilate the fact that now he was May's Charlie.

Charlie kept making fresh pots of tea and May kept crying. He said he'd always loved Sarah, worshipped her. Only one day he saw May in her green taffeta dress and she looked just like Myrna Loy, and she was so pretty and little . . . . "You're still special, Sarah. But May's suddenly different to me now."

Sarah felt betrayed, and so lonely that she didn't see how she was going to get through the rest of her life. "What are you going to do?" she asked.

"We thought we'd like to get married," said Charlie humbly. "If you don't mind."

"It's Anna too," said May. "Anna needs a father, and Charlie's the one man she trusts and loves."

She was going to lose Anna too! She hadn't thought of that. And Anna was her child almost as much as May's.

In the end there was nothing Sarah could do but accept it. Even though Charlie and May were consumed with guilt, they had discovered that they loved each other. It was a warm, cherished, safe love. A Charlie love. The following day Sarah went round to Mr. Bennett and told him she would be his wife.

MAY and Charlie were married three weeks later at Brixton Registry Office. After the wedding they waited—Sarah, Anna, Maxie Dance, and the bride and groom—in the late November wind for the tram to take them up to Kennington where Ma and Pa Dance were giving a nuptial tea.

In contrast Sarah's wedding was to be at home in the village just after Christmas, and was to be the event of the year.

The village couldn't believe it—Sarah to marry a missionary and preach the Lord's word in Baluchistan! Some people were delighted. May's mother because Sarah's marriage allayed her fears that May had "stolen" Charlie from Sarah. That she had chosen a crippled missionary was exactly what one would expect from Sarah. Now everyone was matched—and her granddaughter given a father.

Jonathan also was delighted—almost. His favourite and best-loved child had done more for herself than he had ever hoped. Only . . . when he saw Mr. Bennett he began to worry, just a little.

"It's what you want, lass, is it?" he asked anxiously. They were standing in the garden, looking over the hedge at the shuttered hives. "I'm not against him! Don't think that," Jonathan said quickly. "Just, I'd always thought of someone more . . . younger . . . more like you, lass."

"I'm strong, pa. I can take care of him."

"If you're sure, lass. If you're sure . . . ."

Miss Bennett, on the other hand, had not spoken or looked at her since the evening she had been acquainted with the news. Sarah, knowing Mr. Bennett's terror of his sister, had offered to tell Miss Bennett herself.

"Oh no!" said Mr. Bennett cheerfully. "I shall quite *enjoy* telling her. Now I don't belong to her any more. And you're as strong as she is."

"I see," she answered, but she didn't see at all. Mr. Bennett was such a strange mixture!

Gertie Alexander cried when she heard that Sarah was leaving, and then all the Alexanders came round and cried too. Anna didn't cry, and that was terrible. Her face buttoned tight and she went about being carefully controlled.

Then, the day before the wedding, Gertie Alexander came down to the village on the evening train, bringing a letter from David Baron!

"He comes to see us sometimes," said Gertie nervously. "Only I never mentioned it because you said not to. I told him that you were getting married. And he was ever so upset—said he was going to come down here and talk to you but I said you wouldn't like that. You wouldn't have liked that, would you?"

"No." She had a cold sensation in her stomach at the thought of David Baron storming into the cottage.

She pushed her way out of the kitchen through the hubbub of family and friends. Outside she leaned against the back door for a moment in the light from the kitchen window and breathed deeply. She didn't want to open the letter. While it was still unopened she could pretend that it was a good letter—that it contained warm and comforting news that would somehow make everything come right again. She held it for a little while longer, then opened the envelope and read.

Darling Sasha,
  You can't do this. It's a terrible thing to marry that old man and you mustn't do it. I nearly go mad when I think of you and him. Please, Sasha! Don't make me suffer like this! I beg you, come back to London and see me, talk to me. Don't marry him. Don't go to

India. Please, Sasha! I can't bear it if you marry him!
Please, Sasha, Please!

David

Agony twisted her hands and made her crush the paper into a ball. How could he! How could he do this just before the wedding! Offering no solution, not even saying he was sorry he had married someone else . . . no mention of his son. Just telling her not to do it! Telling her to go on waiting and hoping for something that could never happen! How could he!

Tears began to flow down her cold cheeks. She did not know how long she stood there, but after a while her weeping died away and, her mind emptied of everything, she became quiet—sunk into emotional exhaustion . . . . When she felt her face was less swollen she dried it on her handkerchief. "I don't suppose I shall ever forget him," she said softly to herself as she turned back to the cottage. "I don't suppose I shall ever forget him."

CHAPTER SIX

The one thing she had not expected from Karachi was the scent of roses. Mr. Bennett had told her about the smells of India—urine and scorched earth and spice—but the first smell that had conscious impact on her was the smell of roses.

When the ship docked Mr. Bennett had hung excitedly over the rail, peering down at the figures on shore. "Amos is there!" he shouted suddenly. "Look—down there to the left."

Sarah tore her eyes away from the sails of the native fishing boats that seemed to lie dangerously cluttered all around the harbour in the leeway of liners and merchantmen. She saw, amidst all the shouting coolies, a tall, cadaverous figure in a crumpled suit and solar topi.

"My dear friend! He has come all the way down to meet us!" Mr. Bennett's excitement grew more and more uncontrollable, and when they finally went ashore he grasped her arm so tightly that she could feel his small fingers biting into her flesh. "Amos," he said, when they reached the skeletal figure, "Amos, this is my wife!"

Mr. Scavener lifted her hand in his and stared sombrely into her eyes. "I cannot tell you, my dear Mrs. Bennett, what a gift you are going to be to us in our work. When Bertram wrote me of his excellent notion I felt it was the answer to all our needs." He turned to his friend. "Did you bring copies of the museum records?"

"All here—also some papers I find were previously overlooked."

They wandered on, Mr. Scavener's steel-thin body bent sharply over the frail one of Mr. Bennett. Sarah quickly forgot them, for kites were falling and lifting overhead, big, black birds against the brilliant white sky. A handsome but dirty Baluchi led a trail of donkeys along the road. Behind him walked the draped figure of a woman in a *burqa,* and behind her a small convoy of cars hooted and screeched.

Mr. Scavener found a horse-drawn victoria and helped Sarah up. And it was then, when they reached the outskirts of the city, that she was suddenly overwhelmed with the scent of roses—masses and masses of roses around the suburban villas. She leaned forward and placed her hand on Bertram's knee. "The roses, Bertram! Smell the roses! Who would have thought that India could smell of roses."

Mr. Scavener bared his teeth in polite acknowledgement of her comment, and Mr. Bennett smiled. "You look very happy, Sarah." He pressed his hand over hers as it rested on his knee; hastily she snatched it away.

"Are there roses at the mission, Mr. Scavener?"

"Er . . . no . . . I think not."

"How big is the mission?"

Mr. Scavener's eyes avoided hers. "The mission is small as yet. This is a difficult country in which to spread the Lord's word." He hesitated, then changed the subject. "Tonight we shall stay with friends on the outskirts of the city to compose ourselves before ascending by train to the hills."

THE MISSION consisted of a large one-storeyed building built around a compound. Faded stucco peeled away from the brickwork and the slatted roof was broken in several places. The entire building was shabby, but Sarah loved it because it somehow captured the essence of the northwest India she had imagined. It had once been a Hindu temple, and familiarity was never to remove this first impression of mystery, of something which to incurably romantic Sarah was akin to the Arabian Nights.

The inner compound was bordered by high stone arches. Columns of brilliant sunlight barred the veranda with light, and when one stepped out of the shade the heat was like a blow on the body. Lizards basked in the dust. At night—the huge, beautiful, sad night of India—the moon shone down through the arches, enhancing their mystery all the more.

It had taken two and a half days to get up to the mission by train, and when Sarah arrived she was too ill to do more than glance at the buildings before she lay down in a surprisingly cool bedroom. Mr. Scavener's allocation of separate bedrooms for the Bennetts was his first action to win him any favour in her eyes. She went straight to bed and stayed there, sick and shivering, for three days. Briefly the remembrance of May being sick before Anna was born smote her. Please God, no, not from that one time. Don't let me be pregnant from that one dreadful time!

On the fourth day she woke feeling rested and calm. There were noises outside, but they were the noises of the country, the noise that is really a silence, with insects and birds and animals echoing in quiet air. Sunlight slatted through the blinds. She crossed to the window and looked out on a wild, eerie landscape, sun-scorched, wind-scorched. In the distance, sharp impossible mountains blurred into the blue mist of early morning. It was beautiful.

She dressed quickly, and hurried out through the arches to stand on the road in front of the mission. The countryside was huge and empty. At first glance, everything appeared to be brown and ochre, but when one stared hard the colours changed. There was red, white, and yellow, and here and there the sage green of a thorn tree. To the left the road curved down into the brown mud huts of the village. There were patches of corn and small groves of vines and apricot trees. A goat wandered by, stopping to nibble at tufts of dead grass. A thin, high-pitched wind sang softly. Sarah had to fight a desire to walk forward and lose herself in the strange empty world of hills and white sky.

"Memsahib?"

A fat, cheerful woman in a voluminous skirt and winding robe stood grinning at her.

"I am Lili, Memsahib. You want breakfast with Sahib Scavener and Sahib Bennett?"

Sarah liked the fat, dirty woman on sight, the way she had liked Ma Dance. "Thank you," she said.

When she went into the breakfast room, the two men stood. "You're better, my dear! I'm so pleased." Bertram came round the table and kissed her, a dry brushing of the cheek, no more than a public acknowledgement that she was his wife.

"You must take more care in hot countries," Mr. Scavener said. "Plenty of quinine, and rest when it is too hot."

"I feel quite well now. When may I begin my duties?" She was fired with love and enthusiasm for her new country.

Mr. Scavener waved a knife in the air. "You can attend morning prayers with us, then come along to our study. We will introduce you to the research we shall be doing."

"But when am I supposed to contribute to the school?"

Mr. Scavener looked uncomfortable. "Twice a week we give a little Bible teaching. But the school is as yet hardly established."

"Then what do I do?" She felt confused and disappointed.

Their faces grew animated. "Our research papers on the tribes, Mrs. Bennett, deciphering and studying the old scripts! Your husband tells me you are extremely capable."

"And you can help the doctor," Bertram added quickly. "Dr. Sircar comes down from Quetta once a month."

"But most important," said Mr. Scavener, "is to keep things in the study right." He rose from his chair. "In fact, Mrs. Bennett, when you have finished your breakfast, I will take you to the study."

In the study a desk and three tables were piled with books, papers, old manuscripts, engravings and charts. Avalanches of paper slid off the sides of the table on to the floor, joining the mounds of books and assorted folders already there. Dust, in various stages of thickness, lay over everything. A bookcase stood with the door open. When Sarah picked a book up, a small stream of ants walked out of it, over her hand and up her arm.

"As you see, Mrs. Bennett, we are not very methodical." They laughed jovially together, two scholars against one ignorant little schoolmistress who was nonetheless a good worker. "In time you will understand where the papers must be put."

Bertram stared fondly at her. "You will like that, Sarah. You are so interested in different peoples and lands."

"But of course, Bertram," Scavener said, "we must not chain her to the tribes all the time. I know you ladies like to spend time getting your households in order. If you could begin in the kitchen, my dear, it would be much appreciated. The meals here are not appetizing at all."

She felt a bitter needle of working-class resentment. Bertram had purchased a bargain: in return for her passage and keep, he had bought a secretary, housekeeper, cook, doctor's assistant and—when time allowed—a mission teacher. She had no one to blame but herself.

And there was the other thing too, the extra thing that a husband was entitled to, that had only happened once, before they left England, and that the divisions of the cabins on the boat had prevented ever since.

"And now," said Mr. Scavener, "it is time for worship." He led the way to the cloistered arches in front of the mission, to where fat Lili, a devout convert, surrounded by the staff, by her several offspring and by some who were not her offspring, stood prepared for prayer.

THE MISSION had been founded by Mr. Scavener's father, a minor Indian Civil Servant and a romantic. In Baluchistan he was given the chance for what seemed to him a romantic life, that of the missionaries, offering themselves for an inspired ideal, healing the sick amidst danger and glory.

The chance had come in the strangest way. Presiding over a land dispute between a rich Brahui tribesman and the people of a nearby village, Scavener had refused a bribe from the village headman. The Brahui had taken this as a sign of Scavener's support, and when he died he left this clear-minded Sahib Scavener the old stone temple where Sarah now found herself. The Brahui had no use for the building, and the presence of a Civil Servant lent lustre to their community.

Upon his retirement, old Mr. Scavener took up residence, with his wife and their small band of servants, in the temple. Bitterly he had by now come to realize that he did not have the spiritual strength necessary for mission work. Instead, he decided to make the mission ready for his son, when he came down from Cambridge and entered the missionary service.

So poor young Amos, who had become increasingly absorbed in research into ancient peoples and had no intention of entering the Mission Society, was trapped by the wishes of a dying man. He came back to the temple, bringing his books with him, and took over where his father had left off—giving hospitality to the nomadic tribes, taking prayers every day, and giving the children of the household rudimentary instruction in English—the only tongue common to the Hindus, Punjabis and hybrid tribesmen who made up the staff of the mission. The rest of the time he spent in study. Sometimes, but not often, his conscience troubled him, for he knew he was not doing the work his father had intended. Now Sarah's coming was a godsend. He envisaged a wonderful life, with his very dear friend Bertram working at his side in his research, while Bertram's young obedient wife dealt with the small amount of mission work required.

In her third week at the mission Sarah awoke one morning to hear unusual noises outside: the tinkling of camel bells, donkeys braying, lambs bleating, the clatter of cooking utensils. Peering through the window, she saw a great sprawling mass of people, animals and tents stretching down the hillside. She pulled on her wrapper and hurried out of her room.

"Bertram!" She knocked, and went in. It was the first time she had visited his room, apart from seeing to the cleaning. Bertram was curled into a tiny bundle on one side of the bed. She pulled the mosquito net to one side.

"Bertram! Wake up! The hillside is covered with tribesmen!"

He was instantly awake. He smiled at her, and her nervousness about the tribesmen was instantly replaced by a different fear. He reached for her hand. "How lovely you are with your hair down," he said.

"Come to the window, Bertram. People are pouring into the mission!"

"I expect they're here to wait for the doctor." He began to stroke her hand. "They have come a long way."

She was always surprised at how strong he was. She could not pull away from his grip without turning it into a trial of strength. He was staring wildly, as he had once before, pulling her closer, forcing her down on the bed. "Sarah . . . !"

The pattern of gentle good manners they had built as a basis for living together disintegrated. Perhaps, she thought, perhaps this time it will be all right.

Then she felt his hands release hers and clutch at the neck of her wrapper. She saw his blue eyes, usually kind, take on a maniacal stare. "Sarah!" he screamed, and the nightmare of his clutching hands and contorted face returned.

But then she heard knocking, and Lili calling—oh, blessed, wonderful voice! "Memsahib? You are there?" The door opened and Lili came waddling in, fat, angelic, normal Lili, mother of twelve, all fathered in normal, marital lust.

"Memsahib, the people have come for the doctor. Sahib Scavener asks that you rise and begin to make a list of their complaints."

"I'm coming, Lili." She dared to look at Bertram. His eyes were normal again, kindly and puzzled. "There are so many people out there, Bertram. It would be kind to Amos if we both went and helped him."

"Of course, my dear." He held out his cheek towards her, suppliant for a marital kiss, a signal that he was a normal husband, and she touched his face briefly with her lips.

Then she rose and left, knowing that it would be all right again until something touched the madness in him. For he never came to her of his own accord—some beckoning attitude of hers had to release it.

And, as the last time, he was especially tender to her at breakfast.

Outside, a slight haze hovered over the khaki-brown hills. As soon as Sarah stepped out into the compound, fierce Powindah women surrounded her, pawing at her and screeching each other down. Lili slapped at them savagely and shouted, and the women quietened and giggled. Sarah hurried over to the surgery.

She enjoyed the next two days, though they were occasionally frightening because the women were strong and rough. Under Lili's guidance she began to learn what questions she must ask, and which women the doctor could not help.

"That one cannot be helped," Lili said, after Sarah had painstakingly written down a list of symptoms. "She is ill like my *lumma* was ill. And my *lumma* died."

"But the doctor must decide that, Lili."

"She will not see the doctor. He is a man."

Many more men than women came to see the doctor, and only a few of the women who did come would submit to his ministrations. His nurse would attend to some of the minor ailments, but serious cases went up to Quetta, to the women's hospital.

On the third day, in the middle of the morning, a small dilapidated car jerked down the road towards the mission, and a young Bengali with prematurely white hair alighted from it. Mr. Scavener leapt forward and clasped him by the hand, and introduced him to the Bennetts. Dr. Sircar bowed politely. He wore a crumpled linen suit, and his hair was long and untidy.

"I'm afraid I have had to leave the nurse at an emergency case just outside Quetta," he said. "A Brahui child, badly burned."

Mr. Scavener waved a vague hand towards Sarah. "Mrs. Bennett and the incomparable Lili will assist you."

"Thank you." Dr. Sircar bowed politely again. "Now, with your permission, I should like to begin my surgery."

He was quiet and controlled, thanking Sarah courteously for everything she did. She wrote notes for him, did the simple medical tasks he asked of her, and in two cases acted as liaison—with Lili as interpreter—for a female patient who would not let him examine her but had to be diagnosed and treated from the next room.

Dr. Sircar had the accent of an English public school, and at

dinner exchanged pleasantries about the changing face of
Cambridge since Bertram and Mr. Scavener had been there. Then
the older men's conversation turned, as it always did, to their studies.

They're both dead, Sarah thought. They are only interested in
dead things because they themselves are dead. She looked from
them to the young Bengali doctor. His face, carefully controlled
though it was, somehow suggested a welter of emotions and
energetic conflict. He, at least, was alive.

The following morning Dr. Sircar asked her politely, "Are you
settling in well at the mission, Mrs. Bennett?"

Her frustration burst out. "There is really no mission to settle
at! The only useful work I have done here has been in the last
three days."

Dr. Sircar looked quickly away from her. "What did you expect?"
he asked quietly.

"I thought I was coming to a teaching mission, and I was
prepared to work hard. What I do here is nothing!"

"But you have your husband, and presently your children—"

"No!"

He caught the panic, the concealed fear and disgust in her voice and said no more. He stood up and went to the window. "So you want to be useful. . . ." It was as if he understood that she wanted to be useful because she didn't want to stop and think, to face the full extent of her dreadful mistake.

She was aware that he watched her, politely, inscrutably, for the remainder of the day, measuring her. . . . When he left he shook hands and gave his careful bow. "Mrs. Bennett, if you feel you must work to some purpose out here, talk to the mission authorities in Quetta. If you join Mr. Scavener on his next visit, I will introduce you to the head of the mission."

She thanked him. The car began to trundle away up the hill road, lurching violently over the broken surface. The hills were beginning to be touched very faintly with red.

She would have given all she had to be travelling with him.

EVERY day Sarah walked out as far as she dared away from the mission. The land began to take its grip on her, dry and dun-coloured, but huge and inviting with its sun-scorched landscape and soft sibilant winds. Sometimes, accompanied by Lili, she walked down to the village and was invited into a hut to drink tea and eat sickly sweetmeats. She frequently recognized mission blankets and utensils in shameless display around the huts. It was all part of the mission's price for inviolability from tribal raids.

It began to grow warmer, and when Mr. Scavener spoke of his next trip to Quetta, Sarah asked if she could go with him.

Amos was plainly surprised. "I had supposed," he said, "that you would stay with Bertram and work on the Bugti papers."

"Dr. Sircar suggested to me that it might be profitable if I spoke to some of the missionaries in Quetta."

Amos blinked. "They are splendid folk, of course, but of little use to us on this present phase of our research."

"I was thinking more of the mission work we are supposed to do," she said gently. "At present I do not feel of any great use."

Bertram and Amos were vehement in their protests, partly as an expression of alarm that their assistant might be tiring of her dreary work in the dusty study. But she was stubborn.

"I would like to see the *real* missionaries," she said, pointedly.

Amos looked slightly guilty. "There are the prayers. And your classes . . . ."

"That's not mission work. We're just keeping a houseful of servants who gratify us by coming to prayers and allowing their children to be taught to read."

A shocked silence fell over the breakfast table. Bertram took Sarah's hand. "I'm sorry, Sarah. I believed I could make you happy by bringing you here, but I forgot how strong you are. You must have a purpose, and it was wrong of me to suppose that my purpose could also be yours." His eyes were kind. He looked as if he loved her, and she felt guilty because she could not love him. "Perhaps," he said to Amos, "it would be good for Sarah to visit Quetta. We must not forget that we have a duty to propagate the Lord's word in a heathen land."

Amos muttered agreement. "But we cannot all go to Quetta, so I suggest, Bertram, that you and your wife go together on this occasion. I will go later in the month. You can stay in the house loaned to me by my schoolmaster friend."

"Thank you, Amos." Mr. Bennett made no polite demur as he usually did. Sarah had the ridiculous feeling that she had precipitated a major crisis in the lives of the two scholars.

"I don't want to alter anyone's plans," she said weakly.

"It is decided," Amos announced. "You and Bertram will go to Quetta, and we shall see what will occur as a result of discussion and prayer." He rose and left the table. It was a magnificent exit. Bertram and Sarah followed, Sarah very humbly.

"I only wanted to *talk* to the missionaries," she whispered. But they had vanished into the study and the door had closed.

IT WAS late afternoon when they arrived in Quetta. The three great peaks towering over the city plain were splashed with red and orange and yellow. It was much colder than it had been at the mission, and it was strange to be in a city again.

Quetta was a garrison town, and the streets abounded with military uniforms. Sitting in the antiquated mission car, Sarah could hear the strident tones of the English memsahibs outside the city shops.

Their bungalow was pleasant, standing in a garden filled with sweet peas and irises. The bearer greeted them at the door. "Shall I bring tea now? Or would the Sahib and Memsahib wish to bathe after their journey?"

"You go first, dear," she said to Bertram. "I shall sit in the garden and have some tea, and write to Dr. Sircar."

She watched him bobbing off, a limp, a little jump, not really a walk nor yet a run. Sometimes her pity became an affection so strong it was almost—but never quite—love.

The garden was beautiful, and peaceful, but in the air there was an electric stillness that made the back of her neck prickle. A slight sensation of foreboding descended on her. She wrote to Dr. Sircar that she was in Quetta and would indeed like to meet some of the people at the mission. She gave the letter to the bearer.

Before he went away he bowed and said, "The Memsahib's

luggage has been taken to the Sahib's room. I shall get one of the women to unpack it for you." He glided away before she could ask if there was another bedroom she could have on her own . . . .

In the bedroom her case rested on a stool by the side of the double bed. She was standing, staring at the bed, when Bertram came in. "I feel quite hungry," he said chattily. "I hope Amos's friend has a passable cook." He limped to the table and placed his brush and comb on it. "I think you had better unpack and prepare for dinner, my dear."

It became very cold after dinner on the veranda, and she had to fetch a shawl to wrap round her shoulders. Yet the air was thick, unbreathable. She was struck again by the sinister feeling that had oppressed her earlier.

"How strange," said Bertram suddenly. He leaned forward and peered at the garden. "The birds are all flying away, though it is nearly night and they should be settling. Perhaps we should retire early. The day has not been a relaxing one."

"You go along, dear," she said, striving to speak normally. "I will come in a little later."

He rose, pecked her on the cheek, and stared once more at the birds. "Curious . . . ." Then he went inside.

She drew the shawl tighter round her shoulders, and sat tensed and strained in the cane chair. Everything had become distorted. The trees were bigger, the sky coming down closer over her. She felt a growing terror that she did not understand. She did not think she slept, but certainly she lost consciousness of time because, when the fear abated a little, she looked at her watch and saw that it was almost midnight.

She rose stiffly and walked into the house. When she opened the bedroom door her husband's breathing was deep and regular. She undressed in the dark, pulled on her nightdress, and lay on the edge of the mattress, as far away from him as she could. Scarcely daring to breathe, she drifted into uneasy sleep.

A screaming, horrible nightmare woke her. She couldn't see Bertram's face, but he was shouting, his fingers biting like steel into her flesh. "Be quiet, Amelia! You will do as I say!"

"It's Sarah, Bertram! Your wife!"

He struck her violently across the face, immersed in his terrible, mad dream.

"Leave me alone, Bertram! Leave me alone!"

He was clawing at her as he had clawed once before, on the night she had tried to forget. "I hate you, Amelia! Unless you do as I say, I will kill you!"

Then suddenly a roaring came into the bedroom, a huge noise that drowned out everything else. In the dim light she saw the floor buckle in enormous waves—drop, rise, twist sideways, rear up to heights that threatened to topple over on her.

She saw the walls break, and then the ceiling begin to thunder down on them. "Under the bed!" she shouted, pushing him, throwing herself after him, his madness forgotten. A great crashing avalanche of weight descended, a choking denseness of weight and pain that blotted out everything else.

SOMETIMES it was almost peaceful and she dozed, or fainted, into a hazy dream, cushioned beneath the wreckage of brick and concrete. But then she stopped dreaming, and began to choke, gasping for air. She managed to loosen some rubble, and brushed her hand over her face. The mere contact of one part of her body with another restored a little of her sanity. I must breathe slowly, she thought, and not panic. Recite, that's it . . . Jesus bids me shine . . . Oh God! It's rumbling again. Oh God! Don't let it happen again!

The ground thundered and rocked, then subsided. Jesus bids me shine with a clear, pure light . . . If I'd married Charlie I'd be safe . . . . She was parched with thirst. She put her hand to her face again, and brushed against the iron spring of the bed. The broken bed sloped down over her left shoulder, forming a small tent that gave her a few inches of breathing space. Bertram, she thought, is he under the bed too? But she couldn't feel him.

Then she heard something moving, down towards her feet, and a dim, muffled cry, and a groaning noise of timber. Rubble showered down from the bedstead above her. Now she could hear a wonderful, rough voice. She cried out, "Here! I'm here!"

Dust and cement fell down on her face again but she didn't mind, for her rescuers were just above her. "Can you shout again, lass? So we know where you are?"

"Here! I'm here! Underneath the bedspring!"

In spite of the dust she opened her eyes and saw a small glow of light above her. It was daylight, the bright light of morning. Hands pulled her out through the rubble. There was a moment when she was completely smothered, and then she was through. A kind, weatherbeaten face stared down at her. "You'll be fine now, lass."

She recognized the way he spoke. "You're from Sussex," she said, and began to cry. "You talk just like my pa . . . ."

She started to tremble and someone put a blanket over her. The soldier stroked some of the dirt from her mouth. "I'm from Dormansland," he said. "You'll be all right, love."

"It's near my village, only a little way . . . . My husband! He's still down there somewhere."

The soldier picked her up carefully and passed her to another who laid her on a clear patch of ground. She stared round her, at a vast, devastated wilderness, everything the colour of dust.

"We'll get your 'usband. Don't you worry."

The soldiers were digging at the hole over the bed. She drew the blanket round her shoulders and picked her way over the rubbish. Round the front of the wrecked bungalow a soldier was lifting out the body of a small girl about two years old. Automatically he passed the small form over to her. The child stared soundlessly with huge eyes as Sarah pulled her into the blanket and wrapped it round them both. She sat down on a cement block and rocked to and fro, holding the child against her. Behind her the soldiers were shouting for Bertram. "Over here! I think we've found him!"

Her heart began to pound and the child in her arms stirred restlessly. "Move the bricks to the left. They're keeping the bed down and I can't move him."

A soldier lay face down in the ruins and stretched his arms down into a crater. A head appeared out of the hole, its face dragging in the dust. "Hold his head up," Sarah cried.

When they laid him on the ground he had never looked so pathetic. His body was blackened, his good leg mangled below the knee.

"He's still alive, Missus," a soldier said.

A lorry came up, bumping over the debris. Two Sikh soldiers lifted Bertram into the lorry and another helped her and the child to climb in beside him. Then it trundled on over the shapeless land, stopping to collect the injured and leaving blankets to cover the dead. In the lorry, next to Sarah and the child, a woman with a baby in her arms slid to the floor. Sarah pulled the woman's shoulders back against her knees, but the head lolled to one side and the baby began screaming. Sarah took it out of the lifeless woman's arms, and as soon as she held it to her own tired body it stopped screaming and went to sleep.

The lorry stopped near the still-standing European Hospital, and the two Sikhs lifted them down. The little Indian girl clung to Sarah's legs so, still holding the dead woman's child, she sat down on the ground beside Bertram's stretcher.

When they carried Bertram inside, Sarah stumbled after with the children. There was a doctor who looked exhausted, and a room of chaos and screams.

Bertram was put on a table and the doctor looked at his leg. "Take the leg off," he said shortly.

"No!" The doctor blinked at her. "You can't take his leg away. The other leg is crippled—he won't be able to walk!"

The tired doctor tried to look sympathetic. "Are you all right? Have you any injuries?" She shook her head. "Then one of the ladies will give you some clothes. Perhaps you could help us." He turned back to Bertram's body.

A woman pulled Sarah by the arm and led her away. "I'll give you some clothes, my dear. And there's a bucket of clean water over there." She looked at the baby and the small girl. "I'll see if we've got anything for them. The military are putting up a refugee camp on the racecourse. You'd better take them over there once you've seen your husband is all right."

She handed Sarah an outsize frock, sandals, and underclothes. When she'd washed and put them on she felt better. It didn't seem any time before they brought Bertram in without his leg.

EVEN the fatalistic Indians were horrified by an earthquake which obliterated a city in half a minute. Quetta stood as a seemingly permanent oasis of the British, raj. There were soldiers, and schools, and garden parties on the Residency lawn, the Quetta clubs and the races. And in the space of a few seconds the whole lot vanished. An area seventy miles long and sixteen miles across was swept into a pile of dust. Although the military cantonment was by some miracle untouched, in the city thirty thousand died.

Sarah did what she could for Bertram. When he came round from the anaesthetic he began to cry, and not all her cajoling and pleading would make him stop. On the second day she took the little girl and the baby down to the tents on the racecourse, intending to pass them over to whoever was in charge, but she found chaos there far worse than at the hospital. Every so often the ground would buckle, and the twenty-odd thousand refugees would disintegrate into terror again. So she stayed there, trying to help a small band of women and soldiers to soothe the hysterical and make a little food go a long way.

The children stayed with her, and by the end of the second day she had acquired three more, none of them older than six, and all unable to remember who or what they had been before the earthquake. She went back to the hospital twice a day to see Bertram, but there was nothing she could do for him. At night she slept in a tent, and every morning when she came out there were a few more small children dumped there with nowhere else to go. They were all very young, since the older children, able to explain who they were and where they had relatives, were drawn back into their own clans.

On the fourth day she saw Dr. Sircar. His face was grey and he was wearing pyjamas and a raincoat. She ran after him.

"Dr. Sircar!"

He turned, stared, nodded. "Good. They got you out then. I told the soldiers you were there. I got your note."

"Thank you. We're both safe. But my husband has had to have a leg amputated."

"I'm sorry," he said. He looked at the forty-odd children that trailed behind her. "These are some of the homeless?"

She nodded.

"Provision will be made for them. We cannot expect you to do any more."

His expression was cold, even resentful. She could hardly blame him. All the English women were soon to be sent away, to be soothed and helped to forget their dreadful experience. He had to stay, and watch his own people salvage what was left.

She heard herself say, "They won't leave me. They're afraid, and they've grown used to me. If the authorities permit, I shall take them to the mission until something can be sorted out."

"You think you can care for so many children at the mission? What about Scavener? And your husband?"

"The place is supposed to be a mission," she answered stubbornly. "I shall take them, and ask afterwards."

He smiled at her, a flash of white in a brown-grey face. "There'll be no trouble with the authorities," he said. "I'll talk to them. The army will lend you a lorry. It will only be for a while until things are settled."

Guiltily she remembered Bertram. "What shall I do about Mr. Bennett? I can't leave him, and Mr. Scavener won't be able to manage a lorry load of children on his own."

Dr. Sircar's smile vanished. "The wounded are being evacuated to Karachi," he said impatiently. "You can do nothing for him there."

She knew that the loss of a man's leg was little compared with the overall disaster. "As soon as he goes," she said, "I'll take the children to the mission. I can look after the children here while I wait." After all, the whole point of her coming to Quetta had been to get herself a mission.

ALTHOUGH Amos Scavener had heard about them from Quetta, his reaction to the arrival of Sarah and a lorry load of nearly sixty children was to lock himself in the study. Lili was equally shocked, but brave enough to stand her ground and register disapproval. "Ay . . . eee!" she cried, throwing the end of her robe over her face and rocking backward and forward.

"Don't be foolish, Lili," said Sarah tiredly. "Thousands of people have died, thousands are homeless. The least we can do is take these poor children into our mission."

"But Memsahib, they are native children! Not Christians!" Her round face stared in appalled sincerity at Sarah.

"Well, we can turn them into Christians."

Behind Sarah, soldiers were lifting children down on to the sun-baked earth. They gathered together and did not move.

"They can sleep in the compound until we have sorted things out," Sarah said. "We must get blankets from the village . . . ." She suddenly saw that here was the bribe necessary to line Lili solidly up behind her in the coming battle with Mr. Scavener. "We must buy supplies from the village people, Lili," she said blandly. "You see to that, Lili. And we shall need extra help."

There was a moment's pause while Lili conducted private calculations. "Perhaps the Memsahib will need an extra Christian girl to help with the teaching. My sister's child has been taught at the mission in Lahore."

"We'll talk about it later. First we must feed these little ones."

Lili beamed. "Come unto me!" she said, holding out her arms. She repeated it in Brahui, Hindi, Pashtu and Urdu, and Sarah saw flickers of recognition in faces previously unresponsive. Lili, like Ma Dance, would love and spoil the children once her prejudices had been overcome.

She waited until the children were being washed, and then went to the door of the study. She knocked, and called, "It's Sarah Bennett." The key turned in the lock and Mr. Scavener stared dismayed round the edge of the door. When he saw that Sarah was alone he beckoned her in.

"I had feared, Mrs. Bennett, that some of that *rabble* might be with you."

Sarah braced herself. "The rabble are in the compound being washed and fed."

"They must be gone before Bertram returns to us. He must have perfect peace in which to recover."

"They will not be leaving us, Mr. Scavener. They have nowhere to go. They are part of the new Scavener mission."

A blotchy mauve stole up from beneath Mr. Scavener's starched collar. "Mrs. Bennett, I know you have been under severe strain—and of course poor Bertram's tragedy has affected us all. But even allowing for that, you exceed yourself!"

"I intend to exceed myself. These children need a home. Most of them are too young even to remember what religion or race they are. Once they are settled in we must approach some established missionary groups and ask for their advice and blessing."

Mr. Scavener's face turned purple. He shouted, "This is *my* mission, I shall do what I like with it. You will do as you are told!"

Sarah felt nothing but irritation. "In that case, Mr. Scavener, when Bertram is well enough, I think it better that we leave."

"*Bertram will not leave*," he screeched. "We have waited for years to do our study together and nothing—certainly not you—will make him leave now."

"But he will have to," she said mildly. "He will not be able to walk again, not even on crutches, and from now on I must do everything for him. We stay together, or we go together."

She thought he was going to strike her. "How dare you wreck my life like this."

"Mr. Scavener, thousands of people have died, thousands more are homeless, and you talk of your life being wrecked."

His fury turned to unease. "But I do not like children," he said.

"I shall see they do not bother you."

He glared at her. "You give me no option, Mrs. Bennett. But I shall not forget your impertinence. Bertram made a grave mistake in his choice of partner. You are an ignorant, vulgar upstart."

"Thank you," she said gently. "Thank you for my mission."

CHAPTER SEVEN

Mr. Bennett did not return to the mission for seven months. The stump of his amputated leg became infected, and this was followed by pneumonia. Sarah was truthful enough to admit relief at his absence during this period of trial and confusion. The sheer physical labour of providing food, clothing, shelter and some measure of discipline for sixty children was considerably more than she had anticipated.

Once a month she made the journey down to Karachi to see him, and when she returned she invariably found the children running wild, the younger ones unfed, Lili sulking, Mr. Scavener locked up in his study in a state of near apoplexy.

By the end of the summer, however, they had arrived at some kind of order. The crumbling rooms of the old temple had been cleaned, patched up, and divided into boys' and girls' dormitories. When Dr. Sircar came, he brought four large crates of clothing from the relief fund.

"Do you need any help?" he asked.

"When Mr. Bennett comes home he is going to need a lot of my time. I wish there was someone who could share authority with me then. You see, Mr. Scavener will be delighted if things go wrong and the authorities step in and close us down."

They stood in silence for a moment. A kite circled and wheeled in the hot, white sky. "It is peaceful here," Sircar said. "Even with the children it is more peaceful than Quetta . . . . This is not my country, you know. I am from Bengal, in the east."

A thin, high-pitched wind whined round them, a wind that brought no coolness. Dr. Sircar shrugged his shoulders suddenly. "There's nothing we can do about trained help for you at the moment," he said. "All the missionary groups are strained to breaking point. But later I'll see what can be done. Meantime, I shall resume my medical visits, and naturally I will care for the children. Are they satisfactory at the present time?"

They were not. Two or three had bad sores and one a severe case of dysentery. Sarah led the doctor into the compound for a make-shift surgery.

JUST after Christmas Sarah was able to go down to Karachi and fetch Bertram. The day she arrived was actually their first wedding anniversary, but she tried not to think about it and she hoped Bertram would have forgotten.

The doctor explained to her that Bertram would have to spend the rest of his life in a wheelchair and that, because of the

98

deformity of his spine, movement of any kind would be difficult for him. He would need constant assistance.

"Fortunately, I gather your husband's interests are scholarly," the physician said, "so the adjustment will not be too severe." Then he paused, looking puzzled. "I told your husband about the limitations he must accept, and it was quite extraordinary, he seemed almost relieved at the news."

When Sarah went in to see Bertram she saw that all his depressions had indeed vanished. He was smiling, and seemed overjoyed to see her. "Sarah, my dear! How pretty you look."

"How are you, Bertram?" She kissed his cheek.

"So very well, my dear. And so looking forward to helping you with all the children. We were spared, Sarah, so we must give all we can to those who have lost their loved ones."

"Amos is not too happy with the idea," she said hesitantly.

He tutted in an amused, patronizing manner. "Poor Amos has buried himself so much in the past, he has forgotten the needs of the living. Anyway . . . ." He suddenly took her hand in his and smiled at her. "I have known for some time that there was not enough for you to do. You're such a *shiny* person, Sarah! So alive and full of warmth. I want you to be happy. I like to see you happy."

She couldn't speak. Tears choked her, and they were not just tears of pity. There were times when his perception and genuine affection for her made her wish she could love him, whatever sickness warped his mind. "You're very good to me, Bertram," she managed to say. She kissed him, for the first time with real tenderness. His blue eyes lit up and his little gnome's face was suffused with colour. She sat holding his hand for the rest of the afternoon, talking about the children.

The journey back to the mission was trying, a strain for both of them, so that their arrival at the mission brought a relief out of all proportion to what they could expect to find there. Amos was waiting in the compound, hardly able to contain his anxiety. He now hated Sarah so much that he had quite expected her to whisk Bertram back to England, leaving him alone with some sixty undisciplined orphans.

"Bertram! You cannot know how gratified I am!" The two

friends clasped hands. Then Bertram turned to look at a group of children standing under the stone arches. "Amos, it is good to be back, back to such splendid work! Sarah has told me how you opened the mission to these refugees. At last, Amos, the chance you have been waiting for!"

Amos bared his teeth in a strained smile. "Ah, yes, well . . . your wife looks after all that. We shall conduct our work as usual, Bertram, shall we not?"

Bertram smiled blandly and raised one hand as though blessing not only the children, but also Amos. "The Lord will find time for us to do a little of everything."

The pattern was established, formed round the tiny frail figure of the man in the wheelchair. It became apparent that, of the two scholars, he was the more dominant. When Bertram decided to help Sarah teach the children English, Amos resentfully consented to be present at the classes, and his assistance—bad-tempered though it was—proved very useful for he knew most of the languages spoken by the children.

Life at the mission, though busy and sometimes noisy, was well-ordered. Sarah found that running a class of children in India was not so very different from running a class in England, and sometimes, when she was helping Lili ladle out vegetable curry to a jostling line of children, she was reminded strongly of milk duty at Miss Bennett's school.

During that first year, eleven of the children were reclaimed by distant relatives. No one else was ever claimed, and in the second year they were joined by Dr. Keynes. He was not a medical doctor but an experienced missionary who spoke several dialects fluently. Middle-aged, zealous, he was delighted with the opportunity to form a Christian orphanage, and Bertram and Amos could again spend the entire day in their study.

Dr. Keynes was able to explain to Sarah what a curious and isolated place the mission was. The country all around was full of violence, resentment, tribal wars. The whole Northwest Frontier had found a new battle cry: *J'Hai Hind*, independence for India. They must be careful at the mission, for even their own villagers, who felt proprietary towards the mission, could turn against them if they felt conditions were changing. Sometimes, quite close, they could hear shooting. But the dreamlike quality of the hills blunted Sarah's sense of personal danger.

She had come to love the mission and the sense of space around it, and thought she could never bear to see Quetta again. Yet when at last she made a visit with Dr. Sircar her fear of the earthquake was lost in her stimulation at the sight of the city being rebuilt.

Without ever really knowing Dr. Sircar, she became a colleague and companion to him. The barrier of politeness between them remained, but she learned to know his moods, his passions and his tolerances. On one occasion he brought her mail from home—it was another of the excitements of his monthly visits—and in the evening she sat down in her favourite place looking out over the hills and opened her letters: from her father, from May, from poor old Miss Enderby now retired and filling her penurious and wasted life with the borrowed glory of a missionary friend, and from Gertie Alexander . . . .

"Things is so much better now than they was before because of us all working. It upsets me when I think of how we never had nothing when ma was alive. Remember how David Baron brought her all them things he nicked? He was good to us, he was, and he's been good since. Only he's in trouble now with the police again and is Inside. Took part in one of them fights in the East End—all them fachists or whatever they're called . . . ."

So in all these years he hadn't changed. Still spoiling for a fight, eager to throw himself without restraint into something in which he believed.

"I hope your letter does not contain bad news, Mrs. Bennett."

She turned to Dr. Sircar. "No. Well yes, in a way. Someone I know from the old days is in trouble. He is Jewish, and I gather he assaulted a policeman during a Mosley march on the East End."

"I see."

She wondered if he did see. She could not imagine him understanding why anyone should attack a policeman. "If only he could control his passions," she said quietly. "If only he could learn to fight with discipline."

"Everyone fights the way they can, and to believe in something strongly, is reason enough to fight."

She stared at him in the evening light, but his dark eyes were unfathomable and she was suddenly a little afraid of him.

"You must not grieve for your friend," he went on. "He is happy. He does what he wants to do."

"I think I'll go in now," she said abruptly. "I will be ready tomorrow, as soon as you wish to begin surgery. And perhaps you would be good enough to look at Bertram again. He gets so sore."

"Of course." The simple medical conversation made them mission colleagues once more.

Bertram's sores were bad. He complained very little—he must have grown used to pain in his life—but she knew they caused him constant unease from the way he tried to move his body to a more comfortable position. Dr. Sircar looked at the sores and said, "These will go once you are propped up on rubber rings. I will bring some down from the hospital. And Mrs. Bennett must help you to sit on one side if she can."

"I am so fortunate to have Sarah," said Mr. Bennett. "She looks after me without neglecting any of her other duties."

Dr. Sircar began to pack his things away. "Try to rest a little," he said quietly, and then followed Sarah from the room.

"Is there something wrong with Bertram?" she asked.

"Nothing specifically. But he seems a little tireder, a little less strong, and he is losing weight. Try to make him rest, and make sure he eats well."

She was immediately worried. The time since Bertram had returned to the mission had been so orderly and busy and tranquil that she had allowed herself to be lulled into a sense of purposeful security, forgetting that life always had some unpleasant shock not very far away.

But she allowed herself to be soothed by the promise of extra work in looking after Bertram. At first nursing, washing, helping him with the simplest needs of his body, had proved embarrassing for both of them. By now, however, it no longer embarrassed either of them. She had almost completely obliterated the memory of that other Bertram, and knew only a gentle, perceptive, suffering man for whom she could feel pity, admiration, and deep affection.

She tried to make him follow Dr. Sircar's advice, to rest, and break his long routine of study. But he was childishly sulky about any change to his established pattern. In her concern for him she pushed David Baron so far to the back of her mind that when, a month later, a letter arrived from him, it was with a sense of shock that she recognized the wild, thick-stroked handwriting on the envelope.

Dear Sarah:

I know you hate me, because in all these years you have not once written to me or sent a message. But I am writing to you anyway, because I have no one else to talk to, not in the way that you and I used to talk.

Terrible things are happening in Europe. I have been in prison and this time there was no work for me when I came out, for my family no longer want me. My wife has gone back to her father's house with our son. She says unless I stop getting into trouble at meetings she will not come back. But Sarah, I *cannot* stop.

I am living in a hostel, as you see from the address. A man called Wiseman bought this place for Jews who have escaped but have nowhere to go. Some are children without parents. Write to me Sarah. I have no one to talk to, and at night I cannot sleep when I think of the English who will not believe until it is too late. And I miss my son. Please write, Sarah.

David.

The letter did not upset her, because only the mission and the sun and the wind were real now, and because David made no personal appeal, just the plea that she would write. She told herself that she would make time for writing, but she never did.

When Dr. Sircar returned on his next visit, he suggested that Bertram should be taken down to Quetta for a complete examination at the hospital.

"I do not think there is anything seriously wrong, Mrs. Bennett," he said, "but he is not as he should be. I am shortly going on leave and I think your husband would prefer to go to Quetta while I am still here. I shall be returning to England for a year, to stay with friends."

She was astonished. "You are going to *England*?"

"I have many friends in England. I shall stay for much of the time in Sussex. You know that part of England. Perhaps you have heard of my friends, the St. Clairs of Grantley Hall?"

"No, I haven't heard of them." But she knew what Grantley Hall would be like. It would be like the Fawcetts' house where she had once worked as a parlourmaid. "Sussex is a big county," she said. "I only know the people round my own village."

"Ah, I see." He smiled, and she knew he had mentioned his grand friends deliberately.

"But if you're going to be in Sussex anyway," she said cheerfully, "call in and see my pa. He'll make you very welcome." And then she couldn't help giggling, because she thought of Dr. Sircar sitting in the front parlour under the illuminated text "Repent ye!" with the R of Repent twined about with lilies.

"Why are you laughing?" he asked stiffly.

"Just . . . my family. I don't think you'd like them very much."

"I like courageous people." He gave a bow, intended as a compliment. Then he continued, as if the conversation about Bertram had not been interrupted at all, "So I think it a good idea if your husband come to the hospital with me on my next visit."

"I'll see what he says. I will probably have to persuade him, and I don't want to frighten him into thinking he is ill."

Surprisingly, it was Amos who persuaded Bertram to go. He had himself been a little worried by his friend's health, he seemed thinner, and there had been times lately when he had dozed off even in the middle of a piece of research.

"I think, my dear friend," he said, "that you should sojourn at the hospital for a short while. While you are there, Mrs. Bennett can arrange for you to see one or two people connected with our thesis."

Though he hated to leave the sanctuary of the study, Bertram reluctantly agreed. They left with Dr. Sircar when he had completed his March visit, Bertram propped with pillows and wrapped with blankets in the back seat.

Sarah had made the journey to Quetta several times and knew the route, where the side of a mountain would rear up next to them, where the track would level on to a rolling plain of desert and scrub. It was fortunately on such a comparatively flat stretch that the rear left tyre blew.

Dr. Sircar lost his temper and began abusing the driver for not having checked the tyres before they set out. The driver answered sullenly that it was not his fault if the doctor's car did not function properly. The driver went to the back of the car to get the spare. When he came back he looked frightened. The wheel was in his hand, the three-inch tear in the tyre visible to all of them. Sarah thought the doctor was going to explode.

The driver began to whine. "Not my fault, Doctor. I was not on duty when we left. Joseph had the car last."

Dr. Sircar folded his lips tightly together, and then said more calmly, "We are not too far from Quetta. You must walk to the first village, borrow a donkey or camel and then go to Quetta and fetch a car for us. And at the village you must send men back to collect us."

"It is a long way, and my legs are not good." The driver was young and appeared in excellent health. Dr. Sircar began to lose control again and the driver hurriedly changed his mind. "I go. I go now."

He set off along the road, walking quickly and looking nervously at the rocky hills on either side. Then he disappeared around the wall of a ravine ahead. Sarah climbed out of the car and made Bertram as comfortable as she could along the length of the back seat. "Try to sleep a little, dear," she said. Then she walked over to Dr. Sircar who was staring ahead at the distant ravine. It was late afternoon, and livid colour, orange, scarlet, pink, was beginning to touch the hills. It was very quiet.

"It's strange that we haven't seen anyone on the road," she said. "There's usually an army lorry, or a tribesman of some kind."

"I do not want to be here when it gets dark," he said tensely. "We have no rifle, and the absence of traffic indicates that something is happening in this area."

"But we should have heard if there was any unrest round here.

105

We are always posted about the troubled parts of the country."

"All the country is troubled, Mrs. Bennett," he said tiredly.

Sarah had never worried before when travelling up to Quetta, but it had always been in daylight and the tribesmen had known that the precious person of the mission doctor was in the car. "But all the tribes know you and need you," she said.

"If it is Pathans from the north, to them we are only strangers and a motor car."

She listened with him, straining for the sound of men coming from the village, but the desert remained silent.

The sun moved behind the cliffs and they were in shadow. She shivered and pulled her coat up at the neck. "Perhaps we are a little exposed here. Should we go back to the car?"

"Let us not disturb Mr. Bennett. If they intend to shoot us they will do it wherever we are."

The hills darkened and she was suddenly overwhelmed by the same uncanny fear that she had experienced on the evening before the earthquake. "I'm going," she said, and began to walk across the rocky ground. The last light had vanished and a prickling sensation moved down her back. Abruptly the night was shattered by a blaze of rifle fire from the ravine, ricocheting against rock, flashes of light cutting through the darkness.

Sircar shouted, "Get down!" and she threw herself forward. More rifle shots, then the echoes died and an oppressive silence fell. She heard a rattle of stones behind her.

"It's me, Mrs. Bennett." Sircar was sliding along the ground just behind her.

"We must get to the car," she said. "Bertram will be so frightened."

She felt his hand on her shoulder. "Wait. They are still there."

"But he's on his own."

"We are safer here." She heard him swallow, then whisper, "They are not shooting at us. They are shooting at the car."

"No!" She wrenched away from his hand and scrambled towards the car. There was another wild burst of gunfire. A bullet spat by her leg and she threw herself flat again until the firing stopped. Dr. Sircar crawled up beside her.

"Don't do that again," he whispered fiercely. "They'll shoot at anything moving."

"We must get Bertram out!"

This time he didn't protest. He moved forward with her until they came to the car. He opened the door. Bertram was lying exactly where she had left him.

"Bertram!" She reached out to take his hand. Something warm and sticky was flowing down his wrist. "Oh, God! He's bleeding. Please come and help him."

Sircar leaned in and took the sticky hand in his.

"Bertram!" she called, "it's all right. We're going to get you out."

"He's dead, Mrs. Bennett," Sircar said.

Somehow she had known.

"He's dead. That's right. He's dead."

The air was rent with more rifle fire, making patterns of light and noise. "Come, Mrs. Bennett," Sircar said gently. "We must crawl under the car. It isn't safe here."

They remained there for three hours, until a platoon of Gurkhas arrived. Sircar had said that lying under the car would give them a little protection but, in fact, after that final burst of firing, it remained quiet. They learned later that the raid had been one of several in the area, attempting to wreck cars and military transport. With the exception of Bertram, no one had been killed.

AFTER Bertram's funeral Sarah returned to the mission for no longer than it took to collect her things and say good-bye to Dr. Keynes. He did not even try to make her stay, for he knew how Amos hated her. "I know you cannot continue working here, my dear," Keynes told her. "But we shall never forget that it was your efforts that brought the mission into being. The mission society could use you in other centres."

She thanked him, shook his hand, and left. In her mind was a vision of her Sussex village. Already she could feel it acting as balm to her tired body and spirit. I'm going to lie face down in a field, and listen to the crickets and birds, she thought.

Dr. Sircar had managed to get her a berth on his ship, but it was not due to sail for four weeks so she stayed in Karachi. She was not brooding, or grieving. She was just tired.

She boarded the ship. Ate at the right times. Spent a lot of time leaning on the rail, staring at the wake. When she looked at the water she did not have to think of anything. Sometimes Dr. Sircar stood with her, and mostly he responded to her silence with a silence of his own. On one occasion, however, he refused to remain silent.

"I would like to know, Mrs. Bennett," he said, "if you feel ill or tense. Your behaviour is not normal, even allowing for the death of your husband. I am concerned for your health."

She stared at him. "I'm not ill. I'm just tired."

"But what are your plans for the future? Naturally you will go home first. But after that, what will you do? You are tired, yes. But there are so many things that people like you and I must do! It does not matter if they come to nothing. You and I must attempt the impossible!"

"I can't do it any more. I'm tired." And she walked away from him because she did not want to talk about it any more.

At Naples she received her mail: from the family, Gertie, Miss Enderby, the Dances, and one letter, which she did not expect, from a London solicitor. It told her that she was the sole legatee of her late husband's estate . . . .

She went in search of Dr. Sircar. "Look!" she said, showing him the letter.

He read it. "But of course," he said. "What did you expect?"

"I'm rich!"

"I would hardly say rich, Mrs. Bennett. But certainly you are provided for."

He didn't understand the difference between being poor, and being provided for. No one except the poor understood that.

"Will it make any difference to your plans?" he asked.

"No. Yes. I'm not sure."

Now her pa wouldn't have to worry about money any more. May should have some, and young Anna could go to a good school. I'm rich, she thought, and a joyful leap of excitement shot through her. She was guilty about this excitement, but nothing could stop it.

Her apathy vanished. She talked with Dr. Sircar a lot, discussed the possibility of running a mission of her own, or a school in London, of travelling round the world, of having her hair permed, of buying some land for her father. When she spoke of her pa, Dr. Sircar said surprisingly, "I would like to meet your family, if it could be arranged. I hope the end of this voyage does not mean we shall not meet again."

"I hope so too." She smiled at him warmly. "I'm sure one or other of my family will come to meet me at Southampton."

They all came.

She stood against the rail by Dr. Sircar and watched the quayside grow bigger, and the crowd turn into individual people. There was pa, beloved pa! With shock she saw that he was an old man, white-haired and bent. But now he wouldn't have to work any more. She would look after him, make him happy.

May was there, slimmer and more elegant, a Londoner now; and beside her was Charlie, huger, redder, and with an enormous bouquet of flowers leaning against his shoulder. Anna was gripping May's hand. And behind them Sarah could see a solid phalanx of Dances. A chara, she thought. I bet they hired a chara. And there was Gertie Alexander, and two of her brothers.

Then, standing at the back of the crowd, hands hunched in pockets and face scowling, she saw David. Thin, fierce, no doubt fighting lost causes again. With a jolt to her senses that was almost physical, there came a sense of purpose, of what she must do.

Beside her Dr. Sircar was anxious and uncertain. "I would very much like to see you while I am in England," he said hurriedly. "If you would give me your address I could write to you."

All the Dances had seen her now and were shouting and waving. Dr. Sircar thrust a piece of paper into her hand. "This is my address in Cambridge. I would like you to come and stay while I am there."

"I'll do that." Pa was lifting Anna into the air, but she was really too heavy for him and finally Charlie took her and perched her on his shoulder. The gangplank was down. David had seen Sarah. He was still scowling, but he had seen her. Poor David, she thought, always trying so hard to set the world to rights on his own.

But she was humble enough to recognize that she needed him as much as he needed her. She was good at doing all the practical things, and good, too, at knowing people's hearts. But she was never able, as he was, to mount a gigantic cause, to tackle a wrong so huge that it seemed it could never be put right.

"You will write to me?" Dr. Sircar said. "You will come to Cambridge?"

She turned and gave him a brilliant smile. "Of course I'll come. It is very kind of you to invite me."

And then she was walking towards the gangway with the lift of anticipation she always felt at the beginning of something new. She looked at David. His eyes hadn't moved from her face since he had first seen her. She knew there would be fights and quarrels once again, but she also knew she would enjoy them.

She remembered Dr. Sircar, and waved back at him. Then she forgot all about him. Life was good. It was eventful and unknown, a big adventure. She was still young. It was 1939. And she was going to work with David Baron.

Diane Pearson

Diane Pearson was born in Surrey and spent much of her childhood with her grandmother in a small village in southern England. It is from her grandmother that she gained the sympathetic feeling for the twenties and thirties that makes her books about these years so vivid and memorable. She began writing when she was sixteen, and since then has published several novels and innumerable short stories. Her work has appeared not only in Britain and America, but also throughout Scandinavia and in Germany, France and Holland.

She is now an editor with Corgi Books, and lives with two stout cats in a converted coachman's cottage in south London. In the district she is known to be always good for a free meal (or two) for any down-and-out dog or cat who happens to be passing. In the spare time her job and her doss-house activities leave her she is busily researching for her next book: an ambitious story, gathered from the personal experiences of her friends, of life in Hungary from the turn of the century to the present day.

THE RUNAWAYS
Victor Canning

The Runaways

A CONDENSATION OF THE BOOK BY

VICTOR CANNING

ILLUSTRATED BY THOMAS BEECHAM
PUBLISHED BY HEINEMANN, LONDON

When fifteen-year-old Smiler discovered he was sharing his hideout with an escaped female cheetah, his first reaction was one of terror. But Smiler too was a fugitive—from an Approved School—and once he had made sure he was quite safe, he began to have conflicting feelings about the big cat. On the one hand, a dangerous animal should be reported to the authorities. On the other, she was a fellow runaway . . . .

This story of a "wanted" boy at large in the English countryside, and of the animal for whom he comes to feel a responsibility, is an unusual mixture of suspense, quiet humour and first-class nature writing. It involves some highly original characters, from the resourceful poacher who—like Smiler—had "never done anything really bad", to the eccentric lady dog-breeder who believed that young people should be left to solve their own problems.

How right she was in Smiler's case, and how he solved his problems, readers of this engaging book will enjoy finding out.

One

It HAD been raining all night, and all the morning; raining hard all over Dorset, Wiltshire and Hampshire. It was a cold February rain that spouted over blocked gutters and flooded the low-lying roads so that passing cars sent up bow waves of spray. Now, at half-past eleven precisely, as Smiler was being driven in a police car under the escort of two burly patrolmen, a thunderstorm was brewing overhead. At first it was a few little murmurs, slowly rising to a full-scale roll and rumble. Suddenly there came a great stabbing sword thrust of lightning that turned the whole world into a dazzle of light.

Smiler jumped in his seat and cried, "Blimey!"

The policeman alongside him smiled. "Nothing to be scared of, son. Just think—if we hadn't picked you up, you'd be soaked even more." He glanced at a pile of wet clothes on the floor of the car and then at the blanket-wrapped figure of Smiler.

It was a red-and-yellow blanket and all that could be seen of Smiler was his head sticking out of the top, his fair hair still wet. Smiler—real name Samuel Miles—was fifteen, tallish and well built, with a friendly square face, a pressed-in smudge of a nose, and a pair of angelic blue eyes that made him look as if butter wouldn't melt in his mouth. He had escaped two weeks before from an Approved School, and been picked up that morning by the police. He had been caught because of a tip from a farmer in whose barn

117

he had been hiding (and whose hens' eggs he had been eating, sucking them raw).

Smiler wasn't scared. It took quite a lot to scare Smiler. The lightning had just made him jump, and he didn't much like it, that was all. There were a number of things Smiler didn't like—school, for instance. Particularly he didn't like Approved School—he had run away from it after exactly thirteen days' and four hours' residence. He didn't much care for the country either. He preferred towns, where there were more opportunities for picking up the odds and ends that made living tolerable.

After all, when you were mostly on your own, you had to have a bit of money in your pocket and be able to go to the movies now and then and treat yourself to a Coke in a café when you felt like company. Smiler didn't like being idle; he liked doing things. The trouble was that people made such a fuss about some of the things he did—like pinching a bottle of milk from a doorstep or nicking a comic book from a shop.

Most of all, Smiler didn't like the long periods when his father, a ship's cook, went off to sea. Then, instead of living in lodgings with his father and having a wonderful time, he was dumped with sister Ethel and her husband, Albert. They were all right, but they fussed about their house and their furniture and grumbled when his hands marked the paintwork..

The driver grinned at Smiler's reflection in the mirror. "You look like a red Indian in that blanket. Chief Sitting Bull."

At that moment there was a tremendous clap of thunder and two hundred yards ahead a streak of lightning flared earthward. It seared into the branches of a tree, wreathed its way down the trunk and hit the ground with a crack that shook the earth. A great branch crashed across the road. The police car skidded to a halt twenty yards from the obstruction. A car coming the other way was not so lucky and it slewed sideways into the branch.

The two policemen jumped out of the patrol car and dashed through the rain to give assistance. It took them three or four minutes to climb over the branch and assure themselves that the other driver was in no great distress. It took the driver of the patrol car another few minutes to get back so that he could radio headquarters to report the road blockage and summon help. As he sent out the call he knew that he would also have to report the escape from custody of one Samuel Miles. In the car mirror the policeman could see the back seat. The only evidence that Smiler had ever sat there was a damp patch on the leather.

Smiler at that moment was running up the side of a ploughed field, with his clothes gathered in the blanket. As he pelted towards a crest of woodland, which he could just glimpse through the driving rain, he was smiling because he was free. This time he meant to stay free. Just what he would do with his freedom he didn't know—except that he was going to enjoy it until his father got back from sea. His father would quickly clear up the misunderstanding that had sent him off to Approved School.

Meanwhile the second policeman had returned to the car. He took one look at the back seat and said, "He's gone?"

"With our blanket," said the other. "Do we go after him?"

"In this weather? Not likely. He won't get far when the call goes out for him." The policeman grinned and said jokingly, "Wanted: Chief Sitting Bull. Height five feet two inches, fair-haired, blue-eyed, age fifteen plus, wearing a red-and-yellow blanket. Approach with caution. This man is dangerous." He paused, then added, "Wanted person's face is heavily freckled."

As Smiler reached the cover of the woods, he crashed into the undergrowth like a rocket and put up a couple of pheasants, who flew away, honking and screeching. The noise so startled him that he slipped and fell flat on his face. While he lay there, getting his breath back, he gave himself a talking-to. Smiler was a great one for lecturing himself in moments of crisis.

"Samuel M.," he said (Smiler was other people's name for him and he didn't much care for it), "you got to think this out. You're wet and hungry and half-naked. You are wanted by the police like a real criminal, which you aren't. It was never you that took the old lady's handbag. Thing Number One, then. You got to get warmed up, fed and into hiding. Thing Number Two. You'd better get them wet clothes on. Wearing a coloured blanket is going to make you stand out like a circus Indian."

So Smiler got to his feet and struggled into his wet blue jeans.

As he did so there was a bellow of thunder away to the west and the whole sky was lit with another blaze of lightning. Though Smiler could not know it, this lightning was doing exactly the same for another prisoner as the previous bolt had done for him.

TEN miles away, a little southwest of the Wiltshire town of Warminster, was Longleat, the country estate of the Marquis of Bath. Part of its large park had been turned into a wild-animal reserve. Nearly every day of the year cars brought tourists to see the lions of Longleat and the other animals which were kept in huge, penned-in stretches of the parkland.

The road ran first through the East African section, which held giraffes, zebras, ostriches and antelopes; and then on through the monkey jungle, with its baboons that often cadged free rides on top of the cars; and so into the lion reserve, where the kingly beasts sometimes lay lazily across the roadway refusing to move out of the way. Finally the cars entered the cheetah area.

On this stormy February day there were no more than three or four cars in the reserve. In fact, there were few animals to be seen. The baboons were in their dugouts and the lions in their wooden pens. In the cheetah area all the cheetahs were sheltering in their huts—all except one.

Her name was Yarra. (All the cheetahs had names: Apollo, Chester, Lotus, Tina, Schultz.) Yarra was a full-grown female. She stood nearly three feet high to her narrow, raking shoulders; and from the point of her black nose to the tip of her long tufted tail she measured seven feet and one inch. She was a magnificent animal. Under the rain the spots on her tawny orange coat were as black as wet coals. The dark lines of her face mask, running from inside the eyes down around her muzzle, were boldly drawn charcoal. Her throat and underbelly were creamy white, and her eyes tawny gold.

When the cheetah warden came into the enclosure in his Land Rover, Yarra could jump in one easy long-flowing movement to the top of the cab. Sometimes, to give the cheetahs exercise, the warden trailed a piece of meat from the back of the Land Rover for them to chase. Even when he accelerated to forty miles an

hour, Yarra could easily keep up with the car. If he had gone at sixty, she could have held pace for a while.

Today Yarra was strangely restless. It was not the restlessness that overcame her when her keen sight marked the movement of guinea fowl, pheasant or young deer on the free slopes outside the enclosure; then she would race to the wire fence, longing for the freedom of the hunt and the chase. Yarra did not know what had made her restless, but where normally she would have taken shelter from the rain, she now found herself stalking up and down the long boundary fence. Made of strong two-inch mesh, the fence was over twelve feet high; it was supported on strong wooden poles, with here and there a concrete pillar for added strength. Inside it was another fence, about four feet high, which the cheetahs could have jumped easily, but they never bothered.

There was a low rumble of thunder, and a stronger burst of rain slashed into Yarra's face. She sat down on her haunches close to the inner fence, shook her head and blinked against the rain.

It was at this moment, as Smiler was pulling on his wet jeans ten miles away, that the sky above burst with an earthshaking roar of thunder. A great bolt of lightning was loosed through the low-hanging clouds, hitting the outer fence of the cheetah enclosure a few yards from Yarra. The lightning found the metal bolts in a concrete support, and fence and support were ripped from the ground. The falling top half of the support flattened the low inner fence just by Yarra. She leaped, snarling with fright, into the air and came down on top of the collapsed section of the outer fence. As thunder rolled angrily again she was gone. Impelled by fear and shock, she streaked away up the long grass slope outside the enclosure towards a wood at the top.

It was less than twenty minutes before the cheetah warden in his Land Rover discovered that Yarra was gone. He immediately began to organize a search party. By then Yarra was three miles away, beyond the wood, moving slowly down the lee of a small apple orchard. The land dropped steeply below her. A mile away she could see a road with cars speeding along it.

Yarra watched the road for a while, and then began to work a line across country parallel to it.

IF THERE was an instinct in Yarra to keep away from roads and people, there was the same instinct in Smiler. Dressed now in his clothes, he trotted along the downlands that ran away from the wood, being careful to keep below the crests of ridges. He had no idea where he was; all he knew was that the policemen had been taking him to Salisbury.

He travelled like this for two hours and never did it stop raining. The rain soaked into his thick tweed jacket so that it became a sodden weight. His wet jeans rubbed the insides of his thighs. The water ran down his fair hair, plastering it to his head like thickly spread butter. He was hungry, and beautiful pictures of steaming sausages, hamburgers and golden potato crisps floated before his eyes until he gave himself a smart talking-to: "Samuel M., keep your eyes open for danger, not for food." At the same time he knew he must find shelter for the coming night.

He crossed several roads, hiding first in the hedges and then darting across. Now and then he would sing quietly to cheer himself up—songs he sang when his father played his mouth organ. Sometimes when his father was home they would go out on Ethel and Albert's bicycles and freewheel down hills, both singing madly. Once or twice his father had hired a car and taken him out, and when they were on some quiet road had let him learn to drive.

He was trotting up a river valley, the stream heavy with floodwater to this right, when he saw ahead of him a grey stone bridge. Cautiously he moved out on to it; there was no one in sight. On the far side, set a little back from the water's edge, was a long, low thatched cottage. A board on the garden gate read FORD COTTAGE. Behind the cottage stood a barn.

Smiler eyed the cottage for some time. There was no smoke coming out of the chimneys, and the curtains at all the front windows were drawn. He whistled quietly, speculatively, to himself and then trotted up the road to the yard entrance. Beyond a big five-barred gate, which was padlocked, was a courtyard with a well in the middle, and beyond that the barn with an open car bay at one end. Beside the big gate was a small side gate which was not locked. Smiler went in and walked around the house and barn, peering through the chinks in the drawn curtains and going right into the barn and up the wooden ladder to the hay-filled loft. There were no signs of life, and no recent car tracks on the soft mud at the entrance to the car bay. At the back of the car bay was an old bicycle.

It wasn't difficult for Smiler to get into the house. In his hometown there were certain boys who knew the ways of householders with their keys. Nearly everyone, when he went away, locked the front door and took the key with him, and nearly everyone locked the back door and hid the key where the person who came to keep an eye on things could find it. The back-door key of Ford Cottage was tucked away on a porch rafter.

The door opened directly into a large kitchen. Smiler went in and closed the door behind him. It was a nice kitchen, though now a bit gloomy with the curtains drawn. Smiler flicked the light switch by the door. The centre kitchen light came on. Smiler flicked the light off. He went to the sink and turned the cold tap. Water ran from it.

Five minutes later Smiler was out of the cottage (the back door locked and the key returned to its place) and up in the hay-loft of the barn. He had with him two tins of sardines, a package of biscuits and a large bottle of hard cider. The whole lot he carried in a thick car blanket which he had found in the little hall outside the kitchen.

Smiler picked a spot on the hay bales where he could lie and watch the yard through a dusty, cobwebbed little window. Methodically he stripped off his clothes and spread them over the bales to dry. Then he wrapped himself in the car blanket and began to attend to the inner man. Within fifteen minutes he had eaten all the sardines and most of the biscuits, and had considerably punished the contents of the bottle of cider. Almost immediately he began to regret the cider because it started to make his head spin. He flicked his eyelids up and down to clear his vision so that he could watch the yard. But it was no good. The last thing he remembered before slumping to sleep was giving himself a good talking-to: "Samuel M., my lad, you wolfed your food and swigged your cider like a glutton. If you don't end up being sick, it'll be a miracle."

WHILE SMILER was snoring on his hay bales in the loft, Yarra was about a mile and a half away on the far side of the valley. Her restlessness was still with her and she was also hungry. It was between five and six o'clock in the evening, which was past the cheetahs' normal feeding time. More significantly, this was a Tuesday, which meant that Yarra hadn't eaten since Sunday. In their wild state the big cats hunted and then ate, and hunted again only when hunger returned. To have fed them regularly every day would have dulled their appetites and, in the end, injured their health. So, each Monday, the big cats at Longleat were starved.

Moving along the grass headland at the side of a fenced-in pasture, Yarra caught the quick movement of something white. Immediately she froze in her tracks, her right foreleg poised in mid-air. Beyond the fence was a large wooden chicken house, and scattered around it was a flock of White Leghorn fowls.

Yarra watched them and rich saliva rose to her mouth. She stretched her jaws silently and then dropped low. For all her bulk Yarra moved under the bottom strand of the wire fence like a silent flow of molten gold. Fifty yards away she marked the nearest straggler from the flock, a cock bird with a white, cockaded tail and wattles of shining vermilion. Although she had been captured as a well-grown cub, and had never done much hunting for herself, she moved now as surely as though she had spent all her time in the wilds where she was born.

She was twenty yards from the bird when it saw her. Its head turned with a jerk, and Yarra streaked across the winter-pale grass in two running leaps. The cock screamed in alarm and jumped high, wings slashing the air. Yarra took the bird three feet from the ground, her jaws closing over its lower neck, breaking the vertebrae. A great white explosion of feathers sprayed into the drizzle-soft wind. There was a noisy gust of alarm from the other fowls as they scooted for the hen house.

Yarra, holding her prey high, raced back to the wire fence and cleared it with an easy spring. She found a hollow ringed by gorse and broom bushes and, crouching down, began to eat. When she had finished there were left only the wings, the once boldly arched tail and the stout yellow legs of the proud cock.

Yarra groomed and cleaned herself, then lay for a while on her side, contented.

The rain stopped and the wind began to clear the clouds from the evening sky so that a few early stars showed thinly. Yarra rose, her unnameable restlessness back with her. But this time there was habit with it, too. Each night in the reserve Yarra, with all the other cheetahs, was herded by the warden in his Land Rover into the night pen at the bottom of the enclosure. Night was coming fast now and Yarra moved on to find shelter.

Half an hour later, the dusk thickening, she came down a valley-side and up on to a high bank above a main road. A car went by, but Yarra was used to cars and its movement did not alarm her. She dropped down the bank on bunched feet and was across the main road like a shadow. On the far side a minor road ran down towards the river. Three-quarters of a mile away Smiler was groaning and holding his head, knowing that within the next few minutes he was going to be violently sick.

Yarra padded down the road, flicking a front paw now and then with irritation because the ground was running with water from the overflow of a small ditch at one side. At the bottom of the lane she crossed over a stone bridge and stopped just short of a padlocked gate, which was the barn entrance to Ford Cottage. Although it was almost dark she could see the barn across the yard, with an open doorway cut in its lower weather-boarding. The doorway reminded her of the entrance to her sleeping hut at Longleat. She took one long leap, high over the five-barred gate, and then padded towards the barn.

She was almost at the old wellhead when a figure came through the open barn door. Yarra froze. The figure turned along the side of the barn with a curious stumbling movement and disappeared. Yarra knew it was a tallish human being, one to be treated with respect. It was the very small human beings that roused the killing instinct in her and her kind, the children who looked through the windows of the cars going around the park. To her they were small game to be hunted, like young deer.

She waited for a while to see if the figure would return. After a time she moved slowly across to the barn door.

Two

SMILER had been sick in a little orchard behind the barn. He felt better, but his head still ached and his stomach was queasy and tender. He walked down a small path to the edge of the river, where he knelt and splashed water over his face and head.

Five minutes later he went back to the barn. The ladder that led to the loft was just inside the door. Beyond it the floor of the barn ran back in darkness for about thirty feet. His head still dizzy and throbbing, Smiler turned through the door and groped for the ladder rungs. He did not hear the sudden movement of an alarmed Yarra. She rose to her feet, jaws open, her face mask wrinkled with fear and anger, and gave a spitting hiss of warning—which also went unheard by Smiler as he climbed the steps. He reached the top and dropped the trapdoor with a thump.

Yarra settled again in the straw litter, flat on her side, her head thrown back. She was tired, and she was disturbed by the restlessness in her. She sensed a slight irritation in the dugs along her belly. Her belly itself felt strange and slightly swollen. What Yarra didn't know, and what her cheetah warden would have been delighted to know, was that she was going to have cubs. The father had been Apollo and the mating had taken place thirty days previously. In about sixty days' time Yarra was due to litter. Cheetahs seldom breed in captivity and those at Longleat had shown no signs of doing so—which was perhaps why Yarra's condition had gone unnoticed.

Slowly, her restlessness fading, Yarra dropped away into sleep. Above her, in a nest of hay, Smiler slept too, snoring gently.

JUST before first light Yarra woke and left the barn. She went through the orchard and down to the river, where she crouched and drank. Then she moved slowly up the narrow footpath that fishermen used in the trout season. A hundred yards from Ford Cottage an unwary moorhen got up from a dead patch of reeds almost under Yarra's nose. She took it with one swift pounce.

An hour later Smiler woke, warm and dry and feeling better. He lay back on the hay, looking out of the dusty window, thinking. Since it was impossible for him to work out any grand plan for the future, he had to be content with a short-term view. He must keep out of sight as much as possible and have a base which would give him shelter, warmth, food and drink. Ford Cottage seemed a good base if it were going to be empty for some time. The deep freezer and the food cupboards were well stocked, as he knew. That he would be using someone else's house and supplies didn't worry him very much. After all, he thought, if he had owned the house and there was a young chap like himself on the run—because everyone had gotten everything wrong—he wouldn't have minded if that young chap had helped himself. Thing Number One, then, was to find out if the cottage was really unoccupied and, if possible, for how long it might stay that way.

So from his barn window Smiler watched the cottage all that morning. The only person who came to the house was a postman who pushed some letters through the back-door slot. For lunch Smiler ate the remaining biscuits and drank a little cider.

An hour later he had a shock. An elderly man came walking down the road, stopped at the courtyard gate and looked across to the barn. Smiler saw him shake his head and then come through the side gate and cross to the barn. He heard the open barn door being banged-to on its catch. His heart beating fast, he saw with relief the man moving back across the yard to the lane. Smiler gave himself a black mark for carelessness. The door had originally been closed and he had left it open. The elderly man had closed it, so he must know there was no one in the cottage. After all, you didn't go around shutting a friend's barn door if you knew the friend would be back, say, that evening.

Some time after the man had gone Smiler left the barn—closing the door after him—and slipped across to the back door, which he opened with the key. In the kitchen he picked up the mail from a basket that hung under the mail slot. There were two letters addressed to a Major H. E. Collingwood, Ford Cottage, Crockerton, and a picture postcard addressed to Mrs. B. Bagnall at the cottage. The picture was a view of Mont Blanc and the message on the card cheered Smiler up a lot.

Dear Mrs. B.

I am happy to say Mrs. Collingwood is much improved, though it will be a good month yet before the medico will be able to give her a clean bill of health.

When you next come in will you please check the level of the central-heating oil tank?

Kind regards to you, Mr. B. and family.

Sincerely,
H. E. Collingwood

So, thought Smiler, the major and his wife are away for quite a time. All he had to do was to keep a weather eye open for Mrs. Bagnall. Considerably perked up, he put the mail back in the basket, then made a quick tour of the cottage, promising himself a more detailed one later. This done, he slipped out of the back door and over to his barn, closing the door after him.

He took with him—strictly on loan—a transistor radio which he had found in the major's study. The inside of his shirt was pouched with a tin of corned beef, a package of biscuits and a bottle of orangeade. While he ate he turned the radio on very softly.

Before it got really dark Smiler gathered up the empty sardine tins and other rubbish and, clasping them to his breast, went down the ladder frontward, without using his hands. He jerked the door catch up with one shoulder and slipped out. Because he was only going a few yards to the river he left the door open.

YARRA CAME WRAITHLIKE through the gloom at the top of the garden. She saw Smiler tossing his rubbish into the river, but she moved on without any great interest in him. Had she been hungry and in a bad temper, just the sight of him might have stirred resentment, but she was well fed and wanted only the comfort of warm straw. She had passed most of the day in the river woods, moving away whenever she had heard voices or sounds that disturbed her. Coming out of the woods in the late afternoon, she had put up a hare from a clump of dead bracken. The hare had had fifteen yards start on her but, although it had twisted, zigzagged and doubled back at top speed, she had moved like an orange-gold blur and easily taken it within a hundred yards. She had eaten it, relishing the meat which was strange to her.

Now she passed around the barn and through the open door to drop on to her litter of straw. A few moments later Smiler came in, humming softly to himself. Momentarily Yarra's mask wrinkled and she opened her jaws, but there was no real malice in her.

Smiler closed the door, felt for the ladder rungs in the darkness and went up to his loft. Before going to sleep he listened to the radio, eager to hear whether there would be anything about his escape in the news. He was disappointed; however, there was something about another escape. A cheetah which had escaped from Longleat the day before had not so far been found. Anyone seeing the animal was asked to keep well away from it and to inform the police or the Longleat Park authorities. There was an interview with a man from Longleat Park who gave some general information about cheetahs and mentioned that the escaped one was a female named Yarra.

Smiler lay comfortably in the hay, thinking about the cheetah. From his sister's home at Fishponds, on the outskirts of Bristol, he'd often gone to the Bristol zoo, but he couldn't remember seeing a cheetah there. Actually he didn't care much for zoos. Pacing up and down a cage was no way to live. Being at Approved School was a bit like that. Do this, do that, and being watched all the time, knowing every moment that you were a prisoner. Even having a big enclosure to live in wasn't really good enough, not if you were a wild animal. Yarra . . . that was a nice name . . . same sort

129

of name in a way as Tarzan. He saw himself in a loincloth, swinging through the jungle trees while his faithful cheetah, Yarra, followed him far below. He yawned, switched the radio off and stretched out to sleep.

So FAR Smiler and Yarra had been lucky. No one had sighted either of them. Two wardens from Longleat had tried following Yarra's spoor but found that the rain had washed them out. Nobody had tried to follow Smiler's tracks, but the police had alerted all patrol cars and the local constabulary, giving them Smiler's description. They had also notified sister Ethel, telling her that if Smiler appeared she must report him at once.

Ethel and her husband, Albert, were at this moment in the sitting room of their little villa in Fishponds, having cocoa before going to bed. It was a small neat room, everything shining and brushed and polished and dusted.

Ethel said, "That boy's always been a trouble and always will be. He's got a wild, stubborn streak in him."

Albert knew that everybody had streaks of some kind in them. He was much more easygoing than Ethel and he liked Smiler. He said, "My opinion is he run away from that place because he knew he didn't ought to have been there in the first instance."

Ethel put down her cocoa mug. "He went there because he was a bad one. Knocking an old lady over and taking her bag. And before that always nicking things. Bad company makes bad habits."

Albert sighed gently. "Smiler was light-fingered, yes. But not violent. He wouldn't harm a fly, let alone an old lady. All right, at the time I thought he had done it. But now I don't think he did."

"He was always nicking things and getting into scrapes. The way you start is the way you go on, and you go on nicking bigger things and getting into bigger scrapes."

Albert said reflectively, "It's all a matter of psychology. Smiler was what they call compensating for his homelife—or rather for the homelife he wasn't getting. No mother, and his dad off to sea nine months out of twelve. He was what they call making his protest against what society was doing to him."

Ethel sniffed loudly. "Well, I must say, that's the fanciest notion I've ever heard. And anyway, that old lady stood right up in juvenile court and identified him."

Albert rose. His cocoa was finished and now he meant to go out to his workshop and smoke his good-night cigarette. He liked to sit on his bench and puff away while he dreamed impossible dreams—like being able to smoke in the parlour and the bedroom, to put his feet up on anything he chose and, perhaps now and then, to have a bottle of beer instead of cocoa for a bedtime drink.

He said pungently: "That old lady was as blind as a bat! She couldn't have recognized her own reflection in a mirror!" He moved to the door and added, "Well, I hope the lad's found a fair billet for tonight. It's freezing out."

ALBERT was right. It froze hard all night. When the first light came up over the easterly ridge of the valley, it revealed a world festooned with a delicate tracery of frost. The sun struck gleams of white, gold and blue fire from every branch and twig.

The brightening crack of light under the barn door woke Yarra. She rolled over and sat up on her haunches, tightening the muscles of her long forelegs to ease the night's laziness from them. She sat like an ancient Egyptian lion goddess, her liquid amber eyes watching the light under the door. The door of her hut at Longleat was always closed at night, and the warden opened it early in the morning. She waited for the sound of his feet outside.

Half an hour passed and the warden did not come. Yarra rose to her four feet, walked to the door and sniffed at it. Then she raised herself on her hind feet and scraped against the shut door, rattling and banging it impatiently.

The sounds eventually woke Smiler. It took him a minute or two to remember where he was. When he did, he jumped up quickly. Somebody was down below! His heart thumping, he cautiously lifted the loft trap and peered through. For a moment he watched in amazement. Then he swiftly dropped the trapdoor and shot the bolt across. He sank back on the hay, clapped a hand to his forehead and said out loud, "Blimey O'Bloody Reilly!"

A slow shiver of fear crept along Smiler's scalp as he realized what a narrow escape he had had. When he had come back from throwing the rubbish away *that thing* had already been in the barn! He had closed the door and climbed the ladder and *that thing* must have been watching him! And now *that thing* was down there and he was up here! He went back to the loft trap and raised it a few inches. Down below Yarra was padding restlessly up and down. She caught the slight movement and swung around, making an angry movement with her jaws.

Smiler could see her clearly now. He saw the white shine of her teeth, the restless switching of the tail, and the long, lean length of her forelegs and body. He dropped the loft trap back into place and bolted it. "Samuel M.," he said to himself, "what you've got down there is that escaped cheetah! Yarra. And what you are stuck with right now is that you can't get out until you get her out. That's Thing Number One without any question."

He went to the barn window. Taking a good look at it for the first time, he saw that the window was not fixed in its frame as he had thought. He opened it and looked out. Six feet below him was the top of the barn door. The door latch was a curved handgrip with a thumb press you pushed down to lift the small cross lever on the inside. The door, he remembered, was awkwardly hung; once the catch was free, it swung inward of its own weight.

With his head stuck out of the window he considered his plan of campaign. The window was big enough for him to get through. It was a fair drop to the ground, but not so far that it worried him. Once in the yard all he had to do was . . . Well, what? Press the thumb catch down and then run for his life while that animal came after him like a streak of gold light? Not so-and-so likely. Just drop to the ground, and then tell the police or someone about the cheetah? They'd have him back in that school before you could say knife. No—there was only one way. He had to get the door open from up here and let Yarra go off on her own.

What he wanted was a long stick with which to reach down and press the thumb catch. At the back of the loft he found a hayfork with the head broken off. It was about four feet long and would not reach the door. But in one corner of the loft was an old hen house, its floor made of long strips of wood. Smiler pulled one of the slats free, then lashed it to the broken hayfork with some twine from the hay bales. He pushed his homemade pole through the window and after a couple of attempts managed to bang down the thumb catch. The door slowly began to open.

Before he could get his pole back through the window Yarra was out. She stopped a yard from the open door and looked up at Smiler with her amber eyes. She gave him a quick snapping hiss and then loped away around the corner of the barn.

Three

YARRA passed that day in the area. She went up the river and stopped to drink where a small carrier stream came into the main stream over a low waterfall. In the woods higher up the river she marked the movement of a cock pheasant foraging among the dead leaves. She covered twenty yards of ground before the bird saw her. It was brought down by one sweep of her taloned right forepaw. While she ate she heard the sound of children laughing and playing across the river, and the whine of cars on the main road running from Warminster to Mere.

The frost had held all day, and as the sun began to drop and the air turned colder, Yarra came down from the river woods. She was passing through a thicket when a keeper, shotgun under his arm, stepped out on to the path ten yards ahead. Man and beast saw each other at the same time. Yarra backed away, lowering

133

head and shoulders threateningly, and gave a low snarl. Instinctively, the keeper swung his shotgun to his shoulder and fired.

Although she had never been fired at before, the swift movement of the gun was warning enough for Yarra. She leaped sideways into the cover of a patch of young birches. The keeper fired one barrel and then the other as Yarra disappeared. A few pellets from the spread of shot caught her on the left flank. Then she was gone at top speed through the woods.

Ten minutes later the keeper was telephoning from his cottage to the Warminster police station.

AFTER Yarra had gone Smiler stayed in the loft waiting to see if the postman would call or perhaps Mrs. Bagnall come to do some housework in the cottage. Eventually he saw the postman ride by on his bicycle, but he did not deliver any letters.

An hour later Smiler was in the cottage, the back door locked and the key back on the porch rafter. The door had a spring lock which could be opened from the inside without a key. He had a drink of water, sluiced his head and neck under the tap, and then opened a tin of baked beans and ate them. He tidied up meticulously, then started another inspection of the house.

The hallway running to the front door was red-carpeted and hung with pictures of birds and flowers. A dining room and a large sitting room opened off either side. One wall of the sitting room was covered entirely with bookshelves, and in the window stood a flat-topped desk inlaid with red morocco leather. It was as nice a room as Smiler had ever seen.

On the top floor were three bedrooms. One was large, with two beds in it. The others had a single bed each. Leading off the big bedroom was a spacious bathroom with a mirror-fronted cabinet on the wall. Smiler's reflection confronted him in the mirror: snubnose, blue eyes, his face freckled all over like a skylark's egg, and tousled blond hair. He took a comb from the ledge under the cabinet and tidied his hair.

Then he went down to the sitting room and looked at the bookshelves. There were a lot of books about fishing and hunting, rows of novels, a pile of maps on one shelf, and on the bottom shelf a set of the *Encyclopaedia Britannica*. Smiler liked books. For two hours he sat on the floor enjoying himself. He looked up cheetahs in the encyclopaedia and read that in Persia and India they had been used for hunting small game and antelope. They were hooded, then taken out, and, when the hood was slipped, away they went after their prey. He lay back on the floor, saw himself with a hooded Yarra on a leash, the two of them moving along a great hillside. Then—wheeeh! Off came the hood, the leash was slipped and Yarra was away after a deer!

Smiler sat up and grinned. Some hope, he thought. Anyway, that cheetah was miles away by now if it had any sense. He pushed the book back on to the shelf. As he did so he saw that at the end of the shelf was a large dimple-sided whisky bottle with a slit cut in the cork so that you could drop money through. The bottle was three-quarters full of old sixpences. Smiler picked it up and shook it. He thought there must be at least ten pounds in it.

As he put the bottle back he heard a key scraping at the back-door lock. Smiler was up and out of the front door like a shot. He raced through the garden and up the hillside to a small clump of stunted yews. From here he could look down on the cottage and barn. At least, he thought, he had left no telltale traces in the house. The whisky bottle was back in its place, and all the books. And he had tidied up the kitchen, wiping the sink fairly dry from his washing, and dropping the empty baked-bean tin in the wastebin. . . . The baked-bean tin! What if the person looked in the bin and saw it? That would give the game away. Well, there was nothing he could do about it now.

After about five minutes Smiler saw a woman cross the yard wheeling a bicycle. She was dumpy-looking and oldish. She pushed her bicycle through the side gate and then rode away over the bridge.

Smiler gave her a few minutes to get clear and then he walked down the hill, past the big white gate and on to the bridge. Here he leaned over the parapet and pretended to be gazing at the river. But his eyes were on the house; for all he knew, more than one person might have gone in. It proved a very wise precaution. He had not been there long when the front door opened and a girl came out. She slammed the door behind her and then came on to the road and towards the bridge.

She was a nice-looking girl, with a tanned complexion and shoulder-length black hair, wearing a shiny red plastic coat and high black boots. Smiler didn't dislike girls, but he didn't have a lot of time for most of them. They never seemed to say or do anything that was particularly interesting.

As the girl walked on to the bridge she saw Smiler. She stopped behind him and said, "Hullo."

Smiler half-turned. "Hullo," he said.

"What are you doing here?"

"Just looking at the river," said Smiler. She had a friendly smile, and it occurred to him that he might get some useful information from her. He nodded at the cottage. "You live there?"

"No. Mum does for them. I come with her."

"She the one that went up on the bike?"

"'S right. I comes down with her on the back of her bike. But as it's all uphill going back, I walk. Today she came down to pick up the letters, but I stopped to dust the dining room."

"Don't nobody live there, then?"

"They're away. I haven't seen you around before, have I?" The girl leaned over the parapet beside him.

"No."

"Where you from?"

Smiler hesitated and then he said, "Oh, over Warminster way. Where do you live?"

"Up the hill. 'Bout a mile. Lodge Cottage." The girl picked up a lump of moss from one of the bridge stones and dropped it into the river, saying, "The river's going down fast."

"Plenty of fish in there, I suppose?"

"Trout and grayling. There's some trout over three pounds. My father's the water keeper. What's your name?"

Feeling easier, Smiler said, "Johnny Pickering." Johnny was a boy that Smiler knew but didn't like. "What's yours?"

"Ivy, but I don't like it much. All my friends call me Pat."

"I like Pat best, too. How often do you and your mother come down here?"

"Once a week. Every Wednesday, mostly. But I don't always come." She straightened up and gave him a bright smile. "Well, I got to go. But if you live in Warminster I might see you sometime. I'm starting a job there next week. In Woolworth's. 'Bye."

She walked away up the hill and just before she turned a corner she looked back and waved. As girls went, Smiler thought, she wasn't too bad.

He waited another few minutes and then slipped into the courtyard to the back door. Mrs. Bagnall, for it must have been she, had left the key on the rafter. He went in and found the letters gone from the basket behind the door. His baked-bean tin was still in the wastebin, and he put it in his pocket. Then he took another tin of sardines from the cupboard, some rolls from the deep freezer, and went up to the barn loft.

He put the rolls in the sunshine on the window sill to thaw out and then lay back on his hay to do some thinking, for it was clear to him now that his plan of campaign was not good enough. What he was doing was living from day to day and from hand to mouth. Also, he was living in dangerous territory where he could easily make some silly slip-up that would give him away—like that baked-bean tin, for instance. Or Mrs. Bagnall might spot things gone. . . . No, he had to make himself really safe. It was nine months before his father would be back, maybe a year, and he had to keep from being caught all that time.

Sustained thought was hard, fatiguing work. The hay was warm and soft. After about two hours—with a break to eat sardines and half-thawed rolls—Smiler dropped off to sleep.

AFTER being shot at by the keeper, Yarra kept moving fast. She was angry and disturbed; but her pelt was rough and wiry, and the small shot which had caught her left flank had caused no real harm. She took a line along the valley-side, well above the river, eventually crossing into a plantation of young conifers and moving down through them until she reached their boundary.

She sat on her haunches looking down into the valley. It was growing darker every moment now. Up the river, away to her left, were the bridge and the grey roof thatch and white-plastered

137

end wall of Ford Cottage. To her right, farther downstream and towards the north and Warminster, she could see the lights of houses. Sometimes car headlights swept along the main road.

In a while she dropped down to the river, found the fishing path and walked slowly upstream towards the bridge. She moved like a shadow close to the cottage and then across to the barn. But the door was shut. She could not understand why. Always at Longleat the hut door was opened at night for the cheetahs to enter. She lazily stretched her jaws and gave a low, protesting rumble. Then she rasped at the barn door, rattling and shaking it. When it did not open she snarled and spat angrily.

Smiler came out of sleep with a start just in time to hear Yarra rattle the door again. He was on his feet quickly and at the window. At that moment Yarra moved back, squatted on the ground and sat staring at the door. Smiler saw her clearly. He clapped his hand to his forehead and cried, "Cor, Blimey O'Bloody Reilly— she's back again!"

There was no doubt in his mind as to what he must do. He instinctively accepted that, since Yarra was a fugitive like himself, he could not refuse her shelter. He got his homemade pole and opened the barn window. Yarra heard him and she backed away a few yards, raised her blunt head and gave another rumble.

"All right, old girl," Smiler murmured. "Won't take a moment." He jabbed down in the gloom at the door latch. After a few tries, he hit the thumb press and the door swung back slowly. Yarra looked up at him once, padded in a small semicircle around the open door and moved on into the barn.

Smiler went back to his bed and turned the radio on to the local news. It made no mention of one Samuel Miles, but it had plenty to say about Yarra. The public were warned that she had been sighted that day a couple of miles from the village of Crockerton. She would not attack an adult unless cornered or suddenly surprised. But she could be dangerous to young children, and parents were warned not to let them move about unaccompanied. A cordon was being thrown around the area where she had been sighted. It was expected that she would soon be captured.

Smiler began to get a bit worried. Yarra was no trouble to him, and it didn't bother him that she might go about taking a few chickens . . . but she was dangerous to small children! Oughtn't he to do something about it? Oughtn't he to drop out of the barn window now and find the nearest policeman?

And if he did? "Well, Samuel M.," he told himself, "that would be the end of you. They would say you were a good lad and had done right, but then you'd be shipped back to that school."

It was a difficult problem. Yarra would go off tomorrow and almost certainly she would be caught—and he would still be free. Anyway, he wasn't too keen about dropping from that window right now and having Yarra come out of the barn after him. But if Yarra weren't caught tomorrow? Then she would come padding back here to her shelter. Well, tomorrow evening he would leave the barn door open and he would stay in the cottage, watching. The moment he saw Yarra come back he would go up to the village of Crockerton. Bound to be a public telephone there. He could call the police, say where Yarra was, refuse to say who he was, and then he would have to take off quickly.

Down below, he heard Yarra stirring, and he said aloud, "Old girl, if you got any sense you won't come back tomorrow. And I hope you don't, because I don't want to lose a soft billet."

THE SUN was well up over the valley ridge when Smiler woke. He stretched and yawned, then he got up, unbolted the trap and looked down. The lower part of the barn was empty; Yarra had gone. Smiler went down, peered cautiously around the barn door to make sure that the coast was clear and then, closing the door, he went across to the cottage. In the kitchen he had a drink of water and some biscuits and washed his hands.

Although he had bad habits, like smoking an occasional cigarette, and was no respecter of small items of other people's property when he was bored and idle, Smiler was fundamentally a good sort. When he wished, he could be methodical and industrious. He was also shrewd and far-thinking in an emergency; and he was in an emergency now—the emergency of keeping Samuel M. out of the hands of the police. The previous day he had come to some very clear conclusions:

1. He couldn't hang around Ford Cottage and the barn for nine months, cadging food and shelter.
2. So long as Major Collingwood was away, however, he could just use the barn for a sleeping place.
3. He had to go out and get a job so that he would have the money for food and other things.
4. But to get a job wasn't all that easy, because the moment he showed his face some policeman would recognize him. He had, therefore, to disguise himself somehow.
5. And because people were always full of questions, he had to have answers as to who he was, where he lived, and so on.
6. And sometime he would have to telephone the shipping company offices in Bristol and find out when his father was due back so that he could meet him.

It was a long list but Smiler felt that he had worked out the answers to most of the immediate problems, and he now set about them with a will. He went first into the sitting room and from the dimpled whisky bottle took out two pounds' worth of sixpenny pieces and wrapped them in his handkerchief. Then he went through the pile of maps until he found one with Warminster marked on the cover. He decided to take it with him.

Next, Smiler went up to the bathroom. He had seen two things there which might help solve one of his problems: a bottle of sun-tan lotion and a bottle of hair colouring. Dark Brown, the label on the second bottle said. Smiler read the instructions carefully. Wet your hair and apply the cream as you would a shampoo. Lather it up and leave the foam on for five, ten or twenty minutes, according to how dark you want the hair to go. Rinse, then set hair in your favourite style. Smiler grinned.

He stripped off his shirt and set to work. It wasn't as easy as the instructions made it sound, but after twenty minutes his hair looked dark enough. He then worked the tanning stuff into his face and hands and around the back of his neck. It didn't cover the freckles by any means, but it looked all right. After that it took him some time to clean up the basin. He admired his reflection, then began to explore the house for clothes. He was going to keep his own jeans, but he wanted some shirts and socks, and something to replace his brown tweed jacket which would have been listed in the description of him issued by the police.

Major Collingwood was a small man, Smiler soon realized. He found two old blue flannel shirts that would be a fair fit, three pairs of thick woollen socks, a grey pullover and a well-worn green parka. In a cupboard under the stairs he found, too, a pair of Wellington boots that fitted him.

Conscious of the liberties he was taking, and not overlooking the fact that he *might* be picked up, Smiler felt he must try to square himself with Major Collingwood. He went to the desk in the sitting room, found a pencil and notepaper, and wrote:

Dear Major Collingwood, I hope you find this and will understand that I am really only borrowing and will make it alright when my Dad comes back, like paying for the food and making up the bottle sixpences, if I don't get to do it myself first. I have tried not to make a mess, except for some hair dye on the corner of the bathroom curtins. It is a nice house and I hope your wife gets much better.

Signed, Hunted. (P.S. I can't give my right name, for reasons)

Also the bike, and some other odds and ends, which maybe I will have returned. Signed, H.

He took the letter to a corner cupboard which he had previously looked into. It held bottles and glasses and also a half-empty box of cigars. Smiler reckoned that Mrs. Bagnall was unlikely to open the cigar box, but the major would when he returned—perhaps the first evening. He put the letter in the box.

Back in the barn Smiler stowed all his loose stuff out of sight under a hay bale. Dressed in a clean shirt and socks, his own jeans, the grey pullover and the parka and the Wellington boots, he was ready to tackle Warminster.

Shutting the barn door after him, he wheeled the bicycle from the car bay through the side gate and pedalled it up the lane to the main road. He turned right on the main road and twenty minutes later was in Warminster. He had already given himself a lecture on the importance of acting naturally; people only noticed you if you let your worry about being noticed show. So Smiler rode into Warminster whistling. At a shop in the High Street he bought the local newspaper. He then cycled around the town to get some idea of his bearings and possible escape routes.

He ended up in the free car park near the railway station and went into the cafeteria. He got himself a plate of sausages, two slabs of fruitcake and a cup of coffee, and then sat in the window where he could keep an eye on his parked bicycle.

He drank and ate with relish. He decided that this might turn out to be his lucky day. So far, no one had so much as given him a curious glance, not even a policeman who had walked past him as he came out of the newspaper shop.

In the SITUATIONS VACANT column of the newspaper was a job that sounded right up his street:

STRONG LAD wanted for kennel work, experience not necessary, good wages, free lunch. Mrs. Angela Lakey, Danebury Kennels, Heytesbury

Well, Samuel M., he thought, that sounds all right, particularly the free lunch. For a moment he remembered longingly sister Ethel's Irish stews. Whatever else she was not, she was a jolly good cook. Kennels, eh? But where was Heytesbury? He didn't want to be too far from his barn if he could help it. He consulted his map and soon found Heytesbury. He worked out a route that— if he got the job—would only be three or four miles each way.

A few minutes later Smiler was cycling toward Heytesbury, wondering what Mrs. Angela Lakey would be like.

YARRA, when she left the barn that morning, followed her usual route up the river, keeping just inside the fringe of the woods, but she was unlucky with her hunting. Half a mile from the cottage she put up a drake mallard from the edge of a swampy hollow. The drake went up like a rocket and with him went his mate. The choice of two targets made Yarra hesitate, and when she leaped for the female mallard she missed it by a foot. Farther on in the woods she put up a wily old buck hare.

The hare raced away down the wooded slope. Yarra went after him, but his twists and turns in and out of the trees balked her of a clear, fast run. At the riverbank the hare took off in a long

142

leap. He splashed into the water and swam across. Yarra pulled up on her haunches and wrinkled her mask in disgust. An hour later she was almost at the end of the wooded valley slope when, fifty yards ahead, she saw a lean grey shape at the water's edge.

It was a heron standing in two inches of water just where the flooded river lapped over the bank. A back eddy had cut a deep pool close in under the bank, and it was a favourite fishing place of heron. Yarra lowered her body and began to stalk him, keeping close to the cover of the winter-dry clumps of flags and reeds.

The heron, the wisest and most cautious of birds and possessed of infinite patience, was well aware of Yarra. But he was hungry, as all wild birds and beasts are during the lean months of winter, and he meant to have his meal. Not three feet below him was a good-sized grayling, moving up and down, but so far not rising high enough for the heron to risk a thrust of his beak.

Yarra worked her way forward, flat to the ground. She was bunching her muscles for her leap when the grayling below the heron came surfaceward like a slim airship rising. The heron's beak rapiered down and took the fish. With the movement Yarra sprang and the heron rose, great pearl-grey wings spreading wide, his long legs trailing as he planed away.

Behind him there was a splash. Yarra's right forepaw had missed the heron and, unable to stop herself, she had come down in the water. In a bad temper, she pulled herself back on to the bank. She sat on her haunches and licked at her shoulders and neck mantle, grumbling to herself. It was then that she heard the sound of men's voices and the rattle of sticks against trees.

As Yarra, disturbed by the noise, headed away upriver at a lope, the hunt moved behind her. A long line of beaters had been formed early that morning on the outskirts of Warminster. Now it was moving upriver, and at this very moment the cheetah warden was standing on the bank where the hare had leaped into the water, examining the spoor Yarra had left in the soft mud.

IT WAS two o'clock in the afternoon when Smiler found his way to Danebury Kennels. Danebury House was a large red brick building with an untidy lawn in front of it and stable and kennel blocks at the rear. As he came up the drive Smiler could hear what sounded like a hundred dogs barking and howling.

He rang the front doorbell. The door was opened by a very large woman of about forty who was dressed in a green sweater and riding breeches. She had a big, squarish, red face and an untidy mop of short black hair. She was holding a chicken leg and as she chewed on it she surveyed Smiler as though he were something the dog had brought home. She finished chewing and then said brusquely, "Well, boy?"

Smiler pulled the newspaper from his pocket and said, "Please, ma'am, I've come about the job."

Mrs. Lakey eyed him for a moment. "Oh, you have, have you? Well, let's have a look at you." She took his right arm in a firm grasp. "How strong are you, boy?" Her voice was brisk, but not unkind, and there was a small twinkle in her dark eyes.

"I'm strong enough, I think, ma'am."

"Time will show." Mrs. Lakey peered at his face and said, "You're very sunburned for this time of year, aren't you?"

Smiler said quickly, "My skin's always like that, ma'am."

"Don't call me ma'am—call me Mrs. Lakey. All right, come in and let's have your particulars." She turned away down the hall. As Smiler followed, she called over her shoulder, "Shut the door. Fresh air's for outside houses, not inside."

She led the way to a large, bright room that looked out over the lawn. The walls were hung with fox masks and brushes, glass cases with stuffed fish and birds in them, photographs of horses and dogs. Over the big open fireplace was a large oil painting of a fresh-faced, grey-haired man dressed in white breeches and hunting pink. (Later, Smiler learned that this was Mrs. Lakey's dead father who had been a colonel of the hussars.) Before the fire, between two shabby leather armchairs, was a round table which held a tray of cold food and a glass of dark liquid with a thick white froth on it which Smiler recognized as stout. Just inside the door was an open rolltop desk, crammed with papers.

Mrs. Lakey told Smiler to sit by the fire. She went to the desk and found a pencil and a piece of paper which she brought to the round table. She sat down opposite him, took a tomato from the

144

tray, and said, "Cold snack today. Milly's away shopping. I've got a lot to do this afternoon so, with your permission, boy"—she gave him a smile which suddenly took all the sternness out of her face—"I'll victual up while I take your particulars. Name?"

"Pickering," he said without hesitation. "Johnny Pickering."

Mrs. Lakey wrote it down, and said, "Age?"

"Fifteen and a half."

"Address?"

"I live with my aunt, Mrs. Brown, at Hillside Bungalow, Crockerton. My mother and father . . . well, they're dead. They was killed in a car accident three years ago."

"Sorry to hear it. Damn cars. They're just murder on the roads. Horse and trap—you got a tumble and a bruising and that was that. Never mind. Times move. Any previous job? References?"

"No, ma'am—I mean Mrs. Lakey. I left school Christmas."

"Any experience with animals?"

"No, Mrs. Lakey. But I like 'em. And I had a dog once."

"Willing?"

Puzzled, Smiler said, "Oh, yes, I'm willing to take the job."

"No, boy. I mean are you willing to work hard? Sober, industrious, clean and tidy? Can't have you if you're not all that—and cheerful. And you've got to have a good appetite. Milly can't bear cooking for those who pick and scratch. So what do you say?"

A little out of his depth, Smiler said, "I think so, Mrs. Lakey."

"Good." Mrs. Lakey finished her stout. "You seem a likely number to me. Wages, three pounds a week. Free lunch. Sundays off. Half days to be arranged as work permits. Start at seven-thirty. Finish at five this time of the year. Later as the sun god stays with us longer. Thirty pence an hour overtime. Working overalls provided. Anything in that frighten you?"

"No, Mrs. Lakey."

"Well, it would most of the young lay-abouts these days who want a four-hour day, two months' paid holiday a year, and then wonder why the country's going to the dogs. Which is the biggest slander on dogs ever uttered. And talking of dogs, let me tell you, my bark is not worse than my bite. My bite is terrible!" She winked at him suddenly.

Smiler, who was a bit uncertain about her, was warmed by the wink. He said, with the smile sister Ethel said could charm the birds from the trees, "You seem very nice to me, Mrs. Lakey."

Mrs. Lakey looked at him, slowly grinned and then cried heartily, "Well now, it's a compliment I'm getting! The first for ten years. Right now, run along with you. Be here at half-past seven tomorrow and we'll see how you shape up."

As Smiler let himself out a small Jack Russell terrier darted from some bushes. It chased him all the way down the drive, snapping at his back wheel. But Smiler didn't mind. Going down the road he began to whistle. "Samuel M.," he told himself, "you carried it off like a hero. You've got a job, as easy as kissing your hand." Crikey! Seven-thirty! Ought he to buy himself an alarm clock in Warminster? Yes, he'd have to do that. If he turned up late, he'd have Mrs. Lakey on his tail, biting worse than her bark. But free lunches and three pounds a week! He was in clover.

Four

ON THE plateau at the valley-top Yarra moved out of the trees and began to quarter the ground eastward across the rough amber-coloured grasslands. Near a Forestry Commission plantation of young firs she put up a hare. The hare laid its ears back and went like the wind, Yarra racing after it. At the edge of the plantation

146

the hare found its way blocked by a small-meshed wire fence. It turned right along the fence ten yards ahead of Yarra. She swung across the angle at top speed and leaped for it. Her forepaws smashed down on its back and her hindquarters skidded around to crash into the fence.

As she began to eat her kill a Land Rover came over a ridge to her right and began bumping and swaying slowly along the fence. Yarra stopped eating and watched it without fear. She had seen many like it in Longleat Park. She had chased meat trailing behind a Land Rover, and had often jumped to the cab roof. But now she wanted to eat undisturbed.

When the Land Rover was within forty yards of her, the driver saw her and stopped the car. The man beside him began to speak into his walkie-talkie. Over the air the news of Yarra's location went out to the police cars on the roads, and to the beaters now moving slowly up through Southleigh Wood, the top boundary of which lay a few hundred yards down the slope from Yarra.

When the Land Rover did not move, Yarra began to eat again. Almost immediately, from behind her, the cheetah's quick ears caught the sounds of men coming through the wood. Gripping the big hare in her jaws, she leaped over the fence into the plantation of young firs. She trotted fast across the plantation and kept going until she had crossed the Crockerton road.

A few minutes later she padded into a tall clump of wild rhododendrons and crouched down to eat her hare. As she did so, the first fat flakes of snow began to drift down from the leaden sky, slanting a little in a cold wind that was rising fast.

IN Warminster, Smiler went into Woolworth's to buy his alarm clock. The girl at the counter was amused when he paid for it all in sixpenny pieces.

"I been saving up," said Smiler. "Present for me mum." Riding away down the Crockerton road, Smiler thought that it would have been nice if it really were a present for his mum. She had died a year after his birth, but he knew a lot about her from his father, who worshipped her memory.

Before he reached the cottage it began to snow and blow hard.

Large, heavy flakes filled the air, whirling and spinning in the wind, and he pulled up the hood of his parka for protection. As he neared the cottage he began to think of Yarra. If she came back he would have to do something about her.

He hid his bicycle in the orchard and then, keeping his eyes open for Yarra, slipped around and opened the barn door. The courtyard had an inch covering of snow. The fast-falling flakes rapidly obliterated the footprints he made in crossing to the back door of the house. He let himself in, then went upstairs to the bathroom to watch the barn door. With him he had a packet of biscuits and a pork pie which he had bought in Warminster.

For two reasons he hoped that Yarra would not come back. One, because giving her away when she was on the run like him seemed the act of a traitor, though he knew he would have to do it for the safety of other people. And two, because it was going to give him a lot of trouble. He didn't want to have to turn out and find a telephone, because it would mean that he couldn't come back safely to the cottage until Yarra had been taken.

But Yarra did not come. Sometime after nightfall the snow stopped and the sky cleared, so Smiler could easily have seen her if she had come to the barn. He waited dutifully until the eight-day clock in the hall struck nine (Mrs. Bagnall wound it up once a week). Then he found a couple of blankets in one of the spare bedrooms, rolled himself up and slept.

THE SNOW saved Yarra from being caught. While she was eating her hare, the hunting line swept forward through the young firs and crossed the Crockerton road behind her. She was sighted as she left her clump of rhododendrons. A couple of the men unwisely gave loud shouts which alarmed her. She went away at a gallop, clearing a hedge into a field of young winter wheat and following the line of the hedge. As long as she could hear the men behind her she kept going steadily. When the noises died she slackened her pace.

She was in strange country now and her movement was dictated by the lie of the land. She kept close to the hedges and over open ground trotted fast from the cover of one clump of bushes to the next. Before crossing a road she watched for any sign of humans. The snow and the approach of night were her allies. The snow rapidly filled the tracks she left and made fast going hard for the men who followed. After an hour they had lost all contact with her, and the hunt was called off except for the police cars. Had they but known it, the policemen were wasting their time: Yarra had long since moved out of the area.

The noise of a small waterfall led Yarra to the river, and she began to follow it downstream, parallel to the Warminster-Heytesbury road. Half a mile down the bank a black shape loomed up out of the darkness and the now thinning snow. It was a dilapidated fishing hut with a large plank seat inside. Yarra turned into the hut, sniffed around it and then leaped on to the seat. She groomed and cleaned herself, licking at her muddy, wet thighs and nibbling at her swelling dugs, where the restlessness inside her seemed to be lodged. She was tired and bad-tempered. If anyone had come to the door of the hut at that moment, he would not have had a very warm welcome.

Finally she settled down on the hard board and fell into a light sleep. The river ran by, murmuring quietly. A water vole made a plop as it dropped into the stream and began a night forage down the bankside. A barn owl sailed low on silent wings over the water meadow, quartering the grass for a mouse or shrew. A fox coming up the river caught Yarra's scent and decided to have nothing to do with it; he trotted a wide half-circle away from the hut.

The low-pressure system which had brought the snow up from the west now moved away east, and the temperature rose. The snow melted fast and in a couple of hours was gone from all but the sheltered dips and the north slopes of the high ground.

At three o'clock in the morning Yarra woke, stiff and uncomfortable. She left the hut and continued downriver. On the outskirts of Heytesbury she struck a side road that led over a bridge into the village. She padded through the village, across the main road and up another side road. The night was still and deserted of all humans, but as she passed the entrance to Danebury House the Jack Russell terrier saw her from the bay window of his mistress's bedroom. He jumped up and began to bark. From her bed, half in sleep, Mrs. Angela Lakey reached down to the floor, where she kept a small pile of cushions for the purpose, and hurled one at the terrier as she muttered, "Go to sleep, you old fool!"

Above the house the road ran on to the wide sweeps of Salisbury Plain, which the army used for artillery, tank and infantry training. There was a red-and-white drop post across the road, and a sign which read:

IMBER ARMY RANGE
ROAD CLOSED

Yarra went under the drop post and then left the road for the rough, wild grassland. Ten minutes later she came across an old, rusted Sherman tank which was used for target practice. The turret had been blown askew, and there was a large gap in the side of the empty hull. Yarra looked through into the hull. Somebody had long ago dumped a load of bracken there and covered it with a couple of sacks to make a resting place.

Yarra jumped inside, sniffed around the interior, and then began to tread the sacks and bracken into a bed. When she was satisfied she flopped down, and in a few minutes she was sleeping.

Above her on the inside plates of the tank someone had written in white chalk—*Bombardier Andy Coran, only 5 yrs and 13 days to serve*. Under that, in another hand, was—*Please leave this hotel as you would wish to find it*.

THE alarm bell brought Smiler out of bed with a jerk. Outside it was still dark. He had a quick wash in the kitchen, ate some of the biscuits he had left, and then tidied everything up.

When he went out he found the snow had all gone and there was a fresh wind blowing. He tiptoed over to the barn. He didn't want to leave the door open all day, but he wasn't overlooking the fact that Yarra might have come back during the night. When he came to the door he reached quickly for the handle and pulled it shut with a slam. If Yarra were in there, the noise would have wakened her. He stood listening, but no sound came from inside.

A few moments later Smiler was pushing his bicycle up the hill away from Ford Cottage, and giving himself a talking-to for not having bought a bicycle lamp. Although light enough to see, it was still officially dark enough for him to be showing a light, and the last thing he wanted was to be stopped by a policeman.

Warm and snug in his pullover and parka, he followed the back-roads route he had worked out for getting to Heytesbury. He had a good memory for maps, a "bump of locality" as Albert used to say. Thinking of sister Ethel and her Albert, Smiler decided that he would soon have to get a message to them that he was all right. He didn't want them thinking he was dead and then writing to his dad. The problem of sending a message, without giving himself away, occupied him as he rode.

Smiler arrived at Danebury House at twenty minutes past seven. He was met at the drive by the terrier whose name, he later learned, was Tonks. Tonks gave him a yapping welcome and then trotted up the drive alongside him.

Mrs. Lakey greeted him heartily, smacking him on the back and saying, "Morning, boy. Punctual. That's what I like to see. Begin as you mean to go on." She gave him a cup of coffee in the kitchen and then took him outside to "show him the ropes".

Mrs. Lakey and her sister, Miss Milly Finn, ran breeding kennels for English and Gordon setters, as well as boarding kennels where people could leave their dogs. There was also a small section with room for about eight cats. The cats were Miss Milly's responsibility, though Smiler had to look after them most of the time. Miss Milly ran the house, did the cooking and kept the books with no outside help.

In addition to these animals, there were a chestnut mare, Penny, and a bay gelding called—for some unknown reason—Bacon. These were kept in the stable, and hired out to people who wanted to ride or hunt. In a run at the bottom of a vegetable garden lived twelve White Leghorn hens, known as the Apostles. At the back of the kennel runs was a storehouse where all the hound meal and dog and cat food was kept and cooked.

It was Smiler's job to feed all the dogs and cats and keep their water bowls full. He had to clean out the kennels twice a week, feed and water the hens and collect the eggs, and exercise the setters. He had to groom and brush all dogs twice a week, fetch

in logs for the house, wash down the horse box, and dig the vegetable garden when he had any spare time.

On the first morning, as Mrs. Lakey rattled off all this to him,
his head spun and he felt that he would never be able to manage.
After a few days, however, he was managing easily, though—since
he hated digging—he made sure that he didn't often have spare
time for that.

The most cheering thing for Smiler was Miss Milly, who was
younger than Mrs. Lakey. She was short and plump, fair-haired
and fresh-faced, and jolly and kind. Her kitchen was spotless and
smelled always of baking and cooking. Smiler's first free lunch was
a revelation that outdid even Ethel's culinary prowess. He was
served steak-and-kidney pie, Brussels sprouts and mashed potatoes. For "afters" he had treacle tart with custard and could have
finished up with Cheddar cheese and fresh-baked bread if he had
had room for it.

There was one rather awkward moment for Smiler at the end of
his first day. When he went into the scullery to hang up his working overalls, Miss Milly was there, polishing a pair of Mrs. Lakey's
riding boots.

"How long does it take you to get home, Johnny?" she asked.

"Oh, not long, Miss Milly."

She stared thoughtfully at the sheen she had worked on one of
the boots and said, "I know Crockerton well. Hillside Bungalow?
Can't recall that, Johnny. Where is it?"

Smiler gathered his wits and said, "Well . . . it's sort of past the
post office and then down a side path towards the river."

"Near the old millhouse, you mean?"

"That's right, Miss Milly."

"Well, ride home carefully."

As he wheeled his bicycle out of the yard, Mrs. Lakey came
around the corner on Penny. She pulled up and said, "Finished
for the day, boy?"

"Yes, ma'am . . . I mean, Mrs. Lakey."

"Good. Well, boy, we'll make something of you. You move well.
Should stay the course if your wind holds. Get a good night's rest
and come back fighting fit in the morning."

In Heytesbury Smiler stopped at a garage and bought a bicycle lamp with his last sixpenny pieces. The garage attendant looked at the money, winked at Smiler and said, "Been robbing the poor box, then?"

Five

YARRA left her tank shelter soon after first light. Outside she stretched and then spent some minutes giving herself a good grooming. It was a clear, almost cloudless day, with a brisk wind blowing across the plain from the southwest.

Her grooming finished, she loped down the hill, where she found a pool of rainwater and drank. For the next two hours she circled wide over the eastern portion of Salisbury Plain, an area about six miles long and five deep. The whole plain was some twenty to thirty miles long, a vast expanse of rolling, dun-coloured grass and downland. The land belonged to the Ministry of Defence, and the public for the most part was excluded. When people were admitted at weekends they had to keep to the rough tracks and roads, which were marked with notices that read:

DANGER—UNEXPLODED MISSILES

DO NOT LEAVE THE CARRIAGEWAYS

YOU HAVE BEEN WARNED

When the red flags were flying at the army entrance points to the plain, known as vedettes, nobody was allowed entry except the military personnel engaged in manoeuvres. Land wardens patrolled the roads and tracks in Land Rovers to see that no unauthorized persons came into the area.

Given over by day to the troops, the plain was also the home of many wild creatures—the hare, the fox, the stoat and weasel, the wild deer, the rat and the rabbit. In the air above the plain flew the buzzard, the kestrel and the sparrow hawk, all of them alert for the movement below of pheasant, partridge and the small birds that lived in the tall grasses and thickets. In fact, although the plain looked barren, it teemed with life.

Yarra put up a rabbit from behind a boulder and raced, doubled and twisted with it at her leisure, and finally killed and ate it. At midday she lay in the sun just below a ridge top, her orange-and-black pelt merging into her background so that from fifty yards she was practically invisible. A mile away, on a distant slope, sat an old Churchill tank. As Yarra blinked her golden amber eyes against the sun, there was a loud crack away to her right. Alongside the tank the earth fountained upward in a plume of mud, grass tufts and black smoke. Yarra flinched at the sight, and gave a silent gape of her jaws to show her displeasure.

There was another crumping, cracking noise from the left. This time an anti-tank shell hit the Churchill in the forepart of its hull and a large piece of plating flew into the air. Yarra moved away to seek another resting place. She was at the start of learning many lessons. She would come to know the sounds of guns—from the mad chatter of automatic weapons to the slow, heavy thump of large-calibre shells exploding—the rattle of an approaching tank, the monstrous gnat-song of helicopters in the air above, and to move away from them all. But on most days the plain would be free to her and the other animals during the early morning hours and again in the slow-stretching evening hours, from five to six o'clock onward.

On this, Yarra's first day there, she moved and hunted in comparative peace. She killed two hares in the afternoon and ate them both. Since she only needed about three pounds of meat a day to keep her satisfied, she hunted no more. As the light began to go from the sky, she went back to her Sherman tank. She arranged her bed, dropped to it and settled to sleep.

SEVEN or eight miles away Smiler was settling down for the night in the barn. He now had everything there he needed. He had his clothes, the borrowed radio, two borrowed blankets from the spare bedroom, a small store of food he had bought on the way back, drinking and washing water in a bucket he had found in the barn. The first day of a new regime was almost over.

Back at Danebury House Mrs. Lakey was sitting in one of the leather armchairs, smoking a cigar and sipping a glass of whisky. Tonks was asleep before the fire. Miss Milly sat in the other chair, sipping a glass of sweet Marsala wine.

Mrs. Lakey said, "Well, what do you think of the boy, Milly?"

"He's a good boy, Jelly." Jelly was her nickname for her sister, Angela, and Mrs. Lakey had learned to put up with it.

"Could be," announced Mrs. Lakey slowly. "Tonks has taken to him. That's a good sign."

"I've taken to him, too," said Miss Milly, and added, "And Jelly, for all the work that Johnny has to do, three pounds a week is not enough. He should have four."

"Nonsense, Milly. Boys should work for the love of a job."

"Four," said Miss Milly. "He's got to pay his way with his aunt."

Mrs. Lakey sighed and said, "Toss you for it."

"Right," said Miss Milly. She produced fivepence from her handbag and spun it on the table. "Heads four, tails three."

The coin settled down and showed a head.

"I win," said Miss Milly, smiling.

"You've got a soft heart, Milly."

"And so have you, only you don't show it often. As soon as I get a chance I'll go and see Johnny's aunt in Crockerton. Poor boy, how awful losing his mother and father like that."

WHEN Smiler arrived at work the next morning he was greeted by Mrs. Lakey at the back door and invited in for a cup of coffee. Over the coffee she told him he was showing such promise that she had decided to up his wages to four pounds a week. However, he would have to take on cleaning out the stables and feeding Penny and Bacon. Later, if he liked, she would teach him to ride.

During the following days Smiler buckled down to his job with cheerfulness and goodwill, and soon knew his way around the place. Some of the animals became great favourites with him. He particularly liked a yellow-and-white English setter dog called Lemon Drop and a black-and-tan Gordon setter bitch called Fairy. When he took the dogs for a walk around the paddock and up the little valley beyond it, he always had to keep an eye on Lemon Drop because he had a habit of wandering.

There was plenty of coming and going at Danebury House. Smiler got to know all the calling tradesmen: the butcher, the baker, the milkman; and everyone got to know Smiler (Johnny) and to accept him. Miss Milly fussed over him like a mother hen and he ate like royalty. Outside, Mrs. Lakey kept him hard at work and he grew strong and fit. After two weeks Mrs. Lakey put him up on Penny and gave him his first riding lesson. It ended with his being thrown into a watercress pool in the middle of the paddock; but at the end of the first week Mrs. Lakey said, "Good, boy. You look less like a sack of hay on a seesaw than you did."

On the road between Crockerton and Heytesbury people got to know Smiler and would wave to him as he passed. At Ford Cottage he had fallen into an easy routine. Each night when he got back he went into the cottage and checked the mail in case there was a postcard from Major Collingwood to Mrs. Bagnall saying when he was coming home. On Sunday he would get on his bike and explore the country and, in the evening, go into Warminster to the cinema. He saved the best part of his earnings, slowly amassing a small hoard of pound notes which he kept in a tin box behind a loose board in the barn loft. The rest of his belongings he hid under the hay before he left each morning.

Before the first month was out he found a way to write to Ethel and Albert. One day the dogmeat man asked Smiler to go down to Southampton on a Saturday to see a football match. So Smiler took the day off and went with him. In Southampton he posted a letter which read:

Dear Sis and Albert, Don't worry about me I am doing fine and am shipping to sea for six months. Can't tell you the name natcheraly. Not to worry I am in the pink.

Samuel M.

Albert—forced by Ethel—passed the information to the Southampton police, who made a few inquiries around the docks and shipping companies, but "natcheraly" got nowhere.

The weeks went by. March came, with its high winds and occasional days hot enough to make one think of summer. The catkins bloomed and the snowdrops gave way to daffodils and crocuses. Once or twice smart snowstorms returned to remind everyone that winter wasn't going to pass without a few last skirmishes.

Every fortnight Smiler went into Warminster and bought himself a tube of dye and some suntan stuff from Woolworth's to give his hair and face a new dressing. Every time he did so Mrs. Lakey would look at him oddly the next morning.

Once in Woolworth's Smiler also went to the electrical counter to get a battery for the transistor radio. As he was looking over the display, a voice said, "Hullo, you."

Smiler looked up to meet the dark eyes of Ivy (who liked to be called Pat) Bagnall. "Hullo," he said.

"You're Johnny Pickering, aren't you? Remember me?"

Smiler said, " 'Course I do. Pat Bagnall."

"You still living in Warminster?"

"Yes, sort of. Just outside."

"Ever go to the Youth Club?"

"No. I don't go for that scene."

"You ought to try it. Like to come one night with me?" She said it with a smile and a little toss of her head which Smiler liked. But a youth club was the last place he wanted to visit. People who ran youth clubs asked questions and took an interest in you.

"Can't really," he said. "I work most nights."

"Where?"

Smiler did some quick thinking. "Oh, a garage down Heytesbury way." To change the subject, he went on, "You like it here?"

"So-so. But I'm thinking of getting another job."

Smiler, giving up the idea of buying a battery, said, "Well, see you around sometime."

After work the girl at the cosmetics counter said to Pat, "Who's that chap I saw you talking to? One with a green parka."

"Oh, him. He's just a chap I know."

"Dyes his hair, don't he? And uses suntan stuff?"

" 'Course not."

"He does, you know. Comes in regular once a fortnight." The girl giggled. "And they say us girls is the vain ones."

That night, as Mrs. Lakey and Miss Milly sipped at their after-dinner whisky and Marsala, Mrs. Lakey said, "That boy. He's good with animals. Got Captain Black's brute of an Alsatian right under his thumb. Dog would lick his boots if he said so."

"Animals are good judges," said Miss Milly.

"So would people be if they used their ears and eyes. Anything about him ever worry you, Milly?"

"No. He does his work and he's got a good appetite. Polite, cheerful, and clean—for a lad. Why?"

"I just wondered, Milly. Did you ever get to see his aunt?"

"Not yet. I haven't been over that way."

"Well, don't bother. I met old Judge Renton in Warminster yesterday. He lives Crockerton way. Asked him about the boy and his aunt. Said she was a good, solid body. Spoke well of the boy, too. So don't bother, Milly. You've got enough on your hands already." Mrs. Lakey picked up a newspaper and hid behind it.

By THE beginning of April Yarra was very close to her cubbing time and had grown heavy and full in the belly. Now, when she hunted a hare or rabbit, she killed her quarry quickly because she did not like to run at top speed for long. She found food and water easy to come by. She lived mostly in the Sherman tank, though she now had other sleeping places as well.

At Longleat Park there had been no news of her since they had lost her in the snowstorm. This worried the cheetah warden, who feared she might have had some accident and been killed. Her carcass might be quietly rotting in some lonely thicket or gully. On the other hand, he realized that she might have found her way up onto the plain, and he had asked the land wardens to keep an eye out for her.

So far none of them had sighted her, chiefly because she moved about during the early morning and late evening. However, many of the birds and animals knew Yarra. A carrion crow marked her morning and evening rounds. When she killed, he would circle aloft until she had eaten, and then move down for his pickings. The deer knew her, and moved fast when her scent came on the wind. One or two lucky hares, who had escaped her, knew her.

The only human who saw Yarra during this period was Smiler. One April day, when the fat leaf buds were beginning to green the trees and the sheltered banks held the pale full glow of primroses, Smiler lost Lemon Drop on a walk up the valley. He missed the dog when he got back to the kennels. It was four o'clock and both Miss Milly and Mrs. Lakey were out. So he shut up the other dogs and went in search of Lemon Drop, knowing where he would probably find him. At the top of the valley was a small wood of lofty, smooth-barked beech trees, and Lemon Drop had a passion for squirrel hunting there.

When Smiler was fifty yards from the trees he heard Lemon Drop barking. He could tell he was at the top end of the wood, which was bounded by a wire fence to prevent cattle straying on to Salisbury Plain. He went into the wood and found Lemon Drop at the foot of a tall beech tree growing beside the fence. The dog was looking upward and barking furiously.

Smiler looked upward, too, and immediately stood transfixed. Lying along a thick branch was Yarra, glaring down at the dog from a height of about fourteen feet. She now and again gave a threatening hiss and switched her long tail to and fro.

For a few moments Smiler saw her clearly, the sunlight catching her orange-and-black pelt, one foreleg dangling over the bough. Then she saw him. He was a big human being and she knew better than to stay where she was. She rose and leaped from the branch, clear over the boundary fence on to the plain. She was soon lost over a rise in the ground.

Lemon Drop rushed to the fence, barking and growling. Smiler slipped the lead on to his collar and dragged him away, protesting and whining. He decided that the best thing he could do was to forget that he had ever seen Yarra. He knew that the plain was used by the army, and soldiers, he argued, could well look after themselves. If he reported Yarra to Mrs. Lakey it would bring the police around and attract too much attention to himself.

When Smiler got back to Danebury House, Mrs. Lakey and Miss Milly still had not returned, but Joe Ringer, the dogmeat man, was there. His little green van was in the yard and he was off-loading dogmeat into the storehouse.

"Where've you been then, Johnny? I could have pinched the silver from the house and helped myself to a dozen eggs."

"Lemon Drop went on the loose," said Smiler.

"Itchy feet and a sharp nose he's got. But too big for delicate work like . . . well, let's leave it at that." Joe winked.

Smiler knew exactly what he meant, because everyone knew that Joe was a poacher in his spare time. He was a slight, wiry, middle-aged man who had worked around Warminster and Heytesbury for fifteen years. He lived alone in a small cottage, and he lived like a king. Whether in season or out, Joe fed himself and his friends on the fat of the land—trout, pheasant, partridge, delicious rabbit stews and baked grayling. Also, there was always a large cask of cider just inside Joe's kitchen door. When he had given Smiler supper after taking him to the Southampton football match, Smiler had been so full of food and cider that he could hardly cycle home. Sometimes Joe let Smiler drive the old green van on the road between Danebury House and Heytesbury.

Joe, who was curious about everyone and everything, knew perfectly well that Smiler (Johnny to him) had no aunt living at Crockerton. But because he liked Smiler, he kept what he knew to himself. He said now, "What you doing Sunday next?"

"Nothing," said Smiler.

"Well then, I got an order for some early peewees' eggs. Like to help me collect 'em?"

"Peewees?"

"Lapwings, Johnny. Them birds what nest up on the downs. Could be some laying already. Fifty pence a dozen I get. Give you a quarter of what we make. All right?"

160

"Yes. I'd like that, Mr. Ringer."

"Right then. My place. Eight o'clock. And don't blab it around. The eggs is protected."

"Protected?"

"By law. Shouldn't take 'em. But if nobody did the things they shouldn't the world would stop going round."

When Smiler got back to Ford Cottage that evening, he paid his usual visit to the house to look at the letters which had been delivered while he was away. There was no postcard from Major Collingwood. What Smiler didn't know was that Mrs. Bagnall that morning had received a card at her own house from the major. It said that he and his wife—who was now in good health—were coming back on Sunday afternoon.

WHILE Joe was talking to Smiler, Yarra was making her way across the plain to her new sleeping place. The evenings were much longer now. After the soldiers had gone there was still a good two hours of daylight. She went north for about three miles, then up a long barren slope studded here and there with turf-topped weapon pits. She reached the top of the slope and came out on its ridge.

Below her was a long, narrow valley running away to her right towards the far stretches of the plain. On the far side of the hill and lower down, there was a narrow road and a collection of village houses with roofs and windows shattered, gardens wild and overgrown. Beyond the houses on a rising slope, partly seen through bushes and trees, was a grey stone church. Lost and isolated in the miles and miles of plain, the village held no human life except when the soldiers came.

Yarra dropped down the steep valley-side. Fifteen feet below the ridge grew four or five ash and alder trees. Behind them, perfectly screened by briers and thorns, was an opening just big enough to take Yarra's body. Inside, a narrow passageway curved back a couple of yards and then opened out into a circular den about five feet in diameter. Over the years it had been the home of rabbits, badgers and foxes. It was dry and warm, and Yarra meant to have her cubs there.

She went into it now. In the half-gloom she scraped at the loose chalk floor, then dropped to it and made herself comfortable. She lay, stretched flat out, her legs thrust away from her body. Suddenly she twitched and stirred and gave a little growl. Inside her one of the cubs had kicked and moved.

Within the next forty-eight hours Yarra was due to cub.

Six

YARRA had her cubs at six o'clock on Saturday evening. It had been a beautiful, warm April day. She lay on the patch of chalk just outside the cave entrance, blinking her eyes in the sun. Two cuckoos exchanged calls most of the morning. Once a jay sat in an ash above Yarra and scolded and shrieked at her. The movement in her belly went through her in slow waves and she changed her position frequently to find ease.

As the afternoon finally wore away, Yarra got up and went into the gloom of the cave. Within an hour two cubs were born, a male and a female. They were little larger than kittens. Their eyes were shut and there were only the faintest markings on their grey bodies. Yarra nuzzled the cubs close to her and licked and groomed them. After an hour they found her dugs and began to suck.

Yarra lay happily with them, her head facing the cave entrance, her ears alert for any sound. When darkness came the cubs slept, cradled in the warm fur of her belly. Yarra caressed them with her muzzle. The restlessness had gone from her and she was at peace.

With the coming of dawn she felt hungry. She stood up. The cubs sprawled away from her clumsily and then found one another. They huddled blindly together as Yarra left the cave.

She went up over the valley ridge on to the wide plain lands. Suddenly she caught a familiar scent. As she froze and surveyed the ground, a small fallow deer took to its feet ahead of her and went away like the wind. Yarra's body was lighter now and there was a fierce joy in her that spurred her on as much as her hunger. She ran down the deer within a hundred yards, bowling it over. The two animals rolled in a flurry of flying legs, and when they came to a stop Yarra's jaws were clamped across her quarry's neck. The deer died quickly and Yarra settled to eat.

She ate part of the belly and one of the haunches, leaving most of the hide untouched. Then she left the carcass and turned back towards the valley. High above her the carrion crow had seen the kill. When Yarra left he moved in to have his breakfast.

Yarra did not go straight to her cave. She moved along out of sight of the valley and the deserted village, where yesterday she had seen a land warden's patrol car. When she was directly above the cave, she came back over the ridge, her silhouette low against the skyline, and dropped down the few feet to the opening.

Inside the cave the cubs had become separated and were mewing and shivering. Yarra gathered them into the warmth and shelter of her belly fur. They soon found her dugs and began to suck. Yarra lay back as they fed and purred softly.

SMILER was up early that morning, too. He had a quick breakfast of cheese and biscuits in the barn, washed himself in his bucket and then cycled off to Joe Ringer's cottage.

Joe was waiting for him by the van. To Smiler's surprise Joe drove into Heytesbury and then took the road up to the plain past Danebury House. He stopped at the post-barred entry and had Smiler get out and raise the pole for him. Smiler asked about the notices about unexploded missiles.

"Eyewash," said Joe. "They pinched the land from the public

and now they don't want 'em a-tramping over it. But the officers and their friends shoot and hunt over it. Think they'd do that if there was land mines and such like about? No, me lad, most you'll find is maybe a shell what ain't gone off when it should."

Joe drove along the road for about a mile to an abandoned Nissen hut with both ends missing. He drove the van into the arched iron span and it was effectively hidden from sight.

A few minutes later they were moving over a small plateau hunting for the lapwings' nests. Joe had a pair of field glasses and would sit watching the birds in the air or for bird movement on the ground. The peewits nested right out in the open. They always landed some way away from their nests and then moved through the long grass towards them. Joe had no trouble finding a few nests, but Smiler was far from expert. He was standing looking about him when Joe said, "Go on, Johnny—you got a nest there."

"Where?" said Smiler.

"Right under yer nose," said Joe, pointing.

Smiler looked down. A yard in front of him on the almost bare ground was a shallow depression with three eggs in it. The green-and-brown eggs blended perfectly against their background.

"Only one from each nest, mind," said Joe. "Mother Nature's a generous old gal, but she don't like greedy people."

They spent the whole morning looking for nests and collecting the eggs, which Joe packed into small boxes. Once he caught Smiler by the arm and pulled him down quickly. "Stick your head between your legs and your hands under your arms—like this. And don't move!"

Smiler obeyed. Not far away he heard the sound of a passing car. "What is it, Mr. Ringer?" he asked, head between his knees.

"Land warden. But he won't see us. Not at this distance. White face and hands is the giveaway. Right now we look just like a couple of big molehills." When the noise of the car died away, Joe raised his head and winked at Smiler.

Confident under the protection of Joe, Smiler thoroughly enjoyed himself. He was tempted to tell Joe about Yarra, but in the end he decided against it. If they should come across Yarra by accident, Joe would know how to deal with the situation.

At midday they went back to the van to eat. Joe had loaded aboard cold pork sausages, hard-boiled eggs, bread and cheese, and two bottles of cider. After they had eaten, Joe said, "Now I'll show you where me old daddy was brought up."

He then took Smiler on almost the same line cross-country that Yarra had taken a few days before. When they came to the valley which held the deserted village, Joe sat down on the slope.

"That's Imber village, Johnny. What's left of it. Prettiest village on the whole of the plain it was till the army folk took it. See the church? My grandmammy's buried there. And my daddy grew up in a house that ain't standing no longer."

He told Smiler all about the place: how when the Second World War came, the people all had to leave so that the village could be used for training American and British troops in house-to-house fighting. The same training still went on. "I tell you, Johnny," Joe said, "when the folk had to leave this place it broke many a heart. 'Course, *they* very kindly out of their big military hearts lets 'em come back once or twice a year. Special treat to have a service in the church."

Smiler said, "It must've been nice living up here."

"Well, that's what comes of fightin' and havin' wars." Joe lay back and laughed. "Know somethin', Johnny? A real secret? They took me for the army a long time back. But I upped and run, and they never caught me. Never. I'm a deserter of long standin'—and you're the first one I ever told, Johnny."

"Oh, I won't tell anyone, Mr. Ringer."

"Don't keep givin' me that Mr. Ringer bit, Johnny. I'm Joe to me friends."

Because Joe made him stop and have supper in his cottage, Smiler was late getting back to Ford Cottage. He cycled through the gloaming, and at the river bridge he stopped and looked at the water. Joe had promised to teach him all about trout fishing—in season and out.

"No findanglin' about with flies. You want a big trout—then you want a big worm on the hook." He was going to show him his way around Salisbury Plain, too. The thought of the plain gave Smiler a warm, excited feeling: maybe he'd see Yarra again. At supper he had asked Joe what he should do if he met the cheetah, say, on the plain. Joe had said, "Just stand your ground, lad, and stare it out. She'd go. Specially with a lad of your size. Now, if you was a little nipper . . . well, that might be different. But animals mostly want nothing to do with humans. . . ."

Happy, though tired, Smiler continued on his way.

Within a few seconds his happiness had gone. As he drew level with the courtyard entrance to Ford Cottage, he saw that the gate was open and a car was parked in the yard. From the kitchen window a light shone, and there were lights in the sitting room and the main bedroom. Major and Mrs. Collingwood were back!

Smiler groaned quietly to himself, "Oh, crikey! Oh, holy, smoking crikeys!" At that moment a fat drop of rain splashed on to his hand. In two minutes the rain was lashing down, churning up the surface of the river and sending Smiler racing for shelter—the only shelter he knew.

He cycled back up the hill, hid his bicycle in a coppice, and then slipped around and into the barn. Standing at the dusty window in the loft, he stripped off his parka and watched the house. What was he going to do? *What was he going to do?* Then, pulling himself together, he began to give himself a good talking-to. "Samuel M.," he said, "you've taken a little water aboard, but you aren't sunk yet by a long shot. Just think it all out! Nice and cool! No panic! *No panic!*"

INSIDE Ford Cottage, Major Collingwood was in the sitting room having his coffee after a late supper. He got up and went to the corner cupboard where the drinks were kept. He had had a long travelling day and he felt like having a glass of brandy with his coffee. As he poured himself the brandy, his eye fell on the box of cigars. He reached out for it and then changed his mind. He did not often smoke cigars, keeping them mostly for his guests.

Upstairs Mrs. Collingwood went into the bathroom to set out fresh towels. As she drew the curtains she noticed some small brown stains and frowned to herself. They looked like rust marks, she thought. But how could curtains go rusty? She puzzled over it for a moment and then put it out of her mind.

Downstairs Major Collingwood sat contentedly with his brandy and coffee. He was happy because he was home, and even happier because his wife was fully recovered. His eye fell on the sixpenny bottle on the bookshelf. It looked just the same as when he had left it (which it should have done because Smiler had replaced all the sixpences he had borrowed). When it was full, the major promised himself, he would buy a present for his wife.

SMILER had set the alarm clock for five o'clock, and when it woke him he got up and set about his plan of evacuation. He gathered all his spare clothes into a bundle and put his money box and the clock in his parka pocket. Keeping the light from his bicycle lamp down low, he tidied up the loft. He left the transistor set in full view on a hay bale. Then, not without some sadness because he had come to think of it as home, he left the barn.

He got the bicycle and rode down to the stone bridge, pausing to look back at the cottage where Major and Mrs. Collingwood were sleeping soundly. Sometime, he thought, the major would find his letter and the transistor set, and miss his clothes and the bicycle. What would he do then? Report to the police? Anyway, thought Smiler, there was nothing he could do about it except someday send the major the cost of replacements.

He began to ride slowly to work and reached Danebury House in good time, as he had intended. He knew that Mrs. Lakey never appeared out of the house before half-past seven. He rode around to the stable and put all his stuff up into the loft under a bale of straw. Then he picked up the eggs which had been laid overnight and took them down to the kitchen.

While he was there Mrs. Lakey came in. She gave him an odd look and said, "You're around early this morning, boy. Bad conscience or bad dreams, or both?"

"It was all that rain, Mrs. Lakey. I couldn't sleep."

"At your age you should sleep through a hurricane."

This morning his mind wasn't really on his work. Last night in making his plans he had been confident, but now he wasn't so sure about them. People liked you and were friendly to you, but when it came to doing a real favour . . . well, that was a horse of a different colour. However, he couldn't be gloomy for long. It was such a splendid April morning. Blackbirds and thrushes were filling the air with riotous song, and the paddock, when he exercised the dogs, was a sheet of green enamel.

At the end of the day Smiler rode up the valley to Joe's cottage and left his bicycle and belongings inside the garden gate. He went around to the back of the cottage and found Joe repainting the faded lettering on the side of his green van: JOS. RINGER—DEALER—ALL GOODS HANDLED—LOWEST PRICES.

Joe turned and said, "Hullo, Johnny. Finished for the day?"

"Yes, Mr. Ringer."

Joe frowned. "Joe it is and Joe it must stay. What you hoppin' about from one leg to the other for?"

"I got a bit of a problem, Joe."

"Is it economic, personal or religious? Help offered for all but the last."

Smiler hesitated and then he blurted out, "I got to find lodgings, Joe. And . . . I thought you might be able to help me."

Joe grinned. "Seeing as we're friends, and that's what friends is for, eh? But what you want lodgings for? Don't tell me you've had an up-and-downer with your auntie?"

"No, we haven't quarrelled. It just is . . . well . . ." Smiler didn't like telling Joe a lie, but for safety's sake he had to. "She's gone away. Her sister's very sick. Down in . . . Bristol."

Joe said, "And your aunt only heard about it this morning and had to pack her gear and hump it away to Bristol?"

"Yes."

"Short notice, eh? Who's going to look after the bungalow?"

"The woman next door."

Joe considered Smiler very closely, his face, brown as polished oak, half-thoughtful, half-smiling. Then he said, "Johnny, me lad, I'm a man as likes to keep his own business to hisself. I make a living and the ways I do it ain't always by the book. But I haven't never done anything really bad. You know what I mean by that?"

"I think so, Joe."

"You'd better *know* so, Johnny. I mean like I wouldn't want to help anyone to find lodgings that had, say, pinched money out of the church box, or who'd think nothing, say, of bundling a poor old lady off a pavement and pinching her handbag. So give me a straight answer, Johnny. You ever done anything like that?"

Smiler hesitated. He said, "I pinched a few comic books sometimes, and maybe a bottle of milk or a bar of chocolate. But I didn't ever do anything bad like you said. Not ever."

Joe nodded. "Just like I thought." He stood up. "Well, it just so happens that I like a bit of young company about the place. And it just so happens that there's two bedrooms here and I only uses one. And I ain't out to make a profit from a friend—so you can have the room for a quid a week. Make your own bed, keep your room tidy, help in the house—and the yard! Suit you?"

Delighted, Smiler cried, "Oh, thank you, Mr. Ringer!"

Joe frowned. " 'Nother thing. Every time you call me Mr. Ringer you muck out the pigpen."

"I won't forget, Joe."

"And Johnny, I don't think as I would mention your change of address to Mrs. Lakey and Miss Milly. They mightn't think I was a fit and proper person for you to lodge with."

"Of course they would. You're super."

"All the same, don't let on. What women don't know won't worry 'em. Bring your stuff in, and then we'll go get ourselves a couple of fat trout for supper."

AT THE time when Smiler was taking his belongings into Joe's cottage, Yarra was coming out of her den on the hillside. All day there had been a movement of tanks and lorries through Imber village and the crackle of blank ammunition being fired. Once a badly aimed mortar bomb had exploded on the ridge thirty yards behind the cave. Yarra, touchy now that she had young to protect, had grown angry. She was also hungry, but she would not leave the den until the men had gone from the village.

When at last the valley and village were peaceful, Yarra left the cave and moved swiftly up on to the ridge. The dry, tawny grasses of winter were marked now with new growths. Trefoils and small harebells showed their blossoms on the rabbit-bitten bare patches. Yarra's keen eyes marked every movement around

169

her: the flight of an early bee, the dance of a small hatch of flies above a rain pool, the flirt of wings and the scut of a rabbit's tail.

High above Yarra three pairs of eyes watched her. Two circling buzzards drifted in her wake, waiting for her to make a kill. And sliding crosswind below them, the carrion crow watched her, too. He knew that if she made a kill the buzzards would give him no peace to take a supper from the leavings. But this was the time of the year when Nature began to spread her banquet for the predators. Nests were filling with young birds, and the warrens held young rabbits. The carrion crow, an ancient, weathered bird of the plains, knew that any hole or cranny was likely to hold something good to eat.

For many days now he had seen Yarra coming out of her cave and he was curious. He watched her move away into a fold of the plain, then flapped down to settle on an ash outside the entrance. He cocked his head and listened, but could hear nothing because the cubs were deep in milk-gorged sleep. He sat there for ten minutes, the sun striking turquoise and purple sheens from his tail feathers. Then he uttered a bad-tempered *kwaarp*, flew to the ground and stalked slowly into the cave. When his eyes grew accustomed to the gloom the crow saw a slight movement at the back of the cave as one of the cubs stirred in its sleep. He moved forward cautiously, his great black beak held ready to thrust. One blow would pierce the skull of a young rabbit or kitten.

On the plain Yarra put up a hare from a small hollow filled with dead bracken drift. It was one which she had chased before. Then it had escaped by diving under a derelict tank, but this time there was no such refuge in sight. The hare raced away with ears laid back. He could see Yarra gaining on him, no matter how much he swerved and switched. When she was three feet from him she went into her killing leap. Desperate, the hare produced the only trick he had to offer. As Yarra took off he stopped dead in his tracks. Yarra sailed right over him, overshooting him by a yard.

The hare flashed away. Yarra, angry and hungry, screwed sideways as she landed, her talons tearing up grass and soil. In fifty yards she was on his tail again—and this time she did not miss.

In the cave on the hillside the carrion crow was standing by the cubs. Although he had never seen anything like Yarra before, the cubs were no surprise to him. He had killed many litters of wildcat kittens. These were kittens, young and tender. They were lying a little separated and the crow chose the larger for his kill. He lowered his beak and prepared to jump in and thrust with all his power. At that instant a shadow passed quickly over the mouth of the cave.

The crow swung around to face Yarra as she came quickly into the cave, carrying the hare in her mouth.

It was the last thing he ever saw. Yarra dropped the hare and leaped for him. Her jaws took him under the neck as he tried to fly up. She killed him and then shook him so that long black feathers floated about the cave. Then she dropped him and went to the cubs, waking them as she nuzzled them. They had been saved because, as Yarra had settled on the grass to eat her kill, a new instinct had been born in her. It was the instinct to take food back to her lair for the cubs, though it would be many days yet before they were ready for solid food.

AT Ford Cottage, Major Collingwood came into the kitchen. He had been puttering around the garden and barn. He was a kind, pleasant-looking man, his dark hair well streaked with grey.

He said to his wife, who was mixing eggs for an omelette, "You know, love, some blighter's pinched that old bike from the barn."

Mrs. Collingwood smiled and said, "Then you should be glad. It was just a load of old junk."

"It's funny," said the major. "Not just about the bike. But I got a funny feeling in the barn, as though something's been about."

"Well, perhaps it's the one who had the sardines, because I'm quite sure Mrs. Bagnall would never have taken them."

"You mean you've missed sardines? From in here?"

"Either that or I miscounted before we went away. Six tins, I thought. Now there are only three."

"How could you possibly remember?"

"A woman does. Now go and get cleaned up for dinner."

Major Collingwood went upstairs, looking thoughtful. Since he had done all his service in the Corps of Royal Military Police, he rather enjoyed a puzzle or a mystery. His wife had mentioned the marks on the bathroom curtain, and he now studied them carefully before beginning to tidy up.

IT WAS a few days before the trout-fishing season opened officially, but that made no difference to Joe. He was about to give Smiler his first experience of poaching trout.

They went down to the river below Joe's cottage. Here, across the stream, was a set of hatches that could be raised or lowered to regulate the flow of water to the weir pool below.

Joe tied a hook on the end of a spool of nylon line which had a small stick through the centre of it. Then he threaded several worms on the hook and clipped a heavy lead weight on to the line. He dropped the line into the water and paid it out very gently as the current took the lead weight slowly downstream along the riverbed.

"You sits here like this, Johnny me lad," he said. "And you looks all innocent and enjoyin' the view. Then, if'n a river keeper shows up, you just lets go the spool. The whole lot sinks and you come back next day and fish it out." As he spoke he paid out line slowly. "Otherwise you just pays away the line like this. Sooner or later one of them big trout below the hatch what the fishing gents can't ever get with their little bitty flies will go for the worms. And let 'im take it all. No striking like the fly-fisher folk do. That old trout'll hook himself in no time. Like this one! Whoa!"

The line in Joe's hand suddenly streaked away and downstream a fish broke water in a great silvery jump. Joe held the line firm as the trout dived and darted all over the pool. Then he hauled the fish in without any finesse. He smacked the head of the trout across a wooden post, unhooked it and dropped it into his pocket. He said, "Now then, you have a go. I've got my supper."

Smiler paid out the line as Joe had shown him, and within five minutes he had caught his supper. It was a beautiful brown trout, flecked with red and yellow spots.

"Kill 'un quick. That's a kindness some of these fancy fishers don't always bother about. That's a nice fish. Pound and half. It'll eat like nothing you've ever tasted before."

Later, they both sat in Joe's kitchen, eating grilled trout and drinking cider (Smiler being very careful how much he took, and Joe treating it like water). Smiler, as he washed up the supper things afterwards, remembered how worried he had been about how it would all turn out. And it couldn't have turned out better. Though what he would have done without Joe, he just didn't know. "Samuel M.," he told himself, "don't you ever forget what a good sort Joe is . . . and one day you've got to find some way of paying him back. Say, for instance, you got really rich. Well, then you could buy Joe a new van."

As he stood there daydreaming there wasn't a cloud on his horizon. In five or six months his father would be back.

WHILE Smiler daydreamed in Joe's Cottage, Major Collingwood and his wife were having their after-dinner coffee. The major went to get himself a glass of brandy. This time, seeing the cigar box and feeling extra happy to be back because, after all, there was no place quite like home—particularly when you had a wife like Mrs. Collingwood—he told himself that he jolly well would have a cigar with his brandy.

So he opened the cigar box and found Smiler's letter. As he looked at it, the telephone rang in the hall and Mrs. Collingwood went to answer it.

Major Collingwood liked the tone of the letter. Whoever "Hunted" was, he was a decent sort of chap with some kind of conscience. The major had already found the transistor set in the barn, though he had not yet told his wife. The letter offered him a little detection work which he felt might fill many a long hour. However, because he knew his wife might be upset at the idea that someone had used the house while they were away, he decided to trace Mr. Hunted quietly on his own.

When the major went up to bed he took a closer look at the bathroom curtain, and then a look at the contents of the bathroom cabinet. He smiled to himself. If you used dark brown hair dye it could only be to make your hair darker, surely? But if you used suntan stuff before summer came. . . . Well, that was interesting now, wasn't it? He would have to think that one out.

THE NEXT MORNING Smiler rode to work as happy as a lark. He went about his work humming a ditty that Joe sang sometimes: "Go tell Aunt Rhody the Old Grey Goose is Dead". Every time Miss Milly heard him outside she would smile and nod. Mrs. Lakey said to herself, "That boy's worse than having a canary about the place." But even she was pleased, because the only thing with a long face she liked was a horse.

It was the beginning of two months of bliss for Smiler. April ran into May, and early summer smiled on the valleys and plains. The primroses went and the bluebells came. The trout and grayling grew fat on flies, nymphs and caddis grubs. The fledglings feathered up and felt an urge in their wings that made them restless in their overcrowded nests.

Up on the plain Yarra's cubs opened their eyes, and their pelts began to take on the characteristic cheetah markings. Yarra brought them small birds, mice, and rabbits and hares. They grew stronger and steadier on their feet, and when they were bored they fought one another. The male would sometimes explore towards the mouth of the cave, but Yarra would cuff him back.

Smiler, too, began to know the plain well, for Joe often took him up there poaching. Sometimes of an evening, for the evenings had now grown long with daylight, Smiler would borrow Joe's field glasses and go up on the plain by himself. He came to learn every dip and slope, every hollow and valley-side for miles around the deserted village of Imber. He loved to lie just below some ridgetop and watch the wild sweeps of country. Through the glasses he came to know the foxes and buzzards and, on the fringe of the plain above Danebury House, he saw an old boar badger.

But the thing that really excited Smiler was that he *had* seen Yarra—twice. He had not told Joe, for the reason that Joe often spent the evening at the Angel Inn at Heytesbury. When Joe took too much cider aboard he had a habit of slipping the guard on his tongue, and Smiler didn't want Yarra caught. Her freedom had somehow become linked with his own. He felt in a funny way that it would be unlucky for him if he ever betrayed her.

He first saw her through his glasses on a Sunday evening. She was some way from Imber, hunting. He picked her up as she came quickly over a skyline. She took a hare, and he witnessed the tremendous turn of speed cheetahs can produce. The second time he saw her was from some deserted farm buildings above the village of Imber. He was watching a pair of buzzards circling when one of them suddenly planed downward out of sight. The other buzzard followed. As Smiler brought his glasses down, following the birds, he saw Yarra come over the ridge crest.

She came a few yards down the steep side and then disappeared behind a leafy screen of ash and alder trees. Smiler moved up the opposite side of the valley and examined the trees through his glasses. His observation being now from a different angle, he saw at once the tunnel entrance behind the trees. He guessed that it was Yarra's den, and made a note to keep away from it.

So the days passed for Smiler and Yarra. Smiler grew tanned over his freckles, so that he needed no artificial suntan. But every few weeks he dyed his hair (when it wanted cutting Joe would do it for him in the yard), always choosing an evening when Joe was down at the Angel and being very careful to clear up afterwards.

He knew where Pat Bagnall was now working. He had gone into the food market in Warminster, and there she was, sitting at a check-out point. He met her again one Sunday morning when he was down at the river getting some trout for his and Joe's evening meal. She told him she had come down with her father, who was doing something to the hatches. Smiler was glad of the warning because he already had two fat trout hidden in the bushes.

She wanted to know whether he still lived in Warminster. Smiler shook his head and pointed across the field to Joe's cottage. "I'm staying over there—with my uncle, Joe Ringer."

Pat laughed. "My dad knows him all right. Fancy you being related. Dad says he's worse than heron where fish is concerned."

"Uncle Joe's all right, believe me," said Smiler stoutly.

"Where do you work? Still at the garage, Heytesbury way?"

"Not now. Got a job at Danebury House. With Mrs. Lakey."

"Oh, her. My dad knows her, too." She giggled. "Lash-'em-and-bash-'em Lakey, he calls her. But he likes her."

Smiler grinned at the description of Mrs. Lakey. "So do I."

Then, with a sly twinkle, Pat said, "Still dye your hair?"

Smiler blushed. "What do you mean?"

Pat laughed. "Girl I know in Woolworth's says you used to buy hair dye there—and suntan stuff."

Thinking fast, Smiler said, "What if I did? It wasn't for me."

"For who, then?"

"Well . . . for my uncle Joe."

"What's he want it for?"

Desperate, Smiler said, "I can't really tell you. He mixes it all together and . . ." A brain wave came to him. "Well, if I tell you, promise never to let on to anyone?"

"Promise."

"Well, he uses it on white hens' eggs. People prefers brown eggs and Uncle Joe sometimes only has white ones."

Pat laughed. "What a crook. But I won't tell."

Seven

THE cheetah cubs were well over a month old and no longer stayed all day in the den. Early each morning and late in the evening Yarra would take them out on to the hillside or up to the plain. She would catch a mouse or shrew without killing it, then release it so that the cubs could chase it. They would fight and quarrel as to which one should eat it.

During the day Yarra made sure that they never went far be-

176

yond the entrance to the den. Sometimes when they were out
together she would leave them briefly to hunt down a rabbit or
a hare, and then trot back to the den, where they would all eat.

It was towards the end of May that Smiler first saw the cubs.
One evening when he was watching the entrance to the den, he
saw Yarra come out and stand sniffing the air for a while. She
moved farther out and the two cubs followed her.

Smiler nearly dropped his field glasses in surprise. Tense with
excitement, he watched Yarra pouncing into the long grass after
mice, and chuckled to himself when the clumsy cubs imitated her.

He went back to Joe that evening hardly able to conceal his
excitement. But he managed to keep quiet. It gave him a nice
warm feeling that it was his secret. Also, there was another feeling
in him. Yarra had become a wild animal again and was raising a
family in the heart of civilized England. Smiler, although town-
bred, had now become a country boy. From talks with Mrs. Lakey
and Miss Milly, he knew how the countryside was becoming
spoiled and how hard it was these days for wild animals to survive.
The hedgerows in which the birds nested were being pulled down
and wire fences put in their places. He heard about the use of pesti-
cides and chemical fertilizers that poisoned birds and animals and
seeped into the rivers to kill fish. That Yarra—not even a native
animal—was managing to survive in the midst of all this gave him
a great sympathy for her. He was determined that Samuel M.
wasn't going to give her away.

By now Major Collingwood had discovered the loss of his green
parka and guessed, too, what had happened to the old bicycle.
He had heard about the escaped cheetah, Yarra. He had heard,
also, that a young lad named Samuel Miles, who had run away from
an Approved School only to be caught by the police, had escaped
again in a storm while being taken to Salisbury. This interested
the major very much. Hunted's letter, he felt, read like a young
lad's letter. He went into the police station at Warminster and got
a description of Samuel Miles.

The police inspector, who was a friend of the major, gave him
all the facts, then asked, "What do you want to know all this for?"

The major winked and said, "Sounds interesting. If *you* haven't picked him up yet I thought I'd like to try my hand at it."

"Well—you'll have to go abroad if you want him. He wrote a letter to his sister saying he was shipping to sea."

A few days later the major drove to Bristol to see Ethel and Albert. Ethel showed him Smiler's letter, and the major recognized the handwriting at a glance.

"Do you think he really went to sea?" he asked.

Albert said, "Could have done. It's in the blood. That's where his dad is—and won't be back for several months."

"There's more than the sea in his blood," said Ethel. "There's wildness. Fancy—knocking an old lady down and taking her bag."

"I don't believe it!" said Albert. "Smiler wouldn't 'ave done that. And wherever he is, he won't turn up until his dad's back. Thinks the world of him, he does. Thinks he can straighten it out."

"You must both be very worried about him," said the major.

Albert grinned. "No. If ever there was a boy that could look after himself, it's Smiler."

Driving home the major found himself more than ever interested in Smiler. He decided that if the boy had used the cottage and the barn, then someone might have seen him. He asked Mr. Bagnall and got no help from him. He asked Mrs. Bagnall with the same result. Then one day he met Pat Bagnall pushing her bicycle up the hill from the bridge. He chatted with her for a while and then said, "While I was away did you ever see a young lad— say about fifteen—around the place? Tallish, strong lad, he'd be. Darkish brown hair and very suntanned."

Pat considered. It was an exact description of Johnny Pickering. She knew the major well and she liked him. But she liked Johnny, too. So she said casually, "No, sir, I can't say that I did."

And that—for all his cleverness and professional training—was as far as Major Collingwood got for the moment.

It was about this time that Mrs. Lakey discovered that the boy was living with Joe. Mrs. Lakey was a keen fisherwoman. On two Sunday mornings while fishing the pool below the hatchway she had looked across the field and seen Johnny feeding the pigs in

Joe's ramshackle pen. A few days later she tackled Joe in her usual straightforward manner. "Is that boy living with you?"

"What boy, ma'am?"

"Don't wriggle like a worm on a hook, Joe. The boy. He's living with you?"

"Yes, ma'am, he is."

"Why?"

"Well, 'cos in a way, I'm kind of his uncle. Distantly relationed, you might say, to his aunt."

"Why isn't he with his aunt?"

"The one at Crockerton, you mean, ma'am?"

"I've never heard of another."

Joe smiled. "Oh, yes, ma'am, he's got another. What lives in Bristol. And that's where his Crockerton auntie is right now. Lookin' after her, 'cos she's sick. Got a very bad leg. Plays her up somethin' cruel every summer. Not to mention hay fever. Martyr she is to every ache and pain goin'."

"I'm not in the mood for medical fairy stories. The boy lives with you while his aunt's away?"

"Yes, ma'am."

"And no doubt you're seeing he doesn't get into bad ways?"

"Yes, ma'am."

"Never poaches, does he?"

"Oh, no, ma'am."

"Or worms for trout?"

"Oh, no, ma'am. And he goes to church sometimes of a Sunday." Joe put on a very serious face. "And I really do hope, ma'am, that you don't think I ain't a fit and proper person to bring up me own nephew. Ain't he given you every satisfaction at Danebury, ma'am?"

"He has, Joe. And that's the way I want it to go on. So, you watch your step with him. He's a good boy as boys go."

Mrs. Lakey privately felt that Joe was as fit a person as anyone for a boy to live with. If fishing was dull she wasn't above putting a worm on a hook herself to get a trout. Apart from all this, Mrs. Lakey was a person who—though always ready to help if asked— was a great believer in letting other people, especially young people, work out their own problems. She didn't know what the boy's problem was, but as far as she could see he was coping with it perfectly capably at the moment.

By THE first of June the cheetah cubs were seven weeks old. They could mouse-hunt for themselves, and were sometimes quick enough to take a slow-moving young lark or green plover in the long grasses. Although Yarra still provided the bulk of their food, there were times now when she would cuff them away from the game she brought back. She was deliberately making them hungry to strengthen their own hunting instincts. If she awoke in the night to find them sucking at her dugs she would roll away from them, denying them the little milk flow that remained.

Now that her maternal instinct had been satisfied, there was a new want in Yarra. Like all cheetahs she was a sociable animal and had a need for the company of her own kind. Somewhere in the vastness of the plain there had to be another Apollo to mate with, and other cheetahs to pack and hunt with. It was this that one night took her quartering and hunting into the face of a stiff north wind which was blowing across the plain.

She roamed for an hour, eventually coming out on a high bluff at the northern extremity of the plain. Below, the land fell away into a great valley with cornfields, pastures and patches of woodland. Along the ridge of the bluff ran a barbed-wire fence. Yarra turned left and followed it for a few hundred yards, the wind buffeting at her thick, rough coat. Suddenly a new scent came downwind to her.

She lifted her muzzle into the wind and took the scent. From the edge of a pasture beyond the fence came a low, anxious, bleating sound. Yarra caught the movement of something small and white. Curious, she leaped the fence and began to walk towards the object.

The fence was old and in places had collapsed. Twenty yards from Yarra strands of barbed wire lay coiled and twisted on the ground. Caught by a hind leg in one of the coils was a small Ayrshire calf, white-coated, with a scattering of brown markings. It was no larger than some of the deer Yarra hunted and from its scent she knew it was good eating. Slowly, with her deliberate, high-shouldered walk, she paced toward the calf. Catching Yarra's scent the calf plunged and tugged against the wire.

The movement excited Yarra and she leaped. She landed on the calf's back and brought it crashing to the ground, her jaws clamped across its neck. The calf kicked and struggled under her as she slowly throttled it, worrying and shaking its neck. High above, the wind roared and whistled through the tall beeches, ripping off leaves and small twigs.

From farther down the sloping pasture the calf's mother had heard the distress calls of her young. She came downwind now, seeking her calf. Yarra heard no sound of the cow's movement because it was drowned by the noise of the gale.

The calf died under Yarra. She opened her jaws and released it. As she did so, she saw the cow almost on top of her.

The Ayrshire was a big animal. She had a sleek white hide blotched with red and brown. Like all Ayrshires she had very distinctive horns. They were long, and curved outward and upward—formidable weapons. Under normal circumstances the cow would never have approached Yarra, but now she lowered her head and rushed at her. Yarra leaped sideways but she was a fraction too late. As she rose into the air, the cow jerked her head with a quick sideways slash. One long, curving horn struck Yarra in the side, daggering deep into her belly.

Yarra gave an angry, spitting snarl of rage and pain as she was flung high through the air. She thudded to the ground, rolled over and then raced away as the cow came charging after her. She leaped the boundary fence, blood dripping from her wound, and started back across the plain toward her den.

With every step Yarra took, the pain in her belly increased and she grew more and more exhausted. Once she halted and sat and licked at the wound. Behind her the gale-flattened grasses were spotted with the trail of her lifeblood.

Now and again she stumbled, only to pick herself up and move on. She reached the top of the ridge above the den and half-rolled, half-slid down the slope to the cave.

She stood at the entrance, her flanks heaving, her head dropping lower and lower. She took a step forward to the opening, staggered and fell. As she struggled to rise again and reach her cubs, she died.

YARRA died on a Friday before daybreak. As morning came the wind slewed round into the northwest and brought thick clouds sweeping over the plain. A warm, persistent summer rain began to fall.

The cubs, waking at first light, came out of the den and found their mother. She lay stretched out stiffly, the rain soaking into her pelt. They sniffed around her, not understanding her immobility. The male pawed at her for a moment and butted at her with his head. Then, not liking the hard, driving rain, he trotted back into the den. The female stayed outside longer. She walked around Yarra making small mewing noises and then, getting no response, bad-tempered little spitting sounds. When Yarra still showed no movement, she moved back into the cave.

The rain kept the cubs inside all day, huddled together at the back of the den. Towards midnight the sky cleared and the fresh-washed stars shone down diamond-bright. The male cub, aware of the absence of rain noises in a moment of wakefulness, got up, stretched himself and moved toward the mouth of the cave. He was hungry.

He was two feet from the entrance when there was a noisy, rumbling sound. Something hit him sharply across the neck. He spat and snarled with anger and bounded back to the rear wall of the den—as the roof of the passageway collapsed. Soaked and weakened by the rain, the ancient archway above the entrance had suddenly subsided and sealed up the den.

Outside, the ground above the cave slipped forward in a minor avalanche which half buried Yarra's body, leaving only her head, shoulders and forelegs visible. Later that night a fox caught her scent and came to investigate. It sat for a long time looking at her and then moved on. At first light the two buzzards, spiraling hundreds of feet above, saw her. A white-bellied mouse rummaging in the undergrowth saw her. All of them knew Yarra and all of them kept their distance.

In the cave behind her the two cubs mewed, growled and spat, knowing only their hunger and growing thirst. The male cub found a small puddle of water trapped in a hollow of the passage-way floor. He lapped at it and was joined by the female. By mid-morning their water supply had been exhausted.

Eight

ABOUT noon on Sunday, Smiler cycled up to the plain. He hid his bicycle in a field and took one of his many routes to Imber. Then he climbed to his favourite spot for watching Yarra and the den.

The moment he focused his field glasses on the mouth of the den he saw the half-buried Yarra. The glasses brought up clearly the torn turf and the piled debris closing the mouth of the cave. He jumped up and ran down the valley-side, but when he reached the bottom he stopped. Yarra *might not* be dead. She might just be trapped and unconscious. If she were still alive she could be dangerous. "You've got to go cautious, Samuel M.," he told himself.

He went up the other side of the valley at an angle that would take him clear of the cave. Reaching the ridgetop, he went over it and moved slowly back along it until he judged that he was level with the cave. He crawled to the side of the steep drop and had a clear view of Yarra. From the way she lay he was certain she was dead. Her pelt was matted and dirty and her mouth gaped unnaturally, showing her teeth. Hard against the back of his eyes Smiler felt the sting of tears and fought them back. He and Yarra had, in a way, escaped together. Now Yarra was gone.

Lying there, he buried his face in his arms for a while. Then he slowly got up and went down to the little plateau where Yarra lay. He moved to her and put a hand on her neck. Seeing the blocked mouth of the cave, he guessed how the collapse had happened.

Then he heard very faintly a thin mewing noise. He went to the blockage and put his ear against it. The noise came again, this time mixed with an angry, spitting sound. Smiler scratched his head. The cubs were trapped inside. What on earth was he to do?

"Take it slowly, Samuel M.," he told himself. "Thing Number One is to get them out." They would be hungry, thirsty and frightened—and young animals in that state might be difficult to handle. Then there was Yarra. He had to do something about her.

As he sat there the buzzards up above saw him and swung away. All day they had watched Yarra and had been on the point of closing in for a cautious inspection. A carrion crow watched from a treetop at the valley mouth. Dozens of birds and animals were aware of Smiler as he sat dealing with his problem.

At last he rose and made his way over the ridgetop. Not far away was one of the many fire lookouts which were dotted across the plain. This one, he knew, held an old spade.

WITHIN twenty minutes Smiler was back, digging at the blocked entrance to the cave, working hard and fast. Fortunately the collapsed roof of the den opening was all loose soil and turf. Suddenly his spade went through the last of it and a hole about the size of a man's head opened up.

Inside the cave the sudden sunlight blinded the two cubs. The male arched his back and hissed, half in fear and half in defiance. The female crouched by him and gave a series of small mews.

Outside, Smiler clicked his tongue and made encouraging sounds. In his knapsack was a small roast chicken for his lunch. He broke off one of the legs and held it near the hole. He couldn't see the cubs, but he could hear them moving and crying.

Both cubs suddenly got the scent of the chicken and they ceased their noise. The male cub moved slowly forward towards the daylight. He could see part of Smiler's face, but hunger overcame his fear. He climbed over the loose soil to the opening.

Smiler, shaking with excitement, saw the male's head framed just inside the opening. Behind it, the face of the female appeared. He dropped the chicken leg in front of them. The movement made both cubs jump back a little, spitting and hissing. Smiler, holding himself very still, made soft coaxing noises.

After a moment the male cub came forward slowly, then suddenly pounced, grabbed the chicken leg and disappeared back into the cave, followed by the female. Smiler then tore the rest of the chicken in two and threw one half into the cave. It landed near the female cub, who seized it and ran into a corner.

As they ate, Smiler blocked the opening he had made, piling large turfs and clods of earth into it. The cubs had to be fed and watered, but he could not risk their coming out of the den and escaping. Now that Yarra was dead, *he* had to see that they came to no harm until he could work out a plan for them.

Hating every moment but knowing he had to do it, Smiler dragged Yarra free from the soil that partly covered her. He knew exactly what he must do with her. If he tried to bury her, he could never cover up the evidence of his digging. But scattered all over the plain were old wells which had been dug in years past. The nearest was a quarter of a mile away. Smiler dragged Yarra to the well and pulled aside the timbers which covered it. He let her drop through the gap. As he replaced the heavy planks there were tears in his eyes. It was a moment of great sorrow.

He went back to Imber village and found an old bucket which he filled with water from a spring. He took the bucket to the den entrance and went back again to the village. This time he returned with three short lengths of plank and a battered tin bowl.

For the next hour Smiler worked away, keeping a sharp lookout for any land warden. He enlarged the small entrance to the cave and then tossed the last half of the chicken through to the cubs. They took it and began to quarrel over it. He filled the bowl with water and put that through the opening. To Smiler's delight, both cubs rushed to it and began to lap thirstily, taking no notice of him. He was tempted to reach through and stroke them, but he was country-wise now, and knew that if you wanted to be friends with an animal you never rushed things.

While the cubs ate and drank, Smiler arranged the three short planks vertically across the mouth of the cave. He fixed the outer planks firmly top and bottom, but left the middle one free at the top so he could pull it up to make an opening. Then, knowing that the cubs were all right for the time being, he left them.

All the way back to Joe's cottage, Smiler occupied himself with his real problem. He had to see that the cubs were taken to Longleat, where they would be properly looked after. That meant he had to telephone the police or someone. And the moment he did so he would have to take off right away from this part of the world. Because even if he made an anonymous call, the news would become public and then Joe would put two and two together. Joe knew how much time he spent up on the plain.

He didn't want to move on. He liked working at Danebury House. He liked Miss Milly and Mrs. Lakey, and he liked Joe (better than anyone), and in a way he quite liked seeing Pat Bagnall now and then. "*But*, Samuel M.," he told himself, "no matter what *you* like and what *you* want to do—you've got to tell about the cubs, and that means you *have got* to move on. Not today. Not this week. But pretty soon."

Sadly, Smiler went back to the cottage and counted his savings. He had thirty-odd pounds, a few bits of clothing and a bicycle. All he needed now was a plan.

Meanwhile, he had the cubs to take care of. This was very hard work. He was up and away from the cottage long before Joe was awake. He would ride up past Danebury House, hide his bicycle and make his way across the plain to the cubs. Food was no problem. He packed his knapsack with dogmeat from Joe's store and dropped a shilling into Joe's cashbox now and then to pay for it. He would give the cubs their breakfast, refill their water bowl, and then shut them up and be back at Danebury in time for work. In the evening he would take some dogmeat from the Danebury Kennel's store and go back up to the cubs.

Within three days the cubs got to know him. When he came to the cave door he would whistle to them. The moment he pulled up the plank they would be waiting for him, snapping or spitting with excitement. But he was worried about giving them exercise. Fortunately the male cub solved this problem.

Smiler arrived on the fourth evening to find that the middle door plank had been butted away and both cubs were playing in the undergrowth. He gave his low whistle. The cubs broke into a fast trot through the long grasses, every high-shouldered movement and graceful stride reminding him of Yarra.

Smiler took out a piece of meat and, holding it high, began to move up to the den entrance. Both cubs followed him. Just before they reached the small plateau, the male cub made a sudden leap towards the meat that nearly took Smiler by surprise. It was a higher jump than he had thought the cub could make.

After that it was easy. Smiler tossed two large chunks of meat into the den and the cubs went in after them. He gave them water and then made the door much firmer so they could not get out. On the way back to the cottage he worked out a plan for exercising the little animals.

It worked perfectly. Next morning he pulled up the plank door and held out his meat-filled knapsack. Both cubs came to it. Smiler moved away and the cubs followed him. When he went back to the cave and threw meat inside, they went after it. That was the beginning of their training, and they learned quickly.

At first they would only follow him so long as he had the meat with him. But by the middle of the next week Smiler could hang his knapsack on a branch and walk off; and instead of sitting obstinately under the tree, as they had the first time, the cubs would go with him. It became a firm rule that the cubs followed him for a walk before returning to the cave to be fed. By this time, too, they would let him handle them and massage their necks, which they loved. Though Smiler was always careful when he did this. Twice the male cub had scratched him inadvertently.

Smiler was delighted with all this. So long as the weather was good and the cubs were fed and watered, there was no hurry about settling their future. The days wore into July and every morning and evening he would exercise the cubs up the long narrow valley and across a small stretch of plain at its head. If they strayed a little they would come back at the sound of his whistle.

At the valley head one evening a young rabbit got up from the grass and the male cub went after it and caught it. Smiler realized that it would be dangerous to try and take the rabbit from the cub. So he turned and began to walk back towards the den. The female followed him. He whistled to the male and after a moment the cub followed him, carrying his prey.

Slowly, Smiler learned how to handle the cubs in different situations. And he gave them names. The male he called Rico and the female Afra.

One Friday evening Joe said to Smiler, "Johnny my lad, tomorrow afternoon I'm a-going to give you a treat. And don't tell me you don't want to come because you want to go up on that old plain. What you got hidden up there, anyways? A gold mine?"

"I just like being up there, Joe."

"So do I, Johnny. But a change won't do you any harm. We'll be back by six, so you can slip up for an hour after, if you want."

Joe duly gave him his treat, and when Smiler got back he knew exactly how to solve part of his remaining problem.

WHILE Joe was off with Johnny, Major Collingwood was having tea with his wife at Ford Cottage. They were having it out on the lawn overlooking the river. The major, although he still thought about it sometimes, had long ago come to a dead end in tracing Mr. Hunted. He was feeling rather sleepy from the hot sun, and now and again he dozed off as his wife chatted to him. He surfaced briefly to hear her finishing a sentence. ". . . and although they work him hard enough over there, I thought now in the long evenings he could give you a hand."

"Who, dear?" The major blinked his eyes open.

Mrs. Collingwood laughed. "Why, Johnny, of course."

"Who on earth is Johnny?" asked the major.

His wife shook her head. "Sometimes I think your memory is going altogether. The boy who works for Danebury House, where I go riding sometimes. I've spoken to you about him before."

"Not that I remember."

"Well, he's a nice boy. Tall and strong, with dark brown hair, and sort of freckled under his sunburn. I don't know where Angela found him. She doesn't seem keen ever to talk about him."

The major's old interest in Mr. Hunted had suddenly revived, though he was careful not to show it.

He said, "Oh, yes, I think I've seen him in Heytesbury. Does he wear an old green parka sometimes? Like one I used to have?"

"Yes, he does. Well, I was thinking that if he had the time . . ."

The major didn't hear her because he was thinking, too; thinking that he would like to have a good look at this Johnny.

This he managed to do twice during the next few days. He also met Miss Milly in Warminster the following Monday and learned that Johnny had an aunt, Mrs. Brown, who lived at Hillside Bungalow in Crockerton. The major knew that there was no Mrs. Brown and no Hillside Bungalow, and his certainty grew that Johnny was really Samuel Miles. The major, who was a kind man but one used to army discipline, found himself with a problem. It was more than a week before he came to his decision.

SMILER was never to forget the happiness of his days with Afra and Rico. The movement of the cubs racing and hunting at the top of the valley printed pictures in his mind which he would always remember. Their pelts were taking full colour, the orange, black-spotted coats rippling over their muscles. They caught mice, and twice they packed together and ran down a young hare.

Sometimes Smiler lay in the grass and the cubs would romp over him as they played. He hated the thought of the day that was coming, the day already fixed in his mind, when they would have to part company. He would have liked to stay up on the plain with them forever. They could have lived easily. There was water, food to be found, and plenty of shelter. Even in the winter, he reckoned, they would be able to manage. He saw himself in a commodious cave, a fire burning at the entrance, and Afra and Rico lying together, while the winter wind shrieked outside.

One lunchtime Miss Milly said, "That's a bad scratch on your hand, Johnny. I'll bandage it for you."

Rico had bitten lovingly at Smiler's hand and torn the flesh. While attending to it, Miss Milly said, "Jelly and I are going to dinner with a Major Collingwood at Crockerton on Friday. He asked if you'd care to do a little weekend gardening for him."

Smiler's hair nearly stood on end. "Well, Miss Milly . . . I like to have a bit of time to myself at weekends."

"And you should. I'll tell him to cast his eyes elsewhere."

If he could have told her the truth Smiler would have said that the coming weekend was going to be his last in this part of the world. On Sunday morning he meant to be up early and away in Joe's van with Afra and Rico. It would mean creeping into Joe's bedroom to get the ignition key, but Joe always slept like a log after his Saturday visit to the Angel. Smiler planned to leave a letter for him explaining where he could find the van. The thought of driving the van didn't bother him; under Joe's tuition he had become a fairly confident driver. But the thought of leaving Joe was almost as bad as that of leaving the cubs.

Nine

On Friday evening Mrs. Lakey and Miss Milly went to dinner at the Collingwoods'. They had drinks on the lawn outside the dining room. An occasional trout dimpled the surface of the river and a family of yellow wagtails played along the banks.

Mrs. Lakey and Miss Milly were old friends of the Collingwoods, so the major did not very much relish what he was going to have to do. Being a military man he had decided that it was better to do it quickly. After a few minutes' social chat, he cleared his throat and said to Mrs. Lakey, "Angela, there's something I must discuss with you and Milly. It's about your boy, Johnny."

Miss Milly said, "Johnny's a good boy, Major, but he wants his weekends free. So I'm afraid he doesn't want to garden for you."

"Afraid of a little extra work. Like all boys," said Mrs. Lakey. "Though the boy is furlongs ahead of any other I know."

"I don't mean about working for me," said the major.

"Then what else could you possibly mean, dear?" asked his wife.

"I think I know what maggot has got into your apple," said Mrs. Lakey. "The boy is Samuel Miles, isn't he?"

The major looked at her in astonishment. "You *knew*?"

"Almost from the first. Think I can't spot it when a boy's got something to hide that dyed hair can't cover?"

"*Who* is this Samuel Miles?" asked Miss Milly.

"Johnny," the major said. "He escaped from an Approved School."

"He's a good, kind, honest boy," said Miss Milly stoutly. "I don't believe a word of anything you're going to say."

Mrs. Collingwood sighed. "So far as I am concerned I would just like to know what everyone is talking about."

"Then listen," declared the major almost crossly. "His name is really Samuel Miles and he's been in this house, dyed his hair, and eaten our sardines, and taken my parka."

Mrs. Lakey smiled and said, "And what is more the boy has no aunt called Mrs. Brown of Hillside Bungalow, and if he escaped from an Approved School and from the police, more power to his elbow. Two things better escaped from I can't imagine."

Pompously, the major said, "He stole an old lady's handbag."

"Never!" said Miss Milly. "What an awful thing to say about Johnny! I think I must have some more Marsala."

Mrs. Collingwood, helping Miss Milly to more Marsala, said to her husband, "Darling, take a deep breath, count ten and then start at the beginning. Funny, I thought it looked like your parka."

The major began to explain, telling the story as he knew it.

One afternoon in Bristol an old lady had been jostled off the pavement by a boy, and had her handbag stolen. A policeman, seeing the act from a distance, had gone after the thief. Turning a corner he had spotted a boy running. He had caught him and found that he was holding the old lady's handbag with ten pounds in it. The boy was Samuel Miles. Miles had denied the theft, though he *had* been in some small scrapes with the police before.

Samuel Miles's story, however, was that he had been standing just around the corner when a boy he knew had come rushing past and tossed him the handbag, shouting, "Hide it!" The boy was one Johnny Pickering and they were not friends. In fact they disliked one another. Samuel Miles had said that, when he was caught, he was running after Pickering to make him take the handbag back.

But, the major explained, in the juvenile court Pickering's father and mother had both sworn that their son had been at home all afternoon. One of their neighbours had sworn the same. The court had decided that Samuel Miles was lying to save himself. They had found him guilty and sent him to an Approved School.

At this point Miss Milly said stoutly, "It's not true. Johnny would never do such a thing."

"It's the father and mother of all lies," said Mrs. Lakey.

"I think it's a lie, too," the major agreed. "But the point is, if Johnny is to be proved innocent, we've got to tell the police about him. Then we can have the case reopened and get him cleared. He's worked hard and honestly for you, Angela. He paid back the money he borrowed from me. He's shown resource and initiative in looking after himself and—"

"I think, dear," said Mrs. Collingwood, "that we all understand and agree with you. But it does seem hard to go—"

"Snivelling to the police," said Mrs. Lakey. "But there's some sense in what the major says. How can the law do anything for the boy unless the law has got the boy?" She looked hard at Major Collingwood. "You believe in the boy's innocence?"

"Absolutely. I inquired about the Pickerings. They haven't a good reputation. I think they were lying to protect their son."

"And you think you can clear things for the boy?"

The major said importantly, "Yes. I have friends in the Bristol police. All we have to do is tell them where Johnny is and then I'll lay a hundred to one we can clear things up."

Miss Milly stood up. "You want to ring up the police *now?*"

"Yes, Milly," said the major.

"Then," said Miss Milly firmly, "don't expect me to sit down and take dinner in your house. How could I, while the police are taking poor Johnny to spend the night in a cell?"

"Milly," said Mrs. Lakey, "ease back in the saddle a bit." She turned to the major. "The boy has been free for months. Twelve hours' delay won't do any harm, and he's not going to run away because he knows nothing of all this—"

"And," interrupted Mrs. Collingwood, "I'm not having my dinner party ruined. We've got smoked salmon and then a beautiful piece of lamb, and a sweet it's taken me all afternoon to make."

The major looked at each woman, then he shrugged his shoulders. "All right. I'll telephone them first thing in the morning."

"Poor Johnny," said Miss Milly. She sat down and took a sip of her Marsala. "Never will I believe that he robbed an old lady."

"We'll prove he didn't," said the major. "But until it can be done, he's got to be held in custody by the proper authorities."

At that moment Mrs. Bagnall, who helped whenever Mrs. Collingwood had a party, appeared and said, "Dinner is served."

WHILE Mrs. Collingwood's dinner party was in progress, Smiler was walking down the valley with Afra and Rico towards their den. The light was fading fast. The jackdaws were returning to their roosts. Fox and badger were beginning their night prowls.

When they reached the entrance to the cave, Smiler knelt down and rubbed the rough-pelted necks of Afra and Rico. Afra purred and nuzzled her head against Smiler's bent knee. Rico turned and closed his jaws gently over Smiler's hand. He knew now just how hard he could hold without harming Smiler. In the pale light the golden eyes of the two animals shone softly, their black face markings giving them a faintly laughing look.

Smiler was aware of a lump in his throat. "Samuel M.," he told himself, "Sunday morning, first thing, you'll be up and away with them. They won't see this old plain again, and neither will you."

He tossed some meat into the cave and watched the cubs enter. Then he boarded up the entrance and started for home.

When he reached Joe's cottage, Joe was in the kitchen having a last glass of cider before going to bed. "Been up top, Johnny?"

"For a bit."

Joe gave him a long look. "Anything special happened?"

"No, I'm just tired, Joe," said Smiler.

Joe said, "Sure there's nothin' wrong? Nothin' that you'd care to tell me about?"

"No, really, Joe. I'm all right."

"All right, Johnny me boy," said Joe. "Up you go then, and get your head tucked under your wing."

So Smiler went to bed, and soon afterward Joe did the same.

At four o'clock in the morning Smiler was wakened by a sharp splatter of gravel against his windowpane. He sat up, puzzled, then crossed to the window and looked down. On the narrow path below he could make out a greyish form.

"Johnny?" A pale face was turned up to him. "It's me, Pat."

"What on earth are you doing here?"

"Come to warn you, Johnny. Get dressed and come on down. Hurry, I got to get home before they finds I've been out."

Smiler dressed in a hurry and went quietly downstairs so as not to wake Joe. Pat Bagnall, in jeans and a thick sweater, was waiting for him in front of the house. She came up to him quickly and took his arm. "Now, you listen to me, Johnny, and don't interrupt 'cos I've got a lot to say, and I've got to say it fast."

Then she told him about the Collingwoods' dinner party and how her mother had overheard the conversation about Samuel Miles, alias Johnny Pickering, through the open windows. When her mother had got back that night she had told her husband all about it, full of the gossip and excitement.

"Crikeys!" said Smiler. "What am I going to do?"

"Don't be stupid. You got to get your things and go."

And Smiler saw that he had to do just that. "It's all right," he said. "I was planning to go—tomorrow. Thanks for coming to tell me. But whyever did you?"

"What a question! Because I like you, of course. And because

I reckoned it was up to you to choose. You can stay and face it out if you want to."

"Not likely. I'm off. Only my dad can clear me up. He knows how to deal with Mr. Pickering and that lot. Gosh, it was brave of you to come."

" 'Course it wasn't. You got money, and things like that?"

"Yes."

"Then be on your way. And Johnny"—she came closer to him—"when you're settled you can write to me, if you want."

" 'Course I will when it's safe."

She reached forward suddenly and kissed him. Then, with a little bubble of laughter, she was gone, running across the grass.

Smiler watched her go, not knowing quite how he felt but knowing it was a feeling he had never felt before. Then he turned and went quietly back into the house. All his things were more or less packed for his Sunday-morning departure. Now, he had to go a day sooner and there was a big problem. He *had* to get the key to Joe's van. Joe had not been to the Angel that night, and he might wake up. Well, he would have to risk that.

He collected his things and put them quietly on the floor of the little landing. In the darkness he moved stealthily towards the door of Joe's bedroom. He knew exactly where Joe's jacket would be hanging. Slowly he reached out his hand to the doorknob.

At that moment the door opened, and in the growing light from the bedroom window he was faced by the figure of Joe in a white nightshirt, his eyes shut tight.

Before Smiler could recover from his alarm, Joe began to speak in a faraway kind of voice. He said, "Done it ever since a child. Walks in me sleep. No cure for it. Terrible affliction if you lives on a cliff. When I wakes up I don't never know what I've done or heard. Like I might hear two people talkin' under me window. Like I might know one of them's in trouble and got to get away fast and far. And for which purpose there's nought better'n a car, say a nice little green van. That's always assumin' that the one what wants it 'as the key." His hand came up slowly and the palm opened. In it was the van's ignition key.

"Oh, Joe—" began Smiler, but Joe interrupted him sharply.

"Don't never talk to anyone what walks in 'is sleep. Could give 'em the jumps for the rest of their mortal. Here, lad."

The key was tossed to Smiler, who caught it.

Joe stood there, immobile, but a smile slowly passed over his face. One eye opened and shut in a wink, and he said, "Well, God bless anyone within 'earing at this moment—and send me a post-card sometime just saying—'The old grey goose ain't dead'."

He winked once more and then turned back into the room and shut the door. With tears in his eyes and a lump in his throat, Smiler picked up his stuff and ran downstairs. Five minutes later he was driving towards Heytesbury on his way up to the plain.

Tonks saw the green van go by Danebury House and barked his head off until Mrs. Lakey, half in sleep, reached for a cushion and nearly knocked him from the window seat.

In her bedroom Miss Milly lay awake having a little cry and wrestling with temptation. She wanted to get up and drive to Joe's cottage to warn Johnny. But she knew she could not do it. She was a woman of honour, and anyway in the long run it would all be for Johnny's good. After a while she started to chuckle to herself. Imagine her never guessing that Johnny dyed his hair!

And in Joe's cottage, Joe lay abed and chuckled, too. They wouldn't see Johnny for smoke. No more than they had seen *him* when he had run away from the army. Good lad, Johnny was. Wonder what it was that made him so fond of the plain? Animals, he'd bet. . . . Just loved animals, Johnny did. God bless him.

At the edge of the plain Smiler got out of the van and lifted the road pole. From there the road ran due north to drop finally into the Imber valley. By now Smiler knew all the roads and tracks like the back of his hand.

The pearl-gold flush in the eastern sky was beginning to strengthen with the coming of the sun. The larks were already aloft and in first song. A pair of greenfinches flitted across the road in front of the van. A kestrel hovered over the tank which Yarra had first used as a shelter, watching for the movement of mice around its rusted sides. There was a heavy dew over the grass, and the spiders' webs mantling the small bushes were beaded with glittering moisture.

Within ten minutes Smiler was at Imber. He drove the van under the cover of an open barn. Taking his old knapsack in which he had brought some dogmeat, he walked up the valley bottom. He tried not to think that it was the last time he would go to the den. Going by Danebury House and hearing Tonks bark had been a bad moment. He was leaving all the animals there. Then, as he began to climb the steep slope to the cave, he could think of nothing but Yarra. He sniffed hard. Yarra had gone for good. And now he was going . . .

At the den mouth he pulled up the planks and Afra and Rico came leaping out to him. The sight of them cheered him up at once. They were well grown now and their tawny, spotted coats rippled and caught the day's new light as they moved. Rico's tail was long and drooping and could give you quite a crack if he happened to swing it across your face.

Smiler dropped to his knees and Rico, always the greedier, began to worry and paw at the knapsack on his back. "All right, my beauties," said Smiler. "A walk first and then food."

He started off down the steep slope, back towards Imber. Rico raced ahead and began mouse-hunting from tuft to tuft of grass. Afra found a tattered little white parachute from an old signal flare, picked it up and carried it for a while.

The birds and the beasts of the little valley watched them go. The buzzards, flying low at the ridgetop, soared and hung over them. The carrion crow, dealing with a dead rabbit on the far slope, looked up and watched their movements. A deer couched in bracken followed them with large, liquid eyes.

At the small spring Smiler let the cubs drink. When they had taken their fill they followed him up to the van. He opened one of the van's back doors, took meat from his knapsack and tossed it inside. Rico jumped in immediately, but Afra stood her ground and Smiler wondered whether he was going to have trouble with her. He took another piece of meat, held it briefly under Afra's nose and then jerked it into the van. Afra leaped in after it.

Smiler closed and locked the door. He went around and got

into the driver's seat. The back part of the van was boarded off from the front, but there was a small connecting hatchway. He made sure that it was securely bolted and then drove off.

Some minutes later Smiler was driving down the northern scarp of the plain, not far from the spot where Yarra had been attacked by the Ayrshire cow. In a little while he was off the plain, turning westward along a main road. A mile along the road he drew up. He slipped the hatch bolts and peeped through at the cubs. They both came to the hatchway. Smiler rubbed their masks and then pushed through some meat from his knapsack.

He bolted the hatchway and drove on. He knew exactly where he was going, and he knew all the roads from his many drives with Joe. As soon as he could he left the main road. By now the police might be at Joe's cottage, and if Joe couldn't keep from them the fact that the van was missing they would put out a call for it.

In fact, he need not have worried. Joe had taken Smiler's bicycle to the river and thrown it in. When the police arrived Joe told them truthfully that Johnny and his bicycle were gone. The police never asked him about his van. Joe reported its loss at midday when he went to the Angel.

LATER that morning, not long after Longleat Park had been opened to the public, Apollo, the cheetah male who had been Yarra's mate, was lying along the trunk of a fallen tree. Across the road and the grass two or three other cheetahs were pacing up and down inside the wire enclosure, their eyes on the free parkland over which Yarra had escaped.

A few early cars were beginning to trickle through the animal enclosures. Apollo watched them without interest. He yawned and wrinkled his mask, then snapped at a worrying bluebottle fly.

At that moment a small green van came around the curve of the road behind Apollo and pulled over to the side. In the van was Smiler. He knew all about Longleat Park and its animal kingdom. This was where Joe had brought him for his treat. Smiler had made Joe stay a long time in the cheetah enclosure.

Now he had returned, bringing Afra and Rico with him. Behind

198

him they moved restlessly in the van, roused by the various animal scents that came to them.

Smiler sat for a moment, wishing he didn't have to go on with his plan but knowing it was the best thing for the cubs. Once it was done, he would have to move on because at the entry to the enclosure he had seen one of the black-and-white Land Rovers of the game wardens.

Smiler drew the bolts and opened the hatch wide. Afra and Rico came to the opening. Smiler held up a piece of meat and then leaned over and opened the door of the cab.

As Rico slid through the hatchway after the meat, Smiler threw it out onto the grass. Rico jumped after it.

Afra came through the hatchway and sat on the seat at Smiler's side. "Go on, Afra!" he urged. But she sat on her haunches and rubbed her head against Smiler's shoulder.

Desperate, Smiler pushed Afra off the seat to the floor. She turned, spat-snapped nervously at him and then lifted her muzzle. A mixture of new and familiar scents came flooding through the open door. She jumped down on to the grass to join Rico.

Smiler pulled the door shut and drove off, sniffing and fighting back the tears which pressed against the back of his eyes. As he went he watched Afra and Rico in the mirror. Rico was crouched on the grass, chewing at his piece of meat. Afra was standing up, slowly swinging her blunt head and long neck as she looked around the enclosure.

Even before he saw them, Apollo had caught the scent of the young cheetahs. As the van drew away they came into view. His head jerked up alertly. Slowly he raised himself to a stalking position and began moving along the fallen tree. Cheetahs in captivity do not always take kindly to the introduction of new members. Suddenly Apollo leaped from the end of the trunk in a long, curving spring. He walked slowly, deliberately, across to the young cheetahs. Afra turned and faced him and then opened her jaws in a silent gape, half menace, half fear. Rico looked up from his meat and rumbled a caution for Apollo to keep away.

The other cheetahs began to move slowly towards the young cheetahs in small, exploratory arcs.

Apollo moved to Rico and lowered his head. Rico—Apollo's own son—snapped at the big male to guard his meat. Apollo's right forepaw swept out and cuffed Rico away. Rico rolled over and over for about a yard. He came to his feet, shook himself, and then moved confidently back. Apollo had done to him no more than Yarra had sometimes done.

Apollo watched Rico come back and drop to the meat, almost under his muzzle. For a moment Apollo's paw rose and then he let Rico take the meat. Afra was standing just behind him. Ten yards away the other cheetahs had bunched together, all watching Apollo.

Slowly Apollo lowered his head and sniffed at Afra, who made a small complaining sound. Apollo squatted back on his haunches. He yawned, blinking at the sun, and then he dropped flat to the ground, facing the other cheetahs. Afra squatted a foot from him. Rico ate behind him. The cars passed slowly along the road, and the other cheetahs turned and moved away.

Apollo had accepted Afra and Rico. Father, son and daughter were together.

Joe's old green van was found by the police late that afternoon. It was abandoned in a lay-by on a main road twenty miles from Longleat. Lying on the driver's seat was a note that read: "This van belongs to Joe Ringer of Heytesbury. Say to him the old grey goose is still flying."

Victor Canning

Spy rings, hijackings and political skulduggery are the usual stuff of Victor Canning's novels. His story of Smiler and the cheetah might not have been written but for the postal strike. This, he says, gave him a period of enforced isolation in his Hampshire home, near the area in which the book is set. The idea for *The Runaways* had been in his mind for some time, but he had been waiting for the right moment to attempt what would be for him a very different kind of book. He decided that this was it, and five weeks later the story was complete.

Victor Canning was born in Plymouth, in 1911. Even while he was still at school he had a single, clear ambition: he wanted to be a writer. Or, more precisely, a storyteller. Indeed, the very year he left school—he was sixteen—he sold his first story. His first full-length novel followed a few years later and now, forty-five years, thirty-seven books, eight films and countless TV scripts later, he is still hard at it, telling a good story and telling it well.

His books are enjoyed all over the world, and in many languages—recently one has been translated even into Icelandic. Perhaps one reason for his success is the meticulousness of his research. He writes almost invariably out of close personal experience and is at great pains to make every detail of story and background completely authentic. He is a quiet, methodical man, a family man with four children and six grandchildren, who divides his time carefully between these and his three other obsessions—writing, fishing and golf.

He lives in a tiny village where he has found the fascinating seventeenth-century house he is currently restoring. Apart from the war years, which took him as an artillery officer to North Africa, Italy and Austria, he has chosen to live in the country all his life. "Where else," he says, "could I play golf or fish whenever I needed to?"

NUNAGA
Duncan Pryde

NUNAGA
Ten Years of Eskimo Life

a condensation of the book by

Duncan Pryde

Published by MacGibbon & Kee, London

Once in a while there appears a truly exceptional book of personal adventure—an exceptional story by an exceptional author. *Nunaga* is such a book.

Duncan Pryde, a Scottish orphan, begins his tale in 1955 when, as an eighteen-year-old ex-merchant seaman and disgruntled factory worker, he decided to try his hand at fur-trading among the Eskimos of the Canadian Arctic. Posted to a trouble spot peopled almost entirely with drunks and killers, he found himself committed to a series of breathtaking adventures and extraordinary experiences. For ten years, to earn their trust, he was to enter entirely into the Eskimos' way of life, accepting their magic, their morality, their brutal but realistic attitudes to life and death. He conformed to a world where wife-sharing was traditional, where blood-feuds were inevitable, where hunting was not a sport but the only way to stay alive.

Duncan Pryde's story is much more than an exciting tale of an extraordinary career. It is also a valuable record of a centuries-old civilization that is vanishing at breakneck speed, as the Eskimos move from the tundra to the town. In one of the many reviews that praised the story, the *Sunday Telegraph* summed up Duncan Pryde's achievement in these words: "He has written a book of great historical as well as human interest. He loved the Eskimos, and they, it is clear, loved him."

NORTH TOWARDS
THE WINTER WIND

"Fur traders wanted for the far north," read the advertisement in the Scottish *Sunday Post*, ". . . single, ambitious, self-reliant young men wanted . . . far north of Canada . . . must be prepared to live in isolation . . . willing to learn native language . . . salary: $135.00 per month."

It was 1955. I was eighteen years old, and my only knowledge of fur traders was a vague notion, based on films, that they lived in ramshackle log cabins which were constantly attacked by marauding Indians. But fact or fiction, this was attraction enough for me. Having been brought up in orphanages in various parts of Scotland, I had entered the merchant navy at the age of fifteen. Three years later, after an accident to my left eye, I had been forced to resign. I was now working in a Singer sewing machine factory, and I was thoroughly fed up. I set off down Glasgow's Sauchiehall Street to join the Hudson's Bay Company.

Amazingly, I found my first three years in Canada, fur trading with the Cree and Ojibway Indians in northern Manitoba and Ontario, too soft and civilized for my liking. I actually resigned from the Company and only rejoined on condition that I be transferred to the Arctic, so I was sent to Baker Lake, as an apprentice to Sandy Lunan, the manager of the post.

BAKER LAKE is in the Barren Grounds – the interior of the Arctic continent north of the tree line. It is desolate, rugged country, where blizzards batter the land in winter and mosquitoes hold undisputed sway in summer. In 1958 it was almost trackless as far as the whitemen knew, its native inhabitants nomadic Eskimos, barely out of the Stone Age.

It was late autumn when I flew in. Apart from the lack of trees, the gentle hills and broad valleys looked as if they might almost have been in the Lowlands of Scotland. This variation of topography surprised me. The pictures I had seen of the Arctic had shown fur-clad figures in the midst of a flat expanse of snow and ice. A light rain began to fall as we passed over a distinctive flat-topped hill called Sugarloaf and across the angry waters of Baker Lake. Islands and reefs, almost smothered in foam, winked through the rain, then vanished behind us. The utter gloom and starkness of the scene took my breath away.

The plane came upon the settlement so suddenly that I was caught by surprise. There was a neat compound of buildings painted in the white and red colours of the Hudson's Bay Company, a sprawl of houses along the edge of the lake, and on the slope of a hill a string of Eskimo tents flapping in the wind and rain. We began our descent, and in a few minutes I was being greeted by my new boss.

Sandy Lunan was probably pushing sixty, but he had an unwrinkled face, almost babyish in its smoothness, and his wispy moustache served only to accentuate the essential youthfulness of his appearance. He had a basic honesty and straightforwardness that I found appealing; even more important to a newcomer like myself, he immediately went out of his way to make me feel at home.

On my first morning, he was checking through the official mail in an alcove of the living room that he used as an office, and I was reading on the chesterfield, when we heard the murmur of voices in the porch; then the front door opened and a babble of noise came down the hallway. Sandy pushed back his chair and stood up. He took off his reading glasses, rubbed his eyes, then looked across the room at me. He smiled and said, "Well, I suppose we should go out and show you off to the people. There's no trading today, so I guess they just came to meet you."

We went down the hallway and into the "native room". It was overflowing with people. Women and children sat flat-legged on the floor. One woman was nursing a baby at her breast. The men were packed on the bench alongside the table; others perched on the table itself, while the rest stood against the wall. Everyone was talking and laughing. A smell of unwashed bodies hung in the air.

Sandy looked at them for a moment, smiling, then shouted something in a gruff but good-natured voice. The hubbub stopped, and beaming faces turned towards us. Sandy said something else, speaking in guttural syllables that I could not understand, then pointed his thumb at me. The people all stared in my direction and laughed, then one old woman rose laboriously to her feet and answered Sandy in the same guttural tongue. I stood there with an idiotic grin of incomprehension on my face. She stopped speaking, and more laughter went round the room.

Sandy smiled broadly. He put his arm across my shoulders and explained. "I told them we come from the same country, and the only difference is that you are a lot younger than me and maybe a bit better tempered. The old woman said that you didn't look too bad tempered but you did look too skinny and maybe she should adopt you so that you could be fattened up a bit!"

Still laughing and giggling, the Eskimos surged forward to shake my hand. The Eskimo handshake is quite different from the white-man's, and there was considerable fumbling before I caught on to the difference: my hand was lightly clasped, then raised close to eye level before being released. Sandy and I were almost engulfed in the crush of people, but I knew then that my decision to transfer to the Arctic had been a good one.

THE BAKER LAKE post consisted of our house, a number of ware-houses and a store. This was only about twenty feet square but it held a wide variety of trade goods, from flour, sugar and tea to ammunition and traps—all basic Eskimo stuff. A long wooden counter extended along two walls; pots and pans hanging from hooks in the ceiling gave a cluttered effect to the otherwise neat layout.

I commented on the lack of a heater to Sandy.

"Don't let it worry you," Sandy replied with a broad smile.

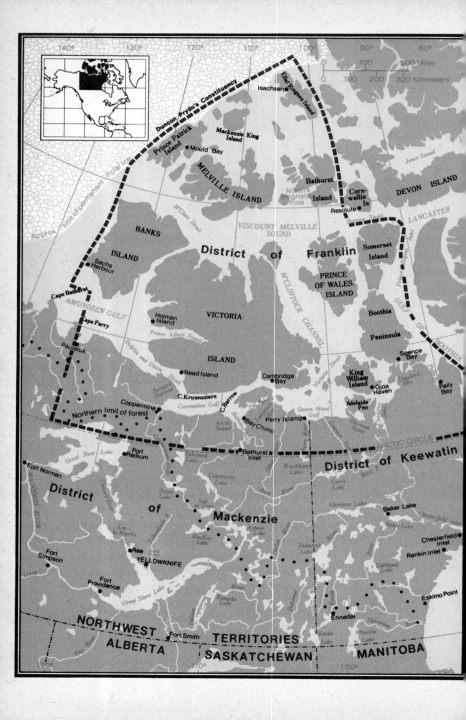

"You'll soon get used to it. This is a trading post, not a supermarket. And what's the point of heating the store when the Eskimos only come in to trade two or three times a year?"

"Still, in the winter—at sixty below zero . . . ."

"Oh, it's not that bad. You'll only be in here for a couple of hours at a stretch, and you can always stand on deerskins to keep your feet warm. Nothing much you can do about your hands, though. If you keep your mitts on you can't write, and if you take them off your hands get cold. The only time you really freeze in here is when the Eskimos come for the Christmas trade. You'll be in here for about ten days or so then, until all the fur is traded off. What you do is trade for an hour or so until your hands are too numb to write, then you come back to the house to thaw out. That gives time for the counterslip book to thaw out, too. The carbon freezes up pretty quickly . . . ."

One of the warehouses at the back of the store was crammed to the ceiling with caribou skins, and my first task was to help sort these out. The prime function of the post was to buy caribou skins from the Eskimos and export them to the coastal ports. The coastal Eskimos had little access to the major herds of caribou that passed by the Baker Lake area on migration and consequently they were always short of skins to make clothing and to use for bedding.

Before bundling, the hides had to be graded; winter skins taken when the hair on the hide was longest; summer skins taken when the hide was paper thin and of little use except for underclothing; clothing skins, the most valuable, taken in the autumn when the hair was lengthening, but not yet too heavy or bulky to be used for winter clothing.

An Eskimo called Naigo was the general factotum around the post. He kept the mess supplied with fish and caribou meat, handled the dogs in winter, and generally acted as a handyman to assist with any chores that might need doing. He was a middle-aged man with a bony, cavernous face, and a set of very bad teeth, which he displayed whenever he smiled, which was often. He always seemed cheerful and usually hummed a little melody to himself as we worked on the hides. He spoke no English, but we communicated with a series of exaggerated gestures involving hands, feet, eyes, lips, and anything else needed to convey meaning.

When Naigo and I graded the skins, he taught me that the Eskimo name for the caribou was *tuktu,* and I scribbled the word down on a cigarette packet and filed it away for future reference. Word number one in the Eskimo language!

I have always felt that not being able to talk person-to-person makes it virtually impossible to appreciate a different culture, and Sandy Lunan encouraged me to learn the Eskimo language and customs. "It's easy to live like a whiteman up here," he said. "I want you to learn the Eskimo way, so you will know how they feel about things."

Sandy spoke Eskimo himself—but with a unique Lunanesque flavour! When I first arrived I marvelled at what I took to be his great proficiency. However, after I had gained some grasp of the language, I realized that there was Eskimo and there was what Sandy spoke! But no matter how badly he tortured the pronunciation, the Eskimos understood well enough; they had long since grown accustomed to his personal variety of their language.

It was hard going at first. There was a small dictionary put out by a Roman Catholic missionary, Father Thibert, but unfortunately the good Father had lived in several places and hadn't bothered to note the dialect from which the words came. There are many Eskimo dialects and the differences between them can be enormous. After I had been using the dictionary for about a month I found so many errors, and the spelling system was so inconsistent, that I couldn't pronounce a single word with any confidence. The only solution was to write my own dictionary.

I constantly pestered poor Naigo, asking "What is this? What is that?" He was unbelievably patient with me and always gave me the word to write down. I had no systematic spelling system at that time, so I simply wrote the words as they sounded to my ear. This created enormous problems, but eventually I worked out a system of transliteration whereby one letter consistently stood for a single sound.

There were difficulties in working out this system. My background made me interpret Eskimo sounds in terms of English sounds, so that in some instances I made too fine a distinction in recording words. In others I failed to hear the distinction between two separate Eskimo sounds and therefore wrote both with the same letter. Eskimo has two types of "k" sound. One is formed at the front of the mouth and is very similar to the English "k"; the other is formed farther back in the mouth and has no exact counterpart in English. It was only after my ear had become attuned to Eskimo that I assigned the letter *k* to the front sound and the letter *q* to the back sound. Indeed, it is common for an Eskimo name to be spelled three different ways. One form might have been spelled out first by a French missionary, another by a Scottish trader, a third by an English mountie. The word "Eskimo" itself is a corruption of an Indian word for the people of the Arctic, meaning "eaters of raw flesh". Eskimos simply term themselves *inuit*—"the people".

Working slowly and on my own, I began to develop a vocabulary. Upon learning a word, I tried to use it whenever appropriate. When I wanted a mug I would say, "Pass me that *tiiturvik*." When I worked out some new grammatical terminations, I would write them out in large letters and paste them alongside my bed. The last thing I would read at night and the first thing in the morning would be what I had written there.

Within a few weeks I was using Eskimo, but mastery of the language came only very gradually. I don't think I could boast fluent Eskimo until I had been in the Arctic three or four years.

The Eskimo's language reveals important aspects of his culture. One word suffices in Eskimo for all the hundreds of species of bright summer flowers in the Arctic—*nauttiaq*. The Eskimo has no use for flowers. On the other hand, he has twenty-five or thirty terms for snow, each meaning a specific type. To a man starting a trip across the Arctic, whose life at some stage of the trip may depend upon finding the right type of snow, it is not enough to tell him there is plenty of the stuff. He must know that there is plenty of *igluksaq* (snow-house-building snow). If someone told him there was nothing but *pukak* (a type of snow granulated like sugar), he would know that he couldn't build a shelter.

My knowledge of snowhouses came with my initial trips out of Baker Lake with Naigo, when he visited his white-fox trapline, for not long after my arrival the winter snow had come, blanketing everything under a soft white layer. From my observation of Naigo,

213

so deft and sure, I concluded that building a snowhouse couldn't be very difficult. So when there was some free time, I took my snowknife, long-bladed like a butcher's knife, and headed out some distance behind the post, eager to master the technique.

I soon discovered that I could not get my snowhouse more than three blocks high, before the whole thing crumbled. I hadn't realized that my failure had been observed until one day Sandy said, "I hear you've been trying to build snowhouses." It seemed that Eskimos passing by with their sleds had noticed and watched me through their binoculars. "Have you been able to build one yet?" he asked. I had to admit that I hadn't.

So one afternoon Naigo went out with me. I think he was inwardly laughing, but too polite to show it. First he taught me how to locate the proper type of snow for snowhouse construction. It had to be firm enough to cut into blocks but soft enough to enable the blocks to fuse together. It should not be multi-layered as blocks cut from this would break along the line between the layers. Naigo could tell the right snow by the way it sounded underfoot; it has a certain creakiness quite recognizable to the educated ear.

Having located a drift of the proper type of snow, he cut out some fifteen blocks, about six inches by thirty-four, with his snowknife. All but the last of these he placed on the surface, leaving him standing in an open trench. The last block went back in the trench a few feet behind him. Using nothing but visual judgment, he placed the blocks around him in a circle about seven feet in diameter, then cutting and shaping each block he fitted one against the other and jammed them with a final blow.

When the first row had been completed, still working from the inside, Naigo made a diagonal cut from the bottom of the first block to the top of the third and removed the upper wedge of snow. This left a sloping ramp, the foundation of the second row of blocks, and the key to the formation of a continuously climbing spiral—the vital constructional feature of a snowhouse which I had previously failed to observe. This was where I had been going wrong in my efforts: instead of forming a spiral of blocks, I had merely placed one row on top of the other.

The more he cut from the trench and the higher the walls rose, the easier the work became. As the blocks inclined towards the centre, they tended to support each other more readily than in the lower rows. In addition, the blocks were cut smaller, making them easier to handle.

Naigo pushed the final block—known as the key block—lengthwise through the gap, turned it horizontal, and trimmed it so that it lowered exactly into place. He cut a low archway in the snowblock left in the trench and emerged. While he had been fitting the blocks, I had been using the soft snow to close up all the chinks between them. Our house was finished.

When I first slept in it my natural inclination was to lie with my head towards the wall, but Naigo laughingly explained why it was better to sleep the other way round. The reason is highly practical; a sleeper with his head towards the centre of the room doesn't have to crawl out of his sleeping bag in the morning to get a fire started. He can just reach out of his bag, light the primus stove, shove some snow into the kettle, and the snowhouse will be warm by the time the tea is ready.

It was Sandy Lunan who taught me to carry a snowknife with me at all times, even around the settlement. If an Arctic blizzard blows up you can then at least cut blocks for a windbreak, for an Eskimo will not try to fight the elements and tire himself out; he will use the snow to protect him.

It may seem excessively cautious to carry a snowknife when simply walking around a settlement where there are houses in every direction, but I saw it snow so hard that one might walk into another man without seeing him. In mid-winter Sandy and I would string a rope between the trade store and our house, no more then fifty feet apart, to keep us from getting lost during a storm.

Over my first few months at Baker, I came to appreciate Sandy Lunan's character more and more. Although he was clearly a man of fixed habits, he had the warm personality that promotes a convivial atmosphere. His slavish addiction to habit merely caused me much amusement.

Sunday night at the post was like watching an old movie run over and over. Invariably Akomalik, the Eskimo woman who cooked for us, served the roast at the stroke of six. After supper Sandy would pat his belly a time or two to show how full and satisfied he was; then he would rise and go to his favourite easy chair. Within about five minutes he was snoring, head back, mouth open. His little dog Tippy always settled down at his master's side by the chair, and when Sandy snored so did Tippy.

At precisely five minutes to seven Sandy would awake, stretch his arms a bit, tug an old turnip watch out of his waistcoat pocket and glance at it. He would then reach for a newspaper, adjust his glasses and settle down to an evening of reading.

Yet every Sunday, on the dot of seven, there would come a rap at the door. Sandy would take his glasses off, squint nearsightedly over at me and say, "What was that noise, Duncan lad? Is that someone at the door?"

And I would say, as though cued, "Yes, that was someone at the door."

Sandy, with his glasses in one hand and the newspaper in the other, would go to the front door, open it and peer out. There, invariably, would be Canon Jimmy James, the Anglican missionary.

"Well, hello, Mr. James, hello! How are you?"

And Mr. James would reply, "Well, good evening, Mr. Lunan. I just happened to be passing by, and I thought I'd drop in."

"Yes, yes, come in, do come in."

Sandy Lunan and Jimmy James had known each other for close on thirty years. Everyone else in the settlement called Mr. Lunan Sandy and Mr. James Jimmy, but between the two old cronies it was Mr. James and Mr. Lunan—two gentlemen of the old school.

Sandy always dressed for Sunday in his best tweeds. He looked like a Highland laird, neatly turned out with a carefully knotted tie. Jimmy dressed, too, for these calls, in his blacks and round collar. They didn't have much to do with each other during the week, and Sandy never once went to church as far as I knew. But on Sundays, the two men would sit there in the fusty old living room with its Victorian furnishings and talk on a world of topics.

Then, at about five minutes to ten, Mr. James would become nervous. He would start rubbing his hands together, his fingers twining and untwining. He knew how dominated Sandy was by the

216

old chime clock on the mantel. He knew that Sandy, come blizzard or caribou stampede, always went to bed dead on ten o'clock. So at about one minute to ten Jimmy would rise to his feet.

Sandy might be speaking, and he would interrupt himself to insist, "Oh, no, no, sit down Mr. James, don't leave yet."

Jimmy would say, "Oh no, really Mr. Lunan, I must get back to the mission. I've a bit of writing to do," or some such excuse. He would be looking at the old clock and waiting for it to chime, knowing that if he didn't get out by ten o'clock he'd be thrown out!

ABOUT the only thing Sandy Lunan didn't do on time was retire. He had earned his retirement, and the Company was more than willing to see that he was comfortably fixed. Sandy had, in fact, retired twice, but found retirement frustrating and boring. Each time he came back to Baker Lake. Fur trading had been his life, and Baker Lake his home for thirty years.

Finally, however, in the autumn of 1959 Sandy made up his mind to leave once and for all. It was comical listening to him trying to rationalize his decision to himself. He kept up a constant grumbling that the place was becoming overrun with whitemen (there were all of twenty or so in the thousand square miles around) and that the country was changing. "It's too civilized around here," he complained, "for an old fur trader."

On the last day, when the plane came for him, the entire settlement was at the airstrip. Sandy uttered barely a word to anyone. He hardly said goodbye to faithful Akomalik, who had taken care of him for so many years. In a loud, hoarse voice he defiantly proclaimed for all to hear: "Well, I've spent thirty years of my life here, and I'm glad to be leaving this place."

He paused and looked around. "I've got some money saved up, I'm going to take a trip round the world . . . . I never want to see the Arctic again . . . ." He sniffed loudly and blew his nose and not a person there was fooled. Everyone could see the old man was on the verge of tears.

Sandy was the finest trader I ever knew in the Arctic. He died just two years after he retired, still an apparently hale man. He would probably have lived another twenty years had he kept working.

After Sandy left, a trader called Bob Griffith came to run the Baker Lake post. He was a first-rate man, but the Company knew I wanted to leave as I had my heart set on a more isolated post. About five months after Bob took over, the Company transferred me to Spence Bay. Spence was farther north, one step closer to the type of isolation I wanted. Part of my new job as a clerk was to go once a month to Gjoa Haven, an outpost of Spence, and help the manager there with his books.

I liked that little chore. I enjoyed the dogteam travel between the two posts. Those trips, which I made with an Eskimo called Takolik, did much to teach me how to handle dogs and live on the trail. The run between the two posts was only three or four sleeps in decent weather, and Takolik had a fine team. Occasionally we made a side trip to one of the Distant Early Warning line radar posts to pick up our mail. In those days there were no scheduled flights to Spence Bay, and if we didn't get our mail at the DEW line post, there was no telling when we might.

Takolik, like Naigo, was a model of patience with the clumsy newcomer. Never showing his amusement, never embarrassing me when I made dangerous errors, he slowly and carefully taught me how to master the Arctic. He would hitch up his team and start us out on a trip, then he would let me take over the dogs. Sometimes we had as many as twenty-three dogs on a fan hitch, and once made seventy miles in a single day. Takolik taught me to navigate by picking out key landmarks on the horizon for each day's travel. When there were no landmarks, at night or in the dark months of winter, he pointed out that the prevailing winds always packed the hard snow drifts in the same general line.

I also learned how important mud is to anyone who wants to run a dogteam. This is because the wooden runners of the sleds are sheathed with a strip of steel to keep them from wearing out. In the bitter cold of winter the steel freezes tight to the ice and snow, and the dogs can't budge the sled.

In the autumn, the Eskimos gather mud, then when it gets cold, they flip the sled upside-down and mix mud with water to make balls about the size of a cricket ball. A mud ball is slapped on the steel runner and pressed down tight. More mud balls are added all along the runner, covering it completely. The mud is then worked up and down the runner so that it is about five inches deep. This is allowed to freeze until it sets almost like concrete. An ordinary jackplane is used to plane the frozen mud smooth, then a pad of bear skin is dipped in water and brushed along the runner, to build up a layer of ice. This is kept up until the ice is half an inch thick, and then the sled is ready to go.

On our trips we ate raw frozen caribou and hardtack biscuits, or else I improvised a kind of homemade instant stew. Before leaving I would set out thirty pie tins with the bottoms greased slightly, mix up a hash out of whatever happened to be handy, corned beef, macaroni, beans and what not, fill all the pie plates and let the mixture freeze solid. Then I would empty those quick-frozen, pre-cooked slabs into an empty flour sack and bash them up with a hammer into a coarse powder. On the trail, when it was time for an evening meal, all I had to do was dump some of the powder in a pot of hot water, and in a couple of minutes—instant stew.

A FIGHT FOR LIFE

I had been at Spence Bay for about a year when the Company asked me if I would like to go to Perry Island, on the Arctic shore west of Spence Bay. They knew I spoke Eskimo well enough to handle a post where I would be the only whiteman, and thought I could perhaps straighten out a problem they had at Perry Island. Apparently the incumbent manager, a young fellow named Neil Timberlake, had somehow got off on the wrong foot with the people and couldn't correct an awkward situation. Accordingly, in February 1961 I flew in to Perry Island to spend a month with Neil before the Company plane picked him up.

The Perry Island people had a very bad reputation. There were seventy-five or eighty Eskimos in the area trading into the post. Not only were they supposed to be a tough bunch and drink a lot, but a large number were believed to have murdered, and many had been involved in blood feuds in other parts of the Arctic and had come to Perry for refuge.

I was fully aware that violence had traditionally been a natural way of life to the Eskimo, who puts a very pragmatic value on everything. Killing, in those days, came more easily to him than to the typical modern whiteman. An Eskimo, after all, lived by killing. One day it would be a caribou, next day a seal or bear, all a simple matter of an infinitesimal squeeze of a finger on the trigger. There was no great difference if it was a man in the sights of his rifle. However, Eskimos do differentiate between murder and man-slaughter. To them it is murder to kill another without provocation or any real justification. The term manslaughter is applied to kill-ings such as those which are the result of a blood feud. There probably hasn't been a blood feud for ten or fifteen years now, but before the Royal Canadian Mounted Police started policing the North in the early 1930s such killings were common, and it was not unusual for eight or nine people to die in the aftermath of one murder.

One major factor that led to murder in the snowhouses was the chronic shortage of women. In the old days when a family could not support an extra child, they practised infanticide. Normally it was the females who were sacrificed, for the simple reason that a girl could not hunt and therefore was not as valuable to the family as a boy. A son was duty bound to provide for his aged parents when he grew up, while the services of a daughter normally passed to another family through marriage. The most common method of infanticide was to put the newborn baby out in the snow for fifteen minutes and allow it to freeze to death. As far as the Eskimos were concerned, that was not murder as long as the child had not been named.

This female infanticide, of course, left an imbalance in the popu-lation. To get a wife, a man often had either to steal someone else's mate or kill the husband and take over the woman. Such a killing often resulted in a feud.

Execution was another form of violence. If an entire settlement considered a killer, or even a potential killer, dangerous, they would nominate one of their number to execute him. I came to know several instances of this at Perry Island. In each case the executioner—usually, to prevent a blood feud, the condemned man's nearest relative—did as the community bid, although in one case the son was greatly saddened. He didn't want to kill his father, but he had no choice. He went to his father and explained the situation, and asked, "Do you want me to shoot you or to strangle you with a thong?" The father just as calmly accepted the community's decision and told his son, "I'd rather you shot me, but shoot me from behind so that I don't have to look at you when you do it." The son took his father's rifle and shot him in the back of the head. In the mores of Eskimo society such killings, and those of old people or people with mental aberrations, were legal executions.

The arrangement when I arrived, was that Neil Timberlake would stay on at Perry for a month before I took over. That month was well spent. I met most of the Eskimos, and with Neil still in authority I had time to observe the difficulties and to consider what moves I might make and how I should make them. Together we went over all the Eskimos in the area, and Neil pointed out the troublemakers. There seemed to be quite a few of them, and I soon saw that Neil didn't know how to handle them.

One of the problems was drunkenness. The Eskimos made their own potent brew, and when they didn't have raisins to make it, they would add a spoonful of methyl hydrate to a cup of tea. All trading posts kept methyl hydrate in stock in those days for use as a primer to light Primus stoves. When it got too cold for the paraffin to catch fire, a little methyl hydrate would fire up at any temperature. So the Eskimos had easy access to the stuff, and they had quickly learned to fire themselves up with it as well. Taken straight, it would burn their guts out or cause blindness. Many Eskimos were blinded or killed in this stupid way.

Anyway, regularly once a week, the Eskimos, well intoxicated, would come across from the snowhouses to the post, ten and sometimes twenty at a time, a pretty rough bunch. Sometimes they would be in a jovial mood, but moments later they would turn ugly, and Neil was plain scared of them.

The basis of much of the trouble at Perry was our post servant, a man named Angulaalik. As post servant he was supposed to do all the odd jobs that were helpful to the manager. He was paid one hundred dollars a month plus fifteen barrels of fuel oil for his house.

The Company had built a house for him about a hundred yards from the post, and he and his family were the only Eskimos not living in snowhouses. On the face of it, Angulaalik's status in the community appeared to be excellent, but it was actually a rather touchy situation for him. He had been in charge of the post at Perry when it had no resident white manager. Then, two years before I arrived, he had been arrested for killing a local man.

He had stood trial and been let off. Some of the Eskimos believed that it was because he was the trader, with powerful friends and money. Others said that no one dared testify against him because they were afraid of causing a blood feud.

Personally I found it hard to believe that Angulaalik was a murderer. He was small, with a charming smile, and basically he seemed a gentle man. Yet an RCMP corporal told me that the force knew of four other killings Angulaalik had been involved in, and I heard higher numbers from other sources.

Neil suggested that the real trouble with Angulaalik was that he simply couldn't take the reduction in status from outpost manager to post servant, and felt the loss of face very keenly. He was now proving his independence by never turning up for work in the mornings. Understanding this, I nevertheless thought it was only right and proper that Angulaalik should work if he expected to be paid, and I intended to make an issue of this, so that not only Angulaalik but all the Eskimos would know just who ran the post.

Accordingly, on the afternoon that the plane arrived to pick up Neil, I made a point of speaking privately to Angulaalik, telling him that I was in charge now and that I wanted him to be at work at nine o'clock the following day.

The plane left with Neil about eight-thirty the next morning. As it disappeared over the horizon, I couldn't help reflecting that there was no other whiteman closer than Cambridge Bay, a good two hundred miles to the northwest. I was alone with a group of Eskimos whose reputation for lawlessness was unmatched in the Arctic.

Quite a number of Eskimos had come to see the plane take off and afterwards they came into the store to trade. Angulaalik was not among them. At eleven o'clock I sent one of the Eskimos up to his house with the instruction, "Tell Angulaalik that if he doesn't get down to the post right away, then he's no longer working for the Company."

Angulaalik finally deigned to appear, all toothy smile as though nothing at all had happened. I jumped him on the spot, in front of everyone. I told him if he wanted to earn his hundred dollars a month and his fuel oil, then he had to be at the post every morning at nine o'clock.

All the other Eskimos stood around, watching and listening in silence, but they were looking sidelong at each other and obviously wondering how Angulaalik would take this. When I had finished laying down the law to him, I looked round for the most lowly chore I could give him, and ordered him to fill my kitchen stove with fuel oil.

Angulaalik hardly said a word. He was jittering with nervousness. He had clearly not expected such a confrontation, and he hadn't realized till then how well I could speak and understand Eskimo.

Angulaalik went to fill the stove and when I had finished trading with the Eskimos, I also went over to my house. With just the two of us there, I quietly explained that if he came late in the mornings, he would be docked a dollar and a half for each hour.

But Angulaalik was determined to show his independence, and he frequently turned up late. Every time he did so I would tell him, "All right, I've docked you three dollars today," or four and a half, or whatever it came to. At the end of the month he wanted to buy some trade goods for his family, but I explained that out of all his month's wages he had only fifteen dollars coming to him. That finally did it; from then on he showed up at nine.

Meantime there was another problem at Perry. Almost all the Eskimos, every family except two, were living at the post. They should have been out trapping but instead they were loafing around and living entirely on welfare. At a small post like Perry, the trader had the additional duty of handling the welfare on behalf of the Government. This matter was something I quickly gave some thought to, feeling that it could and should be corrected. I therefore called a meeting of all the people living in the settlement.

"Now I want you to know that you get no more welfare here." I scolded them: "You're not doing anything but sitting around, making home brew and causing trouble. If you want to drink, go ahead and drink, I don't care. But don't come to my post. Don't cause any trouble for me—get out and go to work."

Naturally there was a lot of complaining, especially from those Neil had warned me were the troublemakers, but there was nothing else for it; they had to go trapping, and finally they all went except Angulaalik, who stayed around the post to earn his money there, even though he was one of the best trappers in the whole region.

With all of them out on the land we at last began to get some fur, the first fur in any quantity for months at the Perry Island post, and I was kept busy trading with the trappers. The Company used a barter system to trade with the Eskimos, using aluminium tokens to get round the rather haphazard way Eskimos had of counting. For example, almost any Eskimo would correctly count up to three caribou, but any more just became "many".

A square token represented one white fox, the fur of which was the prime economic unit in the North. The round token, with an HBC "one" stamped in the middle represented one dollar, and was followed in size by smaller tokens for smaller amounts.

The tokens provided a visual form of counting for the Eskimos that they quickly understood. For example, if a hunter brought in ten white fox pelts, we would lay out one square token for each. Suppose that that year the price for fox was twenty dollars each; we would then take up one square token and replace it with twenty one-dollar tokens. Whenever an Eskimo bought something, the tokens representing the value of his purchase were removed.

There was suddenly a tremendous difference in the atmosphere of the post that was very encouraging. When the Eskimos returned to the post they would spend only a day or so purchasing supplies and then go back out. They would come into my house, and the drinking seemed to be on the decrease. However, it still seemed a good idea to be careful of Angulaalik. After his humiliation in front of the other Eskimos, I sometimes had the feeling that if I turned my back, he might hit me over the head or put a knife into me.

The summer passed without incident, but in the autumn a man named Uakuak moved in with Angulaalik and his wife Irvana.

Uakuak was Angulaalik's stepson, but he had been raised by Angulaalik as though he were actually his own flesh and blood. He had been away from the post for a year, but I knew his reputation as a true Eskimo bully.

Uakuak brought a hoard of rum with him from the DEW line, and the Eskimos at the post went on a drinking spree again. One evening around seven o'clock Uakuak and his wife came to my house. She was a nice girl, very much intimidated by Uakuak. They both were pretty drunk. Uakuak was carrying a bottle, and he wanted to give me a drink.

I declined and he said: "I hear if people have had a drink or two when they come to visit you, you push them out of the house."

"Only if they won't go when I ask them," I replied.

He stuck his chest out and said, "Well, I'm not going to go."

I thought that perhaps I could talk him out of this with my usual line: "Look, why don't you just go home and finish off your drink there and then come back to visit me when you're sober?"

"No, I want some whisky."

We got into a childish argument. I said, "You're not getting any whisky from me, I don't have any whisky."

"I know you do." He looked hard at me. "People don't like you, and particularly me—I don't like you at all. The last manager always gave me whisky."

"Well, that was his business. I'm not the last manager, and I'm not giving you whisky; so you might as well go."

He braced himself and said, "If you want me to go out of the house, you come and push me out like you pushed out those other people."

I tried to be patient with him. "I don't want to push you out." I turned away from him as if the argument were finished, and went back to the stove to pick up my dish towel and finish the dishes I had been washing. But Uakuak leapt in front of me and shoved his arms out wide and wouldn't let me pass.

I was beginning to get fed up, and a little angry, and I snapped at him, "*Taillait*—Get out of the way!"

At this his belligerence flared up. He stuck his face up close to mine and said, "You're scared of me. Come on, take me up like this," and he grabbed himself by the shirt front and repeated the challenge, "Come on, take me like this and put me out."

I said, "No, I'm not going to take you." By this time I was nervous and wary of a real fight coming. He was a big man, as tall as I and very broad in the chest, as hard as a bear.

I thought his wife, who hadn't opened her mouth once all this time, might be able to talk sense to him, so I turned to her. "Tell your husband to go home and not make trouble here."

That was a mistake, it made him furious. "Don't talk to my wife," he said, and the next thing I knew he had grabbed me by the wrist and throat and thrown me back against the wall.

His wife started up and cried out to me, "Don't fight him, don't fight him. He'll kill you!"

I paid no attention to her. My blood up, I let fly and caught him flush in the mouth. He went over on his back. I jumped on him, and hit him once more, another good one.

He lay back on the floor as though he couldn't quite believe he was there with me on top of him. My stomach was churning, for I knew this man was dangerous and all around me were dangerous people. At last he licked his lip where it was cut, and said in amazement, "You made me bleed."

"Yeah," I said. "But you started it."

He licked his lip again. Then he announced, "Well, I'm going to get up and go home," in a strangely quiet voice.

"That's fine. If you don't make any trouble for me, I won't make any for you." I felt relieved. There is an enormous difference between fighting an Eskimo and fighting a whiteman. When two Eskimos get into conflict with each other, ninety-nine times out of a hundred, one man will back down right away and say, "I don't want to fight you."

However, when I got up off Uakuak and stepped back a bit, he at once jumped to his feet and made a lunge for me. Fortunately, just as in a movie, I automatically swung and hit him at exactly the moment he jumped me, catching him flush on the side of the jaw. His head snapped round so hard that his neck made a sharp cracking noise, and he went down cold as if he had been pole-axed.

My heart leapt into my throat; when I heard his neck crack I thought I had killed him. I knelt across him again, shook him, slapped his cheeks and listened for his heartbeat. I had visions of being hauled up in court for killing an Eskimo. Then after what seemed an interminable moment, he drew in a gasp of breath. I was so relieved I could have kissed him.

He lay there on the floor, and as consciousness returned he said, "*Sinnaktulirama.*" ("I feel dreamy.")

He turned his head and looked up at me with a blank expression, as if he were stone cold sober. In a calm, almost casual voice he said, "I'm going to go home, and I'm going to get my rifle, and I'm going to come back here and kill you." His complete lack of expression somehow made it all the more terrifying.

I was properly nervous by now, but I wasn't going to back down. I kept my voice just as low and replied. "O.K. You get your rifle, and if you come back here with it I'm going to kill you first."

He said, "We'll see," and turned to his wife. "Help me up." I stepped towards him to give him a hand.

"Get back from me!" he shouted. "Don't put a hand on me."

I stood back a bit, and he started to rise. He got up on his haunches, then suddenly he kicked out and caught me in the pit of the stomach, knocking me back against the stove. I put my arms back to break the fall and both were burned from elbow to wrist.

Raging mad, I went at Uakuak and smashed him up against the wall, pounding his face again and again. He had no chance to recover his wits or strength. I slammed him repeatedly, scared stiff that he would overpower me or reach for a kitchen knife if he had the chance. I felt I was literally fighting for my life.

There was a patch of blood on the floor and splatters all over one wall and even on the ceiling. All I suffered were the burns on my arms and some skinned knuckles; Uakuak never actually hit me. At last, just as I felt myself beginning to weaken, he went flying sideways, half-knocked, half-slipped over to one side, and caught his head on the kitchen dresser. The sharp edge whacked him right on the temple and he was out cold again.

This time I didn't wait for him to come round. I dragged him out to the porch. Then I took his wife by the arm and shoved her out with him. Figuring that he was going to come to fighting mad, I slammed the door shut and latched it. I raced into my bedroom where I snatched my shotgun and two shells. Sure enough as I raced back into the kitchen, Uakuak had already smashed the window panes of the door and was reaching through, trying to get at the bolt on the inside. His arms were covered with blood from the broken glass.

I shoved the shells into the gun and clicked the double barrel closed. Uakuak froze.

"Get your hands away from that door or I'll kill you right now!" I cried. I do believe I was scared enough to pull the trigger. He took one look and shot off the porch.

I saw him pass by my house in the light from the windows, and then he was swallowed up in the darkness. I kept watching until I saw Angulaalik's door open and Uakuak and his wife go in.

Knowing that there was a party at Angulaalik's house, I dashed over to the store and closed it in case the Eskimos decided to help themselves to the guns. While there, I loaded up a 30-30 rifle, my .22, and another one besides. I was sure that since I had beaten the tar out of Angulaalik's stepson, some of his friends would certainly retaliate. They would be drunk and quite capable of killing me.

I flew back to my house; I put the easy chair up against the front door, pulled down all the blinds and curtains, and doused the lights. I took an axe and my ice dagger and placed them on top of my bookcase beside the door. This would do as a starter.

Then I got on the radio and called the RCMP at Cambridge Bay, explaining that I had had a fight with Uakuak. I told them there had been no serious injuries—yet.

"If he comes through that door with a rifle, however, I'm going to kill him," I said. "I wanted you to know; if something does happen, that's how it started."

The RCMP officer tried to calm me down. "Whatever you do, Duncan, don't shoot anyone unless you're acting in self-defence. We've a plane that could be down there first thing in the morning. So just take it easy. We will monitor your frequency all night; if you have any further trouble, give us a call."

The house was completely dark except for the transmitter's red light, indicating that the radio was on. I was as prepared as I could be, but never felt so alone in my life. It was windy that night, just enough to obscure the sounds outside. I would peek out round the side of the curtain and look towards Angulaalik's house. The moon dodged in and out of the clouds and shadows kept catching my eye. My imagination working overtime, I was sure the whole settlement was about to attack.

An hour or so passed. The shotgun, loaded and cocked, lay across my lap. All of a sudden, I heard a bang at the door. I leapt straight up, nerves jangling. There was nobody to be seen, but I was sure my murderers had come to carry out the deed. In the silence that followed I listened to my heart thumping, then footsteps moving off the porch, then ominous silence returned.

Someone testing me out, I thought, seeing if I was ready.

A couple of hours went by with no more visitors or suspicious noises. I was becoming tired. After taking several empty tins from the dustbin and standing them one on top of each other in front of each door, to act as an alarm in case someone tried to enter, I went into the bedroom. My bed was right in line with the window, so realizing I would be a sitting duck in it, I picked up the pillows and blankets, and put them down in a corner of the living room. Lying down on this makeshift bed with the shotgun between my knees, I tried to calm down.

I had dozed off for perhaps an hour when I was awakened by a banging noise on the side of the house. Once again I came bolt upright, shotgun in hand. It sounded as if someone was banging his hand against the wall of the house. The noise was repeated at intervals, but since nothing happened after that, I went off to sleep again. To my annoyance, I discovered next day that I had been frightened by a broken clothes-line flapping in the wind.

When I next awoke I heard a *chuk-chuk-chuk* off beyond the house. By now it was six in the morning and there was just enough light to see Angulaalik and Uakuak, their wives and children and a pile of gear taking off out towards the bay.

The first man to come across to the post next morning was Tupilliqqut, Angulaalik's son-in-law. He came into the house and looked around. He took it all in, the blood on the wall, the floor and the ceiling, and grinned knowingly at me.

"*Tuktutpit?*" ("Did you kill a caribou?")

"I had a fight with Uakuak."

"Yes, we heard about it." Tupilliqqut sounded pleased. He said, "We were in Angulaalik's house last night when Uakuak came in, and he had two big black eyes, and there was blood all over him. The people are glad because Uakuak was such a bully."

And from everything I heard that day, it seemed that the people were greatly relieved that Uakuak had at last been cut down to size. In fact, he never came back while I was at Perry Island, I suppose because he had lost face.

Angulaalik returned to Perry Island with his family just before Christmas. He seemed quite nervous when he walked into the post.

I asked him where he had been.

"I went trapping down in the Perry River country," he said.

"I hope you don't expect any pay, since you haven't been working here," I told him.

"Oh no," he said. "I wouldn't expect that."

The battle with Uakuak was never mentioned between us, then or ever. Indeed as time went on we became close friends. It was remarkable, in view of our initial relationship, that Angulaalik was the first man at Perry to whom I offered a drink.

Soon after the fight, the Arctic divisional manager for the Company came through the area on an inspection trip. "Would you like another post?" he asked. "I know this is a rough place. If you want to get out. . . ."

I thanked him, but declined the offer. Those first few months had been tough. I had been hard with the Perry people, but once things settled down I didn't have one incident in four years. Before the winter was out they were turning in more fur than posts three times as large. We never distributed another penny of welfare while I was at Perry, and the drunkenness and rowdiness came to a stop. Indeed it was among the Perry Islanders that I was first accepted as an Eskimo. It was there that I learned to travel with dogs on my own; that I became fluent in Eskimo; and it was there that I came to understand shamanism and witchcraft, and shared in many ancient Eskimo ways.

A FUR TRADE BACHELOR

Christmas time in the Arctic is about the only time of the year when a man feels the loneliness of real isolation. By himself in his post, hundreds of miles from any other settlement, perhaps a howling blizzard outside, there sits the trader fiddling with his radio. All he can get are Christmas carols and news of festivities—all over the world he imagines people together, sharing the joy of the occasion with each other. He is all alone.

That is why traders in the Arctic have always gone along with the idea of a big Christmas party for the Eskimos. Obviously before the whiteman came, Eskimos never celebrated Christmas or New Year. They did hold, however, a celebration at about that time, when they first saw *Aagyuuk*.

Aagyuuk refers to two stars in the northern skies which are first seen in the morning when the sky is lightening. There is no sun yet that far north, but the Eskimos know that when they see *Aagyuuk*, it will only be a matter of seven or eight sleeps until the sun reappears—good reason for a celebration in the Arctic.

At Perry Island the tradition at Christmas was well established. The Eskimos came to the post, bringing along any skins they had to trade; their women bought new bolts of cloth and made bright, fresh coverings of calico for their parkas; the men built a *qalgi*, a huge snowhouse where everyone could dance and enjoy games.

My part was to provide a feast for everyone. I borrowed copper vats, the kind used to wash clothes in, from the store, and filled them with rice, caribou and *patiq* (the marrow from caribou leg bones). The women boiled it all up together into enough stew to feed the entire settlement. I also gave the women plenty of flour and salt to make a huge mass of bannock. The feast was held in the *qalgi*, and we played games inside and out—three-legged races, dogteam races for the kids and women as well as for the men. The tangle of excited dogs and yelling children was something to see.

A sealskin thong was stretched across the interior of the big snowhouse, passed through the walls and tied to sleds braced against the exterior. Inside, the thong made an improvised trapeze. Men, women and children vied in performing tricks on the trapeze, one young man even walking it like a tightrope.

Everyone tried a turn at *ayagaq*, which appears tantalizingly easy but turns out to be frustratingly difficult. *Ayagaq* is a hand game in which the player uses a small bone, taken from the flipper of a bearded seal, pierced and then attached by a one-foot thong to a pencil-sized stick. Holding the stick, he tries to flip the pierced bone into the air and catch it on the end of the stick. It's harder than it sounds.

A dozen versions of tug-of-war and tests of strength were played, individually, in pairs and teams, arm tug-of-war, hand tug-of-war and even finger pulls—games that Eskimos had played for generations when it was too dark outside or too stormy to hunt. The greatest of the ancient games is cat's cradle. It was a custom that one never played it in the sunlight, only during the dark part of the winter, but every child, man and woman had mastered hundreds of versions.

When night came it was time for the drum dance. I took over as master of ceremonies and when everyone was seated in the *qalgi*, I said: "Tonight, before the dancing starts, I have devised a contest to find the strongest men among you, but I'm not going to pick them out; it is not for me to say which ones they are." As I knew it would, this created a hubbub. All the men immediately became terribly modest, saying, "Oh not me, I'm not really very strong. So and so's much stronger than I am," the usual way Eskimos politely talk themselves down.

I quieted them and said, "O.K. then, we'll let the women pick out the strongest men," and of course this caused more excitement. Some shouted for this one and some that one until finally they agreed on three of the biggest and toughest.

I got the three nominees out in the middle of the *qalgi*, all looking tremendously husky in their bulky deerskins, but smiling sheepishly, not sure of what I was going to make them do. I brought out a cardboard box and held it up. "Now, the one who finishes first in this contest will be the strongest." They all watched intently as I opened the box and handed each a baby bottle full of milk, nipples all prepared. I gave a bottle to each man. The sight of those three strong, tough-looking Eskimos sucking away on their bottles brought gales of laughter from the crowd. Everyone was soon in a great mood for the dancing.

The significance of the drum dance is not in the beating of the drum, but in the words of the songs. When a person sings a drum-dance song, he sings his own original composition—usually the story of some important event in his experience. A man's wife may sing his song, but other people cannot sing it unless he gives them permission. Sometimes men become song partners and will exchange songs and sing about each other. This is a device to overcome the Eskimos' natural modesty, which would prevent them from seeming to boast of their own accomplishments. Then there is the *atuut*, a general song that everyone can join in.

Before the singer begins a drum dance song, someone will get up and start the dancing. When the singer starts drumming, he holds the drum—like a huge tambourine, one-sided, perhaps three feet in diameter—with the finished side facing out. The performer beats against the skin, keeping the drum close in against his body and beating a rhythm while he bounces up and down and turns from side to side, sometimes in a circle so that everyone can see. When he goes into the actual song, he turns the drum round, and beats on the frame made of bone rather than on the skin. The spectators encourage the drummer with shouts of "*Nivliqtiriarit, nivliqtiriarit!*" ("Cry out with joy, cry out with joy!")

As each drummer took a turn at the Christmas celebration, more people leapt to their feet to dance and, as the temperature rose higher, we stripped to the waist, men and women alike. Everyone was excited and caught up in the noise and I came to realize that an Eskimo drum dance can be highly provocative.

If a man is drum dancing and has his eye on a woman, he will dance for her, the rhythm and the words directed to her. Often her husband will urge her on, saying, "Go on, get up and dance with him." Sometimes the tension and excitement builds up so high that a woman and her drummer will simply leave the scene. The drum dance is a primitive thing, with the beat of the drum throbbing, and at its height the words don't matter very much.

THERE is a widespread belief that a man has only to go to the Arctic, and the first Eskimo he meets will happily turn his wife over to him for the night. There was indeed at one time, and there remains still in some of the more isolated settlements, a system of wife exchange among the Eskimos, but it was rarely established on a casual basis, and there were always certain social boundaries to be observed.

When I was at Perry Island every adult man had an exchange wife, and every woman an exchange husband. There was no question of adultery, or any feeling of "shame". In fact, Eskimos thought it shameful, or at least strange, if a man or woman did not have an exchange partner. In our own society today, if a teenage girl isn't dating, her mother wonders what is wrong with her and pushes her to get into the swim. Similarly, in Eskimo society there was family pressure on young people to obtain exchange mates. The mother of a young bride, perhaps uncertain of her new son-in-law's ability to keep the larder full, might impress upon her daughter the advantage of a liaison with an older, more experienced hunter.

Sound sociological reasons contributed to the growth and perpetuation of the system, and not the least important was self-preservation at a time when blood feuds played a major role in Eskimo life. An Eskimo who was without kin to avenge any wrong done him was exposed and vulnerable. If he travelled to strange territory to hunt or trade, strangers might covet anything from his dogteam to his harpoon, and were sometimes more than willing to kill him to get what they wanted. With no kin to avenge his death, he could be murdered with impunity.

Spouse exchange was evolved as a kind of insurance policy. So, when a man travelled in distant regions he always took his wife with him, and when they reached a strange settlement, the visitor automatically arranged a wife exchange with one of the local residents, thus establishing the all-important kin relationship. It was no longer safe to rob or harm the traveller.

According to Eskimo belief, moulded to fit the circumstances, a "one-night stand" would never result in pregnancy. Accordingly, a single act of intercourse with a non-spouse had little significance to the immediate family.

Whenever wife or spouse exchange took place within the same band or settlement, choice was virtually unrestricted except for the important taboo of incest. As long as a man or woman chose someone outside his or her kinship circle, any arrangement agreeable to the persons concerned was possible, something I was soon to learn for myself.

I HADN'T realized the Eskimos were concerned about my status as a single man until early in the New Year when we were blessed by a visit from a young nurse. White visitors were a rarity and this nurse from Cambridge Bay was the first white woman I had seen in nearly a year. The fact that I was extremely attentive to her did not escape the careful notice of the Eskimos. Two or three days after the girl had returned, I was sitting in my living room writing a letter when Ikpakuhak, one of the friendliest of the Eskimos at Perry, came in to visit me.

Ikpakuhak prepared cups of tea and, after watching my labours, he asked politely, "Are you writing to a woman?"

I said that I was writing to the nurse who had visited us.

"Is that your girl friend?" he asked.

"No, she's not, but I just thought I'd drop her a line."

"Well, why don't you take her as a wife?" he pursued.

"Oh, I don't think a white woman would like to live here," I replied, "it's too lonely."

We talked a little; then Ikpakuhak went home and I forgot about the matter. But, as I was to learn shortly, he did not.

Early the next morning—it must have been no more than five or six o'clock—I was awakened by the sound of my outside door being opened. I drowsily opened my eyes to find that Ikpakuhak and Tupilliqqut, Angulaalik's son-in-law, both dressed for travel in full deerskins, were standing by my bed. Ikpakuhak, seeing that I had awakened, said abruptly, "Yesterday you were writing to your girl friend, weren't you?"

Ikpakuhak was a man who pursued an objective with great singleness of purpose, and perhaps it was knowing this that kept me from finding the juxtaposition of subject and circumstance unduly strange. I said, "I told you, she's not really my girl friend."

235

Undeterred, Ikpakuhak persisted. "Well, do you want to get married?"

As a matter of fact, I didn't particularly. Trying to rub the sleep out of my eyes, and without thinking about it, I just said, "Well, sure I wouldn't mind getting married. It's a tough life when you're alone and a man gets lonely without a woman."

Ikpakuhak was almost quivering with eagerness. He sat down on my bed and said, "Well, I've been talking to Tupilliqqut. We were thinking . . . how would you like to marry my niece?"

I stammered, "Your niece? Which one is that?"

"Tikirluk."

I was thunderstruck. Tikirluk was a very pretty girl—and all of thirteen years old!

I hastily protested, "Oh, I couldn't marry Tikirluk; she's much too young!"

Tupilliqqut straightened that out in a hurry. "Oh, she's not too young," he said. "Her breasts are nicely developed."

Suddenly I realized the disturbing possibility that I might end up a married man. I thought fast how to get out of this and yet not hurt their feelings. After all this was a genuine, honest offer out of the goodness of their hearts, with no strings attached.

So I thought a minute, and then said, with an air of regret but authority, "Well, you know, among the whitemen you can't marry a girl until she's eighteen. Otherwise I wouldn't mind marrying Tikirluk. She's certainly a nice girl, a nice-looking girl too."

Her uncle beamed at this and agreed. "Oh yes, she is, and she's really good at sewing." To the Eskimos this was the clincher; to them a fine stitch is even more important than physical attractiveness. "She's really a good worker," he went on. "She could make you some nice things."

I began to backpedal some more. "I'm sure she could, but if I married her, the police would arrest me."

Ikpakuhak had an easy answer for that. He reassured me. "Well, no one here is going to tell the RCMP, they don't need to know." Obviously feeling that he had scored a decisive point, he rushed confidently on. "I'll tell you what; if you like her and you want her, she can move over here with you today. I'll go now and tell her."

He got up from my bed, and so did I—in a hurry. He said, "You can just use her until she gets older and then you can marry her in the whiteman's way when she is old enough."

A magnanimous offer, but I put a hand on Ikpakuhak's arm to restrain him. "Oh no," I said hurriedly, "don't do that. Don't tell her yet. I mean, she couldn't move in here. . . ." My voice trailed off. I visualized these two well-intentioned Eskimos bringing that sweet little girl across and moving her in with me lock, stock and barrel. The divisional manager of the Hudson's Bay Company enters to find me living with a thirteen-year-old girl!

Quickly I shifted ground. "No," I said, "I couldn't do that. Even if the police didn't find out, my boss from the Hudson's Bay Company, he comes here every year, you know—he'd find out and then I'd be in trouble with him."

Ikpakuhak thought about this; then he shrugged and asked, "Do you want a mug-up?"

I was flooded with relief. "Yes, I would very much."

We sat at the kitchen table with our tea, and Ikpakuhak and Tupilliqqut explained that they were all dressed in their deerskins to go out early for a hunt, but had been worrying about me, a poor single man without a woman, and had stopped by to suggest their solution.

"We'd really like you to stay here," Ikpakuhak said.

That was a gratifying thing to hear. I smiled, but made it plain that Tikirluk was not for me.

So good old Ikpakuhak came up with a new tack of his own. He turned to Tupilliqqut and said, "Hey, Tupiiq, why don't you let him borrow Kuptana?" Kuptana was Tupilliqqut's wife, a girl of about twenty-one and very attractive. Now my ears pricked up.

When Ikpakuhak presented this idea he used the Eskimo word *atullagliuk*, which literally means "allow to use temporarily". Tupiiq would have been a poor poker player: I could read the dismay in his face, and it was easy to see that he didn't think this was a good idea. I was sure that he and Ikpakuhak hadn't talked about this when they planned their little visit. But Tupilliqqut was on a spot. He obviously didn't want to go along, but he didn't want to embarrass his friend either by saying no. So I took him off the hook. I said, "Oh no, I'm doing all right. I can get by without having a wife."

Ikpakuhak didn't buy this. "Oh, no," he said, "you're a real man and you can't live all the time without a woman. A man needs someone to do his sewing, and fix his boots, and cook for him. A man needs a woman to keep him warm in bed."

We finally eased off the subject, and my two concerned friends went off on their hunt. I hoped that the matter was ended, but that evening I saw their dogteams coming back into the settlement, and within five minutes, still in his deerskins, Ikpakuhak stood before me taking up exactly where he had left off.

"We've been talking with the others," he said, "and we heard that a whiteman can marry a girl as soon as the government stops paying her family allowance."

Tupilliqqut, perhaps anxious to keep the talk from turning to any borrowing of Kuptana, was all ready to be helpful.

"That's at sixteen," he said. "You could just get Tikirluk to move in with you until then. It's only two or three years away."

Ikpakuhak added: "We don't know just when she was born."

I could see I was back in it again. Ikpakuhak hurriedly pounded the last nail in: "We asked Tikirluk about it, and she's glad. She's very pleased that she can move in with you." He and Tupilliqqut looked at me expectantly.

Again I could foresee all kinds of trouble. I ticked off in my mind: the Company, the missionaries, the police, everybody I could think of, except Tikirluk and my Eskimo friends here. The time for diplomacy had passed. With a determined look at Ikpakuhak and Tupilliqqut, I uttered just one word: "No."

That, mercifully, ended the matter and I was careful to avoid the subject of marriage for some time afterwards.

However, almost from the time of my arrival at Perry a number of women in the settlement had flirted with me. I was flattered but I realized that I was considered unusual not because of my Scottish face or my splendid physique, but simply because as the only white-man in the place, and as the trader, I had enormous prestige. I was something new, a whiteman who spoke Eskimo and who made it obvious that the attention of girls was pleasing.

238

But I moved slowly. I was unsure of local customs and dared not risk an already precarious position by committing a social gaffe.

However, there was one beautiful and brazen young lady called Niksaaktuq whom I was sure was making a play for me. She was the wife of a young hunter called Nasarlulik. Once when I called to pick up Nasarlulik, Niksaaktuq made a point of joking in a rather risqué way with me, smiling and teasing in little ways that women everywhere instinctively use. When Nasarlulik and I left, I discovered I had forgotten my mitts and went back to get them, telling Nasarlulik I would catch up with him in a minute. His wife handed the mitts to me, and when our hands touched she held on to mine, looked knowingly into my face, and smiled. Neither of us said a word, but I knew for sure that this girl was interested.

I was interested too. Very much. Niksaaktuq was an extremely good-looking girl with a beautiful body, slim and vibrant. Although she was only twenty, she had already been involved with eight or nine different men in spouse exchanges. She had a trick of scratching her instep with the toe of her other foot. I thought she must have a very itchy foot, but later discovered she was using an old Eskimo custom to signal to me that she was interested in a sexual liaison. I was willing all right, but I didn't know quite what to do about it.

Fortunately Niksaaktuq was neither as faint-hearted nor as inhibited as I was. During the next couple of months she made the most of every opportunity to smile at me and try to catch my eye, even when Nasarlulik was there. I didn't object—to be strictly honest, I tried to make it easier for this to happen. The big problem for me was that I really liked Nasarlulik. We got along well, hunting together, joking and laughing to the point where the other Eskimos called us *kipaqatiqiik* (joking partners), which meant we were close friends.

Finally, the situation came to a head. We had been on a trip together, and when we got back I asked Nasarlulik and Niksaaktuq to come over and have a mug-up with me as soon as they had their dogs chained and their gear stowed away. When they arrived I went to the kitchen to get the tea ready. Niksaaktuq came up behind me, put both arms around me and pulled me back against her. Nasarlulik had plopped down on the chesterfield in the living room, barely out of sight from where we stood by the stove. I turned round and Niksaaktuq put her hands to my face and pulled my head down to her and rubbed noses with me. The Perry Island people didn't engage in kissing, but they certainly knew how to rub noses. First this saucy girl just held the side of her nose against mine. That is considered just affectionate; but when she pressed the side of her nose against the side of mine and started rubbing, then that is not only considered passionate—it is!

She was busy leading the nose rubbing, and I was busy trying to see where Nasarlulik was, when she reached into her parka and brought out a little slip of paper which she handed me. On the paper she had written in Eskimo syllabics three words, *"Piyuma-guvit uiga kanngunaittuq."* ("If you want something, my husband won't be embarrassing.")

As soon as I read it I understood that this was a proposal for a wife-exchange relationship. Never before, however, had I asked a man for permission to take his wife to bed, and I started thinking furiously. I well knew Niksaaktuq's reputation as an impetuous and headstrong girl, and I didn't know for certain if this was something she had cooked up on her own, or if, as she implied, her husband knew about it and was in agreement. Besides I didn't want Nasarlulik to suspect I had been friendly with him only because I wanted his wife, which wasn't true at all.

So we sat there and drank our tea in silence, each trying to think of something to say. Every once in a while Nasarlulik and Niksaaktuq would flash smiles at me and make little comments that could be taken two ways.

At ten o'clock I excused myself while I went to the radio room and made my nightly communication with Cambridge Bay.

When I finished, they were both sitting at the kitchen table, and Niksaaktuq had another of her little notes ready. This time it read, "What are you waiting for? Ask my husband!"

I was still too embarrassed, so I folded the note up and stuck it in my pocket. She laughed and said *"Kanngusuktutit?"* ("Are you shy?")

"Oh, no," I replied.

"Well, go ahead, do what I asked you to do."

I didn't know what to do. Somehow Nasarlulik seemed to have become nothing more than an onlooker in this little game. Then Niksaaktuq picked up her pencil and wrote out another little note, and in the next half-hour she wrote six or seven more and passed them over to me while we made small talk. Some of them I looked at and some I just folded over and shoved in my pocket. I was about to stick yet another into my pocket, but Niksaaktuq could take no more.

"Give it to me," she ordered and grabbing the note out of my hand, she gave it to Nasarlulik.

Her husband opened the note, looked up and smiled. Obviously he had known all along what was going on.

He asked me plainly, "Do you desire my wife?"

I still played it cautiously, and said, "Any man would desire a woman as good-looking as your wife."

"Do you want to make love with her?" he persisted.

I was still very cautious. "Well, she's not my wife, you know."

Nasarlulik grinned and said, "Well, Niksaaktuq likes you, and I like you too, so go ahead."

Still uneasy, I tried to be amiable. "O.K., that's great . . . ."

"Fine," said Niksaaktuq, jumping up. "Come on, let's go, let's go."

Off we went while Nasarlulik stayed in the kitchen. The bedroom was just off the kitchen, and there wasn't even a door. It was all wide open. I was in there with Niksaaktuq, not feeling the least romantically inclined, with her husband sitting a couple of arm's lengths away. But Niksaaktuq had no such inhibitions. Down came her pants and bloomers and everything else, and she jumped into bed. So I got undressed and into bed too, but I still had a strange feeling. "What about your husband? He didn't go home."

"Oh, he'll be all right in the kitchen," said Niksaaktuq.

Nature took its course. Then we got up, dressed and went back to the kitchen, and I was a little embarrassed seeing Nasarlulik standing there; he had cleaned up all the dishes and was drying them. He turned to me with a smile. "Feeling better now?"

"Much better," I smiled.

"I'm glad." Then he explained, "Niksaaktuq kept telling me that we should share, because you are such a nice fellow, but I didn't want to say anything, because I didn't know how you felt about her."

We sat down and had another mug-up; then they went home.

By the next day the news had spread. Niksaaktuq was proud to be the first woman in the settlement to "get" me, and in typical Eskimo fashion she described to anyone who would listen the entire event, from beginning to end. Before noon every Eskimo in the settlement had heard all about us.

Every time after that when Nasarlulik and I made a trip, we would wind up at a camp together and we would share Niksaaktuq. Up at his trapping camp there would be Arnayak, his old blind mother, the two kids, Nasarlulik, Niksaaktuq and myself. We would all sleep on the sleeping platform together. At one end would be Arnayak, then me, Niksaaktuq, Nasarlulik, and then the two kids. Several times we made love in that situation. If it seems strange making love to a girl with her husband seven inches from your right knee and her mother-in-law seven inches from your left knee, then that is just another inhibition to be overcome. Everyone politely pretends to be asleep, but all ears are wide open. I can't say it really helped my sexual performance; on the other hand, it didn't stop me.

At Perry Island, two men who share one wife are called *angutau-qatigiik*, and they will become as close as brothers. If, for instance, Nasarlulik had fallen sick, I would have had to look after him and his family. In turn, if anything happened to me it was Nasarlulik's responsibility to see that I was provided for. Indeed we shared every confidence, problem and trouble.

As my exchange wife, Niksaaktuq performed many duties. She had a good ear for the shades of meaning and pronunciation that made so much difference to the understanding of a language and she taught me to perfect my Eskimo. She did a lot of cooking for me, and she took care of my clothing, which is no small matter for a man in the Arctic. Any Eskimo woman will try to outdo the others in making elaborate boots, or the handsomest parka with the best stitching. No one outdid Niksaaktuq. She turned out beautiful clothing for me, including a caribou parka, perfectly tailored.

When she first began sewing for me, like most Eskimo women she simply measured me with her eyes to get the proportions.

Eskimo women have keen eyes for that sort of thing and seldom make a mistake, but Niksaaktuq decided she must measure me more carefully. She said I was a bit lopsided, probably because I was a whiteman, and produced a short piece of string to measure me with. I was puzzled how she expected to get accurate measurements with that, but she tied it around my head, across the forehead. I didn't see how that helped unless she was going to make me a hat. She called me silly and said that everyone knew a man's height is always three times the circumference of his head. That was all the measuring she did and everything fitted exactly.

When, some two years later, Niksaaktuq became pregnant, Nasarlulik and I didn't know which of us was the father. Niksaaktuq just kept smiling and assuring me, "He'll be born with a nose like yours. You wait and see." Eskimos believe that every child takes after the father, so they think they can always tell who the father is.

There is no word in Eskimo for illegitimate child. The child of any union belongs to the mother, so it is relatively meaningless at birth who the father is. The child is raised by the mother and her husband, and when the child is old enough to understand, it is told who the real father is. Everyone knows, and there is no shame. Identifying the real father at that stage enables the incest taboos to be kept.

The Eskimos proved quite right about children taking after their fathers as far as Niksaaktuq's baby was concerned. There was no mistaking; I was the father. Before the birth of the baby, Nasarlulik and Niksaaktuq went to Cambridge Bay and the child was born there, so it was a long time before I was able to see my daughter. But Father Menez, one of the most decent missionaries I ever knew, who saw the child in Cambridge Bay, had no hesitation in confirming my fatherhood to me. "Don't try to deny it," he said gaily. "Everyone knows it is your baby."

The last thing in my mind was to deny it. I was very proud. My daughter was named Utuittuq, which had been Niksaaktuq's father's name, one of the men killed by Angulaalik. But little Utuittuq was weak as a baby. She caught flu and very nearly died. So Niksaaktuq and Nasarlulik renamed her, as the custom decrees when someone has a brush with death. Her new name was Qummiq, which literally means a thing that one grips between one's knees. But Eskimo names are relatively meaningless. They are also all asexual. After our daughter got her new name, her health improved rapidly and she developed into a lovely little girl.

Niksaaktuq's mother, Aaruattiaq, and her second husband, Tupilak, had no children. By Eskimo custom, when a couple want a child and can't have their own, they often adopt a grandchild. Niksaaktuq and Nasarlulik didn't want to give Qummiq to them, but Aaruattiaq begged them; and it isn't good manners for an Eskimo daughter to go against the wishes of her mother; so finally Qummiq went to live with her grandparents and now lives in Cambridge Bay.

MEDICINE - ESKIMO STYLE

In the Spring of 1962, a plane brought nurses from Cambridge Bay to X-ray all the Eskimos in the area. That plane brought trouble in the form of flu germs.

The Perry Islanders had been out of contact with "civilization" all winter, and they had no immunity. After the plane left they went down like flies. At first Alikammiq, the shaman who was Nasarlulik's father, and I went around ministering to the ill. There seemed little cause for alarm—most people just had colds and sniffles; but things quickly became much worse, and sufferers started running high temperatures. Then Alikammiq went down, and of the whole band of eighty or more I was literally the only person on his feet.

I decided to call Cambridge Bay for help, only to find my radio batteries were down. When I went to run the power plant to re-charge them, it failed to start, and for once I couldn't locate the trouble. There was no other way I could contact Cambridge Bay.

By now many people were seriously sick, running fevers up to 105 and 106 degrees. I was run ragged. I cooked up big vats of soup and caribou stew which I put on a little sled and hauled round everywhere I went. All the dogs had to be fed too. I would make my last call at twelve o'clock at night to give penicillin shots;

it would take me an hour or so to get around; then I would have a couple of hours' sleep, and at four in the morning I would make my next round with the shots. I had started out with sulphadiazine but had soon run out of that—we hadn't anticipated a major epidemic. I turned to oral penicillin until that too was gone, and then began giving penicillin intravenously. Then a boy died.

By now, many of the Eskimos had tied a thong around their heads—one of their methods to ward off the evil spirit when the shaman is not available. The shaman himself, Alikammiq, not only had the flu, but he was complaining of severe back pain. Finally, he wasn't even able to answer when I spoke to him.

Somehow the other Eskimos knew that the old shaman was dying and although ill themselves they came to his house. It is an Eskimo custom that if a friend is dying, they will try to see him before the breath leaves his body. When Alikammiq did die the cry from the people in his room was so heartbreaking and full of despair that I myself felt their loss.

On the thirteenth day of the epidemic, an Eskimo arrived from Cambridge Bay by dogteam. I sent him straight back with a message for help and, on the seventeenth day, a plane arrived with a couple of nurses and a man to fix my power plant.

Altogether six people had died in the epidemic and, as a sharing-husband with Alikammiq's son Nasarlulik, I was expected to take part in the death rituals for the shaman.

When a person dies, the body remains in the house on the sleeping platform for four days. During this period neither men nor women may take part in sewing or sawing of any material. They may not hammer anything, and they must not break any bones: this means that if the meat of caribou or seal is eaten, the bones must not be broken to get at the marrow. During the entire period the women must remain on the sleeping platform.

At the end of the fourth day, it was time to "bury" Alikammiq. By this time the body was frozen stiff because we hadn't heated the snowhouse since his death. (If we had the body would have been putrid.) Nasarlulik and I wrapped it in deerskins and lashed thongs around it because the taboo on sewing prevents the women from sewing the body into its caribou shroud. Then we laid the

245

body on a sled with the head in the direction that we would travel towards the burial place.

Eskimos are not buried in the sense that they are put into the ground. No one could dig into ground frozen rock-hard. They are laid to rest at a spot which they pick before death. Nasarlulik knew where Alikammiq's place was and took us to a gravel bar up on the side of the inlet overlooking the sea.

We lifted the shrouded body, just Nasarlulik and I, and walked in a wide circle three times round the place. Then we laid Alikammiq down with his head facing towards the west. His son made a little hole in the caribou shroud close to the head, to allow his soul to escape. Nasarlulik explained to me that it would stay near the body until a newborn child in the settlement had been named for him. Until this was done, Alikammiq's spirit would be restless and make trouble for the band.

Leaving the body, we walked another circle round it, then went back to the settlement. It was taboo to look back. We just left the body there on the bare ground without a marker. Wolves and foxes would clean up the body within a few days, but even after the remains had been scattered the place would still be known as *alikammip iluvra*, Alikammiq's resting place.

ALIKAMMIQ had been one of the greatest of the Eskimo shamans. Oddly enough, it was not his ability to walk on water, nor his feat of flying to the moon, not even his return from the dead that won him fame with his own people. The Eskimos all agreed that the fact that he could casually cut off his own leg, wave it in the air for all to see, then re-attach it and walk away, put him in a class by himself.

Every Eskimo at Perry, even if he hadn't actually seen it happen himself, could at least name one person who had witnessed the feat. Many recalled with considerable glee the time a whiteman, a new police constable, came to Perry Island from Cambridge Bay. Hearing about Alikammiq's particular talent, he went with a group of Eskimos to the shaman's house, and told Alikammiq that he for one knew the self-amputation to be a ruse, and he brazenly suggested that Alikammiq was probably not even a proper shaman.

246

Naturally, Alikammiq could not stand for this, particularly in the presence of seven or eight Eskimos in his own settlement. He grabbed a snowknife and handed it to his antagonist.

"Here, take this," he said. "Now,"—putting his foot up on the sleeping platform so that his leg was right in front of the startled whiteman—"if you don't believe me, go ahead and cut my leg off right here." He pointed just above his knee.

According to the Eskimos who were there, the young constable was so unnerved at this unusual offer that he dropped the snowknife, and from that time on he never doubted Alikammiq again—or at least, never in public.

The Eskimos often cited this incident as proof that Alikammiq could indeed cut off his leg and restore it. But to me the story seemed a beautiful example of the shaman's grasp of practical psychology. Alikammiq had pulled a magnificent bluff—one he knew he would get away with. The chances are the lone whiteman realized that if he had cut into Alikammiq's leg the Eskimos, most of whom were already annoyed at him for insulting their respected shaman, would never have let him escape to enjoy his piece of one-upmanship.

I never ceased to be amazed at the phenomenal range of abilities credited to the shamans. They turned at will into polar bears or birds; they could become small enough to slip through a keyhole or make themselves disappear entirely; they healed the sick; they changed the weather.

Eskimos don't just *believe* that shamans can fly; they *know* it. There is a crater west of Perry Island which, Eskimos will explain, marks the spot where two great shamans collided in midair and fell to the ground. When the United States first landed a rocket on the moon, I thought this a tremendous feat, and I excitedly told the Eskimos about it. They listened to my story politely but I could tell they were amused rather than amazed. Finally one man spoke up.

"Yes," he said, "that is good, but the shamans have always been able to go to the moon." He thought me a bit dull to consider a rocket to the moon so remarkable.

When shamans fly they are careful to take off outside the range of sight of ordinary people, but although they take their leave in secret, they can be seen once they are in flight. The sighting of a meteor or shooting star was sure evidence that Alikammiq was in the sky.

A trip to the moon is never a frivolous undertaking. The most common motive would seem to be to help a barren woman have a child. The shaman takes off on his magical flight, picks up a child on the moon and hurries back with it. His modest remuneration for the service is the privilege of spending the night with the woman in her bed. There are certainly those who would argue that this had more to do with the procurement of the baby than the flight to the moon, but an Eskimo will assure anyone who inquires that babies never result from a single sexual encounter.

Some consider a shaman's "immortality" his most outstanding characteristic. Everyone knew that a murdered shaman would return to life within three or four days and, more often than not, take revenge on those who had slain him. The Perry River people would tell of a duel that Alikammiq fought with two men who "fatally" shot him with their rifles. His relatives took Alikammiq's body and laid it out for the waiting period decreed by the death taboos. Sure enough, on the third day he came back to life, and he and his family hunted down his assailants. One was killed; the other narrowly escaped.

It is this acceptance of the shaman's ability to rise from the dead that has always made it easy for Eskimos to understand the Christian's belief in Jesus's resurrection. They see nothing extraordinary in it. Similarly, walking on water doesn't count for much. Any close observer of Nature—as every Eskimo is—can see insects perform this stunt; it follows quite logically that given the right circumstances, man can do likewise.

Of no small benefit to the shaman's "immortality" is the hole in the centre of his chest, and his ability to move that hole to any part of his body at will. Alikammiq once gave a practical demonstration in a dispute with a man named Savgut. When the argument turned ugly, the two decided to settle their differences with rifles.

Alikammiq challenged Savgut: "Shoot me!"

Savgut did just that. Only a few feet away from Alikammiq, he levelled his weapon at his chest and fired. Witnesses claim that they saw the snow puff up behind Alikammiq where the bullet landed, but the old shaman was unharmed: he had quickly shifted the hole in his chest so that the bullet passed harmlessly through without touching him. What other explanation could there be? Alikammiq in turn raised his rifle and coolly shot off part of Savgut's ear.

But however many tricks a shaman might be called upon to perform, his true role is that of healer. I have spoken many times to Eskimos about shamans, and they have always compared them to physicians rather than to missionaries in the whiteman's culture. During the period I spent at Perry Island, there occurred a case of what proved to be rheumatic fever. At the time I thought it was just a bad case of influenza and so set about treating the man, Qingarullikkaaq, as best I could. I dosed him with antibiotics, but his temperature stayed at 104 degrees and I was at a loss what to do next. Qingarullikkaaq's wife decided he needed the help of the shaman, and invited me to attend a session that night with Alikammiq.

Eskimos believe that all sickness and death are the work of an evil spirit, known in the Perry Island district as the *agiuqtuq*. When someone dies, and his name is not passed on to a newborn child or pup within one winter of the death, then that name turns into an *agiuqtuq*, and will cause sickness and death among the victim's relatives and dogs alike. In a case such as Qingarullikkaaq's, the shaman's first step is to locate the *agiuqtuq*. To do this the shaman goes into a self-induced trance and summons his helping spirits.

That night in Qingarullikkaaq's snowhouse, there were five of us watching the sick man and Alikammiq. Qingarullikkaaq was lying on his back on the snow platform. Alikammiq was crouched on the floor bobbing up and down, bending and dipping from the waist, calling on his helping spirits.

It was remarkable to see the change that came over Alikammiq as he gradually assembled these spirits. In everyday life the little shaman was a somewhat timid man, very quiet by nature. But as his familiar spirits took control of him, he underwent a total personality change. He loudly challenged us to "try him" (by thrusting a knife into his body). Twice he lapsed into an imitation

249

of a polar bear, thus indicating that the spirit of the animal completely possessed him. Each new spirit that possessed him seemed more frightening and dangerous than the last. The watchers grew very tense. Then, when he felt that all his familiar spirits were assembled, he proceeded with the *qilayuq* method (head-lifting) to learn the *agiuqtuq's* name.

Alikammiq tied a sealskin thong round Qingarullikkaaq's head. Standing beside the man, with a tight grip on the thong, the shaman began a series of questions that required a yes or no answer. The sick person would reply, acting unconsciously, by headweight alone. If the answer was no, the head would lift up by the thong easily. If the answer was yes, the head would be difficult to lift.

The questions continued for almost an hour; always the head lifted easily and the answer was no. Finally Alikammiq struck on the name of a dead relative—Qingarullikkaaq's head became very heavy and it was all Alikammiq could do to budge it. The identity of the *agiuqtuq* was revealed.

The tension in the snowhouse was broken by sudden exclamations. Even I could remember that the name of the *agiuqtuq* had not been passed on to anyone in the settlement.

Yet, even with this success, Alikammiq's work was not done. As sometimes happens, Qingarullikkaaq did not get better. It appeared that the shaman must go on to the second phase of the ritual. When a man fails to recover from his illness once the identity of the evil spirit is known, the Eskimos say that his soul has been stolen by the spirit. The shaman must attack the thief for the soul to return home.

Next day Alikammiq once more summoned his familiar spirits. Then he took a long sealskin thong and tied it round the sick man's parka, which was of ordinary caribou skin. He took the parka outside the snowhouse, left it there, and came back inside with the end of the thong. He prepared to fight a tug-of-war with the *agiuqtuq* for possession of the parka. Making himself the anchor man, Alikammiq asked two other men to help pull. Together they would attempt to pull the parka back inside the snowhouse, thereby winning Qingarullikkaaq's soul and assuring his good health. If the thong should break under the strain, the sick man would die.

The latter seemed the likely outcome to me. Qingarullikkaaq's condition was worsening; his temperature was now at 106 degrees. I suspected that the wily old shaman would save face by looping the thong around some steadfast object outside, cut it so as to make it break when pulled, and resign the family to his patient's death in spite of his efforts.

Back in the snowhouse Alikammiq and his helpers had stripped down to their undershirts. They braced themselves as the shaman gave the call to pull. I was sitting not more than three feet away from the porch, where I had a clear view of the parka outside on the snow, the three men inside the snowhouse, and the sealskin thong between them. I was sure that I was about to discover where the sham in shamanism was.

The men pulled with obvious strength. I could see the veins and corded muscles on their arms stand out as they strained, pulling the cord in bit by bit, hand over hand. The thong stretched taut, and I expected it to break at any moment.

Incredibly, the parka eased its way towards the door. I watched it like a hawk, seeing but unbelieving as, heaving and gasping for breath, the men finally pulled it completely into the snowhouse. There was an audible sigh of relief, and the men sank back on their haunches. I casually walked over and picked the parka up. Nothing unusual! It was empty, weighing two or three pounds at the most—yet I had seen three men use all their strength to pull it into the snowhouse.

There is a simple explanation if one accepts Eskimo belief. Pulling hard against the men was the *agiuqtuq*, a strong being composed purely of blood, invisible to all but the shaman's eyes.

Anyway, there was a celebration that night; it seemed as though Qingarullikkaaq would now get well, and by this time I was as strong a believer as the Eskimos. Next day, his temperature had dropped.

Still the recovery was not fast enough to suit Alikammiq. He was not convinced that Qingarullikkaaq's soul had been completely recovered. We returned to the snowhouse a third time, as the shaman prepared to do battle with the evil spirit.

Alikammiq armed himself with a tiny wooden bow and arrow, just like a child's toy, only four inches long, and a wooden dagger. With these he would face the spirit alone in a fight too frightening to be viewed by others.

We sat huddled inside the snowhouse while Alikammiq crawled out on the low snowporch to fight for Qingarullikkaaq's soul. Presently we heard groans and shouts, apparently the sounds of the struggle. Fearful screams followed, and with a shout in his own voice Alikammiq reappeared at the door of the snowhouse, his hands and clothes bloodied. The blood was recognized by the Eskimos as that of the slain *agiuqtuq*, now visible to all. The shaman had emerged the victor.

Within a few days, Qingarullikkaaq, whom I had expected to die in spite of massive doses of the whiteman's medicine and the efforts of his shaman, was on his feet.

A REAL ESKIMO

When the white fox trapping season ended, around the last week in March, all the Eskimos got ready for the annual seal hunt on the sea ice. In my second year I decided to go with them. Although I had been out in my canoe in the summer and killed seal with my .22 rifle, I wanted to learn the Eskimo way of hunting seal with harpoons. Angulaalik had promised to teach me, and this seemed the best opportunity to learn.

By now I had put together a dog team for myself, led by a hefty one-hundred-and-eighty-pound husky named Qaqquq. He didn't look much like Hollywood's idea of an Eskimo husky—he was white with orange patches—but he was a fine lead dog. Unfortunately, he loved to fight, and over the seven years I had him he must have killed thirty or thirty-five dogs. On the other hand, he was an intelligent animal, very affectionate and gentle with people. I've seen kids crawling all over Qaqquq, pulling his tail, sitting on his back just as if he were a pet housedog.

I was lucky in getting Qaqquq to develop into my lead dog. He was only five months old when I got him but he already weighed over a hundred pounds and showed signs of intelligence and aggressiveness. There is no sure way to tell that a pup will make a good lead dog or even a good dog. A buyer has to watch for signs of the traits he will want.

Anyone breaking pups into a team will first let them run loose alongside an experienced team. This builds up endurance. After a few such trips, the pups are put into harness. At this stage, the owner can quickly gauge what kind of working dog the pup is likely to make. When pups are first harnessed they aren't pressured and generally just run along without actually pulling, but gradually the driver will apply pressure, touching them lightly with the whip or a stick, to make them run forward against the harness. Eventually the action becomes habitual, and as soon as they are harnessed in with the team they pull automatically. Some dogs, of course, are natural loafers, like some people. Dogs like that don't last long in the North. As soon as a driver finds a good puller to take his place, the lazy one is off the team and is shot. But even a team of good pullers will go bad with a poor leader; so I worked particularly hard to train Qaqquq.

Training a lead dog as I trained Qaqquq is just a matter of conditioning the animal to do what is required. The dog is harnessed on the end of a trace to a small light sled. By shouting "Haw!" and throwing a stick or a snowball to the left, the dog is taught to turn right, away from the threat. After a bit, a smart dog like Qaqquq turns when he hears the command, and it is no longer necessary to throw anything. The same procedure conditions the dog to turn left when so commanded. From then on if the dog is bright, he soon picks up the little bits of the job he needs to know. For example if the lead dog turns in too short a radius, the swing dogs just behind will overtake him, and there will be a fight. A smart lead dog always keeps the towline taut.

The words and sounds used as dog commands vary greatly in different parts of the North, but if you actually said "Mush!" to an Eskimo dogteam, any Eskimos who heard you would roll in the snow and hold their sides. Eskimos appreciate a good joke. "Mush!" has been getting the job done in the movies for years, but it wouldn't budge a dog an inch in the Arctic. Generally the command to start or go is not so much a word as a harsh, explosive clearing of the throat, something like a bark.

The two key dogs of any team are the lead dog and the boss dog. Because he was a killer and liked to fight, Qaqquq was also my boss dog, the one that keeps order on a team. There is a pecking order on every team. The boss dog is the one that can whip every other dog.

I once bought a huge dog, thinking he would make a good alternative leader when I wanted to rest Qaqquq. I had paid a good price for the new dog—a top-grade fox skin worth about $30. The new dog had plenty of confidence. He and Qaqquq walked stiff-legged round each other, hair bristling, tails straight out, no signs of friendliness, and no indication of surrender. I expected them to fight, but not for long. The fur around a husky's neck is so thick that usually when they attack each other they never get a good grip; they grab a paw or snout and after a few seconds of pain the dog in trouble will give up and the fight is over. This new dog jumped at Qaqquq; Qaqquq got him by the neck and just ripped his throat out. In a few minutes the new dog was dead. I was mad, and gave Qaqquq a good thrashing; but that was the way he was.

Gradually I built a team of thirteen dogs, which was the standard-size team for that part of the Arctic. I owned a good breeding female and eventually most of the other dogs on my team were offspring from the bitch mated to Qaqquq. I'd say that a driver with thirteen working animals might spend three-quarters of his time hunting and fishing to "fuel" his dogs. Having thirteen dogs is like having thirteen people to feed, as the average husky will eat four or five pounds of caribou or seal or fish every day, whether pulling a heavy-laden sled or sitting on his butt howling at the moon.

On the first morning of the seal hunt there was a great bustle of preparations and then the entire settlement simply loaded up their sleds and moved out. We spread out across the landscape, eighteen families, each with its own dogteam and entourage, keeping a proper distance between the teams so there wouldn't be too many dog fights and following the leaders, Angulaalik and another experienced hunter named Kuvluruq.

254

Twenty miles out from the coast and just off the tip of a little island, Angulaalik stopped his team. He knew exactly what he was looking for, of course, and had pulled up by an *aayuraq*. *Aayuraqs* are breaks in the sea ice, caused by the shifting pressures of the ice, which have then frozen over again; they freeze over and break open again many times, but such places usually have ice no more than three or four feet thick. Seal tend to congregate along breaks like this, where it is comparatively easy for them to keep open their vital breathing holes.

Eight families and I stayed with Angulaalik, leaving Kuvluruq to take the rest and search farther out for another good campsite. Each family in our party immediately started cutting out snowblocks and building its own *nallaqtaq*, which is similar to an ordinary snowhouse except that the top snowblocks are not put in place. The warm spring weather would melt those top blocks and cause the whole house to cave in. Therefore a caribouskin sled cover is thrown over the open top to make the roof. I erected my *nallaqtaq* next to Angulaalik's and by evening everyone was snug and content in a new house.

Early next morning all the hunters set out on foot to find the seal. There were ten in our party, including myself and three teenagers who I was sure knew more about what they were doing than I did. We peeled off across the ice, with those dogs that had been especially trained to hunt seal straining and sniffing at the ends of their long leashes. Each of us carried our own harpoon and a caribouskin bag containing our hunting gear. The sun was beating down on us as we tramped across the ice but we were dressed from head to foot in caribouskin because the temperature was actually below zero.

We followed the *aayuraq* farther out to sea, looking for the especially rough places in the ice which make such good hunting places for seal dens and breathing holes. As the seal has to come up to breathe about every five minutes when it is feeding under the ice, it has to make a number of breathing holes, beginning when the ice starts to form and is still thin enough for the seal to break through. The seal keeps each hole open by repeatedly breaking through and scratching at it with its flippers as the surrounding ice thickens. The only way a seal can be killed in winter is by catching it as it comes up for air at one of these holes, or when it is in its den under the snow alongside the breathing hole.

Whenever a dog picked up the seal scent, he was anchored in the snow out of the way while the hunter went forward to check out the spot. We soon found several seal holes this way, but at each, when Angulaalik poked down through the snow with a special snow probe, he found the seal hole too thickly frozen over. "No seal there." He explained to me, "If there were a seal using that hole, there wouldn't be any ice formed over it, or at least the ice would be very thin."

Finally Angulaalik found an open hole. He showed me how to locate the centre of the seal hole under the snow and gave me a special little instrument called a *kaiptaq* (seal indicator) to insert through the snow down into the hole. When the seal came up for air at that hole again, it would cause this indicator to jiggle and alert me, serving, too, as a guide for my harpoon thrust. Then Angulaalik smoothed and repacked the snow where we had disturbed it, so that the seal wouldn't find any change in the light pattern above it when surfacing. Finally, he cut a snowblock for me to sit on, and fixed the harpoon on a little stand made of two Y-shaped sticks so I could grab it up in a second. Telling me once again to keep my eyes glued to the *kaiptaq*, he disappeared over the ice to get on with his own hunting.

I sat there with the harpoon alongside me and my feet on the now-empty caribouskin bag for warmth, and waited. It was a grand way to develop patience. Self-conscious and tense, but determined to be ready if that *kaiptaq* started to move, I resisted all temptation to shift about or even to scratch. I knew that all I had to do was rise silently and quickly when the *kaiptaq* moved, then plunge the harpoon straight down in the snow. Even though I wouldn't be able to see the seal, I knew that if I hit truly along the *kaiptaq* which marked the exact centre of the seal hole, I would smash the cutting edge of the harpoon right into the seal's head, or at worst its shoulder. It seemed ridiculously easy.

The trouble was that the *kaiptaq* never moved. I just sat all day and burned in the sun. Comparing notes as we walked back to camp that night we found that only one man had killed a seal, and although this seemed disappointing to me, the others told me this was about normal. In an average week there, with ten hunters out every day from morning to night, we never had more than nine seals, which provided barely enough meat for ourselves and the dogs. It makes one think how difficult it must have been in the old days when the seal hunt was the only thing between a man's family, his dogs, and starvation throughout the winter.

On the fourth day, still having had no luck, I was daydreaming by my seal hole, my mind off in Scotland. All of a sudden the indicator began to move, and I leapt up in a panic. I plunged with my harpoon—and missed completely! I not only missed the seal but the breathing hole as well, for my harpoon head went right into the ice alongside the opening of the breathing hole.

What a fool I felt! The seal had actually surfaced under the snow and I had heard a sort of grunt as the breath exploded out of its lungs. Then, after I whacked down the harpoon close by its head, I had heard a splash of water as it dived again.

During our after-supper review of the day's activities, I told the others of my fiasco. I really hadn't much relish for admitting my folly, and as I expected, the Eskimos had a good laugh at my expense; but it was understanding laughter and I finally joined in.

Angulaalik said, "Well, don't let it bother you. We're all the same. When I first went seal hunting I became so nervous that I too missed the seal." He grinned at me and added, "I didn't strike the ice, mind you, but I did miss the seal."

So the next day, with my humour and confidence both restored, I went back to the seal hole. Angulaalik had found a hole fairly close to mine and we sat, about four hundred yards apart, like stone figures on the landscape.

I had been there only about an hour, when the indicator began to turn again. I got to my feet as the seal rose and pushed up the indicator. I put all my strength into plunging my harpoon right down alongside the indicator, and with a fierce joy I felt the solid shock all the way up my arm when the harpoon bashed into the seal's head.

I grabbed on the line to pull the seal up, all the while shouting to catch Angulaalik's attention. I couldn't seem to get the seal properly—it was jumping back and forward and was too much for me. It was simply because of lack of experience on my part, and I got too excited. However, before Angulaalik reached me, the seal was tiring. I could hear it grunting under the snow; then it would come out of the water again, and I would pull it farther up with the hand line, until finally I managed to finish the kill.

Seeing this, Angulaalik cried excitedly, "*Quanarunaqtuq! Inuin-nangnguqtutit, inuinnangnguqpiaqtutit!*" ("Well done! You're a real Eskimo, a real Eskimo!")

Now this was a very important moment for me: the first time I had killed a seal with a harpoon. It is one of the milestones in an Eskimo's life. Normally, of course, it takes place at a much earlier age, fourteen or fifteen. But no Eskimo lad could have been more thrilled than this transplanted Scot in his early twenties! Now I could call the Arctic *Nunaga*: my land, my country.

Angulaalik looked upon me as his son in this hunt and was as jubilant about my triumph as he would have been for a real son. As we started pulling the seal up out of the hole, Angulaalik said, "Wait, wait! Don't rush it now. This is your first seal and we have to do things in the right manner. First, lie back."

He pushed at me with one hand. "Lie on your back in the snow, right here beside the hole, and spread your legs. It's what people always do when they kill their first seal."

So I lay back, totally uncomprehending, with my feet just about straddling the opening of the breathing hole. Angulaalik pulled the seal up, soaking wet, dripping with blood, and pulled it right over my body and face as I lay in the snow. "Now get up. We've got to wrestle."

I still hadn't the slightest idea what he was doing. "What for?"

Angulaalik was brusque: "Don't ask questions, you'll offend the seal. Just wrestle with me." He added, "Just make it look good, but let me win."

So we got up alongside the seal, and we wrestled around, and finally Angulaalik threw me on top of the seal, and he cried out to the seal, "There, now you should feel happy!"

As we got up, the other hunters came running in, for once the word got around, everyone was hallooing and hollering. A man's

258

first seal will bring the others to help the hunter celebrate properly. I felt about ten feet tall.

But Angulaalik took me off to one side and scolded me. "Don't smile too much," he said. "Look humble. It's bad manners if you look too proud."

So then, in the Eskimo style, I began to explain to the other hunters how hopeless I was. I said it was purely luck; that if I had been a better hunter, I'd have got a much bigger seal, and look at the size of this poor little seal. Angulaalik looked pleased. An Eskimo must let his father or his nearest relative do the bragging for him.

One of the men ran back to his seal hole where he had a sled. We were in high spirits, all of us laughing and enjoying ourselves as we put the seal on the sled. Away we went; no more hunting for anyone that day, so that everyone could take part in the appropriate celebrations.

Back at camp, we were joined by the families of Kuvluruq's party. The seal was taken into Angulaalik's snowhouse where Irvana stood proudly awaiting us. The first thing she did was to wipe the blood away from around its head. Then she took some water out of a vacuum flask and held the seal's head up, forced its mouth open, and poured in the fresh water. She said this was the ancient custom; after a man's first seal has been killed, it must have a drink of fresh water, because since seals live in salt water the taste of fresh water is a special treat.

Ordinarily a man's first seal is butchered outside by the seal hole, but because I was an orphan, my seal was butchered inside the snowhouse by the wife of my "nearest relative", Angulaalik. As soon as Irvana had finished flensing it, skinning and removing the layer of blubber, Angulaalik said, "It's now time to get your partners." Again I didn't know what he meant.

Angulaalik explained: "When a man first kills a seal, he divides the seal up with his partners." There are many different portions to the carcass, I discovered, about sixteen or seventeen of them, and these portions are given to the hunter's seal partners. My heart partner, my *uummatiqatiga*, was Angulaalik himself, which meant that when the heart was cut out of my seal, I had to give it to Angulaalik as a present. Another man served as my lung partner, and got the lungs. And this went on right through the various portions of the carcass.

Every time I killed a seal from then on, I would share with all my partners. Thus, anyone who kills a seal will get only a few parts of it for himself, but nearly everyone shares in his good fortune. If a hunter has bad luck and doesn't kill a seal at all, the chances are good that if his partners are doing well, he will still get almost a full seal in the course of the hunt.

Another thing I learned about these seal partnerships was that if Angulaalik and I exchanged the hearts of our seals, my son (if I had one) and Angulaalik's son would automatically become heart partners. Among all the numerous real and acquired relationships among Eskimos, this was the only hereditary relationship I found.

We were in that seal camp about six weeks altogether, going out every day. When we brought in seals, they were dumped at the side of the houses where the women butchered them. The entrails went to the dogs, which at that time of the year were fed blubber and entrails, never solid meat. Then, after using the *ulu*, a knife with a fan-shaped blade to flense the skin, the women would remove the epidermis with a scraping knife. The skin was then staked out to dry in the sun.

Generally by the time we got back from the day's hunting, the women were inside the snowhouses, the lamps were burning and the evening meal was cooking. Every house had a blubber lamp made of soapstone, some of them four feet long, which not only gave off a soft light, but also a very soft, low heat. The hollowed-out bowl of the lamp was fed oil from a raised platform where little pieces of seal blubber were laid. These pieces were broken down by tapping them with a musk-ox horn pounder, which released the oil. The Perry Island Eskimos took seeds of cotton grass and put them along the rim of the lamp where they absorbed the oil and could be ignited.

Above the lamp there hung a pot, usually with seal meat in it, but not all the women cooked every night, just one or two. When the food was ready they called in all the hunters and we ate together in one snowhouse. The boiled seal (or caribou), was eaten almost raw. Taken out of the pot, the pieces would still be dripping blood. If dinner was seal flippers, they still had the hair on them.

It was superbly comfortable in the snowhouse when we hunters came in and took off our outer gear and filled our bellies. It was warm and cosy; we brought out our tobacco and rolled a cigarette or pulled out a pipe. The evenings were spent in story-telling and re-enactments of the day's kill. The children of the camp played on the caribou blankets on the sleeping platform, often romping around naked because it was quite warm from the soapstone lamp and the body heat of so many of us in the house.

ONE YEAR at Perry Island the seal hunt proved discouragingly unproductive for those who went out on the sea ice after the fox season was over. After two weeks in the hunting camp, thirteen experienced hunters had only two seals to show for their efforts. Four of them, including Nasarlulik and Tupilliqqut, decided to make a trip up to the north end of Victoria Island and see if they could get some polar bear. They asked me to go with them.

We were as enthusiastic as a bunch of kids. There is always plenty of excitement hunting the polar bear. They are potentially dangerous animals, yet I have known Eskimos who have killed them with hand axes. And not many years ago, Eskimos killed polar bears with a knife tied to the end of a harpoon handle, a weapon they called a *pana*. The use of the *pana* took some courage. They would move in close to the bear, wait until the bear reared up on its hind legs, and then run right in front of it, shoving the butt of the *pana* into the snow and tempting the bear to lunge towards them. The bear's weight impaled it on the *pana*. This way they used the bear's own weight and the ferocity of its charge to make the kill, rather than trying to thrust the weapon into the bear with the puny strength of man.

The rifle, of course, has since made man the most powerful animal on earth. However, handling a rifle in the extreme low temperatures of the Arctic calls for a bit more care than the normal. The gun is prepared beforehand by cleaning all the oil and grease off any moving parts. This keeps the gun from freezing up and jamming. Greenhorns in the Arctic sometimes make the mistake of throwing their mitts off and grabbing the rifle with bare hands, only to discover to their horror that the skin of their fingers has frozen tightly to the barrel. The trick the Eskimo uses is simply to stick his hand into a snow bank until it has cooled so that his skin doesn't freeze to the gun.

Since our trip to the north end of Victoria Island would be a long trip, almost a thousand miles there and back, we left our post with our sleds piled high. After a few days of travelling over the sea ice we hit the coastline of Victoria Island and followed the coast northeast. We had been out nine days when we came across the first tracks of polar bear. We debated whether to follow the trail, but Tupilliqqut, the only one of us who had been in the area before, suggested that if we went farther north we should come into really good bear country.

So we pushed on. Sure enough, when we turned the curve at the top of Victoria Island and started to head west we really hit polar bear country. We were crossing as many as seven or eight individual bear trails a day, so when we found good snow for snowhouses we set up a base camp.

Next morning, we all headed out together, moving out from shore a good twenty miles. We had decided to hunt light, taking just our rifles and a grub box and a couple of vacuum flasks each. For one thing it would be better, when we sighted bear, if the dogs were not hauling a heavily laden sled.

Eventually we came across the fresh track of a bear in some very rough polar-pack ice with large ridges and raised slabs. We proceeded with some caution because if there were bears around they could ambush us.

Nasarlulik took my binoculars, went up to the top of a high hummock of ice, and looked carefully round the country. Quite soon he spotted a bear off in another direction from the one whose trail we had all been following. Nasarlulik and I decided to go for that bear; now we had caught sight of it, we expected little trouble. We descended from the hummock and soon found the bear's tracks. From the way the trail wandered around we guessed this bear was a male, searching for seal breathing-holes in the ice.

Sure enough, when we spotted our bear, it was standing with

its head down a seal hole, as we had anticipated. At the sound of our dogs barking and howling, it yanked up its head and started running like a bat out of hell, with the dogs, the almost empty sled, and ourselves in hot pursuit.

Finally, when we were about three or four hundred yards behind the bear, we came into some more rough ice; the anchor on the sled caught and stopped the dogs. We cast off some of the dogs immediately, but, by the time they caught up with the bear, they were eight or nine hundred yards ahead of us, out of effective rifle range. They began to attack, dashing in and out nipping the bear from behind.

Normally dogs are too agile for a bear and they are careful to avoid being pawed, but as we watched, I saw one of my dogs dart in too close. The bear caught the poor animal bang-on with one swat and knocked the big husky at least twenty feet into the air. The dog was dead before we could catch up, but for the bear, cornered by the other dogs, the chase was over. I walked up and put a bullet into its head.

This was a large bear, a ten- or eleven-footer, and approximately six years old. The age is determined by examining the claws. A light band is followed by a dark band, then a light band again, and so on. A count of these bands will give the age of the bear quite accurately up to about nine years. Beyond that the method isn't reliable because the claws become worn with use.

We skinned out our bear—tough work because it had to be cut every inch of the way. After that, we chopped up the carcass for dogfood, being careful to bury the liver, which was poisonous to the dogs. By then it was getting late and we started back to camp.

Tupilliqqut and the other men came in a bit later. They had had tremendous luck; they brought back seven bears. We now had plenty of meat for dogfood and decided to stay at that camp for another week. At the end of that time, we had twenty-six hides.

The only dangerous incident of the entire hunt came when we spotted a female with two cubs. Nasarlulik and I stopped our sled to cast off two dogs to round up the mother bear who was raging mad, far more dangerous than any male ever is.

The two dogs stopped her for a moment, but before either

Nasarlulik or I could get in a shot, the dogs were diverted by one of the cubs. The cub was just a little thing, about two or three feet long, and the dogs mistakenly took it for easy prey. But the cub turned around and belted the nearest of its tormentors in the chops. Surprised, the dog backed off in a hurry, and then both dogs ganged up, barking ever so bravely at that one game little cub.

Like a white bulldozer, the mother bear came charging in, bowling over the dogs on the way, and dived right at our sled. Nasarlulik and I moved like lightning. With a thousand pounds of white-coated fury coming straight for us, I lunged headfirst right over the top of the sled to get something between me and that mad bear, but Nasarlulik, turning to make a dive in the other direction, got his feet caught in the dog harness and flopped flat on his face right in the animal's path. My hunting partner frantically scrambled to his feet in the midst of what looked like a whirlpool of dogs and bear. I shall never forget the expression of terror on his face. He went flying over the sled with the bear half on top of him and the dogs going absolutely wild. The bear was lashing out right, left and centre with Nasarlulik dodging, the dogs and harness all tangled round him. It was all highly dangerous; yet so chaotic that Nasarlulik had to laugh! Between spasms of laughter he was yelling at me. "Shoot her! Shoot her! I can't shoot! I can't shoot!" When he had fallen the barrel of his rifle had gone plunk into the snow and filled up with soft snow. He didn't dare shoot, because he knew the rifle might blow up in his face with the barrel plugged that way. He had a spare rifle, but it was lashed on the sled, and inaccessible in the tangle. I couldn't get a shot in myself because the bear was jumping all over the place, the dogs were after the bear and Nasarlulik was too close to the fray. At last Nasarlulik managed to scramble to his feet and get his spare rifle off the sled. He dashed nimbly out to one side, completely clear of the mêlée, turned just as the bear charged after him, and coolly shot her right in the eye, dropping her dead on the spot.

We still had a mess on our hands. Some of the dogs were badly beaten up, yelping with pain, others were trying to get up, their legs caught up in the traces. The harness was tangled and torn up. We had to shoot the two cubs before the dogs would calm down enough for us to straighten out the bedlam. It had been a close thing. Luckily Nasarlulik, for all his comedy of errors, had moved pretty fast.

DURING the summer months, many of the Eskimos hunted seal from their canoes. When I first arrived at Perry, we paid five dollars for a large sealskin in good condition. One year all traders got a wire in code from the Company instructing us to pay twenty-eight dollars for a seal. I sent a wire right away asking the Company to verify the price. Back came the confirmation—twenty-eight dollars.

I remember the first Eskimo to come in to the post that summer with sealskins. His name was Paniuyaq and he brought two for which he expected ten dollars. They were both prime pelts so I casually said, "Well, that's fifty-six dollars." Poor Paniuyaq thought I was joking with him, and I had to explain that I was serious, that the Company had indeed changed the price.

The Eskimos went wild! Paniuyaq spread the word, and soon the entire settlement was out on the sea in canoes. In nice calm weather they would stay out all day. We never went seal hunting if the sea was very choppy; shooting from a bobbing canoe was a waste of ammunition. But on a good day that summer, canoes were everywhere. Some of the Eskimos put their transistor radios in the bottom of the canoe and played them at top volume. This, surprisingly, drew in the seals. They would hear the noise, and bit by bit work towards it until they were close enough to give the hunter an easy shot.

When the chores were light at the post, I took off with my canoe myself. Just as the Eskimos did, I based my techniques on taking advantage of the insatiable curiosity of seals, but my method was an older one; I simply picked up my paddle and rapped against the side of the canoe, very sharply. In due course I would see a seal, maybe two or three hundred yards away. As soon as I spotted him I would rap on the canoe again, and the seal would dive and invariably surface about a hundred yards closer. With my .22 rifle now ready, I would rap again, but very quietly, and keeping my head down. The seal would dive again and I never knew which side of the canoe it might surface, but I knew it would be within twenty or thirty yards. As soon as I spotted it, I would take aim with my rifle and then whistle sharply. When it heard the whistle, it would raise its head further to look for the sound, and I would shoot it in the throat.

We tried not to shoot them in the head. A shot in a seal's head kills it instantly; unfortunately it sinks instantly too. Seals shot in the throat, however, take a minute or two to sink, and by that time a good canoe man can reach the seal and haul it in.

I never did learn what vagary of fashion or economy was responsible for the jump in seal prices that summer. Unfortunately for the Eskimos, the remarkable price bonanza didn't last.

The following year brought an uproar over the whitemen clubbing baby seals and skinning them alive off Newfoundland. In the Arctic we never killed baby seals, but I have never really believed there have ever been many cases of skinning them alive. If a seal is alive, it will be harder to skin and a mess will probably be made of the pelt. It would be much simpler to kill the seal pup; a seal skull is very thin and one good blow of the fist is all that is necessary. Still, exaggerated or not, the hubbub knocked the price of seal in the Arctic from twenty-eight dollars down to two dollars. Naturally the pragmatic Eskimos simply stopped hunting seal. The price was not worth the effort.

ONE summer, Angulaalik, Nasarlulik, and eight or nine families decided to go up the Perry River for the fishing. I went with them, and we pitched our tents at the foot of the Perry River waterfalls. Having established our base for the summer, we prepared to place our nets below the rapids. Each net stretched out about one hundred and fifty yards from the bank and we placed one every three hundred or four hundred yards. We caught Arctic char, whitefish and flounder.

At that early part of the summer—mid-June—we could count on birds for food, too, the Perry River being one of the greatest nesting grounds in the world. Every day we saw geese flying overhead, snow-geese, brant, the big Canada honkers, white-fronted geese, and Ross's geese. Perry is the only breeding ground in the world for Ross's geese, the smallest goose known, a beautiful bird like a tiny snow-goose; it has a warty face around the beak and appears to be grinning all the time. There were a myriad other species there, too: sandhill cranes, one of the earliest harbingers of spring along the coast, ducks of all kinds, swans, loons; the country was alive and breathing with birds.

Early one morning when we had been camped for several days, one of the young Eskimos who had set his nets about a mile downstream came paddling back in his canoe shouting, "*Tukturaaluit, tukturaaluit!*" ("Lots of caribou!")

We grabbed our rifles and piled into canoes and headed down the river after our exultant guide. When we reached the spot where he had seen the herd, there wasn't an animal in sight, but we could see the signs and decided the herd had moved inland a bit. We pulled the canoes up on the bank and followed the trail. Four of us went to the left and five to the right; we hoped to encircle the herd in a valley where we expected to find the animals grazing.

After some three hours scouting, we breasted a hill, and there below us in a long narrow valley was the herd—easily five thousand animals.

We didn't know where the other party of five hunters had got to, so we made our own plans. First we sent one man round to the near end of the valley where there was a kind of ravine that the caribou would use as a natural exit. Then Nasarlulik and I moved to positions farther up the valley while Angulaalik positioned himself just below the crest of our hill. We checked each other with our binoculars and were just getting ready to start firing when we heard the sound of shots at the other end of the valley. It was the other five men, who had come over the hill from the opposite direction and were now in a perfect position to drive the caribou straight towards us. We all began shooting then.

A herd that size doesn't scare easily. When there are only ten or twenty caribou in a bunch, they will take off like the wind at the first sign of hunters or sound of guns, but in a big herd, the animals will only become confused and mill around. We simply sat in our hiding places and picked off the targets we wanted.

We picked the biggest and fattest cows, because we knew that most of the females in the herd would be pregnant during such a migration. The unborn calf provides much the tenderest, most succulent morsel of meat anyone could desire, soft like lamb and wonderfully tasty. After I had dropped a couple in their tracks with nice, clean heart shots, Angulaalik and Nasarlulik came running over, scolding me as they came.

"Don't kill them, don't kill them!" they shouted.

Angulaalik, seeing how confused I was, said: "Shoot like we do. Just aim at the rear leg."

I stared dumbfounded at my two companions.

Nasarlulik explained, "Use your head a minute. Just shatter a leg and the caribou can be driven back to the river on his three good legs. We can kill them when we reach the river."

I protested. I thought this was really cruel.

"Use your head," Nasarlulik repeated. "Would you rather carry them back or drive them back?"

Shortly afterwards the shooting stopped. Nine of us had shot fifty-nine caribou in the few minutes before the panicked herd was able to flee over the hills. It had been a good hunt. These animals would give us meat for many weeks and provide us with badly needed hides.

The dead caribou were skinned out and backpacks made. It was then that I understood Nasarlulik's reasoning. Each animal weighed about a hundred and fifty pounds, and this proved a lot of weight to carry back across the tundra. The wounded animals, however, were driven ahead of us.

When we reached the river, we finished off the cripples and loaded all the meat into the canoes. When we brought the meat into the camp the women got out their *ulus* and cut it into thick strips and spread it out over the rocks to let the sun cure it. Meat cured by this old Eskimo method requires no salt, and will keep for over a year.

When we had finished the work, we cooked up a great batch of bannock, and put some caribou heads with the eyes still in and the hair still on in a pot and boiled them up for soup. We made blood soup and caribou stew, and in another pot boiled up some leg bones to be shattered later for the marrow. As we had butchered each animal, we had been careful to save the contents of the stomach, a semi-digested moss-lichen mixture which the Eskimos call *nirukkaq*. The *nirukkaq* was spread out on rocks to dry and then gathered up to be eaten with the meat. This version of Eskimo salad tastes remarkably like a green salad. A meal was enjoyed that night that is not eaten every day!

Watching the women work expertly on the hides we had brought back reminded me of my first winter at Baker Lake when for the first time I saw Eskimos actually dressed in the skins of the caribou. I had been at Baker Lake only a few days when three Eskimos came into the store wearing full winter clothing. To me the Arctic became real at that moment.

The three men looked enormously bulky in their deerskins, though caribou clothing is lighter and warmer than anything yet devised by the whiteman, because caribou hairs are hollow. The men were wearing both inner and outer caribouskin parkas, the inner one with the hair next to their bodies and the outer one with the hair on the outside. Most of the inland Eskimos had their parkas slit up the side to just above the waist and all fringed. The front of the parka came down to about mid-thigh, but the rear was down to the back of their knees. They wore wide, floppy-legged trousers that came down to just above the knee. Underneath were duffle cloth leggings, and a long stocking of soft skin or wool. A caribou slipper, low-cut and soft, was covered by two pairs of caribou boots, the first with the hair turned in and the second with the hair side out. The hair was left on the sole, too, so that the feet were insulated against the snow and cold. Parkas in that part of the North always had a carefully worked design on the back, with insets made of the white belly fur of the caribou, which stands out nicely against the dark skin.

To the inland Eskimos the caribou used to be a staple in the same way the buffalo was to the Plains Indians. The caribou provided food; tools were made from antlers and bones; and the skins went for everything from underwear to bedding to tents in the summer. Today most Eskimos buy canvas or nylon tents from the Bay stores, but one of the advantages of the caribouskin tent was that it stayed dark in the interior, which kept the mosquitoes out, unlike the ordinary, whiteman's tent.

IN OCTOBER I would go with the Eskimos to the little lakes around Perry Island. Most of these lakes are connected to the sea by small creeks or rivers, and are the spawning area for the red Arctic char. Just after each lake had frozen over, with maybe three inches of ice on it, enough to hold a man's weight, we would walk along and look through the ice until we found one of the spawning beds where the female fish pushes small pebbles and gravel together to form a kind of raised bed, where she lays her eggs. When we found such a place, we would chisel a hole through the ice and stand there with a three-pronged fish harpoon called a leister. The female char, which has a reddish tinge, would be swimming around the bed. A male char, his body bright red like a spawning salmon, and his lower jaw extended out like an inverted beak, would be attracted to the spot and come to fertilize the eggs. We would spear the male, never the female, and toss him up on the ice. The commotion would cause the female to shoot away, but she would come back in a few minutes, and then another male would be attracted. A diligent Eskimo could easily get fifteen or twenty char in a day, some up to twenty pounds. As long as he didn't touch the female he had a going business, and it was a good way of starting up a fish supply for the dogs for the winter. I always got a kick out of knowing that the same beautiful Arctic chars we were catching to feed our dogs were selling as a gourmet dish in the top restaurants of Canada and the United States.

THE GREAT WHITE ZOO

In July 1965 the Company asked me to transfer to Bathurst Inlet, a couple of hundred miles or so west of Perry Island. The old Bathurst post was near the closed end of the one-hundred-and-twenty-mile inlet, and the Company wanted to re-establish it near the mouth. While I didn't want to leave the people of Perry Island, I felt it an honour that the Company had asked me to set up a new post. I agreed to go.

By winter, the old warehouses had been taken apart and the new post was established on a site overlooking Baychimo bay, which

e will never be another fur trader in the
dition, nor an Eskimo in the old image."
f and some of my friends before the last
g post was closed.

*Above: An overnight s[...]
house under construc[...]
The third row of snow b[...]
are put into place, [...]
leaning slightly inward[...]
fitted tightly to the [...]
before.*

*Left: Unable to find the
proper snow with which to
build shelter, our hunting
party is forced to keep
moving, though night is falling. Iksik, out in front, is
testing for the distinctive
creaking sound that indi-
cates good snowhouse snow.*

*Right: Icing runners [...]
water, a procedure that [...]
be necessary two or t[...]
times a day. The bu[...]
will be smoothed out [...]
the snowknife.*

Left: The Eskimo canoes could handle almost any sea, and could be manoeuvred safely among the ice floes.

Right: Amid the summer grasses and lichens, I discover the ruins of an old Eskimo settlement.

Below: A mug-up on the trail. The dogs are played out after a hard day's travel on the soft snow of Bathurst Inlet.

Below: Waiting for a seal to surface at a breathing-hole. The harpoon rests on supports, and is attached to a hand-line.

Top left: Polar bears—the largest of the bear family yet, usually, the least aggressive.

Above: A bull musk-ox guards his herd. Musk-ox have been protected for fifty years.

Below: Caribou have provided the inland Eskimos with everything from food and tools to clothing and tents. On migration they move in herds of up to a million strong.

provided anchorage for the annual supply ship. It was in easy reach for the twenty or more Eskimos who lived in trapping camps around the inlet.

Soon after my arrival, the Company sent me an apprentice, a likeable young fellow named Ian Copland. His father had spent eighteen years with the Company and wanted his son to have the kind of training available only at isolated posts. To Ian, barely sixteen years old, sharing in the establishment of a new post was a great adventure. In a different way it was an adventure for me too. I had never had an apprentice before, and I set about teaching the lad all the things I thought he should know: how to handle the dogs, how to grade fur, how to keep the accounts, how to learn the country. As fast as he mastered something I would turn over that bit of responsibility to him and let him gain the experience. He was eager, and turned out to be a good hand.

As a result, for the first time in a long while, I had opportunities to soak up the startling beauty of an Arctic summer. For some reason the Baychimo area seemed to be eight to ten degrees warmer than Perry Island, and accordingly had a much richer vegetation and more wild life. Above the cliffs on the uplands there were long plains spotted with lakes in a great diversity of colours. Mineralization painted them green and blue and yellow-brown, even red.

It was too far north for trees, of course, but some of the willow bushes along the creek were six to seven feet high. Bees buzzed everywhere, and butterflies, six or eight different species, big yellow ones, smaller white ones, and even some huge moths, were all about. And something I have never seen anywhere else in the Arctic—grasshoppers. Walking through the lush grass I heard the harsh sound of their rear legs rubbing together and doubted my ears until I managed to catch a few.

Heather, a blanket of fragrant whiteness spread low over the ground and climbing part way up the hills behind the harbour, put me right back in Scotland. Flowers were everywhere—bright red, brilliant yellow, gay little Arctic poppies nodding in the breeze, a blue alpine blossom and masses of white cotton flowers, tiny blooms smaller than a man's little fingernail, but in great profusion.

The variety of birdlife astonished me—robins, thrushes, ptarmigan, sandpipers, and even sparrows. There were bigger birds too, the Arctic tern, the rough-legged hawk and the marvellously swift peregrine falcon, even a pair of majestic golden eagles. The skies were vibrant blue; the air was bright and sparkly clean, and everything glistened as though just created for my enjoyment.

Now and then I went to Bathurst Inlet to observe the herd of muskox there (the Eskimos didn't bother with them ordinarily because muskox is much tougher meat than caribou), and it was during that summer that a museum asked me to obtain some samples of ground-squirrel skins. These small animals are common throughout Bathurst, so I headed off to the mouth of the Hiukitak River, tied my canoe to a rock and hiked inland.

It was a nice warm day, and I walked along, my .22 rifle strapped on my back, enjoying the scenery. About three miles inland I came to a big eskar, one of those long sand and gravel banks left throughout the North by retreating ice age glaciers. At the end of this eskar was a huge boulder, about three times the size of a house. I was half-daydreaming as I walked around the big rock, and I found myself practically eyeball to eyeball with a grizzly bear. The suddenness of the encounter took my breath away.

Eskimos avoid hunting grizzlies. Quite apart from the fact that the hides are too heavy for clothing, they regard the grizzly as the most dangerous animal in the Arctic. As I stood about seven feet from this one, it flashed through my mind how a grizzly had recently made for a little child who was playing outside a hunting camp near Baychimo. The child's father ran between the grizzly and his son, and desperately began firing. The grizzly charged after the first shot, and the hunter pumped four more bullets right into its chest before the pain-maddened bear literally tore his head clean off his shoulders. Then the grizzly fell dead, and when the Eskimos later skinned it out they found its heart had been shattered by two bullets.

The grizzly now facing me let out an almighty growl, a horrible rumble deep from the stomach, that I can't describe and have no desire to hear again. I stood petrified. What I wanted to do was to run like hell, but I decided that the best thing was to make no motion at all. The bear could catch me in about six bounds and, even if I had been able to swing the rifle off my back and pump a shell into the chamber, a .22 bullet wouldn't do more than sting the bear and make it mad. All I could think was: "I'm going to be killed right here and no one will ever know."

The grizzly growled again and swung its head towards me. It wasn't actually a very big bear, probably no more than nine feet, but its head was monstrous and the characteristic hump on the shoulders appeared huge at such close range. It growled some more and rose up on its hind feet for a moment like a circus bear, then dropped back to all fours and sniffed, trying to decide what kind of threat I was. Then it lifted its head and began to make a queer chomping noise with its back teeth, clacking them together, not a sound that gave me much comfort. It ambled off to one side about thirty feet, turned and walked away from me. The second it turned its back, I scrambled up the boulder. When I got to the top I saw that it had turned again and was charging. I clambered down the other side and started running like mad.

My big friend came round the rock instead of over it, and gave chase. I was running with my head turned back to watch it and I stumbled from tussock to tussock. To my relief, after its initial charge, the bear settled down to an easy lope.

I ran the whole three miles back to the coast with that bear following about fifty yards behind me. I sprinted over a little rise and saw my canoe on the beach and raced over the rocks to launch it. I threw myself into it and let it float out into the inlet. As I lay on the bottom of the canoe I thought my heart was going to pack up with the strain. I had a powerful rifle in the canoe, and could have loaded it up and finished the bear, which had stopped at the top of the rise and was squatting on its haunches, but I didn't have the strength.

IT WAS at Bathurst, too, that one of my most memorable trips with dogs took place. In January 1967 I was restless and seized by a sudden desire to go to Coppermine, our nearest "town". Two Eskimo friends, Iksik and Palvik, came with me—they wanted to find wives.

Iksik had been married, but while he was in hospital with tuberculosis, his wife had been stolen. Palvik, a husky, good-looking man, only twenty at the time, thought a nice Coppermine romance was just what he needed too. Iksik hadn't been able to maintain his own team, but was fit enough to help Palvik with his.

The distance to Coppermine is three hundred and twenty miles by dogteam and we expected the trip to take seven sleeps at that time of year, the dark part of winter. We started out on January 3, with no light to guide us except what starlight filtered through broken clouds. It was forty-eight below zero with a wind from the northwest, the direction in which we were heading.

We were expecting to have the usual rough coastal ice to contend with for a while, but the tortured jumble we saw in the pale starlight looked like a frozen moonscape, a white hell. Rough ice like that is murder. It causes the sleds to drag heavily, and its sharp icy edges slice up the dogs' feet and slash their legs. We decided to stick close to the shore but the ice remained treacherous, and the dogs were having a really tough time of it. Each day that passed saw us more battered. The weather never let up and the sleds were literally being knocked apart, bouncing up and down on chunks of ice that hit between the runners, breaking the crossbars. We spent hours repairing them, eventually having to unload the sleds completely and relash all the crossbars with bare hands in fifty-below weather.

We could tell by the landmarks that we were not making anything like the time we had expected to, and then we came up against a pressure ridge about fifteen feet high. We couldn't cross it, because it was sheer ice, huge blocks welded together where two great beds of ice had jammed together as the sea was freezing over. The only course was to follow along it until some break in the wall presented itself. Unfortunately, when a passage was discovered, I lost control of my sled as it slid down the other side of the ridge. It bounced off a hummock of ice way up into the air and came down with a terrible crash. All the lashings on the crossbars snapped and both runners buckled down flat, spread out like skates on a kid with weak ankles.

We had just relashed that sled, and it had been a hellish job. And now a ground wind had sprung up and was blowing snow right in our faces. There was nothing for it, however, but to unload and go to work on the lashings once again. At the rear of the sled sat a ten-gallon keg of paraffin, our only fuel for the Primus stove. I went back to take the keg off the sled, automatically bracing for the heavy lift. To my surprise, the keg lifted easily, as light as a balloon. With sinking hearts we checked it and discovered that somewhere along the way a sharp pinnacle of ice had jammed right through the sled cover and into the keg, puncturing it. All our precious fuel lay across the sea ice.

This was a crisis. There we were in the middle of nowhere, ten tough days out of Bathurst, and, as near as we could figure, about an equal distance from Coppermine. For us the loss of the fuel meant no more fires for food or warmth. But we were less worried about ourselves than about the dogs. We had decided to carry dry dogfood on this trip because of its lightness, but the dogs wouldn't eat it dry and now we had no way to cook it.

Iksik shrugged, "*Ayurnarmat.* It can't be helped. We've got to decide whether to turn back or try to get to Coppermine."

We talked it over. For all we knew the bad ice might give out in a day or so ahead of us on the way to Coppermine. So we decided it was better to push on than to retrace our route. Since we had stopped anyhow to fix my sled, we decided to camp there and give the dogs a rest. There was good snow along the pressure ridge for a snowhouse. Lashing up that sled again was even worse than the first time. Even taking it in relays, our hands went numb in a few minutes. Our fingertips were black, the penultimate stage of frostbite, before the affected area becomes gangrenous. Iksik's nose and cheekbones were already showing severe frostbite, and Palvik had a patch of frostbite on one cheek.

The next day, the wind was so penetrating that, since I couldn't control the sled anyhow, I just lay back on the sled covers and let it bump along. The dogs were in bad shape with sore paws and empty bellies, and we travelled only a few miles.

When we camped that night, the exertion of building the snow-house, setting up our camp, and putting the dogs out on their chain caused us to sweat, but with no warming stove we couldn't dry out our clothing. We knew that if we took clothes off, damp as they were from our sweat, they would freeze up, we should never get them back on. Additionally, we discovered that the leaking fuel had penetrated most of our meat supply, and all we had to eat was a small chunk of raw, frozen caribou, a few hardtack biscuits and some bannock.

That night a wolf howled. It sounded several miles away but the howling echoed back and forth in the still, cold air, and immediately the dogs joined in. It was a symphony of the North that lifted the short hairs on the back of my neck.

If we were not happy, neither were the dogs the next morning. With no food in their bellies they had no energy, but there was no choice but to hitch up and travel on. At a time like that a driver can't afford to be easy on his dogs; if they don't keep going, then everyone is in trouble. Every now and then some of them would drop in the harness from tiredness or weakness. We would pull them on their feet again, give them a clout and chase them on. They would go twenty yards, catch a paw on a piece of ice and flop again.

One of my best dogs dropped in his tracks so many times that in the end I let him out of the harness so that he would have nothing to pull. He tried to stay up with us, walking very slowly, and every now and then stopping and staring after us. We were leaving him farther and farther behind, so I went back, patted him and talked to him, and put him on the sled right beside me. But he wasn't accustomed to riding, and it frightened him so that he struggled. I couldn't hold him and steer at the same time. He kept falling off and hurting himself all the more. Finally, bitter with the cold, and with what I had to do, I left him behind. I hoped when we made camp that he just might wander in, but I never saw him again.

We had another cold night. When we started the next morning the dogs had run two full days without eating and were starting their third. When they stopped at night they just dropped. Normally a dog will dig down into the snow to protect itself from the cold, but now we had to build windbreaks around them. My lead dog, Qaqquq, and one other kept up their strength, but the others were beat.

We pushed on through the day without losing any more dogs, but we knew it was just a question of time. We didn't make very many miles, and the dogs were visibly weakening. Palvik and Iksik were as worried as I was. That night we tried to feed the dogs the dry dogfood. We held their mouths open and pushed the stuff down their throats, but they just coughed it up.

The next day was a nightmare. If anything, the weather had deteriorated. We were passing through quite steep country now, cliffs along the shoreline and a lot of steep islands. We went around some and then decided to climb one and see if we could sight Coppermine yet, if only for the needed psychological lift. But we couldn't see a sign of lights anywhere. We looked at each other without a word. There was nothing to do but keep going.

Eight dogs died that day, and the survivors were getting frost-bitten. That night we skinned the dogs that had died. After allowing the carcasses to freeze, thereby cutting down the familiar dog smell, we fed them to the survivors, little by little.

It didn't surprise us that the dogs were still very weak in the morning. There was a strong wind blowing and it was obvious that they weren't going to last out the day if we didn't do something. As we sat in our cold snowhouse discussing our situation, my eyes fell on the punctured ten gallon tin. Suddenly an idea came.

I took the empty keg and, by using other tins, I fashioned it into a crude stove with a stovepipe. We put it in the snowhouse, knocked a hole in the wall for the stovepipe to fit through and closed over the gap with a piece of caribouskin, so that we wouldn't melt the snow wall when we got the fire going. Next we took the two battered sleds and with the best parts of each, made one good sled out of the two. The remaining wood we chopped up and set ablaze. We stood there with our mitts off, coughing and choking on the smoke, but enjoying the first warmth we had felt in days.

To begin with it felt great, but soon we were in agony. Our hands and faces, our noses, cheeks and chins had all been frozen, and now they suddenly began to thaw out. Huge frost blisters burst out on our faces. I had blisters down one side of my nose, across my chin, and on both cheekbones. Later they burst, leaving my cheekbones exposed, surrounded by raw flesh.

We knew that the sudden warmth would cause trouble with our frostbite, but really had no option. Much dangerously misleading advice is given on how to take care of frostbite—such notions as rubbing snow on the affected areas. I can't think of anything worse. Snow in the high Arctic is composed almost entirely of frost granules, gritty stuff like sand. It would tear the frostbitten skin and flesh away like sandpaper.

Part of our problem was whiskers. The popular conception of a real Arctic man invariably pictures him with a bushy beard. The truth is that the only people who wear beards in the Arctic are either greenhorns, or men in desperate trouble, for every breath condenses and freezes in a beard. With no hot water, we had been unable to shave for some time, and the ice around our fledgling beards contributed seriously to our frostbitten condition.

But we were happy to get that stove going. The first thing we did as soon as we could stand moving around was to get the kettle out. We drank three or four mugs of steaming tea, dipped our hardtack biscuits in the tea and never enjoyed such a simple meal so much.

Feeling full and warm ourselves, the next thing was to cook up some food for the dogs. As soon as it was ready we went out and fed them, doling out a little bit at a time until they could handle it. Were they glad to get it!

We decided to stay in camp for a day, after which the dogs were much improved. We put the two teams together to pull the one sled, with Qaqquq in the lead, and thus, a few days later, we pulled into Coppermine.

Incidentally, neither Palvik nor Iksik found a wife!

I DID a great deal of hunting and trapping with Palvik and Iksik, and one day Palvik and I discovered that a wolverine was working one of our traplines. One can live a lifetime in the North and seldom see a living wolverine. They are exceedingly wary animals, vicious members of the weasel family with fearful jaws and teeth, utterly unafraid.

This particular wolverine had followed our old sled tracks, and in many cases we would find scraps of a fox in a trap to show that the wolverine had beaten us to the prize. A wolverine often seems to work a trapline not out of hunger, but just for fun. Sometimes it will simply take the fox out of the trap, drag it off thirty yards and bury it. Normally, however, it chews it up enough to ruin the pelt. A single wolverine could reduce our take of fur considerably.

But we had a few tricks of our own. We took an old sawn-off shotgun Palvik had used before on wolverines, dug a little pit in the snow near one of the traps that the wolverine had not yet visited, and buried the gun in the snow so that about two inches of the muzzle stuck out. Then we attached a string to the trigger of the shotgun and to a chunk of raw caribou meat, which we wrapped around the mouth of the shotgun. When we came back on our reverse trip down the trapline, we had our wolverine, minus its head.

Another time a smart wolverine had the best of me. At Perry, Nasarlulik and I had killed some caribou, but couldn't get all the meat in our canoe to take back to the post. We decided to cache what was left. We skinned them out, covered the carcasses with a great pile of rocks, and sloshed water over the cache. The water froze, binding the rocks like cement.

When we eventually got back to pick up that meat, we discovered that a clever wolverine had found a way to outwit us. Unable to tear the frozen rocks away, it lay on top of one rock until its body heat melted the ice around it; it then plucked the rock out and did the same thing with the other rocks, until it was able to get at the caribou.

Wolves will sometimes work a trapline too, but they don't stick with it like the wolverine does. They will follow the scent of the trapper's dog and hit his traps once or twice and then go off after something else.

The Eskimos would often use a forty-five gallon fuel oil keg to make a deadly trap for wolves. They cut a star-shaped hole in the top, bending the points inward to make an opening slightly smaller than a wolf's head. Then they buried the drum in the snow and put a chunk of meat or fish in the bottom of it. When a wolf came along it scented the bait and shoved its head in through the star-shaped hole at the top of the keg. The wolf could get in all right, but when it tried to withdraw its head, it was impaled on the sharp edges of the star-shaped points. Each wolf was worth about seventy dollars—a forty-five dollar bounty and about twenty-five for the fur.

Wolves have long been falsely painted as the villains in the decline of the caribou herds. At one time it was government policy to hire so-called predator control officers, who set out strychnine-packed bait to poison the wolves which invariably accompanied the caribou migrations. The poisoning programme worked extremely well, but has since been mercifully abandoned. Indeed, at Bathurst it was not uncommon to spot wolves just lolling in the sun along with the caribou, not bothering them at all; nor did the caribou seem to worry much about the wolves.

In spite of their reputation for ferocity both male and female wolves are very tender towards each other. A wolf pair, before whelping time, will sit in the sun together and fool around like a couple of dogs. Each pair stakes out a wide territory, and I have never seen more than seven wolves together, although when I was at Baker Lake there were reports of an immense pack of sixty. No pack of that size would stay together long because it would be unable to find food to support itself. The usual pack consists of the adult pair and four or five cubs, which stay with them during the year it takes them to grow to adult size.

One may occasionally see a wolf make a run at a knot of caribou, but if the caribou take off and there appears to be no wounded or sick animal among them, then the wolf immediately quits the chase. It seems to know there is no point in it. Usually the only time wolves make a real run for caribou is when one which is sick or crippled drops back and the wolves have a chance to bring it down. Often in the summer the caribou simply head for the nearest lake and plunge in; the wolves never follow them into the water. Healthy caribou seem to regard wolves more as a nuisance than a danger.

The only time a wolf can expect to bring down a healthy caribou is during the winter, when by sheer persistence the wolf finally wears the caribou down. On one remarkable occasion I saw wolves in winter run a relay system to bring down a caribou. I was hunting with Iksik and we were on top of a ridge from which we watched a complete chase-and-kill sequence down in the valley. A single wolf opened the relay, chasing a cow caribou. There were caribou all over the valley, but the wolf ignored all but the one it had picked out. Caribou and wolf came racing down the valley towards us at top speed. A caribou can hit fifty miles an hour in short sprints when it is in a hurry—and this one was. The wolf couldn't sustain that speed as long as the caribou, so it dropped out and another wolf, which had obviously been lying in wait, sprang up and took over the chase. It seemed to be a family thing, as one wolf after another picked up the run, one at a time, until the last wolf chasing the caribou leaped on it and brought it down by the shoulder.

Yet, even in winter, I would suspect that wolves seldom attack healthy caribou. Every wolf we ever killed in winter was scrawny, thin and badly undernourished. In the summer wolves put on a lot of weight, but when we cut them open and checked their stomachs, nine out of ten had not a scrap of caribou meat in them. Their stomachs were loaded with lemmings, the mouse-like Arctic rodent, and ground squirrels. Lemmings are easier to handle than frisky caribou.

ONE SPRING Palvik and I decided to take my dogteam and make a trip down the inlet looking for caribou. About thirty miles south of the trading post we built a tight snowhouse and spent a couple of days working out of that base, picking up the odd caribou sign here and there, but never actually seeing a herd.

Then one day we were sitting outside the snowhouse in the sun, warming and resting, when suddenly all the dogs began to perk up. We watched them sit up, one at a time, in the snow, their ears pricked, listening, until they were all up and alert. We couldn't hear a thing.

Our camp was on the edge of the inlet, right on the sea; behind our snowhouse a small hill blocked our view inland. It always pays to investigate behaviour out of the norm in the Arctic, so we climbed the hill just to look around, and away off in the distance we could see what appeared to be a greyish-brown flood moving slowly over the land. As far north as we could look and as far south, a flood of caribou was moving east. Then we caught the drumming of their hooves on the frozen tundra, and the clicking noise made by their hooves hitting together. We were right in the path of the most tremendous herd of caribou either of us had ever seen. "What an amazing sight!" I cried. Palvik replied, "*Niqiraaluit!*" ("What a lot of food!") Two cultures!

The churning mass of caribou was advancing directly upon us, tearing up the tundra as they came. I was uneasy, wondering if they might not simply by force and pressure of numbers just run right over us. I thought it might be smarter to leave while we could. But Palvik couldn't see beyond all that meat. He wanted to stand his ground and kill a lot of caribou, enough for an entire winter's supply.

Palvik suggested, "We'd better go back and move the dogteam around in between the hill and the snowhouse and make certain they are securely chained before they become too excited to handle." The dogs were all on their feet, howling and yapping and lunging against the restraining chain. We pulled the entire team around and rechained them so they would be between the advancing herd and our snowhouse. Then we grabbed our rifles and went back up the hill.

We didn't as yet have any really accurate idea of how many caribou there were. At our angle we could see only the first twenty or thirty rows. We knew there were a good number. I thought maybe seven or eight thousand. As we watched from the hilltop they came closer and closer, and through the binoculars we could see that what looked to the naked eye like one undulating wave of animals actually consisted of countless scores of herds of about fifty or sixty animals each.

We stayed up there until the vanguard of the herd actually began coming up the slope of the hill straight towards us. We looked over the animals leading the migration all the way back to the horizon; the whole land just flowed like a brown tide pouring over the snow. When the first of the caribou breasted the hill, we retreated towards the snowhouse, keeping carefully between the dogs and the caribou. The dogs were going absolutely crackers. It was fortunate we had fastened them tightly. Finally we could back up no more, so we carefully shot down two of the leading caribou then several more right behind them. Just as we hoped, the herd split to go around the fallen animals, the flow passing on either side and around the dogs and our snowhouse. This was dramatic evidence of Palvik's practical knowledge. By placing the dogs between the snowhouse and the advancing herd, and by holding our fire until we did, we probably saved the snowhouse and all our gear from being trampled into the ground.

As it was we sat there on our sled and watched the caribou come within fifteen feet on either side of us. Everywhere we looked there were caribou. The stench of the animals was overpowering. And the din of hooves clicking and drumming combined with the hysterical yelping of the dogs was completely deafening. We kept checking the dog chain to make certain the dogs didn't get loose. As it was, half the dogs lunged towards the caribou passing on the right, the other half at those on the left, so the dogs helped to keep the caribou herd split.

We just sat there on the hill and watched in wonder. It was hopeless to even try to get any sort of count. Now and then the pressure of the herd coming on behind would push animals so close to us that we could almost reach out and touch them. From where we stood we could see right down the inlet past our snowhouse; by now caribou everywhere were crossing the inlet. We were a tiny island in a great flood of heaving brown backs, tossing antlers, and pounding hooves.

The migrating caribou kept coming until darkness fell. Then suddenly, they stopped and began to graze. All night long we could smell the strong stench of the animals and hear the clicking of their feet and the whoofing-grunting noise they made as they grazed. Finally, still awed, we went into the snowhouse and fell asleep with the sound and smell of caribou all around us. When we woke up in the morning the caribou migration was continuing. I would estimate that the herd was moving at the rate of about two miles an hour. The animals weren't in any hurry; they simply walked along. This time Palvik and I decided to watch in comfort. We cut a couple of snowblocks for seats and sat right outside our house and watched the caribou go by. Every now and then we would pick out an especially fat cow that was obviously pregnant, and shoot it.

We shot only four or five caribou that day, as we had no space to dry the meat; we decided to hold up any more killing until the tag-end of the herd came by so we could take care of the meat without wasting it.

We had to wait there nine full, unbelievable days, all that time with caribou in every direction as far as we could see. The stench no longer bothered us. Either we had grown immune or smelled like caribou ourselves by now.

When the caribou finally began to thin out a bit, we were able to shoot our entire year's supply in about half a day, carefully picking only the finest animals.

I suppose that if the herd had remained constantly on the move instead of stopping twice a day to feed, the migration would have passed us in three days, certainly no less. If I had to make an estimate, I would put my count at no less than a million. It was the sort of spectacle related by thunderstruck early explorers and fur traders, speaking in awe of millions of caribou. It remains the most amazing sight I have ever seen.

THE HONOURABLE MEMBER

Among the first private entrepreneurs in the western Arctic was an old friend of mine, genial, red-bearded Fred Ross. He had taken over an old construction camp in Cambridge Bay and turned it into a sort of hotel, which wasn't a bad place to stay if you brought your own sleeping bag. I had come up from Bathurst Inlet with my dogs and was staying with Fred. Several other people dropped in, and eventually the subject got round to politics, a subject which frankly bored me.

Fred said that the Northwest Territorial Council had just extended the franchise into the Arctic regions, which were being divided into three constituencies—eastern, central and western Arctic. Then he popped a surprising question. Would I run for the western Arctic?

I just laughed. My impression of a politician was a fellow in a top hat and striped trousers with only the remotest connection with anything human. I had no interest whatever in politics at the territorial or any other level. But Fred and the others said they had talked the matter over and they needed me.

We sat there in Fred's room, half a dozen of us, drinking rum and getting pleasantly tight, and before I knew it I said, "O.K., put my name down." I filled out the nomination papers and back I went to Bathurst Inlet.

I have to admit I didn't give the matter another thought. I never campaigned for a second. On election day in the autumn of 1966 I went out with a pilot and another man trying to find a good fishing spot. Our plane got stuck on a shallow stretch of the river and we had a devil of a time getting it off. When we finally had the plane airborne and the pilot contacted Cambridge Bay, we learned that I had been elected. I hadn't even voted and neither had anyone else at Bathurst Inlet.

In those days the Council of the Northwest Territories met twice a year, once in Ottawa, then still the capital of the NWT, and once in one of the settlements in the territories. It consisted of seven elected and five appointed members.

After I had been elected, there was only a period of a few weeks before the first session at Resolute and I didn't have a chance to make a round of the settlements to find out specifically what the people needed and wanted. However, when the game laws were discussed at the session, I was able to propose a number of changes, based on my own experience.

It seemed to me that one of the major problems concerning the game laws was that these laws were basically drawn up by men who were unfamiliar with the Arctic. The previously-elected members of Council had all come from constituencies within the forest region of the North, men who had little or no knowledge of life above the tree line. They were no more expert in producing good game laws for the Arctic than an Eskimo would be who attempted to make good traffic laws for Ottawa. Now, however, with two Eskimos and myself on the Council, it was possible to make substantial changes for the better.

At our first session we had a major battle with the Canadian

Wildlife Service over polar bear. They expressed concern that the annual kill of polar bear could increase to the point where the animal population would decline. They therefore recommended that a closed season be declared, and that cubs up to two years of age and their mothers be protected by law. The Council agreed with the basic policy of protection of the species, but we differed radically with the Wildlife Service on how best to achieve these ends.

Instead of a closed season during the ice-free period of the summer, I proposed that a quota system be established that would allow the polar bear to be taken at any period of the year—provided that the quota wasn't exceeded. In this way, we could better protect the species in those regions where the bear population was small and the hunter population large.

My counter-proposal to the Wildlife Service's other recommendation was that both mother and cub, regardless of the age of the cub, should be protected if they were found to be still together, but that any cub or adult female found wandering on its own be considered free game without restriction. I pointed out that when a hunter is closing in on a bear with an excited team of dogs, it is hardly a propitious moment for him to check out the bear's birth certificate. I also pointed out that when we were talking about a cub nearly two years old we were not debating the fate of a cuddly little bundle of white fluff, but an animal approximately six foot in length, weighing over 250 pounds, and quite capable of taking a man's head off with one blow. If such an animal were found away from its mother, then it was safe to bet that it was fully capable of fending for itself. So we rejected both recommendations from the service, and substituted our own.

I and other members of the NWT Council had many more battles with the Canadian Wildlife Service, our fundamental objection being that the CWS apparently wanted to protect all the animals all the time whereas we men who lived in the Arctic took the view that with proper game management techniques, the Territory's wealth of game could be harvested like any other resource for the benefit of the people.

Recently, I recommended a sports hunting programme,

for instance, whereby an Eskimo hunter who received an individual quota to kill a polar bear could sell his individual quota to any big game hunter for a fee of approximately $2,000—better than ten times as much money as he would get if he shot the bear himself. Bearing in mind the mutual advantages of such a system to both the trophy-minded sportsman of the South and the needy native of the North, the NWT now permits sports hunting of polar bear.

My election to Council quickly and drastically changed my way of living. After I had been through two sessions of Council I realized that I must make a choice: either leave the Council to which I had been elected, or else leave the employ of the Hudson's Bay Company. I could now see that the time spent on Council work would be quite substantial, and I didn't think it was fair to the Company or to the Eskimos in Bathurst Inlet to be away so much of the time, leaving them, in effect, with no trader in their area. Council met twice a year, and each session lasted approximately one month. On top of that, I would have to travel around to all the other settlements in my constituency. If I were away from Bathurst and someone fell ill, there would be no one to look after him, and in case of serious illness or a medical emergency, no one there to get on the radio and call Cambridge Bay for help.

So, reluctantly, I decided that after eleven years, I would have to leave the Company. I had always been proud to be a Hudson's Bay trader, and I was sorry to leave for another reason. In my last year at Bathurst I was earning approximately $6,000 a year, and now I was getting another $5,000 for being a Council member. When I resigned from the Company, I was left with $5,000 only, and this had to cover all my expenses for travelling around one of the largest constituencies in the world. Even if it did have only eleven towns and at best three thousand people, it covered several thousand square miles. Some of the settlements were a thousand miles apart, and from Paulatuk in the west to Pelly Bay in the east was a good two thousand miles.

It was obvious that I couldn't live and cover my constituency on $5,000 a year, so I went to live off the land with the Eskimos as a trapper. I decided to visit the settlements in my constituency by dogteam in the winter and canoe in the summer.

To my relief I found that I very quickly and easily fell into this new pattern of life. The only problem was that I was soon facing a second election, and this time I was to have opposition for sure—an Eskimo from Cambridge Bay named Qavrana. As a whiteman running against an Eskimo in Eskimo country, I was worried. When I made my way around the settlements, I told everyone: "The choice is yours. You should vote for the man you think will do the most for you, who will work the hardest for you, and if you think Qavrana is that man, then you vote for him. If you think I am that man, then vote for me." Everywhere I went I made a point of explaining to the Eskimos: "I'm not here to tell you what to do. I come here so you can tell me what to do, and then when we hold a meeting with the government people, I can explain to them what you want."

It turned out that I had worried over nothing. I was re-elected by a flatteringly large majority.

ONE DAY early in 1969 I was in Yellowknife for a Council session. I was sitting in a restaurant when in walked Georgina Blondin, who was rated one of the prettiest girls in the North. I had met her only once before, just after she had won the territorial beauty contest and been named the Centennial Indian Princess of the Northwest Territories. That had been in 1967, but I had never forgotten our evening together. The first thing I had done upon being introduced to her was to tell her that "Georgina" was too long and cumbersome to handle, and that she would be "Gina" to me.

Gina now told me that she had been attending university in British Columbia, but had come back to Yellowknife before moving with her family to Fort Franklin, which was about four hundred miles away. If Gina went there, I might never see her a third time.

"You're not going to Fort Franklin," I told her.

"Who is going to stop me?"

"I am," I said, and I did.

We got married in June that year. Friends came from all over the Territories for the wedding, and when we walked out of the church, we passed under an archway—six ivory narwhal tusks brought from the Arctic coast.

EPILOGUE

That was three years ago. Now we live in Yellowknife, but I still spend five months of every year running my own trapline near Coppermine. I gave up my Council work, partly to write this book, but also to make more time for my work as a consultant on major development projects, such as the laying of pipelines and the siting of tourist camps. For me, as for the vast majority of the inhabitants of the Northwest Territories, those days of snowhuts, sealhunts and caribou stew are part of history.

The Eskimos of today, young and old alike, are turning more and more to the whiteman's culture. The image of the cheerful little hunter in heavy fur clothing, so long promulgated in print and film, is perhaps no longer valid for most parts of the Arctic. The people I have known and have attempted to depict had a way of life that was disappearing even as I was getting to know it.

Already the changes are apparent in numerous small ways, such as the Eskimo engineer I saw preparing for bed by putting the cat out and setting his alarm for six o'clock in the morning. The spectacle of an Eskimo setting an alarm strikingly points up the cultural revolution that has swept Canada's twelve thousand Eskimos in a single lifetime. The Eskimo hunter of old ate when he was hungry, slept when he was sleepy, lived a life attuned to his physical needs. He was concerned with the larger aspects of his environment, the arrival of sandhill cranes and the departure of caribou, not with hours and minutes. He thought it strange that a whiteman would look at a clock to find out when he was hungry or would jump up in the morning when the alarm sounded, whether he felt rested or not.

Today that old Eskimo's people live by the clock, just like the whiteman, many of them in government-financed prefab houses with three bedrooms, electricity, oil furnaces and inside toilets. The children are dressed in stretch pants, the women shop at the local Hudson's Bay Store, now as modern as any small super-market, and buy TV dinners that the men, who grew up eating raw frozen food, would complain about if not properly warmed. The youngest children go to school down the block and the older ones are finishing high school, the first trickle is preparing to go south to university, and there is talk of their own university in the NWT soon. Many of those young Eskimos speak English all the time. I have met Eskimos who, when I addressed them in their own language, stopped me with "You'll have to speak English, I don't speak that language."

Yet less than a man's lifespan ago, the Eskimo was a Stone Age man, a nomadic hunter pursuing caribou with crude bow and arrows, a people eking out an existence in as cruel an environment as one could find in the world. Only his remarkable ability to adapt to new conditions, such as the coming of the rifle, has enabled him to survive.

To acquire a rifle and ammunition, the Eskimo had to offer the white trader the only currency in which he showed any interest—fur. So the Eskimo abandoned a life of hunting for a life of trapping, and the difference is greater than might appear on the surface. To trap, a man needed more and more dogs to haul his traps, his furs and his family to the trapping grounds. The average team came to be thirteen animals instead of three. More food was required to fuel the dogs, and so more furs, and the circle spiralled ever upward. Yet within thirty years the era of the big dogteam has risen and fallen, giving way to the snowmobile, now nearly as ubiquitous in the North as the automobile in the South.

People in the South—and whites in the Arctic—who decry the passing of the old ways and customs in the North forget one vital factor—Eskimos are human beings. They don't want, any more than Joe or Mary in Ottawa does, to live in a crummy snowhouse, to be bitterly cold and hungry most of the time. Even worse than this, if the caribou migration misses their area, they could easily starve to death, as I have seen happen.

If they can make a living in a settlement, then most Eskimos will do so. They like gaiety, fun, a busy social life, for they are as gregarious as any white group. They do not want an isolated life out on the land, and are quick to point out that they seldom meet a whiteman who wants this way of life either.

The changes in the brief period that I lived as an Arctic man have amounted to nothing less than the rapid urbanization of the Eskimo. The Bathurst Inlet people are the last to live as a tribe in the old Eskimo way, making their living off the land, existing in snowhouses in winter and tents in summer. The staple food is still the caribou; the winter economy is still the white fox. But drastic changes are in the offing.

In 1970, the Hudson's Bay Company was forced to close down the trading post there. They did so not on economic grounds alone (the post had not made a profit for many, many years) but because they could find no trader willing to live in total isolation. In response to a motion I placed before the Council, a plane flies to Bathurst from Cambridge once a month, and the post is re-opened for trade, but the lack of a resident trader makes it almost inevitable that the people will sooner or later abandon their ancient hunting territory and move to a welfare existence at Cambridge Bay.

There are many dedicated men in the Arctic today who feel as I do that the Eskimo must now be given fair opportunity for employment and for leadership in the North. Whites and Eskimos alike have put tremendous, and I hope justified, faith in the power of education to accomplish this. Prior to 1955 the only formal education available to Eskimo children was from a handful of tiny mission schools. In 1955 the Canadian government belatedly accepted its responsibility for the education of the Eskimos. The government programme was built around a few centrally located residential schools to which children from settlements all over the North were transported.

Bathurst Inlet provides a convenient microcosm of what happened. All school-age children, from six to sixteen, were and still are airlifted nearly a thousand miles to a residential school at Fort Simpson. The old people, barely understanding what was happening but concerned that their children should receive the best education available, swallowed their tears and urged the children to go. Losing their children was like a death to them, but they were concerned with the same things that concern parents anywhere—what would become of the children? Would they grow up to become good people or bums?

Those children were away from home for ten months in the year, during which time they lived in warm, comfortable residences and became accustomed to eating three solid meals a day, and to sleeping on soft beds between clean sheets. Then during summer recess they were flown home to spend two months with their parents. When they came back to Bathurst Inlet they spoke English, not Eskimo. Now there was little or nothing about the way of life of their parents that the children liked.

The old people, many of whom spoke no English, felt at a loss. They couldn't communicate with their own beloved children, who had become strangers. There was now a real generation gap to worry about, much more difficult to solve than the normal age difference between parents and children, because it included a language barrier. It involved a completely foreign way of life, conflicting with every facet of the old way. The children no longer knew how to hunt or trap, and furthermore, they saw no point in learning.

Those of us on Council who observed the frightening consequences of this policy fought to change it. I remember saying at one Council session that, unless the government policy was changed, I intended to go personally to every settlement in my constituency and advise parents to hold their children at home, in short to strike against the school system. Before the end of the week, the federal government announced they were changing their policy and would build schools in every Arctic settlement where the school age population exceeded twenty-five. Many settlements have already got their first schools, and the children thus have a better chance to partake of the whiteman's world without losing their own.

However, the strange paradox remains that the formal school education of the Eskimo children is directly responsible for the massive unemployment of the native people in the Arctic today. On graduation from school most Eskimos are unwilling to return to life on the land but are, at the same time, unable to find permanent employment in the whiteman's labour force, although the very whites with whom they went to school are becoming the managers of the local stores, running local radio stations, getting the best civil service jobs in town. Unless the government provides meaningful employment opportunities for Eskimos on a par with those available to whites in the Arctic, they are going to walk down the path taken by the Indians in many parts of Canada, defeated, resentful, sullen and; eventually, almost certainly rebellious.

Significant changes are also taking place on the land itself. Millions of dollars are being spent in a gigantic search for oil and gas and minerals in the Arctic. Little of this enormous wealth has so far rubbed off on the local people, as their claims to the land and its resources have been disavowed by the federal government. However, the natives are learning, and political organizations are being formed to protect their rights. If future development of the Arctic includes manufacturing and processing industries, then the natives might be able to find employment for which they have been educated and the opportunity to which they are entitled in their own backyard.

Today there are no real fur trading posts in the Arctic. True, the Hudson's Bay Company still does conduct a fur business with the Eskimos, but it is a rather minor part of the concern of its northern division now. The Hudson's Bay posts in the North today are small supermarkets, not fur posts, and the men who run these modern stores are merchandisers, not fur traders. The stores are even heated.

There will never again be a job such as the one which enticed me as a dreamy-eyed young man all the way from Scotland with romantic notions in my otherwise empty head. There will never be another fur trader in the old tradition, nor an Eskimo in the old image. But I cannot quarrel with this. I found the dream I sought, and I have come through those times and like the Eskimos, my friends, I must look forward to new days, new opportunities, and like them, new responsibilities in Canada's Arctic.

THE WINDS OF WAR
Herman Wouk

The Winds of War

a condensation of the book by

Herman Wouk

ILLUSTRATED BY ROBERT LAVIN
PUBLISHED BY COLLINS, LONDON

1939, 1940, 1941 . . . momentous years.
The Siege of Warsaw, the Battle of Britain,
the Nazi march on Moscow: to Britons
these conflicts were vital to the life-or-death
struggle of those terrible days. But to most
Americans then they were mere words in
headlines, distant, none of their business.

It is from this unusual viewpoint that the
story of Commander Victor Henry,
U.S. naval attaché in Nazi Germany, begins.
He wanted command of a battleship, not
pen-pushing missions, even though they
took him to personal encounters with
Hitler, Roosevelt, Stalin, even Churchill.
Only gradually did he realize that Britain's
war was America's, that all civilization lay
in the balance.

Then the turmoil of war caught up with
Victor Henry himself and with his family.
His younger son's Jewish wife trapped in
Fascist Italy. His own wife, beautiful,
restless, left at home in Washington, and
tempted. His older son, a navy flier,
destined to play a courageous part in the
Japanese attack on Pearl Harbor.

It is Herman Wouk's genius to mix the
real and the imaginary in a way that gives
the reader a tingling sense of having been
there. Through the eyes of his characters the
great and the small of those traumatic years
live again. In this book he tells a compelling
human story that surpasses even the high
drama of *The Caine Mutiny*.

This is how it was.

1

Commander Victor Henry rode home from the Main Navy Building on Constitution Avenue in Washington, D.C. in a grey March rainstorm that matched his mood. In his War Plans cubbyhole that afternoon he had received an unexpected word from on high which had probably blown his career to rags. Now he had to consult his wife about an urgent decision; yet he did not altogether trust her opinions.

When she had married him they had talked about the drawbacks of service life and Rhoda had declared that none of them would trouble her: she loved him, and the navy was a career of honour. So she had said in 1915, when the World War was on and uniforms had a glow. This was 1939, and she had long since forgotten those words.

He had warned her that the climb through the system would be hard, but until now his rise had been steady. "Pug" Henry's directness, his dash, his single-mindedness had won him an appointment to the Naval Academy after high school. The same characteristics, coupled with humour and tenderness, had later won him his wife, though she was two inches taller than he, and though her prosperous parents had looked for a better match than a squat navy fullback from California, of no means or family.

Mundane details like a height difference had faded from sight. The real shadow on this couple was that wherever she was, Rhoda tended to fret—about the heat, or the cold, or servants, or shop clerks, or hairdressers—and Victor Henry detested whining. On the other hand, when her spirits were good she could be very sweet and agreeable. Also, she was two things Pug thought a wife should be: a seductive woman and an adroit homemaker. In all their married years, there had been few times when he had not desired her; and wherever they landed, Rhoda had provided clean, well-furnished rooms, fresh flowers, and appetizing food.

But heading home after a day's work, he never knew whether he would encounter Rhoda the charmer or Rhoda the crab. At a crucial moment like this, it could make a great difference.

Coming into the house, he heard her singing. He found her in the living room arranging gladioli in a vase. She was wearing a beige silky dress, and her dark hair fell in waves behind her ears, in the fashion of 1939. Her welcoming glance was affectionate and gay.

"Oh, hi there. Why on *earth* didn't you warn me Kip Tollever was coming? He sent these, and *luckily* he called too." Rhoda used the swooping high notes of smart Washington women. "He said he might be late. Let's have a drink, Pug, O.K.? The fixings are all there. I'm parched."

Feeling better, Pug walked to the wheeled bar and began to mix martinis. "I asked him to stop by so we could talk. It's not a social visit."

"Oh? Am I supposed to make myself scarce?"

"No, no."

"Good. I like Kip. I thought he was stuck in Berlin."

"He's been detached."

"So he told me. Who relieved him?"

"Nobody yet." Victor Henry handed her a cocktail. He sank into an armchair and drank, gloom enveloping him again. "You know that memorandum I wrote on battleships? Well, I got called down to the CNO's office."

"My God! To see Preble?"

"Preble himself." As Pug told her about his talk with the chief of naval operations, Rhoda's face took on a sullen look.

"Oh, I see. *That's* why you asked Kip over!"

"Exactly. What do you think about my taking this attaché job?"

"Since when do you have any choice?"

"He gave me the impression that I did. That I could go to a battlewagon instead, as an exec."

Rhoda hesitated. "Well—naturally I'd adore going to Germany. It's the loveliest country in Europe. The people are so friendly. German was my major, you know, aeons ago."

"I know," Pug said with a wry smile. "You were very good at German." Some of the early hot moments of their honeymoon had occurred while they stumbled through Heine's love poetry.

Rhoda returned an arch glance. "Well, all right, you. All I mean is, if you must leave Washington—I suppose the Nazis are kind of ugly, but Germany's still wonderful, I'm told."

"No doubt we'd have a whirl. Preble says the President wants top men in Berlin now. O.K. I'll believe that. He also says it won't hurt my career. That's what I can't believe. First thing any selection board looks for in a man's record is lots of blue water."

"Oh, Pug, you'll get your four stripes, *and* a battleship command. Are you sure Kip won't stay to dinner? There's plenty of food. Warren's going to New York."

"No, Kip's off to a party at the German embassy. Why the hell is Warren going to New York? He's only been home three days."

"Ask him," Rhoda said. The slam of the front door and the quick firm steps were unmistakable Warren sounds.

"Hi." He came in waving a squash racket. With his hair tousled and face glowing from exercise, he looked much like the lad who, on graduating from the Academy, had vanished from their lives.

Pug envied him the deep sunburn which bespoke a destroyer bridge and duty at sea. He said, "You're off to New York, I hear."

"Yes, Dad. My exec just blew into town. We're going up to see some shows. He's never been to New York."

Commander Henry made a grouchy sound. What bothered him was the thought that a woman might be waiting in New York. A top student at the Academy, Warren had almost ruined his record with excessive playing around.

The doorbell rang and the old Irish houseman answered it. Rhoda stood. "That'll be Kip Tollever, Warren. He's just finished a term as naval attaché in Berlin."

Warren made a comic grimace. "Jehosephat. How did he get stuck with *that*? Cookie pusher in an embassy!"

Rhoda looked at her husband, whose face remained impassive.

"Commander Tollever, ma'am," said the houseman.

"Hello, Rhoda!" Tollever marched in, with long arms outstretched, in a flawlessly cut evening uniform: blue mess jacket with medals, a black tie, a stiff snowy shirt. "My Lord, woman! You look ten years younger than you did in the Philippines."

"Oh, you," she said, eyes gleaming, as he kissed her cheek.

"Hi, Pug." Tollever stared at the son. "Now for crying out loud, which boy is this?"

Warren held out his hand. "Hello, sir. Guess."

"Aha. It's Warren. Byron had a different grin, and red hair. I was told you're serving in the *Monaghan*. What's Byron doing?"

Rhoda chirruped, "Oh, he's our romantic dreamer. Studying fine arts in Italy. And you should see Madeline. All grown up and working in New York."

Warren excused himself and went out.

"Fine arts. Well, that *is* romantic." Tollever sat down, accepting a martini from Pug. "You'll love Germany. So will Rhoda. You'd be crazy not to grab the chance." He drank two martinis in fifteen minutes as he talked.

When Pug probed about the Nazis, Tollever's tone grew firm. "Hitler's a remarkable man," he said. "I'm not saying that he, or Göring, or any of that bunch, wouldn't murder their own grandmothers to increase their power or Germany's. But that's politics in Europe nowadays. We Americans are far too naïve. The Soviet Union is the one big reality Europe lives with, Pug—those Bolos are out to rule Europe, and Hitler isn't about to let them. That's the root of the matter. The Germans do things that we wouldn't —like this stuff with the Jews—but that's not your business. Your job is military information, and you can get a lot of it. These people desperately want our friendship, and they're not at all bashful about showing off what they're accomplishing."

Rhoda asked about the Jews, and Tollever assured her that the newspaper stories were exaggerated. The worst thing had been the so-called Crystal Night, when Nazi toughs had smashed store windows and set fire to synagogues. Even that, the Jews had brought on themselves, by murdering a German embassy official in Paris. So far as Tollever knew, not one Jew had been physically harmed, though a big fine had been put on them for the death of the official. "Now as to the President's recalling our ambassador, that was a superfluous gesture, utterly," Tollever said.

Over more martinis, he began reminiscing about parties, hunting trips, and the like. Great fun and high living went with an attaché's job, he chuckled. Moreover, you were *supposed* to socialize, so as to dig up information. "How on earth did a gunnery redhot like you come up for this job?" he asked.

"Stuck my neck out," Pug growled, "and I also speak German. You know the work I did on the magnetic torpedo exploder—"

"Hell, yes. And the letter of commendation."

"Well, I've watched torpedo developments since. Part of my job in War Plans is monitoring the latest intelligence on armaments. The Japs are making some mighty healthy torpedoes, Kip. I got the slide rule out, and the way I read the figures our battlewagons are falling below the safety margin. I wrote a recommendation that the blisters be thickened and raised on the *Maryland* and *New Mexico* classes. My report's become a hot potato, with memos flying. The blisters *will* be thickened and—"

"And you, Pug, got yourself offered the most interesting post in Europe. Don't pass it up."

"I don't intend to."

RE-ENTERING the house after seeing Tollever to his car, Victor Henry found Warren donning his trench coat in the hall with Rhoda watching him. "Say, Dad, did I mention that a couple of months ago I put in for flight training? Well, it seems I have a chance."

"To become a carrier pilot?" Rhoda looked unhappy.

"Why, Mom, I think it makes good sense. Doesn't it, sir?"

Commander Henry said, "Yes, indeed. The future of this here navy might just belong to the brown shoes."

"Pensacola would be interesting, anyway. Well, back Friday." Warren kissed his mother and left.

Pug Henry consumed his dinner in grim, abstracted silence. He was both proud and alarmed over Warren's casually dropped news. Carrier aviation was the riskiest duty in the navy. The quiet during the meal was unbroken except by the houseman's soft footfalls in the candlelit dining room. When they were settled in the living room, drinking coffee, Rhoda said, "Pug, here's a letter from Byron. He's in Siena doing some sort of research job for a famous author, Dr. Aaron Jastrow."

"I've read his book, *A Jew's Jesus*; it's excellent." Pug read his son's letter. "Well. He seems to be mainly interested in Jastrow's niece."

"She does sound attractive," Rhoda said. "But he's had other nine-day wonders."

2

Byron Henry's involvement with Natalie Jastrow had been much in character. He had drifted into it.

In his junior year at Columbia College he studied fine arts, and the professor, a lover of the Italian Renaissance, took a liking to him. It was the first intellectual friendship in Byron Henry's life. He became a Renaissance enthusiast and finished college in a blaze of B pluses. One year at the University of Florence for a Master of Arts degree had been the plan.

But one rainy November night, in his squalid room in Florence, sick of the bad plumbing and of living alone among foreigners, Byron wrote his friend that Italian Renaissance painting was garish and didn't really interest him.

The professor's reply was cheering: "Obviously art was a false lead. If you can find something that truly engages you, you may yet go far. . . . I've written to Dr. Aaron Jastrow who lives outside Siena. We used to be friends at Yale, and he was very good at bringing out the best in young men. Go and talk to him."

AT FIRST glance, the girl at the wheel of the old blue convertible made no strong impression on him: an oval face, dark hair, enormous sunglasses. Beside her sat a blond man in his mid-thirties, covering a yawn with a long white hand.

310

"Hi. Byron Henry? I'm Natalie Jastrow. This is Leslie Slote, from our Paris embassy. He's visiting my uncle."

As they drove through Siena's narrow streets, Byron asked the Foreign Service officer about his work. Slote told him he was in the political section and was hoping for assignment to Moscow or Warsaw.

Jastrow lived in a yellow stucco villa on a terraced hillside, with a fine view of the cathedral and Siena's tile roofs. As they entered a long, beamed living room, a bearded little man came towards them. "Well, there you are."

"This is Byron Henry, Aaron," the girl said.

Jastrow took Byron's hand then led the way to a table and carefully poured sherry from a heavy crystal decanter into four glasses. He held up his glass. "To Mr. Byron Henry, eminent hater of the Italian Renaissance."

Byron laughed. "I'll drink to that."

It was a spare lunch: vegetables with white rice, then cheese and fruit, served on fine old china. The tall dining room windows stood open to a sunny garden.

"What have you got against the Italian Renaissance, Byron?" the girl said, her dark eyes flashing with bold intelligence.

"Yes, tell us," said Jastrow in a classroom voice.

Byron hesitated. "I started out fascinated," he said. "But now I'm snowed under by all the garbage amid the works of genius. Anyway, what has Renaissance art to do with Christianity? If Christ walked into Saint Peter's, he wouldn't even suspect the place related to his teachings."

Natalie was regarding him with a smile.

Leslie Slote said, "Is your father a clergyman, Byron?"

"His father's a naval officer," said Jastrow.

"Really? What branch?"

Byron said, "Well, right now he's in War Plans."

"My goodness. *War* Plans?" Dr. Jastrow pretended a comic flutter. "Is that as ominous as it sounds?"

"Sir, every country draws up theoretical war plans in peacetime. But as a matter of fact, I think there's going to be a war."

Byron saw the others exchange glances. Jastrow said, "Why?"

"Well, I just toured Germany. You see nothing but uniforms and parades, trucks full of troops, and trains loaded with tanks."

"With such displays Hitler won Austria and the Sudetenland," said Jastrow, "and he never fired a shot."

Natalie said to Byron, "Leslie thinks my uncle should go home to the States. We've had a running argument for three days."

Jastrow was peeling a pear. "This is a comfortable house, and my work is going well. If I tried to sell the house, no Italian would offer me a fair price. They've been dealing for centuries with foreigners who've had to cut and run suddenly. I expect to end my days here."

"Not at the hands of the Nazis, I trust," Slote said.

Jastrow ate a piece of pear and began lecturing. "Leslie, if Hitler were the Kaiser, I admit I'd be worried. Fortunately the old ruling class is destroyed and a tough, able new leadership—Hitler, Mussolini, Stalin—has come up. If Hitler can make it in Poland without war, he'll do it. Not otherwise."

Byron blurted, "Dr. Jastrow, in Germany I saw the anti-Jew signs on park benches and in trolley cars. I saw burned-out synagogues. I'm surprised you talk so calmly about Hitler."

Dr. Jastrow smiled a slow, acid smile. "The tolerance for Jews in Europe is less than a hundred years old, and it's never gone deep. Hitler represents only a return to normal."

"You love to spin such talk," Slote said, "but I wish you'd do it on the next boat home."

"Leslie," Jastrow said, "you rang wild alarms when Mussolini passed the anti-Jewish laws. They've proved a joke. Even if there is a war, the Italians won't fight. Siena may well be as safe a place as any."

"I doubt that Natalie's parents think so."

"She can go home tomorrow."

"I'm thinking of it," the girl said. "But not because of Hitler. There are things that bother me more."

Slote's face reddened, and Jastrow stood up.

"Byron, come along."

They left the girl and the scarlet-faced man at the table, glowering at each other.

BOOKS filled the shelves of a small wood-panelled library and stood in piles on the desk and floor. Over the fireplace hung a painting of a stiff Sienese Madonna and Child. "Now, Byron," Jastrow said. "Sit there in the light where I can see you. Why didn't you go to the Naval Academy?"

Byron sat up in his chair. "I'm just not interested."

"Dr. Milano wrote that you took a naval reserve course, and obtained a commission."

"It made my father feel good."

"It's not too late for second thoughts, you know."

Byron shook his head, smiling.

"Well then, do you want a job?"

Byron was taken aback. "I guess I do, sir."

Jastrow ambled to his desk. "I need a good researcher. Can I interest you, for twenty dollars a week, in the Emperor Constantine?"

"Sir, I've flunked more history courses—but I'll try it."

"Oh, you will? When you say you have no aptitude? Why?"

"Well, for the money, and to be around you." He omitted a third good reason: Natalie Jastrow.

Jastrow laughed. "We'll give it a try."

NATALIE received letters from Leslie Slote two or three times a week in Foreign Service envelopes. Byron hated the sight of them.

He was spending hours every day with her in Jastrow's huge second-floor library. While she typed letters and manuscripts, Byron read up on Constantine, checked facts, and drew maps of military campaigns. Whenever he raised his eyes he saw the smooth face bent over the desk, the shapely bones highlighted by sunshine.

They sometimes drove out in the hills for a picnic lunch, when she would slightly warm to him, treating him like a younger brother. The romance with Slote, he discovered, had begun when Natalie was studying in Paris after graduating from Radcliffe; always stormy, it had broken up once, but she was giving it another try. One picnic day she mentioned that Slote had received orders to Warsaw. She had promised to visit him there as soon as she could get away.

"Natalie," Byron said suddenly, "do you like your work here?"

She cocked her head. "It's a job. Besides, I think Aaron's rather wonderful. And this Constantine book is good." She gave Byron a quizzical look. "Why *you're* doing this, I'm far less sure."

"Me?" Byron said. "I'm broke."

A week or so later, Natalie and Byron were at work in the library when Natalie suddenly looked up. "Byron, would you like to go to Warsaw with me?"

Byron choked back his joy. "What would be the point?"

"Well, Leslie Slote says it's rather old-world and gay. The thing is, Aaron's getting difficult about my trip. He's having a spell of nerves about the Polish situation."

Byron said, "Would my going make a difference?"

"Yes. If you go, Aaron'll stop saying it's too risky."

"And your friend Slote?"

Natalie smiled grimly. "I'll deal with him."

"All right. I guess I'll go."

"Bless you! We'll have fun. I'll see to that."

Later, Dr. Jastrow sent for Byron. "What a load you've taken off my mind!" he said. "That headstrong girl doesn't know how wild and backward Poland is. And Hitler is making nasty noises. Well, I'll be here alone, then."

"You won't go home to America?" Byron said.

"I'm not sure. For one thing, I let my passport lapse, and not being native-born, there's some red tape involved in renewing it."

"You should certainly straighten that out," Byron said.

"Of course. These things used to be simple, but the rules have tightened up. Well, Byron, I hope you'll meet my cousin Berel. You're a capable young man. My mind is much easier now."

3

The gold letters B R E M E N stretched across the stern of the steamship. Above them, an immense red flag rippled in the breeze of the Hudson, at its centre a black swastika circled in white. Because of the practise it would give him with his German, Victor Henry had obtained permission to sail on the *Bremen*.

Outside the porthole the pier girders moved by, and the band far below crashed out "The Star-Spangled Banner". Rhoda threw her arms around her husband and kissed him. "Well! We made it, Pug! Off to Deutschland. Second honeymoon and all *that*! Mmm!"

This mild sexiness in his unpredictable wife was like a birthday present to the monogamous Pug. He pulled her close.

"Well!" Rhoda broke free, with a husky laugh. "Not so fast, young fellow. I want a drink, or two, or three."

In the already crowded bar they found two stools and ordered champagne cocktails. "Well, to whom?" Rhoda said.

"The kids," Pug said.

"Ah, yes. To our abandoned nestlings!" As she polished off the cocktail, Rhoda talked excitedly. "Pug, I wonder if there are any Nazis right here in this bar?"

A man sitting next to Rhoda shifted his glance to her. He wore a feathered green hat, and he was drinking from a stein.

"Let's go on deck," Pug said. "See the Statue of Liberty."

"I've seen the Statue of Liberty. I want another drink."

Pug made a slight peremptory move of a thumb, and Rhoda got off the stool. When anything touched his navy work, he could treat her like a deckhand. In a whipping wind they walked to the stern, where passengers were watching Manhattan drift past. Leaning on the rail, Pug said quietly, "Look, unless we're in the open air like this, you can assume anything we say will be recorded. At the bar, at the table, in our stateroom."

"In our stateroom? You don't mean day and night? Pug!"

"That's what this job is. If they didn't do it, they'd be sloppy, and Germans aren't sloppy. It'll be the same in Berlin. Kip says you can never stop thinking about what you say. Or do."

AN ENGRAVED card, slid under their cabin door before dinner, had invited them to the captain's table. The captain, stiff in gold-buttoned blue, heavily joshed the ladies in slow English or clear German. Now and then he flicked a finger, and a steward would jump to his side. The food was abundant and exquisite.

Also at the table sat a German submarine officer, Grobke, as short and taciturn as Pug himself. On Victor Henry's right sat a small English girl in grey satin, the daughter of Alistair Tudsbury. Tudsbury was the only celebrity at the table, a British broadcaster and correspondent, with a white moustache and thick glasses. He laughed a lot, and smoked too many cigarettes.

It was an awkward meal. Nobody mentioned politics, war, or the Nazis. Even books and plays were risky. Pug tried to amuse Tudsbury's daughter.

"I suppose you're on vacation from school?"

"Well, sort of permanently. I'm twenty-eight."

"I'm sorry. I thought you were younger."

"Many people make that mistake, Commander, because I travel with my father. His eyes were damaged at Amiens; I help him with his work."

"That must be interesting."

"Depending on the subject matter. Nowadays it's a sort of broken record. Will the little tramp go, or won't he?"

Pug Henry was brought up short. The "little tramp" was Charlie Chaplin, of course, and by ready transfer, Hitler. She was saying that Tudsbury's one topic was whether Hitler would start a war. By not dropping her voice, and by using a phrase which a German ear would be unlikely to catch, she had managed not only to touch the forbidden subject but to express a world of contempt for the dictator of Germany.

HALF A DOZEN early morning walkers were swinging along when Pug came out on the cool sunlit deck. He had calculated that five turns would make a mile, and he meant to do fifteen. Rounding the bow, he saw the Tudsbury girl coming towards him. "Good morning." They passed with nods and smiles. At the third encounter he said, reversing his direction, "Let me join you."

"Oh, thank you, yes." She glanced up at him. "Your wife's not a walker?"

"Late sleeper. Well, what does your father really think? Will the little tramp go?"

She laughed, a keen look brightening her eyes. "Talky's come out boldly to the effect that time will tell."

"Talky?"

316

She laughed again. "His middle name is Talcott. Since schoolboy days, he's been 'Talky' to his friends. Guess why!"

"Your father's just published a book, hasn't he? I'd like to read it."

"There's a copy in the ship's library. He sent me to check," she said with a rueful grin. Last night he had not paid this girl much mind, but now he noticed with pleasure the fresh colouring of the heart-shaped face, the expressive green-grey eyes, fine straight nose, heavy brown hair. He wished Warren could meet her.

"You're going around again?" she said. "I get off here. If you do read his book, carry it under your arm. It'll make his trip."

After breakfast, Pug went to the library. The shelves held many German volumes on the World War. Pug found one titled *U-boats: 1914-18* and settled down to see what it said about American destroyer tactics. Soon he heard the scratch of a pen. At a nearby desk the German submarine man sat writing.

Grobke smiled. "Recalling old times?" he said in English.

"Well, I was in destroyers."

"And I was down below. Maybe this is not the first time our paths cross. How about a drink before dinner to compare notes?"

"I'd enjoy that."

Pug put away the U-boat book and took Tudsbury's to read on deck for a while before he went below to work.

The bow wave was boiling away, a V of white foam on the blue sunlit sea, and the *Bremen* was rolling like a battleship. Nostalgia swept over Pug. It was four years since he had served at sea, eleven since he had had a command. He was calculating the wind speed when he heard Tudsbury blare, "Hello there, Commander. I hear you were out walking my Pam at the crack of dawn."

"Yes. I have plans for her to meet a son of mine."

Tudsbury peered through his thick spectacles. "I say, is that *my* book? How far have you got?"

"I just drew it from the library."

Tudsbury's moustache dropped. "You didn't buy it? Damn all libraries!" He bellowed a laugh. "It's a bad book, really, but the part about Hitler's takeover of Austria is not too awful."

He talked about Hitler's rise to power, sounding much as he did on the air: positive, informed, cheerfully ominous. "Did you know that for five years this Führer lived as a seedy tramp in a fat and prosperous Vienna? He was a lazy, incompetent misfit. Then during the World War he was a messenger runner in the German army, a low job, and at thirty he was lying gassed in an army hospital." Tudsbury's voice was beginning to roll in his best professional style. "And then, what happened? Why, this same half-mad little wretch leaped out of his hospital bed and went in ten years straight to the top of the German nation."

"Well, it's the old story of the stitch in time," Pug said. "Your politicos could have stopped him early on. But they didn't. Incidentally, where are you headed? Berlin, too?"

Tudsbury nodded. "Amazing! Dr. Goebbels is letting me in. I've been *persona non grata* in the Third Reich since Munich. But the Jerries are being kind to Englishmen this month, probably so we'll hold still while they roll over the Poles. Haw, haw! I expect we will, too; but if it does come to war, you Americans may have to lend more of a hand than you did last time."

"We've got the Japanese on our hands," Pug said. "They're carving up China, and they've got a growing navy. If they make the Pacific a Japanese lake and do what they want on the Asian mainland, the world will be theirs in fifty years. Compared with that, this Hitler business is just the same old cat-and-dog fight."

Tudsbury sighed. "Possibly you underestimate the Germans."

ON THE last night of the crossing, when orchids were at every lady's place and the champagne was going round, the topic of international politics finally surfaced at the captain's table. Everybody agreed that war was a silly, wasteful way of settling differences, especially among advanced nations like England, France, and Germany. "We're all of the same stock," Tudsbury said. "It's a sad thing when brothers fall out."

The captain nodded. "Exactly. If we'd only stick together, the Bolsheviks would never move. And who else wants war?" Everyone was wearing paper hats and tossing streamers, and Pug observed that a party of Jews were as gay as everybody else, ministered to by polite German waiters. The captain followed Pug's glance.

318

"You see, Commander, how welcome we make them. The exaggerations on the subject are fantastic." He said to Tudsbury, "Between us, aren't you journalists a bit responsible for that?"

"Well, Captain," Tudsbury said, "to foreigners, the policy towards Jews is one of the novel things about your government."

"Tudsbury is not wrong, Captain," Grobke broke in. "That policy has been mishandled." He turned to Pug. "Still, it's so unimportant compared with what the Führer has achieved: Germany has come back to life. The people have work, they have food and houses, and they have spirit. And our youth is just incredible! Under Weimar they were rioting, becoming Communists, going in for sex perversions and drugs. Now they're working, *serving*, happy. My crews are happy. I tell you what, Victor. You come visit our sub base in Swinemünde. It'll open your eyes."

Pug hesitated. "I'd like that, if we can work it out."

"Without formalities!" Grobke waved his arms. "It's a personal invitation from me to you. We're independent in the U-boat command."

"The invitation wouldn't include me, would it?" Tudsbury said.

Grobke paused, then laughed. "Why not? The more the British know about what we've got, the less likely a hasty mistake."

"Well, here may be an important little step for peace," said the captain, "transacted at my table! We will have more champagne on it at once." And so they drank to peace, as the great liner approached the shore lights of Nazi Germany.

4

The Henrys had barely arrived in Berlin when they were invited to meet Hitler. It was a rare piece of luck, the embassy people told them. The Führer was staying away from Berlin in order to damp down the war talk, but a visit of the Bulgarian prime minister had brought him back.

While Pug studied Nazi protocol, Rhoda flew into a two-day frenzy. She had no dress in the least suitable for a formal afternoon reception, she asserted, and three hours before the event she burst into their hotel room clad in a pink silk suit.

"How's this?" she barked. "I hear Hitler likes pink."

"Perfect!" Pug privately thought it was terrible.

Hitler's new chancellery with its opulent stretch of carpet, its high ceiling, the great expanses of shiny marble, all added up to a strained effort to be grand. Blond SS guards in black-and-silver uniforms shepherded the long line of guests towards the Führer, far down the hall.

Hitler was a small man, bowing as he shook hands with his guests, his hair falling on his forehead. His down-curved mouth looked rigid and tense under the famous small moustache, his eyes sternly self-confident. But when Hitler smiled, his face brightened, showing a strong hint of humour and an almost boyish shyness. Sometimes, when he was particularly amused, he laughed and, oddly, jerked his right knee up and inward.

An officer intoned in German: "The naval attaché to the embassy of the United States of America, Commander Victor Henry!"

The Führer's handclasp was firm as he scanned Pug's face. Seen this close, Hitler's deep-sunk eyes were pale blue and remote—a zealot's eyes. To be looking into this famous face was the strangest sensation Victor Henry had ever had.

Hitler said, "*Willkommen in Deutschland.*"

Surprised that Hitler should be aware of his recent arrival, Pug stammered, "*Danke, Herr Reichskanzler.*"

"*Frau Henry!*"

Rhoda, her eyes gleaming, shook hands with Adolf Hitler. "I hope you are comfortable in Berlin," he said in German.

"Well, *Herr Reichskanzler*, I've just begun looking for a house," Rhoda said, too overcome to make a polite reply and move on.

"You will have no difficulty." Hitler's eyes warmed; evidently he found her pretty. He kept her hand, faintly smiling.

"There are so many charming neighbourhoods in Berlin that I'm bewildered. That's the problem."

This pleased Hitler. He laughed, kicked his knee inward and spoke to an aide behind him. The Henrys moved on.

Two days later, Pug was working at the embassy at his morning mail when his yeoman buzzed him.

"Mrs. Henry on the phone, sir."

It was early for Rhoda to be up. A renting agent was in the lobby, she said, saying he had been advised that they were looking for a house. "It's so odd. You don't suppose *Hitler* sent him?"

Pug laughed. "Maybe his aide did. Well, what can you lose? Go and look at some of his houses."

Rhoda called back at three-thirty in the afternoon. "There's this wonderful house in the Grünewald section, right on a lake. It even has a tennis court! And it's not even a hundred dollars a month. Can you come right away and look at it?"

Pug went. It was a grey stone mansion, set on a smooth lawn sloping to the water's edge. Inside the house were oriental carpets, gilt-framed paintings, a dining table with silk-upholstered chairs, and an elegant living room in the French style. The place had five upstairs bedrooms and three marbled baths.

When Pug asked the agent why the price was so low, he explained that the owner was a Herr Rosenthal, and the house was vacant because of a new ruling affecting the property of Jews.

"Does he know you're offering it to us, and at this price?"

"Naturally," the agent said in an offhand tone.

Pug arranged to meet the owner the next afternoon.

Herr Rosenthal, a grey-haired, highly dignified individual, met Pug at the house and invited him inside.

"It's a beautiful house," Pug said in German.

Rosenthal glanced round with wistful affection. "Thank you. We're fond of it."

"Mrs. Henry and I feel awkward about leasing it."

The Jew looked surprised. "If a lower rent would help—"

"Good Lord, no! It's an incredibly low rent already. But will you actually receive the money?"

"Of course. It's my house." Rosenthal spoke proudly.

"The agent said that some new ruling compels you to rent it."

"That won't affect you as tenant." Rosenthal dropped his voice. "It's an emergency decree, which will eventually be cancelled, I have been assured. Meantime this property could be sold at any time, without my consent. However, if there's a tenant with diplomatic immunity, that can't be done." He smiled. "Hence the modest rent, Herr Kommandant."

"May I ask why you don't sell out and leave Germany?"

The Jew blinked. "My family has a sugar-refining business here, more than one hundred years old. I am a native Berliner." He hesitated. "The Führer has done remarkable things for the country. It would be foolish to deny that. I have lived through other bad times." He spread his hands in a graceful, resigned gesture.

Victor Henry said, "Well, we love the house, but I don't want to take advantage of anybody's misfortune. How about a year's lease, with an option to renew?"

At once Rosenthal held out his hand. "We should have a drink on it, but we emptied the liquor cabinet when we left."

Within a few days, the Henrys were in the mansion. From an employment agency came a maid, a cook, and a houseman-chauffeur, all first-rate servants and—Pug assumed—all planted informers. He found no listening devices in the house, but he and Rhoda walked on the lawn to discuss touchy matters.

A couple of whirling weeks passed. The chargé d'affaires arranged receptions for the Henrys and Rhoda made a hit. She liked Berlin and its people. The Germans sensed this and warmed to her.

She was not blind to Nazi abuses. During her first walk in the Tiergarten, the signs on the benches saying JUDEN VERBOTEN nauseated her. Similar signs in restaurant windows made her demand to go elsewhere. Gradually she reacted less, but she kept insisting, even to prominent Nazis, that anti-Semitism was a blot on an otherwise lovely land.

Victor Henry kept off the Jewish topic. He decided instead to dig into a narrow but decisive aspect of Hitler's Third Reich—its military capacity. Was Nazi Germany as strong as the ever-marching columns in the streets suggested? Or was it all a show?

Meanwhile Rhoda's dinner parties increased in size and elegance. She invited the Grobkes, whose home was in Berlin, to one that included a French film actress and the conductor of the Berlin Philharmonic.

That evening Grobke, full of wine, reported that the captain of the Swinemünde navy yard was making difficulties about Pug's visit, but that he was going to push it through. "These shore-based bastards just live to create trouble," he said.

PAMELA TUDSBURY drove Pug Henry and her father to Swine-münde in a rented Mercedes. Tudsbury chatted on the way saying he now thought there might be no war. The British were at last dealing seriously with the Russians about a military alliance; they were turning out aeroplanes so fast that air parity, which they had lost in 1936, was in sight again; and their pledge to Poland showed Hitler that this time Chamberlain meant business.

Commander Grobke met them at the base gate, and when Pamela roared off to a hotel, Grobke took the two men for a long tour through the Swinemünde yard. Viewing the black sub-marines tied to the long piers, the clanking overhead cranes, the grease-blackened men in goggles and safety helmets, Victor Henry thought that he might have been in Britain, Japan, France, or the United States. The differences that counted, the crucial numbers and performance characteristics, were not discernible.

"Well," said Grobke, stopping at a dry dock where a U-boat lay. "This is my flagship. Since I can't have you aboard, Tudsbury, much as I would like to, I suppose we all part company here."

Pug caught the German's meaning. "Look, let's not stand on ceremony. If I can come aboard, I'll come and Tudsbury won't."

"Good Lord, yes," said the Englishman. "I've no business here anyway."

Grobke shook the Englishman's hand. "We want to be friends. We know you have the greatest navy in the world. These silly little boats can do a lot of damage for their size, that's all. One of my officers will drive you to your hotel."

The *U-46* looked much like an American submarine to Pug, although the cleanliness, polish, and order were unusual. "Smells pretty good," Pug said, as they passed the tiny galley, where cooks were preparing dinner.

"Would you care to eat aboard?" Grobke asked.

Pug said at once, "I'd be delighted."

In the U-boat's wardroom he felt completely at home. The four junior officers were shy and wary at first. However, they soon warmed to the American's compliments about the boat, and the joking of Grobke, who got into an excellent mood over the guest-feast of cabbage soup, boiled fresh salmon, roast pork, potato dumplings, and gooseberry *torten*. They told of their early training: exposure to cold and heat past the point of collapse; the cross-country run, wearing seventy-pound loads and gas masks. An officer emerged the better, they said, from such rigours.

The sun was setting when Pug and Grobke left the submarine. "So, Victor, I suppose you join your English friend now?"

"Not if you have any better ideas. I could stand a beer."

"Fine! I'll take you where the officers hang out."

They drove out through the yard. "Damn quiet after five o'clock," said Pug.

"Oh, yes. Dead. Always."

They went to a smoky, timbered cellar where young men in turtleneck sweaters sat at long tables, bellowing songs to a concertina. After a couple of beers, Pug joined in. He had no ear and sang badly off key, which struck Grobke as hilarious. "I swear to God, Victor," he said, laughing, "could anything be crazier than all this talk of war? I tell you, if they left it to the navy fellows on both sides, it could never happen."

The barmaid clacked two more foaming steins on the table. Grobke leaned forward intently. "Do you think the Führer would risk a war against England with seventy-four operational U-boats? No. But in eighteen months we'll have three hundred. Then England will think twice about making trouble." He winked. "Meantime, *Geben Sie gut Acht auf den Osten.* Watch the east."

· IN THE library of the Grünewald mansion, Victor Henry had been typing since midnight. It was now four in the morning. He stopped, yawned, and read over his official report.

COMBAT READINESS OF NAZI GERMANY: AN APPRAISAL

It is common knowledge that since 1933, even before the Hitler régime, Germany has been frankly and even boastfully rearming. Seven years ago this nation was still helpless compared with the Allies. The question is, to what extent has Hitler closed that gap? Two preliminary conclusions emerge:

(1) Nazi Germany has not closed the gap sufficiently to embark on a war with England and France.

Drawing on his own reading and inquiries, Pug presented comparisons of French, British, and German strength on land, sea, and in the air. He concluded that Germany remained inferior in every aspect, except for her air force; and that the edge in the air would rapidly melt away with the British speedup in making aeroplanes. As to land war, the figures proved that France alone could put a larger, better trained and equipped army in the field.

(2) The régime is not making an all-out effort to close the gap.

Hitler had not even put his country on a war-production basis. Pug described the desolate peace that fell over the Swinemünde navy yard after quitting time; there was not even a second shift for constructing U-boats, the key to German sea warfare. Grobke had claimed seventy-four operational submarines. Allied evaluations made it fifty-one. But even exaggerating, as he would to a foreign intelligence officer, Grobke had not gone as high as a hundred.

Then came the crucial passage, which he anxiously read over:

What follows gets into prognostication, and so may be judged frivolous. However, all the evidence indicates to me that Hitler is negotiating a military alliance with the Soviet Union.

Listing arguments in support of his idea, Victor Henry acknowledged that none of it added up to hard intelligence; nor did it impress the professionals at the embassy. The Nazi movement, they insisted, was built on fear of bolshevism and a pledge to destroy it. Reconciliation between the two systems was unthinkable.

Pug maintained, nevertheless, that the move was inevitable. Hitler was far out on a limb in his threats against Poland, but hadn't the combat readiness for a world war. A Russian alliance was a way out. If Russia were to give the Germans a free hand in Poland, the British guarantee would become meaningless. Neither the French nor the British could possibly come to Poland's aid in time to avert a quick conquest.

A week later, Admiral Preble read the report and sent one page of extracts to President Roosevelt. The Nazi-Soviet pact broke on the world on the twenty-third of August, one of the most stunning surprises in all history. On the twenty-fourth, Preble received the page back from the White House. The President had scrawled at the bottom, in strong thick pen strokes: "Let me have V. Henry's service record. FDR."

5

The announcement of the pact shrieked at Byron and Natalie from the news placards in the busy Rome airport. They had set out from Siena before dawn and driven down along the Apennines in golden Italian sunlight. With Natalie at his side, Byron was going to Warsaw in the highest of spirits. Until he saw the bulletins.

At the first kiosk he bought a sheaf of newspapers. The German and Italian papers shrilled that this great diplomatic coup had ended the war danger. The Paris and London headlines were big, black, and frightened.

In a crowded airport restaurant, while they lunched on cannelloni and white wine, Natalie astonished him by talking of going on. To proceed into a country that might soon be invaded by Germans struck Byron as almost mad.

But Natalie argued that they would be in and out of Poland in three weeks, and that even in a war, an American passport spelled safety. And she had promised Leslie Slote.

This last did not cheer Byron. He sat slouched in his chair, contemplating her across the red-and-white checked cloth. The plane was departing in an hour for Zagreb, on the first leg of their flight.

She stared back at him. "Look," she said, "I can understand that for you it's no longer an excursion. I'll go on by myself."

"I suggest you telephone Slote first."

"Nonsense. I'll never get a call through to Warsaw."

"Try."

"All right," she snapped.

Byron pulled Natalie through the crowd in the long-distance office. "That's the number of the American embassy," Byron said, smiling at the operator, "and it's life and death."

He had an odd smile, half-melancholy, half-gay, and the Italian girl warmed to it. She plugged, and argued in German and Italian for ten minutes or more. All at once she nodded violently, pointing to a booth.

Natalie came out red-faced and scowling. "He told me I'd be insane to go on. Our diplomats are burning their papers . . . ."

"I'm sorry, Natalie, but it's what I expected."

She turned on him. "Let's see the plane tickets."

"We can get refunds." He handed her the envelope.

She extracted her ticket and gave the envelope back. "You get a refund. They burned papers before Munich too. Imagine a world war over Danzig! Who even cares about Danzig?"

"But the embassy will be swamped. You won't see much of Slote."

"Then I'll do my sight-seeing alone. I want to see Warsaw, and I have relatives in Medzice. It must be about time for me to check in."

He held out his hand. "Oh shut up, Natalie," he said. "I'll check us both in. Let's have the ticket."

She gave him a playful smile. "Well! Listen to Briny Henry being masterful. The thing is, darling, if anything does go wrong, I don't ever want to feel I dragged you into trouble."

It was the first time she had—however casually—used a term of endearment to him. Byron pulled the ticket from her hand.

THE SCHEDULED eight-hour trip lasted a day and a half. No connections worked. They spent the night on benches in the terminal at Budapest. At Warsaw, their shabby plane turned right around and took off, jam-packed with people fleeing Poland.

Byron ploughed his way through throngs of refugees, found a telephone, and called the embassy. Slote appeared at the airport within the hour in a shiny blue Chevrolet. They piled into it and set off for the city.

Slote reached a caressing hand to Natalie's face. The intimate gesture hurt Byron. He slumped glumly in the back seat. "I'm thrilled to see you, darling, though you're stark mad," Slote said. "Things are looking better tonight. There's reliable word from Sweden that following England's guarantee to Poland, Hitler's calling off his invasion. Don't figure on staying long, though."

"I thought maybe a week," Natalie said. "Then we can go on down to Kraków, visit Medzice, and fly back to Rome."

"Medzice! You *are* insane. Forget it, Natalie."

"Why should I? Aaron said I should visit the family. That's where we're from."

"Don't you understand, darling, that half a million German soldiers are poised at the Czech border at this moment, *only forty miles* from Medzice?"

When Natalie went up in the hotel lift, Slote said to Byron, "This Kraków trip is dangerous nonsense. I'm going to get you on the earliest flight to Rome I can. Don't tell Natalie tonight, though. She'll become unmanageable."

"O.K. You know her better than I do."

IN THE hotel dining room there was no trace of a war scare.

"Sorry I'm late. It's the Jews," Slote apologized when they sat down. "They're storming the embassy. Not that I blame them."

They ate amazingly well. When the waitress put down plates of thick Polish ham Natalie laughed and said they almost made her feel guilty. For the first time Byron dared ask her about her religion.

"It's hardly my religion. I dropped it before I was eleven. It grieved my father, but I just couldn't keep up flummery that made no sense to me."

She cut and ate the rich pink meat with no visible remorse. Later she and Slote got up to dance. Byron thought Slote looked more like her uncle than her sweetheart, steering her clumsily round the floor. But Natalie's closed eyes and touching cheek weren't the ways of a niece.

NATALIE telephoned Byron in his room at seven one morning, after they had stayed up till past three touring nightclubs with Slote. "Hi, Briny!" From her chipper note, she might have had ten hours' sleep. "This is playing sort of dirty, but I have two seats on a plane to Kraków at eleven. If you'd rather just stay here, O.K."

Half-awake, Byron said, "What? Slote's got us on the plane to Rome tomorrow, and those seats were mighty hard to come by."

"I know. I'll leave him a note. If you come, we can go straight to Rome from Kraków, Saturday or Sunday, after I visit my family. Byron! Have you fallen back asleep?"

Byron was calculating the advantages of leaving Warsaw and Slote against these harebrained travel arrangements. He said, "Natalie, this would be a damned wild excursion."

"Why? I'll probably never have another chance to see where my parents were born. Anyway, you don't have to come."

"Well, I'll have breakfast with you."

Natalie was waiting outside the restaurant. She wore a bright Polish dress and had combed her hair down, as the Warsaw women did. Byron joined her, carrying his suitcase. "You're coming!" she said. "Honestly, Briny, you're as goofy as I am."

After breakfast, a taxi took them to the airport. The plane was a real surprise: a squat blue biplane, faded and patched, with three motors. It took off with bumps and shudders and after about an hour and a half they landed in a sunny field. On either side of the tarred landing-strip kerchiefed peasant women were mowing hay.

"Leave it to me," Natalie said. "I can hack out Yiddish after a fashion." She had telegraphed ahead, but had not mentioned the plane, scarcely expecting the wire to arrive.

A brown-bearded Jew in a long dark coat drew near, touching his wide-brimmed hat. "You excuse? Americans? Jastrow?"

"Why, yes," Natalie said. And in Yiddish, "You are Berel?"

"Yes, yes," he said, smiling. "Jochanan Berel Jastrow." He had surprisingly blue eyes with an almost Tartar slant.

After a parley in Yiddish, Berel led them to a rust-pitted orange Packard on the other side of a shed, and they set off. Swerving to avoid a pig or cow, the car bounced along a tar road through villages of thatched log houses. In the sun-flooded fields, women and men toiled with hand implements or horsedrawn ploughs.

"Hitler a big bluff," Berel spoke up in English. "Strong pipple, the Polish. No war."

Medzice was a cluster of houses on narrow cobbled streets sloping down to a winding river. The villagers were almost all Jews and at least half the houses seemed to be inhabited by Jastrows. They swarmed on Natalie and Byron and marched them joyously from home to home. On table after table appeared wine, cake, tea, sweets, vodka, and fish, which there was no polite way to refuse. The visit of the two Americans was obviously one of the grandest events in Medzice since the World War.

What a world! Byron thought. No sight or sound to connect it with the twentieth century. Yet Natalie Jastrow was only one generation removed from this place, and the urbane Dr. Aaron Jastrow had lived here until his fifteenth year!

The sleeping arrangements that night were as novel as everything else. Byron was quartered at the home of the rabbi. The house's second bedroom contained three beds. In this room there were already five tittering girls. After a lot of blushing and laughter Byron ended up sleeping on the floor of the parlour. The rabbi gave him a feather mattress, and he scarcely even remembered falling asleep. But there he was when Berel Jastrow shook him.

"*Der Deutsch*," the Jew said urgently. "The Germans."

Byron sat up. "The Germans? What about them?"

"They come."

6

Shortly before 6.00 a.m. a ring from the embassy woke Victor Henry. The chargé was summoning an urgent staff meeting on the outbreak of the war. It was no great surprise, but all the same, Pug was excited and moved. It wasn't yet *his* war, the one he had trained for all his life, but he was fairly sure it would be.

In the library he switched on the radio. A strident voice was describing the Polish "attack" at Gleiwitz, which, according to the broadcast, had sent the Wehrmacht rolling two million strong into Poland "in self-defence". Radio Berlin's propaganda no longer surprised Pug.

Rhoda came yawning in, tying her negligee. "Well! So he really went and did it. We're not going to get in it, are we?"

"I'm not even sure England and France will go to bat."

"How about the children, Pug?"

"Well, Warren and Madeline are no problem. The word is that Italy won't fight, so Byron should be O.K., too."

Rhoda said slowly, "World War Two . . . it has a funny ring. What happens now to our dinner for that visiting tycoon? What's his name?"

"Dr. Kirby. He may not get here now, Rhoda."

"Dear, please find out. I have guests coming, you know."

"I'll do my best."

The staff meeting was sombre and short. The chargé urged everyone to preserve a tone of neutrality, for the lives of a lot of English and French people caught in Germany might depend on it. After the meeting, Pug told his yeoman to try to track down Dr. Palmer Kirby, the electrical engineer from Colorado who bore a "very important" designation from the Bureau of Ordnance.

Alistair Tudsbury telephoned. "Hello! Would you like to hear the bad man explain all to the Reichstag? I can get you into the Press box. I owe you something for that glimpse of Swinemünde."

"You don't owe me anything, but I'll sure come."

"Good. This is my last story from Berlin, I have my marching papers and we're leaving directly after the speech. Unless we get interned. Well, Pam will call for you at two."

The yeoman came in and handed Pug a telegram. He opened it and got a shock: DO YOU KNOW WHEREABOUTS YOUR SON BYRON AND MY NIECE NATALIE. PLEASE WIRE OR CALL. It was signed AARON JASTROW, with an address and telephone number in Siena.

"Here," Pug said to the yeoman and handed him the telegram, "Try to get a call through to this man in Siena."

He decided not to tell Rhoda. Unable to work, he was about to leave for lunch when the telephone rang. He heard multilingual jabber and then a cultured American voice. "Commander Henry? Aaron Jastrow. It's very good of you to call."

"Dr. Jastrow, I thought I'd better tell you immediately that I had no idea Byron and your niece weren't with you."

"I hesitated to wire, but I thought you could help locate them. Two weeks ago they went to Warsaw."

"*Warsaw!*"

"Yes, Natalie went to visit a friend in our embassy. The second secretary, Leslie Slote. It was risky, I guess, but she has a will of her own. Byron volunteered to go with her. That's really why I refuse to worry. He's a very capable young man."

Pug, dazed by the news, still found pleasure in this good word

for Byron. Over the years he had not heard many. "Thanks. I'll
get on to it right away. If you get any word, let me know."

"I hope we'll meet one day," Jastrow said. "It would give me
pleasure to know Byron's father."

PAMELA was waiting for him in front of the embassy near the
line of sad-looking Jews—would-be refugees—that stretched
around the block. "Well," Pug said, "so the little tramp went."

She gave him a flattered look for remembering. "Didn't he ever!
Here's our car. Directly after the speech we are flying on to
Copenhagen."

She drove in nervous zigzags through side streets to get round
a long convoy of tanks. "I'm sorry to see you go," Pug said. "I'll
miss your fireball driving. Where to next?"

"My guess is the U.S.A. It'll be the number one spot now."

"Pamela, don't you have a young man in London, or several,
who object to your being so much on the move?"

The girl flushed. "Oh, not at the moment. And Talky needs me
since his eyes have got so bad. I like to travel, and—bless my soul!
Look to your left. Don't be too obvious about it."

Beside them, halted at the traffic light, Hermann Göring sat at
the wheel of an open two-seater. He wore a doubled-breasted
business suit, and the broad brim of his hat was snapped down in
an out-of-date, somewhat gangsterish American style. The light
changed and as the open car darted forward the policeman saluted
and Göring laughed and waved his hand.

"How easy it would have been to shoot him," Pamela said.

Pug said, "The Nazis puzzle me. Their security precautions are
mighty loose, even round Hitler."

"The Germans adore them. The way Hitler moves around shows
how solidly they are for him."

Ahead of them Tudsbury stood on a corner, waving. His English
tweed was far too heavy for the weather, and he had a green velour
hat. "Hello, my dear fellow! Pam, be back at this corner at four and
wait, won't you?"

A young German in a business suit took them past SS men up to
the crowded Press balcony of the Kroll Opera House, which the

333

Nazis were using for state meetings until Hitler's new Reichstag was finished. The stylized gold eagle perched on a swastika behind the podium, with gold rays shooting out to cover the whole wall, had an air of theatrical impermanence.

The deputies were streaming to their seats. Göring was already on the stage, in a sky-blue heavily medalled uniform with flaring buff lapels. Pug had heard of the man's quick changes: now he saw one. He stood with feet spread apart, hands on hips, talking gravely with a knot of generals and party men, then took his seat. Hitler simply walked in, holding the manuscript of his speech in a red leather folder.

Pug thought the Führer spoke badly. His speech rehashed the iniquity of the Versailles Treaty, his own unending efforts for peace, and the bloody belligerence of the Poles. He shouted that 1918 would not recur, that this time Germany would triumph or go down fighting. In a while he'd worked up to the flamboyant gestures, and the Germans sat with the round eyes of children watching a magician.

Pug's mind turned to Byron, somewhere in Poland, a speck of unimportance in this big show.

WHEN PUG got back to the embassy after saying good-bye to the Tudsburys, he found a man in a pepper-and-salt suit sitting in his outer office. When he stood up, Pug saw that he was six feet three or so. "Commander Henry? I'm Palmer Kirby," he said. "If you're busy just throw me out."

"Not at all. Welcome. How'd you get here?"

"Well, it took some doing. I had to dodge around through Belgium and Norway." Kirby was an ugly man, with clever wrinkled eyes and a sad look. Pug sized him up as a serious fellow out to get a job done.

The yeoman said, "Sir, two priority messages on your desk."

"Very well. Come in, Dr. Kirby."

The first message had been sent that day from Warsaw: BYRON HENRY NATALIE JASTROW SCHEDULED LEAVE KRAKOW TODAY FOR BUCHAREST AND ROME. ENDEAVOURING CONFIRM DEPARTURE. SLOTE.

This dispatch gave Pug a qualm. Radio Berlin was claiming a

victorious thrust towards Kraków after an air bombardment. The other message was from the chargé: "Please see me at once."

Victor Henry apologized to Kirby and walked down the hall to the chargé's office. "You're wanted at the State Department," the chargé said. "You're to proceed to Washington by fastest available transportation, stay not more than one week, and then return here. You sent in a report, I understand, on the combat readiness of Nazi Germany. That may have something to do with it. Anyway, it seems you're to pack a toothbrush and go."

Pug stood. "Right. I'll leave tonight. What's the late word on England and France?"

"Chamberlain's addressing Parliament tonight. My guess is the war will be on before you get back."

Pug found Dr. Kirby, long legs sprawled, reading a German industrial journal. "Sorry, Dr. Kirby, but I'll have to turn you over to Colonel Forrest, our military attaché. I'm leaving town for a week. Can you give me an idea of what you're after?"

Dr. Kirby handed him a typewritten sheet.

"No problem," Pug said, scanning it. "I know most of these people. I imagine Colonel Forrest does, too. Now, Mrs. Henry has planned a dinner for Tuesday evening. As a matter of fact"—he tapped the sheet—"Dr. Witten will be one of the guests."

"Won't your wife prefer to call it off? I'm not really much on dinner parties."

"Neither am I, but a German's a different person in his office from the one he is after a few glasses of wine." Pug smiled. "So dinners are useful."

Driving home, Pug thought about how to handle Rhoda and whether to tell her that Byron was missing. She was not at home. By the time she got back, he was strapping shut his suitcases. "Now what on earth?" she said breezily. Her hair was whirled and curled. They had been invited to an opera party that evening.

"Come out in the garden." When they were well away from the house, he told her about Washington. "If the Clippers keep flying, I should be back by the fifteenth."

"Oh, Lord. When do you go? Tomorrow?"

"No, they've got me on a plane to Rotterdam at eight tonight."

"Tonight!" Vexation distorted Rhoda's face. "You mean we don't even get to go to the opera? Oh, damn! I'm not going unescorted. And what about that Kirby fellow? How can I entertain a person I haven't even met?"

"The opera may not be on. But I'd like you to go ahead with the Kirby thing. BuOrd wants the red carpet out for him."

They were sitting on a marble bench in the formal garden. Rhoda said in a calmer tone, "All right. I've been planning cocktails out here. It'll be nice at that. Sorry you'll miss it."

"Nobody in this world puts on dinners like yours."

Rhoda laughed. "Oh, well. You'll soon be back. And you can telephone Warren. I'm glad Byron's up in the Italian hills. *He'll* be all right, unless he marries that Jewish girl. But he won't. He seems crazier than he is." She put her hand in her husband's. Clasping her hand tight, Pug decided not to upset her with the news of Byron's disappearance.

7

Byron was changing a tyre by the roadside when he was strafed. He and Natalie were out of Kraków and heading for Warsaw in a rust-pitted taxi, together with Berel Jastrow, the bearded little taxi driver, and his inconveniently fat wife.

Berel had somehow obtained two train tickets from Kraków to Warsaw and had shipped off his wife and twelve-year-old daughter. But air traffic was finished and he could not arrange to get Byron and Natalie safely out of Poland. He had therefore asked his poor relation, the taxi driver Yankel, to take them all to Warsaw. Yankel was willing; and his wife merely insisted on bringing their bedding and kitchenware, roped to the car top.

They spent the first night in a town where Jastrow had friends, and were off again at dawn. The narrow roads were filling with people on foot, and horsedrawn wagons piled with household goods. Marching soldiers now and then forced the car off the road. The clear weather, the smell of the ripening corn, made the travellers feel good. There were no combatants in sight on the road where they'd stopped to change a tyre, when a lone aeroplane dived from the sky, making a hard stuttering noise. It flew so low that Byron could see the painted numbers, the swastika, the clumsily fixed wheels. The bullets fell on people, livestock, and the household goods in the carts. Byron felt a burning and stinging in one ear. He was not aware of toppling into the dirt.

He heard a child crying and opened his eyes. The blood on his clothes surprised him—big, bright stains—and he felt a warm trickle on his face. Natalie knelt beside him, sponging his head with a sodden red handkerchief. Across the road, the child screamed while a Pole in ragged clothes patted her head.

"Are you all right, Byron? How do you feel?" Natalie's face was dirty and smeared with Byron's blood.

"Sort of dizzy, but O.K." He got to his feet. "How does it look?"

"I don't know, your hair is so thick. But it's bleeding a lot. We'd better get you to a hospital and have it stitched."

Byron, followed by Natalie and Berel, walked to the crying girl, whose mother lay with staring eyes. She had caught a bullet in the forehead. Berel spoke to the father, who held the little girl close. Yankel's wife gave the child an apple. She bit into it and her sobbing died away. The man sat down by his dead wife and began to mutter, crossing himself.

Natalie helped Byron into the car, and they drove on. A little farther on there was a good-sized town, where Jastrow told the authorities about the wounded on the highway. At the hospital, Byron's head was stitched by a fat old doctor.

IT TOOK them two days to complete the journey to Warsaw. While it was happening, it seemed to Byron a saga that he would be telling his grandchildren, if he lived through it. But so much happened afterwards that the memory of the three-hundred-kilometre drive soon faded. However, he always remembered how sick he was, and the embarrassment of his frequent excursions into the bushes; and Natalie's unshakeable good cheer as she got hungrier, dirtier, and wearier.

They arrived on the outskirts of Warsaw in the chill dawn,

crawling among hundreds of horsedrawn wagons. The buildings cluttered against the pink northeast horizon looked like the heavenly Jerusalem. At the embassy, sandbags lined the stucco walls, and on the red tile roof an enormous American flag had been painted. "Go in quickly," Berel said to Natalie in Yiddish. "Come and see me later if you can."

When Byron said good-bye, Berel clasped his hand and looked earnestly into his face. "Very much tank you," he said. "America save Poland, yes, Byron? Save de vorld."

Byron laughed. "That's a big order, Berel."

A marine sentry telephoned from a metal box, and Slote came running down the broad steps. "God! Am I ever glad to see you two!" He threw an arm around Natalie, staring at Byron's dirty bandage. "What the devil? Are you all right?"

"Fine. What's the news? Are France and Britain fighting?"

"They finally declared war Sunday, although they've not done anything since but drop leaflets." He led them both into the ambassador's office, explaining that Washington had ordered the ambassador and most of his staff out of Poland when the bombing began.

Over a wonderful breakfast of ham and eggs, their first hot food in days, they described their journey. Slote was appalled. "You two are incredible. Incredibly lucky, too."

"And incredibly filthy," Natalie said. "What do we do now?"

"Well, you're just stuck here, my love. The Swedes and the Swiss are trying to arrange a safe-conduct for neutrals. Meantime you'll have to dodge bombs like the rest of us. I'll cable Byron's father via Stockholm, and he'll pass the word to Siena."

"I'm dying for a bath," Natalie said.

Slote took keys from his pocket. "I'm staying here at the embassy. Take my apartment. It's nearby and on the ground floor, which is the safest."

"Do you mind," Natalie said, "if Byron stays with me?" Both men showed surprise. "Oh, for crying out loud." She turned to Slote. "He's like a loyal kid brother, sort of."

"It's up to you," Slote said, without enthusiasm. "There's a sofa in the sitting room."

SLIVERS of sunlight through the closed shutters made Slote's flat an oasis of peaceful half-gloom. "Want to wash first?" Natalie said. "Once I get in that tub there'll be no moving me. Maybe you should find a hospital first, and get your head examined."

The phrase struck them as funny and they laughed and laughed. "Well, while we still both stink," Natalie gasped, "come here." She threw her arms round him and kissed him. "You damned fool, going to Medzice to visit some dopey Jews."

"My head's all right," Byron said. The touch of the girl's mouth on his was like flowers and birdsong. "I'll clean up first."

Half an hour later, an unmistakable wailing scream sounded outside. Byron, dozing on the sofa, snapped awake and took binoculars from his suitcase. Natalie emerged from the bathroom in Slote's dressing gown. "Do we have to go to the cellar?"

"I'll have a look." From the outside door he spotted big, black planes, showing swastikas.

Behind him Natalie said, "Is that bombing? Those thumps?"

The thumps came nearer. They sat on the sofa, smoking cigarettes. "It's sort of like a summer electric storm coming towards you," Natalie said.

A distant whistling noise grew louder, a crash jarred the room, and glass broke somewhere. There were two more close explosions; then from the street came shouts and screams, and the grumble of falling walls. "Briny, shall we run for the cellar?"

"Better sit tight."

The thumps went on for a while, some so close they could be felt in the floor, in the teeth. Then they died off. Outside, bells clanged, running feet trampled on the cobblestones, men yelled. Byron pulled aside curtains, opened a window, and pointed at two smashed, burning houses down the street.

"Those German bastards," Natalie said. "Oh my God, Briny. Look!" Men were carrying limp figures out of the clouds of smoke. One held a child dangling in each arm. "Can't we help?"

"There must be volunteer squads that neutrals can work in. Nursing, rescue, cleanup. I'll find out."

She turned away. Barefoot, wrapped in the oversize dressing gown, her face shiny with tears, Natalie looked younger and much less formidable than usual. "I got you into it. That keeps eating at me. Your parents must be sick with worry—"

"My people are navy. As for me, I'm having fun."

"Byron! People are dying out there. You saw those kids."

"Look, all I meant was I wouldn't have missed this for anything."

"It's just such a stupid, callous thing to say." She hitched the dressing gown about her closer and stalked to the bathroom.

8

After the blaring pageantry and war fever of Nazi Germany, coming back to Washington was to Pug a bit like coming out of a technicolour movie into a quiet street. Here, where the Capitol dome and the Washington Monument shimmered in ninety-degree heat, the invasion of Poland seemed as remote as Mars.

He sat in the Army and Navy Club breakfasting on kippers and scrambled eggs. His arrival the day before had proved a puzzling letdown. The man in the German section of the State Department had told him to expect a call in the morning; nothing more.

"Well, well, our cookie-pushing friend!" Grinning down at him were three classmates whom Pug had not seen for years. They joined him and began asking naïve questions about the European war. Pug was trying to explain why the Germans were winning in Poland when a page boy called him to the telephone.

"Commander Henry? I'm Carton. Captain Russell Carton. I think we were briefly at the War College together."

"That's right, Captain. 1937." Pug suppressed his astonishment: Russell Carton was President Roosevelt's naval aide.

"When shall I pick you up? Our appointment's at noon."

"How far do we have to go?"

"Just around the corner. The White House. You're seeing the President. . . . Hello. Are you there?"

"Yes, sir. Do I get a briefing on this?"

"Not that I know of. Wear dress whites. Eleven-thirty?"

"Aye aye, sir."

He went back to his table. The others tactfully asked no questions. One of them said, "Pug, don't you have a boy in

Pensacola? I'm flying down there day after tomorrow. Come along."

"If I can, thanks. I'll call you."

Pug donned his whites and ribbons and sat in the lobby until a sailor came in and called his name. He rode the few blocks to the White House in a navy Chevrolet, dazedly trying to keep up chitchat with Captain Carton. Once there, Carton led him through the broad public rooms, along corridors, up staircases, and into a small room. "Wait here a moment," he said. The moment lasted twenty-seven minutes. Pug paced, sat down, and paced again. He was hoping the President wouldn't remember him.

In 1918, as a very cocky Assistant Secretary of the Navy, Franklin Roosevelt had crossed to Europe on a destroyer. The ship's officers, including Ensign Henry, had snickered at the handsome young man with the famous name who made a great show of using nautical terms and bounding up ladders like a sea-dog.

One morning Ensign Henry had done his usual workout on the forecastle and then had hosed himself down on the well deck. Unfortunately the ship was pitching steeply. The hose got away from him and spouted down a hatchway just as Roosevelt was coming topside in a gold-buttoned blazer, white flannel trousers, and straw hat. Pug had endured a fierce chewing out by his captain and the dripping Assistant Secretary.

Now a door opened. "Go on in, Pug," Captain Carton said.

The President waved from behind the desk, then held out his hand. "Hello there! Glad to see you!" The warm, commanding aristocratic voice jarred Pug with its very familiarity. "Drop your bonnet on the desk, Commander, and have a chair." A grey-faced man slouched in an armchair near the President. "By the way, this is the Secretary of Commerce, Harry Hopkins."

Roosevelt seemed unchanged from twenty years ago; he was the same towering man, and a trace remained in his upthrust jaw of the youthful conceit that had made the destroyer ensigns snicker. He looked archly at Victor Henry. "Well, Pug, have you learned yet how to hang on to a salt-water hose at sea?"

"Oh, gawd, sir." Pug put a hand to his face in mock despair.

"I've heard about your memory, but I hoped you'd forgotten *that*."

The President laughed. "Not on your life. Now that I'm Commander-in-Chief of the United States Navy, Pug Henry, what have you got to say for yourself?"

"Sir, the quality of mercy is mightiest in the mightiest."

"Oho! *Very* good, Pug. You're forgiven." Roosevelt's face turned serious. "Well, what's going on in Germany, Pug? Tell me about it from your end."

Victor Henry described the atmosphere in Berlin, the playing down of the war by the Nazis, the taciturn calm he had observed in the Berliners. The President kept looking at Hopkins, who had a long, meagre face but eyes which were thoughtful and electrically alive. Then Hopkins asked, in a soft voice, "How well, really, do you know the Germans?"

"Not at all well, Mr. Secretary. They're hard to make out. But in the end there's only one thing you have to know about them."

"Yes? What's that?"

"How to lick them."

Roosevelt gave the hearty guffaw of a man who loved life. "A warmonger, eh? Are you suggesting we ought to get into it?"

"Not unless we have to, Mr. President."

"Oh, we'll have to," Roosevelt said.

This struck Pug as an amazing indiscretion. The Press was full of the President's ringing declarations that America would stay out of the war.

Roosevelt went blandly on with a compliment about Pug's report on Germany's combat readiness. "How did you foresee that pact with Stalin? Everybody here was stupefied."

"I guess somebody was bound to make that wild guess, Mr. President. It happened to be me."

"Actually, Pug, we also had some warning. There was a leak—never mind where. Trouble was, nobody here was much inclined to believe it." He looked at Hopkins with a touch of mischief. "That's always the problem with intelligence, isn't it?"

Hopkins glanced at his watch. "Mr. President, the Secretary and Senator Pittman are on their way over."

"Already? Well, Pug, this has been grand. If there's anything else you think I should know, how about dropping me a line? I mean that."

At this grotesque proposal for bypassing the chain of command Pug could only blink and nod. The President caught his expression. "Nothing official, of course," he said quickly. "But I liked that thing you wrote. I could just see that submarine base emptying out at five o'clock. Sometimes one little thing like that can tell you more than a report umpteen pages long."

"Yes, Mr. President," Victor Henry said.

"Oh, by the way, here's a suggestion that's just come to my desk, Pug, for helping the Allies. Suppose we offer to buy the *Queen Mary* and the *Normandie*, to use them for evacuating Americans from Europe? It would give Britain and France some much needed dollars, and we'd have two fine ships. How about it?"

"Mr. President, I'd say those ships are major war assets and they'd be insane to sell them. They're the fastest vessels for their tonnage afloat; they can outrun any submarine, and their troop-carrying capacity would be fantastic."

Roosevelt nodded and held out his hand. "Keep in touch, now."

"Aye aye, sir."

Captain Carton met Pug in the anteroom. "Well, that must have gone all right. You went way past the scheduled ten minutes."

Pug hoped he had said something illuminating enough to justify the public money spent on his trip. "What now?" he asked.

Carton smiled. "Well, you're not scheduled here again, but maybe you should check in with CNO." He reached into a breast pocket. "This just came from the State Department."

It was an official dispatch envelope. Pug ripped it open and read the flimsy pink message form: FORWARDED. BYRON HENRY SAFE WELL WARSAW. AWAITING EVACUATION ALL NEUTRALS NOW UNDER NEGOTIATION GERMAN GOVERNMENT. SLOTE.

"HELLO, Dad!" When Pug's plane landed at the Pensacola airfield, Warren was waiting. His firm grip and radiant face expressed all Warren's pride in what he was doing.

Driving his father to the bachelor officers' quarters, he never stopped talking. The flight school was in a buzz, he said, since

Hitler invaded Poland. The number of students had been tripled, and the course cut to six months. He was dying to make Squadron Five, which was fighter training. Finally he remembered to ask his father about the family.

"Ye gods, Briny's in *Warsaw*?"

"That's right." Pug studied his young flier. It was going to be a tough few years, he thought, for men with grown sons.

Warren told his father that Congressman Isaac Lacouture had invited them to dinner at the beach club. Before running for Congress, Lacouture had been chairman of the Gulf Lumber and Paper Company, the biggest firm in Pensacola. "He's anxious to meet you," Warren said.

"Why has he taken such a shine to you?"

"Well, his daughter and I have sort of hit it off." With an easy grin, Warren parted from his father in the BOQ lobby.

At his first sight of Janice Lacouture, Pug decided against mentioning Pamela Tudsbury to Warren. What chance had the mousy English girl against this radiant, assured American? Tall, blonde, with a striking figure, she was one of the belles of Pensacola. She greeted Pug with just enough deference to acknowledge that he was Warren's father, and just enough sparkle to hint that he was an attractive man himself.

Waves broke over the club terrace and splattered heavy spray on the glass wall of the dining room, making the candlelit dinner seem the cozier. Pug never did get clear who all the ten people at table were, but Congressman Lacouture was the one who obviously mattered. "How long are you going to be here, Commander Henry?" he asked.

Pug said he had to leave in the morning.

"Well, I suppose I'll be hurrying up to Washington myself for this special session. What do *you* think of Roosevelt's revising the Neutrality Act? How bad is the situation, actually?"

"I think Poland's going to fall fast, if you call that bad."

Warren said, "I don't see how his revision would weaken our neutrality, sir. That cash-and-carry policy simply means anybody can buy stuff who has the money and the ships. Hitler included."

Lacouture smiled at him. "That's the Administration line, my

346

boy. Except we all know that the Allies have the ships and the money, and the Germans have neither."

"But nobody stopped Hitler from building a merchant marine," Warren came back. "He piled up aggressive weapons instead."

"Warren's absolutely right," Janice said.

"What you kids don't understand," Lacouture said, "is that Roosevelt thinks he's got a mission to save the world from Hitler. Now I say Hitler is just another European politician, a little dirtier than the rest. The way for us to save the world is to stay out of the war, and to be ready to rebuild a decent world when it's over."

When dinner ended, Janice and Warren left the club together. Victor Henry found himself alone with Lacouture over coffee and brandy. "Your Warren's quite a boy," the congressman said.

"Well, thanks. Your girl is beyond words."

Lacouture puffed at a cigar. "No doubt you're glad to see Warren carrying on the navy tradition. Wouldn't want to see him shift over into business, or anything like that?"

"Warren goes his own way, Congressman."

Next morning Warren exulted all the way to his father's room in the BOQ. The assignments had been posted and he'd made Squadron Five, while some of the hottest student pilots had not.

His father listened, smiling, remembering the day at Annapolis when he had drawn his first battleship duty. He said at last that it was time for him to leave.

Warren glanced at his watch. "Gosh, already?" He threw an arm around his father's shoulders. "I feel mixed up. I'm damn sorry to see you go, and I've never been happier in my life."

9

From the German viewpoint, the invasion was proceeding merrily. All over Poland, mile after mile of helmeted Germans marched along, or rode in trucks, or cars, while out ahead crawled the new tank companies, the famous panzers, firing their big shells.

The panzers arrived at Warsaw on September 9. On the tenth the supreme German commander was writing that the war was over. But on the seventeenth Warsaw still stood. Luftwaffe bombers were making unopposed runs over the city, which was also ringed by howitzers. And still Radio Warsaw played Chopin's "Polonaise".

Dawn of September 17 found Leslie Slote at the ambassador's big desk, a pipe clenched in his teeth, drafting a dispatch to the State Department. He was an able and exceptionally clever man, but at the moment he was in the wrong job, because he was a coward. He did not look or act like one, but ever since the first bombs had fallen on Warsaw he had been in a black panic. Every sounding of an air-raid alarm all but deprived him of the power to think. In a way, being in charge was a help. It looked proper for him to move out of his apartment into the embassy, to stay there and set an example of strict compliance with air raid rules. Nobody guessed his trouble.

He was trying to retain the urgency of his dispatch, while editing out traces of his own private hysteria, when there was a knock at the door and Byron walked in.

"I brought the water." Byron's clothes were covered with brick dust and soot. "It's broad daylight. Shall I open the curtains?"

"O.K." Together they pulled back the heavy curtains. "Such smoke! Are there that many fires?"

"God, yes. Didn't you see the sky last night? All red and smoky, like Dante's Inferno. It's the water problem that's going to lick them. Over on Walewska they're trying to put out two huge fires with shovels and sand."

"They should have accepted the German offer yesterday," Slote said. "They'd have had half a city left. How on earth did you fetch the water? Did you find some gasoline for the truck?"

Byron shook his head and collapsed on the leather couch. "Gasoline's finished. I scouted around most of the night till I found a cart and a horse. The U.S. government owes me the one hundred and seventy-five dollars I paid for the cart."

"You'll get paid, of course. Do you want breakfast?"

"I'm not sure I have the energy to chew," Byron said, closing his eyes. "Where's Natalie?" he mumbled. "At the hospital?"

"I daresay."

When the telephone rang, Byron was asleep. The mayor's office was calling; Mayor Starzynski was on his way to the embassy to discuss a sudden urgent development. Excited, Slote phoned the marine sentry at the gate to admit him. This must be news: safe-conduct for foreigners out of Warsaw, or perhaps imminent surrender!

Mayor Starzynski arrived shortly; this thickset, moustached man, whose broadcasts were doing more than anything else to keep Warsaw fighting, looked fresh and combative. Yet he could hardly have been sleeping two hours a night.

"Who is that?" the mayor said, pointing at the couch.

"Just an exhausted boy. He doesn't understand Polish."

Starzynski sat down. "Well. Are your people all right? Is there anything we can do for you?"

"We're fine. We're awed by the stand Warsaw is making."

"Yes? We drove them back in the north last night." The mayor was red with pride. "You'll see. Soon we'll have a battle line again, not a siege. Unfortunately the other news is not so good." The mayor paused. "The Soviet Union invaded our country at dawn. Russians are pouring over the border by the millions! We have been using all our forces to hold off the Germans, and now there is nothing to oppose the Russians." He slapped a paper on the desk. "I have a message for your President. We want to know what we can hope for. The highest speed is crucial."

Slote scanned the dispatch: the pathetic rhetoric of appeal. "I'm not sure how fast I can get this out, sir. I've been encountering long delays via Stockholm."

"I guarantee you immediate transmission. If the great American President speaks a word of hope, the Allies will march to smash the Germans."

"We'll be ready to transmit in half an hour, your Honour."

Starzynski stood up and glanced around the room. "A peaceful oasis. The Luftwaffe respects the American flag."

"Mr. Mayor, is there any word on evacuating neutrals?"

"I did raise the question yesterday when a German emissary came under a flag of truce to demand our surrender." He gave Slote a twisted smile. "He indicated that something would be worked out soon."

When Starzynski left, Slote summoned a coding clerk. Then

he shook Byron. "Wake up! All hell is breaking loose." Byron opened dull eyes. "The Russians invaded Poland this morning. God knows when they'll be here. Go and get Natalie."

Byron sat up. "Holy cow. This thing's getting interesting."

"*Interesting?* Warsaw will probably be blown to atoms! Tell Natalie she's to come here and stay here."

"But what's the rush? The Russians can't possibly get here for a week."

"Of course, but the Germans may decide on half an hour's notice to let the neutrals out. If it happens, there can be no delay."

"Well, I'll try to get her, but you know Natalie."

SOOTY heaps of rubble, craters, and broken sewer pipes pock-marked the way to the hospital. Women were cooking over fires of splintered wood; work gangs were shovelling and bulldozing debris. Almost everybody appeared cheerful. At the hospital, however, Byron met a pitiful scene. Wounded lay crowded on the floor, blood-smeared, with occasionally a red stump of limb showing. Byron hurried down a staircase into a long basement maternity area.

"Is he crazy?" Natalie exclaimed, when Byron had relayed Slote's message. "How can I leave? This is the only maternity ward left in Warsaw. This morning we counted eighty-two women—"

A stoop-shouldered doctor asked Natalie in German what the problem was, and she told him.

"By all means, go," he said in an exhausted voice. "If the embassy sends for you, you must obey."

"But I can get there in five minutes if we're leaving."

"No, no, that's a risk you can't take. You're Jewish, you're Jewish." The doctor pulled off the white cloth that bound Natalie's hair. "You must go."

Tears began to rain down Natalie's face. "The woman with the twins is haemorrhaging. And the baby with the bad foot—"

"I'll see them now. Go to the embassy. Thank you. You've helped us. Have a safe journey."

The doctor shuffled away.

She turned on Byron. "Leslie Slote is a selfish bastard," Natalie cried. "He just doesn't want to have me on his mind. Here." She pulled out a wallet. "I'll go to the damned embassy. But here is all my American money. Please find Berel and give it to him." She paused. "Tell me, Briny, are you still having fun?"

He looked round at the evil-smelling ward, where women were helplessly bringing new life into a dying city. "More fun than a barrel of monkeys. Be careful going to the embassy, will you?"

Hurrying towards the Jewish section, Byron heard the thump of heavy guns and nearby explosions. He muttered routine curses at the Germans. To call this amazing outrage "war" was not to make it any more understandable. And yet in this horrible state of affairs he had been doing the most satisfying job of his life. He was willing to be killed supplying water to the embassy. But the novel thing he noticed was that most people in Warsaw were still going about their business.

Even in the Jewish quarter, where clearly the Germans were raining extra shells and bombs, eager life still abounded. Outside a ruined schoolhouse, boys in skullcaps sat with their bearded teacher, chanting over enormous books. Inside a house, someone was practising on a violin.

Byron found Berel Jastrow inspecting the community kitchen in a huge Romanesque synagogue. People were lined up for a strong-smelling stew being ladled out from tubs on wood-burning stoves.

"The Russians!" Berel stroked his beard, then led Byron into the street, well away from the food queue. "Not such bad news. Maybe two robbers cut own throats," he said.

Byron said the Americans expected to leave Warsaw soon.

"So, we don't see you or Natalie again? Tell her I thank her. I put money for food fund." He held out his hand. "God bless you, and—"

Byron heard the unmistakable whir and whistle of a shell very close. It went splintering through the synagogue roof. The stunning explosion came a second later, giving him and Jastrow time to slap their hands to their ears. Then they saw the whole façade of the synagogue come sliding down, disintegrating as it went. White dust boiled up, and through it Byron could see the carved wooden doors of the holy ark untouched on the far wall.

Berel slapped him sharply on the shoulder. "Go now. And thank you, thank you. A safe journey to you both."

IN THE embassy, all was scurry and noise. The cease-fire had suddenly been fixed for one o'clock. Polish army trucks would take the Americans to the departure point. The Americans still living outside the embassy were being summoned by telephone.

A small dark man named Mark Hartley was sitting beside his strapped-up suitcase. He was a New York importer and his name had once been Marvin Horowitz. He had always joked about the change.

"Ready to go, Mark?" Byron asked.

Hartley shook his head. "I've never been so scared in my life. We're going to the Germans, Byron. The Germans."

"Put that in your bag," Byron said, tossing a worn black book to him as he packed his own bag. "A New Testament. Make a good Christian of you. Now stop worrying."

When the army trucks came rattling up the Americans set up a cheer and sang "California, Here I Come". They piled into the trucks, which then clanked off. A black Chevrolet with American flags on its wings brought up the rear; in it were Slote and his three highest-ranking assistants. Natalie had refused to join them. She stood in one of the trucks, clasping Byron's waist.

He said, "Mark is scared stiff of the Germans. How about you?"

Natalie's eyes flashed. "What can they do? I have an American passport. They don't know I'm a Jew."

The bridge across the Vistula was jammed to a standstill. Byron kept glancing at his watch as German shells boiled up like geysers in the river, showering the trucks. The Germans clearly thought it all in the game if they killed nine-tenths of the neutrals fifteen minutes before the cease-fire.

The convoys finally crossed to a schoolhouse where a Polish colonel stood giving instructions. At one o'clock the guns fell silent. Then in one language after another a loudspeaker bawled final orders: "Please keep together. Do not make wrong turns. The

German command has stated it will accept no responsibility for anybody who is not at the Kantorovicz church by three o'clock. Please, therefore, hurry. Good luck to you all."

The refugees headed into no-man's-land—a strange walk through a fragrant autumnal forest between two silent enemy armies. It took a full hour, and two memories stayed with Byron: the diplomats' cars going by, with Slote waving at him and Natalie; and then, when they first saw the Kantorovicz church, Mark Hartley smiling at him, though his face was terror-stricken.

All at once, there were the German gun crews in the woods, standing quietly by their big new howitzers. Most of the soldiers were so young it was hard to believe they were the villains who had been pouring fire on Warsaw.

The refugees were guided towards clean grey trucks with wooden seats. The loading of the trucks was not quite over when the guns near the church fired a salvo that made the ground shake. Byron's watch read a minute past three o'clock. "Poor Warsaw," Natalie said.

"Are you afraid?" Byron said.

"Not now that it's actually happening. I don't know why."

The refugees were tired, and perhaps cowed by the awareness of being in German hands; hardly a word was spoken in the first hour. The trucks stopped at a convent for the women to "refresh themselves", and Natalie brought back gossip: the neutrals would be offered a choice of flying to Stockholm or taking German trains to Berlin, thence out via Belgium, Holland, or Switzerland.

"You know, I'd sort of like to see Berlin," Natalie said.

"Are you crazy?" said Hartley. "You go to Stockholm, baby, and you just pray they *let* you go."

The ride stretched out to four hours of grinding through forests and farmlands, in what seemed like a peacetime countryside. Natalie put her head on Byron's shoulder and they dozed.

Commands shouted in German woke them. Lights blazed in a square before a railway station. Two helmeted Germans opened the door of their truck. *"Bitte 'raus! Alle in den Wartesaal!"*

The refugees gathered in the station waiting room and were then shepherded into a large hall containing plank tables laden with food. The famished Byron thought he had never seen a more dazzling banquet. There were smoking sausages and sauerkraut, whole pink hams, mounds of potatoes, piles of fried chicken, stacked loaves of fresh bread, immense cheeses.

Then a voice spoke in German over a loudspeaker: "The German people welcome the citizens of the neutral countries in peace and friendship. Relations with Poland have now been normalized. The Führer can now pursue ways to make peace with Britain and France, and then Europe will enter a new order of mutual prosperity. Now we ask you to sit down and eat. Hearty appetite!"

A dozen smiling blonde girls in white uniforms entered, carrying jugs of coffee and beer. There was an awkward, shocked moment. Then first one and then another refugee hesitantly stepped across the space.

Like the rest, Byron, Natalie, and Hartley gorged themselves on the most satisfying meal of their lives. Over the loudspeaker came Strauss waltzes, marches, and jolly drinking songs.

Returning to the waiting room, they saw placards round the walls, bearing the names of their countries. They went and stood under the United States sign. Then men in black uniforms entered and the cheery atmosphere faded.

Slote said soberly to the Americans, "Listen, please. Those are the SS. I'll do any talking to them that has to be done."

The men in black fanned out, one to each group of neutrals. Slote introduced himself to the one who headed for the Americans.

The SS man bowed, heels together. "You have a gentleman named Byron Henry in your party?"

"This is Byron Henry," Slote said as Byron stepped forward.

"Your father is American naval attaché in Berlin?" Byron nodded. "This message is for you."

Byron pocketed the envelope. "I'll look at it later."

The SS man turned to Slote. "Now your roster, please."

Slote's assistant held out three clipped sheets. The SS man glanced through them. "How many Jews in your party?"

Slote took a moment to reply. "I'm sorry, but we make no record of religious affiliation."

"But you do have Jews."

"Whether we do or not I must decline to answer. My country's policy on religious groups is absolute equality of treatment."

"Nobody is suggesting inequality of treatment. The policy of my government is simply to maintain separate records where Jews are concerned. Now, who are these Jews, please?"

"For your purposes you can assume we're all Jews." Slote's voice shook.

The SS officer shrugged, ran his eyes over the group, and stopped at Mark Hartley. "You. Step this way."

"Stay where you are," Slote said to Hartley; then, to the officer, "I protest this procedure, and I warn you that it will result in a written protest from my government if it continues."

The officer gestured. "The officials of all the other governments are cooperating. What is your name, you there?"

"Mark Hartley." The voice was steadier than Slote's.

"Really! Hartley!" The SS man smiled a peculiar, chilling smile. "And your parents' name?"

"That name."

"And they were Jews?"

Byron said, "He's a Methodist, sir, like me. We've been going to church together in Warsaw."

A bald SS man with gold leaf on his lapels now approached the Americans. He took Hartley's suitcase and undid the straps.

Slote said sharply, "Hold on, sir. This is not a Customs point—" But the officer was already spilling the contents of the case on the floor. He came on the New Testament and examined it with a sneering expression. "So," he said in German. "Maybe there are no Jews. Come. The train is being delayed."

Scanning the other faces in the group, the SS man stepped up to Natalie. "You're rather dark. What is your ancestry?"

"I'm Italian."

"What is your name?"

"Mona Lisa," she said, and Byron's heart sank.

"I see. You step forward."

Natalie did not move. Slote quickly said, "She's my fiancée. We'll be married next month."

The bald officer shouted from the door, and the SS man roughly handed the roster to Slote. "Very well. You love your Jews. Why do you refuse to take ours? We have swarms." He walked off.

A loudspeaker called out in German, "All Jews to the restaurant. Everybody else to track seven."

At the train Slote muttered to Byron, "I'll take a compartment. Bring Natalie and Mark. You'll see me at the window."

"A million thanks," Hartley whispered, when they were all seated and Slote had slid the door shut. "God bless you."

"I admit one thing," Natalie said, "I've lost all curiosity about Berlin. Stockholm ahoy."

When the train started, Byron pulled the yellow envelope from his pocket. The message read: GLAD YOU'RE OK. COME STRAIGHT TO BERLIN. DAD.

WHEN the train squealed and clanked into Berlin's Friedrich-strasse terminal Rhoda clutched Victor Henry's arm and jumped up and down.

"My God!" she exclaimed. "Is *that* him coming down those steps? He's a *skeleton*."

The bones stood out in Byron's pale face, and his eyes looked bright and enormous. He was laughing and waving, and Pug plunged towards him. Byron embraced him with a fierce, long hug. Then he hugged and kissed his mother.

"Mom, you look beautiful. About twenty-five."

"Well, you look ghastly. I don't know why the devil you were running around in Poland!"

Leslie Slote, ashen and harried, came up and introduced himself to Victor Henry. "I'd like to call on you at the embassy tomorrow, sir," he said, "once I've straightened things out a bit. But let me tell you right now that Byron's been a real help."

"Come in any time," Pug Henry said.

Rhoda sat beside her son as they drove to Grünewald, happily clutching his arm. She asked about his scar, and he began narrating his odyssey from Kraków to Warsaw, interrupting himself to exclaim at things he saw: a café full of Berliners eating pastry and drinking coffee, a band concert in a park. "It's so damned peaceful!

Dad, what's happening in the war? Has Warsaw surrendered? Have the Allies gotten off their tails yet?"

"Warsaw's still holding out, but it's really over. There's talk about peace in the west, too."

"Already? Well, where was I? Oh yes. Next the fan belt broke. The German planes never stopped. There was a cluster of farmhouses nearby, but they'd been bombed to pieces, so—"

"Farmhouses?" Pug broke in. "The Germans keep claiming that the Luftwaffe attacks only military targets."

Byron laughed. "Anything is a military target to the Germans. I saw a thousand houses blown apart, miles from the front."

Pug was thinking that Byron's story might make an intelligence report. The Germans were publishing photographs of Polish peasants cheering the invaders, and of smiling Jews being fed at soup kitchens. Byron's tale cast an interesting light on this.

At the Grünewald house, they sat sipping drinks while Byron talked on and on, describing the siege of Warsaw.

At dinner he finally stopped talking, and between the soup and the meat courses his head nodded and dropped on his chest.

"I was wondering how long he'd last," Pug said.

Later, when they had got Byron to bed and were strolling in the garden, Pug said, "Quite a change in him."

"It's that girl," said Rhoda.

"He didn't say much about her."

"That's my point. He said nothing about her. Except that she's gone to Stockholm. Yet he went to Poland because of her, and got caught in Kraków on account of her. She must be some girl."

When Pug got home the next day, Byron was reclining in the garden, eating grapes and reading a Superman comic book.

The butler brought out a drink on a tray, and when he went back inside, Pug said, "Briny, that was quite a tale you told us. I want you to write it all up so I can forward it to Naval Intelligence."

"Gosh, Dad, aren't you overestimating it?"

"No. I'd like you to get at it tonight. There's a typewriter in the library."

"Well, O.K." With such casual assents Byron had often dodged his homework, but Pug was hoping that he had matured.

After dinner Byron left the house and returned at two in the morning carrying a copy of *Mein Kampf*. At seven the next evening he was well into it.

Pug said, "Did you start on that report?"

"I'll get to it, Dad."

Byron went out again that night, returned late, and fell asleep with his clothes on, an old habit that ground on Pug's nerves. When he woke around eleven he found a note on his chair: "Write that damned report."

He was idling along the Kurfürstendamm that afternoon, with *Mein Kampf* under his arm, when Slote went hurrying by, halted, and turned. "That's luck. I've been trying to get hold of you. Are you coming back to the States?"

"I'm not sure. How about some coffee and pastry?"

"Why not? I skipped lunch."

They sat in an enormous sidewalk café among potted flowering bushes, with a brass band playing waltzes in the sunshine. "Gosh, this is the life," Byron said, as they gave their orders. "Did you ever see a nicer city? Look at all these polite happy Berliners. The only thing is, these pleasant folks have just been pounding another nice city to a pulp. It's a puzzle."

Slote smiled. "No doubt Paris was as charming as ever while Napoleon was out doing his butchering."

"Slote, the Germans are really strange! I've been reading *Mein Kampf* to try to figure them out. It's the writing of an absolute nut. The Jews are secretly running the world, he says. They're the capitalists, but they're the Bolsheviks too, and they're conspiring to destroy the German people. Have I got it right?"

"A bit simplified, but yes—pretty much."

"O.K. Now, haven't these Berliners read his book? How come they didn't put him in a padded cell?"

Slote said in a low tone, "Are you just discovering the phenomenon of Adolf Hitler?"

"Getting shot in the head sort of called my attention to it. Do *you* understand the Germans?"

"I have an opinion." Slote answered with a wry little smile.

"Can I hear it? I'm interested."

Slote pulled at his pipe. "My view is that Hitler and the Nazis grew out of the heart of German culture—a cancer, maybe, but a uniquely German phenomenon. Others insist the same thing could have happened anywhere, given the same conditions: defeat in war, a harsh peace treaty, ruinous inflation. But—"

The waiter was approaching. Slote drank coffee until he left them. Then he resumed. "But to me Nazism is unthinkable without German nineteenth-century thought: romanticism, idealism, nationalism, the whole outpouring." He shoved *Mein Kampf* back to Byron. "Well, are you coming home?"

"What are Natalie's plans after she leaves Stockholm?"

"I really don't know." Slote hesitated. "I'll tell you something, though, I've had no peace of mind since the day I first met her, at a very stupid Paris cocktail party."

"Why don't you marry her?" Byron said.

Slote had risen. He looked down at Byron for several seconds. "I'm not at all sure I won't, if she'll have me."

10

Rhoda Henry had always enjoyed the attention of men, and, being a beauty, had not lacked opportunities for affairs. But in almost twenty-five years of marriage she had been as faithful to Pug as he had to her.

Nevertheless, during his absence in the States she had tangled herself in a romance.

Dr. Palmer Kirby was a shy, serious man in his middle fifties, a person Rhoda might describe as "one of those ghastly *brains*". At her dinner party, she tried her usual coquettish babble on Kirby over the cocktails. "I've put you on my right, Dr. Kirby, and since my husband's away, we can make *hay* while the sun shines."

"Um. On your right. Thank you."

That had almost been the end of it. But he had mentioned at dinner that he was going next day to a factory in Brandenburg. Because she wanted to see that medieval town and he was, officially, Pug's guest, she offered to drive him. They had lunch on the way and over a bottle of Moselle he started to talk about his work. At an alert question she asked him, Kirby suddenly smiled.

"Do you really care, Mrs. Henry?" said Dr. Kirby. "I have a horror of boring a beautiful woman."

Flustered, she touched a hand to her hair. "Truly, it sounds fascinating. Just use words of one syllable when you can."

Rhoda soon drew out the key facts about him. At the California Institute of Technology he had written his doctoral thesis on electromagnetism. At forty he had decided to manufacture magnetic amplifiers on his own. The long struggle for financing had nearly sunk him, but it was now paying off. War industries demanded "magamps" in quantity, and he was first in the field. He had come to Berlin to study German techniques.

She also learned that he was a widower and a grandfather. He talked about his dead wife, and then they exchanged long confidences about their children. Palmer Kirby ordered a second bottle of Moselle, and they got to Brandenburg an hour late.

When they returned to Berlin, Kirby asked her to dinner and the opera, and it seemed quite natural to accept. The opera was *La Traviata*, which they discovered they both had always loved. Afterwards he proposed a glimpse of the notorious Berlin night life. Rhoda giggled. "Well, thank you very much for a disreputable suggestion. Let's hope we don't run into any of my friends."

So they ended the evening sipping champagne and watching a hefty blonde fling her naked body about in blue smoky gloom. Kirby's long solemn face showed faint distaste. Rhoda, never having seen a nude dancer before, was agreeably shocked.

After that, until her husband returned, Rhoda spent a lot of time with Kirby. In her own vocabulary, she never "did anything", and when Pug came back, the adventure stopped.

A FAREWELL lunch at Wannsee for Palmer Kirby was Rhoda's idea, but she got Colonel Forrest's wife, Sally, to give it.

Midway through the excellent lunch, a loudspeaker crackled and a voice said in German, "Attention! You are about to hear an announcement of the highest importance to the fatherland." An immediate total stillness blanketed the room. "From Supreme Headquarters of the Führer. Warsaw has fallen."

The restaurant rang with cheers. Brass-band music—first "Deutschland über Alles", then the "Horst Wessel"—came pouring out of the loudspeakers. Except for the Americans, everyone rose, most of them making the Nazi salute. Victor Henry's skin prickled as he looked around. Then he noticed something he had not seen for twenty years. Byron had taken punishment dry-eyed since the age of five, but now he was crying.

The seated Americans were getting hostile glares. Their waiter, hitherto all genial, expert service, stood sneering at them. When the songs ended he started removing plates with a jerky clatter, spilling gravy and wine. Sally Forrest gave a little yelp as he struck her head with a plate.

Pug said to him, "Call your headwaiter, please."

"Headwaiter? I am the headwaiter. I am *your* head. We're busy in this restaurant." The man laughed and walked off.

Victor Henry called, "*Stop. Turn around!*" His dry, sharp tone cut through the restaurant gabble. The waiter turned. "*Call your headwaiter. Do it immediately!*" Commander Henry looked straight into the waiter's eyes, his face hard. The man's glance shifted as he walked away. People at nearby tables were staring.

"I think we should go," Sally Forrest said. "This isn't worth the trouble."

The waiter reappeared with a man in a frock coat, who said with an unfriendly air, "You have a complaint?"

"We're Americans, neutrals," Pug said sternly. "We didn't rise for your anthem. This waiter chose to be rude and sloppy. Tell him to behave, and let us have a clean cloth for our dessert."

The headwaiter burst into a howl of abuse at the waiter. After a short tantrum, he turned to Pug and bowed. "You will be properly served. My apologies."

Now a peculiar thing happened. Without turning a hair, the waiter reverted to his former manner. He spread a new cloth and smiled, and bowed, as he took their dessert orders.

"I'll be damned," said Colonel Forrest.

"Well done," Kirby said to Pug, with an odd glance at Rhoda.

"O.K., Dad," Byron said. Victor Henry shot him a quick look. It was the one remark that gratified him.

361

That night after dinner, Rhoda said she was going to the movies, and left the father and son drinking coffee on the terrace. "Briny, how's that report coming?" Pug asked.

"Oh. Yes. The report. Dad, what would you think of my joining the British navy? Or the RAF?"

Victor Henry blinked and took a while to answer. "You want to fight the Germans? I thought a military career was o-u-t out."

"This isn't a career, Dad."

"Briny, I don't think the Allies are going to make a deal with Hitler, but a peace effort's coming up. Suppose you join the British, possibly lose your citizenship—and then the war's off? Why not ask for active duty in *our* navy? You've got your commission. And the reserves who go out to sea now will draw the best duty if and when the action starts."

"And *then* if the war ends? I'd be in for years."

"You're not doing anything else."

"I've written to Dr. Jastrow. I'm waiting to hear from him."

Pug dropped the subject.

Rhoda did go to the cinema, but first she picked up Dr. Palmer Kirby at his hotel and drove him to Tempelhof airport. She felt bittersweet excitement. It was a long, long time since a man had seemed as attractive to her as Palmer Kirby did.

"Well, I guess this is it," he said, as they sat over drinks in the airport lounge. He raised his glass. "Your happiness."

"Oh, that. I've had that." She sipped. "Palmer, tell me what you think of Pug."

"Hm. That's a tough one." The engineer pushed his lips out ruefully. "My first impression was—frankly—that he was a rather narrow-minded sea dog. But he has a keen intellect and he's terrifically on the ball. He's a hard man to know, really."

Rhoda laughed. "After all these years, I don't know him too well myself. But I suspect he's really something simple and almost obsolete. He's a patriot."

"Well, I've come to admire him." Kirby frowned at his drink. "Rhoda, let me just say this. You're a wonderful woman. I've been a sad, dull man since my wife died, but you've made me feel very much alive again, and I'm grateful. Does this offend you?"

"Don't be a fool. It pleases me very much. Oh, damn." Rhoda took out a handkerchief and touched her eyes with it. "Thanks for the drink, Palmer. You'd better go to your plane."

"Look, don't be upset," he said, as they rose.

She smiled at him, her eyes tearful. "You might write, just once in a while, so I'll know you're alive and well."

"Of course I will."

Standing on tiptoe, Rhoda kissed him on the lips.

BYRON at last wrote the report on his adventures in Poland. His father, suppressing his annoyance over the five vapid pages, spent an afternoon dictating to his yeoman everything he remembered of Byron's tale. His son read the seventeen-page result with astonishment. "Ye gods, Dad, what a memory you have."

"Fix it any way you want. Make sure it's factually unchallenge-able and let me have it back by Friday."

Victor Henry forwarded the report to the Office of Naval Intelligence. The cool autumn days went by. Three or four times a week Byron played tennis with his father, and slowly he lost his famished look and regained his strength. He pounced on the mail every morning, searching in vain for a letter from Siena.

When the Führer made his Reichstag speech offering peace to England and France, early in October, Pug took his son along. Speaking in a pedestrian tone, Hitler began with some brazen assertions about the Polish campaign: a powerful Poland had attempted to destroy Germany, but the brave Wehrmacht had punished this aggression.

Byron was stupefied by the pointlessness of the lies. Hitler went on to "offer an outstretched hand" to the British and the French. "Surely if forty-six million Englishmen can claim to rule over forty million square kilometres of the earth, then it cannot be wrong," he said mildly, "for eighty-two million Germans to till in peace eight hundred thousand square kilometres of soil that are historically their own." The British and French could have peace simply by accepting things as they now were, he said. At the end he fell into his old style, howling and shaking both fists as he pictured the horrors of a full-scale war.

The German radio and Press made a great to-do about Hitler's "outstretched hand" peace proposal. Italy and Japan hailed him as the greatest peacemaker of all time. A mighty, popular surge for peace was sweeping through western Europe and America, but "Churchillian" warmongers were trying to stamp out this warm response to the Führer's offer.

Into this confusion came an electric shock of news. A German U-boat had sneaked into the British fleet anchorage in Scapa Flow, at the northern tip of Scotland, and sunk the battleship *Royal Oak*. News pictures showed Hitler shaking hands with the U-boat's captain, Günther Prien.

A small reception was held for neutral military attachés to meet Prien and Victor Henry put his son's name on the list, with the rank "Ensign, USNR". The Henrys dined before the reception at the apartment of Commander Grobke.

Byron, prepared to detest the Grobkes, found them disconcertingly normal. But when the talk got round to Hitler's offer to the Allies, Grobke launched into a tirade about Roosevelt's being the one man on whom peace depended. "If Roosevelt tells Britain and France tomorrow," he said, "'I'm not helping you against Germany', we'll all have a hundred years of prosperity. And it's the only way he can make sure Japan won't jump on your back."

Possibly, Victor Henry thought, his meeting with Grobke on the *Bremen* had not been accidental.

Later Byron listened as intently as his father to the U-boat captain's amazing tale. Captain Prien had gone in on the surface, in the dark of the moon. Inside the anchorage, he had fired four torpedoes, of which one had hit the *Royal Oak*. Evidently not believing that there could be a U-boat inside Scapa Flow, the British had taken the hit for an internal explosion, and no submarine alarm had been sounded. Prien had then made a big slow circle to reload tubes, his U-boat silhouetted by the northern lights. Finally he had shot four more torpedoes.

"We made three hits that time," Prien said. "We blew up the magazines, and the *Royal Oak* went down almost at once."

He did not gloat. Nor did he express regret over the hundreds of drowned British sailors. The odds had been that he, and not they, would die in the night's work. This was not Warsaw, Byron thought, nor the strafing of women and children on country roads.

As Pug Henry and his son drove home, Byron said, "Dad, didn't you ever consider submarines?"

The father shook his head. "No, but Prien's a lot like our own submariners. I almost forgot that he was talking German."

"Well, that's what I'd have picked," Byron said, "if I'd gone in."

"If you're actually interested—"

"No thanks, Dad." The young man laughed.

Victor and Byron spent a week touring German shipyards and factories. Pug enjoyed travelling with his son, for Byron never got angry, and always rose to emergencies: an overbooked plane, missing luggage, a mix-up over hotel reservations. And he could sit for hours listening to plant managers and yard superintendents.

"This is the Germany to worry about," Byron remarked after a visit to the Krupp works in Essen.

Pug nodded. "The German industrial plant is the pistol Hitler is pointing at the world's head. Our own is bigger, by far, but Hitler isn't giving it a second thought, because there's no national will to use it. Germany can run the world, if nobody argues."

A few days after the British and French rejected the Führer's "outstretched hand", a letter arrived from Aaron Jastrow, thanking Byron for looking after his niece while she was in Poland. "Natalie is not here. I've had one letter from her, written in London. She'll try to come back to Siena for a while, she says, and frankly I need her. She feels a responsibility for her bumbling uncle, which is very comforting. You have no such tie, and though I would really like having you, I can't encourage you to come."

Byron found his father sitting in a lounge chair on the porch. "Dad, I've got to talk to you. I've had a letter from Dr. Jastrow. I'm going to Siena."

For a moment his father glowered at him. "Who says so?"

"I do."

"Is that girl there?"

"No, she's in England."

"And you'll do what? Literary research up in an Italian mountain town, with a war on?"

"If I get called to active duty, I'll go."

"That's damned big-hearted, seeing that if you didn't, the navy would track you down and put you in the brig for a few years. Well, Briny, you must do as you please."

Their friendship over the past weeks might never have been.

11

"Byron!" Dr. Jastrow gasped. He sat on the terrace, his writing board and yellow pad on his lap. Across the valley, the red-walled town atop the vineyard-chequered hills looked hauntingly like the medieval Siena in old frescoes.

"Hello, A.J."

"Dear me, Byron! We were talking about you only at breakfast. We were both absolutely certain you'd be in the States by now."

"Natalie's here?"

"Of course. She's up in the library."

"Sir, will you excuse me?"

"Yes, go ahead, let me collect myself—"

She was standing at the desk in a grey sweater and black skirt, looking pale and wide-eyed. "It *is* you! Nobody else galumphs upstairs like that. Why didn't you say you were coming?"

"Well, I thought I'd better just come."

She approached him and put a hand uncertainly to his face. "Anyway, you look rested. You've put on some weight." She backed off abruptly, and returned to her chair. "Well, we can use you here." As though he had returned from an errand in town, she started typing.

That was all his welcome. Jastrow put him back to work, and within a few days it was as though neither he nor Natalie had ever left the quiet hilltop. Her distant manner persisted, and Byron thought he had probably annoyed her by following her here. But he was content simply to be with her again.

One or two letters a week came to her from Leslie Slote, but whereas she used to rush to her bedroom to read them, now she casually skimmed them wherever she was. One day she was reading a letter at her desk when Byron heard her say, "Good God!"

He looked up. "Something the matter?"

She hesitated, her face red. "Oh, hell. I've got to tell someone. Guess what I hold in my hot little hand? A proposal of marriage from Leslie Slote. What do you think of that, Byron Henry?"

"Congratulations," Byron said.

The buzzer on Natalie's desk sounded. "Oh, Lord. Briny, please, see what A.J. wants. I'm in a fog."

Dr. Jastrow sat by the fire in the downstairs study facing a fat uniformed official. "Byron," he said, "ask Natalie for my resident status file, will you?"

Natalie looked worried when Byron told her. She unlocked a small steel file and gave him a manila folder.

At dinner that night, she said, "Aaron, what was that visit about today?"

Jastrow shook his head. "Strangely enough, Giuseppe again." Giuseppe was the assistant gardener, a lazy, stupid old drunkard whom Jastrow had recently discharged.

"How does that man know Giuseppe?" Byron said.

"That's the odd part. He's from the alien registration bureau in Florence, yet he mentioned Giuseppe's nine children and the difficulty of finding work nowadays. When I said I'd rehire Giuseppe, that ended it." Jastrow sighed. "I'm rather tired. Tell Maria I'll have my fruit and cheese in the study."

Natalie said when the professor was gone, "Let's take the coffee to my room." Never before had she invited him there. Byron followed her upstairs with a jumping pulse.

Natalie lit the log fire in her bedroom, and they sat in facing armchairs. "Why do you suppose Aaron's so upset?" Natalie said. "Giuseppe's a good gardener, even if he is a dirty old drunk."

"A.J. was coerced," Byron said. "We're at the mercy of these people, A.J. more than us. He owns property here."

"Oh, the Italians are all right. They're not Germans." She bit her lip. "I've shut Warsaw from my mind. Or tried to."

"I don't blame you. I keep dreaming about it."

"Oh, God, so do I. That hospital, night after night—" Sudden gloom shadowed Natalie's face. She poured more coffee for both of them. "Stir the fire, Briny, I'm cold."

He made the fire flare, and she jumped up and stood by it. "That moment in the railroad station," she burst out, "at least Leslie stood his ground, even if he was shaking like a leaf. What if I'd done something—said I was Jewish, created a scene? It might have helped some of the others . . . ." She threw up her hands in a despairing gesture and dropped into her chair. "Speaking of old Slote," she said, "what do you think of his proposal to make an honest woman of me?"

"He told me in Berlin he might marry you. He said that he hadn't known an hour's peace since he first laid eyes on you."

"But did he tell you the truth about him and me?" Byron shook his head. Natalie said, "I think I'd like a little brandy."

He raced downstairs and returned with a bottle and two snifters. Swirling the brandy around in the balloon glass, Natalie broke loose with a rush of words. It was a familiar tale of a clever older man having fun with a girl and getting snared into a real passion. Resolving to marry him, she had made his life a misery. At last she had him where she wanted him.

Byron hated every word, yet he was grateful. The closemouthed girl was taking him into her life, and this was what he had been starved for. Natalie was the one person who meant as much to him as his father did. His father was terrific. In a different way, so was Natalie.

"Well, there you have it," she said. "What puzzles me is why he's throwing in the towel now."

"It's what you want."

"Well, I don't know. My parents had wild fits when I told them I was in love with a Christian. And then there's Aaron."

"Well, he survived while we were away."

"That's what you think. You should have seen the library and study when I got back. He can't even sharpen a pencil properly." Natalie was talking breathlessly. "And there's still another complication. The biggest."

"What's that?"

"Don't you know, Briny?"

He said, or rather stammered, because the sudden penetrating sexuality in her glance made him drunk, "I don't think I do."

"All right then, I'll tell you. You've done it, you devil; I'm in love with you." She peered at him, her eyes shining. "Ye gods, what a dumb stunned face. Don't you believe me?"

Very hoarsely he said, "I just hope it's true."

He got out of his chair and went to her. She jumped up, and they kissed and kissed. She thrust her hands in his hair, she caressed his face. "Oh, God," she said. "That smile. Those hands. I love to watch your hands. I love the way you move." It was like a hundred daydreams Byron had had, only the perfume of her hair couldn't be daydreamed, nor her moist, warm sweet breath.

At last she pulled away. "I had to do that or *die*. I've never felt anything like this in my life. I've been fighting it because it's no damn good. You're a child. I won't have it. Not a Christian. Not again." She put both hands over her face. "Don't look at me like that, Briny! Go out of my bedroom."

Wanting to please her, Byron turned to go. "You see," she said, "you're a gentleman. It's one of the unbelievable things about you. My darling, I don't want to put you out. I just don't want to make any false moves. I absolutely adore you."

He was dazed with happiness beyond imagining. "Listen, would you think of marrying me?" he said.

Natalie's eyes widened and her mouth dropped. "God in heaven," she gasped, flinging herself into his arms, "you're incredible."

"I'm serious," he said. "I've always wanted to marry you. It seemed preposterous, but if you love me—"

"It *is* preposterous. But where you're concerned I appear to be quite mindless." She kissed him once more. "Good night, darling. I know you're serious, and I'm terribly touched."

Once in his own room, Byron's feverish mind ran on what he must do next. The window was turning violet when he fell asleep in a jumble of ideas, ranging from medical school and short-story writing to the banking business. Some distant cousins of his mother controlled a bank in Washington . . . .

It was almost eleven when Byron hurried into the library. Natalie gave him one ardent glance and went on with her typing. On his desk was a pile of first-draft pages heavily scribbled with

Jastrow's corrections, to which was clipped a note, "Let me have this material at lunch, please."

"A.J. looked in just now," Natalie said, "and made vile noises."

"I'm sorry, but I didn't close my eyes till dawn."

"Didn't you?" she said, with a secret little smile.

He began to type. A hand rested warmly on his neck. "Poor Briny. Type your head off, and so will I."

They did not finish the work before lunch, but by then, as it turned out, Dr. Jastrow had other things on his mind. At noon an enormous white Lancia drew up outside, and Byron and Natalie heard the voices of Tom Searle and his wife. Expatriate Americans, they had lived for years in a hilltop villa not far from Jastrow's. Jastrow often drove down to Florence with the Searles, and Natalie thought they might be fetching him now.

Coming down for lunch, however, they found A.J. alone in the drawing room. He complained that they were late, which they were not, and uttered no further word until lunch was over.

"The Searles are moving back to the States," he said then. "They're worried about the war spreading, so they're abandoning their lease." Jastrow looked morose. "That's the difference between leasing and buying. You just walk away without bothering about the place."

Byron said, "Well, sir, if you think there's any danger your skin comes first."

"I have no such fears," he said peevishly. "We'll have our coffee in the lemon house."

The lemon house was a long, glassed-in structure full of small potted citrus trees. The sunlight that poured in cheered Jastrow up. He said, "I predict they'll sneak back with their tails between their legs, and three furniture vans toiling up the hill."

After he left, Natalie said "He's badly shaken."

"I hope he gets shaken loose from here."

They were sitting on a white wicker couch. Byron started to put his arm around her.

"Stop that," she said, catching her breath. "Briny, I'm twenty-seven. Are you twenty-five yet?"

"I'm old enough for you, Natalie."

"But what are you doing with yourself? You're brave, you're gentle, but you just drifted here, and you're going nowhere."

"How would you like to be married to a banker?" He told her about the relatives in Washington.

"It's absurd. You don't really *want* to be a banker. I'll tell you what I think. If you're anything, you're a naval officer."

"I'm just a lowly reserve. That's nothing."

"If the war goes on, you'll be called up. You'll stay in from sheer inertia and family custom. But Byron, I'm not going to be the wife of a naval officer. I can't think of a worse existence."

"But I'll never be a naval officer—why are you crying?"

She dashed the sudden tears from her face, smiling. "Oh, shut up. This is an insane conversation. All I know is that I'm crazy about you. No, not now, love, really, no—" She gasped the last words as he firmly took her in his arms.

There was nobody in sight outside the lemon house, and inside there was silence and the heavy sweet scent of blossoms.

Later, as they went into the house, Jastrow called from his study, "Natalie, we both have letters from your mother. Your father is sick, and she wants you to come home. But don't worry—he seems in no immediate danger."

Natalie's letter contained a long and somewhat frantic account of her father's heart attack. She showed it to Aaron who shook his head sympathetically. "You had better go at once."

"I think so," she said, sombrely.

He pensively fingered his beard. "You won't come back. Life will get difficult here. Possibly I could go to New Mexico or Arizona. But they're such dull places! The thought of trying to write there!" He gave a deep sigh. "No doubt my books aren't that important."

"Your books are important, A.J."

"Are they? Why?"

Natalie said after a pause, "In a creditable, unsentimental way they are very Jewish in spirit. They've made me realize how much Christendom owes this bizarre little folk we belong to."

Aaron Jastrow smiled. "Well, bless you. I fell in love with the grandeur of Christianity and of Jesus long ago—but it has made me no less Jewish. Nobody else in the family will accept that, your

372

father least of all." He studied her face, and his eyes twinkled.
"How long after you left would Byron remain? He gives me such
a secure feeling, just by being here."

"A raise'll hold him. He's never worked before."

12

"Holy cow!" Byron said. "There's my father, or his double."

"Where?" said Natalie. Her flight was delayed, and they were
drinking coffee in the Rome airport.

"Inside that ring of *carabinieri* over there." He pointed to a
group of men leaving the terminal escorted by six deferential police
officers. "Dad! Wait up!"

When Victor Henry heard Byron's voice he turned, waved, and
asked his escort from the Foreign Ministry to wait for him outside.
"Well, how about this?" he said, clasping his son's hand.

"What's up, Dad? Couldn't you let me know?"

"It happened suddenly. All highly confidential. I intended to
ring you tonight. What are you doing in Rome?"

"Natalie's going home. Her father's sick."

"Oh? Has she left already?"

"No. She's sitting over there. The one with the big black hat."

Victor Henry caught a new proprietary note in his son's voice,
noticed also the confident glance and a straighter back. "I'd like to
meet that girl," he said. He strode towards Natalie.

Shaking hands with her, Victor Henry was taken by this girl with
the dark eyes. She wasn't the Jewish adventuress of his imagination. He said, "I'm sorry to hear about your father."

She nodded her thanks. "I don't know how bad it is. But they
want me at home, and so I'm going."

"Are you coming back?"

"I'm not sure. My uncle may be returning to the States too."

"He'd be well-advised to do that, fairly fast."

Pug was looking keenly at her, and she smiled a wry, puckish
smile, as though to say, All right, I don't blame you for trying to
see what's there. How do you like it? Pug was seldom faced down
in eye-to-eye confrontations, but now he shifted his glance.

To ease the strain, Natalie said, "Byron tells me that you're friends of the Tudsburys, Commander. I knew Pamela in Paris. She's lovely."

"I agree. Maniacal driver, though."

"Oh, I know. She scares me senseless."

"I'd guess it would take more than that to scare you." Pug held out his hand. "I'm glad I've met you, Natalie." Awkwardly, he added, "It explains a lot. Good-bye. Happy landings."

"Good-bye, Commander Henry."

Pug abruptly walked off, with Byron at his elbow, accompanying him to the exit. "You, Briny, you're staying on in Siena?"

"For the time being."

"Do you know that Warren's engaged to Janice Lacouture?"

"Oh, it's definite now?"

"Yes, they've set a date for May twentieth, after he finishes his carrier training. I hope you'll count on getting back by then. I'm working on a leave for myself."

"I'll certainly try. How's Mom?"

"Off her feed. Berlin's beginning to get her down." They were at the exit. "How long will you be in Rome?"

"If I can see you, Dad, I'll stay on."

"Fine. Check in at the embassy with Captain Kirkwood. Could be we'll dine together tonight. By the way, that's some girl. You never said she was so pretty."

"What? I honestly don't think she is. I'm nuts about her, but—"

"She's got eyes you could drown in. However, she's a grown-up woman." He put his hand on Byron's shoulder. "No offence, but you have a way to go." Pug climbed into the waiting limousine.

Natalie's face was tense and inquiring when Byron got back and dropped into the chair beside her. "He fell for you."

"Byron, don't talk rot."

"He said something sappy about your eyes. Too embarrassing to tell you. Say, my brother's getting married in May to the daughter of a congressman. She doesn't seem concerned about marrying a naval officer! Let's make it a double wedding."

"Why not? You'll be manager of a bank by then, no doubt."

They were both smiling, but the unsettled questions between

374

them put an edge in their tones. It was a relief when her flight was announced. Byron carried her luggage into the crowd at the gate. "I love you, Natalie," he said.

"Oh Briny, you know I love you."

Byron kissed her. "Cable if you're not coming back," he said, "and I'll take the next plane home."

"Yes, I'll cable."

"And promise that you'll make no other decisions, do nothing drastic, before you see me again."

"All right, it's a promise. Good-bye, my darling. Good-bye." Her voice rose as the press of passengers dragged her away.

COMMANDER HENRY put on a freshly pressed uniform at his hotel and walked to the embassy. At the café tables along the Via Veneto only a few people were braving the December chill.

Captain Kirkwood had left for the day. His yeoman handed Pug a long lumpy envelope. Two small objects fell out when he ripped it open: silver eagles on pins, the collar insignia of a captain.

Captain Kirkwood presents his compliments to Captain *Henry, and trusts he is free to dine at nine, at the Osteria dell' Orso.*

P.S.—You're incorrectly dressed. Four stripes, please.

Clipped to the note was a strip of gold braid, and the A1Nav letter listing newly selected captains.

The yeoman wore a wide grin. "Congratulations, Cap'n."

"Thank you. Did my son call?"

"Yes, sir. He's coming to dinner. I've got fresh coffee, sir, if you'd like a cup."

Pug drank one cup after another of the rich navy brew, feeling exalted. The big hurdle in the race for flag rank was early promotion to captain. He wished he could share the news with his restless wife.

"Mr. Luigi Gianelli is here for you, sir." The yeoman's voice spoke through the squawk box.

"Very well." Pug swept the tokens of his promotion into his pocket and went out to join the San Francisco banker, friend of Roosevelt, who was the reason for his journey to Rome. He was to act as Gianelli's aide in Italy and Germany.

The interior of the green Rolls-Royce smelled of cologne. Gianelli had the sleekness of secure wealth. "I've already spoken to the foreign minister, Count Ciano," he said, lighting a long cigar. "I've known him well for many years. He's coming to this reception, and from there will take me to the Palazzo di Venezia for a meeting with Mussolini."

Pug said, "This reception is being given for you?"

"Yes. My uncle is a banker here and the reception is at his town house."

About half an hour after the arrival of the Americans, Gianelli and Pug moved into a high-ceilinged library, and the banker talked with Count Ciano. He said that Mr. Roosevelt had sent him to ask a single informal question. The President was alarmed by the drift towards catastrophe in Europe. Was it possible to do something, even at this late hour? Mr. Roosevelt had in mind a formal, urgent mission by a high United States diplomat, such as Sumner Welles, to visit all the chiefs of the warring states and explore the possible terms of a settlement.

Foreign Minister Ciano cleared his throat. "Do the British and French know and approve of this visit?"

"No, Excellency. The President said that he would be making similar informal inquiries at this time in London and Paris."

"I share Mr. Roosevelt's wish to leave no stone unturned." Ciano paused. "If the President sends Sumner Welles on such a mission, I will recommend to Mussolini that he receive him."

Gianelli smiled with delight and pride. The second part of his mission, he said, would be an interview with Hitler, the occasion for which would be a party at Karinhall, Göring's estate outside Berlin.

Ciano smoothed his thick black hair. "Well, Commander, what do you think of the great German victory in the South Atlantic?"

"I hadn't heard of one."

"Really? The battleship *Graf Spee* has caught a group of British cruisers and destroyers off Montevideo, sunk four or five, and damaged all the rest. It's a British disaster that changes the whole balance of force in the Atlantic."

Victor Henry was shocked. "What happened to *Graf Spee*?"

"Minor hits that will be repaired overnight."

Pug was sceptical. "The British have acknowledged this?"

Count Ciano smiled. "No, but the British took a while to acknowledge the sinking of the *Royal Oak*."

ON PUG'S return to Berlin he found Rhoda in a fine fury. Why, she demanded, hadn't she been invited to the Görings' party at Karinhall? In his absence the invitation, addressed just to him, had been delivered by a Luftwaffe staff officer.

"Rhoda, you must take my word that it's a security thing."

"Ha! Security! That old chestnut!"

Pug laughed and said, "Let's have a drink. You look wonderful."

"I do not. The damned hairdresser baked my hair into shredded wheat again. I'm going to bed. Nothing to talk about, since Karinhall is out. I even bought a sensational dress. I'll send it back."

"Keep it. You might just find a use for it."

"Oh? Expect to be invited to the Görings' again?" She went out without staying for an answer.

Pug prepared a couple of highballs to toast the news of his promotion, which he'd been saving. When he got upstairs, her light was out—an old unpleasant marital signal. He drank both highballs himself and slept in the library.

The next day was brightened for him by the German announcement that the *Graf Spee* had heroically scuttled itself after its historic victory, and that its captain had then nobly shot himself in a hotel in Montevideo. Pug heard over the BBC that three much lighter British vessels had in fact beaten the German warship in a running sea fight and sent it limping into the neutral port.

Also, when Rhoda learned of Pug's promotion, she shed her blues. His account of Natalie Jastrow fascinated and appalled her. "Let's hope she'll come to her senses and drop Briny," she said.

KARINHALL sat in a game preserve about two hours' drive from Berlin, behind electrically controlled gates, steel fences, and a gauntlet of machine-gun-bearing Luftwaffe sentinels.

In the vaulted banquet room, amid a dazzling crush of uniformed Nazis and their women, Adolf Hitler was playing with Göring's little girl. The guests were cooing and clapping as their leader in his field-grey coat held the child in his arms and teased her with a cake. Göring and his statuesque wife, both ablaze in operatic finery, stood near, beaming with pride.

"The Führer loves children," said the Luftwaffe officer accompanying the two Americans. "Ach, if he could only marry—"

The Görings escorted Hitler to the long buffet table, and liveried lackeys set up gilt tables and chairs and helped the guests to food and wine. Guided by the Luftwaffe officer, Pug and Gianelli sat at a table with a banker named Wolf Stöller, a man in his fifties who hailed Gianelli as an old acquaintance.

Pug knew that Stöller's bank was the chief conduit by which Göring was amassing his riches. His speciality was acquiring *Objekte,* the term for Jewish-owned companies forced to the wall by restrictive codes of law. Stöller's technique was to find and unite all the buyers interested in an *Objekt,* and to make a single very low offer. The owners had the choice of taking it or going bankrupt. Stöller's group then divided up the firm. The big prizes—metal, banking, textiles—Göring bought up himself.

Clever and cordial, Stöller spoke fine English and made bright jokes. He expressed his deep regard for the United States and melancholy regret that its relations with Germany were not better. Could he not do something to improve them, he said, by inviting Gianelli and the Henrys for a weekend at his estate, Abendruh?

Gianelli declined; he had to leave in the morning. Victor Henry had no stomach for Stöller, but it was part of his job to move about among influential Germans and it might amuse Rhoda. He said he would come.

Stöller took the two Americans on a tour of Göring's vast, flamboyant mansion, but before they had gone far, the Luftwaffe officer caught up with them and whispered to the German banker.

"Ah, what a pity. Now you must go to your meeting," said Stöller. "Captain Henry, my office will telephone you tomorrow about the weekend." He accompanied them to a room hung with antlers. On a settee beside a roaring fire lolled Göring, one thick white-booted leg off the floor, sipping coffee from a gold demitasse. Across from him sat Ribbentrop, the foreign minister.

Göring nodded familiarly at Gianelli. Stöller introduced Victor

Henry, backed out of the room, and closed the door. Ribbentrop stared at the ceiling. "You will have seven minutes of the Führer's time to state your business," he said in German.

Gianelli stammered, "Excellency, permit me to reply in English. I am here in a private capacity, and I regard that much time as an extraordinary courtesy to my country and my President."

Ribbentrop's face remained blank, so Pug translated. The Foreign Minister burst out in English. "This peculiar visitation is another studied insult by your President to the German head of state. Whoever heard of sending a private citizen as an emissary in such matters? Germany did not withdraw its ambassador from Washington by choice. The United States first made the hostile gesture. The United States has allowed a campaign of hate propaganda against the German people. And it has revised its Neutrality Act in blatant favour of England and France."

Gianelli looked shaken at the Foreign Minister's tirade.

Göring said in a milder tone, "What is your purpose here, Mr. Gianelli?"

"Field Marshal, I am an informal messenger from my President to your Führer, and I have a single question to put to him that could have lasting historical results."

"What is the question?" Göring said.

The banker's face was going ashen. "Field Marshal, by my President's order, the question is for the Führer." In the silence that followed, Hitler came into the room.

Göring and Ribbentrop rose as quickly as the Americans. Göring moved from the settee to a chair, and Hitler took his place. He gave the Americans a grave glance.

"Luigi Gianelli, American banker. Captain Victor Henry, United States naval attaché in Berlin," said Ribbentrop in a sarcastic tone.

The banker attempted an expression of gratitude in German for the interview, then, shifting to English, he put to the Führer the question about Sumner Welles. Pug translated.

A bitter little smile moved Hitler's moustache, and he began to speak in clear, Bavarian-accented German. "Your esteemed President, Herr Gianelli, seems to feel a remarkable sense of responsibility for the course of world history. This is strange in that the United States not only failed to join the League of Nations but has repeatedly indicated that she wants no foreign entanglements." German political aims were simple, Hitler went on. Five centuries before Columbus discovered America, there had been a German empire at the heart of Europe. Over and over again, other powers had attempted to fragment the German nation, but each time it had rallied and thrown off foreign yokes.

Victor Henry, translating, was struck by Hitler's steady manner, by his apparent moral conviction, and by his identification of himself with the German nation—"and so I restored the Rhineland to the Reich . . . I brought back Austria to its historical origins"—and by his broad vision of history.

"I share the President's desire for peace," Hitler was saying, gesturing now. "I was born to create, not to destroy. But the British and French leaders call for the destruction of 'Hitlerism'" —he brought out the foreign term with contempt—"as their price for peace. This attitude will doom Europe, because I and the German people are one." His voice began to rise. "How can the English and French be so blind to realities? I achieved air parity in 1937. Since then I have never stopped building planes, planes, planes, U-boats, U-boats, U-boats, tanks, tanks, tanks!" He was shouting now, and sweeping both fists down again and again to strike the floor, bending far over so that the famous black lock of hair tumbled in his face. Then, suddenly, dramatically, his voice dropped. "Let the test of fire come. I have done my utmost, and my conscience is clear before the bar of history."

Hitler stood with an air of dismissal, his eyes burning and distant. Göring lumbered to his feet. "*Mein Führer*, after this wonderfully clear presentation of the realities, you offer no objection to this visit of Herr Sumner Welles, I take it."

Hitler shrugged. "I have no wish to return discourtesy with discourtesy. But until the British will to destroy me is itself destroyed, the only road to peace is through German victory. Anything else is irrelevant." He strode out through the door.

Göring said to Gianelli, "President Roosevelt has his reply. The Führer will not reject the Welles mission."

"I understood him to call the mission irrelevant," Ribbentrop said in a strained voice.

"If you want to press the Führer for clarification," Göring said to him, "go ahead. I think I know him." He turned to the banker. "Tell your President that the Führer will receive Welles, but that unless the British and the French drop their aim of removing the Führer, the result will be the death of millions and final German victory."

"That will be the result in any case. The die will be cast before Mr. Sumner Welles can pack his papers," said Ribbentrop.

With a change to geniality, Göring took each of the two Americans by an elbow. "I hope you are not leaving so soon?"

"I regret that my plane will not wait," Gianelli replied.

"Then you must come again. I will walk out with you."

Arm-in-arm with Göring, the Americans walked down the corridors of Karinhall. He chatted about the U-boat programme and the Luftwaffe; he hoped their President was aware of Germany's industrial strength. By the time they reached the front doors, Gianelli had recovered enough to say, "Excellency, I will have to tell the President that your Foreign Minister does not welcome the Welles mission and has stated the Führer does not."

Göring's face toughened. "If Welles comes, the Führer will see him. That is official. Remember this. Germany is like all countries. Not everybody here wants peace. But I do."

VICTOR HENRY sat up most of the night composing his report to the President. After an account of the facts, he wrote:

> I would guess that Göring wanted it to take place, and that Hitler didn't mind. I got the feeling that he enjoyed sounding off to a pair of Americans who would report directly to you. And I believe Ribbentrop was doing his dirty work for him, expressing what he really feels. I don't think any of them give a damn whether Welles comes or not, though I think Hitler would receive him. All three acted as though the offensive in the west is ready to roll. If the British are as set on their terms as Hitler is on his, you'll have all-out war in the spring.

RHODA hugged Pug when he told her about their weekend invitation. He didn't mention his uneasy feelings about Stöller.

The chauffeur sent by Stöller drove past the colonnaded front entrance to Abendruh and dropped them at a back door, where a maid conducted them up some narrow servants' stairs. Pug wondered whether this was a calculated German insult. But they were given a richly-furnished bedroom and sitting room; and the mystery of the back stairs cleared up when they went to dinner. The curving main staircase, balustraded in red marble, had been entirely covered with a polished wooden slide. Down below, the Stöllers and their guests stood watching an elegant couple in dinner clothes sliding down, the woman hysterical with laughter as her green silk dress pulled up over her legs.

"Oh my gawd, Pug, I'll *die!*" chortled Rhoda. "I can't *possibly!*" But of course she made the slide, screaming with embarrassment, exposing her legs clear up to her lacy underwear. She arrived at the bottom scarlet-faced, amid cheers and congratulations. It was a sure icebreaker, Pug thought, if crude.

After dinner, a string quartet played Beethoven, and a fat soprano sang Schubert songs. Rhoda felt in her element, and when dancing followed, she had one partner after another. At last Stöller took Pug to a library, where a prominent actor and Dr. Knopfmann, the head of an electrical works, sat over brandy.

"Ah, here is Captain Henry," said the actor, in a rich ringing voice. "What better authority do you want? Let's ask him."

"No war talk this weekend," said Stöller.

"I don't mind," Pug said, accepting brandy and settling in a leather chair. "What's the question?"

Dr. Knopfmann said, "I maintain that the Americans will accept the *fait accompli* once England is defeated. When Europe is normalized, we can have a hundred years of peace."

"First you have to lick England," Pug said.

The actor said, "Oh, I think we can assume that's in the cards—providing the Americans don't step in."

Stöller said, "Your President doesn't try to hide his British sympathies, Victor. Would you say the people are against him?"

"Yes, but remember that American opinion can shift fast."

The eyes of the Germans flickered at each other. Dr. Knopfmann said, "A shift in public opinion is manufactured."

"There's the live nerve," Stöller said. "It's where the vast power of the American Jews is such a vital factor in the war picture." He proceeded to reel off a list of Jewish officials in Washington, and he made the usual Nazi assertion that the Jews had American finance and even the presidency in their pockets.

Wearily, Pug gave his stock answers to stock anti-Semitism: the all but solid Christian ownership of banks, industry, newspapers, and publishing houses; the predominantly Christian composition of Congress, the Cabinet, the Executive branch, the Supreme Court, and all the rest. On his hearers' faces appeared the superior smirk of Germans when discussing Jews. Stöller said, "That's always the Jewish line, how unimportant they are."

"Would you recommend that we take away what businesses they do have? Make *Objekte* of them?"

Stöller laughed. "You're well informed, Victor."

"Is it your position," the actor said, "that the Jewish question really has no bearing on America's entry into the war?"

"No. Americans do react sharply to injustice and suffering."

The smirk reappeared on the three faces, and Stöller said, "Victor speaks diplomatically, but his connections are O.K. Congressman Lacouture of Florida is practically in his family. He fought a great battle against revising the Neutrality Act."

This caught Pug off guard, but he said calmly, "You're well informed, too. Our connection's not exactly public knowledge."

Stöller laughed. "The air minister told me. He admires Lacouture. Ach, how did it get to be so late? There's a little supper on, gentlemen. How about an omelette and some champagne?"

ON CHRISTMAS EVE, Victor Henry walked home from the embassy, feeling the need of air and exercise. Berlin's shop-windows offered colourful displays, but very little of what was shown was for sale. Hearing Christmas songs from behind curtained windows, Pug could picture the Berliners sitting around tinsel-draped fir trees, trying to make merry on watery beer and salt mackerel. Suddenly, out of the darkness, a figure approached.

384

"Captain Henry? I'm Rosenthal, the owner of your house."

"Oh, yes. Hello." Shaking hands in the glow of a blue streetlight, Pug saw that the Jew had lost a shocking lot of weight.

"Forgive me. My wife and I are to be sent to Poland soon. We can't take our things, so perhaps you and Mrs. Henry would care to buy something—at a very reasonable price."

Pug had heard of the "resettlement" of the Berlin Jews in new Polish ghettos. "You have a factory here," he said, disturbed. "Can't your people keep an eye on your things for you?"

"The fact is I've sold my firm . . . ."

"Did you sell out to the Stöller bank?"

The Jew's face showed astonishment. "You know about these matters? Yes, the Stöller bank. I received a fair price." He permitted himself a single ironic glance into Henry's eyes. "But the proceeds were tied up to settle other affairs. My wife and I will be more comfortable in Poland with a little ready money . . . ."

"Herr Rosenthal, I must not take advantage of your misfortune."

"Captain Henry, you can't possibly do me and my wife a greater kindness than to buy something." He put a card in Pug's hand and melted into the blackout.

THE NEXT pouch of navy mail contained an A1Nav listing changes of duty for most of the new captains. They were becoming execs of battleships, commanding officers of cruisers, chiefs of staff to admirals at sea. For Pug there were no orders. He stared out of the window at Hitler's chancellery. Then, in a long letter to Vice-Admiral Preble he poured out his disgust with his present assignment and his desire to go back to sea.

A few days later another White House envelope came with a thickly pencilled scrawl. It must have crossed his letter:

> Your report is really grand, and gives me a helpful picture. Hitler is a strange one, isn't he? Everybody's reaction is a little different. I'm delighted that you are where you are, and I have told CNO that. He says you want to come back in May for a wedding. That will be arranged. Be sure to drop in on me . . . .
>
> FDR

Resigned to his stay in Berlin, Victor Henry bought two of Rosenthal's carpets and a set of English china that Rhoda loved. It seemed to Pug that the moral gap between him and Stöller had narrowed. Notwithstanding Rosenthal's pathetic gratitude for the deal, his possessions were *Objekte*.

13

Miami Beach, New Year's Day

Briny dear—

I can't think of a better way to start 1940 than by writing to you. I'm home, typing away in my old bedroom, which seems one-tenth as large as I remembered it. Oh, my love, I had forgotten what a marvellous place the United States is!

When I reached New York my father was already out of the hospital—I learned this by phoning home—so I blew two hundred dollars on a 1934 Dodge coup, and I *drove* to Florida to get the feel of the country again. I found my father fine after his heart attack, but he goes on and on with worry about Uncle Aaron.

I drove down via Washington and saw Slote. When I told him I'd fallen head over ears in love with you, he actually tottered into a chair, pale as a ghost. A conversation ensued that went on for hours, in a bar, in my car, on foot around the Lincoln Memorial in a freezing wind. He kept making the same points: that it was a temporary physical infatuation; that I was an intellectual woman and you just a charming boy, etc., etc. He insisted that he and I would get married once I was over this nuttiness.

Maybe he's right about me and you. I choose not to look beyond the present. I'm still overwhelmed, I still love you, I still long for you. I've never been so happy in all my life.

I adore you.
Natalie

Natalie darling—

You don't have to tell me how good the United States is, compared with Europe. I'm so homesick at this point, I could die. This is quite aside from my yearning for you, which is how iron filings must feel around a magnet. Sometimes when I'm sitting here in my room, the pull gets so strong, I feel if I let go of my chair I'd float out of the window and straight to you.

Slote only *thinks* he's going to marry you. He had his chance.

Getting Aaron out of here seems to be a bit of a project. There was a technical foul-up in his naturalization, way back, that he never bothered to correct. This will straighten out, of course—they've said as much in Rome—but it's taking time.

So I won't abandon him now, but I must come home by mid-April. Aside from my brother's wedding, my father's gotten me admitted to submarine school, where the next officer course starts May 27. However, I'll only enroll if the war breaks wide open.

A.J. and I still have our coffee in the lemon house. I smell the blossoms and close my eyes and there you are for a moment. Natalie, there has to be a God or I wouldn't have found you, and He has to be the same God for both of us. I love you.

Briny

"Well, well, well," Natalie said aloud, as her tears dropped on the flimsy airmail paper. She looked at the date: February 10! This was April 9—two months for an airmail letter! He might be on his way back by now.

Just then a news broadcast came drifting through her open window from the garden where her father was sitting. The announcer's dramatic tones caught her attention:

"The 'phony war' has ended. Nazi Germany has invaded Norway and Denmark. Fierce resistance is reported by the Norwegian government at Oslo, Narvik, Trondheim, and other coastal points. The British navy is moving rapidly to cut off the invasion. Winston Churchill, First Lord of the Admiralty, declared this morning, 'All German vessels entering the Skagerrak will be sunk . . . .'"

Going outside, Natalie was surprised to find that her father had fallen asleep, though the radio was blaring. She touched his shoulder. "Pa?" He did not respond. She thrust her hand inside his shirt; there was no heartbeat. In the instant before she ran in to call the doctor, she saw on her dead father's face a resemblance to Aaron Jastrow that in his lifetime she had never observed.

BIG GERMAN BREAKTHROUGH!
Still Not Our Fight, Declares Lacouture

IN NEW YORK, Janice Lacouture was shopping for her trousseau. Passing a corner newsstand she saw her father's words in screaming headlines. She wondered how they would go down with her prospective in-laws. Rhoda, Pug, and Byron, back from Europe, were due at three o'clock aboard the cruiser *Helena*.

Back at her apartment she dropped her armload of packages and called her answering service, briskly jotting notes on a pad. There was a call from the Waldorf, from a man named Palmer Kirby who said he was a friend of the family.

Janice rang him. "The Henrys were very hospitable to me in Berlin," he told her. "Mrs. Henry wrote me they'd be arriving in New York today, and told me to contact them through you. I'd like to take all of you to dinner."

"That's kind of you, but I don't know their plans."

"Well, suppose I make reservations here? If you can come, I'll expect you at six. If not, just give me a ring."

"Thank you, Dr. Kirby."

Janice found Rhoda waiting by a heap of luggage in the customs shed. "Well, isn't this Janice?" she said, stepping forward. "I'm Rhoda Henry."

"Oh, yes, Mrs. Henry! Hello!"

"My dear, how ravishing you are. Lucky Warren! How is he?"

"All right, I hope. He's sweating out carrier landings somewhere."

Victor Henry came up to them and Janice told the Henrys about Palmer Kirby's invitation. "Well, of all things," Rhoda said. "Of course dinner at the Waldorf would be lovely, take the taste of Berlin out of our mouths! Janice, Germany's just gruesome."

"Matter of fact, I have to talk to Kirby," Pug said.

Byron appeared through the crowd. "Hey, Janice?" he said, shaking her hand. "I'm Warren's brother. I hoped you'd be here." He gave her a small box with a London label.

Janice opened it, and there lay a Victorian pin, a little golden elephant with red stones for eyes. "Good heavens!" she said.

"Anybody who marries one of us needs the patience of an

388

elephant," said Byron. "I'm flying to Miami this evening to see someone I hope will be another member of the family."

Janice kissed him and said, "That must be some girl in Miami. Bring her to the wedding with you. Don't forget."

"*I HAVE nothing to offer,*" said the strong grainy voice, "*but blood, toil, tears, and sweat . . . .*"

"Why, he's a genius!" Rhoda said. Champagne glasses in hand, she, Pug, Janice, and Kirby were listening to the radio.

"*You ask, what is our policy? I will say, it is to wage war, by sea, land, and air, with all our might and all the strength that God can give us: to wage war against a monstrous tyranny, never surpassed in the dark, lamentable catalogue of human crime. That is our policy. You ask, what is our aim? I can answer in one word: Victory —victory at all costs, victory in spite of all terror . . . .*"

When the speech ended, the announcer said, "You have just heard the Prime Minister of Great Britain, Winston Churchill."

Pug said to Kirby, "Can we talk for a few minutes?"

Rhoda smiled. "Champagne and business as usual. That's Pug."

"Come along," Kirby said, leading Pug into the hotel bedroom.

Pug said, "Palmer, are you working on a uranium bomb?"

Kirby turned and looked into Pug's eyes. The silence lasted a long time. Kirby lit his pipe. "I'm not a chemist, and this uranium thing is mainly a chemical engineering problem. Electricity does come into production techniques. A couple of months ago I was asked to be a consultant. The bomb is probably years away, although the nuclear boys say it could be practicable now."

"Do you mind telling me about it?"

Kirby shook his head. "There's a rare hot isotope of uranium, U-235. This substance may turn out to have fantastic explosive powers, through a chain reaction that gives a huge release of energy. The amount of pure U-235 these chemical engineers want will take one hell of a big industrial effort to deliver."

"One last point. Do you think the President should be advised to get off his ass about uranium?"

"The question is, how far along are the Germans? If Hitler gets uranium bombs first, it could be disagreeable."

ON THE flying bridge of the fishing boat *Blue Bird*, moving gently along in the Gulf Stream, Byron and Natalie lay in each other's arms. The sunburned lovers had forgotten the fish, the lines, and the skipper at the wheel below.

The ship-to-shore telephone crackled and there was a loud rapping from below. "Hey, Mr. Henry! Your father is calling you."

"My father?" Byron leapt up and went down the companion-way to the telephone. "What's up, Dad? Is everybody O.K.?"

"Have you heard the radio?" Pug said. "The British Expeditionary Force is hightailing it for the Channel, but it may already be too late. The Germans may actually bag the entire British army."

"Good God," Byron said. "If they do that the war's over! How could this happen in three days?"

"Well, it has. Now," Pug went on. "Warren's thirty-day leave has been cancelled, so he and Janice are getting married tomorrow. They'll have a one-day honeymoon, and then he goes straight out to the Pacific Fleet. So. Number one. You've got to get to Pensacola by tomorrow at ten, to be his best man."

Byron said, "I'll be there."

"Number two. If you want to get into that May twenty-seventh class at sub school, you must take the physical by Saturday."

"Dad," Byron said. "Natalie and I are getting married."

Pug said, "I see. Well, that might or might not affect your admittance. In general, unmarried candidates get preference but I can't hate you for wanting to marry that beautiful young lady. Good-bye. Try to bring Natalie to Pensacola."

14

With a groan, Lieutenant (jg.) Warren Henry woke at seven on his wedding day. Until four he had been in the sweet arms of his bride-to-be in a hotel room outside Pensacola. As he stumbled to the shower, he wondered somewhat about his behaviour. But after all, a one-night honeymoon, and then a separation of thousands of miles, was too much to ask of human nature.

For all his remorse, the prospect of the parting was not bothering

Warren much. Janice would be in Pearl Harbor soon, and the sudden orders to the Pacific had put him in an excited glow. His spirits soaring, he rang for the mess steward, ordered double ham and eggs, and set about getting dressed.

"Come in!" he called to a knock on his door. "Hey, *Briny!*" he said, when he saw who it was. "Gosh, how long has it been?"

Warren ordered more breakfast for his brother. "Sit down. We have a lot to catch up on."

They talked over breakfast and while Warren packed. "What about Natalie, Byron? Did she come?"

"Sure. I parked her at Janice's house. That was decent of Janice, telephoning last night! You know, we're getting married."

"Good for you. She sounds like a marvellous girl. You marrying up now, or after sub school?"

"Who the devil says I'm going to sub school?"

Warren deftly moved clothes from bureau to a footlocker. "Dad's right, Byron. If you wait till you get called up, they'll shove you around and you may not even draw the duty you want. But why in heaven's name do you want subs when you could fly?"

"I got interested in subs." Byron described Prien's talk in Berlin on the sinking of the *Royal Oak*.

"That was a brave exploit," Warren admitted. "But this is an air war, Briny. Planes are the thing from now on." Tossing Byron a large grey book, he said with a grin, "Take a look through *The Flight Jacket*. I'm there in Squadron Five."

Byron opened the yearbook. "Holy cow, Warren, number one in ground school! How'd you do that and court Janice, too?"

"It took a toll." Warren made an exhausted face, and the two brothers laughed.

NATALIE had often visited the homes of wealthy college friends, but the rambling magnificence of the Lacouture mansion unsettled her. Janice scampered to meet her in a fluttery pink housecoat, her blonde hair flying. "I'll never be ready. Let's get you some breakfast."

"Please, just put me in some corner till we go. I'm fine."

In a breakfast alcove facing the water, a maid brought her eggs and coffee on a silver tray. Natalie ate, and then took a letter from her handbag—faintly typed pages; A.J. would never learn to change a typewriter ribbon.

He was now taking his citizenship problem seriously. He had "derivative citizenship" from his father's naturalization around 1900 but difficulties had been caused by conflicting records of Aaron's age at the time. The man in Rome had demanded more and more documents, and Aaron had returned to Siena in deep confusion. The letter concluded:

> What comes next still makes me boil. The American consul here wrote that if I were to apply as a Jewish refugee I probably would have no trouble. The idiot wanted me to abandon all claim to being an American—*which I am*. Of course his letter was opened, and the Italian authorities now know my problem.
>
> Natalie, will you tell all this to Leslie Slote? A noose of red tape can be cut by one word spoken in the right place.

Natalie heard the sound of feet on a staircase, and the bride came sailing in, wheat-coloured hair laced with pearls, white satin clinging to flanks and breasts. "Well, I did it!"

Natalie jumped to her feet. "Oh, you're the loveliest sight!" The bride's eye had an ironic gleam. She felt hardly virginal. "Come on," she said. "You're riding with me."

AT THE church Natalie knew at once that the handsome woman in green chiffon didn't like her. Rhoda's polite handshake, her prim smile, told all.

Pug introduced Natalie to Madeline as "Byron's sidekick on the Polish jaunt", trying to make up for his wife's freeze.

"Oh, yes, wow!" Madeline smiled. Twenty-one, with Rhoda's skin and pert figure, she had her father's determined air. "I want to hear about that! I still haven't seen Briny, you know, and it's been more than two years."

The church was full. From the moment she entered the front pew with Rhoda, Pug and Madeline, Natalie felt uncomfortable. All around her were women in bright or pastel colours, and there she stood in black linen, worn out of a vague sense that she was

392

still in mourning for her father. Perhaps Slote was right, and encouraging Byron had been irresponsible. Slote was a bookish pagan like herself, and they would have been married by a judge.

As the bride paced down the aisle on the congressman's arm, Rhoda started to cry. When Pug took her hand, she clasped his. What fine sons they had, standing up there together!

Byron felt many eyes comparing him and his brother. Beside Warren's uniform his elegant Italian suit seemed frivolous.

As Janice lifted her veil, she and Warren exchanged an amused glance. With the minister beaming, they kissed, and laughed over a war-born joke that nobody else would ever know.

A jocund crowd poured into the beach club for the wedding luncheon. Champagne glass in hand, Byron firmly took Natalie from room to room, introducing her to the wedding party. She met Captain Henry's father, a short, upright man who had travelled in from California; and a knot of Rhoda's kin, Grovers of Washington, D.C., whose polished manners and expensive clothes set them off from the other guests, even the Lacoutures.

Rhoda gathered them up to join a family table. Lacouture was declaring that the President's request for fifty thousand aeroplanes was hysterical. "We have three thousand miles of good green water between us and Europe," he said, "and that's a better protection than any aeroplane. The Germans haven't got one that can fly to Scotland, let alone to America. Roosevelt just wants planes for England and France. But he'll never come out and *say* that."

"You're willing to see the British and French go down, then," Pug Henry said.

"Ask me if I'm willing to send three million American boys to prop up the old status quo in Europe. That's what this is all about."

"The British are propping up our own status quo free of charge, Congressman. If the Nazis get hold of their navy, that'll extend Hitler's reach to Pensacola Bay."

Lacouture said, "Yes, I can just see the *Rodney* and *Nelson* out there, flying the swastika and shelling our poor old beach club."

The war talk over roast beef and champagne had begun to irritate Natalie. She was glad when Byron took her away. "Can we go outside?" she said. "I don't want to dance."

They sat on the low wall of the terrace in the sun. Byron leaned towards her. "Darling, I think I may as well fly up to the sub school tomorrow to take that physical—what's the matter?"

"Nothing. Go on. You're flying to the sub school?"

"Only if you agree. I'll do nothing that we don't concur in, from now on and for ever."

"All right."

"And I'll make sure that a married applicant has a chance, and that if he's admitted he gets to spend time with his wife."

Victor Henry appeared on the terrace and Byron said, "Hi, looking for me?"

"Yes. I hear you're driving Madeline to the airport. Don't leave without me. I just talked to Washington and I've got to scoot back."

"When's your plane?" asked Natalie.

"One-forty," Pug told her, and went back into the club.

Natalie said, "I think I'll go to Washington on that plane."

"Why Washington, for crying out loud?" Byron said.

She put a hand to his face. "Aaron asked me to talk to Slote about his passport problem. While you're away, I can take care of it. What's the matter? You look as if you've been shot."

Byron stood up stiffly. "It's all right."

Warren insisted on coming to the airport too. "How do I know when I'll see you all again?" he kept saying. The upshot was that the Henrys, plus the bride and Natalie, all piled into Lacouture's Cadillac. Rhoda on the way out had snatched a bottle of champagne and some glasses.

By the time the car drove into the airport she was crying into a champagne-soaked handkerchief, stating that these were tears of happiness over Warren's wonderful marriage.

15

As the Battle of France went on, people began to perceive that mankind's destiny now hung on flying machines. The French implored the retreating British to throw all their aircraft into the battle, but Air Marshal Dowding told Winston Churchill that twenty-five squadrons had to be kept intact to save England, and Churchill listened to him. The French collapse therefore became foredoomed.

"I see only one way through now," Churchill wrote, "to wit, that Hitler should attack this country, and in so doing break his air weapon. If this happens, he will be left to face the winter with Europe writhing under his heel, and probably with the United States against him after the presidential election is over."

The German conquest of Europe and the growing menace of Japan posed a danger to the United States. The question arose: If selling aging warplanes to the British would enable them to go on knocking down German aircraft and wrecking German factories, might not that be the best security for America while new, more powerful machines were being built? The answer, from the U.S. Navy, Army, War Department, Congress, Press, and public, was a roaring *No!* Roosevelt wanted to help the British, but he could not sell them so much as a plane without risking impeachment.

IT WAS a shock for Victor Henry to see Franklin Roosevelt out from behind the desk in a wheelchair. The shirt-sleeved President was massive and powerful-looking down to the waist; below that, thin seersucker trousers hung pitifully on the slack fleshless legs. He was looking at a painting propped on a chair—a British man-of-war under full sail tossed on high seas.

"Hello there!" The President gave Pug a hearty handshake. "How about this picture, Pug? Like it?"

"It's fine, Mr. President. But I'm a sucker for sea scenes."

"So am I, but d'you know the rigging's wrong?" The President pointed out the flaws, relishing his expertise. Then he wheeled himself to his desk. "Golly, the sun's going down, and it's still sweltering in here. Would you like a drink? I'm supposed to mix a passable martini."

"Nothing better, sir."

The President pressed a buzzer and a valet appeared. "Let's go," Roosevelt said to him. "Come along, Pug."

All down one long hall, in the elevator, and down another hall, the President glanced at papers and scrawled notes. His gusto

395

for the work was evident, despite the heavy smudges under his eyes. They arrived in a small sitting room, and the valet wheeled a small cocktail bar beside the President's chair.

"Well, how was the wedding, Pug?" asked the President, measuring out gin and vermouth like an apothecary. He laughed wryly at Victor Henry's account of the congressman's arguments. "Well, that's what we're up against. And Ike Lacouture's running for the Senate. He'll give us real trouble if he gets in."

A very tall woman came into the room. "Just in time!" exclaimed the President. "This is the famous Pug Henry, dear."

"Oh? What a pleasure." Mrs. Roosevelt shook hands firmly. Her smile was gentle and sweet, despite the much caricatured protruding teeth. "How do you think the war's going, Captain?"

"It's very bad, ma'am."

Roosevelt said, "Are you surprised?"

Pug took a minute. "Well, sir, in January, all German government war contracts had a terminal date of July first, indicating they were mighty sure the western campaign would be short."

Roosevelt's eyes widened. "That was never brought to my attention. Very interesting."

They talked about the meeting with Hitler at Karinhall. Mrs. Roosevelt interjected in a sharp, serious tone, "Captain, do you think that Mr. Hitler is a madman?"

"Ma'am, he gave a rundown on the history of central Europe that all meshed together and ticked like a watch."

"Or a time bomb," said the President.

Pug smiled at the grim joke.

The President went on in a business-like tone, "That Sumner Welles trip didn't come to anything, Pug, but we made the effort. You were very helpful. What would you think of going to England as a naval observer? Possibly after a month more in Berlin?"

Hoping that the mood was as pleasant as it seemed, Pug said, "Mr. President, any chance of my not going back to Berlin?"

Roosevelt looked gravely at the captain for an uncomfortable few seconds. "You go back there, Pug. I know you're a seafaring man. You'll get your sea command."

"Yes, Mr. President."

"The British are reporting a big success with something called RDF, Radio Direction Finding," the President said. "I'd be interested in your impressions."

"I'll go to London, sir, if that's your desire."

"Now, what's your guess, Pug? Is that man in the White House going to break George Washington's rule and try for a third term?"

"Sir, all I know is that for the next four years we're going to need a strong Commander-in-Chief."

A CRASHING thunderstorm caught Pug as he was leaving the White House. He ducked into a crowded doorway marked PRESS.

All at once a hand thwacked his shoulder. "I say, Henry, you've got yourself another stripe!" Alistair Tudsbury beamed down at him through thick glasses.

"Hello there, Tudsbury!"

"Why aren't you in Berlin, old man?" As he spoke, a small British car pulled up to the entrance and honked. "That's Pamela. Come along with us to the British embassy for cocktails. You'll meet some chaps you ought to know." Tudsbury propelled him into the car. "Pam, look who I bagged!"

"Why, how marvellous." Pamela clasped Pug's hand. "Tell me about your family," she said as they drove off. "Is your wife well? And the boy who was caught in Poland?"

"My wife's fine, and so's Byron. By the way, the girl he went to Poland with is Natalie Jastrow. She says she knows you."

"Natalie Jastrow! Really?" Pamela gave Henry a quizzical glance. "Oh, yes. She was visiting a chap in your embassy in Warsaw, I should think. Leslie Slote."

"Exactly. And now she and my son intend to get married."

"Bless me. Well, she's an extraordinary girl."

"Slote's coming to this party," Tudsbury said.

At the British embassy they joined the reception line, which extended up the wide red-carpeted stairs. The guest of honour stood with the ambassador at the top.

"Captain Henry, Air Commodore Burne-Wilke," Tudsbury said. "Burne-Wilke is here to try to scare up any old useless aeroplanes you happen to have lying around."

"Yes, best prices offered," said the RAF man, smiling.

Tudsbury led Pug through two large, smoky reception rooms, introducing him to many people. They came upon Pamela at a round table with Leslie Slote and Natalie Jastrow. Natalie gave Pug a preoccupied smile, saying, "Small world."

When Pamela had introduced her father to Natalie, Slote said, "Talky, maybe you can settle our argument. What are the chances that Italy will jump into the war?"

"It's too soon. Mussolini will wait until France has all but stopped twitching. Why do you ask?"

Natalie said, "I've got an old uncle in Siena who has to be fetched out. There's nobody but me to do it."

Pamela jumped up. "Will you dance with me?" she said to Pug.

"Why, sure." Knowing she disliked dancing, he was puzzled.

"Thanks," she said as he accompanied her towards the musicians. "Phil Rule was heading for us. I've had enough of him."

Pug took her in his arms. "Phil Rule?"

"He was the man in my life for far too long. He'd been at Oxford with Leslie Slote and was rooming with him in Paris. They're much alike, a pair of regular rips." Then she said more cheerfully, "I'm engaged to be married."

"I noticed your ring. Who is he, Pamela?"

"His name's Teddy Gallard. He's twenty-eight, comes from an old Northamptonshire family. He's a fighter pilot in the RAF."

When the music changed they walked to the foyer and sat under a bad painting of Queen Mary. Pamela was looking, he thought, exceptionally pretty; her hair hung to her shoulders in glossy waves.

"I have a yen to go home and join the WAAFs—our Women's Auxiliary Air Force. What do you think?"

"Me? I approve. Your father can get another secretary. Your lucky RAF man is there."

She coloured at the word "lucky". "It's not that simple. Talky's eyes get tired. He needs to dictate and have things read to him. Is it right to abandon him?"

"He's your father, Pamela, not your son."

Pamela's eyes glistened at him. "Well, perhaps we should return to him now, Captain Henry."

"Call me Pug. Most people do."

"Yes, I've heard them. What does it mean?"

"I was a boxer in school, so I got tagged Pug."

"You boxed? Do you still?"

He grinned. "Too strenuous. Tennis is my game now."

"Oh? I play fair tennis."

"If I ever get to London, maybe we can have a game."

"Is there"—she hesitated—"a chance of your coming to London?"

"It's not impossible. Ah, there they are."

As they reached the table, Slote stood up and offered his hand to Natalie, who rose too. "We have theatre tickets," he said. "We'll have to leave if we're to get some dinner first."

AFTER the theatre Slote took Natalie to his apartment, hoping in a common masculine way to win her back in one evening.

He opened his apartment door and snapped on lights. "Ye gods, a quarter to one. How about a drink?"

"If I'm to search New York courthouses for Aaron's documents tomorrow, I'd better get to bed."

"Let me see his letter again."

Slote studied the letter, then took a government tome from the bookshelves. Finally he said, "Aaron's in trouble on several counts. There's the problem about his father's naturalization. But even if that's all right, there's this rule that a naturalized citizen who lives abroad continuously for more than five years forfeits his citizenship." He held up the book. "Come here."

Natalie sat on the arm of the chair, and Slote showed her a list of exceptions to the five-year rule, some of which seemed to fit Aaron Jastrow's case. "The best thing now, by far, is to get the Secretary of State to drop a word to Rome," Slote said. "I'll get on to it first thing in the morning."

Natalie smiled at him. "It certainly helps to know a man who knows a man, doesn't it? Leslie, will you also get me permission to go to Italy? Without me, Aaron will never pull himself together and leave."

He shook his head. "I told you, the department's advising

Americans to get out of Italy. But I don't think you want to go there to help Aaron. Not really. You're just running away, Natalie. You're in way over your head with your submarine boy."

"Aren't you clever!" Natalie said.

Slote went to the kitchen and emerged with two highballs.

Natalie sipped hers. "My goodness, what a rich drink. I do believe you're nothing but a wolf."

He took her by the shoulders. "I love you. I'll try every way I can to get you back."

"Fair enough. But Leslie, I must go to Italy. My father was worrying over Aaron the day he died. Maybe this is irrational expiation, but I've got to bring Aaron home."

"I'll arrange it, if it's arrangeable."

"Now you're talking. Thanks. Good night." She put down her glass, kissed him lightly, and went.

May 23

Briny, my love—

When you receive this I ought to be in Lisbon. I'm flying to Italy to fetch Uncle Aaron. With luck I'll be back in two months or less. Sweetheart, don't be angry. It's good for both of us to catch our breaths.

Darling—weren't you having sober second thoughts about me at Warren's wedding? Honestly, I could see your mother's viewpoint. Why on earth should her little boy want to marry this dusky Jewess when there are Rhine maidens like Janice around? Should you and I try to bridge such a big gap in background and interest? I'm *not* backing out, Byron, *I love you*. But a couple of months to think this over is not much.

Leslie Slote dropped everything to solve Aaron's mess, and word has now gone to Rome *from the Secretary's office* to expedite Aaron's return. I've told Leslie that I love you and have promised to marry you. You'll be admitted to submarine school, I'm positive, and I think deep down you want it. When I come back, if you still want me, I'm yours.

Love you,
Natalie

400

Natalie had found it surprisingly easy to get a plane ticket into the warring continent, but then tried for five days to fly from Lisbon to Rome, and finally booked passage on a Greek freighter bound for Naples. En route, the ship's radio squawked the BBC stories of the French government's flight from Paris, of Churchill's promise to fight to the end, and of Italy's jump into the war. She arrived in Italy nervous and exhausted, feeling she had better get Aaron out of Siena at once.

But in Siena nothing had changed. Aaron sat reading under a big elm. "Natalie! You made it!" He came stumping towards her on a cane. "Come inside, my dear, you'll want some refreshment."

In his study the piles of manuscript, notes, and the array of reference books were all in the same places. "Why, Aaron, you haven't even begun to pack! Didn't word come from Washington?"

"That was fine of Leslie, but—" He sank into a chair. It seemed that the day Italy entered the war, a man from the Italian security police had come to warn him that, as a stateless person of Polish origin, he was confined to Siena until further notice.

The next day Natalie went to see the young consul in Florence. His nameplate read AUGUST VAN WINAKER II. "I'm sorry I kept you waiting," he said, escorting her to a chair, "but people are scurrying home in droves, and just dumping everything on us."

Natalie told him about Jastrow's new problem, adding, as tactfully as she could, that Italian security undoubtedly knew of his situation from intercepting Van Winaker's own letter.

"Oh, how perfectly awful," gasped the consul. "You're quite right. I didn't have my thinking-cap on when I wrote that letter. Well! I'm blessed if I know, just offhand, what we do now."

"May I make a suggestion?" Natalie spoke sweetly. "Just renew his passport. That would stop this statelessness business."

"Oh, that's not so easy. Congress makes the immigration laws, not the consular service."

"Mr. Van Winaker, the Secretary of State wants Aaron cleared."

"Let's get one thing straight. I heard from Rome, but I have had no instructions from the Secretary. He couldn't go on record as intervening for one individual in matters involving equal treatment under law. I couldn't be sorrier, but it's my duty to—"

The man was getting on Natalie's nerves. "It strikes me that your duty is to help us, and you're not doing it."

He opened his eyes very wide. "Tell you what, I'll comb your uncle's file again. Maybe I'll think of something."

"You will try to find a way to give him a passport?"

"Or to get him out. That's a promise. Come back in a week."

16

Silvery fat barrage balloons, shining in a cloudless sky ahead of Pug's plane, gave the approach to the British Isles a carnival touch. The land below looked very peaceful in the fine August weather. Sheep were grazing, farmers were reaping corn—the pleasant England of picture books and poems.

For Pug it was the end of a tedious journey which had begun with the arrival in Berlin of a letter from the White House:

Dear Pug—

How about going to London now for a look at Radio Direction Finding, as we discussed? You'll get dispatch orders, and our friends will be expecting you. London should be interesting now, if a bit warm. Let me know if you think it's too warm for us to give them fifty destroyers.

FDR

Pug had mixed feelings. Any excuse to leave Berlin was welcome. The blare and boasts in the newspapers, the women strolling the boulevards in French silks and cosmetics, the Polish hams, Danish butter, French veal and wine—it was all becoming intolerable. Because of the worsening of the war Rhoda had stayed in the States when he had returned to Berlin.

"How the devil do you keep looking so fit?" he said to Blinker Vance, the naval attaché who met him at the London airport. Vance's slim waist was as it had been at Annapolis.

"Oh, a couple of hours of tennis a day does it."

"Really? Great war you've got here."

"Oh, the war. It's going on in the sky. Mostly to the south. So far they haven't dropped anything on London."

402

Pug was struck by the serene look of the city, and the cheery, well-dressed crowds. The goods in the shop windows surprised him. Berlin, even with its infusion of loot, was bleak by comparison.

Vance drove him to an apartment off Grosvenor Square, and Pug unpacked his bags, then settled down for a nap. The ring of a telephone startled him out of it.

"Captain Henry? Major General Tillet here." The voice was crisp and very British. "I'm driving down to Portsmouth tomorrow. Possibly drop in on a Chain Home station on the Isle of Wight. Would you care to come along?"

Pug had never heard the expression "Chain Home". "That'll be fine, General. Thank you."

"Jolly good! Suppose I pick you up at five, and we make an early start? You might take along a shaving kit and a shirt."

It was now six in the evening. Pug turned on the radio. In a calm, almost desultory voice, the broadcaster told of a massive air battle that had been raging all afternoon. The RAF had shot down more than a hundred German planes and had lost twenty-five. The fight was continuing, the announcer said. If this bulletin were true, Pug thought, an astonishing victory was shaping up.

He called Pamela Tudsbury's number and another girl informed him that Pamela was a WAAF, working at a headquarters outside London. She gave him the number. He tried it, and there Pamela was.

"Captain Henry! Oh, wonderful! You picked the right day to arrive! Have you heard the news?"

"Yes. But I'm not used to believing the radio."

She gave an exhilarated laugh. "Oh, to be sure. The *Berlin* radio. Well, it's all quite true, though it's not over yet. By the way, if inspection tours are in order for you, I'm working at Group Operations, Number 11 Fighter Group."

"Fine. How's your fiancé?"

"Oh, Ted's fit as a flea. He's on the ground at the moment. Any chance we can see you? We'll be coming to London next week."

"Next week I should still be around."

"Lovely! I'll call you. I'm so glad you're here."

London wore a golden light that evening. Pug walked at random down crooked streets, along elegant rows of houses and through a park where swans glided on calm water. He dined alone on good roast beef. London was a civilian city still, he thought.

The late news that night claimed a hundred and thirty German planes down, forty-nine British. Could it be true?

IT HAD occurred to Victor Henry, after talking to him on the telephone, that General Tillet might well be E. J. Tillet, the renowned military author, and so he was. Tillet closely resembled his book jacket picture: bald, moustached, with a foxy, much-wrinkled face, smoking a stubby pipe. He said almost nothing as he spun his car southward. The farther they went, the more warlike the country looked. Signposts were gone, place names painted out, and great loops of barbed steel rods arched over the roads. "To stop glider landings," Tillet said briefly.

Pug said, "I guess the Germans took a bad beating yesterday."

"I *told* Hitler the range of the Messerschmitt 109 was far too short," Tillet burst out. "He said he'd take it up with Göring, but the thing got lost in the Luftwaffe bureaucracy. It's a mistake to think dictators are all-powerful! Everybody lies to them."

They came to a ruined airfield where burned-out planes stood in skeletal rows and bulldozers snorted along the cratered runways. "Göring's just starting to make sense, going for the airfields and plane factories," said Tillet. "He's wasted a whole bloody month bombing harbours and convoys. He's only got till the equinox—the Channel's impassable after about September fifteenth."

The airfield was miles behind them when suddenly ahead lay the blue Channel, shining in the sun. They got out and, through Tillet's binoculars, scanned the coast of Hitler's France. Tiny images of houses and ships shimmered on the far shore. "That's as close as Jerry's ever come," Tillet said. "Close enough, too."

Driving on westward along the coast, they passed camouflaged pillboxes along the hills and in the towns. On the beaches, jagged iron rods spiked up, festooned with wire. As waves rose and fell, queerly shaped tangles of pipe poked above the water. "You're not exactly unprepared," Pug said.

"No. Adolf was decent enough to give us a breather. Those pipes out in the water are the old Greek fire idea. We set the sea ablaze with petroleum, and fry the Germans we don't drown."

In the hills above Portsmouth they stopped for a snack of sandwiches and coffee. They ate wordlessly until Tillet suddenly gestured with his sandwich. "Look there." A patch of orange was flowering over the city, a barrage balloon on fire. "They're back today. The damned fool's hitting Portsmouth again instead of going inland. Well, shall we get along down there?"

By the time they reached Portsmouth, fire fighters were streaming water on blazes. Tillet said, "Since Jerry does seem to be coming over today, I suggest we go straight across to the Chain Home station at Ventnor. You may find it interesting."

Pug's first glimpse of British radarscopes was a shock. The British had mastered techniques that American experts had told him were twenty years off. The RAF could measure the range of a ship down to a hundred yards, and read that and its bearing off a scope at sight. They could do the same to a single aeroplane, or count a horde of planes, and give their altitude too.

Pug had two immediate thoughts: that the U.S. Navy had to get hold of this equipment, and that the British were far better prepared for war than the world knew.

The group captain in charge was peering at one of the scopes. "Hello, looks like another circus heading this way. Forming up over Le Havre. A couple of dozen would you say, Stebbins?"

"Thirty-seven, sir."

Excitement thickened. A young duty officer wearing headphones strolled from scope to scope, making notes on a clipboard. "This is a major breakthrough," Pug said to Tillet.

"Well, we're grateful that a few Englishmen did stay awake while our politicians kicked away air parity and all the rest. Now, would you just as soon pop back to London?"

"I'm in your hands. If it were possible sometime I'd also like to visit Group Operations, Number 11 Fighter Group."

Tillet blinked. "Number 11? I believe we can lay it on. First of all, though, we must whip up to London. A couple of people there would like a word with you."

OUTSIDE 10 Downing Street a single unarmed bobby paced in the morning sun. Victor Henry smiled, remembering the grim array of SS men in front of Hitler's chancellery. Tillet took him in and introduced him to a male secretary, who in turn led him up a wide stairway lined with portraits of former Prime Ministers.

Winston Churchill stood by the window of a small cluttered room that smelled of old books and dead cigars. He was very short and stooped, and he bulged in the middle like Tweedledum. With a word of welcome, he shook hands and motioned Pug to a seat. He puffed at his cigar. "We're going to win, you know."

"I'm becoming convinced of that, Mr. Prime Minister," Victor Henry said, trying to control his nervousness.

Sitting down in an armchair, Churchill put on half-moon glasses and peered at the American captain. "Your President has sent you here to have a look at our RDF. What do you think, now that you've seen it?"

"The United States could use it."

Churchill uttered a pleasant grunt. "Good! Now have a look at these." He passed Pug several charts showing destroyer and merchant-ship losses, the rate of new construction, and the rising graph of U-boat sinkings. It was an alarming picture. Puffing clouds of smoke, Churchill said that fifty old destroyers were the only fighting ships he would ever ask of the President. New construction would fill the gap by March. It was a question of holding open the convoy lines and beating off invasion until then.

Churchill added—with a grin that reminded Pug of FDR—that some of the President's advisers feared that if the destroyer deal went through, Hitler might declare war on the United States.

"There's not much danger of that," Pug said.

"Not much *hope* of that!" Churchill looked impish. Pug felt that the Prime Minister had stated his entire war policy in one joke.

"I should like you to tell your President," Churchill went on, "that now is the time to get to work on landing craft. We'll need them when we go back to France. We have got some fairly advanced designs, but we shall want a real Henry Ford effort."

Victor Henry couldn't help staring in wonder at this slumping, smoke-wreathed old man who, with almost no guns or tanks left

406

after Dunkirk, with invasion threatened, still talked of invading Europe.

Churchill stared back, his broad lower lip thrust out. "Oh, I assure you we shall do it. Furthermore, we are prepared right now to bomb Berlin till the rubble jumps, if they dare bomb London. Should that occur while you're here, and if you don't consider it foolhardy nonsense, you might go along to see how it's done."

Pug said at once, "I'd be honoured, of course."

"Well, well. Probably out of the question. But it would be fun, wouldn't it?" Churchill pushed himself out of his chair, and Pug jumped up. The Prime Minister held out his hand. "Ask Tillet for all our stuff on landing craft. And remember—we shall require great *swarms* of the things!" Churchill swept his arms wide.

VICTOR HENRY sat in the lobby of the Savoy Hotel, waiting for Pamela and her fighter pilot. Uniformed officers thronged past with young women in colourful summer finery. On the brink of being invaded by Hitler's hordes, England was the gayest place he had ever seen, and not because anyone was blind to the danger. The resolute, cheerful spirit of the people was borne out by a sharp rise in production figures. Now the problem was not so much planes as fighter pilots, for combat was taking a steep toll of men.

"Here we are," chirruped Pamela, floating up in a mauve silk dress. Flight Lieutenant Gallard was short and swarthy; his black hair needed cutting, and his blue eyes were sunken with fatigue. At their table Gallard asked for an orange squash, and grinned. His fingers were beating a tattoo on the cloth. "That's the devil of an order, isn't it, in the Savoy?"

"My son's a carrier pilot. I wish he'd go on orange squash."

"It's not a bad idea. This business up there"—Gallard raised a thumb—"happens fast. You've got to look sharp."

"How good are they?"

"The Jerries are fine pilots and ruddy good shots."

"And their planes?"

"The Messerschmitt 109 is a fine machine, but the Spitfire's a good match for it. Their twin-engine 110 seems to handle very stiffly. The bombers of course are sitting ducks."

"How's RAF morale?"

Gallard lit a cigarette. "I'd say it's very high." His fingers never stopped dancing on the table. "The main thing is learning to live with fear. Some chaps can't. For accuracy, you've *got* to close the range. But nobody blames the chaps who blaze away from afar and head for home. After a while they're posted out."

"Your orange squash, sir," said the waiter.

"And just in time. I'm talking too much."

Pug raised his glass to Gallard. "Thanks. And good hunting."

Gallard grinned. "What does your son fly?"

"SBD, the Douglas Dauntless," said Pug.

Gallard nodded. "Well, my hat's off to those carrier fellows, landing on a tiny, wobbly patch at sea. I come home to broad old Mother Earth, for whom I'm developing quite an affection."

"I have a rival," said Pamela. "I'm glad she's old and flat."

Gallard described the way fighter tactics were evolving on both sides. Pug wanted to remember as much as possible; he drank very little wine. Towards the end of the meal the waiter came to say that Gallard was wanted on the telephone, and Gallard excused himself. He returned in a few minutes and resumed eating.

"Pam, there's been a change," he said, when his plate was empty. "Rest is cancelled." He smiled at Pug. "I don't mind. One gets fidgety, knowing the thing's still going on and one's out of it. I must be on my way now, but there's no reason for you not to go on to that Noel Coward show. I've heard it's very funny."

Quickly Pug said, "I think it's time for me to leave you both."

Gallard looked him straight in the eye. "Why? Couldn't you bear Pamela's chatter for a little while longer? Don't go. Here she is all tarted up for the first time in weeks."

"All right," Pug said. "I think I can bear it."

The three stood up. Pamela said to Gallard, "We'll have a nice stroll alone through the lobby." She started off.

Ted Gallard offered Pug his hand. "Good luck to you, Captain Henry. Come and see us at Biggin Hill airfield."

To Pug the ominousness of Gallard's recall went far beyond the risk of sending up a fatigued, edgy pilot. It could signal that the RAF was coming to the end of its rope.

"MAYBE the Fat Boy's getting low on fighter pilots, too." General Tillet manoeuvred his car through a cluster of black taxicabs at Marble Arch. The hope, he said, was that Göring was already throwing everything in. If so, and if the British could hold on, there could come a crack in Luftwaffe performance.

About an hour out of London they came to a compound of buildings surrounded by a high wire fence. Pug said, "Where are we?"

"Uxbridge. You wanted to have a look at Group Operations, Number 11 Fighter Group."

"Oh, yes." Since Ventnor he had never repeated the request.

They were met by a flight lieutenant who conducted them down to the balcony of a small, strange underground theatre. Below, twenty or so girls in uniform worked around a large-scale table map of southern England. In place of stage and curtain stood a black wall with columns of electric bulbs. And in glassed booths on either side of the room men with headphones scrawled at desks.

"Burne-Wilke, here's your American visitor," said Tillet.

The officer sitting in the middle of the balcony turned.

"Hello there! I was glad to hear you were coming. Here, sit by me. Nothing much doing yet, but Jerry's getting airborne now." Burne-Wilke made room for Victor. "Hello, there's a mutual friend. Didn't I first meet you with the Tudsburys?"

Pamela was walking in to take the place of another girl. She looked up, threw Pug a gentle smile, then got to work.

"This is all fairly clear, isn't it?" said Burne-Wilke, gesturing towards the wall. "Our group is responsible for southeast England. Those vertical banks of lights stand for our fighter control stations." He explained the system. "Going up the wall, you step up in readiness, till you get to AIRBORNE, ENEMY IN SIGHT, and ENGAGED. That's the red row. Oh, yes. Those poor devils under glass on the left collect reports about German planes from our ground observer corps, the ones on the right from our anti-aircraft."

Pug had known of the system's existence; but this close view awed him. "Sir, when did all this spring into being?"

"Right after Munich. Hello, Jerry's on his way. If things warm up enough, the air vice-marshal may come and run the show."

White lights were starting to jump upward. Burne-Wilke talked brisk RAF abracadabra into a telephone, his eyes moving from the wall to the map table. "Chain Home at Ventnor reports several attacks forming up. Two of them are forty-plus, one sixty-plus."

The lights kept moving up the board, and the air vice-marshal appeared. Nobody was excited, and the hum of voices was low.

The first lights that leapt to red were in the column of the Biggin Hill control station. Victor Henry saw Pamela glance up at them. On the table where she and the other girls were laying arrows and numbered discs, a clear picture was forming of four flights of attackers moving over southern England. Within twenty minutes, half the squadrons on the board were blinking red.

"We've got almost two hundred planes engaged," Burne-Wilke said. "The others stand by to cover when these land to refuel."

"Have you ever had red lights across the board?"

"Now and then. It's not the situation of choice."

Pug pictured Ted Gallard, cold sober on orange squash, darting and twisting, squirting his guns at aeroplanes with black crosses on them. Two of the Biggin Hill lights moved up to white: RETURNING BASE.

"These things seldom last longer than an hour or so from the time Jerry starts," said Burne-Wilke. "He runs dry rather fast."

Within a few minutes the red lights had all blinked off. The girls began clearing markers off the table. Burne-Wilke spoke on the telephone, collecting reports. He rubbed his reddened eyes, then turned to Pug. "Would you like to say hello to Pamela?"

"Very much. How did it go?"

"I'm afraid quite a few bombers got through. Both sides lost a number of planes, but the count takes an hour or so to firm up."

The flight lieutenant led Pug to the surface. Pamela stood in the sun outside. "Well, you made it, but not on the best day. Ted's down." Her voice was calm, but her hand was ice-cold.

"Are you sure?"

"Yes. He may have parachuted, but one of his squadron mates reported that his plane dived into the sea." She clung to his hand, looking at him with glistening eyes. "I've asked for a special pass. Would you buy me dinner tonight?"

17

A week passed, and another, and Gallard did not return. Pamela came several times to London. Once Pug remarked that she fought the war only when it suited her. "I am behaving shockingly," she said, "presuming on everybody's sympathy. I shall soon be confined to camp. By then you'll be gone. Meantime you're here."

To cheer her up, Pug took her often to Fred Fearing's apartment in Belgrave Square. Fearing was a celebrated American broadcaster, who was having a marvellous time partying in London. At the same time his broadcasts about England at war were stirring up much U.S. sympathy.

"Aren't you the sly one, Pug?" Fearing remarked. "She's small, but saucy."

"She's the daughter of a guy I know."

"Of course. Talky Tudsbury. My pal, too."

"Her fiancé's an RAF pilot, missing in action. Take it easy, Fearing." The other men who drifted in and out of the apartment left Pamela alone, assuming she was Victor Henry's doxy.

Once, early in September, when they were having a drink in her apartment and joking about this, Pug said, "'Lechery, lechery; still wars and lechery; nothing else holds fashion.'"

"Bless me," she said, "You're a Shakespeare scholar, too. But there's precious little lechery around here. If people only knew."

"Are you complaining, my girl?"

"Certainly not, you leathery old gentleman."

At this point the air raid sirens started their eerie wailing. They carried their drinks on to the little balcony outside her living room. "My God!" she said after a while. "This is *it*. Where on earth is Fighter Command?" Bombers in wide ragged Vs were starkly visible in the late sunlight. Anti-aircraft bursts among the formations seemed to be having no effect.

"Tangling with the fighter escort farther south, I'd guess." Victor Henry's voice shook. The mass of machines was coming on like the invaders in a futurist movie, one V-wave after another, filling the air with a throbbing, angry hum. The muffled thunder of bomb hits boomed over the city, and flame and smoke began billowing up. "Looks like they're starting on the docks," Pug said.

"Shall I get you another drink? I *must* have one." She took his glass and soon returned with the drinks. He put his arm around her and they stood together, watching the Luftwaffe start its effort to bomb London to its knees. It was the seventh of September.

They went to dine in Soho after the all-clear. On the sidewalks strangers talked to each other, laughed, and pointed thumbs up. Distant clangs of fire engines and a heavy smokiness overhead remained the only traces, in this part of town, of the Fat Boy's tremendous attempt.

But after dinner, when they walked down towards the Thames, they skirted roped-off streets full of noise and steam and shouting firemen. Here was an oppressive stench of burning. Reflections of the fires on the other bank flickered in the black water. From across a bridge came a swarm of shabbily dressed refugees.

Pug looked up at the sky. Above rifts in the smoke the stars shimmered. "It's a very clear night," he said. "These fires are a beacon they can see for a hundred miles. They may come back."

"I must get back to Uxbridge," Pamela said. She looked down at her flimsy grey dress. "But I seem to be out of uniform."

Victor Henry watched the start of the night raid from Pam's balcony while she changed. When she came out into the gloomy moonlight in her WAAF uniform, she appeared to him the most desirable young female on God's earth. The severe garb made her small figure all the sweeter, he thought.

Again he held her with one encircling arm. "The bastards just can't miss," he said, "with those fires to guide them."

"Berlin can catch fire, too." Suddenly hate scored her face. "Oh God, they *got* one. Get more, please." A bomber came toppling down, transfixed by two crossing searchlights. And in short order two more fell.

The telephone rang. "Well!" She laughed harshly. "Uxbridge, no doubt, inviting me to a court martial." But she returned after a moment, puzzled. "It seems to be for you."

It was Tillet. "Ah, Henry," he said. "Your friend Fearing suggested I try you here. Do you recall that when you met a portly old gentleman a couple of weeks ago, he mentioned that you might want to go on a little expedition? To familiar foreign scenes?"

A tingle ran down Pug's spine. "I remember."

"Well, the trip seems to be on for tomorrow. I'm to meet you as soon as this nuisance stops, to give you the details—I say, you *are* interested? I must have your answer within the hour."

"May I call you back?"

Tillet gave him a number. "Jolly good."

As he came out on the balcony, Pamela turned to him, her face alight. "They've got two more."

"Come inside a minute," Pug said. They sat in two armchairs near the open French windows. "Pamela, the RAF are going on a foreign expedition tomorrow night, and I'm invited along."

The girl's face went taut. "I see. Shall you go?"

"That's what I'm wondering."

"Decline," she said. "It's not your business and your chances of returning are not good. It's miserably unfair to your wife."

"Those were my first thoughts." Pug paused. Outside, the AA snapped and thumped, and searchlights swayed blue fingers across the blackness. He lit a cigarette. "Well, I'd better call back."

She said quickly, "What are you going to say?"

"I'm going to accept. My job is intelligence, Pam, and this is an extraordinary opportunity."

As he reached for the telephone Pam said, "I shall wind up with Fred Fearing. Or his equivalent." That stopped the motion of Pug's arm. She said, "I miss Ted horribly. I shall not be able to endure missing you. And I'm not at all moral. You have very wrong ideas about me."

The seams in his face were sharp as he peered at the angry girl. "It isn't very moral to hit below the belt, I'll say that."

He telephoned Tillet, while the girl stared at him with wide angry eyes. "Ass!" she said. "*Ass!*"

A YOUNGSTER in greasy coveralls poked his head through the open door. "Sir, the briefing's begun in B-flight crew room."

"Coming," said Pug, struggling with unfamiliar clasps and straps. The flying suit was too big and smelled of stale sweat.

"What do I do with this?" He gestured at the tweed suit he had folded on a chair.

"It'll be right there when you get back, sir."

Their eyes met. In that glance was complete mutual recognition that, for no very good reason, Pug was going out to risk death. Pug said, "What's your name?"

"Aircraftman Horton, sir."

"Well, Aircraftman Horton, we're about the same size. If I forget to pick that suit up or something, it's all yours."

"Why, thank you, sir. That's very fine tweed."

Several dozen air crews slouched in the darkened room where an aerial picture of Berlin was projected on to a large screen. The wing commander was using a long pointer to indicate the primary and secondary targets, the main gasworks and a power plant.

"All right, let's have the opposition map." On to the screen flashed another slide of Berlin, marked with red and orange symbols, and the wing commander discussed anti-aircraft positions and searchlight belts. "Berlin will be on the alert and the flak will be heavy, so look alive." He turned on the lights and changed to an offhand tone. "Incidentally, our American observer will be flying in *F for Freddie*. He's Captain Victor Henry, one of the least prudent officers in the United States Navy."

Faces turned to Pug, and a skinny little man approached him holding out his hand. "I'm Peters, sergeant navigator of *F for Freddie*." He gave Pug his parachute, showing him how to clip it to his chest, and a paper sack with his rations. Then he took him to meet the rest of the crew.

The two pilots were studying and marking up maps of Berlin. Flight Lieutenant Killian gave Pug a friendly nod. Sergeant Pilot "Tiny" Johnson was a large fellow with a ham face. "You're a brave man, Captain," he said.

Outside, the first pilot went aboard the plane. "*F for Freddie*," said the sergeant pilot, giving the fuselage an affectionate slap. From the sound of the slap Pug realized that a Wellington bomber had a skin of fabric. It had never occurred to him that fabric planes could be used as attack bombers.

Far down the field, one plane after another coughed and began to thunder up the dimly lit runway. Soon *F for Freddie* joined them, taking course for the North Sea.

After what seemed an age of bumping through cold air, Pug glanced at his watch. Seven minutes had gone by. The intercom crackled and buzzed in his helmet, but once the plane left the coast the pilots and navigator shut up. Killian gestured him to look through the plexiglass blister where the navigator had been taking star sights. There was nothing to see but black water, bright moon, and stars.

Pug had imagined a long-range bomber would have ample room. In fact, four men sat crowded within inches of each other—the pilots, the front gunner, and the navigator. Crouched and stumbling, Pug dragged himself down the black fuselage to the bubble where Reynolds, the young rear gunner, sat. The boy gave him a thumbs-up and a pathetic smile; it was his first operational flight. This was a hell of a lonely, shaky, frigid place to be, Pug thought. He groped to a clear space, squatted on his parachute, and dozed.

Garbled voices woke him. He was shivering with cold. Someone tugged him towards the cockpit. Suddenly it was bright as day. The plane dived and Pug fell, bruising his forehead. The plane made sickening turns as he crawled forward.

Tiny Johnson, gripping the controls, said in the intercom, "O.K., Captain? Just passing the coast searchlight belt." He waved at a fixture labelled OXYGEN. "Plug in, and come and see."

Sucking on rubber-tasting enriched air, Pug crawled into the bombardier's position in the nose. Beneath he saw grey, moonlit land. The searchlight beams waved behind them. From below, red and orange balls floated up, speeding as they rose. A few burst and showered red streaks and sparks. Tiny said, "Coast flak."

Just then something painfully brilliant exploded in Victor Henry's face. Blackness ensued, then a dance of green circles.

A hand grasped his. Peters's voice said, "Magnesium flash shell, sir. Ruddy close. You all right?"

"I can't see."

"It'll take a while. Sit up, sir."

The plane pounded on, the blindness persisted, then the green

415

circles jerked in a red mist and a picture gradually faded in: faces lit by dials, and the nose gunner in the moonlight. The navigator spoke. "Should be seeing searchlights soon."

"Nothing," said Flight Lieutenant Killian. "Black night."

"I've got Berlin bearing dead ahead, sir."

"Something's wrong. It looks like a solid forest down there."

The strained voice of the rear gunner broke in to report search-lights away to port. After some crisp talk, Killian swung around and headed for them. "*That's* Berlin," he soon said, pointing. "All kinds of fireworks. Well done, Reynolds."

As they neared Berlin, the nose gunner was silhouetted by exploding balls and streaks of colour, and fanning rays of light. Tiny rasped, "The first poor bastards there are catching it."

Killian's voice came, easy and slow: "It looks worse than it is. The stuff spreads apart once you're in it. The sky's a roomy place."

F for Freddie went sailing into the beautiful, terrible display, and as the captain had said, it thinned out, leaving great holes of darkness through which the plane bored smoothly ahead. "See that fire?" Killian pointed. "The others have pretty well clobbered the primary target, so I'm going for secondary."

Shortly thereafter the motor noise ceased. "Gliding approach," said Killian. "They control their lights and flak with listening devices. Navigator's got to take your place now."

As the plane whiffled earthward, Pug made his way to the rear gunner, who was looking down at the city with saucer eyes. Killian ordered, "Bomb doors open." There was a rush of icy air and a roar. The navigator was talking in a drilled cheerful tone: "Left, left . . . too much . . . right . . . dead on. Bombs gone."

Pug saw the bombs fall away, a string of black tumbling sticks. The aeroplane slanted up, the motors bellowed on, and they climbed. Below, a string of small red explosions appeared beside the huge gas-storage tower. Pug thought the bombs had missed. Then in the blink of an eye came a blasting and billowing up from the ground, almost to the height of the plane. In the gigantic yellow flare, Berlin was starkly visible, spread out like a picture postcard —the Kürferstendamm, Unter den Linden, the Brandenburg Gate, the river, the chancellery, the Opera—clear, sharp, close.

416

The cheers in the intercom hurt his ears. He gave a rebel yell. As he did so, *F for Freddie* was transfixed by half a dozen searchlights. In the rear gunner's turret all was blue radiance. The boy suddenly started to scream into his microphone. The plane dived and sideslipped, but the shining blue pyramid of searchlights stayed locked under it. Pug threw his arms around the gun mount to steady himself. The gunner fell against the mount, and his clamour ceased in the intercom. A mass of orange and red balls lazily left the ground and floated up at them, bursting all around in a shower of fire. Pug felt a hard thump. The motors changed sound, and *F for Freddie* heeled into a steep, shuddering dive. Through the frail plexiglass turret Pug watched the fabric wings, waiting for them to break off and flutter away.

All at once the blue pyramid turned black. The dizzying swoops stopped and the plane flew straight. Pug caught a sour whiff. The gunner had fainted and vomit was dribbling down his chest. Black blood welled from the left leg of his flying suit.

Pug stumbled forward shouting to the navigator that Reynolds was wounded. He passed a ragged hole in the starboard fuselage and mechanically he noted the Plough. They were heading west, back to England.

In the cockpit the pilots sat as before, busy at their controls. Tiny shouted, "Ah, Captain. We're going home to tea. You'll tell them you saw that gas plant go up, won't you?"

"Damn right I will. How's the aeroplane?"

"The port engine was hit, but it's still pulling. Heading back overland, in case we have to come down. Looks like we can make it, unless that engine completely packs up."

"Your rear gunner's got a leg wound. Navigator's back there with him."

Tiny pulled off his helmet. "Ruddy asinine way to earn a living. Should have joined the ruddy navy!"

PAMELA knew enough about bombing missions to calculate when Pug would get back. At ten in the morning she went to his flat and persuaded the charwoman to let her in.

Deposited in schools by her divorced parents, Pam had grown

up almost wild, and had had several love affairs before she was out of her teens. In her early twenties she met Philip Rule, a corrupt man with beguiling ways, who would have destroyed her had she not broken with him at last and gone to work as her father's secretary. As such, she had encountered Commander Henry on the *Bremen*, and she had found him attractive from the start.

When Victor Henry had arrived in London two weeks ago, Pamela had been quite ready to marry the fighter pilot, and Pug's visit had not changed that. But since then Gallard had vanished. In wartime, relationships deepen fast and Pamela now thought that, whatever the moral scruples of this very married man, she could get around them if she pleased.

As Pug let himself in, he could hear the twelve-o'clock news echoing in the flat. He called, "Hello, who's here?"

Steps clicked. The girl struck him like a blue projectile.

"What the devil?" Victor Henry managed to say between kisses. "What are you doing here?"

"I'm absent without leave. I shall be court martialled and shot. I'd have sat here for a week." She kissed him again and again.

Dead on his feet as he was, Pug nevertheless began on instinct to respond. "The conquering hero's reward, hey?" he said.

She leaned back in his arms, looking at him. "Just so."

"Well, I didn't do a damned thing except get in everybody's way. However, thank you, Pam. You're beautiful and sweet, and this welcome makes me feel great."

His evident exhaustion, his comical indecisiveness about what to do next, caused a wave of deep tenderness to go through her. "You look absolutely drained," she said stepping free. "Want a drink? Some food?"

"A drink, I guess. But I'd better get some sleep."

"So I figured." He found his bed turned down, his pyjamas laid out. When she took his drink in to him, he was asleep.

THE HAND on his shoulder was gently persistent. "Captain Henry! You've had a call from the embassy."

It took him a few seconds to recollect where he was, and realize why Pamela Tudsbury was standing over him. He sat up in bed and sniffed a delicious odour of grilling meat. "What's that?"

"I thought you'd be hungry by now. It's five o'clock. Captain Vance insisted that you be at the embassy by six-thirty."

As he showered and dressed, he was still stumbling through dreams. He could not get used to the wonder of being alive. A recollection of Pamela's ardent welcome added to that wonder.

"How did you get all this?" he said, when he entered the living room. The salad, the fruit, the long bread, and the bottle of red wine made an attractive clutter on the small table.

Pam was coming in from the kitchen with steaks on two plates. "Oh, I'm a London alley cat. I know where to forage."

Pug attacked the meat and the crusty bread with gusto. "Why, it's the best meal I've ever eaten."

"You exaggerate, but I'm glad. I'm trying to make up for the stupid way I acted before you left."

"Pam, I'm glad I went. It was the right decision."

"Oh, no argument, now that you're back." She was looking at him over her wine glass. "Do you know that I fell for you on the *Bremen*? Did you guess it in Berlin? I'd have tried my luck—only it was impossible. You're so devoted to your wife."

"I guess I'm dumb," Pug said, "but I hadn't the slightest notion."

"Well, it's true. It did me good to be able to like a man so much. I proceeded to go mad over Ted, shortly thereafter." A shadow of sadness flickered across her face. "When you opened the door a few hours ago, I came close to believing in God."

He reached out and took her slim wrist. "Pam, I've developed a high regard for a London alley cat, myself."

"I'm glad. I should be sorry to think my passion was totally unrequited. It's getting on for six o'clock, Captain Henry."

"What will you do? Go back to Uxbridge?"

"What will *you* do? Shall I wait for your call at my flat?"

"Yes, Pam. Please do that."

THE AMERICAN flag flying from the embassy in Grosvenor Square struck Pug with a pang of pride. He sat on a park bench to look at it, suffused with a burning wish to live a long time yet in this radiant world. He felt reborn. Nothing like this had happened to him in twenty-five years; he had fallen in love.

A black Cadillac pulled up at the embassy door and discharged Blinker Vance, two army generals, and Admiral Benton, Pug's old boss at War Plans. Pug hastened across the street.

"Hey, Pug!" Benton offered him a fat hand. "This is General Anderson, and General Fitzgerald here is army air corps."

Vance left the four men in a quiet conference room. "Now damn it, Pug," Admiral Benton began, "the ambassador says if he'd known about this blamed fool flight of yours he'd have stopped you. He's dead right. We don't want to give the army and its air corps" —he gestured at the other men—"the idea that the navy trains goofy daredevils." Benton sounded very pleased.

Fitzgerald said, "I'd like to hear about the bomber ride."

"So would I," said Anderson.

Pug narrated his adventure in a matter-of-fact way. All three officers listened tensely as he described the limping return journey; the jettisoning of all removable weight to maintain altitude; the final thirty miles flown at a few hundred feet.

"Quite a yarn, Captain," Anderson said. "It amounted to a token bombing though, didn't it, after what the Germans have done to the docks here? At this rate, in a week London will cease to be a port. Then what happens? Famine? Plague?"

"Things look worse than they are, General. Their repair and fire-fighting crews are good."

"We've heard, Captain Henry," put in Fitzgerald, "that you've been sending optimistic reports to the President recommending all-out assistance."

"Not wholly optimistic, sir, but yes."

"Well," said Anderson, "possibly you're out of touch with how the people back home already feel about Roosevelt's aid to the British. Now, we have the list of the war matériel the British want. It would strip our armed forces clean. The President has already let them have—in addition to fifty destroyers—several squadrons of naval aircraft, half a million rifles—"

"He hasn't given them away, General," Benton observed. "The limeys have paid cash on the barrelhead."

"Yes, luckily the Neutrality Act compels that, but it was a god-damned lie to call the stuff surplus. We don't have any surplus! And now Congress is passing a draft law. Our boys will be drilling with broomsticks! There's going to be an accounting one day."

Admiral Benton said, "Well, Pug, I've told these gentlemen that any dope you put out is reliable. What makes you think the British will keep fighting, after the way the French folded?"

Tersely, Pug described the British scientific advances, the strength and disposition of their battle fleet, their fighter-control system, the German versus British losses, the morale of the fliers, the preparations along the invasion beaches.

Anderson regarded him through half-shut eyes. "Suppose the British do hold out? What can they do against a man who controls all Europe?"

"I think, General, the idea is to hang on till we get in."

"Now you're talking." Anderson turned to the admiral. "Well, I'll say this, your man makes out a case." He rose. "Let's be on our way, gentlemen."

"I'll be right along," Benton said. When the army men were gone he slapped Pug's shoulder. "Well done. These limeys are holding the fort for us. We've got to help 'em. And since that's what the boss wants, we will. Say, that reminds me—" He brought out two letters. One was in a White House envelope, the other was from Rhoda. Pug slipped them both into his pocket.

In the hall, Blinker Vance handed Pug a dispatch from BuPers: RETURN BERLIN UNTIL RELIEVED ON OR ABOUT 1 NOVEMBER. THEREUPON PROCEED WASHINGTON FOR REASSIGNMENT.

Victor Henry went back to the bench in Grosvenor Square. The sun still shone, the flag still waved. But the strange exaltation was gone. He read the President's pencilled scrawl:

Your bracing reports have been a grand tonic. Thank you especially for alerting us on British advanced radar. They are sending over a scientific mission this month, with all their "wizard war" stuff, as Churchill calls it. There's something heartwarming about his interest in landing craft, isn't there? I've asked for a report from CNO. Get as much of their material as you can.

Rhoda's letter was a strange one. She had just turned on the radio, she wrote, heard an old tune they had danced to on their honeymoon, and burst out crying. She reminisced about his long absence in 1918, about their good times in Manila. With Palmer Kirby, who now kept a small office in New York, she had just driven up to the sub school to visit Byron. She went on:

> Did you know Janice is pregnant? Those kids didn't waste much time, hey? Like father like son! But the thought of being a *grandmother* ! ! ! I'm happy, but it sure threw me into a spin.
>
> Let me give you a piece of advice. The sooner you can come home, the better. I'm all right, but I could use a *husband* around.

He walked to his flat and telephoned Pamela.

"Oh, my dear," she said, "I'm so glad you called. I talked to Uxbridge. They're being very broadminded. If I come back tonight, all is forgiven. Can I see you next week?"

"Pam, I have to leave day after tomorrow. To Berlin for maybe six weeks, then home. Hello? Pamela?"

"I'm still here. You wouldn't want me to desert for two more days and take what comes. Would you?"

"It's no way to win a war, Pam."

"No, it isn't, Captain. Well, good-bye it is."

"Our paths will cross again."

"Oh, no doubt. But I firmly believe that Ted's coming back. I may be a wife next time we meet, which will be easier all around. All the same, today was one of the happiest of my life."

Victor Henry was finding it difficult to go on talking. "I'll never forget, Pamela, not one minute of it. Good-bye."

Fatigued but tense, he went to bed. Restless, he reread Rhoda's nostalgic, sentimental, and troubled letter. Something shadowy and unpleasant was there between the lines.

ON THE way back from visiting Byron, Rhoda had slept with Palmer Kirby. That was the shadowy thing Pug had discerned in her letter; but although her words had been incautious, the thought of infidelity had not crossed his mind.

Rhoda's downfall had been unforeseen. She and Kirby had

stopped for tea at a little tourist house overlooking a charming pond where swans moved among lily pads. They talked of Berlin, of their delight at seeing each other in the Waldorf. Time flowed by, their talk grew more intimate. Then Palmer Kirby said, "How wonderfully cosy this place is! Too bad we can't stay here."

And Rhoda Henry murmured, hardly believing what she heard herself say, "Maybe we could."

They were given a room, no questions asked. Like a declaration of war, that point in time drew a line across the past and started another era. And yet Rhoda felt she had not really changed. She even still loved her husband. She had been trying to digest all this puzzlement when she wrote to him.

In New York, Rhoda and Kirby listened to a Churchill broadcast. Rhoda had chosen her apartment well. Spacious and cheerful, it faced south, across low brownstone houses.

Puffing at his pipe, Kirby slouched in an armchair. "Marvellous phrasemaker, that Churchill."

"Do you think they'll actually hold off the Germans?"

"What does Pug say?"

"He wrote once when he got to London, and not since. I tell myself if anything had happened to him I'd have heard. I do worry."

"Naturally." Kirby glanced at his watch.

"When does your plane go?"

"Oh, not for a couple of hours."

"How long will you be in Denver?"

"Only overnight. Then to Washington. Haven't you got a good reason to go to Washington?"

"Oh dear, Palmer, don't you realize I know everybody in that town? And anybody I don't, Pug does."

He said after a glum pause, "It's not very satisfactory, is it? I don't see myself as a homewrecker."

"Look, dear, I don't see myself as a scarlet woman. It must be the war. With London burning to the ground, all the old ideas seem trivial."

"I didn't tell you why I'm going to Denver. There's a buyer for my house."

"Your house sounds heavenly. Must you sell it?"

"I rattle around in it. It is perfect to entertain in, to have my children and grandchildren come to. If I had a wife, I wouldn't sell it." He looked at her. "What do you think, Rhoda?"

"Oh, Palmer!" Rhoda's eyes brimmed. This resolved the puzzlement. It had not been a crazy slip, after all, but a grand passion. Grand passions were different.

"It can't be news to you. We wouldn't have stayed in Connecticut if I hadn't felt this way."

"Well! Oh, my Lord. I'm proud. Of course I am. But—*Palmer!*" She gestured at photographs of Pug and her children.

He said earnestly, "Pug is an admirable man. But there had to have been a rift in your marriage for this to have happened."

In a shaky voice, Rhoda said, "Before I knew him, Pug was a navy fullback. I saw him play—he was an aggressive, exciting player. And then he burst on me in Washington, and he courted the way he played. The boys I went with were just the old Washington crowd, and Pug was something altogether unusual and wonderful, still is. I know he loves me, but—he is so Navy! Oh dear, now for the very first time I suddenly feel so wretched." Rhoda cried into her handkerchief, her shoulders shaking.

When she calmed down, she said, "You go along to Denver, but ask yourself this. Wouldn't you always be thinking that I'd do to you what I've done to Pug? Why not?"

"Because I believe you've been out of love with your husband for a long time. You feel affection for him. I think you're in love with me." He stood. "I don't think I'll sell the house."

"Oh, sell it, as far as I'm concerned! I only think you yourself might regret it one day." She walked with him to the door, and he kissed her like a husband going off on a trip.

18

September was crisping the Berlin air when Pug flew back there via Lisbon. Compared with London, under the blitz, the city looked at peace, although the air war did show a few traces. Pug tried to see the wrecked gasworks, but the area was cordoned off.

This mindless shutting out of unpleasant facts was prevalent in Berlin now.

One German who seemed to retain some common sense was Ernst Grobke. The submariner invited Pug to lunch, and griped openly about the way Göring had botched the Battle of Britain. "We'll win, though," he said. "Our new, improved U-boats will be coming off the ways next January. Then in four, five months, half a million tons of British shipping sunk a month, and *phfff!*— Churchill kaput."

"Well! Ernst Grobke and Victor Henry! The two sea dogs, deciding the war." The banker Wolf Stöller was bowing over them. "Victor, that is a beautiful new suit. Savile Row?"

"Yes, as a matter of fact."

"Unmistakable. Well, it will be a pleasure to order clothes there again. Ernst, did you tell Captain Henry you're coming to Abendruh this weekend? Why don't you come too, Victor?"

It was clear now why Grobke had arranged the lunch. "All right," Pug said. "Thank you very much."

"Grand. See you on Friday," said the banker.

That same afternoon, Victor Henry's yeoman rang him and said Natalie Jastrow was on the line from Siena.

"Jehosephat! Put her on. . . . Natalie?"

"Oh, *hello*! Is Byron all right?"

"He's fine."

"Oh, what a relief! I haven't had a single letter. I know how impossible the mail is, but I'd begun to worry."

"Natalie, he wrote me that he's had no letters from you, but he's in good shape."

"Why, I've been writing once a week. I miss him so. How's he doing in submarine school?"

"Scraping by, I gather."

Natalie's laugh stirred an ache in him. It was husky and slightly mocking, like Pamela's. "That sounds right."

"Natalie, he expected you back before this."

"I know. There've been problems. Maybe a letter from you will get through; be sure to tell him I'm fine."

"I'll write today."

IT WAS a small gathering at Abendruh—no staircase slide. The other men were a Luftwaffe general and a high official in the foreign ministry. The five pretty ladies were not wives.

Pug sized it all up as an orgy in the making, to get him to talk about the British. So he was surprised when after dinner they went to a music room, where Stöller, the general, the foreign ministry man, and a redheaded lady formed a string quartet. They played the best amateur music Pug had ever heard. After a couple of hours the ladies said good night and left.

"Perhaps we might have a nightcap on the terrace," said the banker, putting his violin in its case. The five men moved outside and a butler passed drinks. "Victor, if you care to talk about England," said Stöller, "we would of course be interested."

"You mean I have to admit I've been to England?"

The banker laughed. "If you prefer, we'll drop the subject. But you're in an unusual position, having been in both capitals."

"Well, if you want me to say you've shot the RAF out of the sky, it might be better to drop it now."

The general said gloomily, "We know we haven't done that."

"Speak freely. General Jagow and Dr. Meusse are two of my oldest friends," said Stöller.

"We say in the Luftwaffe," put in the general, "'The red flag is up.' That means we all talk straight. We say what we think about the Führer, Göring, anybody."

"I like those ground rules," Pug said. "Fire away."

"Would an invasion succeed?" spoke up Dr. Meusse.

"Can your navy get you across?" Pug replied.

"Why not?" said Jagow. "Through a corridor protected by mine belts and U-boats, and under a Luftwaffe umbrella."

Pug glanced at Grobke. "Here's a U-boat man. Ask him."

Grobke said in thick tones, "Very difficult, possibly suicidal."

The general leaned towards him, stiff with anger. "Red flag's up," Pug exclaimed. "I agree with him. Part of a landing force might get through—not saying in what shape. There're still those invasion beaches, which I would hate to approach from seaward."

"What is the bombing of London doing to the British morale?" Stöller asked.

"You're making Churchill's job easier. They're fighting mad now, and they think they're going to win."

"There is the weakness," said Dr. Meusse. "When a people loses touch with reality, it is finished."

Stöller lit a cigar. "Absolutely. The course of this war is fixed. England's shipping is disappearing faster than she can replace it. She will soon run out of fuel and food. When that happens, Churchill will fall. There's no way out."

Pug said, "Isn't there? My country has a lot of fuel, food—and steel and shipyards too—and we're open for business."

The banker smiled coldly. "But your Neutrality Act requires that England pay cash. Well, she started the war with about five billions in foreign exchange. Our intelligence is that she's already spent more than four. By December the British Empire will be broke."

Dr. Meusse put in, "We are sinking ships now at a rate we never reached until the best months of 1917. Do you know that?"

"I do," said Pug. "And that's when we came in last time."

The silence on the terrace lasted a long time.

The rest of the weekend proved cold, and dull, and rainy. Before Pug left, Stöller said to him, "General Jagow appreciated your willingness to talk about England. Most friendly of you."

"I haven't revealed anything. Not intentionally."

Stöller smiled. "We are all struck by your sense of honour. If there's anything Jagow could do for you, I know it would give him pleasure. Installations, perhaps, that you'd care to visit?"

"There is one thing, a little unusual. An RAF pilot, who's engaged to the daughter of a friend of mine, went down in the Channel several weeks ago. Your people may have picked him up."

"That should be simple to find out. Give Jagow his name and rank. If he is a prisoner, you might be able to visit him."

WOLF STÖLLER called him early in October. "Your man is alive. He is in France, in a hospital in Lille, but in good condition. General Jagow has arranged for you to visit him."

After a moment Pug said, "Well, that's good news. The general is mighty kind."

Pug went to Lille by train. Rail travel was surprisingly normal in German-ruled Europe. The train left on time and in the restaurant car, amiably chatting Germans, Frenchmen, Belgians wined and dined amid rich good smells and a cheery clatter. By right of the ability to run things, the Third Reich looked a good bet to last a thousand years.

An emissary of General Jagow, a thin, rigid lieutenant, drove Pug to a grimy stone hospital building in the middle of Lille and left him in a windowless office containing a desk and two chairs.

Soon the door opened again, and a German soldier with a submachine gun tramped in. Ted Gallard followed, his ripped flying suit crudely patched, his right arm in a sling. Behind him came the thin lieutenant.

"Hello, Ted," said Victor Henry.

"*Hello*," said Gallard, with a look of extreme surprise.

The lieutenant told Pug that he would now withdraw, but since British airmen were honour bound to seize every chance of escape, General Jagow could not omit the precaution of an armed guard. The soldier knew no English. He would not interfere, but he was instructed to shoot at the first move to escape. They should avoid gestures that might confuse him. "When you are through, the general hopes you will join him for lunch."

As the door closed, Pug gave a cigarette to the pilot.

"Ah! God bless you." Gallard inhaled deeply. "Does Pam know?"

"Not yet. Telling her will be a rare pleasure."

Flicking the cigarette clumsily with his left hand, Gallard glanced at the guard. "Puts a bit of a chill on the small talk, eh? But I must say, this is the surprise of my life. I thought I was in for a rough grilling. They didn't tell me you were here."

"What do you want me to say to Pamela?"

"First, that I'm all right, more or less. I can't fault the medical attention. The food's been bloody awful—until the other day it mysteriously improved. I suppose that was because of your visit. Tell me about Pam. When did you last see her?"

"I've seen her several times. She'd come to London and I'd take her to dinner. For a while she was peaky and wouldn't eat. But she was coming round. Practically the last thing she told me was that she expected you back and was going to marry you."

The pilot's eyes grew moist. "She's a marvellous girl." He looked at the guard. "He does smell, doesn't he? And that face! Eighty million docile, dangerous swine like this." There was not a flicker in the soldier's eyes. "I really don't think he understands English."

"Don't count on it," said Pug, dry and fast.

"All right. But what's really happening in the war? The Hun doctors say its practically over. Of course that's a lie."

Pug made his account as cheerful as possible. The pilot nodded and brightened. "That's more like it. I don't know how you've managed this talk, but thank you. Now I suppose you'd better be cracking off."

"Take some cigarettes. I'd give you the pack, but Rosebud might think it was funny business and get confused."

"Ha! Rosebud is good." Gallard pulled out several cigarettes. "Look here, this has helped more than you can guess. Tell Pam I'll be seeing her." His firm tone implied an intention to escape.

"Be careful, Ted."

"Trust me. I've got a lot to live for."

THE OFFICE in Wolf Stöller's bank was small but richly furnished. "So, you go so soon," Stöller said, gesturing to a maroon leather couch. "Did you expect this?"

"Well, I thought my relief would be along in a couple of weeks. But when I got back from Lille, here he was waiting."

"Of course you are anxious to be reunited with your very beautiful wife. What do you say to a glass of sherry?"

"That'll be fine. Thanks."

The banker settled in an armchair and lit a long cigar. "Your little trip to Lille was a success, hm?"

"Yes, I'm obliged to you and the general."

"Please. By the ordinary rules, such a trip would be impossible. Among men of honour there are special rules." Stöller sighed. "Well, Victor, I didn't ask you here just to offer you sherry."

"I didn't suppose so."

430

"As a military man you know there are special conversations that sometimes have to be forgotten, obliterated without a trace."

Intensely curious, Victor Henry could not imagine what might be coming next.

"You know what we feel about the tragic absurdity of this conflict between Germany and England."

Pug nodded. At Abendruh Jagow had treated him to a high-flown discourse, foreseeing a new golden age, with America allied to a Europe made orderly by Germany. To this end the United States must above all prevent a war to the death between Germany and England.

"Don't these ideas make sense to you? You do agree that expectation of American help is what is keeping England in the war? This is what stands between disaster for the whole western world and an honourable peace."

Pug took a few moments to answer. "Maybe, but what's an honourable peace? Churchill and Hitler want to depose each other, and both of them represent the national will."

"You are going back to serve as naval aide to Mr. Roosevelt?"

Pug's face registered no surprise. "I'm going back to the Bureau of Personnel for reassignment."

The banker's smile was tolerant. "Well, our intelligence usually gets these things right. Please listen to what I have to say. Between men of honour there is a spiritual kinship. With you, Jagow and I have felt that kinship. You have been impeccably correct, but unlike so many people at your embassy, you don't regard Germans as cannibals. It has been noticed, I assure you.

"Now, you know of our concern about the Jewish influence around your President—" Stöller held up a rigid palm. "Hear me out, Victor. In the circumstances, we need friends in Washington. Simply to present the other side. Roosevelt is a man of very broad vision. He can be made to see that American interest requires a swift, honourable peace in the west. For one thing, only such a development can free him to handle Japan.

"Well, Victor—and remember this is confidential—we do have such friends. Not many. A few. Patriotic Americans, who see the realities of the war. We hope you'll be another such friend."

Pug tried to speak.

"Let me go on," said the banker. "Hermann Göring has established in Switzerland some anonymous bank accounts. His resources are enormous. These bank accounts, after the war, will be the rewards of Germany's honourable friends who have said the right word in the right place when it mattered." Stöller sat back.

"Interesting," Pug said, after a measurable pause. "Tell me, what made you, or General Jagow, or Field Marshal Göring, think that I might be receptive to this approach?"

"My dear chap, the field marshal remembers your visit with the banker Gianelli. His purpose now is exactly what Roosevelt's was then, to avoid further useless bloodshed."

Victor Henry nodded. "I see. That's a clear answer, Herr Stöller. Please tell Field Marshal Göring, for me, that he knows exactly where he can stick his Swiss bank account."

Stöller's teeth showed in an ugly smile. "I remind you, Captain Henry," he said in a new, slow, singsong tone, "that you have not yet left the Third Reich."

"I'm an officer in the United States Navy. Unless I misunderstand you"—Victor Henry's voice hardened almost to a bark— "you've asked me to commit treason for money."

The banker's nasty smile faded. In a placating tone Stöller said, "My dear Victor, how *can* you take it in that way? I asked you just to present both sides, when the occasion arose, for the sake of American security."

"Yes, I heard you." Victor Henry stood. He knew he had hit too hard, but he had reacted on instinct.

"Listen," Stöller said gently. "If the United States is ever in our situation, you may one day make an approach like this to a man you respect, and find it as difficult as I have. I think your response has been naïve and wrong. Still, it was an honourable one. I place a high value on your goodwill, Victor."

He held out his hand. Pug turned on his heel and walked out of the room. Outside, he walked several blocks at a pace that made his heart pound. The first new thought that came to him was that, with his grossly insulting words and acts, he might have murdered Ted Gallard.

19

Travelling to his new post in Moscow in mid-January, Leslie Slote was stalled by a shortage of Lufthansa accommodations from Lisbon to Berlin. While waiting for an air passage, he checked into the Palace Hotel in Estoril, Lisbon's seaside resort, where diplomats, wealthy refugees, and foreign agents congregated.

He was sitting in the crowded hotel lobby one afternoon, when a page walked through calling him to a telephone.

"Leslie? It's Bunky. How goes it by the seaside?" Bunker Thurston had attended the Foreign Service school with Slote, and he was now second secretary in the American legation in Lisbon.

"Mighty dull, Bunky. What's up?"

"Nothing much." Thurston sounded amused. "Only there's a girl named Natalie Jastrow sitting in my office."

Natalie came on the phone laughing, and Slote's heart throbbed at the lovely sound. "Hello, old Slote," she said.

"Natalie! Wonderful! Are you on your way back to the States?"

Natalie hesitated. "Yes and no. Leslie, can I see you?"

"Naturally! Immediately! I'll come right in."

"Wait. I'd rather come to your hotel."

Thurston intervened. "Look, Leslie, I'll put her on the bus. She'll arrive in half an hour or so. If I may, I'll join you a bit later."

SHE STILL had a fondness for big dark hats. She got off the bus and ran to him, threw her arms around him, and kissed his cheek. "Hi! Let's look at you. You look rested."

She seemed peculiarly excited. Slote felt the old snare closing in on him again. He said, "Well, *you* look slightly beat up."

"I've had hell's own time getting here. Let's get out of this wind."

He took her arm and started to walk. "Why are you here?"

"Byron's arriving tomorrow on a submarine."

He halted in astonishment. "He made it through that school?"

"He did. This is his first long cruise. You'll think I'm rattle-brained, but he wrote me to meet him, and here I am."

"Nothing you do surprises me, sweetie. I'm the man you came to visit in Warsaw in August '39. Now, what's Aaron's situation?"

Natalie told him that the impact of the note from the Secretary of State's office had been frittered away, due to the dawdling of Van Winaker, the young consul in Florence.

Slote said, "He's in more danger than he realizes. Perhaps I'll go back to Rome with you and drop in on the embassy."

"That would be marvellous!" He took her into the hotel's crowded lounge. "League of Nations," she said, hearing conversations in many languages. "Except that so many look Jewish."

"Too many of them are," Slote said dolefully.

Natalie devoured a whole plate of sugared cakes with her tea. "I shouldn't do this, but I'm famished. I'm getting too fat."

"Possibly I'm prejudiced, but I think you look like the goddess of love, if a bit travel-worn. There's Bunky Thurston." Slote waved as a little pink-faced man came towards them. "Hi, Bunky. You're late for tea, but just in time for a drink."

With a loud sigh, Thurston sat down. "Thanks. Natalie, here's that list." He handed her a mimeographed sheet. "I couldn't track down Commander Bathurst, but I left word for him to call me."

Slote glanced inquisitively at the paper. It was a list of documents required for a marriage of foreigners in Portugal. "Why, getting all this together would take months!" Natalie said.

"I've seen it done in one month," Thurston said, "but six to eight weeks is more usual."

"Thinking of getting married?" Slote said.

She coloured at his dry tone. "That was one of many things Byron wrote about. I thought I might as well check."

"Who's Commander Bathurst?" Slote said.

Thurston said, "Our naval attaché. He'll know exactly when the submarine's arriving." He tossed off half his whisky when it came, and looked around with a bitter expression. "God, Lisbon gives me the creeps. Forty thousand desperate people trying to get out of the net. I've seen most of the faces in this room at our legation. Many of them still don't believe they can't buy their way into the United States. They keep trying."

Slote nodded gloomily. "Am I taking you to dinner, Natalie?"

"Please, I'd love that."

"How about you, Bunky? Will you join us? Let's all go upstairs to my suite. I want to change my shirt, and all that."

"No, I have a dinner appointment. I'll sit here and have my drink with Natalie. I left word for Bathurst to page me here."

Slote told Natalie the number of his suite and left. Later she found a pencilled note stuck in his doorjamb: "N.—Door's open." She walked into a very large living room, looking out on to the purple sea beyond a long iron-railed balcony. Slote was singing in the shower. She yelled, "Hey! I'm here."

He soon appeared in a plaid dressing gown, towelling his head. "How about these digs? Fit for a rajah, what?"

"It's fine." She sat down heavily. "Bathurst finally called. Briny's sub has been rerouted to Gibraltar. It won't come to Lisbon at all."

"Maybe you can get to see him at Gibraltar."

"Thurston doesn't think so, but he's going to find out. He's being very kind." She took off her hat and tossed her hair. "This is quite a layout. Me, I'm in a boarding-house in town, sharing a room with a poor old Jewish lady from Rotterdam."

"Why not move in here? There's a maid's room I can sleep in."

"Nothing doing. Slote, if I can get to Gibraltar I'll marry Byron. That's what he wants." Her eyes shone. "I want it myself."

"Well, I suppose I should congratulate you, Natalie. God knows, I wish you well."

She smiled tiredly. "I need cheering up," she said. "There's a dress shop downstairs. I'll see what Lisbon has to offer."

Within a half-hour she was back, carrying a box. "I bought a pile of stuff. Maybe it's my trousseau! Byron's eyes will pop out of his head, if he ever shows up. Did you really mean that invitation to stay? That poor old woman gives me the horrors."

"I said the place is yours."

She paused at the bedroom door and turned. Her intense dark glance shook the diplomat. "People wouldn't understand about us, would they, Slote?"

"There's nothing to understand about me. You're the puzzle."

"You didn't used to think I was puzzling."

"I thought I had you figured out," he said. "I'm paying a steep price for oversimplifying."

NEXT morning Slote came out of the maid's room to find Natalie, in a dazzling white wool suit, watching a waiter fuss over breakfast. "Oh, hi," she said. "I ordered eggs for you."

"I'll just brush my teeth. How long have you been up?"

"Hours. I'm supposed to wait for Byron in the bar here at eleven today. That was the original plan."

Slote peered at her. "But his sub's en route to Gibraltar."

"That's what that naval attaché said. Suppose he's mistaken?"

Slote left the room. Soon he returned, fully dressed, and began to eat. "Sweetie, do you honestly expect Byron to materialize at eleven o'clock just on your sheer willpower?"

"Navy signals could get crossed up. I'm going to be there."

When Natalie had gone, Slote called Thurston. "'Morning, Bunky. What did you find out about Gibraltar?"

"Les, that submarine's here. In at dawn, for three days."

Slote had seldom heard worse news. "Then what on earth was Bathurst talking about?"

"He's mighty puzzled. They had orders for Gibraltar." Thurston's voice turned puckish. "Tough luck, Les. Fantastic girl."

Slote hung up and hurried down to the lobby.

"Here, Slote! Look behind you!" Natalie's voice rang joyously. Half-screened by potted palms, she sat on a green plush sofa with Byron. Before them on the coffee table lay a pile of documents.

Slote said, "Well, hello there!" as Byron jumped up to shake hands. "Did Natalie tell you we had some wrong information?"

Byron laughed. "It wasn't wrong, exactly, but anyway, here we are."

Natalie pulled at Byron's hand excitedly. "I can't find your certificate of residence."

"It's clipped with yours."

"Then he's got everything," Natalie told Slote. "And all translated into Portuguese, notarized, and authenticated."

"How on earth did you assemble all this?" Slote asked.

Byron explained that as soon as he had learned of the scheduled cruise to Lisbon, he had obtained an emergency four-day pass and had flown to Washington to find out at the Portuguese embassy what the marriage regulations were. The naval attaché, Captain D'Esaguy, had gone right to work. "It's surprising what those fellows can accomplish when they want to," Byron said.

Slote slipped the papers into their folder. "I'll telephone Bunky Thurston at the legation and ask him what you do next."

When he returned they were holding hands, looking adoringly at each other. He hesitated, then approached them. "Sorry. Problems."

Natalie looked up at him, startled. "What now?"

"Well, Bunky doesn't know what he can do about that twelve-day requirement for posting banns. And the Foreign Office's authentication of the consuls' signatures usually takes a week."

"Right. Captain D'Esaguy mentioned those points," Byron said. "But his uncle's a commodore at the navy ministry in Lisbon, and I stopped off this morning and gave Commodore D'Esaguy a letter. I'm to go back at one o'clock, but he only speaks Portuguese. Could Mr. Thurston meet us there? That might be a real help."

Slote looked from Byron to Natalie, whose mouth was twitching with amusement. "I'll call and ask him."

With some stupefaction, Bunker Thurston agreed to meet them. "I thought you called this ensign of hers a sluggard and a featherhead. He's organized this thing like a blitzkrieg."

"Surprised me. I'll see you at the navy ministry at one."

Outside the hotel, a tall man in navy dress-blues leaned on the fender of an automobile. "Hey, Briny! Is the exercise on?"

"It's on." Byron introduced him to Natalie and Slote as Lieutenant Aster, his executive officer. "Hop in, everybody," Aster said. "Briny, the skipper says you're off the watch list while we're here."

"Great, Lady. Thanks."

Natalie said, "*Lady?*"

The lieutenant's smile was weary. "With a name like Aster, it had to happen."

Driving into the city, Aster described how the *S-45*, a hundred and fifty miles out of Lisbon, had been ordered to Gibraltar. The captain, who knew of Byron's plans, had expressed regrets, but altered course. Within an hour he was receiving reports of malfunctions breaking out all over the boat. Aster recommended an emergency call in Lisbon for repairs. With a straight face the captain accepted the recommendation.

"Nobody was lying," Aster went on. "These old S-boats just gasp and flounder. At practically any moment you could justify an order to abandon ship."

"And you submerge in a wreck like that?" Natalie said.

"Well, the S-45 has made four thousand, seven hundred and twenty dives," Byron said. "It should be good for a few more."

"By the way," said Aster, "everybody's invited aboard after the ceremony. The captain wants to congratulate you."

D'Esaguy welcomed the Americans in his magnificent office; to Natalie he made a deep bow, his black eyes showing admiration. Then he spoke rapidly to Thurston in Portuguese.

"He says these things take time," Thurston reported. "He would like to invite us all to lunch."

Byron glanced at Natalie. "That's very cordial of him. Does he know we only have three days?"

The Portuguese officer's eyes were on Byron as Thurston translated. A flash of fun in the sombre face acknowledged the impatience of a young lover. He rapped an order to an assistant, who jumped up and went out. After a minute he returned with a bouquet of red roses. D'Esaguy handed them to Natalie with a bow and a few charmingly spoken words. Thurston translated: "The dew will not dry on these roses before you are married."

"Good God. How beautiful. Thank you!" Natalie stood holding the roses, blushing. "You know, I'm beginning to believe it!"

The lunch was long and excellent, in a restaurant with a lordly view of the Lisbon hills and the broad sparkling river. At three, the commodore said casually that perhaps they might see now how the "little business" was coming along. In an enormous Mercedes they commenced a whirling tour of government offices.

About two hours later they arrived at the office where civil marriages were registered. It was closed for the day, but as the car came to a stop the door opened. They were taken to a room where a frog-faced man greeted them and spoke to Thurston in Portuguese. Thurston translated his questions; the man scratched with a blotchy pen on many of Byron's documents and kept stamping them. Natalie, Byron, and the two witnesses—Aster and Slote—signed and signed. After a while the man stood up, and with a smile held out his hand to Natalie and then to Byron, saying, "Good luck for you."

"What's this now?" Natalie said.

"You're married," Thurston said. "Congratulations."

"We *are*? When did we get married? I missed it."

Byron said, "Hey, let's have that ring, Lady."

Byron slipped the ring on Natalie's finger, then swept her into his arms and kissed her. Meantime Thurston told D'Esaguy about the American custom of kissing the bride and, with marked pleasure, the commodore did so. Then he left, after handshakes all round.

Slote was the last to kiss her. Natalie said, "Well, old Slote, I seem to have done it, don't I? Wish me well."

"Oh, I do, I do, Jastrow. You know that."

"And now," said "Lady" Aster, "the skipper's expecting us."

"Where will you go after that?" Slote said dryly to Byron.

"Well, I figured—a hotel, something."

"Lisbon's jammed," said Slote. "Why not take my place?"

Byron shook his head, but Natalie said, "Oh, his place is out of the Arabian Nights." She added casually, "I had a drink there last night. *Would* you do such a thing for us, old Slote?"

"Leslie can stay with me," Thurston said. "No problem. Pick me up at the legation, Les. I have to rush."

"It's all set," said Slote. "I'll go to the hotel now and clear out."

"Bless you," said Natalie. "And Bunky, thanks for everything."

WHEN the bellboy opened the door to Slote's suite, Natalie darted in, remembering the negligee she had left hanging in the bathroom. It might take some explaining! But it was gone.

On a table in the living room, beside champagne in a silver

cooler, stood a bouquet of calla lilies, and beside them Slote's small white card. The doorbell rang and a bellboy gave Natalie a box. She hurried into the bedroom and opened it. There lay the grey silk negligee Slote had cleared out.

"What was it?" Byron called from the balcony.

"Oh, some stuff I bought in a lobby shop," Natalie replied airily. Then she saw a note in Slote's handwriting. "You always looked angelic in grey, Jastrow. Confidential communication, to be destroyed. Yours till death. Slote."

The words brought a mist to Natalie's eyes. She tore the note to bits. In the next room she heard a cork pop, and quite forgot Leslie Slote as she showered and perfumed herself. She emerged from the bedroom brushing her long hair down on her shoulders.

. . . Wine, lilies and roses; the dark sea rolling beyond the windows under a round moon; young lovers separated for half a year, joined on a knife edge of geography between war and peace, performing secret rites as old as time, but forever fresh and sweet between young lovers. Such was their wedding night.

20

In Washington, Victor Henry was reassigned to War Plans. Though he had craved sea duty, he was untroubled by the assignment, since he cared also about the future of the United States. Early in January 1941, with a few other planners, he had begun "conversations" with British military men. In theory, Air Commodore Burne-Wilke and his delegation were in Washington on vague missions of observing or purchase. In fact, by the first of March these conferences were finishing up a war operations plan on a world scale. The assumption was that Japan would one day attack, but the key decision lay in two words: "Germany first".

It was clear to Pug that if Japan entered the war, with her annual steel production of only a few million tons, she could not hold out long if Germany were beaten. But if the Germans knocked out the British and got their fleet, they could conquer whole continents, whatever happened to Japan. From his talks in the Army and Navy Club, however, he knew that the "Germany first" decision, if it came out, would create a fantastic howl.

Pug got along well with Burne-Wilke, who had fully grasped the landing craft problem. Among the planners, a laboured joke was spreading about Captain Henry's girl friend, "Elsie", a play on LC (landing craft), the importance of which he kept stressing.

He seldom encountered Pamela Tudsbury, whom the air commodore had brought along as his typist aide. They met for a drink just once and he amplified on the letter he had written her about Ted Gallard. She looked extremely young, and his infatuation seemed distant and hardly believable. Yet any day when he saw her was a good day for him.

Rhoda had received him back with a puzzling mixture of moods —demonstrative affection alternating with spells of heavy gloom over her move back to Washington. She levelled off to a cool detachment, busying herself charitably with "Bundles for Britain", and finding many reasons for trips to New York. In a most casual way she sometimes mentioned Palmer Kirby, now one of the chairmen of "Bundles for Britain".

News about their children intermittently drew them together. Byron's letter about his hasty marriage in Lisbon was a shock. They agonized about it for days before becoming resigned to the fact. Warren sent good news. Janice was returning to Washington to have her baby, and he had been promoted to lieutenant.

Pug turned fifty on a Sunday early in March. He sat in church beside his wife, trying to shake off a sense that he had missed all the right turns in life. He counted his blessings: his wife was still beautiful, still capable of love; his two sons were naval officers; his daughter was self-supporting; he was serving where he was doing some good.

Rhoda was thinking that for the first time since his return her husband would soon be meeting Palmer Kirby face-to-face.

A SNOWSTORM clogged the capital on the night of Rhoda's party. By quarter past seven her guests, including Kirby, had straggled in, but the dinner was still stalled. Pug was missing.

In the kitchen of the elegant little rented house on Tracy Place, Rhoda made a last-minute check and found all in order: soup hot, ducks tender, vegetables on the boil, cook snarling over the delay. She sailed out to her guests. Kirby and Pamela Tudsbury were talking on the big couch, Janice and Alistair Tudsbury had their heads together in a corner, and on facing settees before a log fire, Air Commodore Burne-Wilke was chatting with recently elected Senator Lacouture and his wife: a hodgepodge company, but it was only a hurried dinner before a "Bundles for Britain" concert. Pug's meeting with Kirby was what concerned her.

"We'll wait a few more minutes," Rhoda sat herself beside the scientist. "Then we'll have to eat."

"Where is Captain Henry?" Pamela said calmly. Her mauve dress came to a halter around her neck, leaving her slim shoulders naked; her tawny hair was piled high on her head.

"I'm blessed if I can say. Military secrecy covers a multitude of sins," Rhoda laughed. "That's a divine dress, my dear."

"Do you like it? Thank you." Pamela smoothed the skirt.

The telephone rang, and Rhoda answered it. "Oh, *hello* . . . oh, my gawd . . . of course. O.K. 'Bye, dear." She fluttered her hands at the company. "Well, let's drink up. Pug sends apologies. He's stuck at the White House."

At the table Rhoda put Burne-Wilke on her right and the senator on her left. "Protocol still baffles me," she said. "I'm favouring our foreign guest, Senator."

"Absolutely proper," said Lacouture.

Alistair Tudsbury said, "Air Commodore Burne-Wilke will gladly yield you his seat on this occasion, Senator, if he can take yours when Lend-Lease comes to a vote."

"Oh, done, done," exclaimed Burne-Wilke.

Everyone laughed. Rhoda said, "Well, what good spirits! I was afraid our English friends would eat Senator Lacouture alive."

The senator crinkled his eyes. "You British aren't that hard up for meat yet, are you? But seriously, Rhoda, I'm glad you brought us together. Maybe I've convinced our friends that I'm not a Nazi lover, but just a fellow with my own point of view. If Roosevelt wants to send England arms free of charge, why the devil doesn't he *say* so, instead of giving us all this Lend-Lease baloney?"

"I think the country's going mad," said Janice. "This afternoon, in front of the White House, there was a mob of women, Christian Mothers of America, kneeling in the snow to protest Lend-Lease."

"It just shows how broad the opposition is," said the senator. "Cuts across all lines."

"On the contrary," put in Kirby, "both extremes seem to be against helping England, while the mass in the middle is for it."

The street door opened and closed. Pug came into the dining room. "Apologies," he said, taking off his coat. "I'll just join you, and change later." He walked around the table for handshakes, and came last to Kirby. "It's been a long time," he said.

"Sure has. Too long."

Only Rhoda knew the scientist well enough to note that his smile was awkward. She had a surprising sensation—pleasure and pride that two such men loved her.

Pug took his seat and began chatting to Kirby about Byron, whose submarine had just put in at the Brooklyn Navy Yard. Just then Mrs. Lacouture uttered a shriek. The old steward was offering soup to Burne-Wilke and the open soup tureen was slipping. As it left the tray, Rhoda plucked it out of the air and set it on the table, not spilling a drop.

"Well done," Pug called over the gasps and laughter.

Everybody had a joke or a compliment for Rhoda. She became exhilarated and began reminiscing about Nazi parties in Berlin. Forgotten was her former friendliness to the Germans: she was now the "Bundles for Britain" lady, partisan to the core. The dinner was a great success.

At the concert Rhoda had taken two boxes nearest to the Vice-President's. The orchestra struck up "The Star-Spangled Banner", and then "God Save the King", which, with the nearness of Pam's bare white shoulders, awakened memories of London in Pug's mind, and a wisp of guilt touched him.

During the intermission crush, Victor Henry and Dr. Kirby were left together in the overheated lobby. Pug suggested a breath of air. Outside, he said, "Anything very new on uranium?"

Kirby shook his head, making a discouraged mouth.

"As you know, I'm in War Plans," Victor Henry said. "I'm pushing you because we ought to have the dope, and we can't get it. Could we be doing more about it?"

"One hell of a lot. I'm going to England on this. They're apparently ahead of us."

"As on other things," Pug said. "That's something nobody mentions in this brainless Lend-Lease dogfight. We'd damned well better keep the British scientists on our side."

"I agree." Kirby puffed his pipe. "Are you happy to be home?"

"Happy? Yes, I guess so. Rhoda was sick of Berlin, and being there by myself was certainly grim."

"She's a superb hostess, Rhoda," said Kirby. "That was something, the way she rescued that tureen."

"Rhoda's a born juggler," said Pug.

A BRAHMS symphony was putting Pug in a doze when a tap and a whisper woke him. "Captain Henry?" The usher appeared excited and awed. "The White House is on the telephone." Pug spoke a few words into his wife's ear and departed. When he returned, an hour or so later, the concert was over and the Supper Dance was in full swing. Pug stood in the ballroom glumly surveying the scene: the stage festooned with American and British flags, the jolly queues at buffets laden with meats, salads, cheeses and cakes. The naval aide at the White House had just told him, among other things, of thirty thousand tons sunk in the Atlantic in two days.

Alistair Tudsbury came capering past him with a blonde lady of about forty. "Ah, there, Pug! You're glaring like Savonarola! Rhoda's down at the other end."

"Did Pamela come to the dance?" He needed someone he could talk to.

"She went to the office. She's doing the overworked patriot."

Tudsbury twirled the blonde away. Crossing the dance floor, Pug saw his wife at a small supper table with Palmer Kirby.

"Hello, dear!" she called. "Get a plate and join us."

"I'll get you one," said Kirby, rising. "Sit down, Pug."

"No, no, I have to run home and pack a bag." To his wife, he said, "I just came to tell you I'll be gone overnight." He bent and kissed her cheek. "Sorry, darling. Enjoy the dance."

After he left, Rhoda and Palmer Kirby sat without speaking until Kirby pushed aside his plate. "Well, I leave for New York at seven tomorrow, myself. I'd better turn in. A fine evening. Thanks, Rhoda."

"Palmer, I have to stay another half-hour or so. But I'll walk out with you." In the lobby she said, "I meant to tell Pug as soon as he got back. But he was so glad to be home. I just couldn't."

Kirby nodded, with a cold expression.

"Then along came this awful jolt," she went on. "Byron marrying this girl in Lisbon. It took both of us days to simmer down. And then Janice arrived, all pregnant and whatnot. You've just got to let me pick my moment, dear. It won't be easy."

He said, "I've been very uncomfortable tonight. I really want to get married again, Rhoda. I've never felt that more strongly than I did at your dinner table."

"Palmer, don't give me an ultimatum, for heaven's sake."

"I won't do that." He glanced her up and down with a sudden smile. "Gosh, how pretty you look tonight. I won't get back from London till May. That should be plenty of time, Rhoda."

IN HER mauve evening dress and fancy hairdo, Pamela Tudsbury clattered away at a typewriter. She looked up owlishly when Victor Henry came in, carrying an overnight bag. "You drink it black, with sugar, as I recall." Then she smiled and poured two cups of coffee from the percolator on the desk.

"You look absurd," Pug said, taking another chair.

"Oh, I know, but this has to be ready by eight in the morning."

"What are you working on?"

She hesitated. "I dare say you know more about it than I do. It's the landing craft annex."

"Quite a document." He leaned forward. She was, after all, almost as much of an insider as he was. "This Lend-Lease hubbub isn't helping the President. He's had a bad sinus condition and a fever. He's taking the train to Hyde Park to rest up and strictly on the q.t. I'm to ride with him. I'd hoped he'd forgotten me."

"You're not very forgettable, you know." She rubbed her eyes tiredly. "There's news of Ted," she said.

"Good or bad?" he asked warily.

"Three RAF prisoners at his hospital in France escaped and made their way home. They said that after your visit Ted got special surveillance and was then shipped to a prison camp in Germany."

"It was my doing, then, that he didn't get out."

"That's ridiculous. You relieved me of months of agonizing."

"Yes. At least you know he's alive. Well—I guess I'll go along. He stood up. "Thanks for the coffee, Pam."

"And you for a splendid dinner. Your wife's wonderful."

"Rhoda's all right. Nobody has to sell Rhoda to me."

Pamela peered at the typewriter. "We're finishing up here soon," she said. "Going back to London."

"Maybe I'll see you before you go home."

"That would be nice. I've missed you terribly. More so here than in London." As Pug paused at the door she looked up at him. "Well? Don't keep the President waiting, Captain Henry."

THE PRESIDENT'S carriage, so far as Pug could tell, was a regular pullman parlour car furnished to look like a living room. "Sit down, Pug!" The President waved from a chair. "What'll you have?"

A steward passed a tray of drinks. The President took a tall glass of orange juice. "Doctor's orders. Lots and lots of fruit juice. I want to have a snack, and then try to sleep a little." He fixed Pug with a sharp look. "Pug, the U-boats keep working westward with this new wolf-pack tactic. The sinkings are outrunning the combined capacity of our shipyards and Britain's. You're aware of all that."

"I've been hearing plenty about it, yes, sir."

"The minute Lend-Lease passes, we'll be sending out a vast shipment of stuff, and none of it must land on the ocean floor."

Roosevelt's offhand remark about Lend-Lease surprised Victor Henry. "You think Lend-Lease *will* pass, sir?"

"Oh, it will pass," said the President. "But then what? Seventy ships are standing by. This shipment has got to arrive. The problem is getting it as far as Iceland. From there the British can convoy, but not from here to Iceland. So what do we do?"

Victor Henry said uncomfortably, "Convoy, sir?"

The President shook his head. "You know the answer on that."

In the Lend-Lease fight, the issue of convoying was red-hot. The Lacouture group was screaming that if Lend-Lease passed, the warmongers would demand to convoy the ships that carried the supplies, and that that meant immediate war with Germany.

Roosevelt's grim face took on a mischievous look. "I've been thinking, however. Suppose a squadron of destroyers went out on an exercise, practising convoy *procedures*. And suppose they were to travel with the shipment—strictly for drill purposes—just this once? And to avoid complications, suppose all this were done highly informally, with no written orders? Don't you suppose the U-boats might be a bit discouraged to see sixteen or so United States destroyers out there screening those ships?"

"Discouraged, yes. Still, what happens will depend on their instructions, Mr. President."

"They've got instructions not to tangle with our warships," Roosevelt said harshly. "That's obvious. And the ships may never even be sighted by the Germans before the British take over at Iceland. I'm thinking you might handle this thing."

Captain Henry swallowed and said, "Aye, aye, sir."

"Everything depends on doing it in the most unobtrusive way, with an absolute minimum of people in the know."

"Admiral Stark and Admiral King would have to be told, of course, sir. And Commander, Support Force, and the officer in tactical command of the convoy screen."

Roosevelt laughed. "Well! If you can keep it down to three admirals and one other officer, that will be swell."

"Mr. President, what do we do if a U-boat *does* attack?"

Roosevelt regarded him through wreathing cigarette smoke. "This is a gamble that it won't happen. We *cannot* have a combat incident. Tell me, what do you honestly think of the idea?"

"Well, sir, if those U-boats do see us, they'll radio for instructions. This is a policy decision that will have to go up to Hitler.

That'll take time; I think the ships will get through without incident. But it'll only work once."

Roosevelt nodded. "But it's this first shipment that is crucial. Would you tell the steward on your way out that I'm ready to eat. And Pug, when you come back from that little sea jaunt I want you and your family to come to dinner."

"Thank you, Mr. President. I'm very honoured."

LEND-LEASE passed the Senate by sixty votes to thirty-one. Few Americans followed the debate more keenly than Pug Henry.

Now, he thought, the President had the means to put the United States on a war footing. The new factories needed to make Lend-Lease planes and guns would in time arm the American forces. The day the bill passed, Pug was ordered to fly to the Norfolk Navy Yard and report to Admiral Ernest King, a dragon he had not met before.

King sat behind a desk on the battleship *Texas*, his sleeves stiff to the elbow with gold. Behind him hung a chart of the Atlantic, marked COMMANDER-IN-CHIEF, ATLANTIC FLEET.

He motioned Pug to a seat. "I received a telephone call from the chief of naval operations yesterday," he said, "that one Captain Victor Henry of War Plans would report to me directly from the President of the United States. Well? State your business."

The captain told Admiral King what Franklin Roosevelt desired.

"So! You're prepared to get the United States into this war all by yourself, are you, Captain?" said the admiral.

"Admiral, it's the President's judgment that this exercise will go off without incident."

"So you said. Well, suppose his judgment's wrong? Suppose a U-boat fires a fish at you? What then?"

"If we're fired on, sir, why, I propose to fire back. That won't start a war unless Hitler wants a war."

Admiral King nodded peevishly. "Well, I tend to agree that it very likely won't happen now." After looking Victor Henry over like a dog he was considering buying, King picked up the telephone. "Get me Admiral Bristol . . . . Hello? Admiral, I'm sending to your office Captain Victor Henry. He will visit Desron

Eight and conduct drills and manoeuvres, to test combat readiness. He is to be regarded as my assistant chief of staff."

Staring at Pug, he spoke in a formal drone. "Captain, you are to form out of Desron Eight an anti-submarine screen, and proceed to sea to conduct realistic tests and drills. This includes forming up screens on cooperative merchant vessels which you may encounter. I desire you to keep security at a maximum and paper work at a minimum. For that reason my instructions are verbal."

"Understood, Admiral."

King reverted to his natural voice. "Should an incident occur, it will be a hanging party for all hands. That will be all."

21

Even in the North Atlantic in March, going back to sea was a tonic. Pug paced the bridge of USS *Plunkett* a happy man.

He kept to his official role of observer and left operations to Commander Baldwin, who headed the destroyer screen. He interfered only once. On the second day after the join-up off Newfoundland, after the long columns of zigzagging merchant ships had ploughed into a snowstorm and begun losing sight of each other, Pug called Baldwin into his sea cabin.

"I've been figuring," he said. "We can gain half a day by proceeding on a straight course. Maybe there are U-boats out there. If they really try to penetrate this screen—well, zigzagging won't help much. Let's head straight for Point Baker, turn over this hot potato, and skedaddle."

Commander Baldwin grinned. "Concur, Captain."

Pug called the British signal officer in from the bridge. "Give your commodore a flag hoist: Discontinue zigzagging."

Unmolested, the first Lend-Lease convoy steamed on. Whether U-boats saw it and laid low because of the American destroyers, or whether it got through undetected, Pug never knew.

When they arrived at the rendezvous off Iceland, a feeble yellow sun was just rising. The convoy formed into a pattern ten miles square, waiting for the British. After three hours, the first hulls began to show above the horizon. As the screen of British vessels came on, the leading ship began to blink a yellow light. A signal-man on the *Plunkett* brought Pug a pencilled scrawl: "Thanks Yanks. Cupboard is bare."

Pug grunted. "Send him 'Eat hearty. More coming.' And sign it 'Mother Hubbard'."

RHODA was in turmoil. Kirby had returned from England in April, while Pug was at sea, and she had gone with him on a four-day trip through the countryside. Rhoda came back to Washington committed to leave her husband and to marry Kirby.

The decision seemed simple and natural while Kirby was with her. But when he went off to Denver, the simplicity of the vision, and some of its charm, began to fade.

In Rhoda's own mind, she was a good woman, caught up in a grand passion which consumed all moral law. She still liked—perhaps loved—Pug, but their marriage had long been slightly sour. With such thoughts Rhoda was working herself up to tell Pug that she had fallen in love with another man. But she teetered, ready to be pushed either way.

She missed his return from the convoy trip. He arrived to find the house empty—cook off, Rhoda out, mail overflowing his desk. He put a note on her dressing table—"He's back. Man the bar"—and left for the War Plans office.

There, by chance, he encountered Pamela Tudsbury. She had not gone back to England with Burne-Wilke. Secretaries cleared for Very Secret were rare, so the British Purchasing Commission had requisitioned her. She greeted him warmly. "The sea obviously agrees with you," she said. "You look ten years younger."

All the rest of the day, ploughing through a mound of accumulated paper, Victor Henry felt much better.

That evening Rhoda was waiting for him in a bright red dress, with drinks ready. Her manner struck him as strange. She chattered on about that sore subject, promotions. Finally Pug broke in on her flow of words—this was at dinner—to tell her of the President's invitation. Her mouth fell open. "Pug! Really?" She worried over what she would wear, and gloated about other navy wives' reactions to *this*!

That night Pug recognized familiar signals that he was not welcome in her bedroom. He did not know why; but he had long ago decided that Rhoda was entitled to these spells. It took him a long time to fall asleep. He kept thinking of the callous happy-go-lucky mood he had found in the capital, the sense that by passing the Lend-Lease Bill, America had done its bit. Nobody appeared to care how the stuff was actually to be produced. Under a welter of meetings and talk, Lend-Lease was paralysed.

Meanwhile, the war news was worsening. The Germans had blitzed Yugoslavia in one week. Greece had surrendered, and the Germans had trapped a large British force there. They were sinking ships at a great rate, showering England with fire bombings worse than any during 1940, gaining victories in North Africa, and launching an airborne invasion of Crete. This outpouring of military energy in all directions was awesome. In the face of it, Vichy France was negotiating a deal that would hand over French North Africa to the Nazis. This was a bloody nose for American diplomats trying to keep the Germans out of the African bulge at French Dakar, which dominated the whole South Atlantic.

In War Plans circles, a split was widening between the army and the navy. The navy wanted strong, fast moves in the North Atlantic to save England: more convoys, and the occupation of Iceland. But the army, which now gave England only three months before collapse, preferred a move into Brazil and the Azores, to face the expected Nazi thrust in the South Atlantic. Between these two plans the President was stalling and hesitating.

Then came the scarifying news that the *Bismarck*, a new German battleship, had blown up England's mighty war vessel, the *Hood*.

"WHAT do you think, Dad? Will the limeys get the *Bismarck*?"

It was the evening of the White House dinner, and Byron, perched on the edge of the bathtub, watched his father shave.

"Well, Briny, they claim the *Prince of Wales* winged her. But the *Bismarck*'s a floating steel honeycomb. If she was hit, they probably just buttoned up the flooded compartments and lit out for home. The British are throwing everything into their search."

"I wish I were in that search," said Byron.

"Do you?" Pug gave his son a pleased look.

Byron followed him into his dressing room. "Dad, I got a letter from Natalie. She's pregnant."

Victor Henry put a hand on his son's shoulder. "That's great news, Briny. Great."

"But, Dad, she's stuck there in Italy."

Buttoning his dress shirt, Pug frowned at the mirror. "Why?"

"The same foolishness about when her uncle's father was naturalized. He just can't get that passport renewed. One official makes promises and the next one fudges on them. They're ringed by Germans now. And they're a couple of Jews."

"I'm aware of that," said Victor Henry.

"Dad, I thought you might mention this to the President."

"That's an unreasonable notion," Pug said curtly. He was jarred by the hostility on his son's face. "Byron, I don't think Jastrow's mess is a suitable problem to submit to the President."

"Oh, I knew you wouldn't do it. You're sore at me for marrying a Jew and you don't care what happens to her."

IN THE marble-floored foyer of the White House the chief usher introduced himself to the Henrys. "Mrs. Henry, you will be sitting on the President's left," he said. "Crown Princess Marta of Norway will sit on his right." He led them to the Red Room.

"Oh, dear, think of Warren and Madeline missing all this!" Rhoda spoke in a hushed voice and peered at the paintings of Presidents.

"May I present Mr. Sumner Welles?" The chief usher led in a bald, lean, gloomy man. "And I believe we can go upstairs now."

An elevator took them up. Behind his desk, at one end of a huge yellow room, sat the President, rattling a cocktail shaker. "Hello there, just in time for the first round!" he called. "I hope Mrs. Henry likes Orange Blossoms, Pug. Good evening, Sumner."

In the centre of the room, Eleanor Roosevelt stood with a tall, black-haired woman and a sharp-faced, aged little man. The usher introduced the Henrys to Mrs. Roosevelt, to Princess Marta, and to Mr. Somerset Maugham.

"Anything new on the *Bismarck*, Sumner?" the President asked.

"Not since about five o'clock, sir."

"What do you say, Pug? Will they get her?"

"It's a tough exercise, Mr. President. Mighty big ocean. But if they winged her, as they claim, they ought to catch her."

They drank their cocktails, and then Mrs. Roosevelt left the President and led her guests to the door. When they arrived in the dining room, there sat Franklin Roosevelt, already whisked to his place at the head of the table.

"Well, I had a good day!" he exclaimed as they sat down. "The Ford company finally promised to make Liberator bombers. The business people seem to be waking up at last." He started on his soup. "Mr. Maugham, by next fall, we'll be making five hundred heavy bombers a month. That's hard intelligence."

"Sir, the—hard intelligence is—" Maugham's stammer caught everybody's attention—"that you *s-say* you'll be making them."

The President roared with laughter. "Mr. Maugham was a British spy in the last war, Pug," he said. "Watch out what you say here. It'll get right back to Churchill."

"Mr-Mr. President, I am not a f-f-ferret now, I assure you, but a lower form of life. A-a-a sponge."

"Captain Henry was in the intelligence business, too, Willie," Roosevelt said to Maugham. "He was naval attaché in Berlin. He predicted that pact between Hitler and Stalin before it happened. What is it now, Pug? Will Hitler attack Russia?"

"Mr. President, after that bit of luck, I hocked my crystal ball."

Mrs. Roosevelt said, "Mr. Maugham—if Germany does attack the Soviet Union, will England help Russia?"

The author paused. "I - I can't really say."

"Sumner," said Roosevelt, "do you suppose we could explain it to the American people if the British did not help Russia?"

"I think that would finish off aid to England, Mr. President. If Hitler is a menace to mankind, that's one thing. If he's just a menace to the British Empire, that's something very different."

With a brief look at the British author, the President said, "Well! Shall I slice some more lamb?"

"I will thank you for some, Mr. President," said Princess Marta.

"Of course Hitler may be massing troops in the east to keep Stalin out of the Rumanian oil fields. He needs that oil."

"But it all boils down to Hitler's impulses nowadays," said the President. "And we have here two men who've talked face-to-face with the fellow. Sumner, do you think Hitler is mad?"

"I looked hard for such evidence, Mr. President. But I found him a cool, knowledgeable advocate with considerable charm."

"How about you, Pug?"

"He has a very powerful presence, sir, with a fantastic memory and a remarkable ability to marshal facts as he talks. He gives his people just what they want."

Rhoda blurted, "Pug, when on earth did you have a talk with Hitler? That's news to me." Laughter swept the table. She turned on Roosevelt. "Honestly, to keep something like *that* from me!"

"C-captain," said Maugham. "I bow to a p-p-professional."

Roosevelt said, "My dear Rhoda, you couldn't have paid your husband a handsomer compliment in public."

"I didn't intend to. Imagine!" She darted a tender look at Pug.

"I expect great things of Pug," said the President.

"I always have, Mr. President."

At the other end of the table Byron, between Mrs. Roosevelt and a deaf, very old lady named Delano, sat silent, withdrawn.

The President said, "We haven't heard from our submariner here. Byron, are you ready to go to war?"

"Personally, sir, I'm more than ready."

"Well, that's the spirit."

Victor Henry interposed, "Byron was in Poland when the war began. He was strafed by a Luftwaffe plane and wounded."

"I see," said the President. "Well, you have a motive then for wanting to fight Germans."

"That's not it so much, Mr. President. The thing is that my wife is trapped in Italy."

Roosevelt appeared startled. "Trapped? How, trapped?"

Byron said, "Her uncle is Dr. Aaron Jastrow, the author of *A Jew's Jesus*. He's had some trouble about his passport. He's old and not well, and she won't abandon him."

Mrs. Roosevelt put in with a smile, "Why, Franklin, we both

454

read *A Jew's Jesus*. Don't you remember? You liked it very much."

"Dr. Jastrow taught at Yale, Mrs. Roosevelt," Byron said. "He's lived here most of his life. It's just crazy red tape."

"*A Jew's Jesus* is a good book," said the President, in a flat tone. "Sumner, couldn't you have somebody look into this?"

"Certainly, Mr. President."

"Let me know what you find out." Roosevelt resumed eating.

The door to the hallway opened and a navy commander entered. He handed the President a slip of paper. "Well!" Roosevelt took a dramatic pause. "It seems they've got the *Bismarck*!"

"Ah!" The crown princess bounced in her chair, clapping like a girl, amid an excited babble.

The President raised his glass. "To the Royal Navy."

NEXT morning, when Pug had left, Rhoda wrote a note: "Palmer, dear—You have a kindly heart that understands without explanations. I can't do it. I realize we can't see each other for a long while, but I hope we will be friends forever. My love and ever-lasting thanks for offering me more than I deserve and can accept. I'll never forget. Forgive me. Rhoda."

That same morning, shortly before noon, a buzzer sounded on Victor Henry's desk. "Yes?" he said into the intercom.

"The office of Mr. Sumner Welles is calling, sir."

Welles's secretary had a sweet, sexy Southern voice. "Oh, Captain Henry, suh. The Under Secretary is most anxious to see you today, if you happen to be free."

Pug said, "I can come now."

The sexy voice belonged to a fat old fright. "My, you got here fast, Captain. The Under Secretary is with Secretary Hull just now. He says do you mind talking to Mr. Whitman?"

She led him to an office whose sign indicated a minor official in European affairs named Aloysius Whitman. "The Under Secretary thanks you for taking the time to come over," Whitman said genially. He gestured at a chair. "Well, now, Dr. Jastrow's passport. It's no problem whatever. The authorization was sent out a while ago. We checked by cable with Rome. Dr. Jastrow can have his passport any time he'll come down from Siena to pick it up."

"Good. My son will be mighty glad to hear it."

"Oh yes, about your son. I hope you'll take this in the right spirit. The Under Secretary was disconcerted to have this raised at the President's dinner table."

"Naturally. I was mighty jarred myself."

"I'm glad you feel that way. Suppose you just drop a note to the President, sort of apologizing, and mentioning that you've learned it was all taken care of long ago?"

"But he asked for a report from Mr. Welles."

Whitman gave him the brightest of smiles. "We went to a rather dramatic effort this morning, Captain, just to make sure young Mrs. Henry could get home. In return I really think you should write that letter."

"I'll tell you, I might even write it, if I could find out why Jastrow got stopped by a technicality when he wanted to come home. That's what the President wants to know. But I can't give him the answer. Can you?"

He walked out. From a booth in the lobby Pug telephoned the Norfolk Navy Yard and sent a message to Byron's S-45.

Byron called him late in the afternoon. "Eeyow! No kidding, Dad! How marvellous. Now if she can only get on a plane or a boat! Dad, be honest. Was I right to talk to the President?"

"You had one hell of a nerve. Now I'm damned busy and I hope you are. Get back to work."

". . . THEREFORE *I have tonight issued a proclamation that an unlimited national emergency exists, and requires the strengthening of our defences to the extreme limit of our national power and authority . . .*" Roosevelt's voice rose. "*I repeat the words of the signers of the Declaration of Independence . . . 'With a firm reliance on the protection of Divine Providence, we mutually pledge to each other our Lives, our Fortunes, and our sacred Honour!'*"

"It's far more than I expected," Pug said, when he snapped the radio off. "He finally did it!"

Rhoda said, "Funny. I thought he just pussyfooted around."

"Pussyfooted! Weren't you listening? 'We are placing our armed forces in position . . . we will use them to repel attack . . . an unlimited national emergency exists . . . .'"

"What does it all mean?" Rhoda yawned on the chaise longue.

"We convoy right away. That's for starters."

"If it's war," Rhoda said, "they'll surely give you a sea command." She rose and stretched. "Coming to bed?" she purred.

"Be right up."

Pug did not know why he was back in her good graces, or why he had ever fallen out. He went upstairs humming.

THE YEOMAN's voice on the intercom was apologetic. "Sir, beg your pardon. Will you talk to Mr. Alistair Tudsbury?" Victor Henry, sweating out an urgent report on convoying for the chief of naval operations, growled, "Yes, put him on . . . . Hello?"

"Am I disturbing you, dear boy? That's quite a bark."

"No, not at all. What's up?"

"What do you make of the President's Press conference?"

"I didn't know he'd had one."

"You *are* busy. Ask for the afternoon papers."

"Wait—they're just here now." He reached for the two newspapers the yeoman brought in. The headlines read: NO CONVOYS— FDR and "UNLIMITED EMERGENCY" MERELY A WARNING—NO POLICY CHANGES.

Skimming the front pages, Pug saw that Roosevelt had blandly taken back his radio speech, claiming the reporters had misunderstood it.

Tudsbury said, "Victor, people in England have been dancing in the streets over last night's speech. Now I have to broadcast about this."

"I don't envy you."

"Can you come over for a drink?"

"I'm afraid not."

"Please try. Pam's going home, leaving on a boat tonight."

"Let me call you back."

He telephoned the office of the chief of naval operations and discovered that, following the President's Press conference, the convoy report was no longer needed by that night.

"THE FUNNY part is," Pug said to Tudsbury, "Rhoda said he pussyfooted around. I was taken in."

"Maybe it needs a woman to follow that devious mind. Pam, Pug's here to say good-bye to you."

"Just a minute." They could see her moving in the hall, carrying clothes, books, and suitcases here and there.

Tudsbury, sprawling on a sofa, heaved a fat sigh. "I shall be alone again. There's a girl who is all self, self, self."

"Family trait," called a dulcet voice.

"Shut up. Please, Pug, give me something comforting to say in this broadcast. What's happened to Roosevelt? He *knows* the past three months' shipping losses. He *knows* that with Crete taken the Luftwaffe will come back at us. What the devil?"

"You should be going, Talky," said Pamela, striding in.

He sighed. "I have never been so reluctant to face a microphone. My tongue will cleave to the roof of my mouth."

"Oh, yes. Just as it's doing now."

"I agree with you, Tudsbury," Pug said. "The President's policy is disaster."

"Yes, and it's *your* disaster. This is a contest now between Germany and the United States. We were too slow and too stupid. But in the end we did our best. You're doing nothing." He pulled himself reluctantly to his feet.

"The United States Navy is ready," Pug shot back. "I've been working all day on a general operation order for convoy—"

"Good God, man, can I say that? Can I say that your navy is ready to go over to convoy and expects to do it soon?"

Pug hesitated only a second. "Sure, say it! You can hear that from anybody in the service. Who doesn't know that?"

"The British, that's who. You've saved me." He lumbered out.

Pam sat with her back to the window. The sun in her brown hair made an aureole around her sad face.

Pug said, "It's brave of you to go back."

"Not in the least. I just can't wait to go." Pamela wrung her fingers in her lap. "There's a girl in the office who's gone dotty over a married man. An American. And she has a fiancé in the RAF. I have to live with her maudlin guilts."

458

They sat in silence. Pug rattled the ice in his glass, round and round. "Funny, there's this fellow I know," he said. "Navy fellow. He's been married for more than a quarter of a century, fine grown family. Well, he ran into this girl, and he can't get her out of his mind. There's nothing wrong with his wife. Still, he keeps dreaming about this girl. All he does is dream. He wouldn't hurt his wife for the world. Just as silly as this friend of yours. There are millions of such people."

"He sounds like somebody I might like."

From outside came the sound of a hand organ. "Listen!" Pam jumped up and went to the window. Below, the organ-grinder was almost hidden in a crowd of children. She slipped her hand in his. "Let's go down and watch the monkey. There must be one."

"Sure."

"First let me kiss you good-bye." She kissed him while the music of the hurdy-gurdy jangled. "What is that song?" she said.

"It's called 'Yes, We Have No Bananas'. I love you," said Victor Henry, considerably surprising himself.

Her eyes looked deep into his. "I love you. Come on."

On the street, the children were squealing and shouting as the monkey turned somersaults. The animal ran to Pug and held out its little red hat. He dropped in a quarter. The monkey somersaulted back to his master and dropped the coin in a box.

"If that critter could be taught to salute," said Pug, "he might have a hell of a naval career."

Pamela seized his hand. "You're doing as much as anybody I know—*anybody*—about this accursed war."

"Well, Pam, have a safe trip home." He kissed her hand and walked rapidly off, leaving her among the children.

A COUPLE of days later, Victor Henry received an order to escort to the Memorial Day parade the oldest naval survivor of the Civil War. He picked the man up at a veterans' home and drove with him to the reviewing stand on Pennsylvania Avenue.

President Roosevelt's white linen suit and white straw hat glared in the bright sun as he sat in his open car beside the stand. He gave the tottering ancient a strong handshake.

"How would you like to watch the parade with me?" he bellowed.

"Better than—hee-hee—marching in it."

"Come along. Pug, you sit with me too."

"The navy's my favourite," Roosevelt said, as blue Annapolis ranks swung by. "By the way, Pug, whom can I send over to London to head up our convoy command? We'll call him a special naval observer or something, until we get things started."

"Sir, *are* we going to convoy?"

"You know perfectly well we've got to."

"*When*, Mr. President?"

The President smiled wearily. He fumbled in his pocket. "I had an interesting chat with General Marshall this morning." He showed Victor Henry a chit of paper, headed "Combat Readiness, June 1, 1941." It showed the army ground forces to be thirteen per cent ready and the army air corps zero per cent prepared!

Pug, reading these frustrating figures while the marine band blared out "The Stars and Stripes Forever", in that moment understood Franklin Roosevelt as well as he ever would.

"And here's another figure, Pug. On the day after my speech, *eighty-two* per cent of our people didn't want to go to war. *Eighty-two per cent*. And convoying might just get us in."

The navy veteran, who had been dozing in the sun, was sitting up now, working his bony jaws. "Fine parade. I still remember marching past President Lincoln," he said.

The President waved as a brown mass of Boy Scouts went stepping by.

"Well? What about London, Pug? The fact is, I was considering you. Think about it, will you?"

Pug felt dizzy. "Aye, aye, sir," he said.

He returned the veteran to the nursing home and walked home, to give himself a chance to think. As he strode in at his front door he was humming, "Yes, We Have No Bananas."

"Hey, what the heck?" he exclaimed, as he entered the living room. "Champagne? Whose birthday is it?"

"Can't you guess?" Rhoda's eyes glittered with tears. "It's Victor Henry's birthday."

"Are you potted? Mine's in March."

"Pug, at four o'clock this afternoon Janice had a boy and his name is Victor Henry." Rhoda threw herself into his arms.

They talked about the great event over the champagne. Rhoda had raced to the naval hospital to see Janice and the baby. "The little elephant weighed nine and a half pounds! And he's the image of you, Pug."

"Poor kid. He'll have no luck with the women."

"I like that!" exclaimed Rhoda. "Didn't you have luck? Anyway, Janice won't take him out to Hawaii just yet. So they'll stay with us, and we must find a proper house. Sweetie, let's wither in style, Grandma and Grandpa Henry. And let's always have lots of room for the grandchildren."

Victor Henry stared at his wife for such a long time that she began to feel odd. He heaved a deep sigh. "Well, I'll tell you, Grandma, I couldn't agree with you more. Let's wither, side by side. Well said."

"Oh, I love you! Now let me see about dinner." She hurried out.

Pug up-ended the champagne bottle over his glass, but only a drop ran out, as he sang softly, "We have no bananas today."

Three weeks later the Germans invaded the Soviet Union.

22

The players in our drama were now scattered around the earth. Easternmost, on June 22, 1941, was Leslie Slote. Through the windows of his flat in Moscow, sunlight fell on a letter he was reading from Natalie Henry in Rome.

Natalie had written that Aaron had at last received his passport! She and her uncle were hoping to leave Rome early in July. In his answer, which lay unfinished beside her letter, Slote took modest credit for the success of his efforts, and then explained why he thought the rumour of an impending invasion of Russia was false. Trying to find gracious words about Natalie's pregnancy, he had given up and gone to bed. By the time he awoke, his letter was out of date.

Six hundred miles to the west, at three-fifteen a.m., German cannon had begun to flash along a thousand-mile line from the

Baltic to the Black Sea. At the same hour, fleets of German planes started bombing airfields, smashing Soviet aircraft by the hundred. The morning stars still twinkled over the fragrant fields when the armoured columns and infantry divisions came rolling eastward on the Polish plains that stretched towards Kiev, Moscow, and Leningrad.

In Moscow, shortly after sunrise, Foreign Minister Molotov asked a sad and shaken German ambassador, "Did we deserve this?" The ambassador said that since Russia was obviously about to attack Germany, the Leader had wisely decided to strike first. Molotov's face, we are told, showed a rare emotion—surprise.

Knowing nothing of this, Leslie Slote went off to the embassy with a light heart, hoping to dispose of some overdue work on a quiet Sunday. There he learned that once again the Germans were coming.

NO SUN was visible in Chicago; a storm blanketed the city. Palmer Kirby was riding in a taxicab to a secret meeting of the President's Uranium Committee. The committee's purpose was to find out how soon enough of the rare uranium isotope 235 could be produced to make atomic bombs. Kirby had been asked for a feasibility report on manufacturing certain giant electromagnets.

Kirby knew what the giant electromagnets were for. His opinion on producing uranium for military purposes was definite. Not only could it be done; he thought the Germans were well along towards doing it.

The scientists round the table included Dr. Lawrence, the Nobel Prizewinner. There were also two military visitors, Colonel Thomas of the army, and navy Captain Kelleher. The committee's chairman was Lyman Briggs, director of the National Bureau of Standards and this depressed Kirby. Briggs was a man to whom a thousand dollars was a spectacular federal expenditure.

The committee listened while Kirby read his paper. When he named a feasible date for delivering the first magnets and the prices he would charge, they started glancing at each other.

"Well, that's encouraging," Lyman Briggs said when Kirby had finished. "Of course, the price figures are pure fantasy."

The navy captain put in, "General Electric and Westinghouse project twice as much time and more than twice as much money."

"Are the Germans ahead of us on these bombs?" Thomas asked.

"Well, their present self-confidence isn't encouraging."

"I agree. Then why don't we get cracking?" Kelleher sat up, glowering. "Let's go straight to the President and howl for money and action. I assure you the navy will back the committee."

Briggs said, "The President has more immediate things, Captain, requiring money and action. This is all pure theory." He turned to Kirby with an agreeable smile. "I don't think we need detain you. Your report has been very useful. Many thanks."

Kirby passed the rest of the morning in his hotel, listening to the radio and growing gloomier and gloomier. Finally Lawrence called. "Palmer, you shone this morning. I thought we might manage lunch, but the committee's working straight through. Meantime something has come up. We need one knowledgeable man in constant liaison with business and industry. We've been talking about you."

"Me? No *thanks*."

"Palmer, no job in the world is more important."

"But hell, who would I work for? Not the National Bureau of Standards!"

"For secrecy, you could get a consultant post in the navy. Kelleher's full of fire to get along."

"Where would I be posted?"

"Washington." Kirby was silent so long that Lawrence added, "Something wrong with Washington?"

Kirby had given up a scientific career and gone into industry largely because he had felt outclassed by Lawrence and a few other men unreachably more brilliant than himself. To be urged now by this man to take on a task of this importance was irresistible. He said, "If I'm offered the job, I'll accept."

PURPLE lightning cracked down the black sky, forking behind the Washington Monument in jagged streams. Pug Henry had not yet received his expected posting to London. July in the capital was going out, as usual, in choking heat and wild thunderstorms.

He dived through the rain to a taxicab that drew up at the Navy Building. A tall man was getting out. "All yours," he said. "Why, hello, Pug."

"Well, hi! How long have you been in Washington, Kirby?"

"About a month."

"Come home with me for a drink," said Pug. "Better yet, join me for dinner. I'm all alone this evening."

Kirby hesitated. "Where's Rhoda?"

"In New York. She saw our daughter-in-law and grandson off to Hawaii. Now she's shopping for furniture. We've bought a house on Foxhall Road."

Kirby said, "I must pick up some papers. I'll be right out."

The house stood on a little knoll, topping a smooth lawn and a ravine of wild woods. The rain had stopped and a fresh breeze cooled the back porch, where Pug and Kirby drank their martinis. "It's a nice spot," Kirby said.

"Rhoda likes it."

They drank in silence: "You know, Pug," Kirby said, "I'm starting to suspect that the human race, as we know it, may not make it through the industrial revolution."

"I've had a bad day myself," Pug said. "But I'm feeling better now. You will stay for dinner? Let me tell the cook."

"Thanks Pug. I've done a lot of eating alone lately."

Victor Henry refilled their glasses and took the jug out with him. He brought it back full and tinkling. "I put dinner off. Give us a chance to relax."

"Suits me, though you may have to lead me to the dining room."

"It's not far," Pug said, "and the furniture has few sharp edges. Tell me, what's happening with uranium?"

Kirby looked wary. "Is that why you're feeding me martinis?"

"If martinis can loosen you up, let it happen first with an officer in War Plans, and thereafter don't drink martinis."

"Doesn't War Plans have any information?"

"No. It's still Jules Verne talk to us."

"Unfortunately, it's more than that." The rain was starting again, with a whistle of wind, a rumble of thunder. Kirby went on. "The bomb can be built. With an all-out effort, it might take as little as two years. But we're not making an all-out effort. Tremendous brains are at work on the theory end, but there's no money available and no plan."

"How powerful an explosive are we talking about?"

"In theory, one bomb might level New York City, or even an area like Rhode Island. I frankly don't know enough to be sure."

"Hellooo!" Rhoda's voice rang through the house, and heels clicked on the floor. "Surprise! Anybody home? I'm drenched."

"Hi!" Pug called. "We've got company."

"Hello, Rhoda," said Kirby, standing.

"Oh my gawd!" She froze in the doorway. Her hat dripped, wet strands of hair hung down, and her dress clung to her body.

Pug said, "You finished up fast in New York, didn't you? Palmer and I ran into each other and—" But Rhoda had vanished.

Kirby started to rise. "I guess I'll leave. Rhoda's back, and I don't want to intrude, and—"

"You sit right down." Pug pushed him back into his chair. At that moment the telephone rang. He went in to the marble-floored hallway. "Hello? *Yes*, Admiral. Aye, aye, sir, will do." He hung up, then returned to Kirby, and almost at once Rhoda appeared, all combed, curled, and made up as for a dance.

"Well! Quick-change artistry," Pug said.

"I hope so. I looked like the witch in 'Snow White'."

"Rhoda, I just got a call from Admiral King. I must go. You give Palmer his dinner and maybe I'll get back in time for coffee."

Kirby again offered to leave, but Pug wouldn't hear of it.

When the outside door closed, Kirby sat forward. "Pug doesn't know he's put you in a spot. I'll be going."

Rhoda sat composed, head atilt. "You'll waste some good double lamb chops. Dinner's about ready."

"I really believe you don't feel awkward at all."

"I'm very glad to see you. What brings you to Washington?"

"A defence job, about which I can tell you nothing."

"You mean you're living here?"

"Yes, but I fly to Denver every two weeks or so." With a grin he added, "It's disturbing how well things go on without me."

"And how is that house of yours?"

"Fine. I didn't sell it, and now I won't."

Rhoda dropped her voice. "Was my letter very upsetting?"

"It was the worst blow I've had since my wife died."

Rhoda blinked at his rough tone. "I'm sorry." She sat clasping and unclasping her fingers in her lap. "I'm trying to think how to tell this. I sat next to the President at that White House dinner. He said wonderful things about Pug, about his future career. A divorced man is very handicapped in the service, especially when he's in sight of flag rank. And—well, so I've stuck to him. And I don't intend to apologize."

"Dinner, Mrs. Henry," the maid said.

By the time Rhoda and Kirby had finished the chops and salad and a bottle of wine, the tension was gone.

They had coffee, and more wine, on the porch. A few stars showed in the clearing sky. "I can't tell you how good I feel. This couldn't possibly have been planned, but there's a great weight off my mind," Rhoda said.

Kirby gulped his wine with an abrupt motion. "Now let me ask you something, Rhoda. You told me—and I believed you, and still do—that until I came along there had been no one else. But how come?"

Rhoda's voice was calm. "Of course I know the answer you want—that I'd never met anyone remotely like you. That's true enough. Still, I've had plenty of chances, dear. Mostly naval officers like Pug, and not one has measured up to him." She hesitated. "Even so, I wish he didn't shut me out so much. He's a fanatic, you know, about getting things done."

"That's an American trait," said Kirby. "I'm the same."

"Ah, but in Berlin, knowingly or not, you were courting me. When Pug courted me, I fell in love with him, too. No, there's been no one else. Nor will there be. I'm a quiet grandma now."

They did not speak for a long time. In the darkness, they were two shadowy shapes, visible only by the dim reflection of unseen streetlamps on the leaves.

Kirby rose from the wicker chair. "I'll go now. I feel remarkably better." He bowed over her hand and kissed it. She put her other hand over his and gave it a soft lingering pressure.

466

23

A week after his interview with Admiral King, Victor Henry found himself crossing Nantucket Bay, the choppy water tossing the gig so that he had to brace himself on the seat. The cruiser *Augusta* loomed through the dawn mist, a long dark shape not even showing anchor lights, a strange peacetime violation. Captain Henry mounted the cruiser's ladder; long ramps on the decks and freshly welded handrails were obviously special fittings for the crippled President.

Admiral King, in starchy whites, sat in his high bridge chair querying the cruiser's captain about arrangements for Roosevelt. King dismissed him and turned cold eyes on Pug.

"Henry, are you by any chance a distant relative or family friend of Mr. Roosevelt?"

"No, Admiral."

King lit a cigarette. "Well, be that as it may, the President will want a word with you when he comes aboard. I trust you're prepared with any information he may desire."

"I have my work papers here, Admiral."

Virtually nobody saw the crippled man hoisted aboard. The presidential yacht *Potomac* came along the port side. Sharp commands rang out, the *Potomac* churned away, and the grinning, waving President appeared on the forecastle in his wheelchair, pushed by a navy captain, with an impressive following of civilians, admirals, and generals. The white suit and floppy white hat, the high-spirited gestures, the cigarette holder cocked upward in the massive bespectacled face, were almost too Rooseveltian to be real.

The *Augusta* and another cruiser, the *Tuscaloosa*, weighed anchor and steamed out to sea, a screen of destroyers ahead of them. Pug walked the main deck for hours, relishing the sea wind, the tall black waves, and the slow roll of the ship. But no summons came from the President.

After breakfast next morning a steward's mate handed him a note: "If you're not standing watch, old man, you might look in about ten or so—the Skipper."

At the stroke of ten Pug went to flag quarters. A frozen-eyed marine came to attention outside the President's suite.

"Hello, Pug! Just in time to hear the news!" Roosevelt sat at a table, listening to a radio. He shook his head sadly at a Moscow admission that the Germans had driven far past Smolensk. Then he perked up. President Roosevelt's whereabouts was no longer a secret, the announcer said. Reporters had seen him on the deck of the *Potomac* at eight o'clock last evening, passing through the Cape Cod Canal. "And here I was on the high seas," he said. "How d'you suppose I worked that one, Pug?"

"Somebody in disguise on the yacht, sir."

"Damn right! Tom Wilson, the engineer. We got him a white shirt and white hat. It worked! We didn't want U-boats out gunning for Churchill and me." Roosevelt was searching through papers. "Ah. Look this over, old fellow." It was a typewritten document headed "For The President—Top Secret, Two Copies Only".

The radio announcer was saying that the German propaganda ministry had ridiculed stories of Jews being massacred in German-held parts of the Soviet Union. The President switched off the radio in disgust. "The Nazis are outrageous liars. I hope those stories are terribly exaggerated. Our intelligence says they are. Still—" He took off his pince-nez and rubbed his eyes. "Pug, did your daughter-in-law ever get home with her uncle?"

"I understand they're on their way, sir."

"Good. Quite a lad, that submariner of yours."

"A presumptuous pup, I'm afraid." Victor Henry was trying all this time to read the document, which was explosive.

Roosevelt cleared a space on the table, and he now took up two decks of cards. He moved cards around in silence for a while, then he said, "Well? What do you think?"

"This is something for my navy chief, Mr. President."

"Yes, but he's on the *Tuscaloosa*. And I *don't* want another squabble between service heads." The President smiled with flattering warmth. "Pug, you have a feeling for facts, and when you talk I understand you, two uncommon virtues. So let's have it."

Pug took a while to reply. The document was a scorcher. If it leaked to isolationist senators, it might well end Lend-Lease, even start an impeachment drive.

The half-dozen government agencies responsible for Lend-Lease and war production had tangled themselves and the big industries into paralysis. While their heads jockeyed for presidential favour, shortages and bottlenecks kept munitions production at a feeble trickle. To break this up, Roosevelt had called for a "Victory Program", ordering all the armed forces to list everything they needed to win a global war and to work out new priorities.

For weeks, planners like Victor Henry had been calculating possible American invasions of Axis-held territories; the army and the navy had each demanded the greatest possible share of man-power and industrial output for themselves. Now the army was taking its case to the President in a sharp critique of the navy's demands.

"Essentially, Mr. President," Pug said, "the navy and the army are just using different crystal balls. The army figures it may have to fight the Axis singlehanded after Russia and England fold. So they demand the biggest force our country can field. Fair enough. The main difference is on Lend-Lease. The army says we want to give away too many arms, which the Germans may capture and use against us. Our contention is that every German who dies at Russian and British hands is one less Boche to shoot at us."

"But Lend-Lease isn't the only issue. I notice the navy wants a hefty share of our steel production," the President said.

"Sir, assault from the sea is the toughest battle problem. It's what kept Hitler from beating England last year. The answer is special landing craft that can hit an open beach in large numbers. You throw a large force ashore, and keep it reinforced until it captures a harbour. Then you can pile in with your regular transports, and your invasion's on. But you need swarms of landing craft. We figure something like a hundred thousand."

"*A hundred thousand*!" The President tossed his big head. "Why, all the shipyards in the United States couldn't do that in ten years, Pug, even if they stopped doing everything else."

But when Pug took a sheaf of designs from his briefcase, the President scanned them with zest. There were drawings of every sort of craft, from a big ocean-going landing ship, with tanks and trucks in its belly, to little amphibious tanks. "There's still the shipyard problem, Pug," Roosevelt said. "You're going to have to use factories wherever you can find them—on rivers, and inland waterways." His eyes lit up. "You know? This program could be a godsend to small business." He lit a cigarette. "Very good. Write your notes on that army paper, Pug. Then, once the Victory Program is finished, let's send you out to sea. You're overdue."

Victor Henry saw that the moment was favourable. "Well, Mr. President, I have been yearning to be exec of a battleship."

"Exec? Don't you think you can command one?"

Trying hard to show no emotion, realizing what might hang on the next few words, Pug said, "I think I can, sir."

"Well, let's get you command of a battleship." The President smiled regally at Pug as he dismissed him.

Pug did not see the President again all the way to Newfoundland, but the promise of a battleship command gave him sleepless nights. He tried to crush down his elation. Pug admired the President but he did not understand or trust him. Behind the warm, jolly surface there loomed a grim, ill-defined personality of distant visions and hard purpose. It might be that Roosevelt would remember his promise. It was equally likely that he would revert to his original intention of sending Pug to England to head up convoy operations there.

A PRIMEVAL hush lay heavy in Argentia Bay, Newfoundland, where the American ships awaited the arrival of Winston Churchill.

At nine o'clock, three grey destroyers steamed into view ahead of HMS *Prince of Wales*, the battleship that had hit the *Bismarck*. As it steamed past the *Augusta*, a brass band on its decks shattered the hush with "The Star-Spangled Banner". Quiet fell. Then the *Augusta*'s band struck up "God Save the King".

The President stood under an awning rigged at number one gun turret, one hand holding his hat on his heart, the other clutching the arm of his older son, Elliott, an air corps officer. With them were admirals, generals, and eminent civilians like Averell Harriman and Sumner Welles. Not five hundred yards away,

Winston Churchill was plain to see, gesturing with his big cigar.

Churchill came to the *Augusta* at eleven. Among the staff members with him Pug saw Air Commodore Burne-Wilke. Churchill and Roosevelt met at the gangway, prolonging their dramatic handshake for the benefit of the photographers.

In an odd way the two leaders diminished each other. Who, Pug wondered, was number one man? Roosevelt stood a full head taller, but was pathetically braced on leg frames, holding on to his son's arm. Churchill looked up at him with majestic good humour, older, more assured. Yet there was a trace of deference about the Prime Minister. By a shade of a shade, Roosevelt looked like number one.

The staffs conferred all day. Victor Henry worked with the planners on the level below the chiefs of staff and their deputies. One cardinal point the planners hammered out fast. Building new ships to replace U-boat sinkings came first. No war matériel could be used against Hitler until it had crossed the ocean.

Amid all the grand plans, one pathetic item kept recurring: an immediate need for a hundred and fifty thousand rifles. If Russia collapsed, Hitler might try invading England from the air. Rifles for defending British airfields were needed. The stupendous matériel figures for future operations contrasted sadly with this plea for a hundred and fifty thousand rifles now.

NEXT morning, in bright sunlight, boats from all over the bay came clustering to the *Prince of Wales* for church services. An American destroyer slowly nosed alongside the battleship, and at a point where the decks were level, a gangplank was thrown across. Leaning on Elliott's arm and on a cane, Franklin Roosevelt, in a blue suit and grey hat, lurched out on the gangplank, laboriously hitching one leg forward from the hip, then the other. The bay was calm, but both ships were moving on long swells. With each step, the tall President tottered and swayed.

Here was willpower, Pug thought. Roosevelt could have been wheeled over in comfort. But in his piteous fashion he could walk; and to board the British battleship at Winston Churchill's invitation for church parade, he was walking.

His foot touched the deck. Churchill saluted him and offered his hand. The band burst into "The Star-Spangled Banner". His chest heaving, face stiff with strain, Roosevelt stood at attention. Then, escorted by Churchill, he hobbled across the deck and sat.

As the sailors, massed in ranks around the afterdeck, sang "O, God, Our Help in Ages Past" and "Onward, Christian Soldiers", Winston Churchill kept wiping his eyes. The old hymns, roared by a thousand young male voices, brought prickles to Victor Henry's spine. Yet this exalting service made him uneasy, too. Here were men of the two navies, praying as comrades-in-arms. But it was a phony picture. The English were fighting, the Americans were not. The Prime Minister, with this church parade under the long guns, was ingeniously working on the President. If Franklin Roosevelt could come away from this without promising to declare war on Germany, or at least to give Japan an ultimatum to lay off the British in Asia, he was a hard man indeed.

After the closing prayer, a few British sailors cautiously moved out of ranks. One, then another, sneaked cameras from their blouses. When nobody stopped them, and the two leaders smiled and waved, a rush began. Pug felt a touch on his elbow. It was Burne-Wilke. "Hello, my dear fellow. What is your position on shipboard drinking? I have a fair bottle of sherry."

"I'm for it."

They settled down in Burne-Wilke's comfortable cabin. "I suppose you know that this ship crossed the ocean without escort," the air commodore said. "Our first night out of England we ran into a whole gale. Our destroyers couldn't maintain speed, so we zigzagged on alone."

"Sir, I was appalled to hear about it. You had your good angels escorting you. That's all I can say."

"Oh, well, at any rate here we are. But it might be prudent not to overwork those angels. On our way back, every U-boat in the Atlantic will be on battle alert." Burne-Wilke paused. "We're stretched thin for escorts, you know. We've rounded up another destroyer. Admiral Pound will be happier with two more."

Pug quickly said, "I'll talk to Admiral King."

"You understand it cannot be a request from us. The Prime

Minister would be downright annoyed. He's hoping we'll meet the *Tirpitz* and get into a running gunfight."

Pug found Admiral King on the afterdeck. When he recounted his talk with Burne-Wilke, the lines along King's lean jaws deepened. He nodded twice and strolled away without a word.

Amid much wining and dining, the conference went on for two more days. On the last day, Admiral King sent for Pug. "Task Unit 26 point 3 point 1, consisting of two destroyers, has been formed," he said without a greeting. "It will escort the *Prince of Wales* to Iceland. You will embark in the *Prince of Wales* as liaison officer, and return with our task unit."

"Aye aye, sir."

"In confidence, we'll soon be convoying all ships to Iceland. Hell, our marines are occupying the place now. Now, Henry, how are you at languages?"

"It's a long time since I tried a new one, Admiral."

"Well, a military supply mission will go to the Soviet Union in September, headed by Averell Harriman and Lord Beaverbrook. If Russia's still in the war, that is. Mr. Hopkins has brought up your name. He appears impressed, and the President too, by your expertise on landing craft and so forth. In your service record, it seems you claim a 'poor to fair' knowledge of Russian."

"Admiral, I put that down when I entered the Academy. It was true then. There were some Russian families where I grew up, and we had a Russian-speaking club at my high school."

"I see. Well, upon returning from Iceland you will prepare yourself, with an intensive refresher course in Russian, for a possible trip to the Soviet Union. You'll have interpreters. But with even a smattering, your intelligence value will be greater."

"Aye aye, sir."

King stared at Victor Henry and actually favoured him with a smile. "Incidentally, Henry, I'll soon be needing an operations officer on my staff. After your Russian errand, that's an assignment you may get."

Pug kept his face rigid.

"It would be an honour, Admiral." Compared with a battleship command, it was a crushing prospect.

"I thought you might like it. I mentioned it to the President, and he said it sounded like the perfect spot for you."

A verse from Psalms knifed into Pug's mind: *Put not your trust in princes.*

TO BRASS band anthems and booming gun salutes, the *Prince of Wales* left Argentia Bay. The great conference was over.

In the wardroom, Victor Henry sensed the subtle gloom hanging over the ship. What the conference had accomplished to increase help for England remained undisclosed, and this clearly struck the battleship's officers as a bad sign. They could not believe that Churchill had risked the best ship in their strained navy, and his own life, only to return empty-handed.

Feeling that his presence was an embarrassment to the British officers, Pug went to bed early.

Next day the wardroom was packed for Lord Privy Seal Clement Attlee's broadcast from London. As he read the "Atlantic Charter" —the British and American joint communiqué following the meetings—the faces of the listeners lengthened. For Pug, the American guest, it was a bad half-hour. The high-flown language bespoke not a shred of increased American commitment. Abuse of Nazism, praise of "four freedoms", dedication to future world peace and brotherhood, yes; help for the British, flat zero. Franklin Roosevelt was certainly a tough customer, Pug thought.

The Atlantic Charter pleased almost nobody. Axis propaganda jeered at its rhetoric about freedom, calling it all a big empty bluff.

In the United States, a howl went up that Roosevelt had committed the country to go to war on England's side.

British newspapers implied that what had really been wrought at Argentia Bay had for the moment to be hushed up. And the Russians were disappointed because the Charter mentioned no plan for the crucial second front.

BEREL JASTROW now operated a bakery in Minsk, near the Polish border. Natalie would not have recognized him with his clean-shaven face, his suit dusted with flour. She had met Berel as a prosperous merchant, the happy father of a bridegroom. But

476

Berel's wife and daughter had died in the winter of 1939 of the typhus that had swept bombed-out Warsaw. He and a remnant of his family had joined the trickle of refugees heading east. At Minsk most of the city's bakers were off in the army, so he had learned to bake, and the bureau for aliens had let him stay.

No reaction to the Atlantic Charter was stronger or blinder than the one that swept the immured Jews in Minsk. The Germans had confiscated most of their radios, but a sixteen-year-old boy had heard the Russian broadcast imperfectly on a tiny receiving set rigged in his attic. He had joyously spread the story that Roosevelt had met Churchill and that the United States was declaring war on Germany! The effect of this untruth on the ghetto was wonderful, life-giving.

The spirit of the Minsk Jews had recently been shattered. One night Germans in unfamiliar dark uniforms had swarmed into the ghetto and cleared out two main streets, loading the dwellers into trucks—for "resettlement". According to reports brought back by partisans, the trucks had driven five miles into the countryside. There in a moonlit ravine the Germans had lined the people up and shot everyone—including babies and old people—and then had buried them in a big hole. Now all the houses in two streets stood quiet and empty.

Into this stunned moment came the word that America was entering the war. People cried, laughed, kissed each other, and drank to President Roosevelt. However long it might take America to win, there would be no more insane occurrences like the emptying of those two streets. The Germans would not dare now!

Though the penalty for possessing a radio was death, Berel Jastrow kept a shortwave set concealed in the bakery. At the underground meeting of Jewish leaders that night, he reported the true facts about the Argentia Bay conference as he had heard them broadcast from Sweden. But he was telling the committee what it did not want to hear. Somebody observed that he had probably been listening to the German-controlled Norwegian radio.

A few days later Berel disappeared with his son, and his son's wife and baby.

They went wisely, silently, in the night.

24

Byron and Lieutenant Aster had recently been transferred from the *S-45* to a larger submarine, *Devilfish*, based in the Pacific. Their new skipper, Branch Hoban, possessed a glamorous façade—good looks, beautiful wife, sharp bridge game—backed by performance. During fleet manoeuvres he had sneaked *Devilfish* inside a destroyer screen and sunk a hypothetical battleship. Even now, with his craft on standby in Hawaii, he kept an extra tidy ship. And when Branch Hoban talked, others listened.

In the officers' club several submarine skippers were discussing the possibility of a Japanese strike. Hoban argued that, with the Russians otherwise occupied, the Japs now had a clear field down to Singapore, Java, anywhere, if they moved fast enough. And if the USA didn't pull itself together and interfere.

At a window table Byron sat with his brother Warren, glaring over his shoulder. "Wouldn't you know," he said sourly, "Branch Hoban's right in there."

"You having trouble with Branch Hoban?" Warren asked.

"He's having trouble with me. Look—I drew a sketch of an air compressor for my officers' course book and he didn't like it. He wants me to do it over and I won't."

"That's ridiculous of you."

"Warren, on our way from San Francisco, an air compressor conked and I stripped it down and got it going."

"Three cheers, but did you draw a good sketch?"

"It was a lousy sketch, but I fixed that compressor and that's the whole point."

"No, the whole point is that Branch Hoban decides whether or not to recommend you for your dolphins."

"I don't care about getting dolphins. It wasn't my idea to go to submarine school. Dad shoved me in, mostly to keep me from marrying Natalie. That's why she went to Italy. God knows when I'll see her again. And my baby, if I've got one. That's what I care about, not that phony Hoban."

"Branch is no phony. He has a remarkable record. And you'd

better make up your mind that he's boss man on that submarine."

"Sure he's boss man, and sure he's got a great record, but hell will freeze over before he gets another sketch of that air compressor. When I found out that Natalie was going to have her baby in Italy, I put in a request for transfer to the Atlantic. Our subs operate in and out of the Med, and I might have a chance to see her, maybe even get her out. He lectured me about subordinating my personal life to the navy! He forwarded the request—'Not recommending approval'."

"Don't get me wrong, but it's not the navy's fault that your wife's stuck in Italy."

"I'm not blaming the navy. I'm telling you why I'm not on fire to please Branch Hoban."

Back at Warren's house, Byron read *Time* magazine in a deck chair while Warren and Janice played with the young Victor Henry. After lunch he lay down under a banyan tree and fell asleep. When he awoke, Lieutenant Aster, drink in hand, was shaking him.

"Blazes," Byron said, sitting up. "I was supposed to report back at three, wasn't I? Are you here to take me back in irons?"

"Amnesty. You've got twenty-four hours' leave." Aster grinned. "This just came in from Rome: ENSIGN BYRON HENRY. USS DEVILFISH. CAN YOU THINK OF A GOOD NAME FOR A SEVEN POUND BOY. BOTH FINE LOVE YOU. NATALIE AND WHOSIS HENRY."

Byron bowed his head and covered his face. After a moment he looked up, his eyes glistening. "How about that, Lady?"

"Congratulations, Briny."

Byron got to his feet. "I guess I'll tell my brother."

When Byron got back to base, the *Devilfish* was deserted except for the watch. Byron took out a writing pad and a record of a Portuguese folk song that he and Natalie had heard together in Lisbon. He put the record on the phonograph and started to write: "My darling—the news about the baby just came and—"

He put his head down on his arms, trying to picture his wife and the new baby, a boy who perhaps looked like Victor. Suddenly he got up and stopped the record. The next hour he spent drawing a sketch of an air compressor—a picture clear enough to be printed in a manual. To it he clipped a letter formally requesting transfer to Atlantic duty. He added a scrawled pencil note:

Captain—I deeply appreciate the twenty-four-hour leave. The only thing I want in the world now is to see my wife and baby, and get them out of Europe. I'm sure you will understand.

Next day Hoban congratulated Byron on his sketch, declared his conviction that Natalie and her baby were safe and said he would forward the request, "Not recommending approval."

FROM Moscow, on October 21, 1941, Pug wrote a letter to Rhoda:

"Three hours from now I'll be dining in the Kremlin. How about that? And the rest of this trip has been every bit as fantastic. This will be a long letter—now that we have two grandsons (and how about *that*, Granny?) I feel I should put these things down while they're fresh in my mind. So, after you've read this, tuck it away for the babies to read one day.

"Excuse the typing mistakes, but Tudsbury's typewriter is cranky. Tudsbury's in the next room dictating tonight's broadcast to Pamela. Leave it to Talky to show up where the action is! He got the War Information Office to requisition Pamela for him (his broadcasts are considered ace propaganda), and she's on extended leave from the RAF.

"Well, as to the trip—I haven't had a real night's sleep since I left Scotland in a British cruiser. The run to Archangel is a hot one, in Luftwaffe range almost all the way. At Archangel, the harbour pilot turned out to be a woman! I watched her bring us in; she was quite a seaman, eased us alongside very handily. Then she shook hands with the skipper and left, and all that time she hadn't cracked a smile. Russians smile only when they're amused, never just to be pleasant.

"We flew to Moscow and since we got here we've been in the meat grinder around the clock. When we aren't conferring, we're eating and drinking. The standard fare seems to be a dozen kinds of cold fish and caviar, then two soups, then fowl, then roasts, with wine and vodka going all the time. I think this conference has been a historic breakthrough. When have Americans and Russians sat down before to talk about military problems, however cagily? The Russians don't tell hard facts of their situation, and considering that the Germans three short months ago were sitting where we sit now, I don't exactly blame them. This is a point that our interpreter, Leslie Slote, keeps making.

"I'm not revealing secrets when I tell you the British are yielding some Lend-Lease priorities and even undertaking to send the Russians tanks. It makes some of us Americans feel damn peculiar. We sit at this meeting between men of two countries that are fighting the Germans for their lives, while our Congress won't let the President lift a finger to help.

"Do you remember Slote? He's the second secretary here now. He's the man Natalie went to visit in Poland. He still seems to think she's the finest girl alive, and I don't know why he didn't marry her when he had the chance. Right now he's trying to romance Talky's daughter. She's just sweated out a vigil for her fiancé, who escaped from a German prison camp and hadn't been heard from until this week. He's home, with a bullet in his thigh.

"Now I have a story for you, and for our grandsons, especially Byron's boy. It's grim and puzzling and I'm still not sure what to make of it. Yesterday afternoon I went to see Slote at our embassy with Tudsbury and Pam.

"We were having a drink when another visitor was announced, and in walked a fellow in worn-out boots and a heavy, shabby coat. It was a Jewish merchant from Warsaw. Berel Jastrow, Natalie's uncle! Briny and Natalie were at his son's wedding when they got caught in the invasion. Obviously he has a talent for surviving. How he got his family out of Warsaw, and then out from under the German blitz in Minsk, is a saga. . . ."

Pug went on to tell Rhoda of the Jews massacred in Minsk. Jastrow had given Slote three pictures, and two documents purporting to be eyewitness accounts. He claimed he had risked his life to get to Moscow in order to give some American diplomat the story. He believed that once the American people knew about it, the United States would enter the war. . . .

"When Jastrow had gone," Pug continued, "Slote offered the

481

stuff to Tudsbury for his broadcast. To our surprise, Tudsbury wouldn't touch it. To him Jastrow looked like a plant by the NKVD —the Russian secret police. But even if he knew the story were true, he said he wouldn't use it because it could backfire and keep America out of the war. '*Nobody wants to fight a war to save the Jews,*' he kept insisting. This Minsk story would therefore only play into German hands. Personally, I found it hard not to believe Jastrow, the man has such a keen and dignified manner.

"It's five minutes to six. I have to wrap this up and get on to the banquet. I miss you, busy as I am, but you sure wouldn't care for Soviet Russia, darling, in war or peace. . . ."

25

The knot of Leslie Slote's tie came lopsided twice in his shaky hands. He stretched out on a sofa to calm himself with a cigarette. A German correspondent had abandoned this apartment on June 15, making a hasty deal with him. For Moscow, they were splendid digs. Pamela Tudsbury had cooked many a dinner here for Slote and their friends.

The English-speaking embassy people and correspondents—an isolated, gossipy little band—assumed that the British girl and the American foreign service officer were having an affair. Slote yearned for such an affair, but Pam Tudsbury was being true, she said, to her RAF pilot.

Slote had patiently been biding his time and hoping. But the arrival of Captain Victor Henry changed that. As soon as he saw Pamela with Pug, he knew he was looking at a woman in love. So much for her airman! As for Captain Henry, who looked to Slote like the typical poker-faced military man, one couldn't tell whether he even liked her.

Fate had served him a strange dish, Leslie Slote thought—to be beaten for one girl by the son and then for another by the father. And now he was about to meet the father and Admiral Standley at the Hotel National and interpret for them at the Kremlin banquet. This privilege did not, in prospect, make him happy. He was in a state of general panic.

During the first weeks after the invasion in June, Slote believed the Soviet news, believed that six hundred miles and the great Red Army lay between him and the Germans.

Then Minsk fell, then Smolensk, then Kiev. Air raids started; the Luftwaffe had come into range. Nobody else in the embassy was as alarmed as Slote, but he had learned to live with his own physical cowardice much as other people lived with hay fever or high blood pressure. He thought the other Americans' complacency almost insane. Moscow's amazingly thick anti-aircraft barrage provided a comforting canopy; yet bombs fell. And the terror of the siege guns was still to come.

The Russians had given the Americans to understand that the Nazi hordes were pinned down east of Smolensk. It was true that there had been a lull on the central part of the front, for in August Hitler had diverted some of his panzer divisions to attack Kiev and Leningrad. But now, at the beginning of October, the panzers, back in their positions, were slashing towards Moscow again.

Slote was filled with horror by Berel Jastrow's story. A triumphant Hitler might declare war on Roosevelt. Americans might all be taken to a ravine and shot like the Jews in Minsk. Such were his thoughts as he left to accompany Admiral Standley and Captain Henry to the Kremlin.

BLACK limousines clustered before the hotel, a rare sight. Moscow's auto traffic had dwindled to nothing. Muscovites, taking evening strolls in their usual large numbers, cast inquisitive glances as the cars began to fill with well-dressed foreigners.

"How did you make out on those harbour charts?" said Admiral Standley to Victor Henry, settling into the back seat.

"I got nowhere," Pug replied. "As for operating codes and signals, forget it. Their fellow told me they had none."

"What tripe! Did you give them our stuff?"

"Well, I showed them our general signal book and a few strip ciphers, and almost got into a wrestling match with that fat little rear admiral. He wanted to put them away in his briefcase."

"We're supposed to give, give, give," said the admiral. "I'm damn glad you're along, Pug."

"If we're going to plan convoys to Murmansk or Archangel, we've *got* to swap operational codes," Pug said.

"Russians are obsessed with secrecy," Slote said. "Be persistent and patient."

The cars stopped at a tall gateway under a red stone tower topped by a star, and were checked by uniformed sentries. Then they drove into the Kremlin, past bizarre old churches, to a long building with a majestic stone façade.

The visitors left the cars and mounted the steps. Suddenly the palace doors opened, and they were blinking at dazzling light from globed chandeliers in a long hall, ending in a red-carpeted marble staircase. Young army officers, handsome clear-eyed giants, ushered the visitors towards the staircase. Walking beside Slote, Pug said, "Did you get that Minsk atrocity stuff to the ambassador?"

Slote nodded. "I wanted it to go to Secretary Hull, but the ambassador says it's to be forwarded through channels."

Pug wrinkled his nose. "Your department always drags its feet on the Jews. Show it to some American newspapermen."

"The boss directly ordered me not to."

They passed through one vast room after another, apparently unaltered since tsarist days. "Fred Fearing's in town," Pug murmured. "Suppose you had him up for a drink. He'd steal a scoop from his old blind grandmother."

"Are you suggesting that I disobey orders?"

"I don't think that story should get buried."

In a room grander and richer than the rest, pillared in marble, with a vaulted gilt ceiling and red damask-covered walls, the company of about eighty men halted.

Mirrored doors opened and a party of Russian civilians came in, wearing unpressed flopping trousers and ill-fitting double-breasted jackets. Slote recognized faces that lined Lenin's tomb at May Day parades: Molotov, Kaganovich, Suslov, Mikoyan.

"Look at those guys," Victor Henry said. "They make you feel the revolution was last week."

"That's the Politburo," Slote said. "Very big cheeses."

Introductions began. Liveried waiters passed trays of vodka

and plates of pastry sticks. A moustached little man with slanted eyes and thick, backswept hair, walked alone into the room. No ceremony was made of it, but everyone in the grand state chamber polarized towards him, for he was Stalin.

The Communist dictator moved through the room to Admiral Standley. "Stalyin," he said, putting out his hand. His uniform was superbly tailored, with sharply creased trousers tucked into soft, gleaming brown boots.

Leslie Slote introduced the naval officers. Captain Henry said in slow halting Russian, "Sir, I will tell this story to my grandchildren."

Stalin said pleasantly, "Yes? Do you have any?"

"Two boys."

"And do you have sons?" Stalin seemed diverted by Victor Henry's slow, carefully drilled, mechanical speech.

"Two, Comrade Chairman. One is a navy flier, one is in a submarine." As Stalin kept looking at him, Pug went on, "Forgive my poor Russian. Long ago I had Russian playmates."

"Where did you have Russian playmates?"

"I was born near the Russian River, in California. Some of those early families still remain there."

Stalin smiled a real smile, showing tobacco-stained teeth. "Ah, yes, yes. Fort Ross. Not many people know that we were in California before you. Maybe it's time we claimed California back."

"They say your policy is for one fighting front at a time, Comrade Chairman."

With a smiling grunt, Stalin said, "*Ha*," struck Victor Henry lightly on the shoulder, and walked on.

Soon the company was moving into a stupendous banquet hall of white marble, red tapestries, and shiny parquet, where silver, gold, and glass glittered on the white cloths. "Wow!" Pug said.

Leslie Slote stared round at the walls and ceiling. "It's the Catherine the Great Room. It was her throne room."

"Well, if this is their style of living, by God," said the admiral, "they'll make a Communist of me yet."

The menu was printed in Russian and English on thick creamy paper, with a hammer and sickle gold crest. Attendants began to bring the courses. Others poured wine and vodka. The splendour of it all gave Pug a reassuring sense of Russian self-confidence.

"*Vashe zdorovye!*" (Your health!) Anybody apparently could stand and bawl a toast when he felt like it. Men left their seats and crossed the room to clink glasses when a toast pleased them. Stalin kept trotting here and there, glass in hand.

To Slote it was all marvellously interesting, but he was kept busy, interpreting the sharpening exchange between Admiral Standley and the short fat Russian admiral who had tried to keep the navy codes.

"Tell him we'll be convoying any day," snapped the American, "but unless he loosens up with some harbour data and operation signals, hell will freeze over before we convoy to Murmansk."

The old Russian admiral pushed himself to his feet and held up a brimming glass of vodka. "If you please! I am sitting with representatives of the most powerful navy in the world. These brave men must be very unhappy that while all humanity is in mortal danger their ships ride at anchor gathering barnacles." He paused. "So I drink to the day when this strong navy will get in the scrap and help destroy the Hitlerite rats."

There was a silence as Slote translated. The old man dropped heavily in his seat, glaring round with self-satisfaction. Admiral Standley's voice shook as he said, "It's all yours, Pug. If I reply you'll have an international incident."

Victor Henry rose, glass in hand. All eyes fastened on him while he brought out his response in slow, painful phrases.

"My chief tells me to respond for the United States Navy. It is true we are not fighting. I drink first to the wise peace policy of Marshal Stalin, who did not lead your country into the war before you were attacked, and so gained time to prepare." Slote was startled by the barbed aptness of the retort. "*The wise peace policy of Comrade Stalin*" was the Communist cliché for Stalin's deal with Hitler. "That is the policy of our President. If we are attacked we will fight. I hope as well as your people are fighting. Now as for"—Pug stopped to ask Slote for the Russian word—"barnacles. Any barnacles that get on our ships will have to swim very fast. We don't announce everything we do. Secrecy is another wise

486

policy of both our countries. But let's not keep so many secrets from each other that we can't work together.

"Now, our navy needs some harbour data from you. We need them before we leave, so I also drink to some fast action. Finally, I was a naval attaché in Berlin. I have now travelled from Hitler's chancellery to the inside of the Kremlin. That is something Hitler will never do, and above all I drink to that."

There was loud applause and raising of glasses. Slote reached up to stop Pug from drinking. Josef Stalin, glass in hand, was leaving his seat. Pug strode towards him and they met near the dais. The dictator grinned. They clinked glasses. "I thank you for that fine toast, and in response, you can keep California."

"Thank you, Mr. Chairman," Pug said. "That's a good start, and can you do anything else for us?"

"Certainly. Fast action," said Stalin, linking his arm in Pug's. "American style. We Russians can sometimes do it too." He walked towards the old Russian admiral, who stumbled to his feet, and spoke to him in low, rapid sentences. Then the dictator turned back to Victor Henry. "Well, it is arranged. Tell your chief that I feel the American navy will do historic things in this struggle, and will rule the ocean when peace comes."

Stalin went back to his table. The last toast of the evening was to President Roosevelt. The interpreter was Oumansky, the ambassador to the United States. "Comrade Stalin says 'may God help President Roosevelt in his most difficult task'."

This religious phrase brought a surprised stillness, then the banquet dissolved in handshaking, backslapping, and embracing.

THE LIMOUSINE took the Americans back to the Hotel National. The admiral bade Pug and Slote good night and plodded to the staircase. They followed him up.

"Come in for a minute," Pug said to Leslie when they reached his room. "Stick around. Something may be doing."

Slote asked no questions. His head still reeled from the many toasts. Next thing he knew, knocking woke him. Victor Henry was at the door talking to somebody in Russian.

Pug closed the door. "I'd like you to come back to the Kremlin with me, Leslie, if you will. I have a letter from Harry Hopkins for the big cheese. I didn't think I was going to get to hand it over in person, but maybe I am."

Slote sat up. "Nobody should ever, ever see a head of state without going through the ambassador. How have you arranged this?"

"Me? I had nothing to do with it. Hopkins wanted this letter to go to Stalin privately, and I gather he talked to Oumansky. If it puts you in a false position, I'll go alone. There'll be an interpreter."

Slote began combing his hair. "I'll have to file a written report with the ambassador."

"Sure."

IN A BIG, bleakly lit room lined with wall maps, Stalin sat at one end of a conference table, with papers piled before him. An ashtray at his elbow brimmed with cigarette butts, suggesting that he had been steadily at work since the end of the banquet. He now wore a sagging khaki uniform, and he looked weary. Pavlov, his usual interpreter, sat beside him. There was nobody else.

Victor Henry handed him the letter and a round box wrapped in blue paper. "Mr. Chairman, I'd better not inflict my bad Russian on you any longer," he said in English. Slote translated.

Stalin inclined his head, then opened the White House envelope and passed Pavlov the single handwritten sheet.

Pug said, as Stalin unwrapped the box, "And this is the special Virginia pipe tobacco Mr. Hopkins told you about."

"Mr. Hopkins is very thoughtful," Stalin twisted open the tin and pulled a pipe from his pocket. He puffed fragrant smoke while Pavlov translated the letter aloud. After a meditative silence, the dictator turned coldly to Victor Henry. "This is a strange letter from Mr. Hopkins. We all know how many millions of automobiles the United States manufactures per year. What is the problem, then, with landing craft? Surely you can produce as many as you want to."

Pug opened his dispatch case. "Different types must be designed to land against a fortified coast. We expect mass production in mid-1942, at the latest. These papers may be of interest."

In mid-translation, Stalin uttered a short harsh laugh and began to talk fast in Russian, straight at Victor Henry. "Very fine! This is October 1941. If Mr. Hitler would only halt operations until mid-1942! But perhaps we cannot count on that. Doesn't Mr. Hopkins know that any operation at all that the British mount now might divert enough German strength from here to decide the course of this war? The Germans have mere token forces on the French coast. They are throwing everything on to our front."

Victor Henry said, "Mr. Chairman, I am instructed to answer any questions about landing craft."

Stalin shoved aside Pug Henry's papers. "It is a question of will, not of landing craft. However, we will study the matter of landing craft. Of course, we have such machines too, for landing on defended coasts. Perhaps we can lend-lease some to the British. Mr. Harry Hopkins must use his great influence to establish a second front now in Europe, because the outcome of the war may turn on it. I can say no more."

After the translation, the dictator changed his tone. "Have you enjoyed your stay? Is there anything we can do for you?"

"Mr. Chairman, I have been a military observer in Germany and in England. Mr. Hopkins asked me to go to the front here, if an opportunity arose, so as to bring him an eyewitness report."

At the word "front", Stalin shook his head. "No, no. That we cannot do, in the present stage of fighting. You should understand that the Germans are breaking through in force. We may see the worst hours for Russia since 1812."

Pug said soberly, "In view of this news, Mr. Chairman, I admire your cheerfulness of spirit at the banquet tonight."

Stalin shrugged his broad, sagging shoulders. "Wars are not won by gloom, nor by bad hospitality. Well, if Mr. Hopkins wants you at the front, we will see what we can do."

Leaving the Kremlin, the two Americans spoke not a word. When the car stopped, Pug said, "I'll talk to you tomorrow, Slote."

In his room, Slote brewed coffee and typed a long account of the banquet and the meeting with Stalin. When he had finished, the sun was shining. He took a looseleaf diary from a drawer and wrote briefly in it, ending with these words:

As for the Henrys, father and son, they both have an instinct for action and the presence of mind that goes with it. Byron displayed these traits in moments of physical danger. I've just seen his father, in sophisticated and subtle confrontations with Stalin, act with quick-thinking, hardihood, and tact.

Captain Henry suggested that I disregard orders and expose the Minsk documents to Fred Fearing. Such an act goes entirely against my grain; and entirely for that reason, I intend to do it today.

26

Tudsbury was having five-o'clock tea alone in his hotel suite when Pug came in and told him he was going to the front. The correspondent stopped eating, "Good God, man, you *are*? With the Germans swarming in all over the place? It's impossible."

"Well, maybe," Pug said, sinking into a chair and holding on his lap the briefcase stuffed with codes and harbour charts which he had just collected at the navy ministry. "But my clearance has just come in from pretty high up."

Tudsbury peered at Henry. "I'll go with you."

"The hell you will."

Tudsbury stood up and got his coat. "Lozovsky handling this? I'll just tell him you said I could come. It's up to you."

Pug did not want Tudsbury along, but he was too exhausted to refuse. "O.K."

The intrusion of Tudsbury snagged the trip. Days went by while the Foreign Office stalled. The main trouble, it turned out, was Pamela. Her father had asked to take her along, claiming helplessness without her.

Lozovsky finally telephoned, his voice cheery. "Well, Captain, tomorrow at dawn? Wear warm clothing, a raincoat, and good boots, and be prepared to be out three or four days."

THEY left Moscow in the rain, their little black car grinding along in a thunderous parade of army trucks. Their guide was a mild-faced tank colonel named Porphyry Amphiteatrov. After a few hours he suggested that they stop to eat lunch and stretch their legs.

490

The driver turned off on a side road which wound among fields and copses of birch. At a dead end in wild woods they got out, and the colonel led them to a small, grassy mound where garlands of fresh flowers lay.

"This was Tolstoy's estate," he said, "and there is his grave. Since it was on the way, I thought you might be interested."

Pug stared at the mound. "The grave of Tolstoy? No stone?"

"He ordered it so. 'Put me in the earth,' he said, 'in the woods where my brother Nicholas and I played as boys . . . .'" There was a sound of soft irregular thumps.

"Ah, guns?" said Tudsbury, with a show of great calm.

"Yes, guns. Well, shall we have a bite?"

Under a tree they ate black bread, garlicky sausages, and cucumbers, washed down with beer.

The sun shafted theatrically through the yellow leaves, full on Pamela, sitting with Victor Henry on a bench. She wore grey slacks, fur-topped boots, and a grey fur-trimmed coat and hat.

"Why are you staring at me, Victor?"

"Pam, I've never visited Tolstoy's grave before, but I swear I remember all this, most of all the way you've got that hat tilted." Her hand went up to her hat. "And I remember that movement too."

The colonel called, "Well, Captain, I think we go?"

Whiskered men and stout women, working in fields between stretches of birch forest, paid no attention to the trucks which filled the highway, moving towards the front and returning. Towards evening, the car rolled into a small town and stopped at a yellow frame house on a muddy square. Here red-cheeked children lined up at a pump with pails; others were driving goats and cows in from the fields. German artillery thumped, and flashes flickered like lightning on the western horizon.

The visitors crowded into the dining room of the yellow house with four officers of the regiment and a General Yevlenko, chief of staff of the army group in that sector. At dinner, he talked freely about the war. His army group was outnumbered in this sector and had far fewer tanks and guns than the Nazis. Still, they might yet surprise Fritz. The Germans were taking fearful losses.

"Will they take Moscow?" Tudsbury asked.

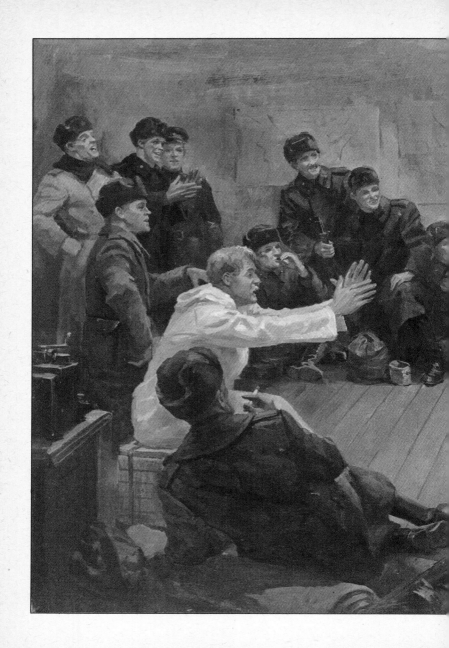

"Not from this direction," retorted the general, "nor do I think they will from any other. But if they do take it, we'll drive them out again, and out of our land. They overestimated themselves and underrated us—a dangerous mistake." He glanced at Victor Henry, "Well, Captain, I suggest you make a start at dawn." He said to Pamela, gesturing upward, "A bedroom has been cleared for you. The gentlemen will bunk with these officers."

"Good heavens, a bedroom? I counted on sleeping on the floor in my clothes," Pamela said. "Anyway, I'm not at all sleepy yet."

Yevlenko's face lit up. "So? You talk like one of our girls, not like a delicate Englishwoman." Offering her his arm, he led them into the next room. Soldiers pushed away desks to clear a space round a shabby upright piano. An officer, cigarette dangling from his mouth, thumped out "There'll Always Be an England". Pamela laughed, then stood and sang it. The general led applause and called for more champagne. The pianist began stumbling through "Alexander's Ragtime Band". With a low bow, General Yevlenko invited Pamela to dance. They made a grotesque pair, he head and shoulders above her, stepping stiffly around in heavy boots, but his face shone with enjoyment.

The pianist began playing Russian music, and Pamela sank into a chair while the officers danced, bounding, squatting, pirouetting. The general danced by himself; he twirled, jumped, then folded his arms and squatted, kicking his feet and shouting, "*Skoreye! Skoreye!*" (Faster! Faster!) The room reeked of men's bodies, smoke, alcohol. When General Yevlenko finished the men roared and clapped, and Pamela jumped up and kissed his big red face, causing laughter and more roars; and that was the end.

AT DAWN, it was raining hard when they left. "In this weather we will go not so far," said Colonel Amphiteatrov. The driver kept the car going through terrible ruts, mounds, and holes, for perhaps twenty minutes. Then it stopped dead. Pug got out with the driver and the colonel. The hubs of the rear wheels were buried in red mud.

The colonel walked off into the woods. Pug heard voices, then engine snorts. The bushes began to move. Pug had been looking

494

straight at a camouflaged light tank. It started towards him followed by the colonel and three muddy men. The soldiers quickly attached a chain, and the car was pulled loose in a moment. Thus they were bogged and rescued several times, and so discovered that the wet, silent forest was swarming with the Red Army.

The lieutenant of one of the rescue squads invited the visitors to stop and refresh themselves, and took them down into a dugout so masked by brush that Pug did not see an entrance until the very last minute. The dugout had a heavy timbered roof that might survive a shell hit. Pug saw men eating chunks of grey bread and dollops of stew from a tureen. They seemed as much at home in the red earth as earthworms, and almost as tough and abundant. Here Victor Henry first got an ineradicable feeling that Yevlenko had told the truth: that for all the Germans' victories, the Red Army would in time drive them out.

"Well, we are not far now from our destination," Amphiteatrov said as the car bumped out of the woods into cleared fields that stretched for miles ahead. The driver stopped at the edge of a grain field. "You will see something interesting." Amphiteatrov gave Pamela an odd look. "Perhaps you will stay with the driver."

"I'll come, unless you tell me to stay."

"Very well. Come." He led them squelching in among the grain. The visitors glanced at each other in revulsion as a stench hit their noses. They broke into a clear space and saw why.

In every direction the grain was crushed flat in great swathes of muck, and tanks lay scattered on their sides or turned clear over, their paint burned, caterpillar tracks torn, armour plate torn apart. German corpses were sprawled in green uniforms on the ground, or slumped in blown open tanks, purple faces bloated disgustingly. Pamela clapped a handkerchief to her face.

"This happened only day before yesterday," said the colonel. "These Fritzes were probing and got caught."

Victor Henry had seen German tanks in Berlin, clanking down boulevards lined with red swastika flags. He said to the colonel, "Aren't these Mark IIIs? How could your T-26s knock them out? They don't fire a shell that can penetrate the Mark III."

Amphiteatrov grinned and led them back into the woods.

"Here we are," he said simply. "This is how we did it."

Dispersed in the thickets, all but invisible under branches and nets, five armoured monsters thrust giant guns high in the air. Tudsbury's mouth fell open. "My God! What are these things?"

"Our newest tank, the KV," said Amphiteatrov.

"Fantastic!" said Tudsbury. "It's a land battleship. What does it weigh? A hundred tons?"

The Russian smiled discreetly. "It's a good tank," he said.

NEXT MORNING the car crossed a white bare plain in a steady snowfall. In about an hour, an onion-top belfry of yellow brick loomed ahead through the veil of snow. They entered a town, and at the steps of the church Pug parted company with the Tudsburys. A commissar in a white leather coat took him off in a British jeep.

The jeep appeared to be heading straight for the front. Pug saw many newly splintered trees and bomb craters. The Germans had been shelling the day before, the political officer said, trying in vain to draw the fire of Russian batteries hidden in the woods.

They came to a line of crude trenches with high earthworks sugared by snow. These were dummy dugouts, the commissar said, deliberately made visible. They had taken much of the shellfire yesterday. The real trenches, dug along a riverbank, their log tops level with the ground and snowed over, were totally invisible. The commissar parked the jeep among trees, and he and Victor Henry crawled towards them.

Down in a deep muddy hole—a machine-gun post manned by three soldiers—Victor Henry peered through a gun slit and saw Germans. They were working across the river with earthmoving machines, pontoons, rubber boats, and trucks. Through binoculars, Pug could see the frost-purpled cheeks and noses of Hitler's men. "You could shoot them like birds," he said in Russian.

A soldier grunted. "Yes, and give away our real position, and start them shelling us! No, thanks, Comrade American."

"If they ever start coming across that bridge," said the commissar, "that'll be time enough to shoot."

"That's what we're waiting for," said the soldier who seemed to be in command of this hole.

496

Pug said, "Can you really hold out if they get across?"

The soldiers' mouths set sourly. "Well," said one, "every man has his time. A Russian soldier knows how to die."

The political officer said briskly, "A soldier's duty is to live, comrade, not to die—to live and fight. Our big guns are trained on this crossing, and as soon as they start coming we'll blast the rats! How about it?"

"That's exactly right, Comrade Commissar."

Crawling through bushes or darting from tree to tree, Victor Henry and the commissar made their way along the thinly held line. The Germans were in view all along the river, methodically preparing to cross. "How far are we from Moscow here?" Pug asked the commissar when they got back to the jeep.

"Far enough. I hope you saw what you wanted to see."

"I saw a lot," Victor Henry said.

The commissar appraised Pug with suspicious eyes. "It is not easy to understand the front just by looking at it."

"I understand that you need a second front."

The commissar uttered a brutal grunt. "Then you understand the main thing. But if we must, we ourselves alone will smash this plague of German cockroaches."

BY THE time they reached the central square of the town, the snow had stopped and patches of blue showed through the clouds. Tudsbury, in great spirits, called to Pug, "Hello there!"

"Where's Pamela?"

Tudsbury flipped a thumb over his shoulder. "Back at the church. An artillery spotter is stationed in the belfry. I couldn't climb the damned tower. She's up there making some notes. How are things at the front? *Brrr!* What frost, eh?"

Amphiteatrov said he was taking Tudsbury to see a downed Junkers-88 in a nearby field. Pug had seen plenty of Junkers-88s; he said he would join Pam in the church. Amphiteatrov made an annoyed face. "All right, but please remain there, Captain. We'll come back in twenty minutes or less."

In the church a strong miasma of disinfectant filled the air; peeling frescoes looked down on bandaged soldiers who lay on straw mats. Pug went up the narrow stone staircase inside the belfry to a wooden platform with big rusty bells.

"Victor!" Pam waved to him as he emerged at the top.

The onion dome was a crude job of tin sheets nailed to a curving frame. Squared around it was a brick walk and parapet, where Pamela crouched in a corner out of the wind. The artillery spotter manned giant binoculars on a tripod, pointed west. Pug surveyed the snowy vista from a corner of the parapet.

"Tell me about the front," Pamela said.

Still scanning the horizon, Pug described his trip. Suddenly he fell silent. "Pamela, pass me the field glasses." One quick look, and Pug tapped the spotter's shoulder and pointed. Swinging the large binoculars halfway around on the tripod, the spotter started with surprise, pulled off goggles and cap, and looked again. He was only eighteen or so and had a lot of curly blond hair. Snatching up a telephone, he jiggled the hook.

"What is it?" Pamela said.

"Take a look." Pug handed her the glasses.

Pamela saw a distant column of machines. "Tanks?"

"Some are armoured personnel cars. But yes, it's a tank unit."

"Aren't they Russians?"

"No."

"But that's the direction we came from." Her red-cheeked face showed fear, but also a trace of nervous gaiety. "Then aren't we in a pickle? Shouldn't we go find Amphiteatrov?"

To the naked eye the armoured column was like a tiny black worm five or six miles away. Pug stared eastward. He felt a flash of anger at Tudsbury's dragging his daughter here. If the worst came to the worst, he felt he could handle himself with German captors. But the Tudsburys were enemies.

"I'll tell you, Pam," he said, "the colonel knows where we are now. Let's stick here for a while."

The spotter made some observations which he marked on a grid map, then barked numbers into the telephone. Animated and cheery now, he grinned at the visitors. "Our batteries are training on them. Maybe you'll see something yet."

"I hear aeroplanes." Pug turned westward. "*Samolyoti!*"

"*Da!*" Swivelling and tilting the binoculars upward, the spotter began to shout into the phone.

"Aeroplanes too?" Pamela's voice trembled.

"That's the German drill. Tanks and planes together."

The oncoming planes, three Stukas, were growing bigger in Pug's glasses. The spotter switched his binoculars to the tank unit again and cheered. Tanks in another column were coming out of the woods about halfway between the Germans and the town, moving at right angles to the panzer track.

"The Stukas are starting their dive. Get down." Pug said. "Crawl up close to the dome and lie still." He crouched beside her. The planes tilted over and dived. When they were not much higher than the belfry, bombs fell out of them. The belfry shook. Dirt and smoke roared up beyond the parapet. Pug noted that the flying was ragged: the three machines almost collided as they climbed and turned to dive again. The Luftwaffe had either lost most of its experienced pilots, or they were not flying on this front.

Pamela, crouched against the dome, gripped his hand.

"Just lie low, this will be over soon." As Pug said this, he saw one of the Stukas dive straight for the belfry. The tin dome began to sing to striking bullets. Victor Henry roughly pushed Pamela flat and threw himself on top of her. He saw the pilot behind his plexiglas, a young fellow with a toothy grin. He thought the youngster was going to crash into the dome, and as he winced, he felt something rip at his left shoulder. The aeroplane scream diminished. The rattling of bullets stopped.

Pug stood, feeling his shoulder. His sleeve was torn open at the top, but there was no wound. The spotter was lying on the bricks beside the overturned binoculars. Blood was pooling under his head, and with horror Pug saw the white broken bone of the skull showing through the torn, shot-away cap.

Picking up the telephone, Pug jiggled the hook till somebody answered. He shouted in Russian, "I am the American visitor up here. The spotter has been killed."

"All right," said the voice, "somebody else will come."

Pamela had crawled beside the spotter and was looking at the dead face. "Oh, my God, my God," she sobbed, head in hand.

Smoke rose from fires in the town, smelling of burning hay. To the east, the two tank units had almost joined. Pug could see five of the KV monsters among lighter Russian tanks. Several German tanks were on fire; the rest were heading back to the woods.

"The Russians are winning out there," Pug said.

Pamela was staring at him with blank shocked eyes. Her hand went to the rip at his shoulder. "Dearest, are you hurt?"

"No. Not at all. It didn't touch me."

The ladder jumped and rapped, and Amphiteatrov's face appeared at the top. "Well, you're all right. I'm glad. That was best to stay here. Many people killed in the town." His eye fell on the body lying in blood.

"We were strafed," Pug said. "He's dead."

The colonel shook his head. "Please, come quickly."

They followed him down the spiral stairs and emerged outside the church. Through the open door of the automobile Tudsbury waved at them. "Hello! There's a monstrous tank battle going on, an utter inferno, right this minute!"

"Yes, I know." Though drained of spirit, Pug was able to smile at the gap between journalism and war. The reality of the two small groups of tanks banging away out there seemed so small-scale compared to Tudsbury's description. "We had a view of it," Pug said. Pamela sank into the back seat and closed her eyes.

"Did you? Well, Pam ought to be a help on this story! I say, Pam, you're all right, aren't you?"

"I'm splendid, thank you," she said, faintly but clearly.

Amphiteatrov slammed the car door. "Make yourselves comfortable please. We are going to drive straight back to Moscow."

"Oh no!" Tudsbury's fat face wrinkled up like an infant's. "I want to interview the tank crews."

Amphiteatrov turned and faced them. "There has been a big breakthrough in the north. Moscow is in danger. All foreign missions will be evacuated to the Caucasus. We must hurry."

Under the blanket stretched across the passengers' legs, Pamela's hand groped to Pug's. She pulled off her glove, twined her cold fingers in his, and pressed her face against the torn shoulder of his coat. His chapped hand tightened on hers.

27

Leslie Slote heard footfalls as he sat in an overcoat and fur hat, working by the light of an oil lamp. He looked up from his embassy desk. "Captain Henry? Why didn't they take you straight to the station? You've got to get out of Moscow tonight!"

"I've been to the station. The train to Kuibyshev had left. The air raid held us up outside the city."

"But that's terrible. God knows when there'll be another train to Kuibyshev." Slote jumped at a sound from outside. "I was at the Kazan station this evening," he went on," seeing off the staff. My God, that station was a spectacle! One bomb hit would have wiped out nine-tenths of the foreign diplomats in Russia—and a healthy chunk of the Soviet bureaucracy too."

"Have all the typewriters been stowed?" Pug asked. "I have to write a report."

"You have no time to write reports, Captain. It's my responsibility to see that you leave—"

Pug held up a hand. "Stragglers like me are to check back at eleven in the morning. It's all been arranged."

"It begins to smell like Warsaw all over again." Slote fussed through the papers on his desk. "By the way, a pouch came with some stuff from Rome." He nervously pulled a photograph from a wrinkled envelope. "Your new grandson. He's handsome."

Victor Henry read the writing on the back of the snapshot—"For old Slote—Louis Henry, aged eleven days, with circus fat lady—" then contemplated the photograph. A plump, hollow-eyed Natalie held a baby that looked startlingly like Byron as an infant. Pug cleared his throat. "Not bad. Natalie's right, she's gotten fat."

Slote said, "Would you care to keep that?"

Pug at once extended it to him. "No. She sent it to you."

"I'll only lose it, Captain. I have a better picture of her."

Victor Henry put the print carefully in an inner pocket.

"Are the Tudsburys stuck here too?" Slote asked.

"I left Talky trying to wangle them a ride to Archangel. The Russians are flying out some RAF pilot instructors. I'm sure they'll get on that plane. Which is why I must get at this report. I want to give him a copy to forward via London."

"Let me have a copy too, won't you? And another to go in the next pouch. *If* there is one."

"You're a pessimist, Slote."

"I'm a realist. I know what the Germans can do. The city's one unholy mess. Have you seen all the barbed wire and steel girders blocking the bridges? And the traffic jams, more cars than I knew were in the Soviet Union, all heading east with headlights blazing, blackout be damned! With those AA searchlights still swinging overhead, it's a real end-of-the-world feeling."

He shrugged, and turned back to his desk. "However, Stalin's staying, and that takes courage. Hitler'll hang him in Red Square. And drag Lenin out of the tomb, too, and string him up alongside."

VICTOR HENRY groped to the military attaché's office. He lit two oil lamps and found a typewriter, paper, and carbons. His fingers were cold and stiff, and the keys clicked slowly as he started his report. He described the air raid he had witnessed that evening, and the impressive display of anti-aircraft fire which the Russians put up against Luftwaffe attacks. Then he went on, "I believe that Moscow has a fair chance. And even if it falls, the war may not end. My outstanding impression is that the Russians are not beaten."

The typewriter was clicking faster now. It was almost one o'clock. Pug was describing the KV tank when Slote came in and dropped a sealed envelope on his desk. "This was also in the pouch for you. Care for some coffee?"

"You bet. Thanks." Pug sat up and stretched before he opened the envelope. There was a letter from the White House and one from the Bureau of Personnel. He opened the one from the White House first—a few sentences in Harry Hopkins's slanting hand:

My dear Pug—

I want to congratulate you on your new assignment, and to convey the Boss's good wishes. He is very preoccupied with the Japanese, who are beginning to get ugly, and of course we are all watching the Russian struggle with anxiety. I still think—and

502

pray—they'll hold. I hope my letter reached Stalin. He's a land crab, and he's *got* to be convinced that the Channel crossing is a major task, otherwise bad faith accusations will start, to Hitler's delight. There's been an unfortunate upturn in submarine sinkings in the Atlantic, and the Germans are cutting loose in Africa, too. All in all the good cause seems to be heading into the storm. You'll be missed in the grey fraternity of office boys.

Harry H.

The other envelope contained a navy mailgram:

FROM: THE CHIEF OF PERSONNEL.
TO: VICTOR (NONE) HENRY, CAPTAIN, USN
DETACHED ONE NOVEMBER PRESENT DUTY. PROCEED FASTEST AVAILABLE TRANSPORTATION PEARL HARBOR. REPORT CALIFORNIA (BB 44) RELIEVE CO. SUBMIT VOUCHERS OF TRAVEL EXPENSES COMBAT FOR PEARL.

In trite navy jargon on a flimsy yellow sheet, here was command of a battleship—and what a battleship! Captain of the *California*! His "grey office boy" service to the President had proved a shortcut after all. Flag rank was suddenly back in sight.

He thought of Rhoda, because she had sweated out the twenty-seven-year wait; and of Pamela, because he wanted to share his excitement right now. But they had parted at the railroad station with a strong handclasp. He might not see her again.

Leslie Slote came back with coffee. "Anything good?"

"New orders. Command of the *California*. A battleship."

"Then I gather congratulations are in order. I'll leave you to finish that report."

When Slote had gone, Victor Henry sat drinking coffee, meditating on the little yellow paper, the sudden verdict on his life. This was the blue ribbon of naval service. Yet there was a shadow on the marvellous news. At War Plans, he had been waging a vigilant fight for the landing craft programme. "Pug's girl friend Elsie" was no joke. With Pug gone, "Elsie" was going to lose ground. But it was absurd, Pug thought, to feel the weight of the war on his shoulders. He was a small replaceable cog; sooner or later America would produce enough landing craft to beat Hitler. Meantime he had to go to his battleship.

Taking a lamp to a globe standing in the corner, he used thumb and forefinger to step off the distance from Moscow to Pearl Harbor. It was about the same to travel west or east; halfway around the earth.

"You look like a mad conqueror," he heard Slote say. "Gloating over the globe by lamplight. We have a visitor here."

A Russian soldier came in, slapping snow from his long khaki coat. He took off his cap, and Pug was startled to recognize Berel Jastrow. His straggly beard was flecked with grey. Speaking German, he explained that in order to get warm clothes he had passed himself off as a soldier from a routed unit. The authorities were collecting such stragglers and forming them into emergency work battalions. "After a while maybe I can find my family," Berel said.

"Where are they?" Pug asked.

"With the partisans, near Smolensk." He turned to Slote. "I heard all the foreigners are leaving Moscow. I wanted to find out what happened to the documents I gave you."

The two Americans looked at each other, embarrassed. "Well, I showed them to an important newspaperman," Slote said. "I'm afraid the story ended up in the back pages."

"Forgive me, sir, but why did you not give those documents to your ambassador to send to President Roosevelt?"

"I did bring them to his attention. I'm sorry, but our intelligence people questioned their authenticity."

"But that is incredible! I can bring you ten people tomorrow who will give affidavits to such stories. Some of them—"

In a tone of exasperation, Slote broke in. "Look here, my dear chap, I did my best. In showing your documents to the newspaperman I violated instructions and received a serious reprimand."

Jastrow answered the outburst in a quiet, dogged tone, "I am very sorry about the reprimand. But President Roosevelt is the only man in the whole world who could put a stop to this crazy slaughter of innocent people." He turned to Victor Henry, "Is there not some way, Captain, to tell him the story?"

504

Pug was already picturing himself writing to the President. It would be just the sort of impertinence that Byron had offered at the President's table. He answered Jastrow by turning his hands upward.

Jastrow nodded. "Naturally, it is outside your province. Have you news of Natalie? Have she and Aaron gone home yet?"

Pug pulled the snapshot from his pocket. "This was taken several weeks ago. I expect they're out by now."

Briefly Jastrow's face became gentle. "Why, it is a small Byron. God bless him and keep him safe from harm." He handed back the photograph. "Well, you gentlemen have been gracious to me. My documents are true, and I pray to God somebody soon finds a way to get them to President Roosevelt."

WHEN his alarm clock woke him after two hours of exhausted slumber, Pug scarcely remembered writing the letter which lay on the table by his bed; he had scrawled it when he got back from the embassy. As he reread it now, it struck him as ill-considered. In effect, he was advising the President to go over the heads of everybody in the State Department, and demand a look at the Minsk documents. The odds against Roosevelt's actually doing this were long.

Pug threw the letter face down on the table as a rapping came at the door. Alistair Tudsbury, enormous in an astrakhan hat and a long brown fur coat, entered and sat down in the armchair. "Sorry to crash in on you like this, but—I say, are you all right?"

Pug was rubbing his face hard with both hands. "I was up all night writing a report. What's doing?"

The correspondent's bulging eyes probed at him. "This is going to be difficult . . . . Are you and Pamela lovers?"

"What!" Pug was too startled, and too tired, to be either angry or amused. "Why, no! Of course not."

"Well, that makes it all the more baffling. Pamela has just told me flatly that she's not going to London unless you are! There's no reasoning with her. Those RAF fellows are flying off at noon, and they've got space for both of us."

"Where is she now?"

"Out for a stroll in Red Square, of all things! Won't even pack. Hell, Victor, it's embarrassing, her trailing after you, a happily married man. And what about Ted Gallard? Why, she sat down and scribbled a letter for me to give him telling him it was all off! I'm having the devil of a time with the girl."

Victor Henry said in weary tones, yet with a glad surge at heart, "Well, take my word for it, I'm utterly amazed."

"I was sure you would be. I've told her till I'm blue in the face that you're a straitlaced old-fashioned man, the soul of honour and all that sort of thing. She simply says that's why she likes you! Victor, surely it's dangerous for a British girl to rattle around in Moscow, with the Huns closing in on all sides."

"Yes, it is." Victor Henry stumbled to the mirror and rubbed his bristly chin. "I'd better talk to Pamela."

"Please, dear fellow, please. And hurry!"

Pug went out to fresh snow, bright sunshine, and a burst of Russian song. A formation of old men and boys, shouldering picks and shovels and lustily shouting a marching tune, was following an army sergeant down Manezhnaya Square.

Red Square was almost deserted. In front of the Lenin tomb, its red marble hidden by snow-crusted sandbags, two soldiers stood as usual like statues. Far on the other side, Victor Henry saw a small figure in grey walking past Saint Basil's Cathedral with the swingy gait he remembered from the *Bremen* deck. He headed towards her, his overshoes sinking deep in snow. She saw him and hurried to meet him. "Damn! Talky went and told you."

"That's right."

"What are your plans? Are you going to London?"

They were walking arm in arm. "I've gotten orders, Pam. I'm going to command a battleship, the *California*."

She pulled on his elbow to swing him towards her, faced him with wide, glistening eyes. "Command a *battleship*!"

"Not bad, eh?" he said like a schoolboy.

"My God, smashing! You're bound to be an admiral after that, aren't you? Oh, how happy your wife will be!" Pamela said this with unselfconscious pleasure. "Where's the *California* based?"

"Pearl Harbor. The Hawaiian Islands."

"Oh. Hawaii. All right. We'll start plotting to get me to Hawaii. No doubt there's a British consulate there, or something."

"Aren't you on leave from the air force? Won't you have to go back on duty if Talky returns to London?"

"My love, let me take care of all that. I'm very, very good at getting what I want."

"I believe *that*."

She laughed. "When do you leave, and how?"

"As soon as I can, via Siberia and the Philippines." He clasped her hands. "Now, Pam, listen. My wife will probably come to Pearl."

"I should think she would."

"Then what have you in mind, exactly?"

"Why, love, since you ask me, to deceive her, decently, carefully, kindly, until you are tired of me and I go home."

This blunt declaration shook Victor Henry. It was so outside the set rules of his existence, that he replied with clumsy stiffness, "I don't understand that kind of arrangement."

"I know, darling. You're a dear nice man. Nevertheless I don't know what else to propose. I love you. That is unchangeable. I'm happy with you, and not happy otherwise. I *don't* propose to be separated from you any more until you dismiss me."

He brushed snow off a bench outside the Cathedral and sat her down. "We're short of time," he said. "For the moment I'll put Rhoda aside and just talk about you—"

She interrupted him. "Victor, love, I know you're faithful to your wife. I've always feared you'd think me a pushing slut. But what else can I do? The time has come, that's all."

Pug sat looking at her. Soldiers, obviously new recruits, began piling out of a long line of trucks that had just pulled into Red Square. After a long pause, Pug said, "I know this kind of chance won't roll round again in my life."

"It won't, Victor. It won't!" Her face shone with excitement. "People to whom it happens even once are very lucky. I know you can't marry me. We must accept that and go on from there."

"I didn't say I can't marry you," Pug said. She looked astounded. "Let's be clear. If I love you enough to have an affair with you, I love you enough to ask my wife for a divorce. But all this is breaking too fast, Pam, and meantime you have to leave Moscow. The only place to go is London. That's common sense."

"I won't marry Ted. Don't argue," she said, as he started to talk. "I know it's a beastly decision, but that's it. Your battleship complicates things, but I'll get to Hawaii myself—sooner than you'd believe possible."

"How about your being needed in England?"

"If I leave old England in the lurch, Victor, it will be because something stronger calls me, and I'll do it."

This was direct language that Victor Henry understood. All at once he felt a stab of sexual hunger for her, and a pulse of hope that there might conceivably be a new life in store for him with this young woman.

"O.K. Then let's get down to realities." He glanced at his watch. "You've got to move in a couple of hours. I do too."

Pamela smiled. "What a nuisance I must be, draping myself around your neck at this moment. Do you really love me?"

"Yes, I love you," Pug said sincerely.

"You're sure, are you? Say it just once more."

"I love you."

Pamela heaved a sigh. "All right. So where to today, then?"

"Back with Talky to London. I'll write or cable you."

"Well, that will be a communication to look forward to," she spoke lightly, then put a hand to his face and smiled at him, her eyes full of love. "O.K. Then I must get cracking. Oh dear, I honestly don't want to travel away from you again."

They rose and began walking arm in arm. Among the recruits they walked past stood Berel Jastrow. He saw Victor Henry, and for a moment put his right hand over his heart. The naval officer raised his cap as though to wipe his brow, and put it back on.

In the unlit hallway outside her suite, Pamela unbuttoned her coat, then unbuttoned Pug's and pressed herself hard to him, and they embraced and kissed. She whispered, "Oh God, how I love you! Will you drive with us to the airport? Will you come in while I pack? Will you stay with me every second to the last?"

"Yes, of course I'll stay with you."

She dashed tears from her face with the back of her hand. "Oh, how glad I am that I dug in my nasty little hooves!"

"Well?" Tudsbury said, as she opened the door.

"I was being silly. I'm going home with you."

"Gad, what a relief! I was about to come looking for you. The RAF lads are being flown out half an hour earlier."

"I can pack in ten minutes."

Pug said, "I must get a report from my room. I'll be right back."

He returned shortly, out of breath from the run, and handed a stapled envelope to Tudsbury. "Give this to Captain Kyser, the naval attaché at our embassy, hand to hand. All right?"

"Top secret?" Tudsbury asked with relish.

"Well—be careful with it. It's for the next Washington pouch."

Into a dispatch case, Tudsbury slipped Pug's envelope which contained two others: the long report for Harry Hopkins and his letter to the President about the Jews of Minsk.

28

Amid a crowd of officers from both services, Pug sat on the back lawn of the Army and Navy Club in Manila. It was three in the morning, and they were listening to a broadcast of the Army-Navy football game from Philadelphia, eleven thousand miles away.

The sticky heat of Manila, the old inter-service jokes and insults, took him back a dozen years. Life here was amazingly unchanged. Only the floodlights blazing across the bay for all-night repair work suggested that it was late in November 1941, and that the navy was bestirring itself for an emergency.

"Pug! I heard you were here." His classmate, Walter Tully, was smiling down at him. Tully was in command of the submarine squadron at Manila. "Mind if I join you?"

"Sit down, Walt. Say, what's the idea, sending the *Devilfish* out on exercises? You think there's a war on or something?"

Tully grinned. "It was Branch Hoban's idea. They're going alongside for two weeks starting today—they're due in at noon—and he wanted to get in some drills. You'll see plenty of Byron."

"I'll only be here till the Clipper leaves for Pearl Harbor."

"Yes. It's great you've got the *California*, Pug."

Tully dropped his voice. "Admiral Hart had a straight war warning today. In July, when the Japs landed in Indochina and then in August, when Roosevelt shut off their oil, we all thought, here goes! We ran dawn and dusk general quarters for a week, till it got kind of silly. Now I'm wondering if I should start that up again. If they do go, we're in trouble. The submarine force is so short of everything—torpedoes, spare parts, watch officers—that it's simply pitiful."

They talked on. When the game ended, many people were stretched out asleep on the grass under a dawn sky. Pug declined Tully's invitation to breakfast and went up to his room for a nap.

He had stayed in a room like it on first reporting to Manila, before Rhoda had arrived with the children to set up housekeeping. It hit Pug with a strong sense of lost time and vanished days. He opened the windows and sat watching the dawn brighten over the broad blue harbour.

He sat so for more than an hour, seeing pictures. Of himself and Byron under a poinciana tree working on French verbs; the boy's thin face wrinkling, silent tears falling at his father's roared exasperation. Of Warren at high school, winning a history medal, and a baseball award. Of Madeline, fairylike in gossamer white, at her eighth birthday party. Of Rhoda crabbing about the heat and the boredom. . . .

Pictures, then, of Pamela Tudsbury in Red Square. Of the dreary mud streets of Kuibyshev while he waited for train tickets; of Siberia on the two-week train ride; the beautiful Siberian girls selling bread and sausage at tiny wooden stations.

Through all these pictures Victor Henry had preserved a happy sense that he was moving towards a new life, a life he had almost despaired of but now within grasp if he'd divorce Rhoda. But in Manila an awareness of his wife began to overtake him. Manila was saturated with her, good and bad memories alike. Above all it recalled to Pug the pleasure he had taken in his children. Those days he looked back on as the sweetest in his life. To divorce Rhoda would be cruel; she had given him an arid, half-empty existence—

he now knew that—but even so she had been doing her best. . . .

He was very tired, and sleep at last overtook him; but his inner clock snapped him awake in time to drive out to the Navy Yard and watch *Devilfish* arrive.

BYRON was on deck, but Pug failed to recognize him. Byron sang out, as *Devilfish* nosed alongside the pier, "Holy smoke, it's my father. Dad! *Dad!*" Then Pug perceived his son's voice issuing from a curly red beard. Byron leaped to the dock while the vessel was still warping in, and threw his arms around Pug.

"Hi, Briny. Why the foliage?"

"Captain Hoban can't stand beards. I plan to grow one to my knees." From the bridge an officer shouted impatiently through a megaphone. Jumping back aboard Byron called, "Hey, Mom says you're going to command the *California*! That's fabulous!"

The *Devilfish* officers warmly invited Victor Henry to lunch at a house they had rented in the suburbs. Pug caught a look from Byron and declined. "I live aboard the submarine," Byron said, as they drove in to Manila. "I'm not in that setup."

"Why not? Sounds like a good thing."

"Oh, neat. Cook, butler, two houseboys, five acres, a swimming pool, and all for peanuts. I've been there for dinner. They have these girls come in, you know, and whoop it up and all that."

"Well? Fine deal for the young, I should think."

"What did you do, Dad, when you were away from Mom?"

Pug glanced at Byron. "I did a lot of agonized looking, I'll admit. But don't act holier-than-thou, whatever you do."

"I don't feel holier-than-thou. My wife's in Italy. That's that. They can do as they please."

"What's the latest word on her?"

"They're at a hotel in Rome. I've got a picture of the kid. Wait till you see him!"

Pug had been poring over the snapshot in his wallet for over a month, but he decided not to mention it.

"It's hell, being this far apart," Byron said. "Can you picture it, Dad? No telephone, a letter only now and then getting through? And the worst of it is, she almost got out through Switzerland.

She panicked at taking a German aeroplane. . . and I don't blame her!" After a silence he changed the subject. "Hot here, isn't it? I guess it was pretty cold in Russia."

"Hot too. If you know what I mean," Pug said.

Over lunch at the Army and Navy Club, Pug decided to probe Byron a bit about Berel Jastrow and about Pamela, for Natalie had mentioned that she'd known Pam in Paris. He described Jastrow's sudden arrival with the documents in Moscow, and his unexpected reappearance in army uniform. Byron exploded at Tudsbury's suggestion that Jastrow might be an NKVD emissary. "Nobody can know Berel for five minutes without realizing that he's a remarkable man. And dead on the level."

"I wasn't that sure. But I wrote to the President about it."

Byron stared openmouthed. "You did *what*, Dad?"

"Well, those documents got shunted aside as probable fakes. I thought they deserved investigation."

Byron Henry reached out and pressed his father's hand. "All I can say is, well done."

"No. A futile gesture is never well done. But I did it. Incidentally, the Tudsburys and I travelled to the front together. Pamela struck me as an unusually brave and agreeable sort."

"Oh, Pam Tudsbury's the original endurer, from what Natalie says. Natalie said she raised Cain all over gay Paree with a character who used to room with Leslie Slote. Then they broke up and she went into a bad spin."

Pug could not help persisting. "How—a spin?"

"Oh, you know, sleeping around, trying to drink up all the wine in Paris—what's the matter? You look upset."

"It's an upsetting story. She seems a fine girl. I'll be here a week," Pug said abruptly. "Can we get in some tennis?"

THEY played early in the mornings to dodge the heat, and then breakfasted together. Pug tried to think of ways to reopen the subject of Pamela, but he couldn't do it. A romance between his staid father and Pamela Tudsbury would strike Byron as a middle-aged aberration—shabby and pathetic.

One day Branch Hoban invited Pug to the house in the suburbs

513

for lunch. Over drinks on the terrace, Hoban and Aster talked reassuringly about Byron. They both considered him a natural submarine man; just now, though, transfer to the Atlantic was his obsession. Hoban pointed out that the squadron was far under complement, and *Devilfish* could not put to sea if it lost one watchstander. Byron had to make up his mind that *Devilfish* was his ship.

Pug brought up this topic at the time of day when Byron was usually in the highest spirits—over coffee on the lawn after tennis. Casually, he remarked, "Natalie's flying to Lisbon on the fifteenth, you said? Think she'll make it this time?"

"She'd better! They've got highest priority."

"Well, that isn't far off. This transfer request of yours—" Pug hesitated at Byron's look which he knew only too well. "Isn't it something you can table, at least until then?"

"Listen, Dad, I've never seen my own son. I've spent the sum total of two days with my wife since we got married."

"There's another side to it. Your squadron is desperate for watch officers, we're in a war alert, and—"

Byron broke in. "What is this, Dad? I haven't asked you to use your influence with Walter Tully, have I?"

"I'm sure glad you haven't." They glared at each other. "Maybe we'd better drop it," said Victor Henry.

"That's a fine idea, Dad."

Victor Henry felt that in the short, bitter exchange he had lost all the ground he had been gaining with his son. Yet Byron could not have been more amiable when he saw him off on the Clipper next day.

He threw his arms around his father, and impulsively Pug said, "Is Natalie going to like all this shrubbery?"

It was a pleasure to hear Byron laugh. "Don't worry. The day I leave the *Devilfish*, off it comes."

As the loudspeaker called for passengers to board the huge flying boat, Victor Henry looked in his son's eyes. He said with great difficulty, "Look, I pray for Natalie and your boy."

Byron's eyes were steady. "I'm sure you do, Dad. Thanks." And when the Clipper wheeled away for the long takeoff the son still stood there, hands thrust in his back pockets, watching.

THE JAPANESE fleet at that moment was well on its way to Hawaii.
The Kuril Islands, a seven-hundred-mile chain between Japan
and Siberia, had made a good secret rendezvous. Japan's six
aircraft carriers had met there first and their fliers had practised
shallow torpedo runs while the rest of the armada gathered. When
the force set out eastward, only a few of Japan's leaders knew where
they were going, and why.

They were not sure the attack would go. The fleet was sailing in
case the Washington talks broke down. The Japanese peace plan
called for the United States to resume sending oil and scrap iron,
and to recognize Japan's right to rule East Asia and China. If the
Americans granted this, the fleet would be recalled. But if they did
not, then the Japanese leaders were determined to fight. In that
case, an enormous simultaneous assault would burst out of Japan
like red rays across the South Pacific.

The three strong points held by the western powers in the South
Pacific were Pearl Harbor, Manila, and Singapore. The plan was to
knock out United States air and sea power at Pearl Harbor from the
air; to capture Singapore by seaborne assault; to land troops in
the Philippines and take Manila, and then to sweep up the chips
in the East Indies; and thereafter to use these new resources for a
strong drive to finish China. The gamble was that Germany would
either win the western war, or would so use up American and
British strength that Japan would in the end keep what she had
seized, no matter what happened to Germany.

And so, on the day before Pug in Manila listened to the Army-
Navy game, the armada had set out for Hawaii. And as the Japanese
task force steamed east, a much smaller American task force headed
west. Admiral William Halsey was taking twelve marine fighter
planes to Wake Island in the *Enterprise*. Japan had long since
illegally fortified every island it held in the Pacific. Only now, at
the end of November 1941, had President Roosevelt managed to
get money out of Congress for counter-fortifying American islands.
At Wake the work was half-finished, but they still had no air
defence.

On the day that the Japanese and Halsey's ships made their
closest approach, Warren Henry flew a search pattern from the

Enterprise—more than two hundred miles straight towards the Japanese fleet. The Japanese routinely sent a scout plane due south about the same distance. But hundreds of miles of water stretched between the two scouts at their far reach, and the two forces passed in peace.

ON Victor Henry's last day in Manila, the Japanese embassy in Rome gave a party for Japanese and American newspaper correspondents. The purpose seemed to be a show of cordiality to counteract all the war talk. A *New York Times* man asked Natalie to come along and she accepted.

Among the American guests was Herbert Rose, a film distributor in Rome who had once worked in Tokyo. He walked Natalie off to a corner, and in a few quiet, nervous sentences, told her to go to Saint Peter's with her uncle the following morning at nine o'clock and stand near Michelangelo's "Pietà". They would be offered a chance to get out of Italy fast, he said, via Palestine. War between America and Japan was coming in days or hours, Herb believed; he was departing that way himself. She told her uncle all this while walking on the Via Veneto in a cold drizzle.

Aaron was in a testy mood. "Palestine!" he grumbled. "Why, it's a hellhole, Natalie, a desert full of flies, disease, and angry Arabs." But he agreed they had better go to Saint Peter's.

Next morning they reached Saint Peter's after nine. "Not my favourite among Italian cathedrals," said Jastrow as they hurried in. "Ah, but there's the 'Pietà'. What a lovely work it is."

"Would you call that a Jew's Jesus, Dr. Jastrow?" said a voice in German.

The man who spoke was rather stout, about thirty, wearing an old tweed jacket with a Leica slung round his neck. He smiled, took Jastrow's book from under his arm, and showed him the author's photograph on the back. "I'm Avram Rabinovitz. Mrs. Henry, how do you do?" Natalie nodded nervously. "Come, let's walk around the cathedral. I'm sailing from Naples tomorrow at four. Are you coming?"

"*You're* sailing? Are you a ship's captain?" Natalie asked.

"Not exactly. I have chartered the vessel. The ship is small, and it's been transporting hides around the Mediterranean, so the smell is interesting. But it'll take us there."

Natalie said, "How long a voyage will it be?"

"Well, the quota of Jews that the British will allow into Palestine this year was used up long ago. The quota keeps Arabs from getting too angry. So we may go to Turkey, and then proceed overland—Syria, Lebanon, and through the mountains into Galilee."

"You're talking about an illegal entry, then, as well as illegal exit." Jastrow sounded severe. "In a situation like this, the first principle is to stay within the law."

"We don't think it can be illegal for a Jew to go home. In any case, there's no choice for my passengers. They're refugees from the Germans, and all other countries have barred the doors to them, including your United States."

"That isn't our situation," Jastrow said. "We have all our documents, and we're flying to America in less than two weeks."

Natalie put in, "I have a two-month-old infant. Could a small baby make that trip?"

Rabinovitz looked her straight in the eye. "Mrs. Henry, you have heard surely the stories coming from Poland. Maybe you should take some risk to get your baby out of Europe."

"If anything went wrong, we'd never get out of Italy," Jastrow persisted, "until the war ended."

Rabinovitz said, "Let's be honest. I'm not sure you will get out anyway, Dr. Jastrow. I don't think the difficulties you've been having are accidental. I'm afraid you're what some people call a 'blue chip'—that the Italians think they can trade you some day for a lot of 'white chips', so something can always go wrong at the last minute. Well, you want to think it over, I'm sure. Mr. Rose will telephone you tonight at six and ask you whether you want the tickets for the opera. Tell him yes or no, and that will be that."

"Good," Natalie said. "We're deeply grateful."

Talking the thing over afterwards, Aaron tended to dismiss it out of hand, but the fact that Rose was going troubled Natalie. Jastrow pointed out that Rose was not as secure as they were. Even if war should break out between the United States and

Italy they had the ambassador's promise of seats on the diplomatic train. Rose had no such assurance.

At the hotel, Natalie found the baby awake and fretful. He seemed frail to be exposed to a sea voyage of uncertain destination. One look at her baby, in fact, settled Natalie's mind.

Rose called promptly at six. "Well, do you want the opera tickets?" His voice seemed anxious.

Natalie said, "I think we'll skip it, Herb. But thank your friend who offered them."

"You're making a mistake, Natalie," Rose said. "I think this is the last performance. You're sure?"

Natalie told him she was positive.

29

Janice Henry left her house and drove towards Pearl City on a cool Sunday morning echoing with church bells. The baby had wakened her, coughing fearfully; he had a high fever. On the telephone, the doctor had prescribed an alcohol rub to bring the temperature down, but she had no rubbing alcohol. So she had set out for town, leaving the baby with the Chinese maid.

On the hill crest she got out of the car to look for her husband's ship. The fleet was in, ranged at its moorings in the morning mist; but the *Enterprise* was nowhere in sight. Janice took binoculars from the glove compartment and scanned the horizon. Nothing; and Warren would have been gone two weeks on Tuesday. What a life!

Since she had come back from Washington, she had begun to realize that Warren was a navy fanatic who made marvellous love to her now and then and otherwise almost ignored her. Janice Lacouture, at twenty-three, a navy baby-sitter! She had spells of deep rebellion, but so far she had been afraid to tell Warren.

Luckily a small store at a crossroads stood open; she might not have to drive clear into town. As she went in, she heard gunfire pop over the harbour, as it had for months in target practice.

As the storekeeper went to find the rubbing alcohol she noticed that the gunfire sounded heavier and planes thrummed overhead.

A funny time for a drill, she thought. From the doorway she spotted the planes, flying quite high, lots of them, in close order. She went to her car for the binoculars. Three planes flew into the field of vision. On their wings were solid orange-red circles. Stupefied, she followed their flight. Below, planes were flitting about the navy base, where the mist still lay pearly pink around the ships. Columns of water were shooting up, a couple of ships were on fire.

Then she saw a strange and shocking sight. A battleship vanished. One instant the vessel stood in the outer row, and the next there was nothing but a big red ball surrounded by black-and-yellow smoke. The ball of smoke and fire climbed high into the air. Then the battleship appeared again, a twisted, burning wreck, sinking at a slant. Men, some with their white suits on fire, were running around and jumping overboard.

"Ess ma'am? Many pranes!" The storekeeper stood beside her, handing her the package with a toothy smile. Janice stared at him. Nearly everybody in the navy assumed the Hawaiian Japanese were spies. Now here was this Jap grinning at her, and Jap planes were actually attacking Hawaii! Horrified, Janice snatched the package and ran to the car. Accelerator on the floor, she raced home.

The Chinese maid sat in an armchair, dressed for church. "The baby's asleep," she said. "The Gillettes forgot to come for me. So I'll have to go to the ten-o'clock mass. Will you please telephone Mrs. Fenney."

"Anna May, the Japanese are attacking us. Can't you hear the explosions? Turn on the radio."

The baby lay on his back, breathing loud and fast. As Janice sponged the hot, flushed little body, she heard an announcer gibbering cheerfully about soapflakes. The maid came to the doorway. "You sure about the war, Mis' Henry? There's nothing on the radio."

"But I saw a battleship blow up. I saw a *hundred* Jap planes, maybe more! Here, take Victor. I'll try to call the Fenneys."

But the line was dead. Tyres rattled the driveway gravel, and Janice ran to the door. Bloody-faced, Warren Henry stumbled in, in heavy flying boots, a zipper suit, and a bloodied yellow life jacket. "Hi, have you got twenty bucks?"

"My *God*, Warren!"

"Pay off the cab, Jan." His voice was hoarse and controlled. "Anna May, get out some bandages, will you?"

Janice paid the driver. In the kitchen, the maid was dabbing antiseptic on Warren's blood-dripping left arm. "I'll do that," Janice said. "You make sure Victor's all right."

Warren gritted his teeth as Janice worked on the raw wound. "Jan, what's wrong with Vic?"

"Oh, a fever. A cough. Darling, what *happened* to you?"

"I got shot down. Those bastards killed my radioman. Our squadron flew patrol ahead and ran into them."

"Honey, you've got to go to the hospital and get stitched."

"No, no. The hospital will be jammed. That's one reason I came here. And I wanted to be sure you and Vic were O.K. I'm going to Ford Island, and maybe get a plane. We'll be counter-attacking, and I'm not missing that. Just bandage it up, Jan."

Janice was dizzied to have Warren suddenly back, bloody, returned from battle. He talked on at a great rate, all charged up. "God, it was weird—I thought those AA bursts were target practice, of course. We never did spot the Japs until six of them jumped us out of the sun. The way those fellows came diving—"

"Hold still, honey."

"Sorry. I tell you, it was rough, Jan. They got my radioman right away. And then our own AA opened up and the flak was bursting all around me. I still don't know whether they got me or a Jap did. All I know is my gas tank caught fire. I popped the canopy and jumped. I landed in a little park off Dillingham—"

"I've got the bleeding under control. Just sit quiet for a minute."

"You should see the sights downtown!" Warren grinned crookedly at his wife. "People out in nightclothes, or less, yelling, running around gawking at the sky. I saw this beautiful Chinese girl crossing Dillingham Boulevard in a bra and pink panties—"

"You would notice something like that," said Janice. "Even if your arm had been shot clean off." With his good arm, Warren gave her a rough intimate caress, and she slapped his hand. "All right! I've got you plastered up, but I still think you should see a doctor at the Naval Air Station."

520

"If there's time." Grimacing as he moved the arm, Warren put on a clean shirt. "I'll have a look at Vic. Get the car out."

A few moments later, he opened the car door. "The son of a gun's sleeping peacefully. He feels cool."

Sightseers stood on the ridge, chattering and pointing. Heavy black smoke boiled up out of the anchorage, darkening the sun. Janice stopped the car. Warren swept the harbour with the binoculars. "Good God, Jan, Ford Island's a junkyard! I don't see one undamaged plane. Hey! They're coming back."

All over the harbour, guns began rattling, and black AA balls blossomed in the blue. Warren peered skyward. "That means their carriers are still in range. Great. Move over. I'm driving."

Warren whistled down to Pearl City like an escaping bank bandit. After a few moments of fright, his wife began to enjoy the breakneck ride. How handsome Warren looked, how competent, how desirable. Her boredom and irritability were forgotten.

THE FLEET landing was a horror. Sailors with blistered faces and hands, with skin hanging in scorched pieces from bloody flesh, were being loaded on to hospital trucks by men in red-smeared whites. Over all rolled the thumping and cracking of guns, the wail of sirens and the roar of aeroplanes. The second attack was now in full swing. Hands on hips, Warren Henry surveyed the scene.

"How'll you ever get across?" Janice said in shaken tones.

He strode to the end of the landing to a long canopied boat, "Coxswain, whose barge is this?"

The immaculate sailor at the tiller flipped a salute, eyeing Warren's gory life jacket. "Suh, this is Admiral Radburn's barge."

"I'm Lieutenant Henry. I'm a pilot off the *Enterprise*. The Japs shot me down. I have to find another plane, so how's for taking me over to Ford Island?"

The coxswain hesitated, then said, "Come aboard, suh. The important thing is to get those sons of bitches. Excuse me, ma'am."

Warren stood in the stern sheets, smiling at her as the barge pulled away. "Get them!" she called. "And come back to me."

"Roger. Don't drive home till these bastards quit, or you may get strafed." He waved, and she wildly waved back.

He ducked as a red-and-yellow plane passed not twenty feet over his head, its motor coughing; then it turned sharply and flew off across the channel. Warren straightened, still grinning, and Janice watched him carried away to the flaming mid-harbour island that was the navy's airfield. She was horror-stricken by what she had seen, yet never had she felt so full of life, or so much in love.

THE SUN poked up over the horizon, painting a red flush on the Clipper's wing. Victor Henry watched the brightening disc rise free of the ocean. The plane had left Wake in the starlit night bound for Midway, the last stop before Honolulu.

The engines changed pitch, rasping at his nerves. The sun moved sideways. The turn was so shallow that Pug felt no tilt in his seat. He walked forward into the galley, where the steward was scrambling eggs. "I'd like to talk to Ed Connelly, if he's free."

The steward smiled, gesturing at the door marked FLIGHT DECK. Pug went through to the dial-filled cockpit. "'Morning, Ed. Why are we heading back?"

The captain passed him a radio message: "CincPac general plain language message quote Air raid on Pearl Harbor. This is no drill unquote. Recommend you return Wake till situation clarifies."

"I never thought they'd do it," Connelly said. "Attacking Pearl! They'll get creamed."

"Let's hope so."

Victor Henry returned to his seat, agitated though far from astonished. Here it was at last, he thought.

At Wake, a marine in a jeep waited for him on the landing. The marine commander wanted to see Captain Henry. They drove along the beach road, then turned off into the brush.

Perfectly camouflaged by scrub, the command post was sunk in coral sand. When Pug saw the radio gear, the crude furniture and freshly dug soil, the war with Japan became a fact for him.

The marine colonel gave Pug an envelope to take to Hawaii. "Put it in the admiral's hand yourself, Captain. Please! It's a list of my worst shortages. Maybe we can hold out till we're relieved if he'll send us that stuff. Radar gear for Wake has been sitting on the dock in Hawaii for a month. For God's sake, ask him to rush it.

522

We'll probably end up behind barbed wire anyway, but at least we can make the bastards work to take the place."

The Clipper passengers were just sitting down to lunch in the hotel when blasts shook the floor and sent broken window panes clinking to the tiles. Fat cigar-shaped planes flashed past the windows, and smoke and fire were already rising from the airfield across the lagoon.

The passengers dived under tables as the planes bombed and machine-gunned the hotel, the repair shops, the radio tower. Then a line of bombers came winging straight for the Pan American compound, and this was what Pug feared. An attack on the Clipper might paralyse his war career before it started. There was no way off Wake Island except aboard that huge silvery target.

When the bomber sounds faded, Pug followed the pilot out on the pier at a run. Connelly clambered all over the flying boat. "Pug, so help me God, I think we can still fly! They didn't hole the tanks or the engines. I'm hauling my passengers out of here now."

The passengers eagerly scrambled aboard and the Clipper took off. Below, smashed aeroplanes flamed and the island poured smoke.

Even in the dead of night, nine hours later, Midway was not hard to find. The flying boat dropped low over dark waters lit by the glare from blazing buildings. The airfields of Midway, they soon learned, had been shelled by a Japanese cruiser and a destroyer. A mob of almost naked fire fighters was flooding the blazes with chemicals and water, generating giant billows of acrid red smoke. Pug found his way to the commandant's office and tried to get news of Pearl Harbor.

"How about the *California*? I'm to take command of her."

The lieutenant looked impressed. "The *California*? There was no word of her. I'm sure she's all right, sir."

Victor Henry slept a little, though he got up well before dawn to pace the cool hotel veranda. Nothing could draw him out of sight of the flying boat, rising and falling on the swells.

The four hours to Hawaii seemed to Pug like forty. As the plane came in from the north over the harbour and hooked around to descend, Victor Henry was struck sick by what his disbelieving eyes saw. All along the east side of Ford Island the battleships of the

Pacific Fleet lay careened, broken, overturned, in the disorder of a child's toys in a bathtub. Pug vainly tried to pick out the *California* in the hideous, smoky panorama.

From the Customs shed Pug went straight to the CincPac building. A pretty woman in a tailored blue suit led him along the corridor to doors labelled in gold, ADMIRAL COMMANDER-IN-CHIEF, PACIFIC FLEET.

"Admiral, here's Captain Henry."

"Hey, Pug! Great day, how long has it been?" Kimmel waved from the window, where he had been gazing at the harbour. He was dressed in faultless whites and looked tanned and fit. "Have I seen you since you worked for me on the *Maryland*?"

"I don't think so, sir."

They shook hands.

"Well, sit you down. Been flying high, haven't you? Observing in Russia, and all that, eh?" This was an outstanding officer, Pug thought, who had been marked for success all the way, and had gone all the way. Now the fleet he commanded lay wrecked in one quick action.

"I know how little time you have, sir," Pug placed the letter from Wake Island on the desk. "Just tell me how the *California* made out, Admiral. I came straight from the Clipper."

In the brisk tone of a report, Kimmel said, "She took two torpedoes to port and several bomb hits. She's down by the bow, Pug, and sinking. They're still counterflooding, so she may not capsize. The preliminary estimate is a year and a half out of action, possibly two."

Victor Henry's voice trembled.

"Admiral, if I broke a lot of necks, including my own, could I put her back in six months?"

"It's hopeless. A salvage officer will take over." The tone was sympathetic. "You'll get another command, Pug."

"There aren't that many battleships, Admiral. Not now."

Kimmel made a curt gesture at the letter Pug had brought. "And there isn't the stuff to relieve Wake anymore, for the simple reason that the Russians and the British have been given it. Mr. Roosevelt was a great navy President until that European fracas started, Pug. But then he got too damned interested in the wrong enemy, the wrong ocean, and the wrong war."

It gave Victor Henry a strange sensation, after Berlin and London and Moscow, to hear from Kimmel the old unchanged navy line about the importance of the Pacific. "Well, Admiral, I know how busy you are," he said.

"Yes, well, I do have a thing or two on my mind. Nice seeing you, Pug," said the admiral, in a sudden tone of dismissal.

JANICE answered Pug's telephone call and warmly urged him to come and stay. Pug wanted to drop his bags and get into uniform to go to the *California*. He took suitable if brief delight in his grandson, accepted Janice's commiseration over his ship with a grunt. She offered to get the maid to press his whites. In the spare room he opened his suitcase to pull out the crumpled uniform, and his letter to Pamela Tudsbury fell to the floor.

He had written it during the long hop from Guam to Wake. Glancing at it now, it embarrassed him. There wasn't much love in it—it was mostly a reasoned case for his living out his life as it was. Their romance now seemed utterly outside reality. Pamela had ignited something in those turbulent hours in Moscow, and in his elation over the *California* he had allowed himself to half-believe in a new life. But now—how finished it all was!

He did not tear the letter up. He did not think he could write a better one. The situation of a man past fifty declining a young woman's love was too awkward and ridiculous. On his way to the navy yard he mailed it, with sadness.

Sadder yet was the trip to the *California*, through a foul-smelling floating mass of black oil-smeared debris. The launch passed all along Battleship Row, for the *California* lay nearest the channel entrance. One by one Pug grieved for these gargantuan grey vessels he knew so well, bomb-blasted, down by the head, down by the stern, sitting on the bottom, or turned turtle.

The *California* listed about seven degrees, rhythmically spouting thick streams of filthy water. The sooty, flame-blistered steel wall leaned far over Pug's head as the launch drew up to the accommodation ladder. The climb up the canted ladder was dizzying.

How often Pug had pictured his reception: side boys in white saluting, honour guard on parade—to be the star, the centre, of this ritual was worth a lifetime of the toughest drudgery. Instead, he met a vile stink as he stepped on the sloping quarterdeck. "Request permission to come aboard, sir," he said to the officer of the day in greasy khakis.

The OOD saluted smartly. "Permission granted, sir." Five sheet-draped corpses lay on the quarterdeck. The smell came partly from them, partly from gasoline fumes, from burned oil, burned wood, broken waste lines. But above the mess on the main deck the superstructure jutted undamaged into the sunset sky, its sixteen-inch guns trained neatly fore and aft. The old "Prune Barge" was alive and afloat—wounded, but still mighty.

"I'm Captain Victor Henry."

"Oh! Yes, *sir*! Captain Wallenstone's expecting you. He's with the salvage officers in the forward engine room."

"I know the way." Walking decks and passageways that were weirdly slanted, Pug got himself down to where four officers, huddled on a high catwalk, were playing powerful handlights on a sheet of oil-covered water.

He introduced himself and joined in the talk about saving the ship. The quantity of water flooding through the torpedo holes was more than the pumps could throw out, so the ship was slowly settling. Pug asked about more pumps, but there were none to be had in the anchorage. Sending down divers to patch the holes or even to seal off the damaged spaces one by one would take too long. In short, the *California* was done for.

Wallenstone took Victor Henry up to his cabin, spacious and intact. It was a blessed thing to smell fresh air streaming in through the windward portholes. A steward brought coffee, which they could not place on the tilted tables. The captain appeared to know a lot about Pug. He asked what Roosevelt was really like and whether the Russians could hold out much longer.

"Oh, by the way," he said, as Pug got up to leave, "quite a bit of mail accumulated here for you." He handed Pug a bulky envelope. "You wouldn't believe what this ship looked like two days ago," the captain said sadly. "She was the smartest ship in the navy."

At the quarterdeck the bodies were gone. "Well, they took those poor devils away," the captain said. "That's the worst of it. At the last muster, forty-seven were still missing. They're down below, Henry, all drowned. Oh, God! *Where* was our air cover?"

"Is that the *Enterprise*?" Pug pointed at a black shape moving down channel, showing no lights.

Wallenstone peered at the silhouette. "Yes. Thank God she wasn't in port Sunday morning."

"My son's a flier on board her. Maybe I'll get to see him."

"That should cheer you, if anything can. I know how you must feel. All I can say is, I'm sorry, Henry." He held out his hand.

Victor Henry hesitated. In that tiny pause, he thought that if this man had been wiser than all the rest—after all, he too had received a war warning—and had ordered a dawn air alert, the *California* might be the most famous battleship in the navy now, afloat and ready to fight, and Wallenstone a national hero.

But could he, Pug Henry, have done any better? The entire fleet from CincPac down had been dreaming. That was an unchangeable fact of history. The sinking of the *California* was a tiny footnote. He shook Wallenstone's hand and saluted the colours.

In the dim dashboard light of the navy car, Pug glanced over his mail; official stuff for the most part, and a letter from Rhoda. He did not open it.

"Dad!" Warren was at home and he had changed into slacks and a loose shirt. He lunged at his father and threw an arm around him, holding the other stiffly at his side.

"How are you, Dad?"

"I've just visited the *California*."

"Oh. Bourbon, then, Dad? And water?"

"Bourbon. Not that much water. What happened to your arm?"

"Just a bit of trouble I ran into. I'm still flying, that's the main thing. Come, it's cooler out here, Dad."

On the shadowy screened porch, Pug bitterly described the *California*'s state. Warren was scornful. The battleship navy had been a lot of sleepy fat cats, obsessed by promotions and ignorant of the air. "We'll get 'em," he said. "It'll be a long hard pull, but the fliers'll do it. Not the battlewagons."

"Seems to me a few aeroplanes got caught on the ground," Pug growled, feeling the bourbon radiating comfort inside him.

"Dinner, fellas," Janice called.

Pug talked straight through dinner about his adventures in Russia. Though he wasn't much of a wine drinker, tonight he poured down glass after glass. Over brandy, back on the dark screened porch, he returned to the subject of the *California* and asked his son what he thought he should do now.

Warren said, "Well, Dad, you'd better go back to CincPac's staff tomorrow and pound desks till you get a command. You'll get what you ask for. But you have to move fast. If Mr. Roosevelt remembers you're on the loose again, he'll send you on some other mission."

"Warren, I never want to get out of sight of ships again, and I never want to see the inside of another embassy." He grinned. "Right now, boy, I'm drunk as a skunk. Thanks for everything and God bless you. Sorry I did so much talking. Tomorrow I want to hear all about your tangle with the Zeros. Now, if my legs will support me, I'll go to bed."

He did not stir till noon. Janice was on the back lawn with the baby when Pug emerged on the porch, carrying his mail.

"Hi, Dad," she called. "How about some breakfast?"

He sat in a wicker chair. "No thanks; your maid's making me coffee. I'll look at my mail, then mosey on down to CincPac."

A few minutes later Janice looked up again. Victor Henry sat staring blankly at a letter in his lap.

"What's the matter, Dad?"

"What? Nothing. Where's Warren, by the way?"

"Went to the ship. He expects to be back for dinner, but I guess we can never be sure about anything anymore."

"That's exactly right."

His voice and manner were queer, she thought. He stuffed his mail back in the big envelope and stood up. "Say, Jan, I'm a little tireder than I figured. I may even crawl back in the sack for a bit."

His bedroom door was still shut when Warren came home. He knocked, then tried the knob and went in. Soon he came out with an empty brandy bottle. "He drank it all, Jan. He's out cold."

"Maybe you should read his mail." Warren glared at her. "Listen," she said, "those letters upset him. You'd better find out what the trouble is."

"If he wants me to know, he'll tell me."

"What are you going to do?"

"Eat my dinner."

30

To military specialists, "Clark Field" is the name of a United States defeat as grave as Pearl Harbor and only a day and a half later. With this catastrophe at the main army airfield on Luzon, the Philippines lost their air cover, and the Asiatic Fleet had to flee south. There has never been a rational explanation for what happened.

The Japanese had no hope of surprising the Philippines after Pearl Harbor. Their bombers took off from Formosa and droned straight in over the main island. Ground observers sent a spate of reports to command centre, tracking the attackers from the coast all the way to their objective. Nevertheless, they got there unopposed, and found, to their own surprise, the fighters and bombers of America's formidable Far East Air Force lined up on the ground. They laid waste to it and flew away. Two days later, a horde of bombers destroyed the Cavite naval base. At the centre of this attack were *Devilfish* and Byron Henry.

When the attack began, Byron was ashore with a working party, drawing torpedoes. With the wail of the siren the overhead crane clattered to a halt and they trotted to battle stations.

Byron's party had four torpedoes in the truck. He decided to load two more before leaving. But with the big crane shut down, it was slow work moving a ton and a half of steel cylinder packed with explosives. The sweating *Devilfish* sailors were rigging a small cherry-picker crane when Hansen, Byron's leading torpedoman glanced at the sky. "Mr. Henry, here they come."

"So I see. Well, let's hurry." The sailor at the wheel of the cherry-picker began gunning the motor, tightening the chains on the torpedo. "Hold it!" Byron yelled, hearing a distant explosion.

More *crumps* sounded closer. Now Byron's ears caught a Warsaw noise—a high whistle ascending in pitch. "*Take cover!*"

The sailors dived under the truck and a heavy worktable nearby. An explosion blasted close to the shed, then a cataract of noise burst all around. Byron had never endured a bombing like this. Over and over he gritted his teeth at the blasts that shook the ground like an earthquake. At last the noise lessened. Flame and smoke were billowing all around and walls starting to crash down. The *Devilfish* sailors came huddling around him.

"Hey, Mr. Henry, it looks kind of bad, don't it?" "Are we going back aboard?" "Should we finish loading the fish?"

"Wait." Byron and Hansen hurried through the smoky shed to see the situation. In the street a bomb had blown a large crater and three heavy navy trucks stood halted by the pit. "Looks like we're stuck, Hansen," Byron shouted.

Hansen said, "Mr. Henry, the fire's gonna spread to this shop and all these fish are gonna go." Byron understood. Without torpedoes, what good was a submarine squadron?

He said, "Well, if you could operate that overhead crane, maybe we could still pull out a few." Byron turned to a truck driver, a Filipino. "Will you guys give us a hand? We want to move some torpedoes."

After a rapid exchange with the other drivers, the Filipino exclaimed, "O.K.! Where we go?"

IN THE bay, meanwhile, Walter Tully's speedboat swooped alongside the *Devilfish*, bringing Branch Hoban back from base. He arrived on the bridge as the speedboat thrummed away. "Lady, what about Briny and the working party?"

Lieutenant Aster gestured back towards the flaming navy yard. "They never showed. I figured I'd better get away from alongside."

"Damn right. Glad you were aboard to do it."

In a short time the speedboat returned and Tully came aboard, white-faced. "Bad business. I think *Sealion*'s a goner—she's on fire and sinking fast. Better go and see if you can help, Branch."

"Aye aye, sir."

A motor whaleboat was puttering towards *Devilfish*.

"Who's this now?" Tully said.

A young seaman scrambled aboard, his face soot-covered. "Captain, Mr. Henry sent me. The working party's all right."

"Well, thank God! Where are they?"

"They're taking torpedoes out of the shop."

Tully exclaimed, "The *torpedo* shop? *Now*?"

"Yes, sir. The fire sort of blew away in another direction, so Mr. Henry and Hansen got these trucks and—"

"You come with me," Tully said, "I'm going back there."

When the squadron commander reached the blazing navy yard, he found Byron Henry, almost unrecognizably blackened, sitting on top of heaped torpedoes in a truck, drinking a Coca-Cola. The three trucks were full of torpedoes, and two cherry-picker crane trucks held more. The *Devilfish* working party lay on the grass in exhausted attitudes, all except Hansen, who sat smoking a pipe.

"Hello there, Byron," Tully called.

"Oh, good afternoon, sir."

"How many did you get?"

"Twenty-six, sir. Then the fire closed in."

Tully looked at the torpedoes. "Suppose you drive this haul around to Mariveles, Byron. I'll want a report on this, with the names and ratings of your working party and of these drivers. And Byron—well done."

Next morning at Mariveles harbour Byron handed the squadron commander a two-page report. Tully glanced at it. "Did Branch tell you what I want you for?"

"Just something about salvage, sir."

"Byron, the Japs are bound to land soon. We probably can't hold Manila, but as long as MacArthur hangs on to Bataan, the squadron can go on operating out of Mariveles. This is a hell of a lot closer to Japan than any other sub base we'll have for a good long while. So—the idea is to clean out of Cavite *and* Manila every single item we can use, and fetch it here. You seem to have a sort of scavenger instinct." Tully laughed, and Byron responded with a polite smile. "You'll work on this until the *Devilfish* goes out on operations. Incidentally, I've written your father about your torpedo exploit."

"Yes, Captain."

Tully irresolutely took off his glasses and looked at the erect impassive ensign. "Byron. Do you still want to go to the Atlantic? With all hell busting out here?"

"Yes, sir, I do want that."

"You do? When there's only our squadron now to oppose the Japs on the sea? Here's where we need you."

Byron did not reply.

"As for your wife and baby in Italy—that's unfortunate, but you know, they'll be enemy aliens now."

"Sir, we're not at war with Italy."

"It's inevitable. Everybody expects Hitler to declare war, and old Musso will follow suit. Your wife will be interned, but after a while she'll be exchanged. I'm sure she'll be all right."

"Captain Tully, my wife's Jewish."

The squadron commander turned a bit red. "Well now, that's a problem. I still don't see what you can do about it. However, Byron," he said, "I'm going to recommend your transfer to Submarine Force Atlantic—as and when the *Devilfish* gets a replacement for you. Not before."

Byron Henry showed no sign of the relief that filled him. "Thank you, Captain Tully."

The squadron commander opened a desk drawer. "One more thing." And he laid on the desk before Byron a gold pin, the dolphins of a submariner.

AT THEIR hotel in Rome Natalie's bedroom door was open, and Hitler's screeching woke the baby. In the sitting room the radio was turned low, but at the Führer's sudden shriek—"ROOSEVELT!" Louis began crying.

"He is a maniac, after all." Slumped in an armchair in a bathrobe and muffler, Aaron Jastrow shook his head. "I confess I never grasped it. I thought he playacted." With a faintly contemptuous glance at her uncle, Natalie went to the baby.

Jastrow had listened to few Hitler speeches. They bored him. History's pages were crowded with flamboyant tyrants who had strutted their brief seasons and passed away. But now, actually hearing Hitler's ferocious ravings, Aaron Jastrow finally lost his philosophic stance and became scared.

"Well?" Natalie said, carrying in the squalling baby.

"He hasn't declared war yet. But listen . . . ." Jastrow waited for the raucous cheers of Hitler's audience and roars of "*Sieg Heil!*" to die down. "I'm afraid that was it. He said he's called in the United States diplomats and given them their papers."

"Well, all I can say is, I couldn't be less surprised." Natalie opened her blouse, and stroked the baby's cheek with a finger, as he began sucking.

Her uncle shut off the radio. "Mussolini still has to talk."

"Oh, Aaron, what choice has he? He'll declare war."

Jastrow sighed heavily. "I suppose so. Natalie, I'm sorry, deeply sorry, for having involved you and your baby—"

She held up a hand. "No, no. Don't rake it over now. I can't stand that."

Subsiding, he sipped a glass of sherry. "I must telephone the embassy, my dear, and ask what we should do."

"That's a good idea, if you can get through. Otherwise, we'd better dress and go there."

"I'll just finish my wine first."

Natalie rose and took the baby into the bedroom to avoid a row with her uncle. She had no patience left for this vain, cranky old man whose blinkered optimism had mired her and her baby in this peril; though in the end—she always came back to this—she herself was responsible. Where had she committed the fatal stupidity? In coming back to Italy? In marrying Byron? In not following Herb Rose to the Palestine ship?

Sometimes, she dreamed that she was out of this, and relief and joy would fill her; cold, sinking sadness would follow when she awoke on the wrong side of the dream line. But at least on this side the baby dwelt. He was becoming her anchor, the most real thing in her life. Beyond in the hotel, in Rome, in Europe—all was danger and darkening horizons. She tucked the infant in bed and dressed to go to the embassy.

"Ah, my dear, you look very well." Aaron reclined grandly on a couch in a handsome blue cape. "Sit down for a moment."

"Aren't we going to the embassy?"

"Natalie, you know Father Enrico Spanelli."

"That Vatican librarian? No. I've never met him. We were supposed to all have dinner, but Louis got sick."

"Oh yes. Well, he's coming to take us to the Piazza Venezia to hear Mussolini. He's getting us into the Press section."

"What! Good Lord, I don't want to go there with the baby in that Fascist mob! What about—"

Jastrow held up a cautionary hand and began scrawling on a pad. They did this sometimes, in case microphones had been planted in their suite. The sheet he passed to her read: "If it's war he'll take us straight to the American embassy. That's the idea. We'll be out of the hotel, where we might be picked up."

The telephone rang. "That'll be Enrico. Get the baby, dear."

They parked in a rubbish-filled archway. The throng in the Piazza Venezia was surprisingly still. People stood around saying nothing. Flag-bearing schoolchildren were huddled in front of the balcony in a docile mass.

They went into the roped-off Press section and somebody produced a folding chair for Natalie. She sat holding the sleeping baby tightly, shivering. The wind was raw.

They waited a long time before Mussolini stepped out on the balcony and raised a hand in salute. A roar cascaded in the square: "Duce! Duce! Duce!" It was a strange effect, since all the people were looking up silently, with blank or hostile faces. Under the balcony, a few Blackshirts, huddled around microphones, diligently manufactured the cheers.

The dictator's brief speech as he declared war on America was belligerent, but he flailed his fists and the effect was somehow ridiculous. While the Blackshirts shouted "Duce!" the crowd began to leave. Mussolini bellowed his last words at thousands of departing backs like an old ham actor scorned by the audience.

The Americans talked in low, tense tones: they now stood on the soil of enemy country. The debate among the correspondents was whether to go to their offices to clear out their desks, or head straight for the embassy. Aaron Jastrow asked Father Spanelli to drive back to the hotel for his manuscript before going on to the embassy. The priest was agreeable and Natalie too shocked to argue.

A block from the Excelsior the priest suddenly braked. Pointing at two police cars in the driveway, he said, "*Professore*, had you not better go to your embassy first? If the worst comes to the worst, I can get your manuscript for you."

"The embassy," Natalie said. "He's right. The embassy."

Jastrow nodded sadly.

But again, a couple of blocks from the embassy, Spanelli halted the car. A cordon of police and soldiers stood in front of the building. Natalie held her baby close, fighting off a feeling of sinking in black waters. "What now, Aaron?"

"We're all in big trouble, kids," said a coarse American voice beside the open windows of the car. "You'd better come with me."

Natalie looked up into the worried, handsome, very Jewish face of Herbert Rose.

FOR a long time after that the overpowering actuality was the smell of fish in the truck that was taking them to Naples. The two drivers were Neapolitan fish dealers. Rabinovitz had hired the truck to transport a part for the ship's old generator; a burned-out armature had delayed the sailing. Now they crouched in the truck beside the burlap-wrapped armature.

When Herb Rose had first brought Jastrow and Natalie to the truck, Rabinovitz had told them a story that convinced even Aaron: he had gone to the Excelsior to offer Jastrow and Natalie a last chance to join them. In their suite he had found two Germans waiting. They had invited him inside, closed the door, and then questioned him roughly about Jastrow. In the end, convinced that he knew nothing, they had, to his relief, simply let him go. Obviously they were Gestapo men, come to pick up the "blue chip".

When the fish truck reached Naples, night had fallen. On its way through to the waterfront, policemen repeatedly challenged the driver, but a word or two brought permission to go on. Finally the truck stopped and the driver said, "Wake up, friends. We're here."

The sea breeze on the wharf was an intensely sweet relief. The vessel alongside was a shadowy shape, where shadowy people walked back and forth.

"Come aboard," Rabinovitz said. "We'll find a comfortable place for you."

"What's the name of this boat?" Natalie asked.

"Oh, it's had many names. Now it's the *Redeemer*. It's Turkish registry, and once you're aboard you will be secure. The harbour master and the Turkish consul have a good understanding."

Holding her baby close, Natalie followed him up the gangway.

As she set foot on the deck, Rabinovitz touched her arm. "Well, relax now, Mrs. Henry. You're in Turkey. That's a start."

31

Janice was awakened by the sound of a shower at five in the morning. She showered too. In the living room, Victor Henry sat reading navy correspondence. His face was ashen, which did not surprise her after his spending the past sixteen hours in a stupor. "Good morning, Jan," he said placidly. "Did I disturb you? Sorry."

"'Morning, Dad. No, Vic often gets me up around now. Is it too early for some bacon and eggs?"

"That sounds good. Warren get back last night?"

"He did, yes." Janice fed the baby and started breakfast. As usual, the smell of frying bacon brought Warren out. Humming and brushing his hair, he grinned at his father, putting on an act. "Hi, Dad. How're you doing?"

"Not badly—all things considered," Pug smiled ruefully. "Did I empty the bottle?"

Warren laughed. "Bone dry. But you picked a good day to sleep through. Hitler and Mussolini declared war."

"They did? They're fools, making things easier for the President. Is that the worst of it?"

"The Japs got the *Prince of Wales* and the *Repulse*."

"What! The *Prince of Wales*!"

"Air attack off Singapore. The limeys are through in this ocean now. Looks like it's all up to us."

Pug half-buried his face in a hand. The *Prince of Wales*. He thought of those tired, gallant men, that deck where Churchill and Roosevelt had sung hymns under the guns.

"Have they hit the Philippines yet?" he asked.

Warren took a moment to sip coffee. "Well," he said at last, "they sort of plastered Cavite."

Staring at his son, Pug said, "Any dope?"

"They apparently went for shore installations."

"The *Devilfish* was alongside."

To Warren's relief, Janice called them to the table.

"What's the plan of the day, Dad?" Warren said.

"Huh? Oh, I thought I might scare up some tennis."

"Tennis?" Warren reacted immediately and forcefully. "You must get on down to CincPac Personnel. Why, you're entitled to the best ship command they've got left; but the navy's not going to come looking for you, Dad. You play tennis and you'll end up back in War Plans."

Warren's energetic tone, so much like his own younger self, drew a smile from Pug. "Jan, hand me the CincPac roster. It's there on top of that pile of mail." He leafed through it. "Hm. 'Personnel —Captain Theodore Prentice Larkin, II'."

"Know him?" Warren asked.

"'Jocko' Larkin? Biggest boozer in my class. I pulled him out of the river once when he fell off a sailboat dead drunk."

"Dad, our squadron's got an officers' meeting at 0700. I'll drop you off at CincPac. Let's go."

At the CincPac building Warren pulled into a parking space. "Well," he said, "don't take no from Captain Larkin, now. Here, better keep the car keys, in case I leave."

"Right. In case you do—good luck and good hunting, Warren." And father and son, looking each other in the face, parted without more words. Victor Henry went straight to the CincPac communications office and looked through the dispatches. In the garbled report about Cavite, he saw the *Devilfish* listed as sunk. He felt ill: nauseated, chilly, yet perspiring. The brandy had done this, of course; but after the letter from Rhoda the only immediate recourse had been oblivion. The *Devilfish* news had struck an almost numb man.

The main thing now was to hold himself together. He did not know, after all, whether or not Byron was dead or injured. Excited first reports were never reliable. The *Devilfish* might not be sunk.

On his wife, however, the straight word was in. Rhoda wanted to divorce him and marry Palmer Kirby.

Far from harbouring any relieved notion that he might be free for Pamela Tudsbury, Pug now fully understood what a strong bond tied him to his wife. That Rhoda did not feel this too—that she could write such a letter, cheerily blaming herself and her long dislike of a navy wife's existence, praising Pug almost as a saint, yet telling him that after more than twenty-five years she wanted another man—this was a stab from which it would be difficult to recover. She was half of him, for better or worse; she was irreplaceable, beautiful, desirable. It had taken a shock to drive these truths home. He could not blame her, for he had come close to writing the same kind of letter. Nor, strangely, did he have strong feelings about Palmer Kirby. The thing had happened to those two people, much as it had to him and Pamela; only Rhoda had gone over the edge.

"Pug! I tried all yesterday afternoon to find you. Where the hell were you hiding!" Jocko Larkin came striding in and sat down in his swivel chair. "That's hell about the *California*, Pug. She'd have had a great skipper."

"Well, Jocko, I'd say my bad luck's rather lost in the shuffle."

"That's what I wanted to see you about," Larkin said. "Admiral Kimmel is going to be relieved. At his own request. His successor will be Admiral Pye and Pye wants you for operations—now hold it, Pug." Larkin held up a hand as Victor Henry violently shook his head. "This is as great a break as a man in our class can have. Remember there are six *Iowa* class battleships building now, due for commissioning in twelve to twenty months. The greatest in the world. You'll probably get one after this."

"Jocko, give me a ship. Now. Not in 1943."

"Listen to me, Pug. *You don't say no to CincPac!*"

"Where's Admiral Pye's office?" Henry stood up.

"Sit down!" Larkin rose too, glaring at him.

"Do I get a ship?"

"*Sit down.*"

Pug sat.

Larkin sighed, and opened a folder on his desk. "The *Northampton* might be available. I say *might*. Most likely not."

"The *Northampton*? God love you, Jocko."

"Pug, a cruiser command doesn't compare with CincPac's deputy chief for operations."

"Jocko, I've shuffled all the high-strategy papers I ever want to. I'm a sailor and a gunner, and there's a war on. If you can't find me anything else, I'll take a squadron of minesweepers. O.K.? *I want to go to sea.*"

"I hear you, loud and clear." He groaned. "One more flap I'll have with the admiral, that's all."

"Thanks, Jockò. If you want me, I'll be at my son's house."

As they shook hands, Captain Larkin said, "When you write Rhoda, give her my love."

He wrote the letter at the officers' club.

Dear Rhoda—

I'm somewhat stymied by the problem of answering your astounding letter. I'm not sure I can set my feelings on paper, not being very good at that sort of thing. I know I'm no Don Juan, but taking the rough with the smooth, you and I have made it this far. I still love you—and in your letter you've managed to say a few kind things about me.

The life we've been leading in recent years has put a strain on our marriage. I've felt that too. We've become a family of tumbleweeds, and lately the winds of war have been blowing us all around the world. Right now it strikes me that those same winds are starting to flatten civilization. All the more reason for us to hang on to what we have—mainly each other, and our family. That's the way I've worked it out. I hope that on further thought you will, too.

I'll probably be at sea for most of the next year or two; so here's how I'm compelled to leave it. I'm ready to forget—or try to—that you ever wrote the letter; or to talk it over with you on my next Stateside leave; or, if you're absolutely certain you want to go ahead with it, to sign the papers and do what you wish. But I'll put up a helluva fight first.

Victor is a handsome baby, and our other grandson looks unbelievably like Briny as an infant. I'm enclosing a snapshot I picked up in Moscow from Natalie's old friend Slote. I hate to part with it, but you'll want to see it, I know. Let's hope to God they got safely out of Italy before Mussolini declared war.

Jocko Larkin sends his love—he's fat and sleek. That's about it. Now I'm to start earning my keep by fighting a war.

Love,
Pug.

He got up and dropped the letter in the club mailbox, and ran into Jocko Larkin coming in for lunch. Larkin said, "I've been trying to find you. Do you know about the *Devilfish*?"

"No." Pug's heart thumped heavily. "What?"

"Well, it was *Sealion* that was sunk. *Devilfish* was undamaged."

Pug had to clear his throat twice.

"That's definite?"

"Couldn't be more so."

"I see. I'm sorry about *Sealion*, but—thanks."

"The thing we talked about, Pug, looks like a pipe dream. I'll keep scratching around, though."

Pug went out of the club into the sunshine. A stone had rolled off his heart; Byron was all right! And one way or another, Jocko would get him out to sea.

Strolling aimlessly through the navy yard, he arrived at the waterfront. There alongside the fuel dock, taking on oil, ammunition, and food, was the *Northampton*. He thought of mounting the gangway and having a look around. But what for? She was a handsome vessel, he thought, but a half-breed, an overblown destroyer, with the length of a battleship, but a quarter its weight. After the *California*, the *Northampton* was a shrunken affair.

Still, Pug thought, he would have been glad enough to get her. It was exciting to see her loading stores for a combat mission. Jocko was right, operations was the inside track. But, for the good of his soul right now, Pug needed the *Northampton* himself.

He drove back to the house. On the desk in his room, clipped to a wrinkled Western Union cable, he found a handwritten note:

Dear Dad,

I'm at the Gillettes. I will be home for dinner. Warren phoned. They sortie at dawn. Yeoman from *California* delivered the attached. Says it's been kicking around for days,

Love, Janice.

He opened the cable.

DEAREST JUST THIS INSTANT HEARD OF JAPANESE ATTACK UTTERLY HORRIFIED FRIGHTFULLY WORRIED ABOUT YOU DESPERATELY ASHAMED IDIOTIC LETTER FORGET IT PLEASE PLEASE AND FORGIVE CABLE ME YOURE SAFE AND WELL LOVE RHO

He could hear Rhoda telephoning it "*utterly* horrified, *frightfully* worried . . . ." He knew Rhoda's burst of contrition. Her impulse in sending the cable might well have been sincere; but the process of repair would be long. He did not know what to reply, so he tossed the cable into the desk drawer.

That night after dinner Pug went straight to bed. At four in the morning he snapped wide awake, and it occurred to him that he might as well watch the sortie of the *Enterprise*. He dressed quietly and drove to the overlook point.

The darkness was merciful to Pearl Harbor. But soon the dawn brightened, and the hideous shame was unveiled once more. Victor Henry turned his face away from it, back to the indigo arch of the sky, where Venus and the brightest stars still burned. In a world so rich and lovely, could men really find nothing better to do than to build grotesque engines for blowing each other up? Yet this madness was the way of the world. He, Pug Henry, had given all his working years to it. Now he was about to risk his very life at it. Why?

Because, with all its rotten spots, the United States of America was not only his homeland but the hope of the world. Because if America's enemies dug up iron and made deadly engines of it, America had to do the same, and do it better, or die. So Victor Henry meditated as the *Enterprise* moved down the channel and out to sea, taking his first-born son into the war.

Back at the house, he found Janice all dressed.

"Hi," he said. "I thought you'd still be asleep."

"Oh, it's Vic's cough. I'm taking him to the clinic, and the earlier I get there the better. You just missed a call from Captain Larkin."

"Jocko? This early?"

"Yes. He said to tell you, 'She's all yours.'"

Victor Henry dropped in a chair with a blankly startled look.

"'She's all yours'? That's the whole message?"

"He said you'd understand. Good news, I hope?"

"Pretty fair, yes. Look, Jan, you'll be passing the Western Union. Can you send Rhoda a cable for me?"

"Sure."

Victor Henry reached for the memo pad by the telephone and scrawled, "Letter coming, am fine, have just begun to fight." Janice's mouth curved in an indulgent female grin.

"What's the matter with that?" Pug said.

"How about 'Love'?"

"By all means. Thanks, Jan. You add that."

When she left with the baby, he was on the telephone, trying to reach Commander, Cruisers Pacific. He responded to her farewell wave with a bleak, preoccupied smile. Janice thought, closing the door on him, that nothing could be more like her austere, remote father-in-law than the little business of the cable. You had to remind this man that he loved his wife.

Herman Wouk

"*The Winds of War* is fiction," writes the author, "and all the characters and adventures involving the Henry family are imaginary. But the history of the war in this romance is offered as accurate; the statistics, as reliable; the words and acts of the great personages, as either historical or derived from accounts of their words and deeds in similar situations. No work of this scope can be free of error, but readers will discern, it is hoped, an arduous effort to give a true and full picture of a great world battle.

"The theme and aim of the book can be found in a few words by the French Jew Julien Benda: 'Peace, if it ever exists, will not be based on the fear of war but on the love of peace. It will not be the abstaining from an act, but the coming of a state of mind. In this sense the most insignificant writer can serve peace where the most powerful tribunals can do nothing.'"

Only Herman Wouk would ever suggest, even by implication, that he is an "insignificant writer". He is in fact very significant, successful and a true professional. Since boyhood he has had no other ambition than to be a writer. Born in New York City in 1915, he graduated from Columbia University and then worked for five years as a gag-writer for one of America's leading comedians. In 1942 he joined the U.S. Navy and served as deck officer aboard a destroyer in the Pacific. After the war he published two moderately successful novels and then *The Caine Mutiny* which became a world best-seller and won him a Pulitzer Prize. His subsequent novels have all been best-sellers.

Now, for the first time since *The Caine Mutiny*, Mr. Wouk returns to the theme of World War II. *The Winds of War*, he says, is "the book I've been aiming towards and planning for twenty years". The work of writing and researching this monumental novel has occupied him exclusively since 1964, when he and his wife and sons settled in Washington in order to be close to his background sources.

Of writing itself, Wouk says: "In the good hours when words are flowing well it seems there is hardly a pleasanter way to spend one's time on earth. Never mind the bad hours. There is no life without them."

SARAH WHITMAN. Original full-length version © Diane Pearson 1971. British condensed version © The Reader's Digest Association Limited 1972.

THE RUNAWAYS. Original full-length version © Victor Canning 1971. U.S. condensed version © The Reader's Digest Association, Inc. 1972. British condensed version © The Reader's Digest Association Limited 1972.

NUNAGA, Ten Years of Eskimo Life. Original full-length version © Duncan Pryde 1971. British condensed version © The Reader's Digest Association Limited 1972.

THE WINDS OF WAR. Original full-length version © Herman Wouk 1971. British condensed version © The Reader's Digest Association Limited 1972.

NUNAGA. Picture credits: Page 271 (top, bottom right), 272 (left), 273 (bottom), 274 (top, bottom), 275 (top): Duncan Pryde; 271 (bottom left), 276 (inset, bottom): Government of the Northwest Territories; 273 (top), 275 (bottom): Art Sorensen; 276 (top): Paul Kwaterowsky.

OO.72